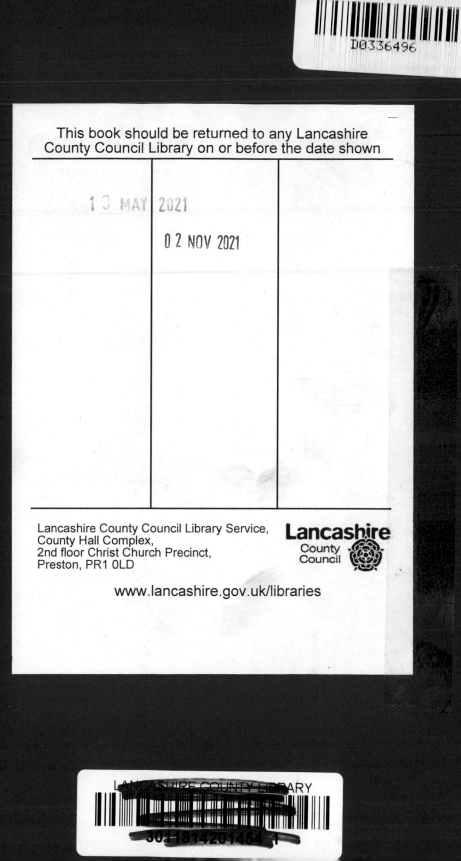

Lie Beside Me

Lie Beside Me

GYTHA LODGE

MICHAEL  JOSEPH

MICHAEL JOSEPH

UK | USA | Canada | Ireland | Australia
India | New Zealand | South Africa

Michael Joseph is part of the Penguin Random House group of companies
whose addresses can be found at global.penguinrandomhouse.com.

First published 2021
002

Copyright © Gytha Lodge, 2021

The moral right of the author has been asserted

Set in 13.5/16 pt Garamond MT Std
Typeset by Jouve (UK), Milton Keynes
Printed and bound in Great Britain by Clays Ltd, Elcograf S.p.A.

The authorized representative in the EEA is Penguin Random House Ireland,
Morrison Chambers, 32 Nassau Street, Dublin D02 YH68

A CIP catalogue record for this book is available from the British Library

HARDBACK ISBN: 978−0−241−36305−8
OM PAPERBACK ISBN: 978−0−241−36306−5

For Rufus, the most excellent and ridiculous of sons. I hope you can forgive the lack of *Fortnite* references.

And you're still too young to read this. Sorry.

Prologue

I felt cold. Cold in the way of night sweats. In the way of a slow waking to damp sheets that stuck to my skin. It was like that time when I thought I had lymphoma but was, in fact, falling to pieces mentally instead. Do you remember that? I would wake up every night, drenched and shivering, having sweated so much that it had soaked half the mattress.

I fought waking up. I was too tired, and too aware of the hangover that was about to descend. I was hating myself before I'd even opened my eyes. Well, hating Drunk Louise, anyway. That irresponsible, crappy version of myself who always seems to screw everything up, just so she can have a good time.

So I was half awake and hating it. And I thought that maybe if I shuffled back onto your side of the bed, then I'd find a dry area, and possibly even the duvet, and I'd be able to go back to sleep.

I couldn't seem to find the duvet. So instead, I squirmed further back to tuck into your body. It's always the warmest way to sleep, with you wrapped around me. But it didn't make me warmer. What had been dampness became shivering wetness. Something was soaking into my nightshirt.

And I remember working out that it wasn't, in fact, a nightshirt. There were thin, hard straps digging into my shoulders and the restrictive feeling of tight fabric. So, clothes. Drunk Louise had gone to sleep in her clothes. And that made me feel a little afraid of what else she might have done.

I opened my eyes a slit, and I turned over. I saw you as a shadow at first. A reassuring, humped silhouette. The window behind you was lit with the orange glow of the street lamp down the road. It wasn't dawn yet.

That light confused me. I've never known you go to sleep with the curtains open. Not once in five years.

I remember I put a hand down to the mattress and then looked at it. I wasn't quite sure whether I could see a darker mark on my palm, but it occurred to me quite suddenly that the wetness might be blood.

It didn't shock me yet. Not even when I saw a . . . *spread* of it between us. It was a dark circle that stretched almost as far as the pillows and down to my knees.

And then I felt a creeping understanding. A realisation that there were none of the normal sounds of sleep coming from you. No breath. No familiar squeak high up in your nose. No gurgling stomach, which always seems to feature in the early hours.

I touched you on the shoulder. And for some stupid reason, I whispered at you instead of speaking properly. 'Niall. Niall.' Like it was possible to check you were OK without actually waking you up.

There were two things that hit me, and I don't know which one came first. I can't quite remember either one being clear before the other.

The first thing was that you were cold. Colder than the sheets. Colder than the feeling of my dress on my skin. A coldness that made your skin feel alien.

And the second thing was stranger. It was realising that *you* were strange. Your silhouette was too big. It was wider at the shoulder than you are. Perhaps thinner at the waist.

By the time I turned the light on and saw the bleached-white face of a stranger looking back at me, I already knew.

It wasn't you. It wasn't you.

I

The call reached Juliette Hanson at 6:46 a.m. It was an ice-cold first of March, early enough that there were still stars out beyond the gap in her badly fitted curtains, and cold enough for an overnight fall of snow to have frozen into bright, glittering crystals. It was also a Saturday, but Hanson was wide awake now. More awake than she'd been on any day this week.

Unidentified male found dead, the DCI had said. It was the most piercing of alarms. She was already swinging her feet out of bed as he went on to read the address.

She'd never heard of Saints Close, but the chief added that it was north-east of the city centre. She was likely to be on-scene before him.

She dragged a clean trouser suit out of the wardrobe, grabbed her toothbrush and toothpaste, and took them all downstairs with her. She snapped the kettle on and dressed quickly while it boiled. She threw instant granules into her thermos mug and dumped boiling water and milk on top, then went to grab her shoes. She'd left her socks upstairs, she realised. It wasn't the weather to do without, and she ran up to grab the thickest pair she could find. She was fully dressed and standing at the front door by 6:53, her blonde hair pulled back into an untidy bun that would just have to do.

She paused with her hand on the bolt of the door. She needed a moment to prepare, mentally, for the few steps to her car. Climbing into the vehicle quickly meant having her keys ready. Her bag looped over her shoulder just right. Her movements planned out.

She was pretty sure there would be nobody out there today. Who would want to hang around her house before dawn on a freezing morning? But she was going to make sure, anyway.

She'd developed a habit of pulling the door shut as she moved off the doorstep, letting the Yale lock click into place, and it was so practised that she didn't even need to think about it today. She checked right and left as she approached the car, too, which she had reversed up as close to the porch as possible. There were no footsteps in the snow, she saw. No sign of anyone close by.

It took five paces to get to the driver's door, and she had the car unlocked on pace number two. By pace number three she was pretty sure that she was alone, but she kept moving at speed anyway. She didn't pause until she was inside the car with the doors locked and the engine running.

She spent a moment, after that, doing nothing more than breathing in and out. She hated that she felt like this. She hated, too, that it was almost worse when he wasn't waiting in the shadows than when he was.

DCI Jonah Sheens was buzzing with curiosity as he pulled his Mondeo into Saints Close. He'd been sad to climb out of Jojo Magos's warm bed, and to miss their one lazy morning together. He also felt a little grubby in yesterday's shirt and trousers. But overriding these considerations was keen interest. An unidentified man at a residential house. A death. All the questions that went with it.

Saints Close turned out to be a meandering little group of

sixties houses off Belmont Road. Chunky detached buildings with decent-sized gardens out at the front. A place of solid salaries. But nothing particularly flashy. No million-pound piles. Volkswagens rather than Audis parked up in driveways.

Jonah noticed that someone had added an apostrophe after the final S of 'Saints' on the street sign, using some kind of sticker that was much larger than the rest of the typeface. He smiled slightly to himself. That kind of a street, then.

He hitched the car half up onto the pavement behind the scientific support van. Three emergency vehicles in total, and Hanson's little Nissan parked further up. The cluster stood out, the only vehicles that were clean and free of snow. He was glad to shrug on his thick padded jacket and pull on ski gloves before he climbed out.

The garden to number eleven was bounded by trees. Snowy firs standing between leafless sycamore branches. At the front an overgrown hedge screened the ground floor from view. It looked like it would be gloomy in that front garden, even in daylight.

Approaching the gate, he struggled to make out much beyond the white forms of the forensics team and a nylon screen being manhandled into place halfway down the garden.

One of the overalled figures moved to meet him. Linda McCullough, forensic scientist for Southampton and the New Forest, and undisputed lead of the scene of crime team. He took a step forwards onto the clear plastic sheeting that had been rolled out from the front door up to the pavement.

'Tell me,' Jonah said.

'We've only just arrived,' McCullough told him, lowering

her mask to speak to him. 'Victim's a young white male. The homeowner called it in. She told us she'd found him just before six thirty.'

Jonah saw that one of the figures was spooling a cable out of the front door, unwinding it towards a pair of wide-based portable floodlights. He couldn't see much within the house. A lighted hallway. Stairs to one side.

'Anyone else in the house?'

'Your constable's here, but nobody else.'

The floodlights burst into brilliant life, dousing the garden with light. He squinted against the sudden brightness, and then followed McCullough behind the screen they'd now erected on the grass.

A young man lay a few feet behind it, his white dragon-motif T-shirt dominated by a large crimson bloom. As McCullough involved herself in angling the lights, Jonah crouched down over the body. He gazed first at the colourless face. A chiselled, high-cheekboned face. It had been handsome, he thought, up until today.

He took in the powerful shoulders and lean abdomen, and a knife that lay close by, sticky with drying blood. Then his gaze travelled to the stained snow beneath the body.

'Not much blood,' he muttered.

McCullough gave an audible sigh as she lifted her mask back into place. 'Sheens . . .'

'All right, I know.' He grinned at her, and straightened up. 'You do your job, and I'll go and make the coffee.'

Ben Lightman arrived after that, only just returned from annual leave and looking as perfectly unruffled and movie-star handsome as ever. He clearly wasn't dressed warmly enough to hang around outside but showed no signs of concern. It was as if the cold was something that affected other people.

He listened in stillness to the sparse information they had so far.

'I'd like witness statements from the surrounding houses,' Jonah finished up. 'You can have my coat and gloves. Juliette's with the homeowner so I'll go and check in with her.'

Lightman nodded, taking the offered coat and beginning to put it on. 'And presumably Domnall can come with me once he's here?'

'He can,' Jonah agreed. 'Give him a few.'

Of the four of them Domnall O'Malley actually lived the closest to the crime scene. But O'Malley had never been a man to hurry unless he had no other choice, and despite a previous career in the military he managed his life in a haphazard, seat-of-his-pants fashion. Jonah was well used to it and was happy to let him do things his way.

Jonah headed inside and found Hanson in a large, beautifully decorated sitting room just off the hall. She'd managed to dress herself formally in a navy suit and cream shirt, and looked respectable, if slightly thrown together.

The woman who sat near her looked unprepared for any of this. She was somewhere in her early thirties, and was swathed in a thick dressing gown over pyjamas. Her feet were bare, and she had the remains of make-up around her eyes. Her very dark hair looked damp, and had been scraped back into an uneven ponytail. She shivered continuously, most likely because there was a dead man in her front garden, but just possibly also because of the blast of arctic air that was making its way through the two open doors.

'Ah,' Hanson said, giving him a smile. 'This is my DCI. This is Louise Reakes, sir. She found the body and called us in.'

Hanson's hint of a Brummie accent had stepped up this morning, and Jonah guessed it was deliberate. An unthreatening regional burr was reassuring.

'Let's get this door closed,' Jonah said, pushing the sitting-room door shut. 'We can at least stop the cold getting in here.' And then, as he pulled up an upright chair opposite the woman on the sofa, he added, 'I'm so sorry for all of this.'

'It's all right,' Louise said, hoarsely. 'Can't be helped. It's not like you put him there . . .' Her mouth twisted slightly in wry humour. For a moment she looked like she might be about to apologise, and then she dropped her gaze to her hands.

'Did you know the victim?' Jonah asked, gently.

Louise shook her head. 'No. I've never seen him before in my life. I'm sorry.'

'Once we've identified him, we'll try to get some images from social media,' Hanson said. 'Sometimes it's hard to recognise someone when . . .' She nodded instead of finishing the sentence.

'OK,' Louise said. 'But I'm pretty sure. I mean, he's big, isn't he? Tall and . . . and strong. I don't know anyone like that.' Again that twist of the mouth. 'And Niall's friends are all middle-aged GPs or lawyers.'

'Is Niall your husband?' Jonah asked.

'Oh. Yes. He's away until later today. Conference in Geneva.'

'Do you work too?' Hanson asked.

'God, yes. I'd never be a housewife. I'd go crazy.' Louise laughed, slightly nervously. Her eyes travelled to Jonah again and back. 'I'm a musician.'

Hanson grinned. 'That's great. Modern or . . .?'

'I'm a harpist.' Louise jerked her head towards the hall. 'My music room's through there.'

'Can you tell me how you found him?' This from Jonah.

There was a clear change of expression. Louise retied her dressing gown over herself before saying, 'Sure.' It was a tight, constricted word. 'I woke up just before six thirty, really hungover. I had my friend April round last night, and she's a massive drinker.' She smiled slightly. 'Terrible influence. I always end up wrecked when we hang out.'

'She didn't stay here?' Hanson asked.

'No.' Louise shook her head. 'She usually goes home.'

'So it was just you last night,' Hanson confirmed.

'Yes,' Louise said. 'Just me.' She paused, finding her thread again. 'So I woke up early feeling like shit. I wanted to make tea so I went to get the milk from outside. We have proper deliveries here. In bottles.' She suddenly shook her head. 'Sorry.'

'It's OK,' Hanson said. 'There's no rush.'

'So I saw this . . . shape on the lawn. And I couldn't quite process it at first. And then I went to see and . . . and I called the police.'

'And you didn't see anyone else out there?' Jonah asked. 'Anyone on the street?'

'No . . .' She shook her head, and then said, 'But I thought . . . Maybe it's not much use, but I think I got woken up in the early hours by a loud car engine.'

'What time was that?'

'I don't know . . .' She looked off to one side. 'I'm not sure if I checked. A while before. Could have been four a.m.'

'The victim wasn't there when your friend left?'

'No, definitely not,' she said, twisting her hands over each other. 'Shit, I could never have gone to bed with . . .'

'What time was that?'

Louise gave him a slightly confused look, and then said, hesitantly, 'I'm not – I suppose midnight.'

'And there's nothing else you can remember?'

'No,' she said. 'Sorry.'

Jonah nodded and rose. 'We'll see if anyone else heard anything. I might have a few more questions at some point, but I hope we won't be too long here.'

'That's OK,' Louise said.

Hanson got to her feet, too, and looked down at Louise's shivering form. 'Let me make you a tea before I head out.'

'Oh, thank you.' Louise's expression was a little pained. 'Are you sure you don't want me to . . .? Everything's in particular places, you know.' And then she made an obvious effort to smile. 'But that would be nice. If you're sure.'

There were people, O'Malley had always found, who could obstruct justice without even trying to. The woman who lived in number nine Saints Close was one of those. A stubborn, slightly self-righteous forty-something named Pamela, she stood on the doorstep, flatly refusing to wake her husband for questioning, and yet simultaneously trying to tease out information on the events next door.

'Well, I suppose it's some kind of violence, then?' she said, as an ambulance drew up slowly behind the paramedics' car.

'I'm afraid we really can't comment,' Lightman said patiently, for what must have been the third time, while O'Malley leaned his substantial frame against the wall with a feeling of his life draining away. He was too old for this stuff, and it was too cold for it as well. 'You said your husband was woken up a lot in the night . . .?'

'Yes. So I'd appreciate it if you'd keep it down.' She peered

12

towards the road. 'Was it Niall, then? Has he attacked his wife?'

'Do you have reason to expect that?' Lightman asked.

The neighbour – Pamela – fixed Lightman with a defensive look. 'Well, it's generally what happens, isn't it?'

In the end, O'Malley stepped in. 'Listen. You can see this is a serious crime. We need your help. If your husband heard anything, we need to know. It could make all the difference.'

At his long, imploring look Pamela finally relented. 'All right.' She opened the door properly behind her. 'But after that, you leave him in peace, all right?' And then she called, 'Phil! Phil, the police need to see you. Sorry, love.'

O'Malley was a little disappointed by the quiet, slightly overweight man in blue tartan pyjamas who descended the stairs. He'd expected someone thuggish and intimidating.

Phil's account was fairly disappointing, too. He'd been woken by a slammed door at some time after two. He thought it had come from Louise and Niall's house, but wasn't sure. He was pretty sure he'd stayed awake until five thirty, and hadn't heard anything else.

'You can bet he wasn't really awake until five thirty,' O'Malley said to Lightman in a low voice, as they left. 'His window's at the front. Surely, if he'd been awake, he'd have heard someone being murdered in the next-door garden.'

'Unless they did it awfully quietly,' Lightman replied with a trace of a smile, 'out of consideration for the neighbours.'

'It's been wiped,' McCullough said, her gloved finger hovering over the handle of the knife to show him the lack of blood over the patterned grip. It would have been a beautiful object without the brownish crust over the blade. A black grip patterned with elaborate silver detailing. A long, tapered blade curved to a hunting point.

There were three of them hunkered over the body of the young man. The pathologist had arrived, and Jonah had been satisfied to note that it was Dr Peter Shaw attending. Jonah had worked with him only once before, but his calm, measured approach had been a key part of achieving a murder conviction. He had turned out to be good on the witness stand, too. Less flappable than Jonah had expected of a fairly young man.

'No prints, then,' Jonah said, looking away from the perfectly crafted weapon. 'But it's pretty distinctive, isn't it?'

'It is. There's a chance you could track down its owner,' McCullough said, and then, to Shaw, 'I'm interested in the smears. It looks like someone wiped the handle clean of prints and deposited it here.'

'He wasn't stabbed here,' Jonah said.

It wasn't a question. It had been clear to him from the lack of pooled blood below the body. He'd seen victims of knife crime before. The extraordinary spread of blood. The way it saturated everything. This looked to him like the end of a journey, one that must have involved a great deal of blood loss along the way.

'No, he wasn't.' It was the pathologist who answered this time. He glanced towards the gate. 'Has your team marked up the footprints yet?'

'Yes, done,' McCullough said, and they made their way carefully out onto the road.

The team had now put a cordon up round the pavement and verge, and McCullough led the two of them to the edge of the road.

'Here,' she said, gesturing to several pieces of plastic that had been skewered into the snowy grass. Alongside each, there was a depression in the snow, and in some places the snow was stained with what seemed to be blood. 'They start at the kerb.'

Jonah turned to look at the road. 'Are they definitely his?'

'They seem to match his shoes,' McCullough replied, 'and I think it would be difficult for someone to carry him.'

'We should look up what time it snowed last night,' Jonah said, thoughtfully. 'There's no snowfall on top of them.' And then he looked towards the edge of the kerb. 'You think he arrived by car?'

'It looks fairly likely,' McCullough said. 'I would say a taxi, except I think they'd have noticed if he was bleeding to death in the back.'

'So someone else dropped him,' Jonah said. 'That person might have carried the knife in some kind of cloth before leaving it next to him?'

'Well, it certainly wasn't pulled out of him in the garden,' Shaw said. He frowned down at the footprints. 'Interestingly, it doesn't look like he was running or staggering.'

'The prints are quite flat-footed and steady,' McCullough agreed. 'So if he was escaping an attacker's vehicle, it doesn't look like he fled in terror.'

'So he might not have known how badly injured he was?' Jonah asked.

'He might not,' Shaw said. 'Though people can exhibit a strange sort of calm when suffering severe blood loss.'

Which was, Jonah decided, too depressing a line of thinking to pursue right now. 'Let me know when I can ID the body,' he said, and turned to take a little reconnaissance of Saints Close.

*

Hanson had boiled the kettle, rooted out a mug and teabag from the cupboards and poured the water before she looked in the fridge and found no milk. But, of course, Louise wouldn't have brought it in. She wouldn't have remembered the milk when she'd seen a body on her doorstep.

Hanson headed outside, treading carefully over the cables that led into the garden, and saw that the milk crate beside the step was empty.

She leaned into the sitting room to say, 'Sorry. I can't seem to find the milk. Did you put it somewhere . . .?'

'Oh.' There was a moment of pure blankness on Louise's face, and then she said, 'No, I was being stupid. There is no milk on Saturdays.' She gave a laugh. 'What an idiot.'

'Well, good work on being an idiot,' Hanson said, smiling. 'You wouldn't have found him so soon otherwise.'

Louise nodded at her, and then said, 'I can have it black. That's fine.' Just as Hanson was turning away again, she asked, 'How long will it be until you know who he is?'

'I'm sure it won't be long.' Hanson tried to make it reassuring, instead of ominous.

'Will you tell me, when you find out?' Louise asked, her stare very fixed. 'I really need to know.'

It didn't take Jonah long to walk to the end of the close and back, and in an effort to keep moving he decided to go back up towards Belmont Road, too. Dawn was approaching rapidly, though the temperature was still well below zero. The sky towards Holly Hill was a warm orange that somehow slid into washed-out blue, and many of the houses had lights on, some showing anxious faces through the window. A whole street, summoned to watch by the flickering blue lights of the squad cars.

'Has someone done her in?'

The voice rang out from a large white-washed house with red-tiled eaves and a protruding porch. A gravel drive led up to it in a sweep, bordered by clipped shrubs, many of them tied with twine.

It was a much older house than any of the others, probably by a good hundred years. Jonah wondered if the land the street was built on had once belonged to this house. It had the look of a small manor about it, with its tall windows and high roof.

The voice came from a figure standing in the porch. He was a man of somewhere between sixty and eighty. Corduroy trousers and a V-neck sweater over a checked shirt were finished off by sheepskin slippers.

Jonah gave him a flat look. 'Sorry?'

'I asked if someone had done her in.' The slippers-wearer raised a slightly crooked finger to point towards the squad cars. 'Wouldn't be such a surprise, with that one.' He nodded in what looked like satisfaction.

'Why do you say that?' Jonah kept his voice neutral. However distasteful comments like that were, they were often useful. Jonah's was a world where every petty, mean-spirited remark was to be hoarded. To be treasured. To be written into his notebook and fed into the workings of the case in the hope that it might point them the right way.

'Well, I've been half expecting it,' the older man said. 'The number of times I've seen her stagger out of a cab in the early hours, barely able to stand. The kind of woman who ends up a victim, don't you think?'

Jonah nodded, almost but not quite as if he agreed. 'Mrs Reakes is fine, luckily, but I'd be interested to know if you saw or heard anything unusual last night.'

'Me? No.' The man in the slippers shook his head. 'Nothing unusual. The standard Friday-night drag race went on, but I don't give them the time of day now.'

'Drag race? You mean fast cars?'

'Yes. The lovely lads who like to tear along Portswood Road and then down past the end of the close.'

'So you heard them last night? What time would this have been?'

'Oh, gone midnight,' the gentleman said. And then he added, 'If something's happened, I'd say they were likely to have been involved.'

'But you don't know who any of them are?'

The gentleman shook his head. 'I'm afraid I'm not in the habit of strolling out at that hour of the night.'

Jonah nodded, slowly. He might not be, but there were traffic cameras not far away. Louise Reakes had mentioned a loud engine, too, which made this account more interesting. 'Just let us know if you think of anything else,' he said. And then he made his way back to number eleven.

Shaw was done with his observations and was in the midst of discussing the removal of the body to the city mortuary. Lightman and O'Malley were hovering near the gate. Presumably they'd finished quizzing the nearest neighbours.

'Am I cleared to look for ID?' Jonah asked.

'Yes,' Shaw agreed. 'Be my guest.'

McCullough pulled a pair of purple latex gloves from her pocket and handed them to Jonah. He slid them on and was immediately hit by their smell. A sex-and-death smell, McCullough had once said. Jonah had laughed, and then felt a little nauseated the next time he'd torn into a foil packet and recognised the scent.

O'Malley crouched next to Jonah as he manoeuvred a

wallet out of the victim's back pocket. He opened it carefully and slid out a credit card, touching it as little as possible.

'A. Plaskitt,' he said, and then continued to look through the cards until he found a gym membership. 'Alex. Alex Plaskitt.'

McCullough held out a plastic bag for Jonah to slide the wallet into, and he shifted so he could reach into the man's right-hand pocket, which looked like it might have a phone in it. It was much harder to pull out. The victim's legs were drawn up so that the phone was wedged against his hip. But by pushing it up from the outside of the pocket, Jonah managed to lever it out.

An iPhone. Fairly new, he thought, and cased in a plastic protector with an elaborate dragon pattern over it that almost matched his T-shirt.

Jonah pushed the home button and it lit up, showing a series of messages from someone saved as 'Sex Kitten Issa'.

Alex's girlfriend, probably, Jonah thought, as he scanned them.

The last one was from half an hour ago and read:

Where the fuck are you?

2

Louise

Niall, there's so much I need to tell you. A whole messy story that surrounds and encompasses the morning I woke up next to a stranger and panicked like I've never panicked before.

I know it might well be too late for any of this. I'm sitting here without you, and I'm not even sure I want you to come back. But after so many stupid secrets, I think it's time to lay everything bare.

And I should probably say here that I'm sorry for my part in it. I really am sorry for what a mess this has turned out to be, and for the actions I took that led us here.

But apologising isn't an explanation, as you've told me before. So here's everything, and it starts a lot further back than you might think. With the night we met, which was obviously also the night I met April. Though, in fact, there were three of you I met that night, and all of you came to dominate my life in a way I could never have predicted.

As much as you might want to believe that *you* started our story, it's abundantly clear to me that it was April Dumont who started it. Even you can't deny the power she has. Everyone was watching her during the wedding, from the moment she stomped in late, with her dress that showed off her midriff (and the side of each breast too, just in case that wasn't enough). They stared at her tattoos. At her high-heeled cowboy boots that were the coolest fucking thing I had ever seen.

I bet you winced at that, didn't you? I bet if you were reading this in front of me, you'd roll your eyes and ask me if that kind of language was necessary.

Well, I'm afraid it is, my darling. This is a *fuck* kind of a story from start to finish, though I honestly will try to spare you whenever I can. I want you to keep reading, Niall. I really do.

So, back to that wedding, when I was still a meek, anxious, painfully shy person. I've often wondered what I would have turned out like if my darling mum had lived a little longer. If I'd spent my teenage years with her, instead of with my increasingly neurotic, messily grieving father. If I'd had someone to tell me how great I was. I might have been a confident, talkative young woman. I might have been *sexy*.

But there's no point wondering about that, really. I wasn't confident, or talkative, or sexy. I was shy and awkward and frightened of attention.

At least I was before April. Before my life was picked up and turned luminous by the cowboy-booted girl who made her noisy way up the aisle, ignoring all the other free seats, and came to sit next to me. Next to mousy little me.

It was me she rolled her eyes at over the truly awful poem the maid of honour read out. It was me she showed her service sheet to, with the word 'cock' circled in the name of some poor composer called 'Peacock'. I was the one who started laughing, to the point where everyone around us turned to look, which made us partners in crime. And to my surprise, I found that I didn't mind being looked at just then. Not when April was on my team.

'Thank Christ that's over,' she said, once the service was done, and if I hadn't already been in love with her, that strident Tennessee drawl would have clinched it. I didn't quite keep up with everything she said to me for the rest of the night, which I'm sure you can imagine. The high tempo and volume of her speech. The sudden low-voiced asides. But it didn't really matter.

She walked with me to the reception, telling me about her baby sister back home, and how I looked just like her. Dee, she said. Dolores, but always called Dee. It seemed to mean something to her, that resemblance.

I asked her, keenly curious, how she'd ended up in Southampton. She seemed just so exotic to me, and so out of place.

'You wouldn't believe it, but I used to work for big pharma, like the groom,' she said, and grinned at me. 'My first husband and I got jobs over here, and then got sick of the sight of each other. He went back home; I stayed. Though I got the hell out of that job.'

'What do you do now?'

She gave me a sidelong look. 'I do a little consulting for some of the pharma firms still. Freelance, you know. So I can tell them where to shove it when I want. But mostly I spend my second husband's money. It's a tough job, but someone's gotta do it.'

I couldn't help laughing. And then, two seconds later, I half tripped on my heels and had to grab hold of someone's garden fence to steady myself, which for some reason made me laugh even harder.

'You OK?' she asked, and looped her arm through mine. 'It's the weirdest thing. You're so like Dee! Almost, if you just had the accent . . . you could be twins.'

'I'll work on it,' I said.

As far as I can tell, she decided right then and there that we were going to be best friends forever.

She put her arm round me the moment we arrived at the reception, and glanced around until she saw someone with a tray of champagne. 'Thank God,' she said, and plucked two glasses from it.

I didn't want to tell her that I wasn't a drinker. It's a difficult thing to admit to someone who clearly sees alcohol as a lubricant to their social interactions. Which is why I never told you, either, Niall. I've consciously hidden the fact that, until that wedding, I was essentially teetotal.

The strangest thing is that I don't think you would have believed me if I'd told you. I'm pretty sure you're struggling to believe it now. You can't even begin to imagine a Louise who doesn't get shit-faced and out of control.

The truth is, I was genuinely afraid of being drunk. Still more afraid of humiliating myself or losing my keys or phone or, I don't know, some part of myself. My sense of control, maybe. I found the idea of not being in command of everything daunting.

But here was April, handing me a glass, and necking hers before I could even start. I wanted, so badly, for her to keep liking me. And so I drank. Quickly. I loved April's approval as she put the empties back and grabbed two more. I loved, even more, the way she smiled at the waiter with a look that thanked him and hinted at a promise of something. And I decided that I was going to be like April, whatever it took.

I felt none of the dizziness I'd expected as the alcohol kicked in. I felt warmth instead. A sense of everything suddenly mattering less. It became easier to act like my new friend. To laugh and even, for the first time ever, to flirt.

April introduced me to all the groom's side of the family. They actually seemed to like me, and that told me I was doing the right thing. I didn't resist when April took me to the bar, or to the washrooms, to touch up my eyeshadow and restyle my hair. Little by little, she managed to erase the Louise I'd been, and replace her with someone shinier. Better.

And, in response, everyone suddenly seemed to want to talk to me. The DJ. That sultry Italian friend of April's. The best man, who was definitely married. They actually wanted to flirt with me and be flirted with. At twenty-eight I finally felt desirable.

Somewhere along the line, I began to imagine that I really *was* a new person. A bubblier, sexier, *better* Louise. I started to feel like I was watching this better person interact, and the loss of control wasn't terrifying, like I'd expected. It was liberating.

In short, Niall, it was the birth of Drunk Louise. She didn't crawl out of some terrible depth like you might imagine; she emerged, butterfly-like, out of the drab, wilted chrysalis of my previous life. And God, I loved her.

You've told me how you felt the first time you saw me. How you were drawn to me, magnetically. Well, when you looked over at me and kept looking, it was this shiny new version of me that you were seeing.

I remember your expression. How you looked a little dazzled. And when you demanded to be introduced, it didn't surprise me as it might have. *Of course* you would like this new Louise. She was so much fun.

Drunk Louise somehow knew what she was doing when she looked at you archly and asked if you were anyone important.

I loved how you laughed. And even more how you said, 'I'm the second most important person in this room.'

'Come on, at least third,' I told you. 'Me, April . . . you can be third.' It wasn't the kind of thing I'd ever said to anyone. But that new me somehow knew that she could.

'I can deal with third,' you told me, which made me feel a rush of warmth towards you. It only got better when we bantered on for a bit and then you asked, 'Shall we do some shit dancing?'

You weren't lying. It really was awful. I remember shaking my head at you in mock disappointment, while I couldn't stop grinning.

In the middle of it I was summoned to perform. I hadn't told either of you that Hannah had asked me to play a harp piece at the reception. I could tell that it added something to your liking for me, the fact that I was a musician, too.

I was getting on for being very drunk as I settled myself on the hard chair and started to flow into the Bach. But, as I have come to know since then, there's a sweet spot that you hit, with alcohol. Where it loosens you up and makes you feel like you're part of your instrument. When *you* get out of the way, and something else takes over. Someone else. *Her.*

And there was that other feeling, too. Of the way your eyes were on me during every touch of every string. I felt beautiful just then. Genuinely beautiful.

When you'd gone to the bar later on, April told me all about you and Dina. About how she'd lasted two months of marriage with you before deciding on an upgrade. April pointed out glamorous, hard-looking Dina and her new man to me. She did it too loudly, though, so that Dina looked over, and I cringed. But of course April didn't care. She just called, 'Hey, Dina! Looking great!' and then steered us both away.

The story about Dina made me feel for you. It also made

me admire you for having the courage to turn up to that wedding, when you knew your ex-wife would be there with her rich new boyfriend. It must all have been so raw. And when you were alone for any time, I could see the way your gaze would slide over to her. Each time it happened, you looked troubled. Confused, maybe.

It's strange how I felt a surge of jealousy erupt in me, even then. Or at least how quickly it erupted in *her.* It made Drunk Louise burn with fury and a desire to win. She didn't like being ignored, Niall. She didn't like it at all.

I asked April if she thought you were a good choice. I was almost afraid of what she might say. I'd already started to think of you as someone in my life, and in spite of the alcohol, I could feel nerves rising as she hesitated before answering.

But in the end, she said, 'You know, I think he's a great choice. He's a kind person. Sometimes too kind, you know? Like I think he's been taken advantage of in the past, because he likes to take care of people.' She gave a grimace. 'And he's probably a little hung up on what watch he's wearing or what car he's driving, but honestly, I think a lot of that came from Dina. I think he could shake it off.'

'He isn't still in love with her?' I asked.

April gave this some thought. 'No, I don't think he is. I mean, I half worry that it's too soon for him to move on, but actually, I think you'll be the best possible thing for him. Someone with a good soul, to make him realise how shallow their relationship was.'

I didn't know quite what to say to her amazing faith in me. But I stored it away and, in the way of stupid people the world over, decided that I could save you.

*

It was late on that the other thing happened. The thing I've always wondered if I should have paid more attention to. It was an argument between you and my new best friend. One I probably shouldn't have overheard, and that I always doubted I'd got right.

The two of you were outside, where April had gone for a smoke. I'd finally, belatedly remembered to congratulate the bride, after realising I hadn't spoken to her once all day. By that time Hannah was reeling, and spent some time hugging me and kissing me on top of the head and telling me how glad she was to know me. Once I'd finally escaped, I came to find one or the other of you, not expecting to find you both together.

April was standing facing the gardens, on that little raised, gravelled terrace at the back of the house. I don't know if you remember it that clearly, but I do. It was beautiful, that place. Part of a night that seemed universally beautiful.

There wasn't as much to see now that it was dark. Just a few solar lanterns scattered through the grounds. But April was looking out at the view anyway, twisting her lower lip to blow smoke into the air.

And I'm positive you were saying to her, 'Whatever you're scheming, I want you to leave her out of it.'

'Oh, please,' April said, dismissively. 'I have a right to talk to anyone I want.'

And I remember that you made a frustrated huffing noise. You said, 'What about everyone else's rights? Don't they matter?'

For a moment April just inhaled and exhaled, and then she said, 'No, not really.'

'Please,' you said next, in what I now know to be a very rare tone of voice for you. 'Please don't.'

And April turned towards you and said, very slowly and clearly, as if she'd been play-acting with her tumbling sentences all evening, 'I'm going to do exactly what I want.'

Then she started to walk inside. And in the fraction of a second I stood there – before pretending I'd just arrived and greeting you both with false enthusiasm – I saw your expression. You looked desolate. Like a man who had just lost something.

3

The team held a miniature briefing outside the front garden of number eleven, their breath billowing into the air. Jonah kept it as swift as possible in the bitter cold, for his own sake as much as theirs.

'I'll take Juliette to see Alex's girlfriend,' he told O'Malley and Lightman. 'Domnall, you take Louise Reakes to the station to give her statement. And make sure she mentions the car engine on the record. I'd like Ben to check with this friend of Louise's to find out if she saw anything strange when she left the house. Louise thinks that was at about midnight. And, Domnall, see if you can find out when it snowed last night. We have footsteps probably belonging to the victim that were made after the snow stopped. Hopefully some of that might narrow our window before we get on to traffic cameras. Currently we're looking at twelve until four, and we've so far got two references to loud engine sounds last night.'

Lightman nodded. 'The neighbour in number nine also says he was woken by a door slamming at two. He thinks it was at the Reakes house, but I wouldn't rule out it being a car door.'

'As far as Louise has said so far, there were no exits or entrances from her house after midnight,' Jonah said. 'So that could be interesting.'

They ran for their cars after that. Jonah started up the Mondeo and watched his two sergeants manoeuvre their way out of the close before he eased out into the road ahead of Hanson. Policing was, as Jojo frequently liked to tell him, a very carbon-intensive job.

The traffic was on the verge of becoming busy by the time Jonah drew up outside Alex Plaskitt's house. It was on Alma Road, barely a mile from where Alex had died.

Jonah always found this part of the city disorientating. Like the Polygon, across town, most of the streets here looked basically the same, with identikit pairs of semi-detached houses set close to the road, each of them red-brick and touched with white details.

They were definitely a step down the ladder of affluence from Saints Close, but Jonah infinitely preferred the effect of these older, more modest buildings. Many of the own-ers on this side of the road had filled their tiny walled front gardens with brightly coloured garden furniture and pots. In today's snow they looked Christmas-card pretty.

Hanson followed him up to the front door, looking less nervous than he had expected. This was only the second time his detective constable had broken the news of a death. Assuming, of course, that Alex's girlfriend actually lived here. The messages seemed to suggest so.

Having to give the worst news possible was gruelling, and it never really stopped being gruelling. You just found ways of distancing yourself.

Hanson seemed to have clocked some of those quickly. She was looking methodically at each detail of the house and street, noting it all, and clearly keeping her mind off what was about to come.

Jonah rang the old-fashioned push-button bell, and

immediately heard rapid sounds from within the house. The door opened with some difficulty. It made a sliding sound and jammed, and whoever was behind it apologised.

When it finally opened, it was to reveal a fairly short, lightly built man of thirty or so, who was in the process of returning some car keys to the top of the hall table. He was dressed quite formally for this early on a Saturday, in an open white shirt with a subtle stripe, and a pair of stone-washed jeans. Dark, tired eyes. Black hair gelled until it stood up. A bronze complexion.

He put his left hand up to the door frame, and Jonah saw that there was a wedding band on his fourth finger.

Issa, Jonah thought, unsure why he had assumed Alex's partner would be a woman.

The dark gaze darted between him and Hanson, and Jonah said quietly, 'I think this is Alex Plaskitt's house.'

Jonah saw the almost non-reaction he had grown used to. The stillness of Issa's body, and the very slight brightening of his eyes.

'Would you be Issa?' Jonah tried next.

'Yes. What is it?'

'Might we come in?' Jonah asked.

Like almost everyone in this situation, Issa already knew what Jonah was going to say. Jonah could see it from the sagging of his body against the door frame, and then the uncoordinated way he turned to lead them into the colourful sitting room.

Any doubt that they had the right person disappeared as Jonah sat on the cushion-laden futon. A chrome-framed photograph on the table beside it showed Issa and their victim in wedding garb. They were grinning at the camera, Alex's head a good six inches higher than Issa's. He had one arm over the smaller man's shoulder. Alex looked about twice as wide as his husband, too.

Jonah focused on Issa and took a breath. 'I'm very sorry to have to tell you that Alex was found dead in the early hours of this morning.'

Issa's brow creased, and he put a hand up to his mouth. 'How?'

'It looks like he was attacked,' Jonah said. 'The pathologist will conduct a full post mortem, but it seems clear that he was a victim of violence.'

Issa took a large, unsteady breath. 'Was it at a club?'

'We're unsure where the attack took place,' Jonah said, carefully. 'He was found outside a residential address.'

Issa gave him a strange, sharp look. 'What residential address?'

Hanson said, soothingly, 'A house on Saints Close. Do you know it?'

Issa shook his head, immediately, and then stood up and went rapidly over to a desk. He picked up his phone, his hand shaking badly.

'He was supposed to come home,' he said. 'I tried calling him.'

And then he started to cry.

'You settle yourself here, so,' O'Malley told Louise Reakes, who was now fully dressed in a jersey dress with a fur-lined parka over the top. He placed an oversized mug of tea down on the interview-room table. 'We'll get your statement done as soon as Detective Sergeant Lightman is back.'

'Thank you,' Louise said to him. Her hand went to the mug, but then dropped to the table. She stared at the steam, unmoving.

'When will your husband be home?' O'Malley asked, thinking of her going back to her house alone after this, and having to walk past the place where the young lad had died. She could do with some support, he thought.

She looked up at him slowly, and said, 'I'm not quite sure. Sometime in the afternoon, I think.'

'Where's he coming from?'

'Geneva.'

'Ah, so a fair distance.' O'Malley nodded. 'He must be worried about you.'

There was a moment where Louise just stared at him, in apparent incomprehension, and then she said, 'He won't be worried. I haven't told him yet.'

O'Malley found himself looking back at her with much the same expression. 'Did you not send him a message or so?'

Louise shook her head, glancing down at the phone she'd placed on the table in front of her, and then, in an agitated movement, folded her arms over herself. 'No. I wasn't sure I should.'

'Well, I'd do that,' O'Malley said, quietly. 'You'll feel better once you've talked about it.'

She didn't look at his sympathetic smile, but instead angled her head to look towards the floor.

'I'll leave you to it,' he said.

Louise's face seemed to grow, if anything, paler as she nodded. By the time O'Malley left, she'd made no move to pick up her phone.

Lightman had tried calling Louise's friend April a few times with no joy. In the end he'd decided to drive over to her flat on Admirals Quay. It made up part of the very modern

Ocean Village development on the dockside, and Lightman knew from having looked idly at the brochure once that the flats were well beyond his price range.

The ground floor was like a hotel. There was a bar, a concierge service, and a lift that you needed a key fob to operate. Lightman persuaded the concierge to rouse April Dumont and grant him access to the lift. The greying man leaned in and pressed the button for the top floor before inclining his head and turning away. The whole process made Lightman feel awkward.

It turned out that April's flat actually occupied the whole of the top floor. He stepped out of the lift into a hallway with a single door. The space was lit in gold colours and featured what Lightman thought of as show-home furniture. It didn't display many signs of anyone living there. This was an entirely different world from Louise Reakes's solid suburban semi, and Lightman wondered what April did for a living.

The door opened before he'd got there, and a messy-haired blonde woman wearing a very short negligee with a silk dressing gown slung over it asked hoarsely, 'What's going on?'

'I'm so sorry to wake you,' he said, coming to stand a little in front of her. He felt the inevitable discomfort of standing in front of a woman wearing very little. So he did what he generally did and reduced the experience to a cataloguing one. He noted her accent, which had the drawl of an American from the deep south or Midwest. He saw the make-up smudged below her eyes. The glazed expression. The tattoo visible just above the line of the negligee. 'I just need to ask two or three very brief questions about yesterday evening.'

'Yesterday?' April asked.

'A young man was found dead in the garden of a house on Saints Close this morning,' Lightman told her. 'I believe you were there last night.'

'What the hell?' April asked. She stood back, suddenly, and said, 'OK, come in for a second. It's just me . . .'

He followed her into a huge, light living area with blocky modern chairs, floor-to-ceiling windows and a view of the harbour on two sides. Like the hallway, it looked almost unlived in. Only a pair of used tumblers, a pack of cigarettes and a lighter on the coffee table spoiled the show-home effect.

April flung herself onto one of the sofas, with a very quiet groan.

'OK. Better.' She brushed some of her hair back out of her eyes. 'Sorry. I may have overdone the tequila yesterday. Please speak slowly.'

'Of course,' Lightman said. 'It shouldn't take long. We just wanted to confirm what time you left the house, and whether you saw or heard anything strange.'

April continued to fiddle with her hair as she thought. 'The cab must've arrived at eleven fifteen. I booked it just before eleven, and there was a little wait.'

'Was there anyone outside at that point?'

'Not that I saw,' April said, and then she looked at him with more focus. 'Hey, is Louise OK? You said this dead guy was in the front yard? Garden?'

'Yes. Louise seems all right, but finding him was obviously a bit of a shock.'

'Jesus.' April's expression was dark. 'I'll drop her a line.'

'Did you hear anyone driving around?' Lightman went on. 'Any strange sounds?'

There was another pause, and April shook her head. 'No.

The cab was sitting there with its lights on and the engine off, so you'd think we would have heard anything . . . Does Louise remember hearing something?'

'Nothing definitive,' Lightman replied.

April nodded, very slowly. 'Shit,' she said. 'This is the last damn thing Louise needs. The last.'

4

Louise

So. You know, now, how Drunk Louise was first born. It may surprise you to know that I almost turned my back on her the next day. I'd never had a hangover before, and this one was so intense that I honestly thought I'd damaged myself irreparably. I was sick all day, right up until four p.m., and for all of that wretched time I could only look back on every single thing I'd done with nauseated regret.

But then April got in touch to arrange a coffee, telling me she needed me in her life. And you messaged me later on, as you'd promised. You told me how much fun I was, and how much you'd like to see me again.

These were two sudden points in Drunk Louise's favour, and as the mild alcohol poisoning receded, I imagined that I might be able to drink again, if I was more careful.

It helped Drunk Louise's case that I was nervous about meeting you when I was sober. I had no idea how to flirt without her help. So having booked in a date, I decided that I'd let myself have a few glasses before we met.

It was such a relief to feel it happening again. To feel her take over. It was like putting on the warmest of coats. If you can imagine a warm coat that somehow also made me look smoking hot.

I still could have kept it under control, I think, even then.

I wasn't inclined to drink most of the time. It was just a few drinks when I hung out with April, which I'd started to do twice a week. Though it was generally more than a few when I saw you.

I think you finally, belatedly need to take a little responsibility for that, Niall. Drunk Louise didn't gain power and frequency without help. She bloomed under your encouragement as much as mine.

I want you to think back to those first dates of ours. To think back honestly, and to ask yourself how they must have been for me. How hard it was every time you told me about Dina, and about the raw anger you felt towards her. The hurt.

It's not the only thing I remember about those dates, of course. I remember learning things about you. Your hatred of ABBA. Your love of Miles Davis and Nat King Cole. Your secret obsession with Star Wars, which nobody from work was allowed to know about. Your equal love of food and your determination to eat organic.

I'm aware of your influence on me, too. It was through you that I started to appreciate really good food. Beyond pizza, I mean, which I've always enjoyed heart and soul. The first time you cooked beef wellington, it was a revelation. It was extraordinary to me that you could make something so good in an ordinary kitchen.

You laughed at me as I gorged myself on three helpings.

'There's a whole other course to come, you know,' you told me.

I said I'd just have to borrow another stomach from somewhere, and you gave me the hugest grin. You told me how happy you were that I enjoyed food.

'It was so frustrating being with someone who was constantly dieting,' you said. 'Dina made food her enemy.'

I honestly didn't know whether I felt good about that, or awful. I washed away any more thought with another glass of Médoc.

I also learned in those early days that you were far more impulsive than I have ever been. Far more likely, too, to put everything off until tomorrow. I remember being fascinated and horrified when you said you'd leave the washing-up until the morning. How I itched to do it, because I knew I would lie awake worrying about it. Though, in fact, by the time we'd spent a good hour in extended lovemaking, I slept like a baby. It was a revelation.

You were far more comfortable in your own skin, too. Watching you speak to waiters and waitresses with warmth and without worry made me feel safe for some reason. And witnessing the way you laughed when you dropped something or screwed up filled me with wonder. Where was the immediate self-loathing that plagued me? And why weren't you angry when I messed up, too?

It occurred to me, for what was honestly the first time in my life, that I didn't actually need to be hard on myself. That there was a choice in this. And every time I broke a glass or lost something, as you rubbed my arm and helped me sort it out, I let a little bit of the dislike I'd long felt towards myself drift away.

In fact, Niall, if only it hadn't been for Dina, you might have been nothing but good for me.

5

'We'd really appreciate any information you can give us on Alex's movements last night,' Hanson said to Issa, quietly, once his racking sobs had subsided into occasional juddering breaths. Jonah was happy to let her be the comforting presence in this conversation. He'd never been sure he was that good at it. 'I know it's hard when you're trying to process this, but the more quickly we start looking for Alex's killer, the more likely we are to bring them to justice.'

Issa nodded, drew in another breath, and then nodded again. 'Yes. Yes, I want to – help.' He turned his eyes up towards the ceiling, gathering himself together. 'Alex was out with one of his – our friends.' He looked at Hanson. 'I was away. I didn't get back until one, and he was still out. I wasn't there to protect him.'

Jonah gave him a nod. The idea of the diminutive Issa protecting the powerful Alex looked a little ridiculous on the face of it, but there were other forms of protection than the physical. There was, for example, the kind that involved persuading someone to stop drinking when they'd had enough. Or that talked them out of aggressive behaviour.

'Do you know where they went?' he asked.

'Yes.' He nodded. 'A gig in the Porterhouse, and then they ended up staying out.' He shook his head. 'The last I heard from him – they were in Blue Underground, and he was quite drunk.'

The tears gained the upper hand for a few moments, and then Jonah asked him, 'Could we have the friend's name?'

He nodded, silently at first, before managing to say, 'Step. Step Conti. He's a Stefano, but he's only ever called Step.'

'You know this friend well?'

'Yes,' Issa said, swallowing. 'He's a good friend to both of us. Alex likes to go out – with Step and a couple of others. I sometimes join them and sometimes leave them to it. I'm not quite such a hard drinker.' He gave a watery smile.

'You don't think he could have . . . argued with Alex?'

'No, of course not,' Issa said, his voice shaking. 'He was his friend. I don't know how . . . If Step had been there, he would have helped. You don't know what happened to him?'

'I'm afraid not,' Hanson said. 'You presumably haven't spoken to Step this morning.'

'No.' Issa shook his head. 'It didn't – occur to me, for some reason. I just thought Alex had got drunk and – and maybe was sleeping off his hangover there.'

'So you can't be certain that Step wasn't involved?' she went on.

Issa's gaze flicked from Hanson to Jonah, and then it rested back on Hanson.

'No,' Alex's husband said in the end. 'I just don't think he could be.'

Hanson gave him a half-smile, one of those expressions that sat uniquely between solemn sympathy and warm support. It was a hard expression to pull off, and Hanson, Jonah thought, did it very well. 'Of course. We'll need to talk to him.'

'Yes. Yes.' Issa picked up his phone from the side table and read out Step's number, and then his address, both of which Jonah wrote down.

'Are there other family members we should inform?' Hanson asked gently, once that was done. 'Parents? Siblings? Or would you prefer to call them?'

Issa's expression made Jonah's chest ache. He was so transparently a man unable to believe he really had to do this.

'His parents live in Surrey,' he said, inconsequentially. 'I'd . . . rather you told them. We never got on all that well.'

Once they had taken their contact details, Jonah told Issa as gently as possible that he would need to identify the body, either in person or over a video link. Alex's husband shook his head at the suggestion of a remote link.

'I have to see for myself.'

'The coroner requested a post mortem,' Jonah said. 'I know it's a hard thing to have to deal with right now, but it will help us. It's standard practice with a sudden death like this. Once that's done, we'll call you in.'

'What if – what if it isn't him?' Issa's eyes were large and dark, and full of a peculiar hope. 'What if you've got it wrong?'

Jonah found himself momentarily unable to think of anything to say. He couldn't tell Issa that he had seen the body, and knew that it was Alex. It seemed unreasonably cruel. And yet to say anything else seemed even crueller.

'We'll make sure we get everything right,' Hanson said, after a moment. 'We'll take every care. We owe it to you and the victim.'

It seemed to be the right thing to say. Issa nodded, and then said, quietly, 'Thank you.'

Jonah sent a swift text to Jojo as they headed back to the car, explaining that his Saturday now looked to be a write-off. She was supposed to be taking him indoor climbing, his first proper introduction to her slightly obsessive hobby. He was sadder about not getting to see her than he was about dodging the session, but he knew she would happily head down there without him anyway. Jojo was never short of climbing buddies.

And then he called Surrey Constabulary through the Mondeo's Bluetooth, asking them to notify Alex's family of the death and to provide his number to call. Jonah disliked sending someone else to break the bad news, but it was a necessity when the trip would take them several hours.

Alex's father called them back only fifteen minutes later, while they were sitting in city-centre traffic. His voice was the full upper-class Surrey gentleman, which was not quite what Jonah had been expecting.

'I'm . . . Edward Plaskitt. I was asked to call you about Alex. About the terribly sad news.'

'I'm so sorry, Mr Plaskitt,' Jonah said. 'I know you must have a lot of questions. As senior investigating officer, I'd like you to feel you can ask me any of them.'

'Well . . .' There was a brief pause, and then Edward said, 'The two who came said it happened in the early hours.'

'That's right,' Jonah agreed. 'Alex was found at six thirty this morning, at a residential property. We're trying to find out when and how he died. At the moment we think it was sometime between one thirty and four.'

'I see,' Edward said, his voice strangely unemotional. 'They implied that it was violent. An attack.'

'Yes,' Jonah said. 'And I want to reassure you that we're going to do everything we can to find the culprit or culprits.'

'Thank you.' There was another pause, and then Edward asked, 'Is there anything in particular that we should be doing?'

'At present there's nothing pressing, but we will need to know anything you think might help us. Anybody who wished Alex harm. Any recent arguments. Any involvement with potentially violent groups.'

'I'm . . . sorry, chief inspector,' Mr Plaskitt answered, 'but I don't think we'll be able to help. We've hardly seen Alex since he moved to Southampton. Perhaps three or four times in five years. He's drifted out of touch, and we don't really know anything about his life.'

'Why might he have lost touch?'

'Well. I suppose he didn't really fit in at home. In staid old Surrey.' There was a note of slightly cutting irony to the remark. 'He changed when he went to school, and then more at university, in Brighton. He fell in with a . . . a group that wasn't what we really wanted. We felt that he'd been led astray. That they'd indoctrinated him.' Alex's father sighed. 'I suppose we let our disapproval be known a little too much, and Alex decided it was easier not to see us.'

'I see,' Jonah said, wondering at Mr Plaskitt's calm. At his collected, unemotional speech, when his son had just been murdered. Everyone dealt with news of death differently, but Alex's father seemed to be barely affected by it. 'So when was the last time you saw him?'

'It would have been . . . the Christmas before last. So a little over a year ago.' There was a trace of emotion this time. Embarrassment, Jonah thought.

'And did anything in particular happen then? A . . . disagreement?' Jonah asked.

There was a pause once again, and then Mr Plaskitt said, 'No more than at any other family Christmas. Emotions ran high, and Alex got upset that we weren't being kind enough to his other half. Which was an unfair accusation. We have always welcomed him into our home, despite the personal pain we've felt.'

Jonah could well imagine why they felt pain at Alex's marriage, and decided to shift the topic of conversation.

'I'm happy to come to Surrey to talk further, but it might be that you'd prefer to come here, to Southampton.'

'Oh. Yes. Well, it doesn't sound like there's any need for that right now, does it?'

Jonah heard a very faint indrawn breath from Hanson.

'It might be more for your benefit, Mr Plaskitt,' he said, gently. 'To allow you to ask questions and talk to Alex's friends.'

'Edward, please,' Alex's father replied. He hesitated before saying, 'I'll discuss it with my wife. It might be better, anyway, for you to see our daughter, Phoebe. She lives in Winchester, so she's much closer to you.'

'Thank you,' Jonah said. 'Would you be able to give us her details?'

He let Hanson write them down, and then said, 'In the interim, I've asked the community support officer to stay with you.'

'I . . . No, that won't . . .' Edward's voice sounded defensive. Almost angry. 'I think we'd prefer to grieve in private, if you don't mind.'

'Of course. I understand. Thank you for your help, Edward.'

Jonah ended the call, and the moment it showed up as complete, Hanson said, 'That was like a lesson in respectable homophobia. That poor lad, having a dad like that! Talking about how "painful" it was, having to socialise with his husband . . .'

'I hope it's more complex than that,' Jonah said, 'but I suspect you may be spot on.'

'Can we arrest him?' she asked. 'Just to ruin his day?'

'If you can think of any reasonable charges,' Jonah replied, grinning.

Jonah was keen to talk to Step Conti, but given he was out in the New Forest, it made no sense for Hanson to drive there separately. They both went via the station and Jonah hovered while Hanson parked up. He fielded a brief reply from Jojo while he waited.

A major incident is a pretty long way to go to avoid getting shown up on a wall, Copper Sheens. But I suppose I'll let you get away with it this once. J xx

Jonah couldn't help laughing, as he so often did when communicating with Jojo. He sometimes caught himself in the middle of it all, wondering exactly how he had become so happy.

This wasn't how any of his previous relationships had gone. Particularly not the slow splintering of his six-year relationship with Michelle. And it was strange remembering that he'd jeopardised a future with Jojo only four months ago, before their relationship had even begun.

He'd known how he felt about Jojo by then. He'd only been waiting for her to come back from Africa before trying to pursue anything with her. It should have been enough to make him resist anything else. But he had bumped into his ex-fiancée while very drunk, and it had been like being hit over the head with past regret. Michelle had been rolling drunk, too, and the result had been pretty inevitable.

The morning after, he'd thought he actually wanted Michelle

back. That was the strangest bit. He'd spent the day after their liaison depressed that his ex-fiancée seemed uninterested.

He could only feel profoundly grateful, in retrospect, that Michelle hadn't wanted to pick things up again. For once in his troubled romantic life, things had turned out for the best. And he knew enough to grab on to that lucky break with both hands and make the most of it.

Hanson took a moment, once in the car, to message Jason. She knew he'd been planning on working today, which meant they would both end up in CID at some point. A slight compensation for a ruined weekend.

Jason, as a detective inspector with one of Sheens's fellow DCIs, generally worked a lot more independently than Hanson did. He was happiest playing lone investigator. And though he was obsessive about his work to the point where he sometimes seemed flat-out moody, he was a kind soul underneath it all.

Their relationship was a strange one. Hanson had certainly never intended to get involved with Jason, and wasn't aware that she'd ever flirted. A sudden invitation for a drink (which had come during the rather heightened emotions at the end of a case) had been accepted, and had turned into a series of drinks. She'd been very reluctant to let those drinks become something more, not least because she wasn't sure how she felt about anything at the time.

But sometimes, Hanson had learned, you ended up falling into things without consciously choosing them. The drinks had turned into dinners, and then, a month after the first one, into going home together for the first time. And it was all . . . nice. Simple, normal, and worlds apart from her abusive relationship with Damian.

The only downside to it all was that she and Ben Lightman no longer seemed to be friends. Things had got suddenly awkward, and it was hard to get her head around given that she and Ben had no history.

There had, it was true, been a weird long hug a few hours before she'd gone for that first drink with Jason, an event that still made her feel embarrassed and strangely sad to think about. But that wasn't really a reason for things to have turned sour, and she was at a loss to explain why everything had changed so quickly. Why she always resorted to false cheerfulness, and why he had become as distant and as detached from her as if they'd never been friends.

Step Conti lived not far from Jojo. He was on the edge of the New Forest, in West Wellow, which was a little less picturesque than Furzley. There were more blocky sixties structures, retirement bungalows and modern touches. The effects of lying just outside the boundary of the national park. Modernity had been allowed to creep in.

Step's house, however, was on a lane that ran south-west out of the village into an open area of heathland. Houses lined one side of the tarmac, with unspoilt land on the other. Today, with a fall of snow over it all, it looked dazzling.

Jonah eased the Mondeo along the lane carefully, trying to stay on the road surface as he manoeuvred round parked cars. There were deep, snowy tyre tracks running down the side, and he had no desire to test out the car's four-wheel drive just now.

Step's house, right at the far end, had a new-looking wooden gate and a thickly gravelled drive. Someone had tied a pair of balloons to the gate, one pink and one blue. Jonah winced, thinking that a murdered friend was not the sort of news to be bringing to a kids' party.

The gravel driveway held only a metallic red Qashqai and a bike rack with one small pink bike in it. Which hopefully meant they had arrived before the party had kicked off.

'Ready for another one?' Jonah asked Hanson, once they'd emerged from the car.

She gave him a wry expression. 'Totally. Can't think of anything I'd rather be doing.'

They approached the house, which bore signs of recent and extensive work. Jonah wondered whether this had once been a seventies bungalow, like a lot of the other homes in the village. Whatever the original building, the finished product was both large and elegant.

He rang the bell, and was rewarded by the sound of thundering feet on stairs. Hanson made an uncomfortable noise, and muttered, 'They are definitely not expecting the police.'

It was a relief when the door was opened by a sandy-haired young woman in a polo-necked jumper instead of any children. The young woman was in the midst of saying, 'Probably the postman,' when her eyes took them in properly, and she hesitated.

'I'm so sorry for coming unannounced,' Jonah said, giving her a slight smile, 'but might we speak to Step? I'm DCI Sheens, with the Hampshire Police.'

He saw her give a shiver, and then nod. She turned to say, 'Just someone for Daddy. Let's finish the banner.'

As she let them in, Jonah had a glimpse of a small girl in a blue ballet outfit and a slightly older boy dressed as what looked like a witch before their small forms disappeared back upstairs.

'Step!' the woman called towards the back of the house. 'For you!'

She hovered in the hallway, watching them, before suddenly saying, 'Karen,' and holding out a hand. Jonah shook it. Karen looked as if she wanted to ask them something, but then decided against it.

A few moments later, a young dark-haired man appeared. He was something of a surprise. His name alone had made Jonah picture Italian flamboyance. Instead he had what Jonah would have described as slightly bland good looks. He was carrying a box full of brightly coloured plastic balls, his expression patient. The whole impression was of a family man.

Step looked slightly puzzled. 'Sorry, is it . . .'

'They're the police,' his wife said in a falsely cheerful voice. She glanced at Jonah, and said, 'Do you want me . . .?'

'That's absolutely up to you,' Jonah answered.

'You'd probably better stay with the kids,' Step said, and gave her a nod. His accent was totally English. Jonah guessed he was at least a second-generation immigrant of Italian parents.

'We just need a quick conversation about Alex Plaskitt,' Hanson said.

'Alex?' Step gave her a blank look. 'Why . . .' He suddenly seemed to remember himself. 'Sorry, why don't you . . .?'

He turned as if to lead them into what looked like a sitting room, and then hesitated.

'Probably quieter in the kitchen,' he said, and walked instead into a room with warm red flagstones on the floor and light-coloured farmhouse furniture everywhere else.

He settled himself at the large wooden table, putting the box of balls down carefully on the floor. While Jonah and Hanson pulled out chairs, he looked on calmly. Patiently.

'I'm very sorry to have to break the news,' Jonah said, 'but Alex was found dead in the early hours of this morning.'

There was a long moment while Step seemed to process this. And then he said, 'Oh, Jesus.' He looked away. 'How did it happen? Was he robbed?'

'It seems not,' Jonah told him. 'As yet, it's unclear what happened. We wondered if you could help by telling us about yesterday evening.'

'Sure,' Step said. 'I . . . God, it might all be my fault.' There was little emotion in his expression, but Step paused again as if working this through internally. 'I went home and left him. I knew he was a bit drunk, but I . . . maybe he was too drunk to look after himself.'

'Can you tell me where the two of you went?'

'I'm sorry,' Step said, lifting a hand towards his head and then letting it fall. 'A gig. A friend's band was playing at the Porterhouse. And then we went to Blue Underground.'

'That's a bar?'

'A club,' Step told him. 'On London Road. Further up past the Wetherspoons?'

Jonah knew London Road well, at least as it had once been. He had spent months doing circuits of the pubs up there at seventeen, eighteen, nineteen. Back when his friends had been in feverish pursuit of university girls, and had abandoned their traditional stomping ground around the quay in order to track them down. There had been clubs back then, too, each of them attempting to seduce those same university girls just as feverishly, because where the women went, the men would follow. And so the road had been awash with laminated boards from nine o'clock onwards. Two Malibu and Cokes for a quid. Two-for-one Blue Lagoons. Free entry for ladies before eleven.

That part of it probably hadn't changed, even if the prices had.

'How long were you there?' he asked Step.

'We went at about ten thirty, and I was there until . . . twelve? Maybe just before?' Step swallowed hard. 'I had to get back. It's Lisa's birthday today. We had a lot of prep to do for the party.'

'You weren't to know,' Jonah said, quietly. 'What was Alex doing when you left?'

Step lifted his head. 'He was dancing. In the – in the eighties room.'

'With anyone?'

'No.' Step shrugged. 'He generally just dances by himself. He loves it. He's a great dancer.' And then Step tailed off, halted by the inevitable clash between tenses; between someone who *is* and, quite suddenly, someone who *was*.

'He definitely wasn't talking to anyone else?'

Step thought for a while and then said, 'No. No, he was definitely on his own.'

'Had he . . . talked to anyone earlier in the evening?'

'Not at any length,' Step said, with a shrug. 'Brief chats with the bar staff, that kind of thing. Nothing that would make me think . . . that implied he might have argued with anyone.'

'There was nobody in the club who seemed to recognise him?' Hanson asked.

Step shook his head, slowly. 'No, I don't think so.'

Jonah nodded, his eyes roaming the orderly kitchen before coming to rest on Step again.

'Can you tell me what Alex was like?' Jonah asked. 'Was he patient? Boisterous?'

Step fixed him with a slightly bright-eyed gaze. 'You mean

do I think he brought it on himself?' Step shook his head. 'He was a profoundly gentle person. And a kind one. Even when he was trashed, he was always a good guy.'

'Did he get drunk a lot?' Hanson asked.

'Every so often.' Step gave a shrug. 'Like most guys in their late twenties. Probably less than most, really. He believed too much in his health.'

Jonah gave him a nod. 'How's his relationship with his husband been recently?'

'Good,' Step said. 'It's never been anything other than good. Issa and he were . . . They were close from the moment they met. They look after each other.'

'There's nobody Alex has had any disagreements with recently?' Hanson tried. 'No involvement with any groups that might have wanted him dead?'

'No,' Step said, shaking his head more quickly. 'He was likeable, and definitely law-abiding.'

'Thank you,' Jonah said. 'I'd really like to know anything else you think might help. People he might have met up with. Messages he sent. Anything.'

'Of course,' Step said, and then he leaned forwards, so that his elbows rested on his knees, and asked, 'You don't have any ideas, do you? Who it was?'

'We're doing our utmost to find out,' Jonah said, as soothingly as he could.

'OK. OK.'

During the drive home, Jonah found himself wondering about that last question of Step's. Questions like that could come from wanting a loved one's killer brought to justice. But they also might come from a fear of being found out.

*

'It's a little weird,' O'Malley muttered, as he and Jonah stood looking in at Louise Reakes from the observation room. 'I don't know if she's called him now, but when I mentioned it she looked like the thought made her ill. It made me wonder about him. Maybe he did know the guy. Maybe Alex was a friend of his. Could be nothing, but could be some kind of criminal involvement, if she's scared of him. Ben's looking him up on the system to see if there's anything.'

Jonah nodded, considering. 'I guess criminals can live in suburban bliss, too. I'll talk to her.'

'I've told her you just wanted to drop in before she goes. We've got the statement. I didn't push her.'

Jonah smiled. 'I can do the pushing. Anything else?'

'I was looking at the weather for last night,' O'Malley said. 'It's tricky to be positive, but as far as I can make out from a number of sites, it snowed somewhere between one thirty and four a.m. across most of the city. We'll probably know more if we get CCTV footage, though that won't be local to Saints Close.'

'Potentially useful,' Jonah said. 'If we could at least rule out him dying after 4 a.m., that's a start.' And then he let himself into the interview room and sat in front of Louise, who moved ever so slightly away from him.

'Thank you for giving your statement,' Jonah said. 'There are just a few things I wanted to check.'

Louise fixed her eyes on him, and nodded. 'Sure.'

'Going back, first, to this question of the victim's identity,' he began. 'It seems strange that the young man would have ended up in your front garden if he was unknown to you.'

Louise lifted her hands, a helpless gesture. 'I know. I have no idea why he'd come to us, unless it happened to be the nearest house, and he was desperate. If it were me, I suppose

I could see myself aiming for the porchlight, hoping for help.' Her lips twisted. 'Poor fucker. Bleeding out his life without . . . without anyone even knowing.'

'Someone knew,' Jonah said, quietly.

The sharp look she gave him made him reassess her. Louise might be hungover and afraid, but she wasn't in any way stupid.

'Mrs Reakes,' he said in a harder tone, 'I'm sure you're aware that we'll need to speak to your husband directly. It would save us time if you could pass on his contact details.'

There was a curious twist to Louise's face as she said, 'But I haven't – been able to get through to him yet. Do you mind if I try again before you call? Just so he doesn't lose his shit?'

Jonah nodded, slowly, finding the occasional peppering of profanities a little disconcerting. They were a strange contrast to her otherwise meek manner.

'We'd appreciate it if you'd call him as soon as we're done here. Straight afterwards.'

'Yes,' Louise said, and swallowed. 'Of course.'

Jonah watched her for a few seconds, happy to let her discomfort increase. He agreed wholeheartedly with O'Malley. Something about contacting her husband concerned her. Was it possible that he wasn't, in fact, away? That he had murdered a man at their property and then gone to ground?

'When did you last speak to him? Your husband?'

'Yesterday,' Louise said. And then, when Jonah watched her without replying, she added, 'Before April turned up. Probably . . . five?'

'Can I take your friend's full name?'

'It was just over the phone, though. My chat with Niall. Why do you want to know?'

Jonah allowed the silence to build, considering his options, and then he decided that pushing her now, while she was tired, hungover and anxious was probably his best option. 'Is your husband really away, Louise?' he asked.

She gave him a genuinely startled look. 'Of course he is. I wouldn't have got drunk with April if he . . . Niall's been in Geneva since Thursday.'

'And this was a work trip?'

'Pharmaceuticals conference,' she said. 'He's a rep. He does this a lot. Takes GPs to nice places and spoils them.' She suddenly gave a strange half-smile. 'Look, he has nothing to do with what happened.'

'Then why are you afraid of contacting him?' Jonah asked, his eyes fixed on her face.

He saw a blush creep up Louise's neck, and then she said, quietly, 'Because Niall is . . . he can be a tad self-righteous. He'll be angry with me for getting drunk. He'll think this is my fault.'

Jonah gave a small, involuntary smile. 'I think he'd be hard pressed to make a dead man in your garden your fault.'

Louise looked up at him, with that half-smile back on her lips. 'You haven't met my husband.'

6

Louise

The first night that really fucked things up for us was my birthday. Though it wasn't the night itself. It was, of course, Dina. Your gorgeous, hideous ex.

God, I hate remembering it. Dina suddenly *had* to meet you for lunch that day. And it was incredibly clear to me what she was going to say. I suspect it was to you, too. You went along hoping she wanted you back.

And of course that was what she was going to say, whether it was true or not. It was my birthday. What better time to ruin things for both of us? I can imagine how she let delicate tears slide down her cheeks as she told you she'd made a mistake. That she missed you. It was deliberate and predictable and thoroughly, thoroughly cruel.

I've never quite been able to admit to you how much I hate Dina. How could I, when you cycled so regularly through fury at her and sudden loyalty? When it was OK for you to call her a horrible human being, but absolutely out of the question for me to do the same?

That day justified every thought I'd had about her. It was abundantly clear after you'd met her that you were halfway to being hers again, and my birthday party became a hollow, bitter experience when it should have been fun.

I drank more than I've ever drunk before. I started early on, with April. I had never valued more her freedom to sack off work and drink whenever she felt like it. And although I didn't tell her why I was so determined to get shit-faced, she drank with me through the afternoon anyway, and managed to make me laugh a few times in spite of everything.

I kept going once we all met up for cocktails. While you hunkered over your phone at the bar instead of mingling with my friends, I drank. I waited for Drunk Louise – *her* – to take over so I didn't have to feel. But that happy-go-lucky, irresponsible version of myself somehow stayed away, no matter how hard I chased. It was the first time she'd let me down.

So I kept chasing her. I chased Drunk Louise so hard that I eventually vomited into the toilet for twenty minutes.

When I emerged afterwards, stumbling and probably smelling of vomit, you looked horrified. Appalled. Like you were wondering what you'd been thinking. I wasn't the wonderful, fun Drunk Louise: I was a mess. I was so ashamed, and so very much aware that April was now watching, too.

I honestly thought I'd lost both of you.

But then my best friend took my hand, and turned to face you. 'What the hell are you doing, Niall?'

You looked genuinely taken aback. '*Me?*'

'Yeah, you,' she said. 'You have a girlfriend you don't deserve. She's gorgeous and talented and smart. And on her birthday you've been standing at the bar and messaging your ex-wife. I'm not surprised she wanted to get blind drunk. I'd have done the same, only I would have dumped your lousy ass first.'

For a moment you just stood there looking at her with your mouth slightly open. And then you looked away, gathering together what I fully expected to be anger. I thought you were going to tell us both to get lost.

But when you turned back again, it was as if something had given way in you instead. You looked so guilty, and so sad. I think that expression was what saved us just then. What let us carry on.

'I'm – I'm really sorry, Lou. She's just . . .' You shook your head. 'It's all messing with my head, but I'll sort myself out.'

'You need to know something about Dina,' April added. 'You need to realise that she would throw you under a bus without even thinking about it. She's actually tried to do it already, Niall. It's me who stood in the way.'

And I saw the way your expression changed. How your mouth dropped slightly and your eyes fixed on her.

'What do you mean?' you asked.

'What the fuck do you think I mean, Niall?' she asked, with a raised eyebrow.

I watched your expression as you looked down at your phone, and then slowly put it away. And after that, when you folded me into a hug, and told me you were being an idiot, all my anger and distrust seemed unimportant. I let it all go, and let you look after me.

But the damage had already been done, I think. The slide had already started. I began to obsess over what you'd been saying to Dina and, unable to cope with those feelings, I drank. I couldn't think of any other way of dealing with them.

On top of that, my fear that you didn't really like my sober self grew. Everything you told me that you loved about me was really about Drunk Louise. The fun. The laughter. The way I made your life better. I knew it was Drunk Louise you'd fallen in love with.

So the more time we spent together, the more she bloomed. And although I'd got to know April better by then, in sober times as well as drunk, I developed a profound fear that she might decide I was boring, too. Which meant that I never turned up sober to see either of you.

I was aware, though, of a growing disconnect between Drunk Louise and me. I would occasionally be alarmed at things she'd done. Like the time she talked you into getting sexy in an office at your work Christmas party. Like when she and April stole a bottle of champagne from an unattended hotel bar in London. And there were increasing blanks in my memory, too. Whole hours or parts of evenings where I didn't know what she'd done, and felt nervous about finding out.

I thought it was all OK, though. It was only later that I began to be afraid of her.

7

Lightman was making good progress with checking up on the Reakes family. He had so far established that neither had a criminal record, and that Niall Reakes had a strong and respectable internet presence through his drug rep work. He'd worked with several of the bigger pharma companies, and was currently listed with Pollai as a clinical sales special-ist in the field of arthritis.

His LinkedIn photo was a classic black-and-white headshot, with Niall coming off as both impressive and approachable, an effect helped by his slightly chubby face and beaming grin. There was nothing to suggest any criminal involvement: no articles in which he featured, and no apparent sackings, though that didn't mean they hadn't happened. It wasn't the policy of big firms to broadcast bad hires.

Louise Reakes had her own slick-looking website. It advertised her services as a wedding, event, film and TV harpist, with an impressive list of past work. It was a hugely visual site, with slowly fading images of spring sunshine and Louise herself playing while draped in long, floaty dresses.

He'd just about finished looking the site over when a call came in on the team's line. Hanson was immersed in some-thing on-screen, headphones in and eyes following some video, so Lightman picked up and found himself talking to the duty sergeant.

'I have a caller. He says he's the dead man's husband.'

Issa Benhawy, Lightman remembered from Hanson's brief update.

'Put him through.'

There was a click, and then a very precise voice asked, 'DCI Sheens?'

'This is DS Lightman,' he said. 'I work with the DCI. He's just tied up, but perhaps I can help?'

'Oh, I see.' There was a pause, and then Issa said, 'I just wondered about Alex's things. I don't want them getting lost.'

'I understand your concern.' Lightman pulled his notebook closer and clicked his pen out. 'We do label and store everything carefully during enquiries, so everything will be kept safely and returned to you as soon as possible. Was there something in particular . . .?'

There was another pause, and Issa said, 'There's a ring that I gave him. And – and his phone.' When Lightman didn't immediately reply, he added, quickly, 'It's full of photos. I don't want them getting lost.'

'Of course,' Lightman replied, writing carefully in the notebook. 'With the phone, it's hard to say exactly when that will come back. Our tech team won't delete anything, but phones often reveal a lot about who's been in touch with the victim.'

'I can help you with that,' Issa said, immediately.

'That's very good of you, but there might be people you weren't aware of.'

There was another silence, and then Issa said, 'All right. Just . . . be careful. With the photos. And please don't pry into our messages.'

'It's never our intention to do that,' Lightman said, gently.

Once Issa was done, he wrote another sentence in his notebook.

Particularly anxious about the phone and their messages.

And then he underlined it.

Alex Plaskitt's life turned out to be quite a public one. He had more than three hundred videos uploaded to YouTube, all of them dedicated to helping people achieve a healthier lifestyle. He had twelve thousand subscribers, and clearly used the account to drum up business.

Hanson had started with the most recent video, from a week before. Alex appeared immediately, his head and shoulders visible on the camera and some kind of fitness studio setup behind him.

'You should never feel embarrassed about the level of fitness you're starting from,' he was saying, his blue eyes fixed on the camera. 'Most of my clients start out struggling to run at all, and I don't worry about it. Fitness is for everyone and it's my job to encourage and support you until you start to love it as much as I do. The trick isn't to go at it hard and feel like a failure. It's about making small gains. If that's running for a hundred metres without stopping for the first time in years, then that's a huge achievement, and I want to be there to celebrate that with you.'

Hanson continued watching and then loaded up a few more. Alex's YouTube vlogging was miles from the narcissistic fitness clips she'd seen on her Facebook and Twitter feeds. He came across as warm, supportive and one hundred per cent genuine. With his Queen's English, big blue eyes and chiselled cheekbones, he also came across as a little bit upper class. Where in other people it might have seemed obnoxious, Alex's laughing apologies for his love of good wine and his trips to Lords were endearing.

She tried not to think about the fact that he would never upload another video, and scrolled down to look at what his viewers had written on some of the latest. She half expected to see tributes to him, but knew it was too soon. News of his death had not been officially announced.

Instead there were lots of profoundly grateful comments. Viewers told him how much weight they'd lost since starting his fitness plan. Others were clearly direct clients, referencing sessions with him and recipes he'd recommended.

And then, of course, this being the internet, there were other comments, too. The kind that made the human half of Hanson burn with anger, and the cop part sit up.

After fifteen minutes of scanning the abuse, Hanson felt in need of a gin. Or at least, she thought, a coffee. She slid her headphones off, but before she could move, the chief came over for an update. Lightman dived straight in.

'We've checked for criminal records for the victim, his husband, and Louise and Niall Reakes. Nothing for any of them, and the husband seems fairly high-powered.'

'Nothing linking the Reakeses to Alex?' Sheens asked, looking between him and Hanson.

Hanson shook her head. 'They aren't Facebook friends or following each other on anything, and it doesn't look like Louise was a client of Alex's. But his online presence is actually pretty interesting.' She swung her screen round to face him square on, showing a still of Alex Plaskitt's face from one of the videos. He was caught grinning at the camera, his mouth half open as if he'd been in the middle of speaking. 'Alex is a minor vlogging celebrity. Twelve thousand subscribers, so not huge. He seems to use it in part as a way of drumming up business, and in part to inspire people to become active.'

'So he had a chance of being recognised while out,' Sheens said, thoughtfully.

'Yes, and some of these are interesting.' She scrolled down to the comments on the video, letting her mouse rest on a comment from someone called S88*burger, whose comment was five homophobic slurs in a row.

'Are there more like this?' the DCI asked.

'Quite a few. There are a few other videos that feature Issa briefly, or where he talks about him. They attract quite a bit of attention. But most of the accounts seem to be throwaways.'

The DCI's phone rang, a summons from the pathologist to attend the post mortem. There was a nervous twist to Hanson's stomach as Sheens glanced around at his team. She'd managed one post mortem in her career so far, and knew she would survive another one if necessary. But that wasn't to say that she would ever feel positive about them.

Sheens's eye eventually fell on Lightman, and Hanson slid away to make coffee with a slightly shameful sense of relief. She was safe for today, free to dig into the murky world of internet trolls.

Louise waited until the door to the interview room was shut before she opened up her contacts list. Her thumb hesitated over Niall's name. It was right at the top, with a star next to it. Her favourite. Her husband. God, she didn't want to do this.

But it was like pulling off a wax strip, she thought. It might sting at the time, but it was never as bad as you imagined.

Which was a shit analogy, she realised. Because this might

turn out to be infinitely worse than she'd imagined. The stripping away might never stop.

As she hesitated, her phone buzzed. April, sending another message of support, and obeying her request to text instead of calling.

> I can't even imagine how awful that must be. I'm so sorry! I want
> to call so let me know as soon as you're out of there, OK? I have
> the mother of all hangovers but I'm here. Xx

It was a good message to read before dealing with her husband. Unquestioningly supportive. Kind. Normal.

Niall was none of those things. At least not now. And that thought made her feel even worse.

She sighed, minimised the text, and pressed the call button. She rubbed at her right temple as the phone rang. She should have asked for paracetamol. No. Not for paracetamol. For codeine. Morphine. Something strong enough to knock her out until everything had somehow improved.

'Hey sweetie! How's it going?' Niall asked, over background noises of people talking. Presumably he was still at the conference, and she'd caught him in a gap between meetings. She almost wished she hadn't.

'Fine,' she said, automatically, and then corrected herself. 'Well . . . not really fine. There was . . . Someone was killed right outside the house. I found them this morning.'

There was a silence, and then Niall asked, 'Are you serious?'

'Yes. Sorry.' Louise gave a short laugh. 'I wish I wasn't.'

'Killed how?'

'Stabbed,' she said. 'In the stomach.'

'Who – what, a teenager?'

'A bit older, I think. He looked quite big.'

There was another silence, and she felt her heart rate speed up as he asked, 'So just . . . some stranger? Not someone you know?'

The post mortem of Alex Plaskitt was uncomplicated, but it left Jonah feeling sombre. He and Lightman had watched Shaw's initial examination of the knife, and listened to his quiet voice describing the three-inch, slightly tapered blade. He'd noted that it had a decorated metallic grip. This was not a utensil, but a weapon, and one that almost certainly had a sheath that had not yet been recovered.

'McCullough's putting us in touch with a weapons specialist she knows,' Jonah told Shaw. 'We may get something useful back from him.'

The pathologist moved on to look at the hands, which showed bruising on the knuckles, but no abrasions.

'Would you still say they were defensive wounds?' Jonah asked.

'They could be, but they could equally well have happened a little earlier in the evening,' Shaw said. 'Slight swelling and visible bruising has begun to appear, which would have taken at least some minutes. But then he would have taken some minutes to die.'

Shaw moved to look at the knife wound and surrounding tissue. Removing organs in turn, he explained the damage to the upper part of the large intestine and the splenic artery.

'The entry wound has cut the wall of the large intestine just below the stomach. However, it slid fairly neatly between the spleen and stomach above.' He lifted an elastic pinkish-grey strand. 'The damage to the splenic artery, which is what almost certainly caused his death, happened when the knife was removed.'

'You're sure?' Jonah asked.

The pathologist gave a small smile. 'I always am.'

It took Jonah a moment to get the joke: that he was always Shaw.

When he gave a small laugh, in spite of himself, the pathologist went on, 'You can see here that the back and underside of the artery has been damaged, while the upper and forward parts remain intact. The cause looks to be upward movement of the blade as it was pulled out. The rupture would have caused extensive bleeding, which would have resulted in death within fifteen or twenty minutes.'

Jonah asked quietly, 'Any indication of whether it was removed by his attacker?'

Shaw gave a slight shrug. 'It's not clear, but if you're asking whether he might have pulled it out himself, then yes, it's entirely possible. I don't know how that ties in with it being wiped, though, unless the killer deposited it there later.'

Jonah glanced at Lightman and nodded. They had both been part of investigations into knife attacks before; and both remembered a teenage boy who would probably have made it if he hadn't pulled a blade out of his chest before going to get medical help.

It was all odd and dissatisfying. If Alex had removed it, he must have done it elsewhere or there would have been more blood. If the killer had deposited it next to him, there should have been footprints. Whichever way he looked at it, the series of events was muddy and unclear.

'We could really do with some witnesses,' he said to Lightman, once Shaw had finished with the other organs and taken blood samples. 'I'm going to head over to that nightclub.'

*

Louise Reakes was allowed to go home at twelve fifteen, which felt to Hanson like at least six p.m. It looked like Louise's involvement in this enquiry was done. A quick follow-up call to the Reakeses' neighbours at number nine Saints Close had produced no suggestion of any rows or strange behaviour. Louise, they said, was generally free to do her own thing, and did so. They gave their opinion that the two would be fine if only Louise would stop drinking.

This filled Hanson with relief. The idea of having to delve into a case that involved an abusive partner had made her feel distinctly sick. It was too close to the past, and to the present, too. Too close to everything she was trying so hard not to think about.

On top of that, it felt like a dangerous topic for her own relationship. She was four months into dating Jason, and she'd never quite got round to telling him about Damian, the abusive partner she'd tried to leave behind in Birmingham.

Jonah dropped Lightman back at the station and picked up O'Malley, who had printed out photos of the victim. His Irish sergeant was generally the preferred choice for casual meetings with witnesses, assuming he was actually somewhere to be found and not off pursuing his own leads. There was a warm humour to him that both disarmed the more obstructive folk and encouraged the more helpful ones to bend over backwards.

'Are we headed to Blue Underground for some moody daytime drinking?' O'Malley asked, once he'd levered himself into the car.

'You know it?' Jonah asked, with interest.

'I met a witness there once.' O'Malley shrugged. 'It's OK. Cocktails and a pretentious DJ one floor down, and an eighties disco cheese-fest the floor below. But it's not drugged up, and there's not a lot of brawling, either.'

Jonah nodded, remembering that it was the expensive, exclusive Midnight Bar that had been closed down a few years ago after a drugs bust. The most likely clientele for party drugs were, it turned out, wealthy men and women in their forties.

Twenty minutes later, Jonah pulled into a pay and display space a few yards down from the club. The doorway to Blue Underground lay between an estate agent's on one side and an oriental food shop on the other. The sign above it spelled out the name in cursive lettering on a midnight-blue background, and almost managed to look classy.

They made their way down the stairs and turned the corner to find the entrance barred by a security door. The sound of a vacuum cleaner came from just beyond it, and Jonah rapped sharply.

The vacuum cleaner grew louder and then ceased, and a middle-aged Latino man wearing a black polo shirt and matching trousers opened the door.

'DCI Sheens,' Jonah told him. 'I spoke to Charlie earlier.'

He let them into a slightly featureless corridor and pointed them down to a bar at the far end. Bright overhead lights had turned what was presumably a dimly atmospheric night-time grotto into a slightly tatty-looking cellar. The chairs were all up on the tabletops, and there were boxes of beer standing on the bar, where a tall thirty-something man with a Mediterranean look was discussing stock with a diminutive girl in another black polo shirt.

'Would you be Charlie?' Jonah asked him.

The man turned, revealing a cheerful, tanned face marred by a bruise on his cheekbone.

'Yes. You're the police?' He moved to the end of the bar and walked round it. 'Come and have a seat. We've got coffee if you want it?'

His accent was pure Sheffield, and the chirrupy manner was encouraging. He liked their chances of getting as much help as they needed out of Charlie.

'No coffee, thanks,' Jonah said.

'Joanne, could you make me a cappuccino?'

The diminutive Joanne disappeared through an archway, and Charlie took three chairs down off a table with a 'Here.'

'We'd like a little help from you and your staff. We're looking for anyone who can remember this man,' Jonah told him, handing over a photo. 'He was here last night.'

Charlie took the photo and studied it, and O'Malley added, 'He's a big guy. Six three and quite stacked.'

'Yeah, he was definitely here,' Charlie confirmed. 'I sort of know him. He's been a few times. He had a friend with him. Also a regular.'

'Do you remember any incidents involving him?'

The sound of a coffee grinder started up beyond the archway, ridiculously loud in the brick-walled space. Charlie spoke loudly over it. 'Nothing major. He's a nice enough guy, I think. He got a bit tetchy with one of the bar staff, but that's pretty common.'

'He didn't do that?' O'Malley said, nodding towards Charlie's cheek.

'Sorry? Oh.' Charlie put a hand up to the bruise and gave a rueful laugh. 'No, that was the arsehole who didn't like being told he'd had enough to drink, and went for one of the guys before I stepped in. Fortunately doesn't happen too often, and the bouncers were on it pretty quickly.'

'Did he get kicked out?' Jonah asked, thinking that an

71

aggressive and aggrieved man hanging around outside the club could well be involved in attacking Alex.

'Your guys picked him up,' Charlie said. 'He wouldn't stop lashing out, even when a squad car got here, so he ended up getting himself arrested.'

That almost definitely put him out of the picture, Jonah thought, since anyone arrested for assault late on would probably have spent the night at the station. But he made a mental note to check last night's arrests.

'And there wasn't any brawling involving Alex at any time?' O'Malley asked.

'No, nothing like that,' Charlie said, with a laugh. 'Just some bitching about being ignored in the queue.' Joanne reappeared from the archway carrying a coffee in a tall glass. 'Jo, was it you or Mark who had the big guy being a bit of a twat to you?'

Joanne glanced up from her focus on the glass. 'Mark, I think.'

Charlie turned back to them with a shrug. 'Like I said, not major.'

'But he was quite drunk?' O'Malley pressed.

'Yeah, fairly.'

'Did you see him talking to anyone else? Particularly late in the evening?'

Charlie gave an uncertain look. 'I'm really not sure. I mean . . . I think he was chatting to a girl for a while, but I'm not . . .' He turned towards the bar, where Joanne was back to stacking shelves in the fridge. 'Do you remember him chatting to someone, Joanne? I feel like it might have been that brunette who was all over the place.'

She glanced up, and then paused to think. 'I think that might be right. In the queue, and then for a bit afterwards.'

Charlie frowned and turned to them. 'There was a girl who kept falling off her chair, or into people. She was absolutely shit-faced, and I was quite worried about her but she did take herself off home in the end. It's not . . . this isn't about her, is it?'

'We don't really know,' Jonah admitted. 'All we do know is that Alex Plaskitt ended up dead.'

'Him?' Charlie looked shocked. 'I figured this must be about something he'd *done*.'

'I'm afraid not. So if there's anything more you can remember . . .' Jonah suggested, gently.

Charlie looked at Alex's photo again, and then shook his head. 'I don't think so. But I can ask the others if he had any arguments.' He shivered. 'Fucking hell. How did he end up dead?'

'It looks like he was attacked,' O'Malley told him. 'We'll know more soon.'

'Could you give an estimate of what time he left?' Jonah added.

'Not really . . .' Charlie pulled a slightly helpless face. 'You don't really clock-watch when it's busy, and people drift around. He could have headed downstairs and been here until closing, and I probably wouldn't have seen him.'

'You mentioned CCTV on the phone . . .'

'Yeah, we've got one by the door. The data files go to my computer. I'll be heading home in an hour, so I can pick it up. It's a bit erratic, to be honest, but if there's anything at all, I'll send it over.'

'Thanks,' Jonah said. 'That would be appreciated.'

As he and O'Malley climbed into the car, his sergeant said, 'I sort of see everyone's point, about Alex not being an obvious victim.'

73

'Yes, though he could have been incapacitated by drink,' Jonah commented. 'Or –'

'Taken by surprise,' O'Malley said, nodding. 'Yeah. Which implies an attack that came from an unexpected quarter.'

'Are you thinking of the apparently shit-faced brunette?' Jonah asked him.

'They wouldn't be the first to pull off a sting,' O'Malley said. 'There was a couple I helped arrest when I was a DC who had a whole routine worked out. They'd go to a bar, she would be all over some guy, apparently very drunk, and then at some point she'd either slip his wallet out or lead him outside, where the boyfriend would act drunk and aggressive and extort money.' O'Malley shrugged. 'Could be something there.'

'Yes,' Jonah said, thoughtfully. 'An extortion gone wrong is possible. But then anything is possible at this stage.'

He just hoped that there was some working CCTV somewhere between the club and Saints Close. Something to explain how Alex Plaskitt had ended up dead in a suburban garden.

8

Louise

The fear began to kick in long before you noticed anything. At least, long before you started to question me about what Drunk Louise had got up to. Before your reaction to me changed.

We'd had eight increasingly happy months. Dina had receded into the background a little. Your work was going well, and so was mine. I'd finally succeeded in joining the Mother Pluckers after two of the members put me forwards to audition, and although a couple of others were patronising as hell towards me about not being a parent, it was generally a kind and talented bunch that I liked spending time with.

Then came the anniversary of the day you'd married Dina. Which was also the night we found out that Dina was now engaged to her new man.

I'd watched you descend into a foul mood the day before, already steeped in resurging resentment at how quickly Dina had left you. I'd started to understand, by then, that what other people thought of you was more important than you claimed. It was the real reason for the expensive clothes and the flashy car. In the way you liked to mention the specifics of the eye-wateringly pricy wine you bought.

It had taken me a while to really put my finger on it, though. I suppose the constant effort to hide my own insecurities made me blind to yours. Perhaps I'd seen you acting up a little around your posher friends. Suddenly booking tickets to the opera just before we met up with Patrick, and then talking at length about it. Insisting we had to have monkfish parcels and tuna carpaccio when he came for dinner.

But it didn't really hit home until the time you brought the wrong credit card to dinner and then couldn't pay at the end of the meal. I'd never seen you humiliated before, and I'd never have guessed that you could sink into seething self-laceration as bad as mine. My breezy statement that I was delighted to pay my way for once did nothing to lift you out of it.

I began to reinterpret what had happened with Dina, and to see it as a massive blow to your sense of self-worth. I tried to reassure myself that you felt nothing for her now. But it didn't really convince me that I was safe, and I woke up on the morning of your anniversary with the heaviest of depressions hanging over me.

Your morose silence that day did nothing to lift it. You didn't tell me about the engagement. You barely put a whole sentence together all day.

April clocked that something was up when we spoke on the phone that afternoon, and despite feeling profoundly humiliated by it all, I told her what was going on.

She responded with a frustrated sigh. 'He needs to let it go, and realise she's just a waste of space.' Being April, she then moved straight on to, 'Let's go out. You and me. Let him sit and wallow and miss you, and we'll have some fun. Forget all about it.'

It seemed like the perfect plan. Instead of sitting around and being the stressed-out girlfriend, I was going to get dressed up and have girl time. Laugh about it all, and maybe flirt harmlessly with a waiter or two.

You were happy enough for me to go. From your slumped

position at the kitchen table you managed to stir up a small smile as I kissed you goodbye.

'I'll see Drunk Louise later,' you said. Do you remember that? You found it cute, still, that whole Drunk Me, Sober Me thing.

I gave you a grin I didn't really feel. 'You'd better have water and Nutella ready.'

The night out started out all right. April was her usual hilarious self, and it made everything feel better. But then she showed me Dina's engagement announcement on Facebook, and asked me what I thought.

It was a nauseatingly perfect picture, one that had, in all probability, been filtered to within an inch of its life. Dina was cuddled up to her handsome, clean-cut new man, her left hand displayed on his chest, with a frankly ridiculous diamond on the fourth finger.

'Look at the background,' April said. 'That's Florence. They've been back almost a week. She's saved it up just for today.'

'Oh my God.' I felt, for some reason, more sickened than I had on my birthday. It felt so calculated. Evidence of such a long game, and one I was certain I would lose.

I knew, right then, that I was going to get drunk. So drunk that I had no recollection of anything, and felt nothing. Drunk Louise would handle the night from here on in.

It must have been late on when I suddenly snapped back into myself. I guess I'd had a gap in the drinking, and sobered up just enough to surface.

And it was the worst awakening. I found myself pressed up against a man I didn't recognise, with his hands moving up the back of my thighs towards my backside and his face close to mine.

77

It took me a second to retreat. And then, when he came with me instead of letting go, another few seconds to push at him.

'Hey!' I could hear him say, over the music. 'What the fuck?'

And then I was screaming at him and lashing out, my hands connecting with his upper arms and chest. I was telling him to get off. To let go. And, eventually, he did, with an angry shove that sent me reeling backwards.

For a moment I thought about hurting him. I had a crazy, off-beat idea that I could smash a glass over his head. But it ran through me in an instant and vanished, leaving me shaking.

I had no idea where I was going. It was sheer good luck that I stumbled on April, who was chatting to a couple of guys in the queue for the bar. I was so worried she would think badly of me for wanting to go home, but she responded with concern. She gathered me up and took me to get my handbag and coat, then climbed into a taxi with me. She waited, patiently, for half the ride without saying anything. By that time I'd got myself together enough to tell her what had happened.

'I must have led him on,' I told her, tears starting to work their way out. 'I must have made it happen.'

'I don't think you can assume that,' April said, gently. 'There are a lot of assholes out there. And even if you did . . . Well, I don't think anyone could blame you.' She put a hand out to my arm and rubbed it.

'But I feel like . . . like a shitty cheat.'

I regretted saying it immediately. I'd been with April while she'd kissed other men, and while her second marriage fell apart as a result. Now on to her third, and only one year in, she was just as willing to be unfaithful.

'Sorry. I'm being a twat,' I said.

'You're just being a human being who's had a rough time,' she argued. 'There's only room for one twat around here, and that's going to be me.'

I felt a little better about it all after that, but then fell back into awful guilt the moment I walked through the front door and found you half asleep on the sofa.

'Hey, Lou-Lou,' you said, sitting up and taking my hand. You drew me to sit next to you, your eyes and body drowsy. I was shaking hard now, from the alcohol withdrawal and the guilt of it all. 'Come here.'

Wrapped up in your hug, I felt even more profoundly stupid for having risked this. Us. All of it.

But it was you who apologised.

'I'm so sorry for being an idiot,' you murmured into the top of my head. 'It really, honestly isn't that I miss Dina. It's that I – I feel stupid for having ever thought she was a good person. She's just announced that she's engaged. Today. And she knows what bloody day it is. I'm sure she does. It's all designed to hurt, and I . . . I just feel like such a dickhead for falling for her.' You sighed, and I loved being able to feel the movement of your chest underneath me. There was something soft and all-encompassing in it. 'And the last thing I should have done was get grumpy with you. You're so different to her. So wonderful. I love you.'

'I love you too,' I said, and I didn't tell you that the tears that oozed out onto your shirt were nothing to do with Dina, and all to do with a man in a nightclub.

9

Hanson was trying to get a response from YouTube about two of Alex Plaskitt's most persistent trolls when Jason appeared in CID. He gave a resigned shrug that very clearly asked why they were spending their Saturdays here. She shook her head wryly in return, but found herself smiling.

Jason winked at her as he settled himself at his desk, and then gestured with his hands to make the letter T, before holding up five fingers. Hanson gave him a thumbs up. Tea in five minutes, and an opportunity to tell him about the murder enquiry, sounded good to her. He was always great to talk policing with. He loved his job as much as she did hers.

Her phone buzzed a few minutes later. The DCI messaging to say that Alex Plaskitt's sister was free to talk this afternoon. He suggested that she and Ben should head over there.

The idea made her stomach drop slightly. The address was up near Winchester, a good forty-five minutes away. She wasn't sure she felt equal to three quarters of an hour in a car with Ben Lightman just now.

She glanced across at Ben, who seemed to be very much involved with something. She'd leave it a little while, she thought. They could go after she'd had a cuppa and a chat with Jason.

She put her phone back on the desk, and found that there was an email waiting from one of the YouTube technical team. He'd come back with another email address for another part of the company, and then added that, while they might be able to help, anonymous accounts could be very difficult to trace.

Hanson sighed and briefly replied to say she was aware of that, and then thanked him for his help. She'd been to a talk just before Christmas on how digital footprints were making the detection of criminals easier and easier. She wondered when that might actually start to influence her day-to-day work for the better.

Lightman finished his phone call to the duty sergeant and typed up his findings in the database. After that, he rang the DCI back to confirm that they could rule out any involvement from the aggressive drunk at the nightclub.

'He was picked up before one and kept in until seven this morning,' Lightman confirmed.

'Thanks,' Sheens said. 'Are you and Juliette on the road to Phoebe Plaskitt's?'

He glanced over at Hanson, who gave him a thumbs up.

'About to leave, I think.'

'I'd particularly like to know what she thinks of Alex's husband,' the DCI told him. 'Any issues between them. How she thinks they were doing.'

'Sure,' Lightman agreed.

He hung up, and decided he could do with a coffee before their journey. He was about to suggest making one when Hanson rose, gave him a vague smile, and headed towards the kitchen. He glanced across at Jason Walker's empty desk, and nodded to himself. He'd wait a few minutes.

Jason was already waiting in the kitchen with two mugs of fully made tea on the counter. He was leaning against a cupboard, one arm folded over his stomach and his phone out.

It was a note of disappointment that he'd already made the tea. Hanson hadn't yet had the heart to tell him that she liked it brewed for about twice as long as he ever gave it.

'How goes?' she asked, touching his shoulder lightly.

'Not too bad.' He smiled and squeezed her hand, putting his phone back into his pocket. The two of them had their office-level displays of affection worked out precisely. It was all about brief, non-intimate touching. 'I've been looking for more of this stolen sound gear on eBay,' he went on. 'You'd be amazed how many of the exact model of amp are for sale on there.'

'I thought you'd already found all of them?' Hanson asked, picking up the slightly less anaemic of the two mugs of tea.

Jason had spent some weeks digging into a network of housebreakers. It had taken time. The group had been extremely careful, and they had sold their stolen items carefully. They'd listed them individually, through numerous different eBay and Gumtree accounts.

'I thought so too,' Jason said. 'But the audio theft at the uni and all those bikes at the sports centre weren't sold on any of the accounts we've identified.'

'Oh, that's a bugger.'

'It's OK.' Jason gave a brief shrug. 'I'll get there. Even if it means no arrests today.' He straightened up and picked up his mug of tea. 'How about you? Murder?'

'Yup.' She gulped some of the weak brew. 'Stabbing.'

'How's it going?'

'Slow so far.' She shrugged. 'Not a lot of people hanging around residential areas in the early hours of the morning.'

She suddenly found herself thinking of Damian sitting in his car outside her house, watching her through the kitchen window, and she could feel a cold sweat sweeping over her.

She tried to take another sip of tea, but the mug banged into her teeth, painfully.

'Are you OK?' Jason asked, reaching out to squeeze her arm. She glanced at him, seeing his concern. It occurred to her that she really could just tell him about all of this. Share it.

She couldn't even explain why she'd resisted telling him in the first place. She justified it to herself that it was to avoid overshadowing their relationship. Though she knew it was more complicated than that, and tied up with shame for what she'd put up with. And the more she'd put off actually telling him, the harder it had become, until it seemed like a huge thing that she was hiding from him.

She teetered on the edge of just telling him everything, but it seemed the wrong time and place. So she put the tea down, quickly, and tried to smile.

'Just a young guy,' she said, 'dying like that . . . He seemed really nice, from his YouTube account. Murders are shit, aren't they?'

Visiting a suspect. That was all Hanson needed to think about. Not about the forty-five-minute journey to Winchester with Ben Lightman. Not about the awkwardness, or her confusion over their lost friendship. And definitely, definitely not about the night before she'd started seeing Jason, when she and Ben had gone to a bar. When he'd seemed for a very intense moment like he might tell her what was going on under the unruffled facade, and then had suddenly shut her out and left.

The first five minutes of the drive went past in absolute silence. There was nobody on a par with Ben for keeping quiet. In contrast, Hanson felt an increasing sense of pressure to say something.

She sighed without meaning to, and then tried to turn it into a yawn. And then, barely a minute later and with her gaze firmly fixed out of the window, she said, 'I meant to ask about . . . your dad. Ages ago. I'm sorry for being rubbish.'

'Oh.' She thought she caught a good-natured shrug out of the corner of her eye. 'You aren't rubbish. There's not much to say. He's been in and out of hospital, and it's been a bit . . . shit. There isn't a lot anyone can do.'

'I could be a better friend,' Hanson countered, glancing at him and then away again. 'A bit more supportive.'

Lightman seemed to think for a moment, and then replied, 'It's difficult. I don't always find it easy to take offers of support. I hate thinking about my dad, so I avoid talking about it, too, and it always feels . . . awkward.'

Which wasn't entirely unlike how she felt when it came to telling Jason about Damian, she thought, surprised both at finding some point of similarity with Ben's reticence, and at his willingness to volunteer that much information about himself.

'Makes sense,' she said, and then she added, with a slight grin, 'I mean, you being awkward.'

She heard Ben's slight laugh, and it made her smile properly. It had been months since she'd made him laugh. It always felt like a victory, with Ben. And not just, she thought, because he looked like the school heart-throb she'd grown up trying to impress.

'But what about you?' he asked her. 'How are things?'

'Oh, they're all right,' she said, feeling the beginnings of heat in her cheeks. 'I'm overdue spending time with my mum, and I seem to be incapable of doing laundry at the moment. Other than that, fine.'

Ben nodded, glancing over to her and then back at the

road. She was poised for him to ask about Jason, but instead he said, 'What about the awful ex? Has he been making life difficult?'

'Oh . . .' Hanson found herself lost for anything to say. How had he known to ask that question? Hanson hadn't mentioned Damian since late last year, and she hadn't told anyone about the way her life seemed to have imploded. Not anyone.

She was still framing an answer when her phone buzzed, and she grabbed it like a lifeline.

'Just Domnall,' she said, opening her messages with a forced laugh. 'He wonders whether we'd like to get some Krispy Kremes for tomorrow on the way home.'

Ben shook his head. 'Not unless there's pizza waiting for us when we get back.'

'Yeah, good point.' Hanson took her time typing out the reply, and then, once finished, she turned away from Ben to look out of the window, as if they'd never begun a conversation about Damian. As if things were absolutely fine.

Jonah sat in one of the comfortable beige chairs in the entrance hall to the mortuary, wondering about Issa. There was grief there, and it currently took the form of denial. Six or seven times on the drive over, Issa had begun a sentence with, 'If it's not him . . .' and Jonah had struggled to find the right words in reply.

He would have been more comfortable asking him formal questions. There was a lot to ask him at a better time. It was difficult to ignore that Issa had sent at least two extremely angry messages to Alex.

Anger at one's partner was clearly not always a motivation to commit murder. Men were also murdered by their partners less often than women were, though it happened more frequently in same-sex partnerships. Added to that, Issa's messages had seemed to suggest that he hadn't known where Alex was.

But Jonah wondered whether there were more messages from Issa, and exactly what they said. Following proper procedure, he hadn't made any attempt to unlock or look at the phone itself. That was a job for the tech team. So the only messages he'd seen were the ones on the lock screen.

He'd already made a request through Detective Chief Superintendent Wilkinson for the technical team's work to be fast-tracked. The DCS had agreed that would be appropriate, and Jonah hoped they would have data about Alex's whereabouts and communications later this afternoon.

With that thought, Jonah's phone buzzed. He'd switched it to vibrate while they were in the mortuary, but he felt that he needed to be in contact with his team. When he checked the screen, it turned out to be not his team but his significant ex, Michelle.

He felt an uncomfortable squeeze in his stomach at the sight of her name. An unwelcome reminder of the last time he'd seen her, and the guilt he'd felt about it all since.

Her message was brief and apparently casual.

Hi. Would you be free for a quick call today at some point? I could use some advice.

He let out a sigh, strongly suspecting that it was an excuse to make contact again. If he had to guess, he'd say that Michelle had probably just gone through a break-up and was feeling vulnerable. She was reaching out to him because he'd shown himself to be interested, even after a year apart.

He wondered whether he should reply at all, and if so,

what the hell he should say, but before he could decide anything, his phone buzzed again with the insistent vibration of
a call.

He glanced towards the door into the rear part of the building. There was no sign of Issa returning from IDing the body,
so he made his way to the front door to take the call.

'This is Charlie,' he heard, in the nightclub owner's unmistakable Sheffield accent. 'We spoke earlier at the club? I've
looked through the footage, at the door, and your victim left
at one thirteen.'

Jonah nodded to himself. 'That's great, thank you. Is he
with anyone?'

'No,' Charlie said, 'but you know I mentioned the brunette? The really drunk one? She left just before he did. It
looks like he may have been following her.'

Jonah glanced towards the rear room of the mortuary,
where there were sounds of movement. 'Can you send me a
still of the girl? We'll need the video too, but if you could get
that straight over, I'll see if anyone recognises her.'

'Sure,' Charlie said. 'I'll do it now. Is your email . . .?'

'On the card I gave you,' Jonah said. But he told him what
it was anyway.

As he hung up, Issa was being led to one of the chairs by
the manager of the mortuary, a woman Jonah had unbelievable respect for. Issa's face was white, pinched and terrible,
and Jonah felt an awful lurch of vicarious grief.

'Take a few minutes to rest,' the manager said, as Issa sat,
heavily. He looked close to vomiting, and Jonah wondered
whether it was the physical sight of Alex that had done it, or
the sudden and complete loss of his desperate illusions. It
was no longer possible to ask if it might not be Alex; Issa had
seen his husband's body with his own eyes.

Jonah wondered, too, whether denial had been Issa's way of escaping what he had done. He wouldn't be the first killer to convince himself he hadn't hurt anyone.

'I . . .' Issa turned his head, and stood again. 'I need . . . some air.'

'Sure.' Jonah watched Issa leave by the main door, and went to fetch him water in a paper cup. As he was filling it from the cooler in the corner, an email arrived from Charlie. It had two large video attachments, which he knew his phone would take a while to download. But there was also a still, presumably of the drunk brunette.

It was clearly too soon to show Issa an image of someone Alex may have known, but Jonah was curious to look anyway. He opened it, his left hand pressing the button awkwardly and his right hand on the cup.

He came close to dropping his phone as he opened the attached image. The girl leaving the club was, unquestionably, Louise Reakes.

IO

Louise

You probably want to know why I didn't stop drinking straight away. Right after I realised there was a strange man pawing at me, and that I had no idea how it had happened.

I did actually stop, for a while. I managed a week. But it was torture. Every time you and I saw each other, I felt stilted and awkward and dull. After the third time you'd looked at me strangely and asked if I was feeling OK, I told you I'd been under the weather, and then I sank three glasses of gin.

I decided I'd have to wean myself off the sauce more slowly, and learn to behave the same way around you once I was sober. But I didn't really believe I could.

I did, at least, cut down on drinking the rest of the time. I explained to April that I couldn't get blind drunk ever again because the guy in the club had scared me. It was easier, I told her, just not to start drinking in the first place. She genuinely seemed to understand, and not to think I was boring. She told me she'd look out for me better in future, but that she respected my decision.

That didn't mean she didn't keep tempting me, though. Every time it was her round, she'd arch an eyebrow at me before paying, as if to ask if I wanted a shot in that non-alcoholic cocktail. The shameful truth was that I did. I really did. But I didn't trust myself.

It's possible that I didn't quite trust April, either. I knew

89

some of her behaviour was bad for me. The way she would sometimes arrive to meet me in what she liked to call Predator Mode, which I've never once told you about. I didn't think you'd want me to spend so much time with a serial cheat who would periodically home in on some guy while we were out and leave me to get a cab home.

But I didn't worry all that much about it. I was more responsible now. I didn't need her to stay the whole night and keep an eye on me. I wasn't drinking, and I was in control. There would be no more guys with their hands all over me.

It all seemed manageable until, three weeks after Dina got engaged, you proposed to me.

I'm not blaming you for proposing. I'm really, truly not. My first rush of unbelievable happiness on that Iceland trip, when you dropped down in front of me in the shadow of Gljúfrabúi (I had to look up how to spell that again) was one hundred per cent real. You looked beyond handsome, more so because you were clearly nervous. You cared so much that I accepted you.

And that ring you chose. God, it was wonderful, Niall. It was like you'd somehow been there every time I'd sighed over someone else's sparkles, and understood that I would want something slim enough and small enough to wear when I played. You hadn't gone for some great big, flashy stone like the one Dina was waving around, but for something I would genuinely love.

I've never told you quite how grateful I was for that, Niall. It was that, as much as anything else, that made me cry as I said yes.

That night was without doubt the most wonderful one I've ever spent. Discussing where we would hold the wedding, and what we would do with decor; who the bridesmaids would be and who you'd like as your best man. And, beyond that, talking about kids for the first time. About having the child I'd craved for more years than I'd like to admit.

You told me, that night, that I'd make a wonderful mother. That you could see me already, teaching them music and juggling my part of the childcare with work. I loved how you added that you'd take paternity leave too. That you wanted to be part of it all.

When we wandered out into the cold night and stood wrapped round each other, I felt as if everything was perfect. Everything.

It was only later that panic started to set in.

It actually started a little while after you'd dozed off half on top of me. I felt a sudden rush of sadness at not having my mum around to tell, and then I imagined how she'd react if she were still alive. And for some reason, in my head, my wonderful, deeply missed mum asked a terrible thing. She asked if you'd thought of proposing before Dina got engaged. Whether you were just doing it to make a point.

My real mum would never have been so cruel. This was purely my subconscious talking. Or perhaps it was *Her*, because I'd certainly had enough champagne that night for my drunk persona to make something of an appearance.

It only took that thought to drive me straight from contented joy to total paranoia. I started imagining that these two proposals were really just some kind of conversation between you and Dina. A dialogue that I had no part in. You were toying with each other, I thought. And her new fiancé and I were just collateral damage.

By the time I arrived back in the UK I was a wreck. I think you put a lot of it down to the overexcitement of our engagement. I was grateful that you did. There was no way I could talk to you about this. I knew you would be furious with me, and I was more than afraid that you might call the whole thing off.

All this was in my mind the night Drunk Louise did something truly terrible. Something that might still, to this day, turn out to be worse than I thought.

And I knew none of it at first. I knew only that April and I had gone out, and that I had woken up in pieces, with what must have been the worst hangover I've ever had. Worse even than that first one.

You spent the morning laughing at me and making me tea. You weren't angry, even then. You were happy with my explanation that April had bought us a lot of champagne to celebrate, that I just hadn't eaten enough to cope with it. You were cheerfully accepting of it all, until we were curled up on the sofa watching *Lawrence of Arabia*, and my phone buzzed.

I saw the message flash up on my home screen at the same time you did.

Hi Louise, it's Matt. It was so great to meet you last night. Let me know if your free to hang out later. I'd love to see you again.

However bad you felt right then, Niall, I can guarantee that I felt worse. It felt like my whole world was falling apart. I couldn't help looking at you, and I saw when your cheerful face became hard. Cold. Furious.

'What the actual fuck, Louise?'

It must have been bad, for you to swear like that. I mean, even with your slightly gendered view of the appropriateness of swearing, I've almost never heard you do it.

I was silent for a long time, and then I shook my head. 'I don't know. I don't know who that is.'

The silence was terrifying. And when you said 'Give me your phone', it didn't sound like you.

I was actually too frightened of you to argue. Even though I knew it might make everything worse.

I was shaking as you opened my messages, and something awful happened to my heart as I saw that I'd messaged this guy first, with the word 'hello'.

I watched your face, and I cringed away from you. There was nothing in your expression except rage. It twisted your face into something else, and for the first time I thought you might do something violent. Did you teeter on the edge of it, Niall? Because it looked like you wanted to put your hands round my throat. I'd like to know if I'm right.

It was words you lashed out with in the end. Asking if I was a drunken whore. Asking why the hell I'd said I wanted to marry you when I really just wanted to screw around. And on, and on, until eventually, crying so hard I could barely say it, I told you to ask April what had happened.

I was terrified when you called her, but I also desperately needed you to stop. To pause.

April reported what she'd said later on. She told you to stop being stupid, apparently. That obviously it was just some asshole taking my phone. No, of course I hadn't given any-one my number. No, I hadn't flirted with anyone. There had just been some guy who was keen on me and he had clearly crossed some lines.

I know it helped, what she said. But nothing was ever quite the same after that. Not for you, and not for me. Because April admitted to me, privately, that she had no idea whether I'd given him my number. She'd been too busy with his friend. That's something I never told you, either, and I feel like it stands against me now, a terrible judgement on my character. Or at least on *her* character. On Drunk Louise's.

That message from a strange man was the beginning of

your interrogations. My alter ego suddenly lost her charm in your eyes, and my hungover, sober self lost all your sympathy. You waited for me to overdrink, and you attacked me for it, though I tried so hard to stay the sober side of the line and almost always succeeded. I really did try, Niall. But I couldn't cope without it. I was so afraid you would see through me, and leave me. And simultaneously afraid that you'd never wanted me, and that everything was still about Dina.

And, of course, the more you criticised, or gave me the silent treatment, the more anxious I became, and the more I needed the alcohol.

I say anxious, but what I really felt was a combination of fear and profound sadness. My life started to look hopeless.

The worst part was when we talked about kids again, two weeks after that incident. You were so cool. Unemotional. You said we obviously weren't going to be ready for that for a while.

I could see in your expression that you didn't trust me to have your children any more, Niall. And it felt like you'd driven a knife into me.

The DCI's phone call came half an hour into the journey, and Hanson felt nothing but relief. She wondered whether Ben, who had driven in silence for the last twenty minutes, felt the same. There was nothing in his expression to suggest that he was uncomfortable. But then there never was.

'Chief,' Lightman said.

'It looks like Louise Reakes may not be as unconnected as we first thought,' the DCI told them in a slightly muffled voice. 'She was in the same club as Alex Plaskitt last night, and he left shortly after her.'

'Interesting,' Ben said, at the same time that Hanson said, 'Wow, OK.'

'I'll be asking O'Malley to bring her in,' the DCI went on. 'Where are you two now?'

'Still fifteen minutes from Phoebe Plaskitt's house,' Hanson said, with a sudden lift in her spirits. 'Do you want us to come back?'

'No, you carry on,' Jonah said. 'She's expecting you, and, whatever happens with Louise Reakes, I want to know more about Alex.'

'Right,' Hanson said, her brief hope shattered. 'Can do.'

The silence felt worse once the phone call was done, and, after a minute, Hanson leaned forwards and pressed the button for the radio. 'Are you OK with Radio Four?'

'Sure,' Lightman said, equably. 'Whatever you like.'

*

Louise Reakes's manner was a little defiant. She seemed genuinely outraged to be back in the station. But Jonah was certain he detected a note of panic beneath the affront.

'I don't understand why I'm here,' she said to Jonah, as soon as the tape was running. O'Malley, alongside him, was tapping on a laptop, and Louise gave him a look of irritation before she gazed back at Jonah.

'You're here because we think you lied to us,' Jonah told her.

'I've told you nothing but the truth,' she said. And yet Louise looked close to breaking. It was clear that she was hiding something from them.

'What about when you told us you didn't know the victim?'

Louise gave him a look that seemed genuinely confused. She glanced towards O'Malley, who gave her his warmest smile.

'I didn't know him,' she said, after a beat. 'There's nothing untrue in that.'

'My sergeant is going to show you a video clip taken from the entrance to a club called Blue Underground,' Jonah said. He could see the sudden step up in tension in Louise's body.

He turned towards the side wall, where the ceiling-mounted data projector shone its image. As a bright rectangle lit up across the wall, O'Malley rose and dimmed the lights.

The CCTV footage began, a moving version of what Jonah had seen once before, but just as silent. Just as grey-scaled. Just as stark.

Louise Reakes appeared, with the fixed gaze and wavering gait of the very drunk.

'This is you leaving Blue Underground at just before one

twelve a.m.,' O'Malley said, his voice still affable. It jarred with the starkness of the image.

Even in the dim light it was obvious that this had hit Louise hard.

'Oh my God, I'm . . .' She gave Jonah a slightly desperate look. 'I don't remember leaving the house. She – we must have decided to go out. I'm so sorry . . .'

Jonah looked back at the screen, and asked O'Malley to rewind it and play it again.

'I can't see any sign of April Dumont in this image.'

There was a brief silence, and then Louise said, 'No.'

'When did April go home?'

'I don't know,' Louise said, unsteadily. 'I don't remember any of it. I thought I'd stayed at home. Like I told you.'

O'Malley paused the image as Louise was about to vanish off screen, and they both waited, looking at Louise instead of the projection.

'Maybe I felt too drunk, and left,' she said. 'Or . . . I guess she could have been . . . with a guy.'

Neither Jonah nor O'Malley said anything.

'I'm sorry,' she said, looking at the screen and then back at them. She squeezed her hands together, and Jonah could see that they were shaking. 'But I really wasn't trying to hide anything. And it doesn't mean anything. I wasn't out with some gang or with the victim or anything.'

O'Malley and Jonah remained silent, but O'Malley pressed the play button.

There was a short pause, while all that showed on-screen was the bouncer shuffling closer to the desk to say something to the woman who was manning it. All they could see of the latter was the top of her head, her parting a bright, white line in her dark hair.

And then another figure appeared. Taller than the bouncer, and slightly wider across the shoulder, though he was
definitely a great deal slimmer around the waist. He slid his
feet a little, a sign of drunkenness perhaps less severe than
Louise's.

When Jonah glanced at Louise, she looked dumbstruck.
Horrified.

'What . . .?'

'This is Alex Plaskitt leaving at just after one thirteen. He
was only a minute and a half behind you.'

There was absolute silence as O'Malley let the video play
for a short while longer, and then paused it once again.

Louise eventually turned towards Jonah. 'But I didn't
know him.' She put one of her shaking hands flat out on
the table between them. 'When I saw him in – the garden,
I didn't recognise him. I can't have met him. Please believe
me.'

'But you claim not to remember major details of the night,'
O'Malley said. 'How can you be sure?'

'Because I'd surely have felt some . . . hint of recognition,'
she said, her eyes very wide.

'You didn't talk to him earlier in the evening?' O'Malley
went on.

'Please listen to me.' Louise sounded close to crying, but
she took a deep breath and went on. 'It's the world's worst
coincidence, him being there and us being there too. But I
promise you, I didn't know him.'

'So please enlighten us as to how he ended up dead in your
front garden,' Jonah said, his voice dripping with acid.

'I don't know,' Louise said, with something between frustration and earnestness. 'It's so fucking mad, and – and
horrible.' She shook her head. 'Maybe . . . maybe he followed

me for some reason. Maybe he was attacked outside the club, and he stumbled after me. I don't know if that's even possible, but I'm telling you I don't remember him at all.' She balled her hands into fists. 'April will tell you. She'll remember more.'

'You left without her,' Jonah reminded her. 'You could well have met up with Alex Plaskitt without her knowing.'

'But I'm not like that,' Louise said, loudly. She suddenly sat back, put her hands up to her head and tucked a strand of hair behind her ear on each side before folding her hands together in front of her. Jonah wasn't sure if it might be calculated, but the effect was somehow more respectable. The tucked-back hair and the folded hands. Age-old signals of self-containment. Of virtue. 'I'm a married woman, and I don't go flirting with men I don't know.'

Jonah considered this in the light of what she had said about her husband. About his ability to make everything her fault. He thought that a married woman who felt criticised might well try to flirt. And the flip side was that Niall Reakes might have had reason not to trust his wife.

Louise was holding his gaze, that earnestness still there. *Believe me*, she was saying silently. *You have to believe me.*

Jonah broke the gaze. He looked towards the wall, which still showed the last frame of the projected video.

'Detective Sergeant O'Malley is now going to show you an image. I'd like to know if you recognise this knife.'

Louise's head dropped in exasperation. But she looked at the screen, where O'Malley had put up a photo of the bloodied knife with its elaborate ornamental handle.

'No,' Louise said, firmly. 'I don't. Except from when I saw it next to . . . to Alex, on the ground.' And then she shuddered and looked away.

'It's fairly distinctive,' Jonah said.

'I can see that,' Louise said, slightly more quietly, her gaze on the table. 'And that makes me one hundred per cent certain that I'd never seen it before.' She gave a long breath out, and then lifted her chin a little. 'Look, I want to help you. I want to know who killed him. It was right – right where I live. I want them to be caught.' Her jaw trembled slightly. 'But I can't, because it wasn't me. I don't know him, and I'm sorry that I can't help.'

Jonah watched her. Read her expression, and wasn't quite sure what he was seeing there.

Phoebe Plaskitt's house, out in much snowier Winchester, was named The Dovecote. It had clearly started out as its name implied, before someone had decided to turn it into a dwelling. As a result, it had been extended in a style that was basically in keeping but which had left it looking off-centre. The cote itself was to the far right, with the front door at the other end.

The young woman who opened the door to them was probably twenty-five, Hanson thought. She was a lot shorter than Alex, and lacked his muscle. But the cheekbones, eyebrows and chin were almost identical to their victim's.

'I'm DS Lightman,' Ben said. 'And this is DC Hanson. I wonder if we could come in?'

The young woman seemed dazed, though they knew she'd been expecting them. The raw redness of the skin under her eyes looked like a sign of recent crying. Perhaps someone in Alex's family had cared about him.

Phoebe nodded slowly and backed away. She tucked her hands into the ends of her overlong cardigan sleeves as she waited for them to enter and then shut the door behind them.

'Do you need tea? Anything?'

'I'm OK, thanks,' Hanson said, and Ben shook his head too. 'We stopped off on the way.'

'Sitting room, then,' Phoebe said.

'Are your parents coping all right?' Hanson asked, as they were led along the varnished wooden floor to one end of the house. It was hopefully an easier question to answer than one about Phoebe's own grief.

'I think so,' Alex's sister said, pausing very briefly with her hand on the last door. She turned the handle and opened it, letting them into a bright room that had a view of the garden through tall windows. It was all pale colours and long, low sofas. All of it looked, Hanson thought, expensive.

There were a few photos scattered around. Hanson's eye was caught by a formal family portrait of the Plaskitt family propped up on a bookshelf. It was probably close on twenty years old. Alex was recognisable even as a boy in trousers, shirt and tie. He looked the perfect little heir. Phoebe was starchily dressed and probably somewhere between four and six.

Of particular interest to Hanson was the vision of Alex's father in what must have been his mid-thirties. He looked so very like Alex looked in his training videos, except with all the warmth taken away. He was unsmiling, and the hand resting on his wife's shoulder looked heavy.

The wife was very pretty, Hanson thought. Dark-haired and brown-eyed, with skin a lot more tanned than her husband's. Perhaps of European heritage.

Hanson dragged herself away from the photo and found a seat. Phoebe looked even smaller as she folded herself into an armchair. She must have been a good foot shorter than her brother.

Lightman began as soon as they were seated. 'We'd really like to know what Alex was like.'

'Well . . .' Phoebe's eyes moved sideways and it was clear that she was trying not to cry. 'He was . . . very kind. Very patient. Hugely into sports, but always . . . a great sportsman.'

'So not particularly competitive?' Hanson said.

'He . . . no,' Phoebe said. 'Well . . . he was fairly competitive. He wanted to be good, and he was very driven to improve himself.' Her mouth twisted slightly. 'When Alex was very young, he was a bit of a mummy's boy. At least that's what Daddy used to think. Sport became Alex's way of proving himself to him. So he's always been quite . . . fierce about it.'

'Did they end up bonding, then?' Lightman asked. 'Your father and Alex?'

Phoebe shrugged. 'I suppose so. They were quite close for a few years. But Daddy's struggled with . . . a few things.' She shrugged. 'I wish he could get over it all, but I don't think he's programmed that way.'

'With Alex's sexuality?' Lightman queried gently.

'Yes, and . . . some of the boys he's fallen for.'

'Like his husband, you mean?' Hanson asked.

Phoebe grimaced, and looked down at her sleeves. 'I think he was the last straw, really. A very unmanly Muslim. The last in a long line of people Daddy felt to be inappropriate . . . He kept asking him why he hadn't settled for any of the women he'd dated. Why he couldn't try harder to make things work with someone female.'

'So Alex had dated women, too?'

'Not for any length of time,' Phoebe replied. 'The only people he'd ever loved were men.'

'How did you feel about Issa?'

Phoebe looked slightly surprised. 'Totally different. I was relieved. Issa isn't drugged up or violent or anything.'

Lightman glanced over at Hanson, clearly as interested in this as she was. 'Alex had violent ex-boyfriends?'

'Not violent like hurting anyone,' Phoebe said, quickly. 'Not murderous. And only the one, really. Most of them were just no-hopers. But at school he fell for a troublemaker called Danny, who was – who was sweet, really, but riddled with issues. He would do destructive things because he was unhappy. He took a lot of drugs, and he sort of took Alex with him. They got into constant trouble, and Alex and Daddy really fell out.'

It was surprising, Hanson thought, that Phoebe was willing to talk so openly about all of this. Particularly with such an emotionally closed-off father.

'Has Alex been in contact with this Danny recently?' she asked.

'Oh no, Danny's – Danny died.' She looked at Hanson with an expression that seemed genuinely regretful. 'He overdosed while they were at uni. It was pretty shit for Alex. Maybe it was good for him, in the long run, but it was horrendous too.' She shook her head. 'Poor Danny.'

Hanson nodded, feeling a dip in her spirits at the closing off of this obvious line of enquiry. 'Did Alex and Danny have any mutual friends who might be on the scene?'

Phoebe thought for a moment, and then shook her head again. 'Alex pretty much started over after Danny's death. It broke him, and then he had to put himself back together. He stopped seeing that whole crowd, found a new group, and ultimately met Issa. He's been a lot healthier and happier since.' Phoebe gave a small, humourless smile. 'My parents don't know that we still see each other. Saw each other. He messaged me sometimes, too.'

'It's OK, we're not about to tell them,' Lightman said, smiling. 'Have any of his recent messages contained anything strange?'

'No,' Phoebe said, definitely, and then asked, 'Was it not – random, then? That's where all this is going, isn't it? You think someone singled him out. Someone he knew.'

'I'm afraid we have no theories as yet,' Lightman said, gently. 'We need to cover everything.'

Alex's sister took a long breath in and then breathed it out. 'OK. I don't know much. He just sent occasional updates. We last talked on the phone a couple of weeks ago . . .' There was a pause, as Alex's sister once again tried to swallow down rising tears. 'He seemed – fine. Normal. Whatever happened wasn't – I don't think he was in any weird trouble.'

'And he didn't mention meeting up with anyone new?' Hanson asked, thinking of Louise Reakes. That she had been at the nightclub, and might be hiding the fact that she knew Alex. 'A female friend?'

Phoebe focused on her. 'He's never really had female friends.' She shrugged. 'I know it flies in the face of the stereotype, but he's always been more comfortable around other men. I'm the one exception, really.' Her eyes narrowed slightly. 'When you say "friend", are you . . .? You think he was seeing someone? A woman?'

'We really don't know,' Hanson admitted. 'We're just trying to work out who the people at the club with him were, and if there were any connections.'

'Well, I don't think he was having an affair, if that's what you mean,' Phoebe said. 'He loves Issa.'

'Are you close to Issa, too?' Ben asked.

There was a brief pause, and Phoebe said, 'We're all right. We used to be closer, but then we argued. Issa wanted Alex to do less social media stuff and I told him to stop interfering.'

Hanson sat forwards slightly. Issa had completely failed to mention Alex's sister. Could this be the reason? 'He doesn't like him doing it?' she asked.

'No, not after the trolling started.' Phoebe pulled a face. 'It's been predictably awful for both of them. Alex is open about having a husband. He's put clips of Issa on there, too. Some people are totally hideous. I'm sure you know this. But anyway, Issa got to the point where he couldn't stand seeing himself and his husband abused and threatened, and he told Alex to stop. Which really upset him. It's his job, and the trolls are in the vast minority.'

'Which you thought too?' Ben asked, quietly.

'Yes,' Phoebe said. 'He – Issa – came round and tried to tell me I had to weigh in on his side. I told him I wouldn't, because it would damage Alex's business. So he got angry and read out some of the comments, and said I was heartless when I wouldn't budge. I thought he'd get over it, but he's stayed angry with me.'

'Do you think any of those trolls could have really wanted to harm your brother?' Hanson asked.

Phoebe gave her a bleak look. 'I didn't think so. And I don't really . . . I mean, it's just people with no lives. Nothing better to do. They do it online because they're too cowardly to do it for real, don't they? I read about it.'

'That's generally true,' Hanson agreed. 'But we obviously need to check every possibility.'

Phoebe looked away, her face screwing up. 'God. How much will – will he hate me, if it's – if it was one of them who killed him and I could have stopped it?'

12

Louise

It sometimes surprises me, looking back, that we ever made it to our wedding day. There was so much resentment building, and so little trust.

Though, of course, that isn't to say that there weren't good patches. After those shaky weeks where you looked at me as if I was some kind of criminal, things gradually returned to an easier state, if not to a blissful one.

There was a good month where we managed to talk more about wedding plans than suspicions. But I can remember, clearly, how hard I tried to suffocate all the rising doubts. The number of times I turned away from you with a feeling of desolation.

So many people told me how happy I looked in the weeks before our wedding. I suppose I must have done a good job of pretending. As time went on, I even started to believe the facade. At the dinner with our families the night before, when you kept putting your arm round me and kissing me, I remember clearly thinking that everything was perfect, and would be wonderful from then on.

And the day itself, which is a little hazier in my memory, seemed to be a long-awaited prize. Some kind of confirmation that you did love me and hadn't got engaged to piss your ex-wife off. I felt fierce love for you. Pride, too. You were so charming and gentle with my friends. And I think I

actually loved you still more when I saw your obvious embarrassment in your very ordinary family, and the way you'd
schemed to keep them away from your middle-class friends.
I saw it all through a haze of adoration, where every part of
you now belonged to me.

But I also remember the next day. When I asked you how
it felt, and you said you couldn't remember that much of it,
but you were glad we'd done it.

Glad we'd done it.

I remember laughing at your unromantic ways, while
inwardly I felt like I was being crushed. I knew you had a
capacity for romance. It had been clear from the little things
you'd done early on, and from your proposal. I had somehow
just stopped stirring it in you.

I was glad when the subject moved on to April and what
she'd said at the wedding reception. How she'd drawn you
to one side and said, unusually slowly, that I was the best
person she knew, and she'd kill you if you ever hurt me. I
remember the sheen of sweat on your brow as you told me
about it, even a day later. I could see it had shaken you
more than you wanted to admit. But you were angry about
it, too.

Who does she think she is, saying that to the man who loves you?

I remember feeling for you when you said that. I would
have been angry, too, I thought. But now I think not. I think
I would have assumed April just cared about her best friend.
I would probably have forgiven it.

Maybe your anger came from somewhere else. From guilt.

Those are the only really strong memories I have of our
wedding. The photos seem to be of some fantastical dream I
once had.

I sometimes wonder whether I would have gone through

with it if I'd known everything I do now. In particular, if I'd known about the money.

I'm being honest when I say that I never even suspected it. The truth only hit home three months after our wedding, during that strange, rather disappointing time when the ceremony and the party were all done, when the gifts were all opened and had been used a few times or put away, when life had returned to normal and I'd really understood that marriage was never going to make me feel secure.

I remember trying to move things on. To think about the next thing. To bring up the subject of children again. And it was only on the fourth of these occasions, a Wednesday evening when we were eating a Greek salad and flatbreads that I'd thrown together in the hope of pleasing you, that you finally seemed to grow angry.

I remember the expression on your face as you put your fork down and said, 'I don't think you're responsible enough to have a child, do you?'

I shouldn't have asked what you meant. I already knew.

'Come on. Anyone who gets blind drunk and can't remember what they've done isn't responsible.' Your voice was loud. Full of outrage. 'You lost your handbag and keys a week ago, Louise. At a nice restaurant. God knows what you're like when I'm out of the country. How would you look after a kid?'

I felt breathless with hurt. We'd got drunk *together*. You'd been just as shitfaced as I'd been. And I'd been so, so well behaved the rest of the time. With April. When I was on my own.

'But I don't do anything when you're away,' I told you, my voice tight. Choking. 'Not any more. Not after that – that horrible man . . .'

You got to your feet at that point, pushing your kitchen chair back so hard that it made a screeching sound on the lino.

'Look, I don't want to talk about this right now. OK? I'm tired. It's been a long week.'

And it had, of course. It had been like every other week. You'd been away for three days, and I'd been either performing or rehearsing around that. This was the one night we'd had together, and I suddenly felt awful for having ruined it. So I let it go. I swallowed the hurt, and I cleared up the remains of our dinner in silence.

But I didn't forget it. I dwelled on it for the next four days, until the morning I opened your bank statement instead of mine. There are probably a lot of truths discovered about spouses this way, though I imagine that some husbands or wives are clever enough to open them on purpose.

I'm happy to admit that I wasn't clever at all. I assumed that your lavish gifts and lifestyle were based on a serious salary and savings. I thought I could sit back and enjoy it. That the amount we spent on our wedding had been entirely justified given how much you earned. I really did think this, Niall. It was never wilful ignorance on my part.

And then I read that statement, with its fully used overdraft of thirty thousand, and it filled me with horror.

It pulled the rug right out from under me. You were so *together*. So *grown-up*. How could you possibly have let this happen?

But as I looked at the payments in and out, I started to have some idea. The clothes you wear so well are all designer, aren't they? And those company nights out where you lavish free drinks on everyone are costing you thousands per year. And then there's your car, which I right then discovered wasn't 'a really good deal'. I know now that it costs you nine hundred a month. It costs a mortgage, Niall. A *mortgage*. And I find it incomprehensible that a week ago you mentioned swapping it for a newer model when you are so deep in debt that it's terrifying.

The money coming in was almost as worrying. It was clear that you were taking out loans. The sums were too big and too round to be anything else. And I know what those kinds of loans cost in interest.

The more I saw, the more I started to doubt everything you'd ever told me. More than anything, I doubted that you actually liked yourself. How could anyone who felt comfortable in their skin be so desperate to have so many symbols of status? Because there was status written all over every single payment you'd made.

I went pretty quickly from being frightened of those numbers to being searingly angry. Four nights ago, you'd held up my erratic behaviour as a sign of inadequacy. As definitive proof that I couldn't cope with having a child. And while you were punishing me for that, you were busy being as irresponsible as it was possible to be.

I know you'll wonder why I said nothing. I could so easily have confronted you.

But as I sat there with that statement in front of me, and I thought about having an open conversation, I felt everything in me protest. I wasn't strong enough. Not just then. And part of me worried that you would react defensively, and tell me off for snooping. I don't know even now if that was unfair of me.

So I took that statement, envelope and all, and I hid it in a copy of Handel's *Messiah*, which I slid back onto the shelf in my music room. It was somewhere you would never look.

We were three months married, and you had already lost interest in my music. It had become, if anything, an irritation to you when I played. I'm pretty sure it was before this that you first came and shut the music-room door while I was practising, so you could continue your evening uninterrupted.

It took three glasses of wine to stop me worrying about that bank statement. And then another three to make me calm enough to be normal when you got home. To make you dinner and to listen with a smile as you told me about the rheumatologist you'd converted into a champion for your drugs. I did my job well, I think, because you came over to me as I was clearing away, and smoothed my hair back out of my face. Your eyes studied me, and you said, 'Love you, Lou,' for the first time since our honeymoon.

And then, instead of having a difficult conversation, we made love, then put crap comedy on the upstairs TV and lay next to each other. It felt like a dangerous corner that I'd managed to swing into and out of. It felt like I'd made the right decision.

Perhaps I was wrong to hide it. Perhaps you had actually been waiting for a chance to talk about it. It might have been a massive relief for you, and it would have become *our* problem instead of *yours*. You might have thanked me for forcing it out into the open, instead of telling me I shouldn't have been looking at your mail.

But I feel that your behaviour since Alex Plaskitt's death has proved all my fears justified. Don't you?

13

O'Malley agreed to take April Dumont's information over the phone. What the DCI wanted from her now was a simple account of what Louise Reakes had done the night before.

'Ask me anything you want,' she said, firmly. 'I can tell you she has no earthly thing to do with some poor guy's death.'

Anyone, O'Malley thought, who described Southern US accents as soft or lilting needed to talk to April Dumont. This Tennessee twang was all hard edges and rapid rhythms. There was nothing remotely lilting about it.

'What makes you say that? Has Louise told you she feels under suspicion?'

'She messaged to say you'd dragged her into the station again,' April said. 'So I guess there's something going on.'

'Not so much that,' O'Malley said in a soothing tone. 'We just need to check things. That's all. Due diligence and all that. Could you tell me if you'd arranged to meet someone at the club?'

'No, we didn't,' she said. There was a momentary pause and a murmur. O'Malley caught the words 'whisky sour', and realised she must be in a bar somewhere. 'That's never what we do. It's always just the two of us. And Louise wasn't even that keen at first. I insisted we had to go out. I thought she needed cheering up, and, to be honest, I did, too.'

'Why would Louise need cheering up?'

'Because her life's been increasingly depressing.' April made another impatient sound. 'Look, I don't want . . . This is Louise's business. But . . . it's hard when you want kids and don't seem to be making any progress with having them. OK?'

'Sure, OK,' O'Malley answered. 'And I know it seems intrusive, but all this stuff is useful so we can stop looking at someone who wasn't involved.'

'I guess I get that,' April said, sounding a little less combative.

'Louise's husband was away, so you felt free to go out? Is that right?'

'Darn right. Niall's not too fond of his wife drinking anything these days.' April gave a short laugh. 'And he thinks I'm a bad influence, too.'

'So he'd be angry with her if he knew?'

'He'd be preachy,' April corrected. 'And that's enough of a pain in the ass. Look, I've got about ten minutes before a meeting and I thought you wanted to know about last night.'

'That's fine,' O'Malley said, easily. 'Can you tell me when you arrived at the club?'

'I guess . . . eleven thirty or something?'

'And you were with Louise the whole time?'

'Well, I went to the bar and the ladies a few times,' April said. 'And then I – sorta hit it off with this guy . . .'

'And you didn't see Louise talking to a young man?' O'Malley asked. 'He was tall and obviously athletic. He probably would have stood out.'

'No, I didn't,' April insisted. 'I didn't see her talking to anyone except the bar staff all evening.'

'And while you were with this fella . . .'

'Louise went to get drinks.'

'And then?'

'And then I guess . . . I'm not sure after that,' April

admitted. 'She would have queued a while. You always do somewhere that serves cocktails.'

'When was the last time you saw her?'

'On her way over there. So I guess . . . before midnight.'

O'Malley paused slightly. 'So you left with this . . . guy? You didn't say goodbye to Louise?'

'I know I should have,' April said, with a touch of defensiveness, 'but I was rolling drunk by that time. And sometimes you don't make great decisions in those circumstances.'

O'Malley waited a moment, certain that April would feel compelled to say more. He wasn't disappointed.

'Look. Whatever Louise did after that, she didn't end up killing some guy,' she said, sounding frustrated. 'She's this warm, loving, kind person. I felt bad this morning because I worried something could have happened to her, understand? I would never in a million years worry she'd hurt someone else. So you need to send Louise home so she can sleep and recover. She probably feels like a heap of shit right now, and she should be in bed, not being grilled by some drama-hungry cops.'

'I'm sure she'll be heading home soon,' O'Malley said, not too concerned whether or not this was true.

'You'd better listen to me and let her go home,' April said, with a little steel, 'or I'm going to come down there myself.'

'We'll bear that in mind,' O'Malley told her.

Jonah tried to fill some time while waiting for his team to update him. As much as he valued the space to think during investigations, there were too many gaps in his knowledge to get to grips with it all, and the two other cases on their books from the week before were at similar stages, without the sense of urgency of a murder.

He decided to look at some of the earlier video footage sent over by Charlie as a starting point. It was all filmed from the same spot close to the door, and caught everyone entering and exiting. It was largely uninteresting, except for a brief brawl at eleven fifty. Then, at twelve ten, Step Conti appeared. He was markedly more sober than anyone except the staff. Jonah noted the time down and switched the video off a few minutes later.

At three he decided to chase up the technical team about Alex's phone. He suspected that they would now be waiting another day. Getting the civilian parts of the force to come in on days off and work swiftly was a constant challenge. Only Janet McCullough would generally show willing, thanks to her obsessive attitude towards her work.

'We're nearly done,' a begrudging Intelligence officer told him. 'I'll send it to you as soon as it's ready.'

Jonah hung up with a rare feeling of satisfaction. DCS Wilkinson must have done a good job of leaning on them.

He spent a few minutes writing up his notes on Louise's interview, and headed back out to CID. Lightman was back at his desk, and Hanson was making her way back over with Jason Walker, who had presumably met up with her outside rather than going along for the ride.

Jonah arrived at Lightman's desk at the same time Hanson did, and watched in some amusement as Jason melted away, and Hanson blushed very slightly.

'How was the sister?' he asked them both.

'She had a few things to say,' Lightman said, thoughtfully. 'She's not on great terms with the victim's husband because Issa apparently wanted Alex to stop doing his fitness videos. He disliked the trolling. Phoebe Plaskitt refused to take Issa's side.'

'She described her brother much as Step Conti did,' Hanson added. 'Alex was a patient, protective person who generally defused fights rather than getting into them.'

Jonah nodded again, digesting this, and then asked O'Malley for an update on April Dumont.

'Everything matched what Louise Reakes said most recently,' O'Malley told him. 'April copped off with a guy she'd met there. She then left with him, at around midnight. She's positive she didn't see Louise talking to anyone who looked like Alex Plaskitt. She's also pretty keen that we let Louise go immediately. A concerned, mildly threatening friend.'

'Well,' Jonah said, getting to his feet, 'she gets what she wants. Louise is going to have to be released while we work out if we want to arrest her.'

'I'll drive her home,' Hanson said, swinging her chair round. 'She's tired and hungover, and it's possible she might say something she shouldn't.'

'Good,' Jonah said. 'Was there any update on CCTV on London Road?'

'Sod all,' O'Malley said. 'I'll ring them again.'

'Thanks,' Jonah said. 'I'd like to chase the traffic cameras up, too.'

He collected Louise from the interview room, glancing at her sweat-sheened face. She'd put her coat on now, and the white fur lining made her look both younger and even more off-colour. But she'd been out drinking last night, so there wasn't necessarily anything suspicious in looking nauseous. He'd been there himself on other occasions.

'Detective Constable Hanson has offered to give you a lift home,' he said, once they were close to his team.

Louise faltered. 'Oh. That's OK. I can get a cab.'

Hanson grinned at her. 'It's no problem. I want to grab a sandwich, anyway.'

Louise's expression was clearly unenthusiastic, but she let Hanson walk her out. Jonah, watching Hanson's very slight smile, felt almost guilty for handing Louise over to her. Almost.

'I'm so sorry about this,' Hanson said quietly, once they were out of CID. Up close Louise looked, if anything, worse than she had from a distance. There was a heavy look to her eyes that spoke of barely being able to keep awake and she was gleaming with perspiration. 'I know it's not much consolation, but it's just the DCI doing his job.'

Louise gave her a doubtful look. She said nothing.

'I've got some ibuprofen and co-codamol,' Hanson tried, once they'd climbed into the ice-cold Nissan. 'Would you like some . . .?'

'God, I'd love some,' Louise said, with sudden feeling. Hanson grinned and rifled through her handbag until she'd found them. Louise held out a hand and let Hanson squeeze four tablets onto it, two sugar-coated and two chalky. 'Oh, do you have any water . . .?'

Hanson reached round to the back seat and retrieved a half-full bottle of Evian.

'It's only from yesterday,' she said, 'and I promise I don't have the plague.'

Louise seemed unconcerned by the idea of germs. She tipped all four tablets into her mouth and then drank all of the remaining water as she swallowed them down.

'Such awful timing, having to deal with this on a hangover,' Hanson commented, as she started the ignition and began manoeuvring the little car. The steering wheel was painfully cold. She wished the heating worked better. If she turned it on now, it would blow cold air at them and then never really get hot. The only answer was to leave it for a good ten minutes with the engine running and then put it on full blast.

'It's horrible,' Louise agreed in a low voice, and then added in a rush, 'I don't know where the hangover ends and the shock starts. I wish he'd, you know . . . gone somewhere else.'

'I'm sorry,' Hanson said. 'It must feel completely unreal, him turning up like that with no warning.'

Louise nodded, but said nothing else. A short while later, she made a sniffing sound, and when Hanson looked over at her, there were tears tracking down her cheeks.

Saints Close was back to its quiet state, free of ambulances, squad cars and forensic vehicles. In fact, it was quieter than it had been before the flashing blues had arrived. Many of the other cars were now missing. Louise's neighbours had presumably gone to spend their Saturday afternoons in pilgrimages to the shops or kids' sports clubs.

Hanson pulled up outside number eleven. There was little to show what had happened here aside from the craze of footprints and trampled snow left by so many crime scene investigators.

'Thanks for the lift,' Louise said, and started to lever herself out of the car hurriedly. As she stood, her eyes went to her front gate, and she faltered.

Hanson could well guess what she was imagining. The dead man lying on the grass. Perhaps the screens that had been set up, and the white overalls moving around it all.

Hanson undid her seat belt. 'I'll walk to the door with you. It can't be easy, after . . .' She gave a shrug.

Louise paused for a moment, and then said, 'Thank you.'

Hanson climbed out onto the pavement. She let Louise through the gate first, and then, as she followed, moved to block any view of where Alex Plaskitt had been lying a few short hours ago.

Louise kept her gaze fixed ahead, and unlocked the front door hurriedly. As she pulled the keys back out, she fumbled them and dropped them onto the doorstep with a noisy jangle.

'Do you need anything?' Hanson asked, as she picked them up and moved to step into the house. 'Tea? Company?'

'I'm . . . I'm fine,' Louise said, her face pallid and sick-looking. And then she suddenly lunged forwards, dropping her bag and running for the stairs.

Hanson heard her climb to the first floor and trip. She instinctively stepped forwards to help, but Louise seemed to have recovered and rushed further into the house. 'Louise?' she called.

The sounds of Louise vomiting were loud enough that Hanson could hear them from the foot of the stairs. Hanson hesitated for a moment, and then went to the kitchen and pulled open the cupboards until she'd found a pint glass. She ran the tap cold, filled it, and then quietly moved upstairs.

There were still isolated noises of retching going on, but it sounded as though there was little coming up now. Hanson followed the sounds into a large double bedroom at the front of the house, where she had a view through into an en suite. She could just see Louise's feet, soft and grey in her boots where they rested on the tiles. She was clearly kneeling over the toilet.

The human side of Hanson was both sympathetic and hesitant. She wasn't entirely sure Louise would want a police officer intruding while she was being ill, but she wanted to offer help in case it was needed.

And then there was the copper in her, which was alert to everything else. It was taking in the details of how Louise lived, from the perfectly made-up bed to the spotless surfaces. From the severe Scandinavian colours to the obvious high quality of everything she was looking at.

It was the copper in her that picked up on the one small imperfection. The tiniest spot of dark red on a pale grey carpet, just under the edge of the large double bed.

Hanson paused momentarily between one step and the next. Her mind went through the options. It might be nail varnish. Coffee. Some flaw in the carpet.

But Hanson had learned enough of Louise to doubt it. She was clearly obsessive about tidiness and order, and it seemed impossible that she would have let a mark spoil that carpet.

Hanson could see more of Louise now. She was facing almost entirely away from Hanson, slumped on her arms, which were folded across the toilet seat. The picture of misery.

Hanson was only too happy to use that misery to her advantage. She moved over to the bed, and then crouched. Close up, the spot on the carpet was rusty red, and Hanson felt a shiver run through her. It looked very much like dried blood.

She ran her eyes along the bottom edge of the bed, which was a pale grey velvet. And then, glancing towards the bathroom again, she put a hand out to a point just above the stain on the carpet and lifted the very edge of the sheet.

It took one glance to tell her everything she needed to know, and she felt dizzy as she tucked it in again and got back to her feet.

She took another two steps towards the bathroom, and Louise turned, her eyes bloodshot and her expression stricken.

'Have some of this,' Hanson said, gently, and handed her the water.

She stayed with Louise for ten more minutes, helping her to her feet and back down to the kitchen, where she made her another cup of tea without milk and talked cheerfully about how much better Louise would feel after a nap on the sofa.

And then she climbed back into the car and called the chief as she manoeuvred back onto the main road.

'We need a search warrant,' she told him. 'As quickly as you can.'

14

Louise

There are a few events that I look back on now and see as turning points for us. The crossroads that sent us down this crappy path. There was a darkness to realising how much money you owed, and how easily you had lied to me. It made me more willing to believe that you'd lied about other things, too. But it wasn't what did for us. There were still signs of hope afterwards.

One of those was your reaction the first time I slipped up and got really drunk again with April. I hadn't meant for it to happen, but I'd had a mortifying experience at rehearsals with the Mother Pluckers. Helen, whose smiling viciousness I'd already experienced in the past, had asked me why I looked so tired.

'You aren't pregnant at last, are you?' she'd said in a low voice, while we were getting set up.

'No,' I told her, blushing. 'No. I'm pretty sure not. We've not had any accidents . . .'

I saw the way her eyes narrowed. The next bit was said much more loudly. 'But I thought you said you were trying? Has something changed? Niall got cold feet?'

It was clear that the others had all heard. Their conversations tailed off into silence.

I've never felt so mortified. I had no reply, because that *was* what had happened. I could feel myself going scarlet until kind-hearted Lyn joked that Niall was sensible. That she'd just spent a morning with a vomiting toddler and wouldn't wish it on anyone.

Things then moved on, but for the whole rehearsal I felt their gazes on me. The one non-mother of the group, who perhaps had only been allowed in because they all thought I'd have kids soon.

I pretty much launched myself at the wine when April and I met up. She soothed me and told me they were all pathetic, but none of it helped. The only thing that made me feel all right was sitting back and letting Drunk Louise take over until late, late into the night.

I remember how you looked at me the following morning, with none of the anger I was expecting. You seemed concerned for me. Caring.

'Do you think you should go and see someone?' you asked, having come to sit on the bed next to me.

It knocked me back, that suggestion. Even then, I didn't really think of alcohol as a problem. If anything, it seemed like a solution I was no longer allowed to take.

I shuffled up in the bed until I was sitting, trying to turn this into a conversation between equals.

'I hardly drink at all now,' I told you. And it was true. Even when I was with you, I'd cut down. I wanted so badly to prove to you that I had everything under control. That I could be a fantastic mother. 'I go days and days. I drink less than you most of the time, too. I'm really all right. I just didn't eat enough last night, that's all.'

I saw your reaction. Your expression changed, to something between exasperation and desolation. You nodded and gave a strange half-smile. Then you rubbed my shoulder and got up. It looked like I'd damaged you somehow, and thinking of the hurt I might be inflicting did more to wake me up than anything else.

I went out a few days later. It was the Sunday afternoon after the big concert, when the Pluckers had agreed to meet for lunch. I'd promised myself that I'd only have a couple of glasses. But somewhere along the line, beaten down by more snide remarks from Helen, I'd had a few more, and let Drunk Louise take the reins again. I have a hazy memory of being hilarious, and of the nicer Pluckers telling me how great I was.

But then I remember it being six p.m., and it being me, the other Louise, who was at the helm. I remember that my hand was firmly round a glass of Pinot Noir, and I had no idea how it had happened. It was like I'd been pinched awake again.

It was your heartbroken expression that I thought of just then, Niall. I suddenly saw the wine as the cause of it, and I put it down. I took a breath, and then I went to the bar for water and a few packets of crisps.

For three hours I drank nothing but water and juice. I ordered myself a plate of pasta, and I sat and waited for sobriety to return. I felt strangely proud of myself. And determined to turn this all round.

At nine I smiled at all of them and said I was going home for crap TV and cuddles with my husband. I left imagining you telling me how well I'd done. I ached to hear you say it.

I let myself in at nine fifteen, and felt an immediate dip as I realised that the house was empty. I was pretty sure you'd said you were at home, and it puzzled me. But then I doubted myself and sent you a message. I asked you what you were up to. That was all.

I got myself another glass of water and put my coat and

handbag away, and while I was doing that you messaged back cheerfully to say you were on the sofa watching *Game of Thrones* and accidentally falling asleep.

And, you know, I think that was the first time I'd ever known you to outright lie to me. I mean, there was the money thing, it was true, but you'd never actually told me that you were solvent. You'd just let me assume. And you hadn't hidden what Dina had said to you, either, even if you hadn't been quite open about how you felt.

But now here you were, telling me a stark untruth. And, in this case, I was certain it was for a really, really bad reason.

I desperately wanted to know where you were, but I had no way of knowing without alerting you to the fact that I was home. And for some reason that was the scariest thing of all.

So I did a crazy thing instead. I went back out there, in another rip-off cab ride, and I started stalking your favourite bars and restaurants. At first I told myself I'd just check a couple. I figured you might be at La Mejican or the Pitcher and Piano. When you weren't there, I thought of a few more. And a few more.

I was out there for three hours, and when I finally gave up because the blisters on my heels were too bad for me to walk any further, it was after midnight. You still hadn't messaged me to tell me you were going to bed. You'd only sent a query at eleven, asking if I was still having fun, which I replied to with a thumbs up, because I had to reply somehow.

I was so sure you were still out there by the time I gave up. I was certain you were meeting up with someone. Cheating on me. I cried all the way home in the cab.

The house was still empty when I got in, and I couldn't face being in the sitting room or in bed when you returned.

I just couldn't. So I went to the music room and huddled on the sofa in the dark.

You actually didn't get back that long after I did. An hour at most. But it felt like years had passed. I'd been unable to sit still.

I heard you arrive home, then make yourself tea before you went up to bed. I had all my things with me, so there was no reason for you to know I was there. I listened, hardly breathing, to the sounds of running water. You showered for a long while. Were you washing off traces of whichever woman you'd been with, Niall? Is that what you were doing?

I stayed where I was that night, unable to face curling up next to you. So when you woke me, you thought I'd stumbled in and slept right there on the music-room sofa.

The fact that you were angry with me about it was the unfairest part. You gave me a cold look when you woke me and asked if I wanted breakfast, as if I'd been the one who'd done wrong.

God, I wanted to throw it in your face. But I was too scared to find out that we were over. Isn't that pathetic?

So I said nothing when you got at me. I didn't apologise. I didn't argue. I ate the breakfast you gave me and said nothing at all, and I think something in that eventually got to you, didn't it? Because after I'd gone to shower and got myself dressed and told you I was going out, you suddenly turned to me and wrapped me in a hug and apologised. You said that you loved me and it was concern that made you act like an arsehole sometimes.

Later on, you saw the blisters on my heels and bandaged them up. You kissed me gently and told me you'd fix me up somehow.

I guess you remember that bit, and how we had two weeks after that which felt like the old us. Two weeks where we were fine. Happy. The best of friends who told each other everything (except not quite everything).

But it was all false. I was sure that your good behaviour was nothing but guilt. I wanted desperately to look at your communications but was too frightened, and so, as a coping strategy, I became increasingly obsessed with tidiness and order. I would sometimes catch you watching me clean, an expression on your face like you wondered what on earth you were doing with me.

And, as the two of us fell apart, the other me returned, too. It was just one night at first. A single night off while I let myself enjoy Drunk Louise taking over.

But the thing I've now learned about her is that it's never just one night. Once Drunk Louise has me again, she doesn't like to let go.

Damian punched the steering wheel again, letting fury seep into him. Revelling in the rage.

Everything about his relationship with Juliette had made him feel worse about himself. He could see that now. That was why he'd needed to spend so much to feel better. And it was why he'd been messaging other women.

Juliette was poison. That was what it came down to. Her apparent sympathy for him had quickly been revealed as cold judgement. Every decision he'd made had been resisted, bloody-mindedly. And she'd belittled him in public, too, by flirting with other men.

The trouble with that kind of poison was that it was addictive. It wasn't his fault he'd been unable to get her out of his system. Two girlfriends had already walked out on him for still trying to contact her, and earlier today a girl he'd only been on three dates with had told him she didn't feel comfortable about his attitude to his ex.

He'd told her to go fuck herself and climbed into the car. It was inevitable that he'd ended up driving towards South-ampton and that bitch Juliette.

He'd made the trip several times recently. He'd been try-ing to work out whether Juliette was shagging someone. She'd changed phones, so he could no longer check her messages using the apps he'd installed on the old one. He had to be there in person to find out.

She'd definitely stayed away overnight multiple times in

the last few months. His immediate assumption had been that she'd got together with the perfume-model cop she worked with. But having followed him home, he'd seen no sign of Juliette visiting.

It was only today that he'd put everything together and realised that the moody-looking bloke she'd sometimes walked to the pub with was now her boyfriend. It had sent a strange, sick electricity through him watching her turn to give him a peck on the lips in the station car park.

God, she was a bitch. She'd clearly never cared about him at all.

What she needed to learn was that she couldn't do whatever she felt like and get away with it. He was going to get even.

And the thought made him smile.

Louise Reakes's arrest ended up being quite a public event. The forensic team arrived at a little after five thirty, just as the sun was setting. Numerous families were at home, and others were able to gawp on their way out for the evening. Jonah had been aware of at least ten people stopping to watch as the squad car and scientific support van had pulled up behind him.

It had taken an hour and twenty-five minutes to procure a warrant for the search of the house. Which was, in fact, terrifically fast, while also feeling infuriatingly slow.

He was profoundly grateful that Hanson had acted so carefully. She must have been tempted to arrest Louise Reakes. She could have used it as a justification for searching the house immediately. The power to search on arrest was a grey area that had certainly been exploited that way in the past. But whole cases had sometimes collapsed in the courts as a result. A good barrister could argue that such searches had not been carried out legally, and some judges were inclined to agree.

Hanson had played it perfectly, however. She'd requested the search, and been calm and collected giving her evidence to the magistrate via video link. She hadn't even mentioned the blood. Instead she had explained that Louise had previously lied about her whereabouts that night. She had then expressed concern over Louise's reaction on arriving back at the house. Vomiting, she felt, was likely to have been the result of guilt or anxiety.

The magistrate had agreed.

Hanson had asked to be there while the search took place, and Jonah had been more than happy to bring her along. If they ended up making an arrest, he wanted Hanson to have the satisfaction of doing it.

It was hard not to feel a little sorry for Louise as they converged on her front door, however. Her neighbours were unlikely to forget this particular scene. Though at least the front of the house was fairly well screened. Louise herself wouldn't be on full display.

Jonah knocked loudly, reverting to the loud rapping they'd been taught when he'd first become a constable. Knocking that was too loud to ignore. Too loud for 'I didn't hear you'. The kind of knock used only by policemen or bailiffs.

Louise's eyes were very wide as she opened the door. She said nothing as Jonah showed her the warrant and told her that they had the right to search the property. She did no more than nod, and then move slowly aside.

Janet McCullough had already been primed to search the bedroom. She left three of her overall-covered team downstairs and headed upwards with just one of them. Jonah gestured for Hanson to follow them, while he prowled around downstairs. Louise retreated to the far end of the house, and Jonah left her to it for now.

What was to follow was both thorough forensic work and a little play-acting. They had to let a reasonable amount of time pass for it to look like the blood had been discovered organically. So Jonah drifted in and out of rooms, asking the three forensic staff to look at a few things. A faint mark on the wall next to the stairs. The laundry hanging out on a rack in the tiny utility room.

McCullough left it fifteen minutes before she called him upstairs. Jonah was in the music room at that point, where Louise was sitting with her legs pulled up on a futon. In that position she was largely hidden behind her harp, but he could still see the side of her face through the strings.

It was clear from her expression that she knew what McCullough had found. Her legs moved instinctively, as if she were about to get up, before she froze in the act and tried to sit back naturally.

Jonah left her there. He climbed the stairs and entered Louise and Niall's bedroom. McCullough and her assistant had stripped the sheets back from the bed, exposing a tide mark of brownish red. Hanson was standing to one side, a satisfied expression on her face.

Despite having been prepared for this, Jonah found himself a little nauseated at the extent of the blood. It had soaked through most of the mattress. The only white details remaining were the little plastic buttons dented into its top.

'I'm confident we'll be able to get DNA,' McCullough said. 'The underneath hasn't entirely dried yet.'

'Good,' Jonah said. 'And quantity . . . You'd say it looks enough for him to have died here?'

'I'll get you a volumetric estimate,' McCullough said, 'but on a visual reckoning it looks more than enough.'

Jonah gave her a small smile. McCullough was renowned for being difficult to pin down. She hated committing herself to theories, and tended to offer stark fact with no interpretation. For her to give him that much meant she had no doubt at all.

Hanson went back downstairs with him. He let her walk into the music room first. Louise's expression looked hopeless. Her fear was stark and obvious even viewed through the strings of her harp.

'Louise Reakes, I'm arresting you for the murder of Alex Plaskitt, and for perverting the course of justice,' Hanson began.

'I'm sorry for lying,' Louise said, before she could go on. 'I'm really sorry.'

'Did she say anything else?' Lightman asked an hour later. His eyes were on the pale, sick-looking face of Louise Reakes.

He, Jonah and Hanson had gathered briefly in the observation room. Louise's solicitor was on his way over. Jonah had gone into the interview room to tell her, but Louise had said nothing. Done nothing. He wondered whether she had really understood him.

'Not a word,' Hanson murmured. 'We both tried asking her why she'd lied, but we only got head shakes.'

'Any news on the husband?' Jonah asked.

'No reply from his mobile,' Lightman told him. 'Presumably in flight.'

Jonah nodded. He didn't go on to say anything more yet. About the significance of the blood being in Louise and Niall Reakes's marital bed. About the fact that Alex Plaskitt had been married to a man and yet had almost certainly died in bed with a woman. There were too many questions that needed answering, and no way of making sense of any of it without making a lot of strange assumptions.

'Juliette, I want you and Domnall to go and see April Dumont. And we should talk to Alex's husband again as soon as we can. It's high time we found out whether Alex and Louise actually knew each other before that night, and I doubt Louise will tell us.'

The pressure was now on to pin this thing down, and soon. They might only have twenty-four hours to charge Louise Reakes with murder. But Jonah had already applied to the superintendent for an extension to the standard twenty-four-hour limit. He was asking for an initial thirty-six hours, but fully intended to apply to the magistrates' court for the maximum after that, which was ninety-six. Given the seriousness of the crime, with the added charge of perverting the course of justice, it was highly likely they'd be granted their request.

If, in the next ninety-six hours, they could prove that the blood on the bed was Alex's – which was the only reasonable explanation – then they would almost certainly have passed the threshold for Louise to be prosecuted. They could charge her knowing that the prosecutor would be happy to work with them to obtain further proof. Which was satisfying, but it wasn't enough.

As far as Jonah was concerned, within those ninety-six hours they needed to know whether she really had killed him and why. Because although the circumstances and her actions pointed that way, there were an awful lot of unanswered questions.

*

'I've got something for you,' Lightman said, quietly, a few minutes after he and Hanson had returned to their desks.

Hanson looked at him in surprise as he smiled at her. Was this banter? With the exception of their car journey, Ben hadn't offered anything like that in months.

Recovering, she asked, mock-seriously, 'Is it a cake? Please let it be a cake.'

Ben smiled more widely, and shook his head. 'Sadly not. But it is great.' He leaned across the desk. 'As well as being a solo harpist, Louise Reakes is a member of a harp ensemble. They're called, get this, the Mother Pluckers.'

Hanson gave a delighted laugh, in part at the name and in part because he really was bantering again. 'All right, that is genuinely almost as good as cake. Are they all mums or something?'

'Looks like it,' he agreed. 'There are loads of cheerful and not-at-all-posed pictures of them with their children. Louise seems to be the odd one out.'

'I have to look at this,' Hanson said, and was in the process of typing it into Google when the DCI emerged.

'Louise Reakes's solicitor's just arrived downstairs,' Sheens told them. 'I'll give them a quarter of an hour to get their ducks in a row and then we can head in, Ben.'

Hanson watched him return to his office, still a little disappointed at missing out on Louise's grilling. Not that she didn't have plenty to be getting on with. She needed to put together a new social media post asking for information on Louise Reakes, and ask her colleagues in Intelligence to circulate it to the public in case someone had seen her on her way home. It would also be up to her, as the team's constable, to appear in front of the magistrates tomorrow to ask for their custody extension. But before doing any of that, she finished loading up the Mother Pluckers' website. She shook her head as she flicked through their pictures.

'Oh my God, look at this one,' she said, turning her screen so that Ben could see. It was an aggressively arty black-and-white image of the group posing in leather jackets. 'It looks like a poorly thought-through eighties album cover. I love it.'

Ben nodded. 'Fo sho, motherplucker.'

Hanson laughed so loudly that Jason looked over from the far side of CID with a frown. She mouthed at him, 'I'll tell you later,' a little guiltily, and then, still grinning, started to get their case against Louise Reakes moving.

Patrick arrived a little over an hour after Louise had called him, and her feelings as the dashing, ever so slightly chubby solicitor was let into the interview room were entirely mixed. Relief made up a big part. She had someone to fight her corner now. But on top of all that, she felt a nauseous, squirming sense of shame. Patrick was the last person she wanted to be going into all this with. She wished, helplessly, that he could have been simply her lawyer, and not Niall's best friend.

Patrick's smile was warm and confident, and she tried to return it. She wondered how he would look at her once she'd explained everything. Once he knew.

He settled himself into a chair opposite her, and placed his dark brown leather case, which looked like it cost about the same as Niall's car, on top of the table. Then he drew out a notebook and a silver fountain pen, as though they were his weapons.

'How are you holding up?' he asked her, all brown-eyed charm.

'All right,' she said. And then she added, wanting to make

sure he really did like her before the shit hit the fan, 'Better now that you're here.'

'Good. Good. I've managed to get through to Niall. He's just landed. He won't be long.'

It was supposed to be comforting, Louise knew. Instead the threat of Niall arriving drove her anxiety up to a critical level. She'd thought she'd have more time.

Patrick unscrewed the lid of his fountain pen. 'So. Tell me.'

'OK,' she said, and then without meaning to she gave what was almost a laugh. 'Please brace yourself because it sounds – it sounds fucking awful, and I'm a little afraid you're going to think exactly the same as the police.'

'Of course I won't,' he said, soothingly.

'Well, I went out drinking last night.' She swallowed. 'I remember almost none of the later part of the evening. Nothing about how I got home. When I woke up early this morning, there was a dead man lying next to me.'

Patrick's writing hand went absolutely still, and he fixed his gaze on her. 'Cause of death?'

'He was stabbed,' she said, feeling heat in her eyes and then wetness tracking down her cheeks. 'And they think – they think I did it. But you have to believe me, Patrick. I don't know who the hell he was, or how he got there. And I'm – I'm sure I could never have stabbed anyone. I'm so very sure.'

Sometimes you had to attack. To be relentless and without mercy. It was clear to Jonah that this was what he had to do today, to get in there and shake Louise up in the seconds before her solicitor could intervene and distract or calm or deflect. And so he took Lightman with him, told him to play it cold and clinical, and began as he meant to go on.

136

'Alex Plaskitt died in your bed,' he said, harshly. 'Not in the front garden, as you tried to lead us to assume. In your bed. This man that you apparently didn't know.'

'My client's statement that she didn't know this man stands,' Patrick Moorcroft said, easily and loudly. 'Did you have an actual question, or just a series of statements to make?'

Jonah had dealt with Mr Moorcroft once before. Only the once. He was too expensive for most of the people Jonah interviewed. And he was expensive because he was bloody good. Or, to put it from Jonah's perspective, bloody infuriating. But Jonah couldn't help feeling a grudging respect for him, however frustrating it was to have an interview essentially dictated by a solicitor.

'How did a man you don't recognise end up in your bed?' Jonah tried instead.

'I'm afraid I don't know,' Louise said, with a glance at her solicitor. And that was all she said. Louise seemed collected now. Focused, in a grim sort of way, and less afraid. Presumably because her expensive solicitor was now there.

Patrick gave him the smallest of smiles, and Jonah shared a momentary glance with Lightman, both exasperated and amused in spite of himself. Lightman's expression in return was, of course, unreadable. Jonah turned back to Louise.

'I'd like to know how Alex Plaskitt died.'

She glanced at Patrick Moorcroft, and then said, 'I want to be able to help. I wish I could, because what happened to him was awful. But I don't remember anything about the later stages of last night.' She looked down. 'I've tried. I've tried over and over again. But there's nothing. All I know is that I've never done anything violent, and I don't believe I would have harmed Alex Plaskitt or anyone else.'

137

Jonah kept his gaze on her. 'Why would he have been in your bed?'

Louise's expression changed slightly. A note of discomfort crept in.

'I can't think of any reason at all. In five years there's been nobody in that bed except me, my husband or, on a few occasions, his parents.' Her mouth twisted slightly. 'I wasn't out on the pull, if that's what you might be thinking. I've never cheated on my husband and in the memories I have of yesterday night I was talking to April, not to any men.'

'And yet Alex ended up there,' Jonah said. 'In your bed.'

Patrick leaned over to murmur to her, and Louise said simply, 'I've told you already that I can't explain it.'

'You claim never to have met him before,' Lightman commented.

'I hadn't.'

'It seems unlikely that you would have invited an unknown man back to your house, to sleep in your bed, unless you had a sexual motivation,' the sergeant went on.

'Who says I invited him?' Louise asked, coldly. 'For all I know he took advantage of me.'

'Was there any sign of that?' Jonah asked.

Louise's face flushed a deep red. 'I don't – I don't know.'

Jonah expected another murmur from her solicitor, but Patrick, surprisingly, said nothing. He kept his gaze on his papers.

'If you need an examination,' Jonah said, more gently, 'we can get you one. If that's what happened, then it's important for us to know, as well as for you.'

Louise shook her head, rapidly, and then said, 'I don't want an examination.'

Jonah nodded, not without frustration. It wasn't uncommon for possible victims to panic at the idea of an examination. But Louise could equally well know that she hadn't been assaulted, and still want to keep the possibility open.

'Do you often experience complete blackouts after nights out drinking?' Jonah asked, changing tack.

'What relevance does that have?' Patrick Moorcroft asked.

'It gives us an idea of whether her apparent failure of memory stands up,' Jonah replied, giving him a level stare. 'In addition, Mrs Reakes has suggested that Alex Plaskitt might have sexually assaulted her. If she makes a habit of going out and becoming incapacitated through alcohol, it's possible that she and Mr Plaskitt had met on another occasion, without her remembering it.'

The solicitor leaned over to mutter to Louise, and she said in a quiet voice, 'I do lose . . . time, sometimes. Some events. Not normally quite so much, but . . .'

'Do you often drink alone?' Jonah asked.

'No,' Louise said. 'I don't.'

Jonah signalled to Lightman, who brought up the slide containing the photo of the knife.

'I'd like to ask you once again whether you recognise this weapon.'

'No,' Louise said. 'I told you that before.'

'Then how did it end up in your bed, alongside the body of Alex Plaskitt?'

'I don't *know*!' Louise said, suddenly half shouting. 'It isn't mine, and I didn't stab him!'

'Then who did?'

Louise dropped her head to her hands and let out a growl, but Patrick stepped in smoothly to say, 'It is the duty of the investigating officers to suggest other suspects. It isn't my client's responsibility.'

Jonah had to smile slightly. He gave Patrick a nod.

'Well, at the moment, our theories are fairly limited,' Jonah said. 'We have a murder weapon found in your bed, a dead man likewise, and a frantic attempt to cover up the crime scene.'

'It wasn't how you're trying to make it sound,' Louise said, angrily, before her solicitor could say anything more.

Jonah nodded again, in satisfaction, this time. He was getting to her, and if he kept on prodding her into speech, then her solicitor wouldn't be able to help her. 'So how did he wind up in your front garden when he died upstairs?'

Louise took a deep breath, as though she'd realised that she needed to calm down. To keep to the script. Her voice was much more measured as she said, 'When I woke up this morning, I was still very much under the influence of alcohol. I was terrified when I found a bleeding man in my bed. At that point I wasn't certain that he was dead.'

'It wasn't obvious from the quantity of blood?'

'I'm not a doctor,' Louise said, with a slight spikiness back in her voice. 'I don't know how much blood loss would kill someone.'

'So your reaction would have been to call for help,' Jonah said. 'To call an ambulance.'

'It might have been if I'd been in a more rational frame of mind,' Louise countered, 'but unfortunately I panicked. I think it was a combination of the alcohol clouding my judgement and sheer fear. I thought I needed to get him to someone. A neighbour. Anyone. So I dragged him outside, telling him it would be all right, and not understanding that it really wasn't all right until he was lying on the grass. I realised – I realised . . .' She waved a hand in what looked like frustration, her eyes filling with tears.

Jonah sat back, watching her for a moment, absolutely certain that this was an account her solicitor had rehearsed with her. They might even have rehearsed the tears. The problem for him, and the prosecutor, would be that it *could* just about be true, and therefore was difficult to disprove. Despite its unlikeliness. Despite all the obvious doubts that her actions raised.

'I'll admit that I'm finding that hard to believe,' he said, after a deliberate pause for consideration. 'Particularly given the care you took to clear up any traces of Alex being in your house.'

'However hard it is to believe, you need to start trying,' Louise said thickly. She drew in a slightly ragged breath. 'I didn't kill him, and somebody else did. I want to know how he ended up there, too. I really, really want to know, so I can prove to my husband that I wasn't shagging someone else.'

She descended quite suddenly into actual sobs, and dropped her head into her hands, the heels of her palms squeezing into each eye socket.

Jonah glanced towards Lightman, whose face was as neutral as ever as he sat up to ask, 'Do you know a man called Issa Benhawy?'

Louise raised her head slightly, and her mouth twisted, as if she hadn't expected any kindness and was almost satisfied to have it confirmed. 'No,' she said, from behind her hands. 'I don't think so.'

'What about Step Conti?'

'No,' she said, pulling the hands away and scrabbling in her handbag until she found a tissue. Her eyes looked raw and red. Perhaps the tears had been real this time. 'Definitely not.' She looked towards Patrick, and then asked, 'Why? Who are they?'

'Alex Plaskitt's husband and his best friend.'

There was a profound silence for a moment, while Louise stared at Jonah, her mouth ever so slightly ajar. And then she said, 'His *husband*?' at the same moment that her solicitor said, 'Are you serious?'

'Indeed,' Jonah said, answering both of them with a very small smile.

'Let me just clarify this,' Patrick said. 'You are attempting to suggest that my client was involved in some sort of one-night stand with a gay man, and . . . what? I'm not quite clear. Decided to stab him? Without motive?'

'What your client and Alex Plaskitt were doing in her marital bed remains unclear,' Jonah said, his voice and expression hard. 'The outcome is, however, exceptionally clear.'

There was a slight pause, and then Louise said, 'Do you think . . . he might have been trying – to rob me?'

Jonah glanced at her in surprise. The theft angle was on his list of possibilities, but he hadn't expected Louise Reakes to think of it. Unless, perhaps, Louise remembered more than she was letting on.

'What makes you ask that?'

'I suppose we have money and . . . the only thing I remember about the later part of the night is that at some point I was afraid. I have this . . . fragment of a memory, and there's a man's voice in it, hushing me.' Her eyes took on a slight sheen. 'It might have been him.'

Jonah looked at her expression, which seemed halfway

between eager and agonised. As if Louise both wanted to believe this and desperately didn't all at once.

The highly anticipated data from Alex's phone arrived just after they'd left Louise to eat sandwiches with her solicitor. Jonah forwarded it to Lightman and, before leaving to speak to Issa, asked his sergeant to run a quick check for Louise Reakes's phone number.

'Nothing,' Lightman said, after running a search. 'And no Louise listed in his contacts.'

'OK. Any messages sent last night?'

Lightman scrolled through the records. 'Quite a few to and from his husband, plus one two-minute phone call at a bit before midnight. A couple between him and Step Conti, but that's it.'

'OK.' Jonah put a hand on his shoulder. 'I'd like a full report, if you're OK to wade through.'

'Sure.'

Of course he was OK. Ben Lightman was always OK with the kind of in-depth, laborious work that would have driven most people mad. There was a reason two of the new Intelligence staff had now nicknamed him the Cyborg. Though there was another related reason, too. One of them had been infatuated with him and had made a move on him at a retirement party a couple of months ago, but Ben hadn't been interested. He never was.

Jonah turned to Hanson and nodded towards the door. His constable rose readily, grabbing her jacket and handbag.

'Issa is at home and ready to talk. I'm stopping at Costa on the way,' he added. 'In case you need anything.'

'God, yes,' Hanson replied. 'I could murder a ham and cheese melt.'

The traffic was still heavy. Travelling back and forth across the city was a time-consuming element that Jonah could have done without, but he specifically wanted to talk to Issa at home. He wanted access to any recent videos Alex had made and to his email accounts, if possible. Anything that might contain some form of contact between him and Louise.

'What went on with Louise Reakes in the interview room?' Hanson asked between mouthfuls, once they were back on the road and attempting to eat hot sandwiches without letting any cheese ooze anywhere.

'She's not admitting to anything except moving the body,' Jonah replied. 'And even then, she says she thought he was alive and was dragging him to the neighbours' for help.'

Hanson gave a slight laugh. 'I'm sure we'd all immediately try to lift a ninety-kilo man down the stairs.'

'My thoughts entirely,' Jonah agreed.

'Has she told us anything about last night?'

'She claims she remembers nothing at all beyond talking to her friend April.' Jonah tried to squeeze the rest of his sandwich further up the cardboard pack and then swore as one of the pieces of bread slid up and out, landing in his lap.

'I've got baby wipes,' Hanson said. 'You can have some once we get there.'

'Thanks,' Jonah said, with a wry grin. 'I clearly need some kind of nanny.'

'Oh, don't worry about it,' Hanson answered, cheerfully. 'I'm the same. You'd be amazed how much a baby wipe will clean off. I actually sometimes worry about what they put in them.' She took another mouthful, chewed thoughtfully and said, 'She remembers nothing? As in, there's a complete blank?'

'Yes. From when she was at the club with April, who snogged some other guy, until the morning, or so she says.' Jonah shook his head. 'There's clearly a lot she's hiding. I need to find some way of pushing her, but it's going to be hard getting anything past her solicitor.'

There was a brief silence from Hanson, and then she said, 'But maybe she really can't remember anything.'

Jonah glanced at her. 'Because of how drunk she was?'

'Yes, or because her drink was spiked.' She was gazing somewhere towards the dashboard, obviously thinking this over. 'What if it was nothing to do with Alex, and he just walked her home? Then somewhere down the line she freaked out and thought he was trying to attack her.'

Jonah considered. 'There's some point to that.' He nodded. 'Let's get a blood test.'

He put a call through to Lightman, asking him to get Louise Reakes's consent to blood testing.

'Sure,' Lightman replied. 'And while you're on the line, you might want to ask Issa Benhawy about the messages he sent his husband in the early hours of the morning.'

'Are they aggressive?'

'I'd say so,' Lightman replied. 'And one of them strongly implies that Alex had form for going home with other people. I'll send Juliette some screenshots. I'm not surprised he was keen to get Alex's phone back untouched.'

He heard a quiet 'Wow,' from Hanson a few moments later as the screenshots arrived on her phone.

'Interesting stuff?'

She read out three messages in turn, the last Issa's vicious threat to end it if Alex had gone home with a 'slut'.

Jonah took this in, lining it up with everything else they had so far. Alex had died in Louise's bed. That much was certain. Issa had accused his husband of sleeping with somebody else. In isolation Jonah would have assumed he meant another man. But the term 'slut' could be applied to someone of either gender.

Was it worth seriously considering Alex's husband as a suspect? They couldn't be certain that Louise had been the one to kill Alex, even taking into account her frantic efforts to cover things up. As Hanson had suggested, Alex could have walked Louise home, an action that was open to misinterpretation. Or he could, in fact, have gone home with Louise for sex. There was no reason to assume that Alex was only interested in men.

The question was whether his jealous husband could have made his way to Saints Close. Could he have tracked Alex through his phone? Or gone to the club to confront his husband, and then followed them to Louise's house? Killed him, assuming he was being unfaithful, and then . . . what? Left him in her bed to punish her?

It was one solution to the bizarre discovery, but it was still all a bit of a stretch, Jonah thought. And proving any of that theory to be true was highly unlikely to be easy.

Lightman was alone in CID when the team's phone rang. The duty sergeant, whose voice Lightman didn't recognise, sounded a little harassed as he explained, 'I've got a Niall Reakes here. I believe you're interviewing his wife. He'd like to see the senior investigating officer immediately.'

'I'll come and get him,' Lightman said, before adding, 'but he's going to have to make do with me for the moment. The chief's out on an interview.'

There was a pause, and Lightman could imagine the sergeant asking why, exactly, a DCI felt it necessary to go out and interview people. But after the pause he just said, 'OK. Not sure that's going to go down well.'

Lightman made his way down to reception quickly, fully expecting a tirade from Niall Reakes once he got there. But Mr Reakes looked stressed out rather than angry. He was pacing the waiting area with clear agitation, looking strangely like a fair-haired, neurotic version of his wife's lawyer. Niall, too, had boyish good looks, and was slightly running to fat. He was also impeccably dressed in a blue-grey suit and a white shirt. Despite having been travelling for half the day, they showed very few creases.

He shook Lightman by the hand when he introduced himself, and said, 'Sorry for blazing in here, but this has all really . . . It's knocked me back. You know?' He looked over at the duty sergeant. 'I've not been able to talk to Louise and my – her solicitor says there might be a murder charge.'

'It's clearly a very stressful situation,' Lightman said. 'I'll do what I can to help. Do you want to come on up to CID?'

'I . . . guess so.'

Once they were in the stairwell and out of earshot of the duty sergeant, Niall asked in a quiet voice, 'Why has she been arrested?'

'You're aware that a young man was found dead in the garden of your home,' Lightman said, sticking to the rule of giving away as little as possible at any given moment.

'Yeah, but she said it was a stranger,' Niall said, as he waited for Lightman to use his swipe card on the door of CID. 'Nobody she knew.'

Lightman glanced at him, able to divine that this was as much a question as it was a statement. Niall Reakes was looking for reassurance, and Lightman would not be giving it to him.

'We need to clear up a few things with both of you,' he said, evenly, keeping his expression absolutely neutral. 'I'm sure the DCI can tell you more as soon as he's back.'

He opened the door, and was surprised to feel Niall's hand on his upper arm in a clumsy grab.

'Please,' Louise's husband said in a desperate voice, 'please tell me if she was screwing someone else. I need to know.'

A narrow garden with a high fence ran from the back door of Alex Plaskitt's terraced house down to a blue-painted single-storey building at the far end. The green-brown skeletons of climbing plants and a few rhododendrons gave the only signs of life. The rest of the garden looked bleak in the spotlight over the back door. Half-melted snow lay over patches of grass and mud, and the rest showed no sign of disappearing.

'It's a lot nicer in daylight, and in summer,' Issa said, with a note of apology. 'Alex spent half of last summer out here, either filming or doing . . . workouts.' He faltered, his eyes fixed on the widest part of the grass, as if seeing Alex there. His expression was desolate.

'So that was his studio?' Jonah asked, gently, nodding towards the building at the end.

'Yes.' Issa looked up at it. 'His gym. I've got the key . . .'

He led Jonah and Hanson to the side of the building, planting his feet carefully on each of the slippery moss-covered stepping stones that meandered down towards it. The door was locked by a simple padlock through a ring with a metal flap. 'It's not a real building,' Issa said, apparently still feeling the need to apologise. 'We just bought a really big summer house for a grand and a half and assembled it. Alex did most of it on his own.'

Issa leaned in to flick a light switch. Jonah stepped in first, and said, 'It's impressive,' in part to make Issa feel better. But also in part because it was. Along one wall were racks containing stacks of free weights. At the rear were a rowing machine, treadmill and spinning bike. The centre of the space was covered in rubberised matting, and sported two fit-balls of different sizes.

The desk occupied the wall nearest the house, and had windows on two sides that presumably gave quite a bit of light during the day. Perched on top were a desktop computer and a freestanding webcam with a tripod. It was pointed towards the centre of the shed.

'Did he edit his videos in here, too?' Jonah asked, glancing at the desktop. It was cold enough in the studio that his breath fogged in the air, strikingly lit by the two overhead lights.

'Yes,' Issa said.

'Would you be happy for us to look through the hard drive?' Hanson asked, with a sympathetic smile.

'I don't . . . mind.' Issa gave a tearful shrug. 'But why do you want to?'

'His YouTube videos often include mentions of what he's been doing that day, or is planning on doing later,' she explained. 'They also show some of his clients. Though the ones with them in are normally filmed at a public gym, I think?'

'It's the SimpleGym,' Issa told her. 'When he goes, he takes the camera with him and plugs in his laptop. You might need to look on there for anything recent.' His gaze wandered, and then came to rest on Hanson again. 'Do you think this wasn't random, then? That it was someone he knew?'

Jonah nodded to Hanson, a sign that he would take over

149

again. It was only fair that he should be the one to break the news to Alex's husband.

'It seems that Alex didn't die in the garden, as we at first thought,' he said. 'He was inside when he died, and his body was removed to the garden to mislead our team.'

Issa's mouth moved, an involuntary twitch. 'What was he doing there?'

'We don't know, but it's clear that he died in bed. The woman who lived there with her husband was with him, though we don't know in what capacity.'

Issa turned his head away, and the twitching of his mouth became a chewing on his lip that looked hard enough to hurt.

'Would you have any reason to expect Alex to have been in bed with a woman?'

Issa's voice was half choked as he said, 'He's done it before.'

16

Louise

I hid my gradual slide down the slope of alcoholism for some while. I would save it for when you were away. I'd get obliterated, and then set alarms for myself that went off at seven in the morning, just so I could send you a cheery message proving I was up and at 'em. The irony being that you, in most cases, were hungover as anything following conference dinners or client piss-ups. That didn't count, did it? You didn't have previous form for terrible drunken behaviour.

I would also delete every message that might have incriminated me, and scour my phone for new contacts or apps each morning. There was always something that needed deleting. A harsh message about you to April. A mortifying website I'd visited. A really grim meme I'd shared. I began to feel like Drunk Louise was working as hard as she could to fuck my life up.

I have a video somewhere of the two of us, me and April, on one of our nights out. Except of course it's not me. It's Her. Anyway, I found it on my phone the next day and it's just April and Drunk Louise with the phone held overhead in what I think is Drunk Louise's hand, shouting, 'We hate you, Sober Louise!' And watching it made me feel ill, like I was seeing my friend and my worst enemy united. Stabbing me in the back.

And then there was the time I found the Tinder app on my phone one morning, which felt like a trap laid especially for me by Her. There's a chance she downloaded it for innocent reasons. It might have been so April could show me some guy she was sleeping with. It might even have been a bizarre moment of curiosity, just a way of understanding what so many people talked about. But it might also have been for a much worse reason. I deleted it, googled whether it might show up in my phone's history, and then deleted my searches, too.

But you grew wise to me in the end. When you walked in late in the afternoon after a trip, and found me looking drawn and fragile, I could see that you knew. It was during this time that you started to make cutting remarks about April, or to grow angry whenever she was brought up. I knew you'd never really liked her, but the animosity stepped up and up, until I stopped mentioning her at all. But your silent, icy disapproval spread to encompass everything I did after that. It became, in fact, the one constant in our marriage.

The neurotic side to my personality got completely out of control during this time, too. I became unable to stop cleaning. Tidying. Perfecting. And I could see that you hated this just as much. You saw it as another character flaw, one that you'd failed to fix.

And so we come, inevitably, to last Friday. To the night when every one of my worst nightmares came true.

I thought it would be safe enough. I'd talked April into coming over to the house, because I was tired and hadn't quite shaken off the cold that had been lingering since Valentine's Day. The other thing that had lingered was depression. Another festival of romance had come and gone with the two of us barely talking. It had felt, for most of our dinner out, like you would have preferred to be elsewhere.

April arrived all made up, caffeine-psyched and chewing on bubblegum. The bubblegum was a surprise, even for April. When she 'Hey, sistered' me at the front door in full-on Tennessee drawl, with the candy-pink gum rolling over her tongue, I wondered for a moment how she was going to fit in the talking and the chewing at once. But of course she managed it.

She talked, and I lined up wine glasses and bowls of nuts and olives while I laughed at her. I'm sure you can imagine the swiftness with which the plastic cork came out of the grim Rioja she'd brought with her. God knows why she can't spend some of her streams of alimony on something nice to drink. But for some reason that's just not her style.

I remember her asking about you.

'He behaving, that old Niall?'

She was leaning on the breakfast bar across from me. Her gauzy black top drooped low enough to show a line of hot-pink bra and the scrawled tattoo across her left breast. I didn't bother telling her she was flashing. She always knows exactly how much tit she's got on show. She must have got dressed up to meet someone for lunch.

She asked if you were behaving. I tipped back some of the cheap crap and shrugged at her. 'Niall's fine. Back tomorrow.'

She fixed me with a very grey stare. 'And do you miss him these days? When he's away?'

'We're married,' I told her. 'We don't do missing each other any more.' And it was so deliberate, that comment. It was one of those things I say to pretend. To make out that I'm in the kind of relationship where we can joke about our marriage and not mean it.

And then, in my memory, it was later. We were no longer in the house, but in a club I didn't remember going to. It didn't worry me, because I was no longer me. I was Her. I could tell because of the warmth in me. Because of the satisfaction I felt with myself and my life.

For some reason Drunk Louise was telling April that she'd made a decision. That she was just going to get goddamn pregnant, whatever it took, and you, Niall, would have to deal with the consequences.

'We still have sex,' I was telling her. 'I'll just manufacture an accident. Once it's done, he can't force me to get rid of it, and then he'll realise it was all I needed to motivate me to stop drinking.'

It seemed like the best plan I'd ever had. I was so convinced it was going to sort my life out for good. I felt fantastic. Powerful.

Which all vanished when April leaned towards me and said, 'Honey, I saw Niall with his ex-wife.'

I don't know how I would have reacted if I hadn't been fairly merry already. As it was, even with the shield of a few glasses of wine between me and this truth – even with Drunk Louise ready in the wings – I wanted to be sick.

'What do you mean, *saw*?' I was wondering if she could have walked in on the two of you having sex, and at the same time I was thinking she must have made a mistake. The power of denial is strong, isn't it?

'I saw them drinking wine at Domo and they were . . . It was obvious something was going on.' She gave a long, frustrated sigh, and jabbed at her drink with her straw. 'Look, I've had suspicions for a while. But I do actually like Niall and I wanted to give him the benefit of the doubt. I know they work in the same field, and it's good if they can get on, but this is clearly not right. If you're genuinely going to have a child together . . . You can't go into that blind. It's too important.' She gave me a very serious look. 'Did he tell you they were meeting up?'

I actually hated her a little bit in that moment, for making me admit that you hadn't told me anything. Isn't that the worst? That the person I hated was not the person who'd been lying to me?

I couldn't admit to her, either, that I'd long, long suspected that you were seeing Dina again. Worse, that I was certain you'd been seeing someone, and just put my head in the sand and hoped your affair had died a death.

'When was this?' I asked her.

'Last Saturday,' she said.

I'd been away all weekend, at a concert in Edinburgh. One of those rare occasions when I'd travelled and you'd stayed at home. You'd gone to meet Dina while I was away overnight, when you must have thought you were safe.

'You said it looked wrong . . . Wrong how?' I could hear how tight and stupid my voice had suddenly become. How *shrill* I sounded. I hate that word, but it's still the best description for it.

'They looked like a couple,' she said, simply. 'I came in and stood at the far side of the bar, and I could see them across from me. They had a table by the wall, one of the high-up ones, and she was all coiled round this high stool, wearing a jumpsuit that was slit real low down the front. She was laughing a lot and touching his arm all the time. You know.'

I remember that shivers started to run through me. And fucking Drunk Louise, who I needed so badly right then, was nowhere to be found. She'd clearly scampered away to the bar and left me to deal with this shit.

I didn't want to know any more, but I felt unable to stop asking questions.

'How did he look?'

April shrugged. 'I don't know. I guess like he was enjoying it.'

'Did they . . . kiss?'

'Not that I saw, but it was all there in the body language.' April gave me a look that was full of sympathy and anger in equal measures. 'What you need to know is that he's a fucking idiot, OK? You deserve so much more, and he deserves hell. She's the vainest person I've ever met.'

I nodded, and folded my arms round myself. 'Do you think she wants him back? You know . . . properly?'

'For now,' April said, 'yes. But only so she can *win*. She feels like she lost.'

'How?' I asked. I could feel myself getting tearful, and I decided to swallow it down with vodka, which was what we seemed to be drinking now. 'How did she lose? She left him.'

'She lost because he moved on,' April told me. 'She lost because her fantasy of him pining after her for years got overturned in a few months, and she didn't like it.'

'She got *married*,' I said.

'That doesn't matter a damn,' April said. And actually, April's pretty good at weighing people up, something I think even you would admit. I trust her on Dina. 'Winning is everything. She didn't want to actually *be with* her new guy. He was a rich married man, and she wanted to prove she could break apart his marriage. And now she wants to prove she can break yours apart, too.'

All of it chimed with everything I'd always thought about your ex-wife, Niall. The stuff I'd never wanted to let on to you. If you've ever doubted why April has always meant so much to me, you could put a lot of it down to her taking my side. *Mine.* She sees through your ex-wife like she's transparent.

Something bubbled up in me, then. A huge feeling of resentment, all of it directed at you, not her.

'She didn't force him to go for a drink and – and whatever else . . .' I shook my head. 'He's a fucking arsehole, too.'

April lifted her glass. 'I'll drink to that.'

After that, I tried not to think about you, or the fantasy of our happy family that had well and truly died. I tried so very hard. But there was a burning feeling in my stomach, and I spent the next hour or so checking my phone constantly, to see if you'd looked at WhatsApp recently. Whether you might be messaging her instead of me.

And I drank. I drank to dampen that feeling, and to welcome my drunk self back. To let her take over and stop me from feeling anything.

So this time, it wasn't actually an accident that I ended up obliterated. I did it with a sense of grim purpose. I wanted to destroy myself with drink and turn into Her. And then I wanted, actively wanted, to become that pathetic wreck you always get so angry with, as a huge *fuck you*. I even thought about finding some guy and screwing him in the toilets. About finally, totally ending our marriage. Not by waiting for you to leave me, but by doing something unforgivable and then telling you all about it.

I half remember a little more, from later on. I remember the moment I realised April was gone. It was definitely Sober Louise who realised, and not the other one. I know because of how frightened I suddenly felt. So afraid of being alone that I thought about calling you. I really thought about it, despite how drunk I was and how much worse I'd feel about myself.

I remember pulling out my phone and finding your name. I remember staring at it and wanting so much to have you there with me. Caring about me instead of Dina. Taking me home and looking after me.

And then nothing.

Well, nothing I'm certain about. There is a memory that hit me while I was trying not to doze in a chair between interviews.

It began with me walking through a tiny garden. But that garden turned quickly into an endless, awful forest, and there was someone behind me. I knew for a long time that there was. I kept turning round to look at him, but every time I did, he was smiling at me like he was innocent and trustworthy. And every time I turned away and then looked back again, he was closer, without ever seeming to move. His smiling face seemed to float somewhere in front of his body, which horrified me.

I tried to run, but my legs felt limp. Out of my control. I kept tripping over. Time after time, I found myself on the grass or the frozen earth, and he caught up more quickly each time, until he was right behind me. I was screaming and trying to run, and then falling again.

And I don't know why I didn't wake up at that point, because that's what should have happened. I should have woken up when I fell and he'd got me, but I didn't. I couldn't. I could only lie there, and feel him on top of me. Then he was pressing something sharp into my back, further and further, until I knew I was dying.

I had to wake up, because if I didn't, I would die in that dream. I knew that. I would die for real.

And somehow I dragged myself back. I woke up.

I'm glad I'd been left on my own for a while. It took me a long time to stop crying. I could still feel that pain in my back, and I remembered suddenly that it had stung when I showered that morning, along with all the other grazes I couldn't identify. So I stumbled to the reflective glass at the side of the interview room, feeling like I might be sick. I pulled my top up a few inches and turned my back, craning my head to see my reflection.

And there it was, on my back, right where I'd felt it in the dream. A scab where a cut had been, and around it dark, purplish bruising.

I felt like I was falling.

The conversation with Issa was, from Hanson's perspective, hard going. He had sobbed his way through an angry, hurt, grief-filled account of Alex's past infidelity, while she and the DCI had begun to shiver in the unheated studio.

'She was one of his clients,' he told them. 'The daughter of a baronet who'd grown up in all-girls' schools riding ponies. She was a Plaskitt family sort of person, and it felt like – like the worst kind of betrayal. I couldn't believe *that* was the kind of woman he would go for.'

'Was Alex bisexual?' the DCI asked.

Issa had nodded. 'Essentially yes. But he told me he'd only ever fallen hard for men. Just me and a boyfriend at school. It would have been easier for him to have married a woman, and I know it got to him sometimes. If he'd just decided on a nice young girl, it would have meant reconciliation with his parents. Grandkids for them to dote on. Seeing his sister more often. Mummy and Daddy would have approved and come to visit, and probably bought them a nice big house. Who knows?' He made a lunge for a drawer of the desk, and after some rifling pulled out a packet of tissues. He blew his nose into one, before saying, 'I knew that part of him was there, and it drove me mad. He wasn't the one whose family hasn't spoken to him in eight years. He wasn't told he was an abomination.'

'Is that what your family did?' Hanson asked, quietly. 'Cut you off?'

'You bet they did.' Issa's mouth set into an angrier line. 'I was raised an Ahmadiyya Muslim, with all the preaching of how forgiveness is everything. That we must be tolerant, and seek peace, because those are the true teachings of Islam.' He gave a bitter smile. 'It turned out that there are exceptions, according to my parents. Tolerance is only for those of other faiths, not those of other sexualities.'

Hanson winced. 'I'm so sorry. That's a terrible thing to go through.'

Issa gave another one of those not-quite-smiles. 'It goes on being pretty rough, but I've made my peace with it.' He gave a very long sigh. 'I suppose it was hard to feel sympathy towards Alex for what was a much easier situation.'

Hanson nodded, and let the DCI take over again to ask, 'When he cheated, was it a one-off? Or a . . . relationship?'

'He said it was a one-off,' Issa said, a note of doubt in his voice, 'and I didn't have any reason to think . . . They hadn't been working together that long, and he seemed devastated by it. He really did.'

'Do you recall her name?'

'Yes.' He gave her a defiant look. 'I sometimes look her up, just to make sure she's really, you know . . . moved on. She's called Sarah Lang. But she lives in Monaco now. I doubt she's going to be of any interest to you.'

Hanson pulled her notebook out and scribbled the name down anyway.

'Did you ever get the impression he might be pursuing other young women?' the DCI threw in.

Issa gave a strange shrug. 'I got angry with him a few times for staying out later than he'd said he would. I didn't – I didn't like him hanging around with Step.'

'You felt he was a bad influence?' Jonah asked.

'Maybe.' He looked upwards, the expression of a man try-ing to stop himself from crying. 'Whenever they went out together, Alex seemed to want to party for longer. I had this – this feeling that he was flirting with girls.'

Sheens took out a glossily printed photo of Louise Reakes from his pocket. It had been taken after her arrest. She looked pale and slightly sick-looking. The lighting wasn't exactly flattering, but she looked like someone who knew she was in big trouble.

'Do you recognise this woman?' the DCI asked.

Issa took the photo, and glanced at it before shaking his head. Hanson caught a twist at his mouth, and asked, instinct-ively, 'Does she look anything like the woman he slept with?'

'Yes,' Issa said, in what was almost a whisper. He looked up at her. 'There's quite a similarity.'

Sheens pulled out another photograph. It was the murder weapon in all its gleaming glory.

'What about this? Might this have been Alex's?'

Issa's face grew visibly paler. It wasn't something Hanson had seen very often, a draining away of blood. One of those often-described and rarely experienced occurrences.

'No, it's not his.' He swallowed. 'Why are you showing me this? Was this what killed him? Of course it wasn't his. Of course it wasn't. Why would he have a knife?'

'It's surprisingly common for people who carry knives to end up killed by them,' the chief said in a sympathetic tone.

'He's never carried a knife in his life,' Issa said. 'He was a hardcore pacifist.'

'He wouldn't have bought it just for the look of it?' Sheens asked. 'It's a beautifully made piece.'

'That isn't beautiful,' Issa said, his eyes gleaming and his jaw set. 'That's a monstrosity.'

Lightman managed to get through to the DCI some fifteen minutes after leaving Niall Reakes in a relatives' room with a cup of black coffee. The call was picked up quickly this time, and he could hear background engine noises. He explained that Mr Reakes was demanding to see both his wife's solicitor and the DCI.

'Let him talk to Patrick Moorcroft,' the chief said, after a moment of thought. 'But inform him that any conversation between them will not be protected under client–solicitor confidentiality, as the solicitor is not, in fact, representing Mr Reakes.'

'And presumably you'd like me in the observation room while they talk?'

'You bet I would,' Sheens confirmed. 'We'll be back in twenty or so minutes and I'll probably talk to him then. And keep me posted if the super calls through to the office. I want to know if we have our thirty-six hours. Thanks, Ben.'

Louise Reakes and her solicitor were sitting in what seemed to be a strained silence. The solicitor was reading something that presumably pertained to her case, while Louise was brushing a strand of hair back and forth across her mouth, her eyes wide and unfocused.

'Mr Reakes has arrived,' Lightman said, and Louise immediately stood, her chair making a loud, low-pitched screech across the lino floor. 'He's asked to see you, Mr Moorcroft.'

Patrick looked up at Lightman, his brow creased. He glanced briefly at his client, and then said, 'In what capacity?'

'An unofficial one.'

Louise stared at her solicitor while he reflected. As he moved to rise, she said, 'I need to see him. I'm the one who needs to talk to him.'

'I can explain the details of your case to him,' Patrick said, soothingly. He lifted his briefcase onto his chair and began methodically sliding his papers back into it.

'That's not the same,' Louise countered. 'He'll think . . . I need to explain it all to him.'

The solicitor looked up at her for a moment, and then said, gently, 'It would be extremely unusual for contact to be allowed between you while you were in custody on such a serious charge. I know how concerned you are about his reaction, but I really will put forward everything you've said, and I'm sure he'll understand that you are as bemused as the rest of us.'

Lightman listened to this in faint surprise. He hadn't expected sympathy from the hotshot lawyer. He might have anticipated a cheerful dismissal of her concerns, but the quiet, soothing voice was unexpected.

It seemed unexpected to Louise, too, who gazed at him, blankly, and then said, 'All right. Thank you – so much – Patrick.' And then she turned away, her hand over her eyes.

The lawyer said nothing as Lightman took him to the relatives' room. His expression looked pensive, and Lightman wondered what he was working through in his mind.

There were still traces of tears in Niall Reakes's eyes as they entered. His reaction to the solicitor was somewhere between relieved and angry.

'The chief has agreed to let you speak to Mr Moorcroft,' Lightman said. 'But he remains your wife's solicitor.'

Niall Reakes, who had been in the process of getting

up, looked sharply at Lightman. 'What's that supposed to mean?'

'It means that we can speak, but without the privilege of solicitor–client confidentiality,' Patrick Moorcroft explained.

'I'll leave you to it,' Lightman said. He caught the solicitor's wry look. He was clearly aware that their conversation would be listened to.

By the time Lightman had shut himself into the observation room, Niall Reakes was saying, heatedly, '. . . why in the hell she called you. You're my friend, not hers.'

'I'm also the only solicitor you both know,' Patrick said in a measured tone. He placed his briefcase upright on the table. 'She probably didn't know who else to call.'

'Well, she'll have to find someone else,' Mr Reakes said, his voice high-pitched and unsteady.

'She's asked me to represent her, Niall,' Patrick said, slightly more firmly. 'I'm her solicitor.'

'You're joking,' Niall said, half laughing in disbelief. 'They've arrested her. They think – they must have a reason. Why are they holding her if she hasn't done something?'

Patrick looked, momentarily, almost awkward. And then he said, 'The question over what she may have done rests on where the young man died. He was found to have died in your home, rather than outside it.'

'Oh my God,' Niall said, putting his hands up to his face. 'I knew it. I knew she was . . .' He suddenly turned to Patrick. 'She was sleeping with him, wasn't she?'

'That remains unclear,' Patrick said. 'He died in – in the bed alongside her.'

'For God's sake!' He shook his head, violently. 'You can't represent her. There's no way.'

'Niall . . .'

'There was another man in our bed!' He leaned forwards to point somewhere towards the door, as if the bed lay in that direction. 'Some stranger who's now dead!'

'It's clearly a horrible thing to find out,' Patrick said. 'I'm so sorry, Niall. But from the moment she hired me, I became her legal counsel as well as your friend.'

'She doesn't effing deserve legal counsel,' Niall Reakes said through gritted teeth.

Lightman found himself smiling slightly at Niall's non-swearing. His wife seemed to be much happier with colourful language.

'Everyone deserves it, Niall,' Patrick said, quietly. 'Everyone.'

'Well, I'm going to hire you instead,' Niall said in sudden triumph. 'You won't be able to represent her, because it'll be a conflict of interest.'

Patrick sighed. 'I'm afraid the way it works is that I wouldn't be able to represent *you*. But then you aren't in current need of counsel, are you?'

'Yes, I am,' Niall said. 'I need counsel to explain to me what the hell happened.'

'I can help you with that, up to a point.'

Niall turned away, waving a hand in clear frustration, before he asked, 'Did she take some – some – some bastard home and then find out too late he was violent?'

'Your wife can't remember a lot of the evening,' the solicitor said. 'She went out with her friend, April. The two of them ended up drunk. April left with a man she'd picked up, and Louise was left alone, and has a large memory blackout covering the later part of the evening.'

'Oh, really?' Niall almost laughed again.

'It may be worth knowing,' Patrick Moorcroft said, evenly,

'that the young man who died was married. To another young man.'

There was absolute silence. Niall moved his head, opened his mouth, and then seemed to falter. 'What?'

'The details of the case are clearly complex. However easy it is to jump to conclusions, I think you need to be patient and let the truth come out. Louise has assured me that she doesn't recognise the man in question, and is certain she couldn't have been violent towards him or anyone else.'

'And do you believe her?' Niall asked. He came to stand close to Patrick, his hands in his pockets and his body leaning slightly forwards once again. 'Do you think that's true? Do you?' There was a brief pause, and then Niall said, much more quietly, 'Please, Patrick. Please tell me. I'm losing my mind.'

'I know, Niall,' the solicitor said, quietly. 'And I do believe her. She's clearly been through an awful day as well.'

Niall shook his head, for some reason unwilling to accept this. 'Of course she has. She tried to hide some – some kind of murder.'

'Niall,' Patrick said, his voice suddenly sharp. 'I've told you everything I know. Perhaps it's worth you considering what you know of your wife's character, and whether she is capable of this action, before you damage her defence.'

Niall's expression went momentarily slack. He looked, just then, like a chastened child. 'I'm not . . . I'm . . . I'm sorry.' He looked down, towards the floor. 'I didn't mean to – I'm not accusing her of anything.'

'Good,' Patrick said, nodding. 'I'm glad.'

Another silence grew between them, and then Niall asked, 'So what's next? What do I do?'

'Perhaps you should go home,' the solicitor said.

Niall shook his head. 'I want – I need to see the police. I want to talk to them. Myself.' He looked up at the solicitor. 'I found out that – that she'd been arrested from the bloody news.'

'I called you as soon as I could, and I think the police have been trying to reach you –'

'Yeah, I know,' Niall snapped. And then he added, in a quieter voice, 'I'm sorry, Patrick. I should be . . . grateful to you. It just feels suddenly like there are sides. My side and hers.'

'There are no sides as far as I'm concerned,' Patrick told him, reaching out to put a hand on his friend's shoulder. He gave a small smile. 'In my official position as your best friend, I'm here for both of you. All right?'

Hanson spent the remainder of the journey back mulling over what Issa had told them. It seemed possible that Alex and Louise had gone home together for sex, but they had no proof that a liaison had occurred at the club. Nothing on any of the cameras. Nothing from the bar staff or Louise's friend. And the two of them had technically left separately.

She was still thinking it all over as they drew back into the car park at the rear of Southampton Central. As she climbed out of the chief's Mondeo, she found herself looking at a black BMW 3 Series that was hovering up near the entrance to the station. She felt her heart squeeze in immediate response.

It's not him, she told herself, as she removed the laptop from the car and closed the door. But she couldn't look away from the car. She thought she could make out the driver's shape in the light from the street lamps, and in her mind he became Damian, sitting at the steering wheel and watching her.

He'd still been driving the BMW the last time she'd seen him. The car that she'd paid the deposit on, stupidly believing that he would pay her back. A car that was far, far too expensive for Damian's modest salary and immodest debts. But of course Damian had to have it. He had to have the best of everything, always, as if the world owed him luxury.

She lowered her head and started to follow the DCI, refusing to look towards the car. It probably wasn't even him.

Lots of people have black BMWs, she told herself.

But she was still shaking as she stepped into the rear lobby.

She wished they hadn't built the place with so much glass. She could feel her skin crawling until she'd closed the door of CID behind her.

Jonah's call from the superintendent came as he was halfway to his office. He deposited the desktop computer he was carrying on O'Malley's untidy desk in order to answer it.

It was a mercifully quick call. The superintendent agreed that a custody extension was warranted, and approved a further application to the magistrates' court for longer if needed. Technically, this meant that only Hanson, as the team's constable, would be required to take Louise Reakes to the court the next day. But Jonah would go too. It was useful to have a senior officer there to answer any difficult questions, and kinder to support his junior officer.

'Right,' Jonah said, with the call done. 'We have our thirty-six hours, and we'll plan for a court application. Can I get a download on what Niall Reakes said to his solicitor, Ben?'

Lightman told him in his measured, precise way about the conversation. He outlined Niall Reakes's doubts over his wife and his demand for Patrick Moorcroft to represent him instead.

'They are clearly friends rather than solicitor and client, and Mr Reakes seems to feel betrayed by his friend's decision to represent his wife. He implied that it pits her against him somehow, though exactly how that works isn't clear. It was a fairly heated conversation,' he added, in such a cool voice that it was slightly comic.

'So he found it easy to imagine his wife cheating, and even killing,' Jonah said.

'Yes,' Lightman agreed. 'That's a good summary. He's now demanding to see you. His wife, meanwhile, is demanding to see him.'

Jonah gave a wry grin. 'Well, I'm demanding coffee. Let's see which one of us gets what we want first.'

O'Malley took a thermos and went to do a Costa run. 'You don't need a crappy disposable cup, so,' he said, waving the thermos at Jonah. 'Those things last for centuries before rotting down.'

It made Jonah grin. This was clearly a new concern for O'Malley, who was well on the way to being a takeaway coffee addict. He noted that O'Malley's hectic desk had three disposable cups sitting on it, their contents in various stages of moulding over.

He took a few minutes to retreat to his office and mull things over before he spoke to Niall Reakes. Though, in fact, when he sat down and woke his desktop, he found a note in O'Malley's sloping scrawl asking him to call Janet McCullough. The call had clearly slipped his sergeant's mind.

Their forensic scientist answered swiftly, and with clear enthusiasm.

'I've talked to my guy about this knife of yours,' she said. 'And it's actually pretty good news. Unless it's a copy, which he doesn't think it is, it's a Ukrainian import. At the moment there's only one firm in the UK that sells them.'

'Wow, great work,' Jonah said, not really surprised that McCullough had contacted him herself instead of just putting them in touch. It was very much her style to go beyond her brief. 'Can you give me the name?'

'It's Steel and Silver, and they're an online retailer with shops in Newcastle and London,' McCullough told him. 'Let's hope they don't sell so very many of them.'

'Let's hope they don't,' Jonah agreed.

18

Louise

You won't want to read about this next part. I know you won't. But it's vital that you know. If I don't explain the sheer, heart-twisting panic I felt when I woke up on Saturday morning, then you'll never understand why I did what I did. Even now, I hate that the picture you have of me in your head is all wrong. All distorted.

I've told you how it was, when I found him there next to me. But I need you to understand, now, the awful, awful things I began to think. I imagined that Drunk Louise had seduced and then killed him, and that she'd done everything she could to make sure I suffered for it.

You're probably thoroughly sick of all this talk of Her, aren't you? By this point you must be railing against it, wanting to shout that it's all *me*, and this artificial distancing of myself from Her is both childish and pathological.

But to say that is to misunderstand the nature of me and Her. It is to trivialise the dissociation that happens each and every time. I can see, now, that there is something more profound at work in my psychology than simple alcoholism. And, in part, I can see it more clearly because of another version of me that I met that morning.

It was the anxiety that triggered it. Fear like I have never known before. It reached an unbearable crescendo, and then something snapped. I vanished, and another me came into being. She was – well, she was unstoppable.

That new Louise knew more than I did. She knew she had to get the body of this man out of the house. She could see herself being jailed for something she had no way of defending herself against. She had to stop it happening.

And, as a side point, isn't this refreshing? An alter ego that is actually looking out for Sober Louise. One who clears up the mess instead of making it. I can't help liking her.

It felt very much like watching someone else as she set to work. She knew she had to do it while it was still dark, and that it would be better to do it naked, so she stripped off, and put my going-out clothes into the wash. She noted, as she did it, that I was missing a diamanté earring but dismissed it. It didn't matter if it turned up somewhere on the streets if the crime scene was going to be in my front garden.

She put on a pair of disposable cleaning gloves, and heaved him out of bed. He was unbelievably fucking heavy but she did it anyway.

Did you wince again just there? Did you feel more revolted by the swearing than you did by this vision of your wife dragging a well-muscled dead man out of our marital bed? I almost want to know.

Anyway, she was a determined person, this newly born Louise. After a good twenty minutes, she'd made it outside with the body. And having Dettol-ed the knife in case she'd touched it at some point, she put it down next to him and stood back to take a look.

There wasn't enough blood, she realised. Nobody would believe he'd been attacked there. She needed to make it look like he'd come from somewhere else.

So she took his shoes off him, soaked them in blood off the mattress, slipped them on to her own feet (over some socks) and left a fake trail from the pavement to where he lay, making sure to step only on the marks she'd already left on her way back.

Doing it, she thought about dead men's shoes, and it made her laugh. She actually laughed, out there in the bitter cold, with the threat of discovery hanging over her. And that isn't the black mark against her character you might think. There is a great, terrible absurdity in having to handle a dead body, and I defy most people not to be hit by it at some point.

After she'd put his shoes back on to his feet, she started to clean everything up. And I bet at this point you're laughing a little bitterly and thinking, *Of course she cleaned.* But it was absolutely needed. It turns out both versions of me were born for this.

Cleaning everything took us until twenty to six, a good hour and a half after I'd first woken up and found him. Getting up early is clearly the first habit of successful justice perverters.

The final and biggest problem we both had was the mattress, which was still steeped in blood. She was equal to this, though. She used my hair dryer on a cool setting to blow-dry it. By the time she'd finished, it left only a smudge on her hand if she pressed it hard. None of it showed once she'd got the spare duvet and pillows out and made it up again.

That other version of me stayed right up until the police arrived. She was there with me, telling me what to say. Guiding me. Stopping me from messing everything up.

And I know you're going to be certain, now, that there's

something wrong with me. That this constant dissociation with myself shows that I'm deeply damaged. But I'm starting to understand that these parts of me come into being out of necessity. That life, and the people in it, sometimes just push me too hard.

So whatever you think of my other personas, I'll tell you this: I miss them intensely now that they've left me. Each of them did, in their way, what I so badly wanted you to do, Niall. They made me feel like everything would be OK.

19

With Lightman volunteering to check up on Niall Reakes's trip to Geneva, and O'Malley on coffee duty, Hanson was free to investigate what she chose. She needed to take her mind off that black car in the car park and, more particularly, off her own adrenaline-filled reaction to it. Off the way it was all getting to her.

Alex Plaskitt's tower computer was still on O'Malley's desk, sitting at an angle on top of some paperwork. She had his laptop case perched on her own. Between the two machines, they had all of Alex's videos to work through, and she might as well get on with them.

She hesitated over which to start with and chose the laptop. This was, presumably, where any more recent, unedited footage would be found. She knew finding something significant was a long shot, but at the very least she hoped to understand more about the man and his frame of mind. Something to tell her whether he might have wanted to sleep with Louise Reakes, and whether he could ever have been violent.

She loaded up the laptop, half listening to Ben in the background. He was now talking to a second person at Niall Reakes's pharmaceutical firm to ask them about the conference. She had the strong suspicion that they were being difficult from the way he was repeating his requests extremely politely. She'd never known him get angry with anyone. Not a witness, or a suspect, or a colleague. Though she often wondered whether he felt more underneath it all.

She pulled her headphones out of her desktop and plugged them into the laptop, hoping that she wasn't about to get a telling-off from the cyber team for accessing the files before they'd had a look.

It took her a few tries to locate Alex's personal videos. There was nothing in his documents, but eventually she thought to look for online storage folders and found a batch of them sitting in Dropbox. Ben had finished his call and started another by the time she'd loaded the most recent one up.

This video had been recorded the day he died, and Hanson took a long, steadying breath before pressing the play button.

Alex appeared in excessive close-up, having clearly just pressed the record button on the camera. His expression, even in that unplanned moment, was warm. Excited. Open.

Alex backed away until he was standing in the middle of his studio, and then, after a brief pause, he launched himself into a greeting.

'This is Alex Plaskitt, your health and fitness coach, and today I'm looking at how to do a really great core-workout session. Now, a lot of people will use plank holds as their core training, without movement. What I want to show you today is taking that position and turning it dynamic, because your core will always be trained better when you move.'

He hunkered down onto the ground and put himself into an easy plank position, his feet on the floor and his body supported with enviably straight forearms.

'Now, trying to hold a static plank for longer and longer to try and get better core is like weight training by holding a car over your head. It's likely to cause injury, and it doesn't really help. Like with weights, we need movement.'

Alex began to demonstrate a series of moves, all based on forward and side plank, and Hanson found herself taking mental notes. This was good stuff, which made her think again of what a stupid waste his death had been.

The clip ran smoothly for five minutes, and then Alex got up to turn off the camera. There was nothing in there about his life. Nothing to suggest why he might have ended up dead.

She tried the previous four videos, which were much shorter, and it turned out that these were all out-takes of the same short segment. In the first one, Alex fell over his words, made a burbling sound, laughed, and went to turn the video off. In the second one, he made it through the intro, and then tripped over trying to move into the plank. He collapsed into a fit of giggles that was infectious and, for Hanson, achingly sad.

The fifth clip was less engaging. Alex was filming himself doing 2k on the Concept 2 rowing machine. He gave a brief introduction, saying he was filming it for posterity, and then he turned some pounding music on and started.

Hanson skipped on twice, seeing nothing much of interest. And then, at five minutes in, Alex suddenly faltered, and came to a stop. He let go of the handle, breathing heavily, and then he let out a roar. He undid his foot straps with a furious rush, and staggered to his feet, swinging close to the camera.

'For fuck's sake, you fucking pussy!'

Hanson actually flinched as he shouted. It didn't seem possible that it was the same voice as those cheerful, encouraging comments on the other videos.

His movements were no less aggressive. He started to kick the wheel of the Concept 2, lending a rhythm to his shouts of, 'What – the – fuck – is – wrong – with – you?'

The anger went on for a good minute, and then Alex collapsed onto the floor and began to cry, still half raging between the tears. Calling himself a useless twat. A pathetic fag.

Hanson paused it, wondering for a moment where the rage had come from. Then she remembered what Phoebe had told them.

He was a bit of a mummy's boy. At least, that's what Daddy used to think . . .

She felt slightly sick as she moved on to look at the other videos.

'Niall Reakes's alibi seems to hold up,' Lightman told Jonah, after tapping on the door to his office. 'His firm has sent over a few social media photos of the conference and forwarded on his flight bookings. He was on the twelve-forty home today.'

'OK, thanks,' Jonah said, reflecting that this would make things simpler. If Niall had been abroad, Louise alone had been responsible for moving Alex Plaskitt's body, and quite possibly for killing him, too. But that didn't mean that speaking to her husband was any less important.

Jonah braced himself for something of a confrontation, given Niall's earlier blustering, but, in fact, the interview went smoothly. It was clear that Niall had burned off a lot of energy while he'd been waiting. By the time Jonah entered the relatives' room, he was sitting meekly at the table, his expression mild and eager to please.

Jonah explained to him, briefly, why they needed to hold Louise. About the terms of custody and their application to the magistrate.

'You can make this a lot easier, however,' Jonah went on.

'If, for example, there's any previous behaviour of this kind you can tell us about . . .'

Niall gave a slightly helpless expression. 'Behaviour like – like being involved with a dead man and then . . .' He gave a short laugh, and then shook his head. 'She's never been in trouble with the law before. I don't know if that's what you want to hear.'

'And she's never brought anyone else home?'

'I don't think so,' Niall said, a little hoarsely. Niall looked a lot like his friend Patrick, but, as he spoke, Jonah could hear differences. Where Patrick was clearly public-school-educated, Niall's accent was neutral south-east England. He seemed more open, too. Less in control of his emotions. Easier, Jonah thought, to provoke.

There was a brief silence, and Jonah raised an enquiring eyebrow.

Niall looked uncomfortable, and added, 'When I'm away, I guess . . . I wouldn't know if she was . . .'

'You've never had reason to suspect?'

Niall hesitated, then shook his head.

'But the drinking?'

'I guess . . .' He sighed, briefly and sharply. 'Yeah, it's a bit of a habit. I mean, not often. A couple of times a month. But it's always a mess.'

Jonah nodded. 'Is that to imply that you've had to step in at times?'

'I usually just have to pick up the pieces,' Niall said. 'Although these days she mostly waits until I'm abroad, so all I get to see is the terrible hangover. And she's – she's a night-mare, hungover.' He shook his head. 'Just deeply self-pitying and guilty.'

'Has she had things to really regret?'

Niall gave a tight laugh. 'Nothing most people would worry about. She can beat herself up over having said something a bit impatiently, or having lost her keys. Just not . . . you know. Terrible.'

'You didn't get the sense she was hiding worse things? Thinking back to the last few times this has happened?'

Niall paused for a moment and then shook his head. 'It's hard to say, but . . . I don't think so.'

'Has she often been unable to recall much of the night before?' Jonah tried.

Niall gave him a long, considering look before he said, 'I honestly don't know. She normally remembers some things, at least. I'm not sure she'd tell me if she had huge blackouts. She said she had once, but . . . '

Jonah watched him, briefly, and then said, 'Your wife would like to see you. It's not standard practice to allow suspects to see family while in custody, but I'm prepared to make an exception, given that you've been away from her for several days.'

He saw Niall stiffen slightly. And then, to Jonah's surprise, he said, 'I don't want to see her.'

Jason ambled over to Hanson's desk while she was writing up her notes on the video footage.

'I'm done. They're screening the game at the Hammer and Tongs so I'm going to head over there. See if I can catch the end and then eat something unhealthy.' He gave her a slightly ironic look. 'Your perfect evening.'

Hanson laughed. She had admitted to Jason early on that the Hammer and Tongs was her least favourite pub. It was devoted to sports Hanson had no interest in, had a generally sticky floor, and served only one type of cheap gin alongside the countless lagers. But Jason was a huge rugby fan, and part of a group of detectives and uniforms who used it as their local. They went there three or four days of the week and often watched obscure matches streamed off a PC. Hanson had dutifully gone along with Jason a few times, but avoided it when she could.

'Thanks,' she told him. 'I'll be here a while, and then I might find myself just too tired for such a fantastic event. You can come to mine afterwards if you like, though. I may have beer.'

'I'll see how I go,' he said, throwing his car keys up and catching them. 'Don't work too hard.'

Jonah ducked back into Interview Room 1, where Louise and her solicitor were still waiting. Louise was gazing at nothing, her whole pose defeated. Patrick Moorcroft rose from his chair the moment Jonah was inside the room.

'I need to get back home to my family,' the solicitor said. 'I assume there's nothing more for me this evening.'

'No,' Jonah agreed. 'We'll continue tomorrow.'

The solicitor collected up his coat and briefcase, and spoke to his client quietly. 'I'll check in tomorrow morning. I'll work out what time I need to be here.' Louise nodded without looking at him. Patrick glanced at Jonah. 'I assume you're pushing for a magistrates' court hearing.'

'Yes. We should know by mid-morning.'

'We'll discuss that tomorrow,' Patrick told Louise, looking at her with an expression that might have been slight concern. 'You'll be here for the night, but it should be relatively comfortable.'

Louise nodded again, and then looked up at Jonah. 'Has Niall gone?'

'Yes,' Jonah said, quietly. 'I'm afraid he wasn't feeling equal to seeing you.'

Louise's mouth twisted, and she looked down at her hands. 'Poor Niall.'

'There's a constable on the way to take you to a cell. She'll get you sorted with some food, too.' Faced with her desolate expression, he added, 'They aren't bad, the cells. They have TVs, and the beds are OK.'

It was always an odd thing, holding a suspect in custody. They were at once the enemy and within your care. The fact that Louise Reakes may have killed a man and then tried to hide it made Jonah feel no less concerned for her welfare than if she had done nothing wrong. She would clearly be having a hard time for the next few days, whatever happened.

He left the interview suite along with Patrick Moorcroft, allowing the solicitor to walk ahead of him. Neither of them spoke as they made their way across CID, but as Jonah held the door open for him, the solicitor turned briefly and said, 'Niall may well regret his decision not to speak to her. If he does, would you be willing to grant him access?'

Jonah studied his expression, wondering if his question was down to his friendship with Niall, or reflected concern that Louise's husband might undermine her defence.

'I'd certainly be willing to consider it.'

'Thank you,' the solicitor said, and left.

Jojo gave Jonah her version of the third degree while they drove to dinner at Roy's house. He'd had to push the timings back by an hour and a half, and felt lucky to be making it at all. Fortunately Roy and Sophie were unshakeably relaxed about that kind of thing, and Roy had even said cheerfully that it might mean the house ended up tidy before they arrived.

Jojo's form of interrogation always started with, 'Did you manage to arrest anyone today?'

'No,' Jonah replied. 'Massive fail.' He grinned at her. He'd stolen one of Jojo's current favourite phrases, which she'd stolen from the younger climbers and a good portion of the people she followed on Twitter.

'God. It's a wonder they pay you at all, Copper Sheens.' She shook her head, and started scrolling through radio stations out of a general disgust with his allegiance to Radio 2. 'You said it was a murder?'

'Yes. A stabbing.'

'Young person or old?'

'Young.'

'That's cruddy,' Jojo said, more seriously.

'It is,' he agreed. 'And it's definitely more complex than a random on-street attack. The body was moved, by someone who may or may not have killed him.' Which was as much as he could say to her about it, however greatly he trusted Jojo's discretion.

She gave him a sidelong look. 'Sounds like just your cup of tea.'

'You may be right,' he agreed.

They arrived a few minutes later in Lyndhurst, where Roy and Sophie had now bought themselves a fairly substantial marital home. The parking was alongside grass on an unlined, very rural-looking road. He took care not to let the tyre dip down off the tarmac. He'd made that mistake last time and then spent ten minutes getting it unstuck again.

He cut the engine and turned to look at her. 'I like that dress,' he told her, reaching out to tug the material further off her shoulder. 'Particularly the way you can see the strap of your bra. It's got a kind of . . . rebellious-chic thing going on.'

'Oh, really?' she asked, moving in on him. 'That's interesting, because I'd say you've got a sort of slutty-authoritative vibe.'

'I always have that vibe,' he said. 'It's what they say about me after my press appearances.'

'Yeah.' She kissed him, and then sighed. 'They're all over you. It's so hard dating eye candy.'

He pulled her towards him for another, longer kiss, before releasing her. Four months in, he was still hugely proud of taking her out to see his friends. But that didn't mean he wasn't equally impatient to get her home at the end of the evening.

Hanson checked the car park several times before heading to her car. There was, luckily, no further sign of Damian, or of any idling cars. Her Nissan was only ten feet from the door, and she climbed into it thankfully. It may have been freezing in there, but it was a safe space.

She set the engine running before doing anything else. She found herself looking across the road towards the Hammer and Tongs, wondering whether she should go and find Jason. She knew he'd appreciate it, for all his facade of independence. And maybe afterwards they could go home and have a proper talk, and she could tell him about Damian at long last.

But the idea seemed too much just then. With her mind half on the murder enquiry and having worked six long days this week, she was tired and fragile. She could also feel a headache coming on and knew that a loud pub would be the worst thing for it. It would be better to find time when things had calmed down a bit.

Decided, she plugged her phone in, hit the play button on some of her running tracks, and pulled out onto Southern Road. By the time she'd got most of the way home, the music had worked out some of the tension in her head.

She backed the Nissan into its customary position as close to the front door as she could manage and killed the engine. The silence left by the music seemed worse than usual. And then she realised that it wasn't the quiet that had hit her; it was the darkness.

She turned her head to look back at the house, where the security light usually came on when anyone came up the driveway. She could see its outline, faintly, but it was in darkness.

She felt a rush of unease, and thought about driving away again.

But this was her house. She needed to go home. To shower and change. To sleep.

She hesitated, and then picked up her baton. There was no point being unprepared. Hefting it, she climbed out of the car slowly. She tried to look everywhere as she walked, letting nothing escape her notice. But it was hard to make anything out in the tiny front garden. She was suddenly aware that it was riddled with hiding places. Behind the conifer. Round the corner of the house. By the side gate . . .

God, she hated this. Hated how rattled she felt at a simple light not working.

But as she trod towards it, her feet encountered the unmistakable crunch of broken glass. She looked up at the light, her heart jumping. It had been resoundingly smashed, in what looked like a frenzied attack. The light itself was hanging off at a sad angle, trailing wires behind it.

There was a sound up by the gate, and she spun wildly, her baton held out in front of her. But the shape crossing her view turned out to be a chihuahua. It paused at the far gate-post to lift its leg, and then her neighbour appeared after it, his eyes on the illuminated screen of his mobile.

She lowered the baton in case he turned and saw her, though she needn't have worried. He was too engrossed in the screen and must have been totally night-blind.

Trying to force herself to breathe steadily, she reached into the car and picked up her bag and coat. Her hands were shaking as she let herself into the house, and they kept shaking as she shut the door and checked every room.

There was no broken glass. No forced entry. Nothing to be afraid of. And a quick glance outside showed her that the big, fake but realistic security cameras higher up the wall were still intact.

She moved back into the hall and finally put her bag down. But she kept the truncheon in her hand and used it to hit the carpeted stairs as hard as she could. The sound was loud and satisfying, but not as satisfying as when she yelled 'Bastard!' at the top of her voice.

The Hammer and Tongs was, predictably, crowded. There weren't many places that screened club matches, and this had been Southampton playing. They'd played well, too. As a result, a lot of groups had stayed after the match and there had been a long wait for food.

Jason had caught some of the second half of the game and was feeling as cheerful as most of the other punters. Queuing for the bar when it was finally his round turned out to be a slog, but one that had become strangely companionable. Everyone was either enthusing about Southampton's performance or talking about the upcoming Six Nations.

He eventually made it to the front of the queue, and found

himself squeezed in a little uncomfortably next to a strapping bloke in a Hackett shirt. He made an involuntary noise, and the guy said, 'Sorry,' and shuffled away a bit. 'I'm fatter than I think.'

'You're all right,' Jason said, with a nod.

A barman came over to him and he managed to get his order in before anyone else. Once he was done, the bloke next to him asked, 'Are you guys coppers?'

He turned to look at this man a little more carefully, trying to work out why he was being asked. The guy didn't seem to be angry. Just cheerfully curious.

'Yeah,' Jason answered. 'We are. But off duty.'

'Oh yeah, obviously.' The guy shrugged. 'You have to have time off. I used to tell my ex that. She was always on the job. Though actually —' he gave a laugh — 'it turned out it was bullshit, and she was on a different job.'

'Ah, I'm sorry,' Jason said, his eyes on the first almost-poured pint. 'That's tough.'

Jason had never known why he gave off such a strong aura of 'tell me your problems'. He was tempted to blame the psychology degree, though it had happened to him as a teenager, too. Somehow people found him approachable whenever he didn't actively give them fuck-off vibes. And sometimes even then.

'I was pretty cut up at first,' the guy said in a lower voice. 'But actually it was the best thing for me. I was tired of the games. And, oh my God, Juliette loves to play games. She got me to move here, and then was stringing some poor bastard in her team along, too.'

Jason found his pulse quickening. It was no different to the feeling when a witness said something incriminating.

He glanced at the big bloke, who was holding on to the bar with one hand now, bouncing his other fist off the surface. He was clearly in his late twenties. Quite expensively dressed. Attractive. And his accent was decidedly Brummie. He was from Birmingham, like Hanson.

'Your ex was called Juliette?' Jason asked, as the two pints arrived in front of him.

'Yeah,' the guy said, glancing at him and then away. 'I'd worry she might come in here, but this isn't Juliette's kind of place.'

'What kind of an officer is she?' Jason asked, lifting one of the drinks with a hand that felt cold. 'Uniform?'

'No, a detective,' the guy said. 'She came here to become one.'

Jason took a long, steadying breath in through his nose, and then said, 'Let me buy you a drink. What was your name?'

'Damian,' the strapping bloke said, looking a little taken aback. 'You really don't have to . . .'

Jason cut across him, with a very determined smile. 'I'd like to hear more about your ex, if that's OK with you.'

20

Louise

I owe you something of an apology, Niall. In all of this, I haven't been quite honest about a few things. Though it's not that I've actively lied, really. It's more that I've failed to tell you significant details.

I don't even know why I care what you think any more, but for some reason it's still hard to admit a few things to you. Perhaps because it's hard to admit them to myself. It could be that. But I'm starting to realise that the only way I'm going to feel better is to blast every secret out of the water, and leave the truth standing bare. Probably dripping onto our spotless fucking carpets.

So, the first untruth by omission. It's a longstanding one, and I know that you're going to hate it.

You were not the first man I kissed at Hannah's wedding. More than that, I almost ended up going home with someone else entirely.

I told you that April's Italian friend had flirted with me. I don't remember anything he said to me. Or much else about him. Just that he was tall, attractive, and didn't really sound all that Italian.

And, in fact, I don't really know how it happened. One minute I was talking to the bride, and the next I was in a corridor, pressed up against a wall while this handsome man slid his tongue into my mouth and his hand round my back.

I'd never done anything like that before. I've already told you how hard I used to find it to attract attention. Alpha men, in particular, used to look straight past me. So it was extraordinary to me. Wonderful. I was a willing participant as he drew me into an empty bathroom and locked the door behind us.

A more experienced, more self-possessed woman might have taken it further. There might be another reality where I am that person, and where you and I never got together because I decided pushy Italian men were my thing. Maybe it's an inverted reality, where Drunk Louise is the real person and Sober Me is the snivelling creature who only comes out after I forget to drink enough.

But that isn't how it was. As he pinned me against the counter and started to lift my dress, Sober Louise made a comeback. I suddenly felt like it was too much. Too fast. Like I shouldn't be doing this with a man I didn't know, and particularly not with one who was so very much in control.

I went from desire to panic. I found myself fighting to be free of him. He was asking me what was wrong, and then someone started banging on the door. They must have seen us go in there.

We separated and straightened our clothes. When my almost-lover opened the door, he pretended I was ill. That he'd had to look after me. The middle-aged man outside looked like he didn't believe a word of it. I was almost grateful that he was there, though. It meant I could hurry away from the hot Italian without looking at him. It meant I could pretend not to have been frightened.

So when I came to find the two of you outside, you and April, I wasn't walking out fresh from a nice conversation with Hannah. I was doing it with the taste of that man still on my tongue, and with a feeling between relief and regret that I'd run from him.

Does that make you re-evaluate everything about us, Niall? Does it make you look back and ask how you'd been so blind?

I really hope it does, darling, because I'm beginning to want nothing more than to hurt you.

The magistrates agreed to their request for a custody extension early on Sunday morning, which meant it was now up to the team to build enough evidence for a prosecution within a total of ninety-six hours. Jonah shut himself away in his office on his return from the court, equipped with supplies of coffee and three caramel digestives from O'Malley's rapidly diminishing supplies.

Sundays were often a frustrating grind of a day, when businesses were closed to enquiries, Intelligence staff were largely at home, and labs did not process results. The unique value of being at CID on such a deadbeat day was that it allowed him downtime to reflect.

In this case, he had a strange collection of hard facts and large questions. The fact of Alex dying at the Reakes house, compared with the question of how and why. The fact of Louise Reakes moving the body outside, placed alongside uncertainty as to exactly what she had been covering up, and for whom.

He spent a while looking at a map of the area between Louise Reakes's house and Blue Underground. Then he pulled out the printed photo of the knife from his paperwork. After a few minutes looking at it, he rose and asked his team to make their way into one of the meeting rooms.

He got his laptop set up and connected to the data projector, and then settled himself on the edge of the central table while the team trooped in. He waited until Hanson had closed the door behind them all before he said, 'There seem to be three things all this hangs on, at the moment.'

He clicked on a Google Maps tab on his laptop, bringing up the London Road area. He zoomed out and manoeuvred it until they had Louise Reakes's street visible to the top right.

'The first,' he went on, 'is how – and why – Alex Plaskitt ended up at eleven Saints Close. What happened on the way could tell us everything we need to know about how he died. Was there someone else who made their way to the house with Louise and Alex? Did Louise wait somewhere for him? Did he stumble after her in confusion? There might have been an altercation on the way. They also might have been seen together at some point, though we've not had anything useful back from our appeals to the public.'

He paused for a moment, letting the three of them finish writing all of that down, and then went on, 'Related to that is point two: whether we believe that Louise Reakes suffered a total blackout, or whether she's hiding a crime. We probably want to approach both of these questions in the same way.' He highlighted the bottom of London Road with the laser pointer. 'We still haven't had CCTV back from the Wetherspoons to the south of London Road, or the kebab shop further north. I want to prioritise getting footage from those two places, and anywhere else between the nightclub and Louise's house. Either or both of Louise and Alex might have gone south to pick up a cab from the taxi rank on the corner of Cumberland Place. Alternatively, they might have gone north, and then either continued up London Road or headed east along Bellevue.'

'If they did cut through Bellevue, they probably would have gone up Onslow Road afterwards,' Hanson said. 'There are loads of places along there that'll have CCTV. I'll get on it. I can chase up the other ones, too.'

'Thanks, Juliette. The third thing,' he went on, 'is the knife.' He brought up an image of it on the screen, and then glanced at Lightman. 'Do we have any updates from the makers, before I go on?'

'I've left messages with Steel and Silver,' Lightman said. 'Emails, voicemails and web contact form. No reply as yet. Head office is in Newcastle, so hopefully they'll get back to us before we end up having to visit.'

'OK, thanks,' Jonah replied. 'So, my thinking. That knife isn't something you'd happen to have with you. It's a weapon, and it was presumably being carried for a reason.'

O'Malley gave him a speculative look. 'Criminal involvement?'

'Of one sort or another, possibly,' Jonah replied. 'If Louise Reakes is telling the truth, and had never seen the knife before, it could be Alex's. But if he brought it out with him, that implies premeditation. Do we think Alex Plaskitt went out that night with the intention of threatening, raping or hurting a young woman?'

There was a momentary silence, and Hanson said, 'If he had predatory intentions, why didn't he leave with her? She was drunk enough. Do we even know she was still in sight once he'd left?'

Jonah gave a wry smile. 'You think the predatory male idea doesn't fit?'

'Not really,' Hanson replied. 'And to be honest, no kind of violence seems to fit with what we know of his character. It's hard to even imagine him fighting to defend someone. I mean . . . I've seen him throw a strop on camera at his own uselessness, but I just don't see him attacking Louise.'

'There's also the high quality and high price tag of the knife to consider,' Jonah added. 'Those features point to something.'

'Someone who owns it because they get a kick out of it,' O'Malley said, immediately. 'They enjoy using it.'

'Or at least someone who enjoys the idea of using it,' Lightman offered. 'A gang member might own a weapon like that to up his power to intimidate.'

Jonah nodded again. The city's gang culture was depressingly strong, and it was generally an angle they considered in most cases.

'Can we match any of that up with any of our suspects?' Jonah asked.

There was a long silence, and Jonah knew they were mulling over Louise Reakes, Step Conti, Niall Reakes and Issa Benhawy with the same lack of conviction that he was. None of them seemed likely to be criminals of any kind.

'What about April Dumont?' Lightman asked, thoughtfully.

'As a gang member?' O'Malley asked. 'I mean . . . maybe, but I'd doubt it.' He paused, and then went on, 'She is awfully protective of her friend, though. She might have thought Alex was threatening her.'

'But then,' Hanson replied, 'if she killed him to protect her, why would she leave Louise to deal with the body?'

'Fair point,' O'Malley said, with a shrug. 'But it would make sense of Louise trying to cover it all up.'

'So,' Jonah said, 'that basically leaves us needing to know a lot more about our group of involved people. But it also means we should keep the possibility of an unknown attacker in mind. If Alex Plaskitt really was stabbed by someone with a fetish for knives, it could have happened while Louise

Reakes was unconscious. She might only have left the door unlocked and suffered the consequences.'

Jonah could feel his team's reaction to this idea. Or at least O'Malley and Hanson's reaction. It would be a huge blow if Louise turned out to be uninvolved when they'd worked hard both to bring her in and to win as much custody time as possible.

'Ben,' he went on, 'I'd like you to see Step Conti and April Dumont again. I want to know what sort of a person Step is. And I'd like you to press April on whether she really left with another man.'

'Sure,' Lightman agreed.

'Domnall,' he added, 'I want you back on those traffic cameras. Make sure we have licence plates for Niall Reakes, Step Conti and April Dumont. Does Louise Reakes have her own car?'

'I'll check it out,' O'Malley replied.

'OK. Let's go to it.'

'So we're not viewing Louise Reakes as prime suspect?' Hanson queried, as she got to her feet.

'I feel we should be viewing her as the first option of many,' Jonah said. He gave her a slightly wicked smile. 'Business as usual.'

Hanson went to pick up her coat, keys and phone, relieved to be getting out of the station again. The sun was out in force today, and yesterday's snow was almost gone. It was bright and pretty out there, even if it was still freezing, and she wanted to be out in it.

She checked her phone before putting it away. She had an eBay notification on a jacket she'd bid on, but no messages. Nothing from Jason.

And actually, now that she thought of it, she hadn't heard

anything from him last night. She hadn't genuinely expected him to come round after the rugby. He generally got stuck into the beers and ended up going for a late-night curry. He was too considerate to roll in drunk only to pass out on her bed. But it was a little odd that he hadn't messaged her to say so. Or to check in this morning.

She took a moment to send him a quick greeting, asking how he was doing. She might be too busy to reply until later if he did get back in touch, but she'd like to know that he was alive and well.

She grabbed the big square wool scarf that she'd looped over the back of her chair, and nodded to Lightman, who was putting down the phone without having spoken. She felt a need to keep the amicable conversation going. To keep things friendly with him.

'No response from April Dumont?' she asked.

'No,' Lightman agreed. 'And nothing from Step Conti, either. Though I've got stuff to be getting on with until one of them replies. The company that sells those knives finally emailed. Apparently one of the managers should be in from two.'

'On a Sunday?' Hanson asked, winding the scarf round her neck.

'I suppose if they have orders in, they can probably ship them with a courier,' Lightman said, with a shrug. 'I'm guessing it's a pretty small enterprise.'

'I hope they keep proper records.'

'Yeah, I was thinking the same.' Lightman gave a very short sigh. 'It's so rare to have a weapon that might be traceable. It'd be supremely shit if it came to nothing.'

'Supremely,' Hanson agreed, and left the building feeling a little better about everything for some reason.

*

After some time spent banging on the door, Hanson had at last been shown into the cluttered office at the kebab shop and let loose on its old desktop computer. The hard drive had all the shop's CCTV footage, broken down into three-hour chunks.

She sat on the battered foam of the chair and loaded up the file from twelve a.m., wondering what sort of view they were going to get. The answer was, unfortunately, not a great one. The camera was placed at the door, and pointed downwards fairly steeply to catch the faces of everyone coming in. The view of the pavement was limited to a distance of about twenty feet along, and to the near side of London Road. Anyone walking on the other side wouldn't be caught at all.

She scrolled through to one thirteen and then hit play. To her relief, Louise Reakes entered the frame after two minutes. Hanson noted the time down and added a comment that Louise looked as drunk as she had on the nightclub footage. She had the unmistakable straight-legged gait of someone who was having trouble balancing, and in the few seconds of footage they had she veered sharply from left to right.

Hanson wondered if Louise might have been so out of it that she could have gone too far in defending herself. Though whether she could have been coordinated enough in that state to take a knife off someone and stab them was less clear.

Hanson started the video again, guessing that Alex wouldn't be far behind Louise. He'd been less drunk. He was probably walking in straight lines.

And there he was, coming onto the screen seventeen seconds after her. Hanson immediately froze the clip, and wrote the time down with a suddenly accelerated pulse. On the still she had, he was moving aside to let someone out of the

199

kebab-shop door, but his gaze was fixed down the street. As if he was looking at Louise.

Hanson breathed out, and then pressed play. Alex began to move again, and then unexpectedly faltered. His hand went to his pocket.

Hanson found herself fixated. Were they about to see the knife, and end all speculation over whose it had been?

His hand emerged, but it was holding something smaller. Something concealed easily by his palm. Hanson refroze the image, trying to tell what it was, but it wasn't clear enough. It was definitely too small to be his phone.

Frustrated, she pressed the play button once again. She watched as Alex turned, and then, in a move she really hadn't expected, walked into the kebab shop. He disappeared from view, and as time ticked onwards, the truth dawned on her. Alex had been looking to see if he had his bank card. He'd gone to buy himself food.

Seven minutes later, Alex emerged clutching an open kebab in a wrapper. Although Louise Reakes wasn't in sight at this point, it was clear she would be long gone by now. Alex and Louise hadn't met up outside the club, and it didn't look like he could possibly have followed her.

So how, Hanson thought, *had he ended up dying in her bed?*

Patrick Moorcroft made it to Southampton Central just after midday. He was wearing a different but equally expensive-looking suit-and-watch combination, and to Jonah's thanks for coming in he responded with a terse, 'Let's get on with it, shall we?'

Louise's expression was more resigned today, though Jonah suspected that part of that was tiredness. Few people slept well during their first night in the cells.

With the preamble done and Lightman ready next to him, Jonah began the interview.

'In your account of Friday night, you insisted that you remembered nothing from the later part of the evening.'

'That's right,' Louise said, her voice lifeless.

'Louise,' Jonah said in a low, urgent voice. 'I want to be clear on this. We aren't interested in condemning you for your behaviour. We want to know what resulted in the death of a young man. Whatever happened, it is vital that you tell us the truth.'

'I have,' she said, her eyes gleaming slightly.

'My client has expressed no wish to alter her statement,' Patrick Moorcroft said. 'She has also explained her lack of memory to you.'

'Understood,' Jonah said, without looking away from Louise. 'But there may be confused, hazy memories that you haven't told us about. Perhaps things that make no sense to you.'

Jonah saw, clearly, the way Louise reacted. It was the expression of someone who has been seen through.

'I don't think I . . .' Louise shook her head. 'There's only been a dream. And . . . and a few . . .'

'We need to know.'

Louise turned to Patrick. Her solicitor looked torn, as well he might. It was unclear whether anything Louise said was likely to incriminate or exonerate her. But it was important to show that his client was cooperating where she could. He glanced at Jonah, weighing things up, and then nodded.

Louise gave a long sigh. 'I think I remember someone chasing me. Not him. Not Alex. But it's a dream, so maybe it was meant to be him. I knew they were a threat, and they kept coming, and I kept falling.' She gave a sudden, loud sniff, and then continued with an unsteady voice. 'I fell, and they were suddenly on top of me, hurting me. There was – there was a pain in my back, and when I woke up and looked in the mirror, there was a bruise where – where I remembered it.'

'OK,' Jonah said, with some satisfaction. He felt instinctively that she was telling them the truth. 'It's important that a female officer photographs any bruising. Any injuries at all.'

'I know.' Louise's cheeks were wet with tears again.

He watched her, briefly, as she rubbed at one of her cheeks. 'You said you fell onto the grass. Was there anything else to your surroundings?'

'Trees,' she said, indistinctly. 'I thought there were trees. But I don't – I don't think I was in the woods, after a night out. I don't think that's right.'

Jonah glanced at Lightman, who was writing notes with unusual energy. He suspected that Lightman's thoughts mirrored his own. That with a large blank in her memory it was possible she'd ended up almost anywhere.

'Was there anyone else, in the dream?'

Louise's expression grew distant. She tried to speak, swallowed, and then said, 'I don't know. There could have been someone else. At some point in the evening someone was angry. Maybe with me, or maybe – maybe I just saw a fight. But I don't – I don't know. None of it's clear.'

Jonah nodded. 'That's all right. And what else was there? You said you remembered a few fragments?'

Louise paused for quite some time, her eyes on her hands, before she said, 'I think I talked to the victim. In the club. I don't know how long for. I just have this memory of his face as he's saying something and I have no idea what it was.' She gave Jonah an anguished look. 'I only remembered that this morning. I'm sorry.'

Lightman glanced at Jonah, and then asked, 'You think this was after your friend April had left?'

'I suppose so.'

'And what else?'

'Nothing else.' She sounded dejected rather than combative. 'I'm sorry.'

Jonah waited a moment before he asked, 'You mentioned that Alex Plaskitt might have tried to rob you.'

'I wouldn't have hurt him,' Louise said, immediately.

'And yet you tried to hide his death,' Jonah argued. 'That was not the action of an innocent person.'

'I told you –'

'Who were you covering up for, Louise?' he asked, cutting across her, his voice steely.

Louise looked upwards, as if trying to find strength somewhere. 'I didn't know what I was covering up. I panicked.'

'Why were you so afraid of telling your husband what had happened?'

'I wasn't –' Louise gave a short, strange laugh. 'I already told you.' Patrick leaned over to murmur something, but she shook her head, impatiently. 'He hates it when I drink, and I thought he'd think it was my fault somehow. That's all.'

'That's a strange idea,' Lightman said, interjecting. 'That the death of a young man was somehow your fault.'

'I didn't – what I meant was, he'd say I shouldn't have been that drunk, or maybe I would have seen something. Stopped it.' Louise looked close to the fine edge between coping and not coping at all.

'I would caution you against overanalysing comments made by my client in a state of shock,' her solicitor said.

'Did he have some reason for thinking that you were

having an affair?' Lightman pressed, not acknowledging the solicitor.

'No!' Louise's protest was a gasp of outrage. 'Why would he? I'm bloody devoted to him.'

'What did he say when you told him what had happened?' Lightman went on, with an untouched coldness that was impressive.

Patrick Moorcroft shifted in his chair, his gaze moving from Lightman to Jonah. 'How are these questions related to your inquiry into Alex Plaskitt's death?'

'That will become evident,' Jonah said, firmly, his gaze fixed on Louise. 'Please carry on, sergeant.'

'Would you tell us what he said, please?' Lightman said, evenly.

Louise shook her head, in small, quick, jerks. 'I don't know. He just asked – what had happened.'

'I'm sure you can be more specific,' Jonah said, his voice a great deal less measured than Lightman's. Where his sergeant did a wonderful line in being relentlessly unemotional, Jonah's real skill had always lain in attack. In suddenly bringing out such harsh, scathing tones that it broke suspects down. The deep marks left by his father's abuse would always have their uses. 'You claim not to be able to remember Friday night, but yesterday morning, when you called your husband, you were stone-cold sober. So what, *exactly*, did he say?'

'He asked – if it was someone I knew . . .' Louise said, and then she stopped, and he saw one of those rare, intensely telling expressions. She wasn't looking at Jonah, though. She was looking towards the wall, with her face a mask of shock.

22

Louise

I realise that telling you about the Italian man at the wedding was something of a sidetrack. If we're going to continue chronologically, then the next thing to address is the revelation that hit me like a bus earlier today.

I'm not sure quite how it took me so long to realise. I've thought back to the phone conversation we had so many times. I've thought how heart-breaking it was that you were so ready to believe this was my fault, before there was anything to point in my direction.

It occurs to me, having written this all out, that I understand you better tonight than I have ever understood you. I understand why you've been so angry with me for so long, and that it hasn't really been about my drinking, or my desperation for a child. It's had nothing to do with the times I couldn't help tidying when you just wanted to relax.

It explains not only your anger, but also your swift belief that I'd cheated. That I'd killed. Because if you could be angry with me, it exonerated you, didn't it, Niall? Nothing that you'd done could ever be as bad as that, and that left you free from guilt.

But anyway, back to that phone call. The bit I kept forgetting about was the start of it, when I waited for five rings for you to pick up. Waited with a dial tone in my ear that was not the long, irritating beep of an international call, but which was instead the standard double-chirrup of a bloody UK one. Long before you should have even boarded a plane home, you were back in this country, and had probably been back before any of this shit even happened.

You lied, and it took a police interrogation to make me realise the truth. I wonder how I can have been so slow.

23

Louise hadn't even tried to hold out on them. When Jonah asked her, sharply, what it was that she'd realised, she had looked at him, her eyes large and unfocused, and said flatly, 'Niall wasn't in Geneva.'

They'd got a few more words out of her before Patrick Moorcroft had intervened and demanded a private conversation with his client. But they had heard enough.

'We need to get confirmation from the airline,' Jonah said to Lightman, as they walked rapidly back to CID. 'Find out when he did actually arrive back, and see if we can trace him to Southampton on Friday night. Get O'Malley on to it.'

'Of course,' Lightman answered, a little awkwardly. 'Sorry. I've dropped the ball. I should have pushed the airline earlier . . .'

'Hindsight is a wonderful thing,' Jonah said. 'We'd already taken steps to prove he was at the conference and it seemed to tie in. He went to great efforts to cover his tracks. The big question is why.'

'Given his immediate assumption of an affair,' Lightman commented, 'could he have been trying to catch Louise out?'

'It is possible,' Jonah agreed. 'An attempted trap that went wrong. I think she was telling the truth about someone attacking her, and I want to find out where it happened. Louise remembers falling face first onto grass, and trees around her. If the ANPR cameras haven't picked up any of our suspects' cars in the area, then our search radius is fairly small.

As far as a drunk woman could stumble.' He paused outside his office door. 'Do we know when Juliette's going to be back?'

'I'll find out,' Lightman replied.

'I want the two of you to work out any likely places for an attack. And when you have any, get Linda McCullough to meet you there.'

As Lightman wrote himself a note, Jonah briefly updated O'Malley and asked if he'd had any joy with the traffic cameras.

'Louise Reakes's car wasn't on the road,' the older sergeant answered. 'April Dumont I've only picked up much earlier in the day. She must have got a cab to Saints Close, which means any movements later would have been in a cab, too. I'm checking Step Conti now.'

'When you're done with the airline, I want to look for Niall Reakes on those cameras,' Jonah said, tersely. 'Someone attacked her, and Niall wasn't where he said he was. We need to know where he went, and what happened to his wife.' And then, realising that this was a little sharper and more melodramatic than his usual style, he added, 'Please.'

'I'm so sorry,' Louise said, quietly, as soon as the officers had left the interview room. She couldn't bring herself to look at Patrick. 'I didn't . . . I'm too tired to think. I'm not trying to get Niall in trouble.'

There was a moment of silence, and then Patrick said, 'Of course not, and I'm sure he isn't in trouble. It's sensible for you to explain everything that casts doubt on this idea of you as perpetrator.'

There was another pause, and then Louise said, 'I think it'll be OK for Niall. I'm pretty sure I know what he was doing. And who he was doing it with. It isn't what they're thinking.'

After another moment, Patrick said, 'Perhaps you should tell the police what you think. But I'll be sorry if it's that, too.'

Jonah picked up the phone to Hanson twenty minutes after leaving the interview room.

'So we definitely have no sign of a meet-up between Alex Plaskitt and Louise Reakes on London Road,' she summarised. 'And he was too far behind to be following her. So either they met at the house by prearrangement, or something else went on.'

'That's very interesting,' Jonah said, not sure how to fit this into everything else. He briefly imagined Louise letting Alex into her home, and Niall arriving back to find them there together. Had Louise been lying about the attack? Or had something else happened on her way home?

'I've also travelled along her most likely route home,' Hanson went on. 'If she was attacked, I think it must have been on Asylum Green. It's bang on the way, it's the only real green space, and once she was under the trees, she'd be pretty much invisible from the road. Can we get someone out there?'

'I'll send Linda's team,' Jonah told her. 'Are you on your way back?'

'Yes, almost there,' Hanson confirmed.

'Good. Pick Ben up and meet Linda at the scene.'

O'Malley leaned in through the door of Jonah's office. 'Niall Reakes is on his way in. And I've tracked down his movements. He ditched the doctors and came back late on Friday night, from Zurich instead of Geneva. He landed at Gatwick at ten twenty, and could easily have been back here by twelve thirty. Time enough to work out the house was empty and go out and find his wife.'

Jonah gave him a grin. 'That's excellent news.'

As O'Malley let himself out, though, Jonah became thoughtful. If Niall had found Alex and Louise in bed together, he might well have killed them. But how did Louise being attacked on the grass fit? Had Alex stumbled on an attack and thwarted it? Or was Louise Reakes, who had proven adept at hiding the truth, still sending them on a merry dance in order to protect her husband?

Even that made little sense, though, Jonah thought. Why would she protect the man who had killed her lover and left her to deal with it? Unless Niall had threatened her. Or unless Louise had been involved from the start.

Hanson decided to park at the magistrates' court, which was right by Asylum Green. It limited the amount of walking they'd have to do in the freezing wind, even if they did end up standing around in it.

Driving into the car park gave her a strange feeling of déjà vu. It had only been a few hours ago that she'd come here to ask for a custody extension.

She'd been in a very different frame of mind then, her anxiety limited to the tiny flicker of nerves at having to speak in front of the magistrates. There had been no constant panic that was like a siren somewhere in the background. No feeling of everything having gone wrong.

She knew it could be nothing, even now. Jason could have read her message and forgotten to reply. She did that, sometimes, only to be told off for it later. But this was Jason. The man who always messaged back, and dropped her a line at bedtime. Which meant something was really wrong.

Ben seemed to be oblivious to her mood, thankfully. He climbed equably out of the car, stretched his shoulders slightly, and began to amble back up the road towards the green. As Hanson caught him up, pulling her scarf up as high as it would go to protect herself from the wind, he said, 'I wonder if she walked this way often during daylight hours. Louise Reakes, I mean. You'd probably avoid going across a deserted area at one a.m. in the normal run of things. But if it was a frequently used route and she was drunk, she might default to it.'

'Yes,' Hanson said. Then she added, 'She looks like someone who runs. Could be a route she uses for that.'

Lightman gave her a sidelong look. 'Do I look like someone who runs?'

'Probably.' She glanced at him. 'Do you not run?'

'Only under duress,' he said. 'If there are no pools open anywhere, or tennis courts or anything.'

Hanson shook her head, trying to bring some kind of banter to mind now that it seemed to be back on the menu. But she felt as though it had been drained out of her, and she wondered, suddenly, whether this feeling really had anything to do with Jason, or whether it was just the long-term effect of Damian's persistent presence in her life. Whether she'd actually just reached some kind of breaking point.

They crossed the Avenue, the two-lane road that described a long, thin loop like a racing circuit. Asylum Green sat in its centre, a narrow strip of park land that bulged at its southern tip. Linda McCullough's scientific support vehicle was parked up at the bottom, near the green's widest point. She emerged from the driver's door, white-clad and ready for business. A male assistant climbed out of the other side and gave them a nod.

'What are we looking at?' McCullough asked.

Lightman glanced at Hanson, and she realised he was letting her do the talking.

'Thanks for coming so quickly,' she said, grateful that her voice seemed to sound normal in spite of everything. 'We're looking for evidence of some kind of attack on our suspect. I've been looking at routes. If she crossed the green, it's likely to have been at this end. She would have emerged from London Road, and it's likely she'd cut across the diagonal path to get onto the far side of the Avenue.'

'OK,' McCullough said, pulling a set of latex gloves out of her pocket and handing them to Hanson. 'You two may as well look too. Any scuff marks, dropped items, signs of discolouration of the soil or obvious blood on the grass or paving, call me over.'

So Hanson and Lightman began treading the frozen grass, stepping slowly and carefully. They moved in and out of the sunlight between the trees. It was strange how quickly they got into a soothing rhythm, despite the freezing air. There was nothing to do except look at their feet and make occasional remarks.

When she glanced over at Ben a few times, she realised that he looked less neutral than usual. There was an aura of brooding about him.

'You aren't beating yourself up about Niall Reakes's flights, are you?' she asked him, quietly. 'If you are, you're being an idiot.'

There was a note of surprise in his expression as he looked at her, and then he gave a very small smile. 'I've never denied being an idiot.'

'You spoke to the conference organisers,' Hanson said. 'You spoke to the airline. It's not your fault they hadn't bothered checking properly.'

'But I always work on the assumption that people don't bother,' he said, with a shrug. 'It's how I make sure of things. And I should have chased them up.'

'It didn't make any difference,' Hanson told him. 'Niall Reakes is still going to have to explain himself. So cut yourself a bit of slack. Otherwise it makes the rest of us feel worse.'

Ben's smile turned into a laugh, and she was pleased to note that he seemed a little less morose as they trod onwards. It made her feel incrementally more useful and in control of things, and that was important right now.

After ten minutes, Lightman found an empty cigarette packet in a patch of remaining snow. Linda came over and bagged it up, despite the low chance of it meaning anything. Five minutes later, Linda's team found a single glove that looked like it might belong to a woman. It was navy fleece, the cheap kind you got in petrol stations, and it was sodden with melted snow. It got bagged up too.

A few minutes later, at a midpoint in the green, Hanson caught a glint of reflected light. Crouching down, she saw an earring nestled into the grass. Its triple rows of hanging diamantés were set into silver squares. It looked, to Hanson, like the sort of thing Louise Reakes might well have worn on her night out, and she tried to remember whether earrings had shown up on the CCTV.

Lightman stepped carefully past her where she crouched, and then stopped.

'There's blood,' he said.

Jonah's working of Niall Reakes began the moment he walked through the door of CID. Assuming a mantle of full-blown officialness, he dispensed with any conversation at all as he took the drugs rep quickly and angrily through to the interview suite. O'Malley was already waiting for them by the door, and Jonah almost felt tempted to laugh at the pitying expression his sergeant gave their suspect.

If Niall had looked anxious on arrival, he was actually shaking by the time Jonah introduced them all for the tape. Jonah gave him nothing but a piercing stare once the introductions were done, and Niall caved within seconds.

'I need to tell you something,' he said, putting a hand out to the table as if to steady himself. 'It isn't – it's got nothing to do with the death of that guy, but I know you're going to think it does.'

'Would this be about your whereabouts on Friday night?' Jonah asked, whip-sharp.

'Yeah.' Niall swallowed. 'Yeah, it is. I flew home early from the conference. I told Jessie, my assistant, that my wife was really ill, and she said she'd cover the final night and morning.'

Niall's accent seemed to have slid a whole step less middle class, making it clear that he spent much of his life acting. Trying to be more than he was. It elicited a surge of sympathy in Jonah.

'And yet you didn't go to look after your wife,' he said.

'No. I lied.' There was an ugly-looking sheen to his face, and Jonah focused on that instead of his sympathy. On how distasteful this man was. It made it easier to go on the attack in the short window they had before Niall requested a solicitor. 'I flew back to meet up with my ex-wife.'

Jonah glanced over at Lightman, and said, 'I find that difficult to believe.'

'It's – true.' Niall looked desperate. Sick-looking. 'It isn't the first time, and Dina can back me up.'

'You're telling us you were having an affair?'

'Not even an affair,' Niall said, clasping his hands together. They were trembling uncontrollably. 'Though I – she's been pushing for one.'

Jonah gave a short laugh. 'You're asking us to believe that you lied to your employers and your wife, and then spent a great deal of money flying home early to meet up with your ex-wife, all purely for a platonic chat?'

'She's getting me a job,' he said, just before Jonah had finished. 'A VP role at Glaxo. A friend of hers there is on the board. She told me about it back in June and I – I really wanted it. It's where I've wanted to work forever.'

'Why not simply tell your wife about it?' O'Malley asked. 'If a perfect job was being offered.'

'Because . . . Look, Dina obviously seems like a threat to her,' Niall said, trying for some sort of boys-together tone and not achieving it. 'I knew Louise would tell me to stay away from her, which would have meant no job.'

'So let me understand this,' Jonah said. 'You've been carrying on what might as well be an affair with a woman who has promised you a job on the basis that, what, you sleep with her after it's all sorted? Is that it?'

'No,' Niall said, his expression pained. He clearly thought this unfair. 'There's never been any agreement of any kind. I never would.'

'How did your marriage to your ex-wife end?' Jonah asked.

'I . . . She left me. For someone else.' Niall Reakes looked, for some reason, more awkward admitting this than he had at any point so far.

'Why would she now want you back so desperately that she's found a way of offering you your dream job?'

'She misses me. She realised it was a mistake breaking

things off the moment I got married to Louise. But . . . but I love my wife. Very much.'

'Despite the ease with which you believed she was having an affair,' Jonah countered. 'Despite your swift assumption that she is guilty of murder.'

'I never assumed that!' Niall said, looking angry. 'I was eff-ing furious with her because – because all of this is probably going to screw everything up.' There was a pause, and he said in a more measured voice, 'I lied to my company, and now I probably don't have a new job to go to. It's all been forced out into the open because – because Louise got pissed again.'

Jonah felt overwhelmingly tempted to ask whether Niall thought that might be karma, but instead he asked, 'Where did you stay on Friday night?'

'At the Gatwick Hilton.'

'And you met Dina in your room?'

'No. In the bar.'

'Until what time?'

Niall considered for a moment, and then said, 'A bit after twelve, I guess.'

'What car do you drive?'

Niall looked wrong-footed. He sounded a little defensive as he said, 'A Jaguar. An F-TYPE.'

'That's a nice sporty car,' Jonah commented. 'So you could easily have driven back home by, say, quarter to two. Prob-ably even earlier if you'd floored it.'

'I didn't,' Niall protested.

'You didn't arrive back and find your wife in bed with another man?' Jonah asked. 'You didn't decide to do away with him and leave her comatose to wonder if she'd done it? I mean, it would be a pretty effective form of revenge, wouldn't it?'

There was a silence for several seconds, and then Niall said, 'I want my solicitor now.'

'So I'll call the ex-wife now?' O'Malley asked, following Jonah back into CID.

'Yes,' Jonah said. 'Though I strongly suspect that he's made some sort of arrangement with her.'

'You don't believe him?'

Jonah glanced at his sergeant. 'There's a small chance that it's true. But looked at rationally, he went to a hell of a lot of trouble just to meet up about a job offer.'

'Agreed,' O'Malley said. 'And I'm interested in why he flew from Zurich. He must have driven for two or three hours to get there. I'm going to look up whether there were other flights he could have taken without the long drive.'

'Yes,' Jonah said, trying and failing to picture where the two cities were on a map. 'That's probably the weirdest part of it.' He paused for a moment, thinking of the distinctive murder weapon. 'It might also be worth checking whether there's a retailer who sells those knives in Zurich.'

'I'll get on it,' O'Malley answered.

'The blood tests from Louise Reakes are sitting with the lab, aren't they?' Jonah went on, thoughtfully.

'Yup,' O'Malley said. 'Also useless until tomorrow.'

'Unless we work on the good nature of our colleagues,' Jonah said. He pulled his phone out and dialled Linda McCullough's number.

There were traffic noises in the background as she picked up.

'We're on site at Asylum Green,' she said, immediately. 'And we have blood.'

'Blood?' Jonah asked, dumbly.

'Yes, Sheens. You'll know it as the red stuff that runs through most people's veins.'

Jonah half smiled as he replied, 'I'll look it up.'

'There isn't a lot of it. Did your female show any signs of injury?' McCullough asked.

'Nothing she showed us,' Jonah said, thoughtfully, 'but she mentioned pain in her back, which we're going to get photographed.' He glanced up at O'Malley, who nodded. Presumably that was already being sorted by one of the female PCSOs.

'We've got a few personal belongings bagged up, too,' McCullough went on. 'They may or may not have anything to do with an attack.'

'Thanks,' Jonah said. 'How long do you think you'll be there?'

'Why do I suspect that this question isn't about my mental health?' McCullough asked.

'I have no idea,' Jonah countered. 'But we've got a blood test for Rohypnol I badly want back, and a non-functioning lab.'

True to form, McCullough complained loudly, and then agreed. 'I'm still waiting for all those pints you owe me, Sheens,' she added.

'Just say the word,' Jonah replied.

The temperature was now just above freezing, and Hanson was suffering. Even with her coat zipped up to her chin and her hands shoved in her pockets, she was shaking with cold.

'Should have brought another four or five layers,' she said to Lightman, as the two of them huddled beneath one of the trees on Asylum Green. Or at least as Hanson huddled. Lightman looked as unaffected by everything as usual.

'Do you want to wait in the car?' he asked her. 'There's no reason for us both to hang around here.'

'That's extremely kind,' Hanson said, meaning it, 'but my pride would never recover.'

McCullough came over a few minutes later to announce that they were packing up, and Hanson sighed with relief.

'We've got blood and soil samples and we've taken cuttings of the grass,' she said.

'Can you tell how much there was?' Hanson asked. 'Like whether it was a serious injury or just, I don't know, a nose bleed?'

'It's not a lot,' Linda said. 'A splash only.'

'And I suppose we don't even know if it was connected,' Hanson went on, more quietly.

'No, we don't,' McCullough said, cheerfully. 'Welcome to my world.'

Lightman and Hanson walked briskly back to the car after that, and Hanson turned the engine on immediately in the hope that it might warm up. She pulled her bag off over her head and felt her phone buzz as she did so. Pulling it out, she saw a message from Jason. It began with the words, I don't quite know what to say to you . . .

She opened it up with an unreal feeling. She read his words, feeling as though she was slipping sideways out of the car as she did.

'Everything all right?' Lightman asked from beside her after a moment.

And to Hanson's absolute humiliation, when she tried to answer, nothing but a ragged sob came out.

O'Malley had both a mobile and landline for Dina Weyman and managed to reach her on the latter. The call was originally answered by a disgruntled-sounding man who was presumably Dina's husband.

'Why do you want to talk to her?' he asked, gracelessly, when O'Malley explained who he was.

'We want to corroborate a story given by a witness,' O'Malley told him. 'We're told your wife can help.'

There were movements on the other end, and a ferocious-sounding muttered conversation followed by the slam of a door. O'Malley wondered whether he'd called in the middle of some sort of domestic.

Eventually, Dina said, 'Hello?' in a voice as cheerful and unconcerned as a child's.

'Is that Dina Weyman?'

'Yes,' she said. 'I understand you're with the police.' There was a slight sigh to her voice, as if talking to the police was immeasurably boring.

'Detective Sergeant O'Malley,' he told her. 'I want to ask you about Friday night.'

'What about it?' The question could have been rude, but she managed to inject just enough lightness into it to save herself.

'Niall Reakes tells us that you met up with him at a hotel,' O'Malley said. 'We just wanted to confirm the details.'

There was a pause, and Dina said, 'I'm sorry, Niall said I met up with him?'

'Yes.' O'Malley found himself sitting up very straight. 'On Friday night.'

There was another pause, and then Dina said, in a much less light tone, 'I'm very sorry, but we didn't end up meeting. Niall asked to see me, and then he stood me up.'

24

Louise

I want to tell you about the one other memory I have, one I'm not even sure is real. But I need to tell you because it scares me every time I think of it.

In my memory, or my dream, because I'm no longer clear on which it was, I remember crying. Lying on my side on what feels like cold ground with my hands in my hair. I'm sobbing and sobbing, and somebody is shushing me.

It's the thing that makes me panic more than anything else, remembering that gentle hushing noise. It sends blades of fear running through me, and I don't understand why.

Jonah found it hard not to laugh as O'Malley summed up his conversation with Dina Weyman. It was partly a laugh borne out of victory, and partly a reflection of the absurdity of it all.

'Did it sound like she was expecting us to ask about Niall Reakes?' Jonah asked, once O'Malley was done with his brief summary.

'No,' O'Malley said, 'but then I got the impression she'd be good on the stage. Very much in control of how she comes across, you know?'

'So there might have been some kind of an agreement,' Jonah said, thoughtfully. 'One she then went back on. OK. Well, we have a new prime suspect. Any news on Niall's solicitor?'

'Nothing yet.'

'I'd like to have more to throw at him before going in there, anyway,' Jonah went on, thinking as he spoke. 'The guy up the road talked about being subjected to boy racers gunning their engines late on Friday. Niall Reakes drives an F-TYPE. That's a good audible, racy-sounding engine.'

'But we didn't find him on any of the ANPRs,' O'Malley pointed out.

'Can we check further afield?' Jonah asked. 'He might have gone home by an unexpected route.'

'I'm pretty sure I've got all the routes to Saints Close covered,' O'Malley said, doubtfully, 'but I'll check. We've got to check up on those knives, too,' he added. 'Which may take a while . . .'

'Let's get Ben on that as soon as he's back,' Jonah suggested.

'Ah, he'll like that,' O'Malley agreed, with a grin. 'A good bit of careful checking.'

Jonah glanced at his watch. It was gone half past five. They needed to make some real progress before heading home for the day. They couldn't hold Niall Reakes overnight without arresting him, and Jonah wasn't going to arrest a second suspect without strong evidence.

He felt slightly frustrated, too, that he had no clear picture of how all this might hang together. Louise's attack might tie in with Alex being stabbed somewhere other than Saints Close. But if Niall Reakes had attacked them, how had they both ended up at the house?

He felt an urge to get out of the station. To do some active investigation. But there was nothing specific for him to follow up on.

The phone on O'Malley's desk rang, and Jonah was still trying to work out his own next move while O'Malley answered it. He saw his sergeant wince slightly at what was obviously a tirade. Though as Jonah watched, his expression changed from long-suffering to alert.

'I'm very sorry to hear that, Mr Derbyshire,' he said, after a few moments. 'We'll get someone out to take a look.'

He hung up and said to Jonah, 'That was one of the residents of Saints Close. He wants to know when someone's going to come and clear up all the blood.'

'The blood?' Jonah said, blankly.

'Apparently, now the snow's melted, you can see pools of it all the way down the road.'

'I'm so sorry.'

It must have been the tenth time Hanson had said it. Each time she intended for it to be the end of the tears. But they kept on oozing out, as Ben gently persuaded her to swap seats so he could drive, and then pulled the car in at the drive-to Starbucks so he could pick up tea. He let her sit in the passenger seat to try to compose herself while he went to buy it, but nothing had changed by the time he got back. And it was still the same after several scalding mouthfuls of Earl Grey.

'There's nothing to be sorry about,' he told her again. And then he said, 'You don't have to tell me anything, but it might genuinely help.'

She would have kept on resisting if everything hadn't felt so terrible.

She handed Lightman the phone and let him read for himself all the horrendous things Jason now thought about her.

I bumped into your ex, a man I didn't even know about. A man you were still seeing up until last week . . .

She tried to swallow down the tears along with another mouthful of tea while he read. It took Lightman a good thirty seconds to finish reading. She wondered if Ben would take it all at face value, too, and it made her feel desolate.

Damian had even woven Ben into his lies, a fact that added its own extra turn of total humiliation.

He told me that you'd been making moves on another colleague too, and bragging about it to your female friends because he was good eye candy. I assume he meant Ben Lightman, and I only hope he realises what he's letting himself in for.

And the real clincher, of course, was the way Damian's lies had used truths and then twisted them to make them work against her. That had always been the way it worked with him. Genuine, incontrovertible facts that he grossly, hideously misrepresented.

Jason had been putty in his hands.

I might have questioned it if it hadn't explained so much. The fact that you claim to be busy so often in the evenings, and to like your own space. The fact that you've never introduced me to any friends, or suggested a visit to your home town. It must be exhausting keeping all the lies going, Juliette, and I feel sorry for you.

The sad fact was that Juliette *had* no real friends in Southampton. And Damian was the prime reason she now avoided going home to Birmingham. But her ex knew exactly how to retell it all.

And if Jason believed it, what was to stop Ben believing the rest of it, too?

But once he'd finished reading, Lightman lowered the phone and said, 'Jesus. That's . . . what a total manipulative bastard.'

She felt such a rush of gratitude that it made the tears worse, not better. But she managed to smile at him, shakily, and say, 'Oh, he's a real keeper.'

'Which one?' Lightman asked, with a raised eyebrow, and Hanson actually laughed slightly.

'I can definitely pick 'em, can't I?'

Ben took a gulp of tea, the phone held loosely in his other hand, and then said, 'I take it this isn't the first time Damian's tried to wreck your life.'

Hanson shook her head, feeling the truth rush to make its way out. 'He's been messaging me. Constantly. All from anonymous accounts.' She swallowed, feeling strangely all right about saying it now that she'd begun. 'And turning up at

225

my house. Sometimes watching me from his car. Never quite often enough to constitute harassment, and not always – not always close enough for me to be certain it's him before he leaves.' She gave another humourless smile. 'He's a clever bastard like that.'

Lightman nodded again, slowly. 'Have you written it all down?'

Hanson started to nod, and then shrugged. 'I started doing. More recently I've been – I've been a bit lax. It's been getting to me.' She took a large, steadying breath. 'I wrote down some of the worst times, though. Like when I got outside and found all my tyres slashed. And the – the mutilated Barbie doll he left on the doorstep. And the smashed security light last night.'

Lightman shook his head. 'The man has problems. You reported all of those?'

Hanson nodded. 'Not the security light. Not yet. But the other two. I couldn't prove it was him, though. I did put up two big, noticeable, completely fake CCTV cameras off Amazon, but he still took out the light. Looks like he stood at the end of the drive and threw rocks at it until it went.'

'I'd say the odds are definitely in favour of it being him,' Lightman said, drily. 'You don't generally go around pissing people off that much.'

'Hey,' she protested. 'I work pretty hard at being annoying.'

'Granted.' He hesitated for a moment. 'I should probably say that this isn't the first defamatory bullshit I've read from your ex.'

Hanson's shaky sense of certainty took another dip. 'What do you mean?'

'A month after you joined, I got an email,' he said. 'An anonymous one. It tried to claim that you'd been dismissed

from your last role for gross malpractice, but that Birmingham had hushed it up.'

'Oh my God.'

'I thought I should take it to the chief, and it turned out
he'd had an email too.'

Hanson turned away from him, a reflexive instinct based
on defence. She hadn't thought she could feel any more humiliated by her ex-boyfriend. But, of course, Damian could always
sink lower. Could twist the knife in that little bit further. She'd
never met anyone with such a gift for hurting people.

'I would have told you,' Ben said, with a note of apology,
'but the chief was convinced it would just stress you out,
even if you knew he didn't believe a bloody word of it. And I
thought he was probably right.'

'You're sure he didn't believe it?' she asked. The thought
of it made her cringe. This must have been, what, a week or
two after she'd had a showdown with the DCI over his own
behaviour in an investigation? What must he have thought
of her?

'Come on,' Lightman said, with a grin. 'He's too smart for
that. What he actually did was have a quiet word with our IT
department, asking them to filter out any similar content and
report it to him. He was hoping to catch the perpetrator out.
And by the way, his immediate guess was a disgruntled ex,
which was what I thought, too.'

There was a short pause, and then Ben said, 'I guess the
question is what we do about all this.'

The word 'we' made Hanson feel indescribably better.

'You aren't starting to wonder if Damian's actually telling
the truth?' she asked, trying to keep her voice light. 'Whether
I am actually a deeply manipulative, deceptive psychopath
who's been stringing everyone along?'

Lightman out and out laughed at this. 'Don't give yourself airs, constable.'

'Yes, sarge.' Hanson found herself grinning, a genuine grin that almost broke into real laughter.

'So we're going to sort this.' Ben gave a nod.

'Do you think so?' she asked, a little less cheerfully. 'I mean, I've seen how this stuff goes. Women being stalked and harassed. The full weight of the law means nothing in so many cases.'

'Agreed,' Lightman said. 'But there might be better ways than the law itself to stop him.'

'Maybe you're right,' she answered, thoughtfully. She'd thought that herself, early on, before it had all seemed to pile up on top of her.

'I can explain things to Jason,' Lightman said, after a moment. 'If it comes from me, he's not going to end up dismissing it.'

Hanson felt her face growing hot. 'You don't need to do that.'

'I honestly think it would help.'

'It's OK,' she said. And then she swallowed. 'The speed with which he chose to believe it is . . . well, I think it tells me something. I mean, he's the one with the bloody degree in criminal psychology. He's the one who's supposed to know what to look out for.'

'I assume your ex-boyfriend played on his feelings,' Ben said, quietly. 'I wouldn't blame him too much.'

'And yet here you are,' Hanson countered, 'not in a relationship with me, and refusing to believe a word of it.'

'Well,' Lightman said, 'as you'll know, I don't have any feelings to play on, so . . .'

Hanson gave a real throaty laugh at that. 'Fair point.'

*

'And can you turn to your right?'

The female officer was softly spoken. She sounded like she came from Swansea, and she seemed sympathetic. Kind, even.

Louise turned as directed, feeling strangely like she was back at her engagement photo shoot with Niall. Though they'd been in the grounds of a National Trust property that day. Not in a small bare room in a police station. She'd been wearing a brand-new wool sweater and jeans, too. Not just her bra and leggings.

And it had only been her constantly smiling mouth that had ached on that day. Not her back. Her head. And somewhere difficult to pinpoint in her chest.

The soft flash of the camera came three times, and the officer asked her to extend her left arm out to the side. Louise twisted, trying to see the arm herself. There must be bruising that she hadn't discovered yet.

'If you could just look forwards . . .'

Louise straightened her head, having caught sight of nothing more than a purplish-yellow tinge on the back of her arm. The camera flashed again.

And then suddenly Louise was not in that room, but face-down on icy grass, the taste of mud and leaves in her mouth. She was fighting to move. To breathe. There was pain in her back, and in her left arm, where his hand was pushing her down.

That's a knife, sweetheart, he was saying. *You feel it? I'm going to squeeze down on it every time you move. So you'd better keep fucking still, hadn't you?*

And then she was crouching on the floor of a brightly lit room, her breathing rapid and shallow, begging them to let her have some air.

*

With Hanson and Lightman back in CID, Jonah called a briefing in the big meeting room before doing anything else. The one advantage of being in on a Sunday night was that they had their choice of rooms, which meant they were back in the much-coveted conference room, complete with big windows and comfortable chairs.

He gave them all a moment to settle, his gaze resting briefly on Hanson. It looked as though she'd been crying, and very recently. She now had the hesitant, careful air of someone just holding it together. He needed to check in with her again. It was frustrating that it might have to wait, though. They had two people in custody, both potentially to be charged, and a limited time frame to do something about it.

He loaded the map up on to the projector again and began.

'Having established that Alex Plaskitt died in Louise Reakes's bed, it now looks fairly certain that he wasn't actually attacked there. There are significant splashes of blood down Saints Close, none of which were visible until the snow melted.'

There was a brief silence. Then O'Malley said, 'It might scupper our theory about Niall Reakes finding them in bed together and going mad.'

'It might,' Jonah agreed. 'Though it still remains possible that he went out hunting for his wife, found something going on and went on the attack.'

'We have blood found at Asylum Green,' Lightman said. 'It could be Alex Plaskitt's. We also have an earring and a glove. If Louise identifies either as hers, we can pin down some kind of event happening there. Possibly an attack.'

'If it was Louise's husband,' O'Malley commented, 'is it

possible she's still covering for him? Out of a sense of guilt for having cheated?'

'Would he really have risked refusing to see her if so?' Hanson asked, doubtfully. 'Surely he'd want to keep her sweet.'

'Unless refusing to see her is just an act,' O'Malley countered, with a shrug. 'They're pretending to have rowed when they were both in on it.'

'We'll have a clearer idea once those bloods are back,' Jonah said, aware that he was, as usual, slightly damping down the general enthusiasm. 'We need to work out whether Niall really was in Southampton. I want to check public transport. Trains. Buses. Taxis.'

'I'll get on it,' Hanson offered.

'And then there's Niall's strange trip to Zurich,' Jonah went on. He switched tabs to bring up a zoomed-out version of the route from Geneva to Zurich. 'We've got the receipt for the new flight he booked, and it cost him a small fortune. Zurich is also a three-hour drive from Geneva. O'Malley's looking to see if he went there to purchase the murder weapon.'

'And I've confirmed there were spaces on flights from Geneva,' O'Malley commented. 'For less money, generally. He could have flown straight home.'

Hanson glanced up. 'But if he went to buy the knife, then the attack was premeditated. That doesn't tie in with him finding her with another man.'

'It could, if he was already convinced his wife was cheating,' O'Malley countered. 'He may not have known Alex Plaskitt, but he might have had reason to think there was infidelity going on. He could have been planning this for months.'

Lightman shifted slightly, and Jonah asked, 'Thoughts, Ben?'

Lightman breathed out for a moment. 'It's . . . strange behaviour. If it really was all planned, then it seems unlikely that he would have left the ticket purchase until the last minute. He was running a big risk that he might not get one.'

'Yes,' Jonah said, thoughtfully. 'He was.'

'Doesn't it read,' Hanson asked slowly, 'more like a sudden crisis? That ex-wife of his . . .'

'Dina Weyman,' Jonah said.

'Are we positive she isn't lying?' She glanced at Lightman. 'Maybe she did summon him for an urgent conversation.'

'It's hard to say,' Jonah told her. 'Perhaps we need to see her in person. But Niall Reakes's story about a job offer is more than a little far-fetched. As you say, his actions sound more like a crisis.'

'So our hypothetical situation would be that Dina needed to see him in a hurry,' Lightman said, slowly, 'for some reason requiring him to get to Zurich first. He was doing something for her, maybe. And then, once they'd met, Dina denied it.'

There was a brief pause, and then Jonah said, 'Talk to her. And to anyone who knows her.' He glanced at O'Malley. 'Didn't you say April Dumont knows the ex-wife too?'

'Yeah, she does,' O'Malley said, and gave a grin. 'And she doesn't seem much of a fan of hers, either.'

'Talk to her, as soon as you can,' Jonah said.

'I've arranged to see Step Conti again shortly,' Lightman commented. 'Should I keep that appointment or bunk it?'

Jonah hesitated. Their priority seemed clear: to dig into everything to do with Niall Reakes. But the possibility of Niall having planned his attack shifted things. It made him wonder whether they were missing a link between him and Alex Plaskitt.

'I think see him,' he said in the end. 'Show him photos of the Reakeses and see what he says. O'Malley, let's go and talk to Niall Reakes. Juliette, see if you can book us in to see Dina Weyman later this evening.' He gave her an apologetic smile. 'Happy crap weekend.'

'Ah, I have nothing to do except watch shit TV,' Hanson said, with strange cheerfulness. 'It's all good with me!'

Hanson was glad that their investigation seemed to be going somewhere, and not just for its own sake. It meant she could get her head down and work, and not think about Jason and how awkward it was going to be seeing him every day from now on. This, she thought, was why you should never date someone at work.

And also, she added to herself, *why you should get yourself an actual social life*.

She woke her desktop up, and her eyes drifted over to where Jason sat on a normal working day. She thought of Louise and her husband, who had been so quick to condemn her. And she thought how, in a way, Jason had done exactly the same.

She suddenly found herself coming to a decision. Pulling out her phone, she typed him a brief message.

Thank you for that essay. I have nothing to say in reply except that I want your things gone from my house before I get home later.

And with that done, she was ready to work.

Jonah hid himself away to prep for the interview with Niall Reakes. He knew he needed to be on form. Niall had ended up being represented by Daniella Hart, who was with the same firm as Patrick Moorcroft. Like him, she was expensive, and Jonah's one encounter with her had been exhausting.

He'd dropped in on the solicitor and her client to give them warning and found the atmosphere a little tense. It was clear that having someone who wasn't Patrick was galling for Niall. It was equally clear that Daniella Hart didn't like being second choice. He couldn't help smiling as he left them again.

Midway through getting his notes together, Jonah's landline rang. McCullough, with the blood results.

'Her blood tests are negative for Rohypnol,' McCullough said, her voice slightly raised to speak over music she had on in the background. 'There was still alcohol present, indicating that she'd drunk more than twenty-four units that night. Enough to explain serious memory loss. But perhaps more interestingly, she's showing traces of Viagra.'

'That's . . . slightly odd . . .'

'They do say it's the modern man's drug of choice,' Linda commented, drily. 'There are lots of rumours online that it can be used to make women aroused. If true, that would be a score for any potential rapist. It's pretty easy to defend rape if the victim was clearly horny as hell in the earlier part of the evening.'

'And is it true?' Jonah asked, with interest.

McCullough gave a derisive laugh. 'I'd say it's pretty unlikely to do anything at all. Viagra works by increasing blood supply to the groin. Men who take it don't need it because they can't get horny. It's because they can't get an erection.'

'Right,' Jonah said, not sure quite why he'd thought this conversation a good idea. 'So it's more than a little odd that Louise Reakes had it in her system.'

He thought of Niall and decided that this was a strong sign against his involvement. Unless he'd somehow spiked something that he knew Louise would drink. Viagra tablets could presumably be crushed and added to most things. But that would be a bizarre move. Could he really have got himself into such a twisted state that he'd *wanted* his wife to cheat so he could take revenge?

'I've also taken prints from the articles we found at the park,' McCullough said. 'Obviously no analysis run until tomorrow, but if you need to show them to your suspects, they're now yours.'

'I'll get one of the team to pick them up, thank you.'

Jonah ended the call feeling as though nothing quite added up. The only theories he currently had to explain everything seemed more than outlandish.

Which meant they had to go for hard facts, however small, he thought. There were things they could pin down.

He ducked back out into CID, and told O'Malley he'd be ready in a minute, then asked Hanson if she'd had any response from Dina Weyman, Niall's ex-wife.

'She's going to call back,' Hanson replied. 'She's supposed to be at some important meeting but will see what she can do.'

'OK, great. I'd like you to show Louise the items you picked up at the park. They're ready to collect from Linda.'

Hanson nodded and rose, her expression still distant, but not bleak or on edge, he thought. Whatever was going on, she seemed to be holding it together.

'Is everyone hanging in there OK?' he asked O'Malley once she'd left, trying to say it lightly.

'Ah, sure, I think so,' O'Malley said, with a shrug. 'I mean, sure, it's Sunday night and we'd all rather be at home, and I think Juliette got hypothermia at the park, but, you know.'

Jonah nodded, and glanced over at Lightman, who was on the phone.

'Is Ben on the line to Step Conti?'

'Yup,' O'Malley agreed. 'Just started the call. Do you need something from him?'

'Nothing that can't wait until we've seen Niall Reakes,' he said. 'Let's go.'

'Sorry about this,' Lightman told Step, once his wife had fetched him to the phone. 'I know Sunday evenings aren't the best time.'

'Are you kidding?' Step said. 'You got me out of the world's longest *Peppa Pig* marathon.' He added, more seriously, 'And I'm happy to do anything I can to help. Alex was the closest thing I ever had to a best friend.'

Lightman thanked him. 'There are a few things we need to ask you. The first is whether you saw Alex with a woman on Friday.'

There was a long pause, and then Step said, 'I'm sorry. I should have said before. Karen – my wife – was angry with me for not telling you about it. I just . . . Yes, I did see Alex with someone.' There was an audible swallowing noise down the line. 'There was a woman who was – well, she was hitting on him quite hard. And – he ended up kissing her.'

'Why didn't you mention this before?'

'Because it happened much earlier on,' Step said. 'A long time before I left. And he clearly immediately regretted it. He backed off, and she was angry with him about it. I actually had to get involved, to try and calm things down.'

There was a note of defensiveness in his voice, one that was possibly understandable in the circumstances.

'She felt rejected?' Lightman asked.

'Yes.'

'How did she react after you talked to her?'

'She calmed down after a few minutes,' Step said. 'I think she was just drunk, you know? Anyway, she left him alone after that. I saw her talking to another couple of guys before I left, and she looked like she was having fun.'

'I'm going to share a photo with you,' Lightman said. 'If that's OK. A woman we know to have been at the club. Do you have your mobile on you?'

'Yes, I can look now,' Step offered.

He waited in silence as Lightman forwarded both the arrest photograph of Louise Reakes, and then another image of her captured from the CCTV. He heard a faint chime in the background as they arrived on Step's phone.

'Can you let me know if that's the woman Alex kissed?'

There was a brief silence, and then Step said, 'No, it wasn't her. Sorry.'

Lightman found himself momentarily at a loss. Given everything that happened later that night, how could it possibly have been anyone other than Louise Reakes?

'That's fine,' he said, as smoothly as he could. 'Could you describe the woman you saw him with, perhaps?'

'Sure,' he said. 'She was pretty noticeable. Blonde. Really tall in her heels. She had tattoos. One across her chest and another one on the small of her back.' He looked away for a moment. 'Oh, and she was American. Southern. Really, really hard to understand.'

'Thank you,' Lightman said. 'I think we know who that is.'

Niall Reakes seemed a lot less panicked than he had during their last interview. It seemed, to Jonah, that he was expecting Dina to have backed him up. That this would all be

237

cleared up shortly. He even smiled when Jonah apologised for the delay.

Daniella Hart, next to him, was all cool self-possession. She watched him with a faint hint of a smile, and Jonah returned it. He remembered this from the last time he'd met her. This slightly mocking air. He felt tempted to tell her he was immune to it now. He'd spent the last four months dating someone who mocked him incessantly.

Jonah decided to keep things friendly during the preamble, allowing Niall to remain confident that everything was running smoothly. And then, once the interview had officially started, he said very calmly, 'So, we've now spoken to your ex-wife about the meeting at Gatwick on Friday night. Dina denies having met you at any time in the last few months.'

There was a momentary pause, and then Niall gave a short, almost explosive laugh. 'Sorry?'

'Dina Weyman has denied that you were with her on Friday night,' Jonah repeated. 'She said you asked to meet, and then stood her up.'

'We'd like to know where you really were,' O'Malley said.

Niall shot a glance of desperation towards his solicitor, who leaned to murmur rapidly in his ear. But Niall shook his head, violently.

'I did meet her! What the hell is she . . .? Look.' Niall leaned forwards and clenched his fist on the tabletop. 'I don't know what she's trying to do, but I bloody met her.'

'Why would she tell us she didn't?' O'Malley asked, conversationally. 'It seems like a strange thing to do.'

Niall looked between them, his jaw visibly tightening. 'You can't . . . This is what she does.' He shook his head, and Jonah could see a shake running through him now. 'She

238

plays games. I don't even know why she's saying it, but . . .'
He tailed off, and Jonah watched, in satisfaction, as some
thought occurred to Niall.

'I think you know exactly why she'd do that,' Jonah said.

'Asking my client to speculate on the motivations of his
ex-wife seems counterproductive when you are able to ask
her these questions yourself,' Daniella Hart said.

'It's never counterproductive to respond to someone's
expression,' Jonah replied, smiling. 'That's just good police
work.'

Niall started to shake his head, and then laid his hands flat
on the table, as if trying to control the situation and
himself.

'What about your little jaunt over to Zurich?' O'Malley
asked. 'Why didn't you fly home from Geneva? There were
flights available, and they were a lot cheaper. You could have
been home for dinner.'

Jonah watched Niall carefully, and was fairly sure that he
lost a little colour just then.

'Were you on your way to buy something?' Jonah asked.

'I'm not . . . going to say any more,' Niall said, with difficulty. 'Just talk to Dina again. Please. And tell her . . .' Niall
paused, almost as though the act of speaking had become
difficult. 'Tell her you know we've been meeting up for
months. Maybe it'll help jog her memory.'

'We have two items we'd like you to look at,' Hanson said,
glad of the presence of the female PCSO. Louise Reakes
looked a fraction closer to falling apart every time she met
her. Her nervous movements and darting gaze were
unsettling.

Hanson handed the first evidence bag over to Louise. It

contained the woman's glove they'd found on Asylum Green. There was condensation on the inside of the bag, presumably because the glove was still damp. But the shape was relatively easy to make out even so.

Louise took it, and examined it for a moment, before shaking her head. 'It's not mine, and I don't recognise it.'

'OK,' Hanson said, and then passed the earring over. This time, Louise's reaction was immediate. She nodded and ran her thumb over the length of the earring through the plastic.

'It's mine,' she said. 'I was wearing them on Friday. Where did you find it?'

'On the route we think you took home,' Hanson replied.

Louise nodded, and put a hand up towards her left ear, her gaze distant. Something changed in her expression. And then she said in a dull voice, 'It got caught on his sleeve. When he pinned me down.'

Jonah left the interview room with the conviction that there was a lot more going on between Niall Reakes and Dina Weyman than he yet understood.

'Can you run a check for Dina's licence plate, too?' he asked O'Malley. 'If Niall Reakes didn't drive himself to Southampton, maybe she gave him a lift.'

He took himself back to his office, wondering how this was connected to Alex Plaskitt's death, if at all, and why Niall had looked so sick when they'd mentioned his journey to Zurich. And, on top of that, why he was so set on them talking to Dina again.

Lightman tapped on his door, and Jonah nodded him in.

'Ben. How's it going?' he asked.

'Interestingly,' Lightman told him. 'Alex Plaskitt did, in

fact, have a romantic liaison in the club, but not with Louise Reakes. It was with April Dumont.'

Jonah gave a slight, shocked laugh. 'You're kidding.'

'His description didn't leave much doubt,' Lightman said.

'OK,' Jonah said, growing more serious. 'I want her here, as soon as possible.'

'She's unfortunately now in Leeds until late tonight so I told her nine o'clock tomorrow. Sorry, chief.'

'Nine tomorrow will have to do. Did Step have anything to say about Niall Reakes?'

'No, nothing,' Lightman said. 'He didn't recognise photographs of either Niall or Louise when I sent them over, either.'

'That's useful. Thanks, Ben.'

Ben let himself out again, and Jonah's thoughts bounced between Louise Reakes, her husband, and the sudden introduction of April to the proceedings. He mentally balanced up the time they still had in which to charge Louise Reakes, and his determination not to arrest her husband until they absolutely had to. If they were going to mount an entire new case against him, Jonah didn't want to be rushing to make another custody deadline.

He approached O'Malley again, where he was still working at his desk, his eyes bloodshot.

'You've definitely drawn a blank on Niall Reakes's car?'

O'Malley nodded. 'He's not on any cameras until Saturday morning. Dina Weyman likewise.'

'Louise has identified the earring as hers,' Hanson chipped in. 'And she's added to her statement. She says she remembers a man holding her face down on the ground and pressing what he said was a knife into her back. She remembers the pain of her earring catching on his sleeve as he adjusted his grip, and it coming free.'

'Anything direct about an assault?'

Hanson nodded, her face a little grim. 'He pulled her dress up and dragged her underwear down. That's all she has, but assuming her account is true, it sounds highly likely that she was raped. She's accepted an examination this time.'

Jonah tried to fit in this idea of rape. Could Niall have raped her after finding her with Alex Plaskitt? Had he stabbed Alex and raped his wife? What, then, had happened to Alex while the rape was happening? And was it really nothing more than coincidence that Alex had kissed Louise's best friend only an hour or so before?

'Have we managed to raise Dina Weyman yet?'

O'Malley shook his head. 'Sorry. I've tried both numbers. Want me to send a uniform round there?'

Jonah looked at his watch and let out a long sigh. 'It's seven forty-five. That might have to be one for the morning. We can't keep Niall much longer without arresting him.' He nodded to himself. 'OK. I want to get Louise Reakes released on bail as soon as the examination is done. I'll tell her husband he's free to go, too, and ask him back in here tomorrow. The house has been thoroughly searched, so there's no evidence there to destroy or dispose of. I suspect we may have more to gain by letting some kind of confrontation happen between them. And we're going to be there to see it.'

O'Malley grimaced. 'And there was I thinking you might be about to send us home.'

'I don't mind being on stake-out,' Hanson said. 'In case that helps.'

Jonah nodded. 'I'll see whether Ben can go along, too. If you can manage until one, that'll probably cover it. We'll get some uniforms to do the night shift. Domnall, perhaps you can take over in the morning. In place by eight?'

'Thanks, chief,' O'Malley said. 'Very kind of you.'

'Boss of the year, me,' Jonah agreed.

Hanson had another message from Jason as she was getting herself ready to leave and felt impatient with it. There was paperwork involved in getting Louise Reakes out of the station, and Hanson needed to be in the car park by the time she and her husband left, ready to ease out into the traffic after them. Assuming, of course, that Niall drove his wife home.

She thought about ignoring whatever Jason had sent. She didn't want to read anything more from him. Right now, she didn't want to lay eyes on him again.

But she wasn't going to get her wish. She had to sit in the same room with him tomorrow, and on all the upcoming tomorrows. And so, once she had her coat and scarf on and her bag looped over her head, she opened up the message.

> So you don't want to tell me your side? To actually discuss this like adults?

It was a good thing Jason wasn't here in person. The anger she felt towards him then was a fierce, blistering thing. She felt her thumbs punching at her phone screen as she messaged back.

> I don't have anything to discuss with someone who's willing to take a conversation with some guy he's met at the pub as absolute truth when it is so very much at odds with the person you claim to know I am. There has clearly been no point to the time we've spent together. If there had been, you wouldn't have been so ready to believe the incredible manipulations of a man I have been trying to block from my life for a very long time.

Her eyes were teary again, but the tears were angry ones. She was so very, very done with feeling betrayed.

Louise stood silently as they handed back her personal effects. They weren't returning her earring. She supposed that was still some kind of evidence. But her handbag, keys and phone were there. She signed for them and slid everything into its slot in the bag, taking comfort in organising it. It was good to think of that, and not the probing examination that had happened a while before.

Niall was a wordless, looming presence over her shoulder. He seemed unable to bring himself to say anything to her. Which suited her just fine. She couldn't bear to talk to him. The thought of being trapped in his stupid flashy car was horrible and she was considering telling him to leave. That she would prefer to pay for a cab.

But then she realised how it would look to the police. She was being judged on everything. She knew that. From the clothes she wore to the way she spoke; the way she treated her husband to the way he treated her in return. And so she walked out alongside him without speaking, and climbed awkwardly into the low passenger seat of the Jaguar, her body feeling stiff and underused.

She needed some exercise, she thought, as she closed the door. A run. A swim. And then she needed to play something. God, she needed that. To let her hands move over her harp strings, and blot out the last nightmarish forty-eight hours.

They were halfway home when Niall broke the silence, and he did so hesitantly.

'We need to talk about – things,' he said.

'Do we?'

She saw the way he grimaced before he said, 'Yes. We do. I think we both owe each other some kind of an explanation.'

'I tried to give you one yesterday,' she said, coldly. 'But you wouldn't see me.'

'I know,' he said. 'I wasn't quite . . . You need to understand what a shock it was.'

She found herself looking at him in dumb shock. 'You want me to understand how shocking it all is for you? To find out that your wife had woken up next to a dead man? You want me to sympathise with that?'

'How do I even know that's true?' Niall countered, loudly. 'I have no idea what happened.'

'And neither do I,' Louise told him, wondering why she didn't feel more as she said it. 'And we should both have faced it, together. We should have been a team. But we haven't been a team for a long time, Niall. And I'm so sad that I've wasted so much worry over us when we were dead in the water months ago.'

He stopped trying to talk, after that, and Louise turned sideways to lean against the door. There were so many things she should have been asking him, really. Whether he was in love with Dina. Whether they'd agreed to get back together. And what the police had asked him about, too. But she felt too tired for all of it.

Tailing a vehicle was both easier and more challenging than people thought. It was easier because most people were so poor at checking the rear-view mirror. You could be behind someone for miles without them even noticing, and even when they did notice, they didn't necessarily think anything of it. Cars generally followed major routes, and if you peeled off at some point before their destination, you were usually forgotten pretty quickly. Assuming, of course, that they weren't looking out for you.

The difficult bit was keeping them in sight. At each junction there was a chance of missing them, and the one thing that would bring attention to you was to hustle through a set of lights on their tail when they were already changing.

Luckily, there were only a few cars around tonight, so it was easy enough for Hanson to keep behind Niall's Jaguar. To him and Louise, she was probably nothing more than an anonymous set of headlights.

It was going well enough that she was able to spare some thought for the traffic around her. She noticed that the car behind had one badly adjusted headlight. It was much brighter than the other, and occasionally struck dazzling reflections off her wing mirror. It was irritating, and she waited impatiently for it to turn off onto another route.

But it stayed where it was, resolutely following her every move. And, after a few miles, it occurred to her that she might not be the only person following.

And she thought again of Damian, who had taken unreasonable steps to wreck her life, and who loved nothing more than to frighten her. And she wondered whether she actually ought to be growing frightened.

26

Louise

All of this has brought us, inevitably, to tonight. To our silent, unhappy return from the police station. To a home that feels like it's made of nothing but paper. As if it's about to float away.

I keep imagining I can hear you moving around upstairs, even though the door shut behind you hours ago. The fact that you've gone makes me rage and hurt even while I wanted you out of my life. I'm a mess of conflict, and I wonder if you are, too, or whether that silence of yours was the mark of someone who's already moved on.

I spent almost an hour cleaning a house that was already clean, and then I suddenly just ran dry. Poised with a cloth in my hand, I felt the urge to move drain away, and I felt really, truly bereft.

It was you I was thinking about. You and Dina. I found myself finally wanting to know everything. Every detail of what's been going on between the two of you.

And so, for the first time, I loaded up the desktop computer in your study, grateful that it had been inconvenient to take to a hotel with you. I'd always been afraid of looking at it, despite how many times it had occurred to me.

There turned out to be a mine of information on there thanks to it synching with your phone. Hidden amid innocuous photos of us and of your work events and of scenery you'd enjoyed, there were photos of Dina. Images she'd clearly taken of herself and then sent you. They spanned years, these images. Terrible, painful little points scattered through stills of our everyday lives.

There was only one of the two of you together. It had clearly been taken by Dina, evident from the edge of her bronze forearm in the frame. She'd lifted the phone over her head and snapped the two of you next to each other, your head close to hers and a slightly dazed expression on your face. The two of you were illuminated by the camera flash, in sharp contrast with the dim lighting of what looked like a nightclub scene behind you.

I looked at the date and location on it and felt a slight tremor of unease. It had been taken last summer, in Southampton. And I remembered being in a club like this. With April. And how I'd gone to find her with a couple of drinks and been absolutely positive that you were standing next to her when I caught sight of her.

I was so sure it was you. You, who were supposed to be in Birmingham but were for some reason in the same club we were, talking to April.

You were out of sight by the time I made it over, and when I handed April her drink and said, 'Was that Niall?' she gave me a strange look.

'Niall? No.' She glanced around, considering. 'I guess he looked slightly like him. Which makes me feel weird for flirting with him.' She laughed and took a long sip of her drink. 'But definitely not your husband. Jesus, can you imagine what he'd say if he saw us here?'

I remember my certainty that I'd recognised you evaporating, chased away by relief that you hadn't caught me out drinking. And I suppose, after that, the drink did a good job of making me doubt it had ever happened.

But it did happen, Niall. I've saved the photo that proved it. You were there, with Dina. And April . . . lied about it.

It left me feeling like you've poisoned everything, that realisation. I couldn't even trust my best friend, could I? She hid your affair from me, when I thought she'd always been honest. Particularly about Dina and all of her bullshit. Particularly about that.

I felt lost, and furious. And desperate to call you up and yell at you. There was so much I wanted to say, but my pride wouldn't let me even think of it. I'd told you to get out, and I was going to stand by that if it killed me.

But then the idea of writing to you came to me, and it seemed like the answer. I could pour all of it out on paper, and then decide whether to send it to you, or burn it. So for an hour, that's what I did. Right up until now.

I expected it to be cathartic, but I feel as angry and as empty at the end of it as I did at the start. Perhaps because you haven't read it, and may never do so. Perhaps because what I really want is answers.

You've explained nothing. And although part of that might be my fault, because in my seething sense of betrayal I shut you down, you should have tried. You should have bloody tried. After five years, I think I deserve it, Niall.

Hanson was now certain that the car was following her. The little three-car procession had turned down too many side roads for there to be any doubt about it. They were all weaving whatever complex route Niall Reakes had decided was the quickest. Hanson had been keeping well back on the almost deserted streets.

The car behind, however, had done no such thing. It had stayed close on her tail, as if willing her to notice it, and that had started to make Hanson angry.

Half a mile from Saints Close, she signalled left and pulled suddenly into a single parking space, forcing them to go past. She was confident that she could keep track of the Reakeses from here, even with a car in between.

She turned her head to watch the vehicle, expecting to see the sleek black form of the BMW. But the silhouette was all wrong. This was a smaller, older car. A Vauxhall Corsa, she thought. Or something like it. And it didn't slow down as it passed, either. It accelerated.

Hanson let out a long breath, and moved back out onto the road. Sometimes coincidences happened, she thought. It looked as though this had been one of them. A car that just happened to be making its way along the same route.

She could just see the lights of the two cars up ahead as they turned into Saints Close. And that made her feel slightly doubtful again. Was it really likely that both drivers happened to live on one tiny close?

She slowed down as she pulled onto Saints Close. She could see the bright red illumination thrown by Niall Reakes's Jaguar, which he'd pulled up half on the pavement outside number eleven. Further up the road, there were headlights in the act of manoeuvring. The Corsa must have driven past.

Hanson pulled in a little way from the house, close enough to give her a good view, and switched off her headlights. She watched as the Corsa completed its turn and pulled up against the kerb. Its lights died at the same time the Jaguar's did.

Niall and Louise emerged from their car, and Hanson tried to pay attention to their manner with each other while half her attention was still on the Corsa. Nobody got out of that second car, and the lights remained off while the couple moved silently to the door.

From what she could see of them, things were not rosy between Louise and Niall Reakes. By the time she lost sight of them past the trees, they had neither looked at nor spoken to each other.

And then, finally, it occurred to her that she'd got that car wrong: that it had been following them, and not her, from the moment they'd left the station.

Jojo messaged at eight twenty-five to ask whether Jonah would like takeaway at his house, and his response was the largest thumbs up he could get his phone to send. His team had stake-out duty covered, with a couple of Heerden's uniforms covering the graveyard shift.

That left Jonah free to see his girlfriend, which inevitably made him feel guilty, but was sometimes how things went. He messaged to say he'd be there in twenty minutes, and then sent Hanson a quick text to tell her he was heading home but would have his mobile on at all times.

O'Malley had already left, and Lightman was filling a thermos to take with him. Jonah was waving to him when Hanson messaged back to say that there was another car there, and that the driver appeared to be watching the house. She asked if he wanted her to go and talk to them.

Jonah sighed, and messaged back quickly to tell her to stay where she was.

'Do we know anyone involved with Alex Plaskitt or the Reakeses who drives a Corsa?' Jonah asked Lightman, as he returned from the kitchen.

'O'Malley might know,' Ben said, picking up his coat. 'Or I can look it up. Why?'

'Juliette's got another car parked up on Saints Row watching the house.'

'Tell her I'll be there in fifteen,' he said, transferring his keys to his coat pocket. 'We can go and see who it is once I'm there.'

'It should really be me,' Jonah argued.

'Well, you're currently the only one of us with a girlfriend waiting, so I think you should leave it be. You can pay me back once I've sorted my love life out.'

'Thanks, Ben,' Jonah said, with relief. He doubted Jojo would give him a hard time if he cancelled on her, but letting her down again would have made him feel crap. 'Keep me posted on what happens.'

'Will do.'

*

Hanson was fixated on the other car. The Corsa was perhaps twenty feet from her, its lights out, but without doubt still occupied. She could just make out a dark shape behind the wheel, an ominously still, unsettling unknown.

Ben had messaged her to say that he was on his way too, and asked as an afterthought whether her psycho ex drove a Corsa. She'd grinned at that.

He wouldn't be seen dead in anything less than a Merc.

Ben's reply had been a thumbs up, and then a comment about her amazing taste in men. And although she didn't feel she needed him to be here to watch out for her, she was glad that he was on his way.

The first sign she had of any movement from the Reakes house was the sudden bright red illumination of the Jaguar's tail lights. It was followed afterwards by the throaty growl of the engine, and the car began to manoeuvre. Niall must have left the house while she'd been focused on the other car. Was he alone?

Hanson picked up her phone and called Ben.

'We've got movement,' she told him. 'The Jaguar again.'

'I'm just about to turn into the close,' Ben answered, his voice a little distant over his car's Bluetooth.

'You might want to hold off and tail him,' Hanson said.

'Are you definitely OK there with the mystery driver?' he asked.

'I've got my baton and my stab vest,' she said, only half joking. 'I should be fine.'

The Jaguar had finished its turn out onto the road, and as it came level with Hanson she was granted a clear view of the driver. It was Niall Reakes, and he was alone.

'Looks like you've just got Niall,' she told Ben. 'Which

means Louise is still in the house, with our mystery driver still at large. I'd definitely better stay put.'

'OK,' Ben said. 'I'll let you know where he goes. Keep me posted on events there.'

Louise had thought that she needed music. At every other low point in her life she had played. When her mother had died. When her father had suddenly flipped from neurotic overprotection and moved to the other side of the world, as if determined never to see his daughter again. Louise had got through it all with music.

As the door had finally closed behind Niall, she'd made her way to the music room and gone to her chair. She'd drawn her harp towards her and leaned its reassuring weight onto her shoulder. Her hands had found their positions for the start of the Donizetti.

And then she'd thought once again of the first time she'd played for Niall, and she faltered. She found herself replaying conversations with him. And, seamlessly, those thoughts turned into words she might have exchanged with Alex Plaskitt. Whole conversations she might have had with him, at the bar of Blue Underground.

Minutes later, she was still sitting where she had been, a heavy feeling in her chest, and her hands equally heavy on her lap. The only music she could hear in her head was the pounding beat of a dance track, drumming its way into her memory two days later.

She felt hopeless as she returned the harp to its place and left the room. How could she deal with this if she couldn't play?

She found herself in the kitchen, switching on the kettle. There were a few crumbs on the top of the stove, and she went to find a cloth. And then she saw that some of them had ended up around the kettle itself, and behind the bread bin. Niall had always had an expressive way of cutting bread, one that littered the kitchen with detritus.

She started to move things onto the table so the surfaces were clear enough to wipe properly, and, once she started, it became difficult to stop. She took out sprays and gloves and cloths, and began to clean away every trace of dirt. She moved from the surfaces to the floor to the fridge. The oven. The utility room.

Her thoughts narrowed themselves down to finding the next imperfection and removing it. And, in spite of half hating herself for it, she began to feel comforted at last.

Hanson was now very much on edge. With the Jaguar gone, she felt as though something else had to happen. She'd expected the other driver to either follow, or move again. But the car remained motionless. A full hour passed, and then most of another.

The lack of action was excruciating, not just because her car was now freezing cold. She was at the point of going to see who was in the bloody Corsa when there was movement at last. The driver's door opened, flooding the interior with blue-white light, and a figure stepped out. One who was huddled in a scarf, hat and high-necked coat, and was frustratingly hard to make out. She couldn't even guess their gender.

Hanson picked up her phone and started to take photographs, willing them to turn towards her. The figure made its way over to number eleven, and Hanson climbed out of her car as quietly as she could to follow. Her breath fogged in the freezing air as she trod carefully along the pavement.

She paused at the end of the drive, in sight of the Reakeses' front door.

The figure was now on the doorstep, and she could hear the bell chiming from here. She could also see Louise Reakes's face clearly as she opened the door.

'You know who I am,' Hanson heard.

28

You know who I am.

Five words that fed into all the mass of uncertainty and fear Louise had been feeling, and sent her heart rate into overdrive. She didn't want to know what he had to say, this crumpled man on her doorstep. She didn't want to know anything more about the awful things she'd done.

'I'm so sorry,' she said. 'I don't. I need to go to bed. Please . . .'

And she started trying to close the door, but he was pushing against it.

'I spoke to you,' he said. 'I spoke to you. Don't you remember?'

'No,' she said. 'I don't.'

But that didn't mean it hadn't happened.

'I need to talk to you,' the man said, and then suddenly he was crying in an awful, ugly way. She was revolted by him. Repulsed. And yet she also felt for him. She'd cried a lot over the last two days, and she didn't want him to feel as bad as she'd felt.

And then she realised who he must be, and she stopped trying to push the door closed. 'You're Alex's — Alex's husband.'

He nodded, and Louise let out a long breath. As hard as it was going to be, she knew that she owed him a conversation. She opened the door and let him walk inside.

*

'He's still there,' Hanson told the DCI. 'I saw her making tea while he stood there, and now they're in the sitting room, where we spoke to her yesterday. Unfortunately, the curtains are shut, so there's not a lot I can see.'

'Did they seem to know each other?' Sheens asked.

'I was supposing so,' Hanson said. 'But they spoke for a minute and then he walked in. So I suppose it could have been an introduction.'

'And you think he was following you from the station?' Jonah said.

'Yeah, I do. So he might not previously have known where she lived.'

There was a brief silence from the other end of the line. She could almost hear the DCI thinking.

'If you can get the car close enough and a window down, I'd like you to listen out for any raised voices. Beyond that, if he leaves, stay with Louise. It looks like her husband is checking into a hotel, so I've sent a couple of uniforms to take over. Ben is coming back your way. He can go after Issa if needed.'

'Roger that.'

Hanson started the engine and began to manoeuvre her car, not relishing the idea of sitting with her window down in sub-zero temperatures. But she relished even less the idea of missing something important, and so she pulled the car up, and dragged her stab vest and a jumper from the back seat.

Issa took the tea from her, his hand closing round the hot mug instead of the handle without any apparent reaction. He seemed to be too distracted to feel it. His eyes were darting everywhere around the room. They took in the furniture.

The paintings. The photos of her and Niall. His scrutiny made her feel exposed.

She settled herself on the sofa, experiencing the same sense of unreality that had gripped her in the police station and then again in the car on the way home. How could she be sitting in front of a dead man's husband?

'I wish I could tell you more about that night,' she said, quietly. 'I know you must want to know.'

His eyes focused on her, slowly. 'Did you meet him at the bar?' he asked. 'Or was it before that?'

Louise shook her head. 'I didn't know him. I only remember speaking to him briefly. I can't remember anything else at all.'

'Do you remember talking to me?' he asked.

She shook her head again. 'Were you there?'

'On the phone,' he said, and she detected anger in his voice. 'You must remember. I tried to call him, and you answered instead.'

Louise could feel her forehead creasing with anxiety. It threatened to bring back the headache that had only recently abated after two whole days.

'I don't remember that,' she said, and then, suddenly badly needing to know, 'What did I say?'

Alex's husband's mouth pursed in distaste. 'Nothing that can help me. That it was Alex's phone, but he was tied up right now. And then he got it off you and apologised. You sounded drunk. He did, too.'

Louise felt a swelling of shame. She could imagine Drunk Louise doing that. Drunk Louise always wanted to have fun, no matter who it hurt.

'I'm so sorry,' she said. 'I don't think I was myself on Friday. I was . . . upset. And I got really drunk.'

But Alex's husband seemed not to be listening to her. He was looking at her belongings again, his brow wrinkling in what looked like frustration. Perhaps confusion.

'I expected you to be . . . richer,' he said.

Louise almost laughed. 'Richer?'

'That's what he liked,' he said, his gaze flicking to her and then away. 'The rich country girls. The ones his dad would have loved.'

'Look,' Louise said, feeling an increasing sense of unease, 'I don't know . . . I don't think that's what happened. I don't think he was chasing me.'

But then she listened to herself and thought of the man who had pursued her in her dream. Of the pain in her back and the dirt in her mouth. And she felt ill.

'Any kids?' he asked.

And Louise shook her head, and said, 'No,' wondering why he would ask that. 'Sorry, I . . . what's your name?'

'Issa,' he said, his voice quiet. Slightly child-like. And then he suddenly asked, 'What is it you have?'

'I don't . . . understand,' Louise said. He was staring at her as though she had personally betrayed him and it made her feel that she must have done it somehow. Must have been a traitor.

Alex's husband continued, his voice low with hatred. 'What is it you have that made him want to risk everything? Just so he could fuck you?'

'I don't . . . I don't have anything.'

Issa surged to his feet, and, as he stood over her, she felt a return of her earlier fear. There was something not right about the way he was looking at her, and the heavy mug in his hand became a possible weapon.

'Whatever you tempted him with, it destroyed everything.'

Louise flinched away from him, and then said, her voice as firm as she could make it, 'I think you need to leave.'

It was ten forty by the time Ben arrived back at Saints Close. Once Issa had left the house and she'd seen Louise Reakes moving around in her kitchen, Hanson had closed the car window again. But it was still freezing in the little Nissan and she was beyond grateful to see that Lightman had brought fast food and hot coffee with him.

'Oh my God,' she said, as he climbed into the passenger seat and passed it to her. 'This might be the best thing you've ever done.'

Ben smiled, lifting his coffee to his mouth. And then he paused and said, 'There was that thing a few months ago where I took a knife off a psychotic woman . . .'

Hanson took a large bite of cheeseburger and swallowed it before she replied. 'Nope. This is much better.'

'Well, that's good to know. For future reference.' He chewed for a few moments. 'What did you think of Issa, when you met him?'

'By the time we turned up on Saturday morning, I'm pretty sure he hadn't slept at all,' Hanson said, considering. 'And I don't think his mental state has improved with news of Alex's death. I'm not sure I'd trust him to be rational right now.'

'Yeah, I'm not sure sitting in a freezing car outside some-one's house for hours is rational behaviour,' Ben said. 'Not if somebody isn't making you do it, obviously.'

'Obviously,' Hanson said, and then sighed. 'I really want to know what they were talking about. Half of me thinks there's some kind of conspiracy going on between them, and the other half thinks Louise Reakes might actually be in danger.'

*

From his position on the sofa, with Jojo's legs wrapped round his and her head resting on his shoulder, Jonah felt a momentary resurgence of guilt. Ben and Juliette would be sitting in a cold car right now.

He stretched out to grab his phone, dislodging Jojo slightly, and she gave a quiet growl of protest.

'I was comfortable, Sheens.'

'Last message of the night, I promise,' he said, getting hold of the phone and typing out 'All OK?' to Hanson.

'Last message unless something kicks off,' Jojo countered, as he sent it.

'Er, well, I was sort of hoping something else might kick off here . . .'

Jojo shifted around until she was lying directly on top of him. She gave him a narrow-eyed look, her mouth twisting in humour.

'That can probably be arranged,' she said, and ran a hand down his chest until she found the waistband of his trousers.

Louise couldn't stop shaking. She felt so angry with every man on the planet. With Issa for his horrible, piercingly painful remarks. With that bloody DCI for not believing her, and not finding out what had really happened, either. With Niall, for fucking *everything*.

And it was only now that the truth of her situation really hit home. That she was never going to feel safe. Even if she somehow avoided jail, Issa would still be out there, thinking she'd done it. Possibly trying to get revenge. And what if it hadn't been Alex who attacked her? What if it was someone else, who was still out there, faceless and awful?

She put a hand into her hair and squeezed it until it hurt.

She felt as though she'd worked herself into a place she couldn't get out of. She should have told Issa about the rape, or attempted rape, or whatever it had been. God, and she should have got them to test her earlier.

After the awfulness of that truth came another one. It came more slowly, in a cold creeping sensation down her spine.

They thought it was her. Not her husband, who she was now sure had lied to hide an affair with his ex. He'd probably admitted it all to the police. They might even have brought Dina in to back him up, a thought that only made her feel more sick.

So they didn't suspect Niall any more. They thought it was her, the woman who had slept next to a dead man and then tried to hide it. Of course they thought that.

Which meant they weren't looking for whoever had attacked her. They weren't even looking.

The early part of the night had passed uneventfully for Hanson and Lightman, hunched in the freezing-cold car. The two of them had spent much of it in companionable silence, though they'd played a few pointless word games, too.

They had spoken only briefly about Damian, after Ben had suddenly commented, in a voice full of humour, that this must be how her ex-boyfriend felt half the time.

'Just imagine how many hours he must have spent sitting waiting in his car, just for a few seconds of making you feel uncomfortable.' He'd shaken his head. 'The man seriously needs to get a life.'

Laughing at Damian had been a very good thing. As soon as she started thinking about him as a sad individual, she felt enormously better.

It was only at twenty to twelve that they'd seen a taxi draw up slowly outside number eleven. Louise had emerged a minute later, her hair twisted up into a bun and her dress and leggings exchanged for jeans and high heels. With a sigh, Hanson had asked, 'Any wagers on where she's going?'

29

Louise

I didn't think I'd be writing any more, at least not yet. But more has happened. I *made* it happen. I suddenly found myself unable to sit alone and let this all just build and build beyond my control.

With the awful realisation that nobody was looking for whoever had attacked me, I felt like I needed to do something. With no other obvious paths open to me, I tracked Alex Plaskitt down online and discovered a treasure trove. A YouTube channel full of fitness videos.

I found myself watching video after video, watching obsessively for signs of his character. What I hadn't really been prepared for was the reality of him. For how much of a punch to the gut it would be to see him alive, and animated, and likeable. He seemed less and less like a predator and more and more like a victim whose death I had helped to cause.

And as I watched, a suspicion that's been creeping up on me for the last two days crystallised into certainty.

What I finally faced up to was that I did spend time with Alex Plaskitt that night. Every time I denied having met him, I was lying, and I think some part of me knew it. *She* knew it.

I don't think I just talked to him. I think I flirted, and I think it was entirely deliberate. Not just something that Drunk Louise wanted to do, something *all* of me wanted to do.

At some point on Friday night I sat beside him at the bar.

I have a fleeting memory of imagining I was Dina. I remember consciously imitating what April had told me. I remember putting my hand on his arm as I laughed at something he'd said.

But that was all I could remember. Everything else was still a yawning void, and it was driving me to agitation. I couldn't calm myself, even with more cleaning. I felt certain that I'd done something awful.

I knew I needed to know what I'd said to him. Whether I'd agreed to meet up with him at our house. I needed to know how much of this shit I'd brought on myself.

It was a momentous thing, leaving here alone, just before midnight, with a destination in mind that intimidated the hell out of me. But I did it. I had to.

You know what the worst part of it was? That I had to do it basically sober, because I needed to remember everything. I couldn't leave it all up to Drunk Louise and go along for the ride. I had a one-and-a-half-strength gin and tonic while I waited for my cab, and I walked up to the door of Blue Underground feeling basically myself.

I almost got turned back right then. The bouncer asked for my ID, and I looked all through my handbag without being able to find it. I came dangerously close to crying. Why had I been IDed tonight, of all nights? It only happened once in a while, when I somehow gave off the effect of being a teenager instead of an adult.

'I didn't think to bring it,' I told him, with a note of desperation. 'I'm thirty-three.'

The bouncer sighed, and after another, more careful inspection of me, waved me into the club. I gave him a smile and hurried past.

The inside of Blue Underground looked vastly different in

reality to every memory I had. A combination of it being only quarter full tonight, and Sober Louise now being the one to see it. The clientele were different, too. Most of them looked like students or postgrads. Lots of them were non-English. And the music was more poppy. Less *club*.

I didn't really care about the music or about anyone else who was in there, though. I was looking at the staff, searching for someone I recognised.

It didn't take me long. A guy of probably twenty, down at the far end of the bar from me, one with curling hair and an eyebrow piercing, turned to give a customer his drink. He'd been there on Friday. I knew he had. I'd spoken to him.

It turns out that it's surprisingly easy to get served quickly by a particular person when you don't care what anyone thinks of you. I shoved my way in and got his attention with a smile and a lift of my credit card. He came straight over, overlooking three or four people who'd been there first.

'Kronenbourg, please,' I said, choosing something that would keep him standing still in front of me while he poured. As he flipped a glass up and into place under the tap, I added, in a voice that sounded strangled to my ears, 'And I need some help. I was in here on Friday. Do you remember?'

The guy glanced at me, and then I saw something change in his expression. He looked uncomfortable. Worried.

'I don't know . . .'

'I was with a loud, blonde American woman,' I went on, trying to pretend I was confident Drunk Louise instead of myself, 'with lots of tattoos. And after I left, something terrible happened. The police must have been here asking questions. They were here, weren't they?'

The barman glanced around, and then gave a slow nod. He'd almost finished pouring the drink.

'Sorry, that should have been two Kronenbourgs,' I said.

I could see from his face that he didn't like that. He stayed still while someone squeezed in next to me, and then he grabbed another glass with bad grace.

'Please just tell me what I was doing,' I begged him. 'I need to know. I was so drunk, I don't really remember.' I swallowed, feeling a flickering, sick beat to my heart. I was so afraid of what he was going to say. 'Was I talking with a guy? A . . . tall, athletic sort of guy?'

The barman started to pour the second pint and gave a slight sigh. I could see it from the way his body moved, even though I couldn't hear it over the music.

'Yes,' he said in the end. 'You were sitting just along there with him.'

'Over there?'

He nodded to the end of the bar that was furthest from the door. There were a few stools down at that end, but nobody serving.

'Was I . . . flirting?'

The guy shrugged. 'I'd say so. But . . . you didn't go home with him or anything. He was a bit pissed off that you left in a hurry.'

I felt another twist of my heart. 'He was? Did he say anything?'

'No,' he said. 'But you notice this stuff, you know.' He looked towards a barmaid working further down. 'Look, you need to pay, and I need to get on with work. You didn't do anything while you were here that might have . . . I heard about what happened, but I can't help. I'm sorry.'

And then he was placing my two unwanted beers on the bar and holding his hand out for my card. And no matter what I asked, he said nothing more.

268

30

'So what do we make of her?' the DCI asked, as Hanson wrapped up her brief report on their stake-out. It was eight forty-five in the morning. Sheens had just returned from his early caseload meeting and, with the weekend done, CID was busy once again, though their team was down on numbers. O'Malley was on stake-out at the Reakes house, and Lightman had been sent to see April Dumont again.

'Of Louise?' she asked. 'It's hard to say. Ben couldn't catch much of her conversation in the club, but if she really was doing her own investigating, it strongly implies that she's been telling the truth about not remembering anything.'

'Agreed,' Sheens said. 'Though whether she was involved in Alex's death is still, frustratingly, up in the air.'

'I want to look more at the knife,' Hanson told him. 'Surely that's still our firmest piece of evidence. If I can link it to any one of our suspects, we'll know who to press.'

'I think you may be right,' he said, nodding slowly. 'See if you can work out what Ben's done on that so far.'

Hanson found Ben's work to be as meticulously logged as she'd been anticipating. It took her no time at all to continue what he'd started, and she quickly immersed herself in cross-checking delivery addresses with their suspects. It was perfect work to avoid thinking about anything. Lots of facts and attention to detail.

It took her a while to notice someone loitering next to her desk. And when she looked up, she tried not to grimace. She'd momentarily forgotten that Jason would be here today.

But she was prepared for this even so. She'd decided how to play it.

She gave him a bright smile and said, 'How can I help, sir?'

Jason visibly flinched at the deliberate use of rank. 'Juliette, could we – could we please talk?'

Hanson glanced at her screen. 'I've got quite a lot to do.'

'So have I,' Jason said, with slight frustration, 'but it's going to get done a lot more quickly if we can clear this up. I can't think like this.'

Hanson was sorely tempted to ask whose fault it was that he couldn't concentrate. But this was still Jason, the man she'd cared about up until yesterday. The man she'd spent a great deal of time with. Even if there had been little passion in their relationship, she'd at least felt she could trust him. It was hard not to want him to think well of her on some level.

'All right,' she said, standing. 'I may as well do a coffee run.'

She left a note on Lightman's desk, picked up her coat, and walked out just ahead of him. She didn't volunteer anything. She might be willing to talk, but there was no way she was going to kick things off. It was up to Jason to say his piece, or apologise, or whatever it was he wanted to do.

They were crossing the car park before he said, 'So. Your ex. Damian.'

'Yes,' she said. 'My ex.' She stressed the word slightly, but that was all she was giving him.

'When did you stop seeing him?'

'Several months before I moved here. Would you like to know why I stopped seeing him?'

'Yes.'

'Because he was an abusive narcissist,' she said, with as little emotion as she could. 'The humiliating thing is how long it took me to see it.'

There was a pause, and then Jason asked, 'Abusive how?'

Hanson let out a sigh. 'In every possible way. As soon as he'd moved in with me, he stopped paying rent. He claimed he was having a temporary money problem thanks to a previous girlfriend who'd run up bills in his name. Then he borrowed off me on top of that. Thousands in total. I had to borrow off my mum to cover it and he kept claiming he had a bonus coming up at work that would sort it out, only it never came.'

Jason said nothing, but he nodded when she glanced at him.

'He tried to tell me what to wear. He told me my clothes made me look like a whore. He also accused me of *being* a whore because I'd once told him, when he asked me, that I'd tried an open relationship.' She took a breath. 'He resented every good thing that happened in my life and tried to undermine it. Roughly every two days he would say something so unbelievably nasty to me that I cried. As it progressed, I increasingly ended up screaming at him in rage, too. But in the end, he always broke me down. Anger turning into misery.'

They came to a stop at the pedestrian lights, and Jason pressed the button. Hanson looked away from him before she went on.

'And then he would apologise. He would tell me he was trying to get help. That he had trauma, and it got the better of him sometimes. It should have been clearer earlier on that he apologised because he'd got exactly what he wanted, which was to know how much he could hurt me. He got his kick out of breaking me down, and then he needed to reel me back in to stop me actually leaving. So it was all "my trauma, my trauma, poor me".' Hanson gave a small snort of laughter. The lights changed, and they started to cross. 'The irony being that he dealt out trauma like nobody else. Oh, and he cheated on me with multiple women, which I damn well knew but couldn't prove because he deleted every message between them. One of them was a good friend of mine and I lost her because of it.'

'When you say he deleted his messages . . .' Jason said, carefully.

'I saw him delete them in front of me,' Hanson snapped, knowing what he meant. Asking her if she'd been checking up on him all the time, as he'd probably told Jason that she had. 'If I asked to see any messages he got angry and told me I should trust him, whereas my own messages were continually hacked. He sometimes got my phone and said terrible things to my friends, while they thought it was me. I caught him a few times and I can only imagine what he said that I didn't see. That he deleted.'

'How long were you with him?' Jason asked.

'A year and a half.'

'Why did you stay with him?' The question was asked with such disbelief that Hanson almost laughed.

'Do you really need me to tell you how abuse works?' she asked him. 'How they turn on the full force of their charm every time they apologise, and make you feel like it's all right now? How when you do break up with them, they find ways of making you feel guilty? They point out all this stuff they are doing "for you". The therapy sessions that, coincidentally, you are paying for. Do I need to tell you how you defend their behaviour to all your concerned

friends and family so many times that you become compli-
cit in it?'

'But you're smart,' he argued, stopping, and turning
towards her. 'Surely you could see through him.'

'Like you did?' Hanson asked.

There was a very long silence, as Jason looked into the distance somewhere. 'I'm sorry. It's just . . . I didn't see any
reason not to believe him, when he said it.'

'Except for four months of getting to know me better
than anyone else,' she said, quietly, and turned to continue
walking.

O'Malley had stocked up well on breakfast materials. He
liked to complain bitterly about stake-out duty whenever it
cropped up, but he generally used it as an excuse to treat
himself to unhealthy food. As a result, he almost looked forward to it.

Today's haul had come courtesy of the Greggs in the petrol station, which had the good sense to be open from seven.
He'd arrived at Saints Close just before his clocking-on time
equipped with everything he needed for a long stint. The
blinds and curtains in the Reakes house were still drawn.

Having eaten one sausage roll and a chocolate croissant, it
was clear that he was going to have to vacuum the car later
on. But it had been well and truly worth it.

There was still no sign of movement by nine. O'Malley
guessed that musicians weren't required to be up all that
early. He was quite happy with that situation, as it meant he
got to drink coffee and mull pleasantly on his upcoming
holiday to Morocco. He was holding out for that week of
sunshine.

The daydreaming was rudely interrupted at ten past nine

by the arrival of a metallic blue Corsa. So Issa was back. O'Malley wondered what his business was, and whether it was by arrangement.

Issa parked right outside number eleven, seemingly unaware of O'Malley's Astra perched on the kerbside opposite. He climbed out with the look of a man on a mission and strode up to the door.

O'Malley watched him ring on the bell, and then, after a minute, ring on it again. After that, when there was no sign of life, he started to move round the side of the house, peering into the windows. O'Malley was on the verge of going to intercept him when Issa turned and walked back to his car. Instead of driving away, however, he let himself in and then sat in the driver's seat, his head turned towards the house.

'Who does he think he is?' O'Malley muttered to himself. 'A fecking copper?'

Louise was barely functioning today. Another night of terrible sleep and ceaseless worry seemed to have finished off her ability to perform even the simplest of tasks efficiently.

She'd thought she'd be exhausted enough to sleep. But it hadn't come, and she'd found herself, at three, switching on her laptop and returning to Alex Plaskitt's YouTube channel.

The urge came out of an equal blend of guilt and determination to know more. Here was a man whose death she might have caused, but also one who might have pinned her down and raped her. She needed to work him out, and this was all she had.

She'd eventually dozed off some time after five, only to dream of Alex. In her dreams, she had tried to save him, and then realised that he was a predator who was doing nothing more than tricking her. And later, at some confused point, she was pregnant with his child and about to marry him.

She woke again at eight feeling as though she'd been scoured out by emotion. She was so tired of being haunted. By Alex in the fullness of life, and then by his lifeless form. By memories of the club. Of attack.

And now, this morning, by Alex's husband, who had returned to lay siege to her.

She'd watched him from the upstairs hall window as he'd walked towards the house. She was glad of the muslin she'd hung there, despite Niall's complaint that it was as bad as a net curtain. She was able to see him without being seen, to watch him, with her heart in her throat, as he got tired of ringing on the bell and began to move round to the side gate.

What was she supposed to do if he tried to get in? Call the police? Call Niall?

But she couldn't call Niall. She could never call Niall again. And she felt as though the police wouldn't believe her. Why would they believe a suspect? They thought she was a killer.

Issa had eventually retreated again, and she felt a sag in her shoulders as he went back to his car. He climbed in, but the car stayed where it was. She couldn't see him from up here, but she felt certain that he was watching the house.

And then, of course, the obvious answer came to her. She could call the one person who always took her side.

Except, she thought, with a sudden drop in her stomach. Except that April had lied to her, and she needed to know why.

*

The walk back to the station had felt painfully long. Hanson had to hold herself aloof for all of it, and even ten minutes of it had been draining.

Jason had asked her, while they'd stood waiting for the coffee to be made, whether things could be all right between them. Whether she could look past the things he'd said in that message. She supposed that meant that he believed her. A small victory.

But she'd said no.

'How can I be in a relationship with someone who doesn't trust me?' she'd asked. 'How would I feel confident and comfortable knowing how easily he talked you round? What if he came back more persuasively?' He shook his head, but she went on, 'And all of those little frustrations he played on. That you don't like it when I go back home after seeing you. That I don't message often enough. That I still want to do Friday pub trips with my own team. They'd all still be there, and what Damian has done is to make it blindingly obvious that I don't make you happy.'

Jason had had no answer, and she'd felt a heavy certainty as she had turned to begin walking back. He'd come to walk next to her, his own tray of coffee the match of hers, and the silence had lasted all the way to the station.

It was only when they reached the bottom of the stairs to CID that he suddenly seemed to wake up.

'Juliette,' he said, and his voice had been so . . . so *sad* that she'd felt she had to look at him. 'I know you think this was all based on lack of trust, or dissatisfaction with you, but it wasn't. It really, really wasn't. I was taken in by him, and I know you were, too. Can you not understand that he can be as charming to a man as he can be to a woman?'

He gave her a long, beseeching look, and it was deeply

uncomfortable because she knew that he was, on some level, right. And yet other people hadn't fallen for it. The DCI hadn't. Ben hadn't. They'd known her for less than a month, as a new colleague, when Damian had first tried to twist their view of her. And they'd dismissed it out of hand.

Jason took a step towards her suddenly, bringing his beseeching gaze that little bit closer.

'Just take a while to think about it. Please. I don't want to lose you. I probably haven't made it clear enough how much I care about you. Or how much it hurt when I thought all this shit was true.' He squeezed her free hand, briefly. 'I'm sorry for being so stupid, but that's all it is. Stupidity.'

As he let go of her hand, Hanson felt as though her defences were being burrowed under. And it made her feel a sick, dizzy sense of déjà vu. This was what Damian had done to her, over and over.

She'd never thought of Jason as being anything like him. How had he managed to poison this so completely?

'Of course I'll think about it,' she said, as he gave her a questioning look. 'I've always cared about you too. But I need to work now.'

She entered CID ahead of him, and although she held the door for him, she didn't walk alongside him as she returned to her desk.

Lightman returned to the flat on Admirals Quay and parked up in the underground car park of April Dumont's building. The rigmarole with being allowed up in the lift was repeated with a new concierge, and he was deposited once again on the top floor.

April emerged into the hallway, dressed in a loose white top over a very visible black bra, and distressed silver and black leggings with biker boots. She looked unashamedly out of place in the ultra-sleek apartment.

'Dan's at work,' April told him, as she sprawled on one of the sofas.

'Right,' Lightman said. 'Dan is . . .?'

'My husband,' April said, and then laughed at the surprise on his face. 'Oh, you thought I was footloose and fancy free? No. Some marriages run better on a little spice, if you want the truth.'

Lightman nodded and decided not to write this down at present.

'You want a drink or something?' April asked, with a slow smile.

'I'm fine, thanks,' he said. 'I need to ask you a few things about Friday night.'

'I want to ask some things first,' April said, sitting up. 'Why did you arrest Louise? She isn't the kind of person to hurt anyone.'

'I can understand your worry,' Lightman said, nodding. 'There were various circumstances around the finding of the body that are of some concern. But we are investigating –'

'I know Louise,' April said, cutting across him. 'She's not going to go home with some man she's never met. That is not her MO. Not her MO at all.'

'You're saying that Louise . . . had nothing to do with any-one at the club?'

'Damn right I am,' April said. 'She was drunk and hurting and the most I saw her do was talk to a couple guys nicely.'

'Could you tell us who you went home with?' Lightman asked.

April gave a short laugh. 'Not really, honey. Except his name was Adam, I don't have much.'

'You went back to his house?'

'Yeah, I did. It was just a little fun. Dan and I've been hav-ing troubles. Like some others.'

'Do you have an address for the house?'

'Hell no,' April said. 'I got a cab there with him, and I made him call me a cab after, too.' She shrugged. 'It was somewhere this side of town is all I know. Kind of a nice place.'

Lightman gave a vague smile, thinking that this meant no provable alibi for the time of Alex Plaskitt's death. And regardless of what Niall Reakes was hiding, April Dumont was still a suspect.

Lightman watched her for a moment, and then said, 'I'm a little confused, if I have to be honest, about your behav-iour.' He let her turn round and face him before he went on. 'You clearly feel protective towards Louise. And yet you apparently left her while she was extremely drunk.' He tipped his head slightly to one side. 'It seems out of character that you simply abandoned her.'

April's expression dropped. She looked deeply uncom-fortable, and slightly angry. 'I didn't just abandon her. I was – I was drunker than I should have been. I'd been there for her, helping her, you know.' She looked at him with eyes that were slightly reflective, even in that bright light. 'I got her water and I hugged her when she looked like she might cry. And I tried to help look for her drivers' licence for a good twenty minutes. I did all the things a good friend does, up until I got too drunk and forgot I was supposed to be looking after her.'

Lightman studied her for a moment. 'She lost her driving licence? In the club?'

'Yeah,' April said. 'She not tell you? She'd had it out ready, because she looks awful young when she's dressed up, and then later she realised she didn't have it any more.'

'And did you ever find it?' he asked.

'No,' April said, shaking her head. 'No, it stayed lost.'

'OK,' Lightman said, writing that down. He wondered, briefly, whether Alex Plaskitt had found it.

'So tell me what motivated you to leave with this man.'

'Because fuck Dan if he was going to be an asshole.'

'I believe that this Adam wasn't the first man you'd had some kind of romantic liaison with that evening,' Lightman said, quietly.

He had expected an expression of surprise or anger, but April gave an immediate smile of amusement. 'Romantic liaison? Who in the hell talks like that?'

'Just us,' Lightman replied, smiling slightly in return. 'As far as we know, you kissed someone else that night.'

April shook her head, still grinning. 'Yeah, I did. Tall, upper-class kind of a guy with a six-pack. Who wouldn't have?'

'But you moved on pretty quickly?'

'Yeah,' she said, the smile fading slightly. 'Turned out he was married, and had a guilty conscience about it.' She gave a shrug. 'Which I guess is up to him.'

'You weren't angry about it?'

April rolled her eyes. 'Not really. I mean, I was a little pissed off for a second. He'd been so obviously keen. And his friend was all interfering, too. I was more annoyed with the friend.'

'You didn't try to follow this man?' Lightman asked. 'Or meet up with him later?'

'I can take no for an answer,' April said, beginning to look offended by his questions.

'Did you find out who he was, this other guy?' Lightman asked.

'No,' April said, 'I didn't. Why would I? And why are you so obsessed with it?'

'Because that man was Alex Plaskitt,' Lightman told her. 'The man who died in Louise Reakes's bed.'

There was a long beat. 'Shit. Seriously?' she said.

'I'm afraid so,' Lightman replied.

April turned away from him, looking out of the picture windows towards the sea. 'That's a hell of a shame,' she said. 'He was quite something. Even if he was a prude.'

'You didn't see anything later on that evening?' he asked. 'Anything to suggest why he might have been killed?'

April shook her head, slowly. 'No, I don't think . . . I guess the only thing I thought was how weirdly possessive his friend was.' Lightman realised that April must mean Step Conti, and it gave him pause for thought. 'When I kissed Alex,' April went on, 'it was almost like he was jealous.'

31

Louise

It's morning now. I left my account where it was last night, wondering if I'd actually write any more, or if I was done. I felt like there was nothing more for me to tell you. There were, instead, a lot of unanswered questions.

But I hate leaving anything unfinished, as you know. And after talking to April, I felt an itch to write more of it down.

I called her this morning, in spite of my sudden doubts. This is the first time I've ever distrusted her. Perhaps that sounds ridiculous, when she's so willing to sack me off in order to chase the man of the minute, and when she clearly has her own secrets. She's perpetually vague about her job, and who's paying her, and even more so about life back in Tennessee. But she's always essentially been there, a strong, dependable rock for me to grab on to.

It was a vast relief to hear her voice. It was like an instant return to normality. She spoke, and the earth righted itself.

It didn't matter if I was still under investigation for murder, or that you'd left, probably for good, or that she'd lied a while back, or that I felt like I might never be able to sleep again without dreaming of a smiling man following me. The moment she said, 'Lou, honey, I'm just the gladdest to speak to you,' I felt like I was back in my own skin.

'You too,' I told her. 'Everything's been such a fuck-up.'

'I hear you, honey,' she said. 'I've just spoken to that

insanely handsome cop. Who is completely, one hundred per cent immune to any kind of flirtation and it's heartbreaking.'

I couldn't help smiling. 'The older one or the younger one?'

'Well, he's a sergeant, I think he said,' she tried. 'Probably thirty-something and with cheekbones like knives and the most incredible blue eyes.' She sighed. 'But nothing there, you know? Not a hint of sexuality.'

'I know the one.'

And God, the relief of talking about the police like that. Of not thinking of them as terrifying figures of authority.

'So,' April said, 'are you OK? I've been going crazy with worry.'

'I know,' I told her. There had been fourteen missed calls and eight messages from her on my phone by the time I got it back. Which was a lot, even for April. 'I wanted so badly to talk to you. I'm back home now. Feeling like shit but on the up.'

'Where's Niall?'

I flinched slightly. 'I – I asked him to go.'

'You did?'

April sounded genuinely surprised, and I rushed to defend my actions. 'If you'd been there . . . in that fucking cell . . .' I swallowed, trying to be angry and not tearful. 'He let me down so badly, April. He jumped to the immediate conclusion that I must have slept with someone else and then killed him, and he refused to see me to even ask about it.' I used my thumb to wipe each eye, frustrated that I was once again tearful. I wanted to be stronger when I talked about you, Niall. To be the kind of woman who stands up to her awful husband and walks away with no regrets. 'Even Patrick believed in me more than Niall did. And do you know what he was actually doing on Friday night? He was with Dina.'

283

April hissed between her teeth. 'So there really was something going on with those two.'

'Yes,' I said. 'I've had zero other explanation. He couldn't even look me in the eye when we were released. How fucking dare he stand there and judge me after that? And I should just be angry but I'm so fucking sad.'

'Honey,' April said, warmly, 'I am positive he will come to his senses and realise what he's ruined. But that doesn't mean you have to take him back. Anyone who can do that to you – well, I'd be wondering if he was the right man to spend the rest of my life with.'

'Too right.' I said it so rebelliously, but I was still feeling lacerated by what you'd done, Niall. Whatever you felt when Dina abandoned you, what you've put me through has been infinitely worse. Trust me.

April sighed. 'He's not the only man out there, you know. Hey, you remember that Italian bambino from Hannah's wedding? My friend Chez? He's still single.'

'Oh . . . I think it might be a little soon, but thanks.' I didn't tell her that the idea of seeing any other man was crazy right then, when I could close my eyes and remember someone pressing down on me. And beyond that, that I might be about to go to jail for a crime I was certain I hadn't committed.

And then, just after that, I remembered that I needed to talk seriously to April. About that other time in the club. And I felt my stomach drop further.

'Why don't I come over?' she offered. She sounded enthusiastic. As if there was nothing better she could think of doing than cheering me up.

I couldn't ask her about that lie just then. I just couldn't.

32

The DCI was on a call when Hanson returned to the office, so she parked her tray of Costa coffee and settled herself at her desk. She began looking through the spreadsheet once again. She identified another address that might be of interest a few moments later. A knife identical to their murder weapon had been sent to a firm of mortgage advisers based in Winchester. The addressee was a Mr Marc Ruskin. She started looking to see if any of their suspects had anything to do with this firm, and the careful, methodical work was the perfect antidote to everything else she was feeling.

She'd only meant to fill a little time, but ended up so absorbed in it that she didn't notice the DCI coming to find her until he said her name from a few feet away.

'Sorry,' he said, as she started. 'Didn't mean to break your concentration. How's it going?'

'It's going OK, I think,' she said. 'There are a couple of addresses on the list from Steel and Silver that look promising. I'm just wading through any connections to the first one. And I got you coffee.' She gestured to a cardboard tray from Costa. 'I hope it's still warm. Flat white. Is that all right?'

'Oh, thanks. That's actually perfect.' Sheens manoeuvred the cup out of the cardboard holder. 'So. If it's not a bad time, I wanted to bounce a few thoughts off you.'

Hanson sat back from her computer. 'Fire away.'

'There's no way I buy Niall Reakes and Dina Weyman

meeting about a job,' he said. 'But equally, if it was simply an affair, it seems bizarre that he wouldn't just admit it to us, as it provides a perfect alibi.'

'Particularly since his fake alibi relies on his ex-wife anyway,' Hanson added.

'Exactly. I doubt his wife would believe him about the job idea in any case, so there's no benefit to it. Unless both he and Dina are covering up for something else that's been going on.'

Hanson looked away, towards her screen. Her mind was grinding through this, slowly. 'He seemed quite sure that Dina would cover for him. But then she clearly decided it was better to scapegoat him instead.'

'Which suggests something criminal,' the DCI agreed.

'Niall Reakes drove to Zurich before he flew home. He booked the ticket at the last minute. As if he'd suddenly been summoned . . .'

The DCI gave her an odd look. 'And he's a drug rep.'

'His ex-wife,' Hanson said quickly, 'manages a whole team of reps at another big pharma.' The DCI met her gaze. 'Could it be that simple?'

The chief stood, his face in a half-smile. 'If it is, it may have nothing to do with Alex Plaskitt. Let's bring Mr Reakes back in.'

O'Malley had finished most of his food and was feeling over-sugared, in need of a comfort break, and a little nauseous. Neither Issa nor Louise Reakes had gone anywhere, and the inside of the car was now bitterly cold. Which made it about standard for a stake-out, in O'Malley's experience.

On the better side of things, he was now three and a half hours through his five-hour stint, and he had identified a petrol station round the corner that had a customer toilet.

Naturally, he was within moments of taking a brief break when a Lotus came noisily down the road and hesitated outside number eleven. O'Malley had his camera phone out and ready, and had a clear view of April Dumont as she looked around for a space.

He took three photos and then waited as she found a spot further up the already-crowded close. She left the car half on the pavement and half hanging out diagonally into the road as she strode towards Louise Reakes's house. But instead of going towards the door, she moved across the road. For a moment her gaze swept over his car, and he thought he'd been seen. But she walked on past him, heading for the Corsa.

O'Malley hastily switched on the ignition and put the window down far enough to be able to hear any conversation, though the first sound was just a sharp rapping as April knocked on Issa's window. O'Malley couldn't see Issa himself, just April, her hair swinging down over her face as she leaned towards him.

'Hey,' she said, her drawl loud and piercing. It seemed that Issa had not opened the window to listen to her. 'So I know that you're grieving and all, but you need to leave. Louise has been through enough shit, and this is not reasonable behaviour, OK?'

O'Malley found himself holding his breath slightly. He wasn't too clear on how Issa was going to respond. He imagined him erupting out of the car and trying to injure her. But there was silence until April said, 'Hey! You getting this?'

And then the engine started up, and April backed away as Issa drove his car down onto the road. She stood and watched the car disappear from sight, and then she turned and walked towards number eleven.

O'Malley grinned to himself, deciding it was time for that comfort break.

Niall Reakes no longer looked anxious. He looked defeated. He moved slowly and without apparent care into the interview room and sat heavily. There was none of the self-righteousness that had characterised his first interview in this room, and Jonah was caught between satisfaction at his fall from grace and genuine empathy at his situation.

Daniella Hart, here as Niall's solicitor again, looked rather more cheerful. She threw a slightly combative smile in Jonah and Hanson's direction as they ran the tape. Jonah smiled back, guessing that Niall hadn't told his solicitor what he'd really been doing with Dina Weyman.

'Thank you for coming in again, Mr Reakes,' Jonah began. 'I'm afraid we have yet to communicate with your ex-wife.' He saw Niall's expression tighten very slightly, but it was almost as though he'd expected this. As though he had come prepared for betrayal. 'There are, however, a few more questions that need some answers in the interim.'

Niall did nothing more than nod, and Jonah glanced over at Hanson, who was primed to take the questioning from here.

'We've arranged to liaise with the Swiss police in order to trace your movements during Friday afternoon,' she said, with perfect coldness. 'Before we pin down exactly where you went in Zurich, and prove what you were picking up, we want to give you the opportunity to cooperate fully with our investigation.'

Niall's eyes were on the table, his jaw working. Daniella Hart's eyes were fixed on Jonah now, her pen poised over her notebook. The silence went on for a good few seconds and felt a lot longer.

And then Niall said, 'Shit.'

Hanson adjusted her pose, and spoke more quietly. 'This doesn't have to be an unmitigated disaster, Niall. You aren't kingpin in this.'

'I'd like to speak with my client alone,' the solicitor said.

'I didn't want to get involved,' Niall said, lifting his head and ignoring her. 'They entrapped me.'

'As serious an offence as drug smuggling is,' Jonah said, 'we're only interested in whether it relates to Alex Plaskitt's death.'

'Of course it doesn't!' Niall said, immediately. 'There's a big difference between shipping stuff around and killing someone. I wasn't even in Southampton on Friday.'

'Mr Reakes,' Daniella said sharply, 'we need to have a conversation.'

And this time, Niall nodded silently. Jonah switched off the tape.

It took the solicitor and her client fifteen minutes to establish that Niall was going to cooperate fully. When Jonah and Hanson returned and ran the tape again, he told them, in great detail, about the new friends he'd met at a conference in Dallas eight years ago. Two wonderful new people who had turned out not to be who he thought they were.

'They were a GP and his dermatologist wife, they said. They struck up a conversation in the hotel, and they were just so . . . cool. The kind of people you immediately want as your friends.'

Niall had met up with them again late on the second night of the conference, and they'd fed him a story about her having stage two breast cancer. 'The one experimental drug that looked like it was going to work wasn't on the market in the

UK yet, which was why they grabbed any opportunity to come to the States. They said they'd been buying it for a fortune and shipping it to the UK, and had ended up with massive debts. They had to find a solution, or they were going to have to sell their house, they said.' He sighed. 'Somewhere down the line, I admitted I had debt problems, too. And that I hadn't told anyone, least of all Dina, who was my fiancée back then.'

It was clear how much Niall hated talking about this, and his shame added to Jonah's conviction that this was the truth. He signalled for Niall to continue.

'The wine was flowing and it seemed really . . . natural to talk about it all. They seemed like they were being so open . . .'

Jonah nodded. He could imagine it well. Successful hustlers often had a particular ability to connect with people. Or to fake it, at least.

'The next night,' Niall went on, 'they told me they thought they'd found a solution to the cancer drug issue. A way of making it affordable. They looked so ecstatic that I actually felt happy for them. They went off to bed, and we agreed to see each other on the last night. We partied late after the conference and rolled to bed. I didn't think I'd see much of them after that, but she – the wife – turned up at my room before breakfast on the last morning, freaking out, apparently.'

'Their scheme with the drugs had gone wrong somehow?' Jonah asked.

'Of course it had,' Niall said, bitterly.

He explained, tightly, everything she'd told him. That their flight had been cancelled and their airline was rerouting them via Boston, an airport where they used sniffer dogs.

They'd picked up a large batch of her cancer drugs at a much cheaper price here, not actually legally. They knew they couldn't risk taking them through US customs in Boston.

'She said, "We can't afford to jettison them," and she looked so . . .' He sighed. 'So desperate. I didn't even stop to think about it all properly. When she asked what they should do, I just – I just said to give them to me. I was taking drug samples myself so it wasn't a problem to take theirs home too.'

'And these drugs . . .' Jonah said.

'They weren't cancer drugs,' Niall said, flatly. 'They told me later that they were MDMA. And, no, I didn't check before I shipped them. I went to their hotel room with my case, and I let them thank me over and over as they gave them to me. They hugged me and cried a little, both of them, and I never even stopped to wonder if the bag sitting on the bed had a concealed camera in it. I guess I just don't think in the right way for that stuff.'

'So what happened when you arrived home?'

'They came to get the drugs, and they said, "Come on, Niall. You know they weren't cancer drugs." Then they played me the little video they'd taken of me putting the drugs in my suitcase and pointing out my fake paperwork. They'd obviously edited out the rest. And I felt just so . . .' Niall's body sagged as he sighed. 'I thought I'd made some lifelong friends. When all they'd done was recruit me.'

'Did they pay you?'

'Yes,' Niall said. 'They paid me a lot. And they told me not to worry, because their organisation would keep on paying me. They said they really were going to be friends to me. I was going to get right out of debt, they said.' He glanced up at Jonah, and then added, tightly, 'I wish I could give you their real names, or some way of contacting them, but I can't. They became just the collection people, and the numbers they gave me were never answered by them. Always by someone else.'

'Another team here will need to ask you about all of that,' Jonah replied, not without a little sympathy. Jonah knew that the National Crime Agency would have a lot of questions for Niall about his contacts, but Jonah's interest was a lot narrower. 'What we need to know about now is Friday. Is Dina involved in all this somehow?'

'Of course she is,' Niall said, his mouth twisting. 'I'd stupidly let slip in those early conversations about my fiancée who worked in pharma too. They didn't touch her while we were together, but then I turned up at a drop-off and it was Dina instead of the couple. She became . . . They used her to recruit reps. She's risen up the ranks crazy fast. I guess she was in an ideal position to manage a whole group of runners. And she's ruthless enough to help dig dirt on her employees and then force them into it. The part that got to me the most was that she was suddenly above me in this scheme. I've spent the last four and a half years being answerable to my ex-wife, and having to walk this constant line. Avoiding sleeping with her but keeping her sweet.'

'But you kept doing it,' Jonah said.

'What choice did I have?' Niall asked. 'They had the video, and I had money troubles. They seemed to know exactly how to keep me tied in. There was never enough money to get me totally out of debt, and a lot of their deals meant going to expensive hotels or bars, which made it worse.'

Jonah nodded. 'So tell us what happened on Friday.'

Niall's mouth twisted into a slight smile. 'That was a massive balls-up. But it wasn't actually mine. One of Dina's reps in Zurich was supposed to take a shipment and got himself arrested.' He shook his head, his hand coming up to rub his face as he thought about it. 'I don't even know who he was, but you could probably find out. He got picked up in a bar for sniffing coke in the middle of the effing afternoon. He rang one of our group, who told me they were extracting his stuff from his hotel room, but I needed to get my ass over there, or their buyer was going to be seriously pissed off.'

'So you changed flights and collected it?'

'Yes,' Niall said. 'And it was bloody stressful. I could just see everything crumbling, which it did. Just . . . for a different reason.'

'Where did you go once you were back in the UK?' Hanson asked him.

'Oh, I met Dina at Gatwick airport, like I said.' He looked between them. 'I wasn't lying about that. The stuff was supposed to go to her . . . She could have just bloody lied for me, and this would all have been fine.' Niall made a slightly disgusted sound. 'You know, I don't even think they told her to throw me to the wolves. I've been thinking about it, and it's much more dangerous to have me questioned under pressure. I think denying it was all her idea. A way of making me know that she had power over me. She probably thought she could leave me to sweat for a few hours and then admit that she saw me.'

'So you met her at Gatwick,' Jonah said. 'And the hand-over went as planned?'

'Yes.'

'And then?'

Niall looked disconcerted. 'Well, I stayed at the hotel, so Louise wouldn't find out I was back early, and I hung around there on Saturday morning. Went to the gym, had coffee and read the papers . . . I was just killing time. And then . . . and then Louise called and told me what had happened.' He shook his head, his expression angry. Even after everything he'd done, he still seemed aggrieved at his wife's actions.

'So you weren't in Southampton on Friday night?' Jonah asked, his voice hard. 'You didn't make your way home, thinking to catch Louise out for drinking?'

Niall shook his head, very definitely. 'Why the hell would I do that? I was trying not to get caught out myself.' He shook his head, slowly. 'I'm sorry, but I don't have a clue what happened to that guy. It had nothing to do with me.'

'Do you believe him?' Hanson asked, as they returned to CID. She wasn't quite sure why she was asking. Perhaps because she wasn't sure what she thought about it all.

'Not necessarily,' the DCI said. 'The people Niall works for are exactly the kind of people who might stab someone using a custom-made weapon. It's possible that Alex saw something he shouldn't have done, and Niall ended up reacting violently out of desperation. But it does seem unlikely that he'd then leave the body in his own house. Or frame his wife, for that matter. It's too close to home.'

'But he still could have had a knife like that and flipped out because he found Alex with his wife,' Hanson countered. 'I still want to try and link Niall Reakes to that weapon. Possibly his ex-wife, too.'

'Good,' Sheens said. 'I agree that we shouldn't rule him out.'

They came to a stop next to Lightman's desk. Ben was typing up a report, presumably of his interview with April.

'What did April Dumont have to say?' Hanson asked.

'A few things,' Lightman said, thoughtfully. 'She agrees

that she kissed Alex Plaskitt, but had no idea he was the victim. She doesn't think Louise would have gone home with Alex, either. She says it's not what she does. Interesting observations on Step Conti, though.'

The DCI raised an eyebrow.

'He was apparently very upset when Alex and April kissed. April thought he might actually be jealous that Alex had kissed someone else. She saw some intense conversations going on between the two of them afterwards.'

Hanson cast her mind back to Alex's self-contained friend. He had seemed genuinely upset at Alex's death. Surprised, too. Or at least good at pretending to be.

'He did seem close to Alex,' she said, thoughtfully. 'Might he have been secretly obsessed with him? Or even seeing him behind Issa's back?'

'Nothing has pointed in that direction so far,' Sheens said. 'But it's worth looking at.'

'I suppose,' Hanson went on, 'if he was obsessed, then if he'd seen Alex get together with yet another woman, that might have driven him to do something stupid.'

'I wouldn't mind getting other views on Step Conti,' the DCI agreed. 'Let's try Alex's sister.' He turned to Ben. 'Anything else from April?'

'Yes. A small but potentially interesting other thing,' Lightman said. 'Louise lost her driving licence in the club. I wondered if Alex might have tried to return it to her.'

'Interesting,' the chief agreed. His expression was thoughtful. 'I need some more coffee and some time to think. Anyone want anything from Costa?'

'As many chocolate twists as they have,' Hanson said. And then she added, 'God, and I'd better do some exercise later. I've done nothing for days.'

She didn't add that she'd largely stopped running because of Damian. It had lost a lot of its charm once she'd started looking over her shoulder for him. She'd ended up running in the gym instead, and she didn't enjoy it in the same way. Getting there was also needlessly time-consuming, so she inevitably went less often.

But as she settled herself at her desk, she decided that a run would be a good idea. She was going to face up to being alone, in darkness, and enjoy it. The threat of her ex had become less real. More ridiculous. She wished she'd told Ben about it earlier.

She loaded up the spreadsheet of knife orders again and spent a good half-hour trying to link either Niall Reakes or Dina Weyman to the address in Winchester where the knife had been sent. And then, in the end, as she finished up one of the DCI's newly bought chocolate twists and threw the bag in the bin, she realised that the obvious route would be to call the firm and ask to talk to this Marc Ruskin who had apparently taken the delivery.

It didn't take long to raise him.

'This is Marc Ruskin.' His voice was brittle, his cheerful, northern-accented speech not quite steady. 'Is this . . . about Alex?'

Hanson had a momentary floating sensation. 'Sorry, you mean . . . ?'

'My – friend? Who was murdered?'

Hanson tried to make sense of this. 'Yes, I . . . Could you tell me how you knew him?'

'Through my cousin,' Marc said. 'Through Step. We were a group. Me, Step, Alex. Occasionally my brother, when he wasn't working.'

'You used to go out together?'

'Yeah, we did.' He gave a slightly emotional-sounding laugh. 'I know we seem like a weird bunch. From finance people to personal trainers and everything in between. But we were pretty close.'

Hanson made an effort to get mentally back on her feet. To take control of this interview. 'When did you meet Alex?'

'A little while after he met Issa,' Marc said.

'Were Alex and Step particularly close?' she asked next, April's comments about him very much in mind.

'Yes, I'd say so,' Marc agreed. 'The two of them meet up a lot more often.'

'There's never been any . . . jealousy issue, has there?' she tried. 'Between Step and Issa?'

There was a brief silence from Marc, and then he said, 'I don't know. I think Issa can be a little bit resentful of Step sometimes.'

'And the other way?' Hanson went on. 'Does Step resent Issa?'

'Oh, I don't think so,' Marc said. 'Not really. Only when he tells Alex not to see him.'

There was a silence as Hanson wondered how to move the conversation round to the knife. She decided there was no gentle way of doing it, so she went on, 'Can I ask about a package that was sent to you, a while back?'

'Uhh . . . a package?'

'Yes,' Hanson said. 'From a company called Steel and Silver. This was in January last year.'

There was a brief pause, and then Marc said, 'Oh, you mean that Alex sent over? Yes, the knife for Step's birthday.'

Hanson paused, very much aware of her heart beating in her throat. 'It was a present for Step Conti?'

'Yes,' Marc said. 'Beautiful thing that Alex had found. It was just Step's kind of thing.'

'So . . .' she said, as her brain attempted to catch up with this. 'So why didn't Alex have it delivered to his house?'

'Oh, because Issa would have lost his shit,' Marc said, with a laugh. 'He's an absolute pacifist. I mean, Alex is, too, but . . . you know. He wanted to get Step something he would love.'

'Is . . . Step into weapons?' Hanson asked.

'Well, he likes anything with workmanship, but he's got a particular thing for hunting knives and ceremonial swords, that kind of thing. Has a huge display in his house.' There was a brief pause, and then Marc said, 'Was there a particular reason . . .?'

'We were just wondering what was in it,' she said, as calmly as she could. 'Did Step like it?'

'Yes,' Marc said, more slowly. 'He loved it.'

'Perhaps you could describe the knife, just so . . .?'

'Well, it had a long, tapered blade,' Marc said. 'And lots of . . . of black scrollwork round the handle.'

'That's great,' Hanson said, with a breezy, final note. 'Thanks so much for all your help. We'll probably need to talk to you again later, but that's all for now.'

'OK,' Marc said. 'Thanks.'

There was something in his voice that told her he'd started wondering about that knife. She lost no time in heading to the DCI's office.

'A knife that matches our murder weapon was delivered to the workplace of Marc Ruskin,' she told him, before he'd had a chance to say anything, 'who turns out to be Step Conti's cousin. Alex ordered it himself, as a gift for Step Conti. He gave it to him for his birthday.' There was a brief pause while the chief looked at her, and she added, 'Marc described it perfectly to me, and I think he'd started to cotton on to why I was asking. He might warn Step about it.'

Sheens's expression was unreadable at first, and then he said, 'Right. We'd better get over there.'

Step Conti's house looked just as picture-perfect on a gloomy day as it had in clear sunlight. Though there was a keen, cold wind blasting across from the heath that hit Jonah and Hanson hard. It had snowed again out here, too, a hardened layer that had immediately frozen on top.

Jonah couldn't help laughing slightly as he and Hanson both slipped and nearly fell at almost the same time, and then moved flat-footed across the icy driveway towards the front door. They both looked, he suspected, a little ridiculous, and not much like the stern forces of justice they represented.

He waited for the two uniforms from the squad car to catch up with them before he rang the bell. One of the officers was already heading to the side of the property to make sure Step didn't do a runner out of the back.

Step Conti's expression was contained as he answered the door. It was hard to tell whether he felt under pressure as Jonah greeted him.

'We've been given some information about a gift you were given for your birthday,' Jonah said. 'A knife. Do you have it with you?'

Step looked from Jonah to Hanson, and then behind them to the second uniformed constable. And then he said, 'The one Alex and the guys gave me? Sure. Come in.'

Jonah caught Hanson's gaze as Step moved to let them in. She looked wary, which matched his feeling. He nodded to her, a silent agreement to be on their guard.

Step led them through the sitting-room door this time.

Jonah remembered how he'd nearly taken them into this room during their last visit and then changed his mind.

They found themselves in a large space with exposed brickwork and bifold doors at the far end. The left-hand wall was mainly given over to a series of display cabinets, built around a big flat-screen TV.

The locked cabinets were all full of weaponry, though most of it was old-fashioned. Old muskets or fragments of them. Ceremonial swords. Daggers. And, at the far end, a much shinier collection of blades that looked to be new. It was no wonder, Jonah thought, that Step had hidden this from them on their first visit.

Step went straight to the far end and waited while Jonah and Hanson caught up. Jonah could feel the constable at his heels, and hoped he was on his guard. Their suspect was standing in front of a whole arsenal. But Step made no move to open the case.

'It's this,' he said, gesturing.

And there, sitting neatly between two less elaborate hunting knives, sat what looked to be their murder weapon. Only this one was clean, unbloodied and gleaming.

33

Louise descended the stairs again, a little self-conscious in her very low-cut black dress. She dropped her rucksack down by her feet and tried to grin at April.

'Great,' April said. 'You look much more like you again.'

'I'm still me when I'm wearing a dressing gown,' Louise countered.

'No, we're all slobs in a dressing gown,' April argued. 'This – this is the strong, mouthy, fun person I know. This is Louise.'

'I don't feel strong,' Louise said. And then she pulled a face. 'Sorry. I sound like a self-pitying idiot.'

'That is exactly why we need to get you out of here.' April gave her a grin that was full of mischief. 'A change of scene is going to do you so much good. We can book you a massage, drink cocktails crazy early, and then party. OK?'

'That sounds good,' Louise agreed.

'So you're ready?'

'Yes, I . . .' Louise paused. She didn't really want to ask April this. She didn't want to break the spell. 'Look, there's something I need to know.' She hesitated, still dreading the consequences of this, but then ploughed on. 'When we went clubbing last summer, and I said I thought I'd seen Niall. I . . . I did see him, didn't I? I know it was him.'

April pulled a wry face. 'Ah. I . . . Sorry.' She gave Louise a doubtful, slightly humorous look. 'That was the first time I saw him with Dina. I didn't know whether to tell you. I was just – I was so goddamn angry with him that I stormed over, but when I got there, they weren't kissing or anything, and I overheard them talking about money. Dina left the moment she saw me, and Niall begged me not to say anything. He said she'd offered to get him a job. That it really, genuinely wasn't more. And I thought, you know, that might have been what I heard.' April sighed. 'I told him to get out of there, but I said I'd be keeping my eye on him. I felt really crappy for lying to you, but it sort of seemed more like a business arrangement than a date. You know?'

Louise studied her for a moment, and then said, 'You still basically trusted him?'

'Yeah, I did.' And April nodded. 'Ever since I first met Niall, I've thought he was decent. You know, the first time we met, out in Dallas, he thought I was in trouble, and he just straight off tried to help. It wasn't sleazy like every other guy in the world. He never flirted or made any moves on me. He just – saw a human being suffering, and he decided to try and fix it.' She gave a small smile. 'I mean, he was flat out wrong. I didn't need any help. But it made me like him. And I've always liked the way he tries to help you, too.'

Louise gave her own sigh. 'I suppose he does. Up to a point. So . . . when you told me on Friday about seeing them together . . .'

'Oh, I'd seen them again, like I said,' April replied. 'She was just all goddamn over him like a rash. Whatever political manoeuvrings in the world of pharma may have been going on, he was clearly enjoying it. I felt so torn about telling you. I thought maybe I should just give him a warning and see which way he jumped. And then you told me you were going to get pregnant . . .'

Louise could feel herself blushing a deep red. 'Oh, God. I don't know what I was thinking.'

'You were thinking it was how you'd sort your life out,' April replied with a shrug. 'And if Niall hadn't been lying to you, then maybe it would have fixed things.'

Louise shook her head, mortified. 'A child would never have fixed our fucked-up marriage. It was over years ago.'

April pulled her into a fierce hug. 'I'm sorry, honey. But you're going to find yourself a really great guy. One who knows you'll be an awesome mother, and who hasn't got some crappy ex-wife Rebecca-ing in the background without having the good grace to be dead.'

Louise found herself caught between laughing and crying. She took a long breath in, trying to tip herself towards laughter, and said, 'Thanks, April. For everything.'

'You're welcome,' April said, releasing her with a half-smile. 'Shall we go?'

'Yes,' Louise said. 'Let's go.'

34

Step Conti was the picture of unruffled calm. Even while he was stuck in a low armchair, with the DCI in full attack mode and two uniformed officers loitering in the background of his sitting room, he was calm and clear-headed. Hanson found herself wondering, idly, whether this was how Ben would be under interrogation.

Step explained that he had only ever had one copy of that knife. He also hadn't shared with anyone where it had come from.

'I couldn't have done, because I didn't know myself,' he said. 'Alex just told me he'd had it imported from Poland, and I didn't try to find out. It's beautiful as it is, without needing any history.'

Hanson wasn't positive that she believed him. As strange as it might be to buy a second version of a very distinctive knife in order to kill with it, it wasn't beyond the realms of the possible.

The DCI seemed to be thinking along the same lines and carried on with his questioning. Midway through, he suddenly changed tack.

'Tell me,' he said. 'Did you have feelings for Alex Plaskitt that went beyond the purely friendly?'

And at that point Step had finally shown some kind of reaction.

'Feelings for him? But I'm not – no, of course I didn't.' He shifted in the armchair and looked from Hanson to Jonah and back. 'I've never fancied anyone male, and the only person on earth I'd get jealous about is through in the kitchen.'

'Why were you so angry with him about kissing a woman at the club, then?'

Step shook his head. 'Obviously because he was risking everything for something stupid and meaningless. I was angry because I know how much Issa means to him. Look, he's screwed up before, and it was awful for both of them. Alex felt . . . If you'd seen how broken he was after he cheated on Issa . . .'

'So you were acting as his conscience,' the DCI said, with heavy scepticism. 'Why is Issa so distrustful of you?'

Hanson expected Step to become frustrated, but he gave a slightly weary smile. 'Issa thinks I encouraged him the last time round, or maybe even matchmade him, because I was the one who put them in touch. Alex and Sarah. I had zero idea anything would happen. I'd just met her at work, and she'd told me she was unhappy with her weight and fitness.' He shifted very slightly again, leaning forwards and resting an arm on each knee. 'If Issa wants to believe that Alex's straying only happened because of me, then in some ways I'm happy for him to think so. Alex just had fleeting moments when he wished he'd fallen in love with a woman instead. Deep down he knows – he knew – that any acceptance from his family would be hollow, and he wanted to make a life with Issa.'

'So you didn't feel jealous when he hooked up with someone?' Hanson asked.

'No,' Step said, back in control now. 'Alex was a really wonderful friend, and I miss him like crazy. But I never in a million years thought of him as anything else.'

Step asked if they'd checked the time of his return on

Friday evening with his wife, which Lightman had done previously. But the chief asked Hanson to put the question to his wife again, so she left them in the sitting room while she went to find her.

Karen Conti was trying to bake cookies with two kids who seemed more interested in eating smarties out of the packet. She answered over her shoulder, looking worried by the question. But she seemed quite definite that Step had been home by twelve thirty.

This all meant there was no justification for bringing Step into the station. Given that his own knife was sitting there, unused, and that they had little more to point at him than an observation from April Dumont, they had to leave it.

The other members of Step and Alex's group knew about that weapon, too, Hanson thought. That was where they needed to look.

As soon as they were back at the station, Hanson opened up the data file from Alex's phone. By Step's account, the knife had been given to him on the nineteenth, so she set her date range from January the tenth to the nineteenth.

She vaguely heard Lightman tell the DCI, 'Issa Benhawy was in Blue Underground on Friday, looking for Alex. One of the bar staff spoke to me.'

Hanson's head snapped up. She hadn't thought about Alex's husband in some while. He seemed such an unlikely violent killer: a pacifist who hated any kind of aggression. So much so that his husband had hidden that he was buying a knife for Step.

But his pacifism could be as hypocritical as the next person's, Hanson thought. He might believe in non-violence until pushed, and it sounded as though Alex had done a lot of things his husband might have objected to that Friday night.

'Issa has also been spending a lot of time hanging around Saints Close,' the chief said. 'O'Malley had him back there this morning, until April Dumont arrived and chased him away.'

'Did we check for his car reg on the ANPRs?' Hanson asked.

'We did,' Lightman said. 'His car wasn't flagged anywhere on Friday night, but I'm going to check Alex's car, too. He would have had access to it.'

There was a pause, and the DCI said, 'OK. I'd like to look at him more closely. There could be reasons for his behaviour other than grief.'

Hanson nodded, and returned to what she had been doing with a new sense of significance. If Alex had sent a message about the knife before they'd given it to Step, Issa might have known about it. Particularly if, as a jealous husband, he was looking at Alex's phone to see if he'd cheated again.

There were thirteen WhatsApp strings on Alex's phone on the right dates, she discovered. He'd been a fairly heavy phone user.

Several of the strings, she dismissed immediately. One to Issa she hesitated over, but then moved on. Alex wouldn't have sent his husband a photo of a knife he was hoping to hide. It made no sense.

And then she saw a group chat from the twelfth with the names Marc and Chez, and she opened it with a feeling of buzzing excitement.

There were only a few messages on it. The first was from Alex to the rest of the group, and said:

Look at this Polish beauty! Absolutely psyched for Saturday.

Beneath the words, an icon showed that there was an image attached to the message. Hanson clicked on it and sighed as her screen was filled with a large photo. The knife was identical to their murder weapon.

With perfect timing, the phone on her desk rang the moment she opened her mouth to tell the chief.

'DC Hanson,' she said, trying not to sound irritable.

'Hi,' a woman's voice said. 'It's – it's Phoebe Plaskitt. I hope it's OK . . . I have something I really want to tell you.'

There was a shake to Phoebe's voice, a sense of stress that cut through Hanson's annoyance.

'Of course. Anything you have to say is helpful,' she replied, pulling her notepad towards her.

'I've been looking at Alex's videos,' Phoebe said. 'I got – I actually got a little bit obsessed with the trolls. Some of them are repeat offenders, and the things they say are really vicious. One of them started a little while before the row I had with Issa about Alex stopping it all. It's got a ridiculous username but . . . but I looked back through the posts from that account, and there was basically nothing much before the trolling, but the account's been up a while.' She took a shaky breath. 'I looked at the comments this person had made three years ago, when it was first opened, and they're totally different. A couple of nice comments on some music. And one of them is on the music of a friend of mine, and I remember that comment. I read it at the time, but the username was different then.'

'You recognised it?' Hanson asked.

'Yes. Because it was a band I recommended to Issa and the comment was from him.' She gave a strange, tight laugh. 'The troll was Issa.'

*

Two things happened rapidly after Hanson finished her call with Phoebe Plaskitt. The first was that Lightman found Alex's car on the ANPR file. It had been driven down London Road at three minutes past one on Friday night, and then past Asylum Green at one thirty-seven. He reported his findings quickly to Hanson and the DCI, whose expression was distant and, she thought, slightly troubled.

Before the chief had said anything, his phone buzzed, and he switched it to speakerphone before he said, 'Domnall. Anything to report?'

'I'm afraid so,' O'Malley said, his voice tinny. 'April Dumont has managed to smuggle Louise Reakes out of the house. She drove past me a good ten minutes ago and I'm positive Louise is no longer in the house. I'm ready to pursue, but I have no idea at present where they've gone.'

'I'll get Heerden's team on it,' the chief said and rang off. As he was striding back towards his office, he called, 'I'd like you to get Issa Benhawy on the phone and find out where he is, too.'

Hanson nodded, her hand already going to her mobile. She could sense Lightman's eyes on her as she made the call and waited through eight full rings before it went to answerphone.

'No reply,' she said.

It was Chief Inspector Yvonne Heerden's team who tracked Issa down. It took them eight minutes to flag him on a traffic camera at the junction with the M27 Eastbound. Two minutes later, as Jonah and Lightman were walking towards the Mondeo, Heerden called to inform them that April Dumont's car had been picked up slightly further along the same road.

'They're headed in the general direction of Portsmouth,'

she told him. 'And they're about fifteen seconds apart on the camera. It looks like pursuit to me.'

As soon as she rang off, Jonah dialled through to O'Malley, who was already on the correct side of town. 'Get after them if you can.'

'Thanks, chief,' O'Malley said. 'I'm sure I can close the gap, Lotus or no Lotus.'

'We shouldn't be too far behind you,' Jonah said, picking up his coat. 'We're going to leave now.'

'Do you have any thoughts about what Issa Benhawy is trying to do?' Lightman asked him, after the call was done.

'Lots of them,' Jonah said grimly. 'And none of them are good.'

'Done,' April said, leaning in through the driver's door to pick up her suede handbag. The car was full of the smell of petrol, a scent Louise had always loved. 'Need anything from the store?'

'Vodka?' Louise asked.

'Hell yes!' April replied, and manoeuvred herself back out of the car. She slammed the door hard enough to make Louise's head ring. For some reason April seemed incapable of closing doors quietly.

Louise followed her progress across the petrol station forecourt, hugely relieved to trust her again. What April had told her about that strange moment in the club had rung true, not least because April had been endlessly loyal to her from the moment they'd met. She, unlike Niall, had proved herself over and over.

April passed by a young guy, probably only in his twenties, as she stalked her way in, and he stared after her with obvious admiration. The April effect.

Louise smiled, and then yawned. She was beginning to feel genuinely tired now. She guessed the adrenaline was finally wearing off. There was no longer any reason to feel keyed up. She was out of the city and accompanied by her best friend.

She cranked her seat backwards, and then shifted until she'd found a comfortable position. She felt as though she might, finally, sleep. Her eyes were half closed as she looked lazily at the rear-view mirror and watched an old Ford Fiesta pull into the station forecourt behind them. She could see the driver looking ahead as he pulled into the small queue of cars waiting to fill up. She caught his face just before he turned and vanished behind the bulk of a Qashqai. Sleepily, she thought she recognised him.

It was Issa, she realised, with a sudden jolt. What was Alex's husband doing here?

Then she remembered that she had flirted with Alex. That she had, in all probability, gone home with him. That his death was her fault.

She turned to look behind her, and saw Issa climbing out of his car. There was something really wrong in his expression. Something that went beyond grief. And he was holding something under his jacket. Something bulky.

She was suddenly no longer sleepy. Not sleepy at all.

She hurried to undo her seat belt, and then pushed the door open. She scrambled out in a crouch, hoping to be hidden behind the SUV until she could make a run for the shop and the tills. She could feel every inch of her flesh crawling as she scooted forwards and round the front of the car, not caring that a woman leading a small girl back from the shop was staring at her.

'Hey!'

It was Issa's voice. He'd seen her.

She stood up and ran for the shop. She didn't notice a car trying to exit the petrol station until she was already in front of it, and she gasped as it jolted to a stop. But she ran on. And then she cannoned into the heavy swing door, feeling the time it took to open as if it were an age. But she was through, into the shop, where April was. Strong, dependable April, who would somehow stop whatever it was that Alex's husband was trying to do.

Except that there were only two customers in the shop, and neither of them was April.

35

'We're coming up on Junction Eight,' Jonah told O'Malley.

'I've already passed Nine,' O'Malley answered. 'I haven't seen either of them yet. Are they still on the M27?'

'I'll check with Yvonne's team.' Jonah rang off and listened to the phone ring four times. 'Come on,' he muttered.

And then Yvonne Heerden was there, telling him they had the two cars thirty seconds apart going past Junction Nine. 'They were still on the road eight minutes ago, but we haven't picked them up since.'

The toilets. April must be in the toilets. And there were locks on the doors. They could hide if they had to.

Louise saw an open door at the rear left of the shop and ran towards it. She almost tripped on the mop and bucket that were propping it open, but then was through.

She was so busy running forwards, totally fixed on escape, that she was slow to realise there were no toilets here. They must have been through another door. Out here there was just a small staff kitchen and a storeroom. Boxes of confectionary spilling out into the hall.

There was nobody here, and nowhere to lock herself away.

She could feel her pulse twitching madly in her chest and neck.

Shit. What do I do?

There was a way out. A heavy grey door with a bright green lever. She barely paused before bolting towards it.

She slammed it open, and felt as if she were leaving some form of hell behind her as she ran out into the bright sunshine again.

She closed it behind her as quietly as she could, and then moved to her right, along the blank back of the shop. What next?

She took a breath, knowing she just needed to stay calm and try to find April.

But at the thought of moving past the bins and round to the front a vivid image of Issa stalking towards her struck her, and she leaned back against the wall for fear of falling.

O'Malley slowed just before the entrance to the petrol station, his eyes scanning the forecourt. He was almost past it by the time he saw the back of April's Lotus. It only became visible as a large vehicle pulled out from behind it.

Cringing at the thought of being rammed, he stepped on the brakes, and felt the car begin to skid as he turned the wheel. The Astra hung for a moment, as if unsure whether to let him live through this or not, and then suddenly gained grip, and lurched towards the forecourt. He pressed the brakes harder and managed to bring the car into a controlled entry with a few feet to spare.

Breathing hard, he drove round the queue waiting to fuel up and dumped the Astra in the space reserved for putting air in the tyres. A quick glance showed him that the Lotus was empty. He tried to remember what kind of car Alex Plaskitt had owned. The one Issa might be driving.

His eye fell on the Fiesta that was now sitting two spaces behind the Lotus. It was empty, too, despite the fact that the driver hadn't made it to a pump.

O'Malley checked his waistband for his baton, and then jogged towards the shop.

The clunk and squeak of metal as the back door opened was one of the most terrifying sounds Louise had ever heard. She should have moved. She should have gone round to the front of the shop.

And then Issa's quiet voice said, 'Louise,' and her flesh crawled. She was trying to remember. To remember if this was the voice she'd heard that night, even while she pushed herself away from the wall and tried to stumble away from him.

'I'm so sorry,' he said.

And Louise found herself stopping. Turning. He was crying again. She could only remember ever seeing him in distress. Even when he'd been angry with her.

He was putting his hand into his pocket, and she tried to back away further. Had he armed himself with another knife? With a gun?

And then he pulled his hand out and it wasn't a knife. It was a box of some kind. Dark wood inlaid with gold.

'I found this in Alex's car,' he said.

He was holding it out to her, and she didn't want to come closer to him. It must be a trick to get her to come over, so he could attack her. The knife would come out from another pocket, and he would kill her.

But watching him hold it out to her, with such pathos, she found that she couldn't refuse to take it. She took two steps and stretched to cross the gap between them until it was in her fingers.

And then she opened the hinged lid, while trying not to stop looking at him.

What she saw made no sense at first. There was nothing in

there but hair. Strands and fragments of hair, all of them dark. Two of them so dark as to be almost black. All of them coiled up and slotted into neat squares.

And then her hand went to her own hair, and she suddenly understood.

'You must have been one of many,' Issa said, quietly. 'You must have been just one of a long list. It wasn't your fault.'

Louise took a large, shaky breath. 'It is my fault. I was angry. And hurting. And I flirted with him.' Her vision had become fragmented as her eyes filled with tears. 'I sat at the bar with him for half an hour. An hour. I'm not sure. And I sank drink after drink with him and I laughed at everything he said, and I put my hand on his knee, and I told him – I told him that I'd like to take him home with me.' She gave a great, heaving sob. 'And I didn't even mean it. I didn't mean it.'

Issa's jaw moved. For a moment he looked angry. But then he said, 'I think he would have followed you anyway.'

There was a long silence, which wasn't really silence because of the rush of cars from the motorway.

'I think I killed him,' she said, a little later, remembering the slick feeling of hot blood on her fingers. Remembering that he had made a strange laughing sound that had turned into a groan. 'I think I killed him.'

And Issa, to her profound sadness and humiliation and relief, said, 'It's OK.'

The back door of the shop opened so hard that it banged back against the wall, and the rotund police sergeant cannoned through it, followed quickly by April, who looked so terrified it was almost funny.

'It's all right,' Louise said, holding out a hand. 'He just needed to show me something.'

And then April flung her arms round her, and Louise felt

as though her legs had turned into string. Perhaps harp strings. And she laughed as she slid through the embrace and sat heavily on the tarmac.

'We'll need to know about Friday night,' Jonah told Issa an hour and a half later. 'You went to find him, didn't you?'

'Yes,' Issa said. 'I thought he might cheat again. When he didn't reply to my messages on Friday, I called him, and a woman answered instead. So I went to find him. I couldn't get my car out so I took his. I should have told you . . . but I never found him. I looked for him up London Road, and then between there and home. But I didn't catch sight of him.' He put his hand onto the table edge, very carefully. 'I must – I must have driven right past them, mustn't I? While he was attacking her.'

'It's possible,' Jonah agreed. 'They would have been out of sight.'

'Why do you think he ended up at her house?' Issa asked, his gaze fixed on his own fingers. 'Do you think she ran and he kept following?'

'That's the most likely explanation,' Jonah agreed. 'Alex may even have forced his way into the house after she injured him fighting him off. We think he might have taken her driving licence earlier on. So he would have known where she was. But by that point he had suffered extensive blood loss. Whatever he planned by way of revenge or . . . well. It may not have happened.'

Issa gave a small, hiccupping sob. 'It's – I still feel so sad that he – that he just curled up and died. Alone. And I don't know how I can feel that now that I know . . .'

'It's still possible to feel for people,' Jonah said, gently. 'Even those who have done terrible things.'

Issa looked up towards the ceiling, but he nodded.

'Do you have any idea why Alex might take hair from these women?' Jonah asked. 'Was there some reason for it?'

'I don't – I suppose all these women were – they looked a little like Alex's mother.' He rubbed at each of his eyes in turn. 'I think he felt more betrayed by her, when she turned on him for his sexuality, than he did by his father. Maybe they all represented her. Or just . . . the women he told himself he should desire. I don't know.'

There was a silence in the interview room for a few seconds, and then O'Malley, his voice full of sympathy, asked, 'Could you explain to me, too, why you were trolling your husband?'

Issa's empty expression briefly shifted. Fleetingly, he looked as though he hated himself.

'I wanted him to take it seriously,' he said, quietly. 'I was so frightened that something would happen to him. I mean, I was frightened for myself, too, but he was the one who was going to get recognised. He'd – he'd done some TV appearances and it looked like he might get to be a regular fitness adviser on a lifestyle show. It was all dangerous for him.' He gave Jonah a long stare out of gleaming eyes. 'I know it was an awful thing to do. And it didn't even work. He was a lot tougher than I am, I guess. Or maybe he just knew he was capable of – of hurting people.'

Jonah nodded, and then said, 'We'll need to hold on to Alex's car for a few days.' When Issa said nothing, he went on, 'We'd also like your help with a few dates from Alex's diary. To make our search for the women whose hair he had easier.'

'We have a shared diary on our phones. You can – can you see it on Alex's?'

Jonah glanced at O'Malley, who said, 'Yes, we should be able to. Thank you.'

There was another silence, and then Issa said, 'Do you think he . . . hurt . . . any of them?'

Jonah knew he was asking whether Alex might have killed anyone, a question Jonah badly wanted an answer to as well. All he could say in reply was, 'We'll find out.'

Hanson felt flat. Flatter than she had felt at the close of any case.

She had been wrong about Alex. Really, truly wrong. He wasn't a kind, supportive person. He was a bloody monster. A man who had stalked and abused women out of, what, a warped revenge on his mother? And then had kept trophies of them in his car. Memories of his victories.

Their job now, hers and Lightman's, was to find them. To find the women he had attacked before. And that was depressing, too. Scanning case after case to find women who might have been Alex's victims rather than anyone else's.

It hadn't taken her long to find one that seemed to fit. Just over a year ago, a student named Gianetta Jilani had been left huddled in a heap in Portsmouth with almost no memory of an assault that had left her bleeding. The one thing she remembered was a knife.

That attack had happened on Step's birthday, six days after Alex had sent a photograph to the WhatsApp group. Six days after he'd talked about the knife as a Polish beauty.

36

The inevitable flurry of work that came with trying to tie up their investigation kept the team at their desks until late. O'Malley and the DCI spent a good hour shut away with DCS Wilkinson, going over and over the upsides and down-sides to pursuing a case against Louise Reakes. Lightman spent the time writing up a preliminary report, which would be used to create a press release the next day. Hanson, mean-while, finished compiling her list of assaults, rapes and murders across Southampton and major cities within a potential day trip or overnight distance, and started compar-ing Alex's diary and messages with them.

Gianetta Jilani's attack was almost definitely a match. The database revealed that the student had originally gone to Rain in Portsmouth. Earlier in the same WhatsApp thread where Alex had posted the photo of the knife, she found that this was the club his group had arranged to meet at.

She'd found other possibilities, too. One of which she didn't quite want to connect to Alex. A thirty-four-year-old Londoner named Laura Stevenson had last been seen at a bar in Camden Town in May. Her body had been found in the canal four days later. She had been stabbed twice in the back.

She'd had long dark hair, like Louise Reakes. Like Alex's mother. It was much like all the hair they'd found in that box. And blood tests had showed traces of Viagra in her system.

Alex had, it turned out, been away that night. A lads' night in London. It matched up too well.

Hanson sent McCullough a summary of the report and asked if she could look at the post mortem. They needed to know whether the weapon that had killed Laura Stevenson might have been the same as the knife that had killed Alex. The next step would be to DNA test the hair strands in the box and compare them with any DNA of the victims of attacks.

Their theory on the knife was that Alex had ordered a second one to a different address. They were confident they would connect him to another order in the end, even if it meant going to the original makers of the knife in Poland and checking up with them.

At nine fifteen the DCI announced that he'd spoken to the Crown Prosecution Service. The CPS were not enthusiastic about charging Louise Reakes with either the more severe charge of murder or the lesser charge of manslaughter. There was an ongoing debate about whether the perversion of justice charge should go ahead, but they had two more days in which to make a decision.

'I know what she did was pretty sneaky,' Hanson told them all, 'but I hope they let it lie.'

'I hope you aren't expressing a personal opinion that isn't in line with the letter of the law,' O'Malley said, giving her a grin.

'Of course not,' Hanson replied, deadpan. 'Wouldn't ever.'

'So with that, I think it's time to call it a night,' the DCI told them. 'I'll see you all in the morning.'

Hanson ended up walking down to the car park with Lightman, who asked, once they were on the stairs, how she was doing.

'I'm OK,' she told him, with a shrug. 'Feeling a little flat at the outcome of all that, but not as anxious about Damian and all his bollocks. Having talked it all through has helped a lot. So thank you.'

Lightman nodded. 'We should have a plotting session,' he said. 'Tomorrow or Wednesday. A plan of action for dealing with the ex.'

'That sounds good,' she said, holding the door for him as they walked outside. 'Thank you.'

They stepped outside, and then Lightman paused on the pavement. 'He, um . . . he was here when we got back from the service station. Damian. He was hanging around out here, presumably in an effort to scare you.'

'Shit,' Hanson said. She shuddered, an involuntary reaction she wasn't proud of. And then she asked, 'Are you sure it was him?'

'Yeah, I looked him up yesterday,' Lightman said, with a trace of a smile. 'I dug up *all* the dirt on him.'

Hanson gave a shocked laugh. 'You didn't use the police database for this, did you?'

'I haven't so far,' Lightman said. 'But I'm bearing it in mind if I feel he merits further investigation.'

Hanson glanced around and tried to ignore a crawling sensation up and down her spine. 'I hope he's got bored and buggered off.'

'Well, he didn't hang around,' Lightman said, carefully not looking at her, 'after I had a quick word.'

'*What?*' Hanson realised it had come out a little sharply and pulled a face. 'Sorry, but . . . What did you say?'

'I addressed him as Damian, and he reacted, so I asked if he would like to come inside and talk to us or vacate the premises. He chose to leave.' He shrugged. 'The DCI was about five feet away, watching, so I think he felt a little outgunned.'

'Right,' Hanson said. 'Right.' She wasn't sure if she thought this was high-handed or actually the best thing anyone had ever done for her.

Lightman looked at her, his eyes clearly trying to read her expression. 'Was that all right? I really don't want to interfere. I just . . . well, I hoped it would help. Make him realise you aren't on your own.'

Hanson thought about what Damian had probably wanted to say to her. She had no doubt that he'd wanted to see her reaction to his shit. To everything he'd told Jason. He would have wanted to crow over it. She could imagine his smug, awful smile without needing to see it.

'No, it was a great thing to do. A great thing.' Then she gave a small tilt of her head from side to side and added, 'Surprised you managed it, to be honest.'

Ben grinned. 'Glad you salvaged that one. I was worried you might have actually said something nice to me.'

'Nah, you know me. Only ever a compliment sandwich.' But she went on, 'Thanks, Ben. I'll see you tomorrow.'

Ben made his way across the near side of the car park, waving briefly as he went. Hanson's car was parked almost at the far end, away from the bright lights of the building. It was in such darkness that she felt the need to switch her phone on to flashlight mode and check between the cars as she walked past.

She fully expected to find her tyres slashed again. If Ben had chased Damian off, there would be some kind of revenge. She was certain of it.

But the car was fine. Perhaps Damian had been worried about doing it at the police station. She knew there would be some kind of retribution on the horizon, though. Something petty and damaging. It made her feel weary.

*

Louise hadn't expected to be allowed to leave. Not now they knew what she'd done. However kind to her they were, she knew that she had to face the music on this one. That she had killed a man. She'd done it in fear for her life, and in what could be termed self-defence, but she'd still killed him. That memory of hot blood spilling onto her hands was real.

Patrick had been with her from the moment she walked back into the station, and she'd felt such uncomplicated relief at seeing him this time. There was nothing for him to suspect her of any more. Nothing except what she'd done, and she might have killed Alex Plaskitt, but she hadn't gone home and slept with him. She was, in some bizarre sense, cleared.

He'd put a hand to her arm when he first saw her. His touch had been firm. Reassuring.

'We'll get this sorted,' he said.

'Thank you.' She grasped his hand, just for a second. And then she found herself asking, 'Is Niall all right?'

Patrick gave her a funny little grin. 'He's fine. And relieved that you're OK.'

And then, a matter of hours later, they were suddenly releasing her. Patrick told her she could go home, and that he was happy to drive her there.

'Am I not under arrest?' she asked.

'Technically, you still are,' he explained, 'but with no fresh charges, the situation reverts to your previous bail conditions.'

It took no time at all for his Jaguar to drive them the few miles home. The roads seemed absurdly quiet, but then she remembered that it was nearly ten p.m. on a Monday. Of course it was quiet.

Patrick climbed out to help her with her overnight rucksack, which had gone with her to a service station and then back without being opened. And then he gave her a brief hug and told her to get as much rest as she could. It was only as he'd backed away again that he said in a low and surprisingly uncertain voice, 'You know, I felt tempted to say earlier, but . . . I never liked Dina. At all. I was very glad . . . when you and Niall got together. I would very much like to think there was still a chance for you two.'

She couldn't find any response, but she nodded at him, and he smiled before getting back into his car. She felt a trace of sadness after he left. Niall's best friend had turned out to be a great deal more loyal to her than she'd had any right to expect.

She let herself into the house, and wondered, suddenly, whether she would continue to live here. Whether she might find herself in jail, or whether she and Niall would sell the place in order to go their separate ways. And all those uncertainties were far too much now, so she dumped the backpack and let herself into the music room, where her harp was waiting for her.

She sat, and leaned it against her shoulder, and felt its comforting weight for a moment. And then she started to make music, a flow of unwritten melodies that seemed to pour out of her without thought.

It was still hard for Hanson to feel safe in her home, but it unquestionably felt better than it had. Sharing all of it with Ben had given her more comfort than she could have expected.

She glanced up at the mock CCTV camera over the door, with its big, bulky black box and its cable that actually didn't go anywhere. She'd tucked it back in on itself within the box before she'd mounted the thing. There was another one on the first floor, too, looking out towards the road.

Hanson went through her usual routine of locking up, though less quickly, and decided that a glass of wine and catching the end of *Last of the Mohicans* was in order. And then sleep. Hopefully good sleep.

She dozed off quickly, keeping thoughts of Damian firmly away and thinking instead about the work she would do tomorrow. How she would go on tracing other women who had been victims of Alex's need for revenge. How she would also re-engage with drug dealing in a pub on the Highfield estate on O'Malley's behalf. There was a lot of catch-up to do on their other casework.

The thoughts were satisfying, if not actually cheerful. They soothed her. Though just before she slept, she found her mind drifting briefly to the image of Ben talking to Damian outside the station, with Ben as unflappable as ever and Damian suddenly on the back foot. No longer in control. It made her smile.

And then she was awake. Fully awake and half out of bed, because there had been a sound. A sharp, loud, heart-clammering sound from downstairs.

She staggered as she tried to stand, her body not yet catching up with her mind, which knew that the sound had been the kitchen window shattering.

Weapon, she thought, hearing sporadic crashes of glass as more fell out of the pane.

She'd got this one covered. She'd been sleeping with her truncheon next to her for months now. She'd rehearsed this situation for months, too. She picked up a pillow off her bed and clutched it in front of her, an instant guard against knives when she had no time to put on her stab vest.

She knew, without question, that the intruder was Damian, and part of her was glad. Whatever he was trying to do, she'd back herself in a struggle over him. He was taller, and per-haps a little stronger, but also out of condition. Too self-indulgent to keep himself toned or to go to any of the martial arts classes he'd always talked about.

She opened her door as silently as she could, determined not to flinch with every fresh sound. Was he in the kitchen? Or had he already moved into another part of the house?

She became aware, as she went slowly down the stairs, of a strange light and smell. It was a hot, Bonfire Night smell, and the colours on the walls were a faint, unsteady orange.

Shit.

She ran the last few steps and dropped the pillow in order to open the hall cupboard and haul out the foam fire extinguisher. She kicked the cupboard door back out of her way and walked into the kitchen, where little sprays of fire were burning away merrily on different objects. The fridge. The table. One of the chairs. The sink.

In the centre of the floor was the source of it all, a fiercely burning heap of glass and petrol that was melting the lino. And she dropped the baton without regret, pulled the pin out of the extinguisher and began to douse every one of those little fires.

She was lucky that there wasn't more flammable material in the kitchen. Lucky, too, that the Molotov cocktail had landed centrally and not any closer to the hallway. The carpet had remained untouched, and once she'd drowned everything in foam and stopped spraying, there was silence.

She looked around at the burned and blackened room, and she smiled grimly to herself.

37

'You look perfect,' April told her. 'Stop fiddling and drink.'

Louise applied another smudge of eyeshadow before she put the brush down on the bathroom counter and picked up the glass of Prosecco.

'Something doesn't look right,' Louise said, looking back at the mirror.

'It *all* looks right.' April was definite.

'But it doesn't look like me,' Louise said, trying hard to pinpoint what was wrong.

'You know what I think?' April said, coming to put an arm over her shoulder and giving Louise's reflection a considering look. 'I think you're normally drunk when we get ready. What you're seeing is Sober Louise in her going-out clothes, and it's freaking you out because you've never seen her like this before.'

Louise gave a laugh and wondered if April was right. She studied herself again, and thought about all the times they'd done this, when she'd looked at herself through a haze of alcohol and felt fantastic.

She realised that she wasn't smiling, either, and that was a wrong note. Drunk Louise always smiled. She was fun, and she never cared if her lipstick wasn't just right.

Sober Louise took the Prosecco and swallowed a large mouthful. 'I'm not going to be Drunk Louise tonight, but I definitely don't want to be Sober Louise.' She gave a small belch as the bubbles came back up and laughed again. 'Allow me to introduce you to Tipsy Louise. Tipsy Louise is a lot of fun, too, but she knows her limits.'

'I want to be like Tipsy Louise,' April said, and then drained her glass. She was already pouring another one before Louise had managed another mouthful. 'Only I guess I don't want it that badly . . .'

Louise watched her, thoughtfully. At this point in the evening it had always been about April bringing Louise out of herself. It was always her lively, dominant friend insisting that they needed to drink so that Louise could feel better. And for the first time, Louise wondered if that was really why April brought wine over and ordered round after round of tequilas.

'How are *you* doing?' Louise asked. 'What's going on with you?'

'Oh.' April gave a shrug. 'All OK.'

'You don't seem . . . happy, now I have time to think about it.'

April laughed, but then she tipped the glass back again and swallowed, and Louise had the impression she might be swallowing back tears.

And then she said, 'I don't know. I guess I've just been . . . missing my sister. And worrying that things are changing without me somehow.' She shook her head.

'You haven't seen Dee for a long time, have you?' Louise asked her, gently.

'No,' April agreed. 'No. Not for a long time. I had a dream about her the other day, about going on a road trip with her, and when I woke up, I felt . . . bereft, I guess.' She gave a frustrated sigh. 'I'll get over it. I'm good at picking myself up.'

'You don't have to get over it, you know,' Louise said gently. 'You can talk about it properly, if you want.'

April rolled her eyes, but said, 'Thanks, honey.' She put her arm round Louise and pulled her into a hug. Then she reached for her phone. 'I want a photograph. To commemorate this fine occasion.'

She held the camera out at arm's length, studying them both on the screen for a few seconds before she smiled and took the shot.

'You know,' Louise said, 'Tipsy Louise loves you just as much as all the other Louises. And she'll still be here for you.'

'I know she will.' It looked like April might say something else, but she looked at her phone instead. 'OK, the cab's here in five. We'd better drink up.'

Louise felt a twist in her stomach. She wasn't sure she was ready to do this. However much she wanted to tell the horrors of the last week to go screw themselves, the idea of going to another club on another Friday, of seeing men there who might want to flirt with her . . . it was horrifying. It had been hard enough going on her own last Sunday, before she knew for certain that an apparently kind man had pinned her down and raped her.

But April was a firm believer in getting back in the saddle. She'd rebooked the hotel they'd never made it to on Monday, and had insisted on paying for Louise to spend two full hours on a massage table. She'd also booked them a VIP area at a club that was run by a friend of hers.

'We won't be standing at the bar with everyone else,' April told her. 'You'll have a safe space at the table to retreat to if you feel bad, and if it's awful, we'll just go.' She'd raised an eyebrow. 'But this is going to be a night we'll remember for years. I can feel it.'

'Oh, will it?' Louise had said, and then found herself

capitulating. April was essentially right. She shouldn't be hiding away because some psycho had attacked her. She was stronger than that.

But she could still feel the pounding of her heart as she put her coat on and looped her large handbag round her, holding it close in front of her like a shield. And she wondered, a little wistfully, whether Drunk Louise would have been a little tougher.

For the first time in six weeks, the team did pub night. The DCI always took himself off after the first forty-five minutes, in some sort of deference to them wanting to kick back and enjoy themselves. Before he left, however, he caught Hanson on her own.

'I don't want to pry into anything,' he said, 'but it's come to my attention that you may be having a few issues with an ex-boyfriend.'

Hanson could feel her cheeks heating up from the moment he started speaking. But it was right that he should know what was going on.

'Unfortunately he's been stalking me, slandering me and vandalising my property, so I've had to report him,' she said.

Hanson guessed that Chief Inspector Heerden had mentioned the case to the chief. Heerden had probably felt that she had to. Hanson was eager, however, for the whole situation to be handled by the uniformed police. The idea of it landing somewhere within CID, with the people she worked with every day, was agonising.

There shouldn't be any need for them to get involved, anyway. There was little investigating that needed to be done. Jason had written a summary of his conversation at the pub, including all of Damian's allegations about her. It had been awkward asking him for it while they existed in such an unresolved state, but he had been eager to help. Ben had, of course, provided an account of Damian's presence on the evening of the arson. And Hanson also had her own diary entries, detailing almost all of the grim reality of being harassed.

None of which might have been enough if Damian hadn't petrol-bombed her house. She still found herself smiling whenever she thought about it. It was the one real mistake he'd made, presumably triggered by anger that she still had her job and was being protected by her colleagues.

She'd asked for a quiet chat with Lightman the morning after. It had been hard not to grin at him as she shut the door of the meeting room behind her. Despite a large hole being smashed in her window, and a similar hole bored through her night's sleep, she'd felt more energised than she had in months.

'I'm going to report Damian,' she said. 'Today, if possible. Would you be able to write up the conversation you had with him outside the station yesterday? I'd like to link his behaviour with it.'

'What behaviour is that?' he asked.

She told him, in a few words, about the night-time vandalism.

'Which means we've got him,' she said, her eyes bright with exhilaration. 'I caught the whole thing on camera, by making him feel clever.'

Lightman narrowed his eyes at her. 'The fake cameras . . .'

'I opened them up and put real ones inside.' She laughed with total glee. 'It cost me a fortune, but I knew it would work. He's such a smug, egotistical arsehole that he was congratulating himself on knowing they were fake. The best bit is, they're the same ones he put up when we lived together in Birmingham. He knew for sure that they were fake because he recognised them and was too arrogant to realise that I knew exactly what I was doing.'

She held her phone out to him, which featured a close-up image of Damian's face. He'd actually turned to look, in satisfaction, at what he believed was the fake camera over the doorstep.

'The upstairs one got his car, too, and his approach to the house. Add that in to the lesser crime of smashing my security light, and we've got a pattern of violent and destructive behaviour.'

'God,' Lightman said, taking it with one of the largest and most open smiles she'd seen him give. 'That's absolute genius.'

She'd filed her report with the crime desk three and a half hours later. And although she hadn't felt quite as upbeat since – had, in fact, had moments of squeezing anxiety at what Damian might do when he found out about the charges – she'd generally felt as though she'd been cut free from a heavy weight.

'Well,' the DCI said to her now, with an expression that was somewhere between wary and warm, 'I may not be able to get involved, but that doesn't mean I can't offer support. Just tell me if you need time, or space, or a rant, or – I don't know, alcohol – to get you through it.'

Hanson gave him a grin. 'Thanks, chief. I will. And, um . . .' She shifted a little before going on, 'thank you for the, er, help with the emails he sent. Ben told me about it. It means a lot. Knowing you have that kind of faith in me.'

'Well, you know,' Sheens said, with a shrug, 'I sort of had to. Otherwise it'd make me look like I made a bad hiring decision, so . . .'

She gave an out-and-out laugh at that. 'Yeah, true. Well, thanks anyway.'

Jonah was enjoying the pub more than he'd expected to. He generally had trouble relaxing in these situations. He was too conscious of being the boss. And despite liking his team a great deal, he half expected them to exchange a look about something he'd said, or to quietly hint that he should go.

But tonight he was finding his team's company genuinely helpful. The lack of resolution to their case had made him dissatisfied. He couldn't quite let go of it all. Something in him didn't really want to believe that Alex Plaskitt had been so twisted, and he'd found himself picking over it all with a feeling of depression.

The moral grey area over Louise Reakes's actions had also left a sour taste in his mouth. He supposed it was in his nature to look for certainties and endings. To keep pushing until an investigation felt rounded off. Closed. Finished. And yet, as he well knew, life was rarely like that. There wasn't always a definite conclusion about who the bad guy was. And when there *was* a bad guy, there was usually a reason. Like Alex Plaskitt's awful parents, or Louise Reakes getting drunk because of a faithless husband, and then lashing out as she was attacked.

The great thing about his team was that they understood. They got that he might feel a little melancholy right now, even though it seemed like time to celebrate. Their expressions were full of that same feeling, and it soothed him.

But at quarter to nine his phone buzzed with another text from his ex-wife.

Did you get my text last Saturday? I really need to talk to you. Can you ring me, please?

He felt strangely depressed reading it. He really didn't know what to do. Ignoring Michelle felt like unnecessary cruelty, even if she was angling for nothing more than an ego boost. But talking to her felt like a betrayal of Jojo. And, worse still, it reminded him uncomfortably of how badly he'd slipped when he'd seen his ex four months before. Of how stupid he'd been to sleep with her.

He looked at it for a minute and then put his phone away. He'd call her tomorrow. Tonight, he needed to see his girlfriend.

Hanson watched the DCI go, thinking it a shame that he couldn't stay out and be one of them.

'It must be lonely,' she said to O'Malley, 'being the chief.'

'Ah, you'd think so,' O'Malley agreed, 'but don't feel too sorry for him. He has a burning-hot girlfriend and a house that's three times the size of yours.' O'Malley leaned forwards. 'And a proper pension, too.'

'OK, fair point,' Hanson agreed, picking up her beer. 'He's clearly an arsehole. Who's getting the next one?'

Louise had actually made it to a club again, one that looked not unlike Blue Underground. She wasn't blind drunk, and she was almost having a good time. The 'almost' part of it was less to do with anxiety, as she'd expected, and more to do with the fact that drunk people turned out to be incredibly annoying.

It was strange to think that she'd never really seen other people getting this drunk before. Sober Louise had always headed home before it got too late, and Drunk Louise didn't seem to see anything that wasn't rose-tinted.

'Oh my God, look at the state of him,' she said to April,

safe in their little cordoned-off area and watching as one of the other punters staggered over to the bar and then managed to drop all the cards out of his wallet onto the floor. He'd already tried to slobber over some poor girl and been told to sod off. 'Please, please tell me I'm never like that.'

April glanced over at him stooping to pick the cards up, seemed to weigh it up, and then said, 'Hell no. You're way less coordinated.'

'You can go fuck yourself,' Louise said, with a laugh.

One of the bar staff came over and asked if they wanted anything, which felt bizarre to Louise. This was a crowded club. They ought to be elbowing their way to the bar. This VIP thing was strange.

'I'd like another screwdriver,' April said. 'You should have one too,' she added to Louise.

Louise looked at her doubtfully. 'I'm not – I'm probably OK. I had the Prosecco.'

'You sure?' April asked it a little slyly, as if the only right answer was to change her mind. The inevitable pressure drinkers applied to those who were not drinking.

Louise let out a sigh. Truthfully, she felt a bit over-sugared. The three non-alcoholic cocktails she'd sunk had all tasted like variations on Um Bongo and she would really have killed for something to cut through it a little.

'OK. A single gin and tonic. But that's all. That's me done for tonight.'

'Great,' April said, and then, to the guy taking their order, 'Is Charlie here yet? He's supposed to come say hi.'

'Oh yeah,' the guy said, glancing around. 'I think he's here. I'll tell him.'

'I'd love you to,' April said, giving him a look that was one hundred per cent Predator Mode.

336

The guy grinned back at her as he walked away, and Louise shook her head. 'I don't think he's your type.'

'But that's the thing,' April argued. 'Maybe my type needs to change.'

Louise narrowed her eyes at her. 'What about this Charlie, then? Your friend? You seem quite keen to see him?'

April gave her a slightly wicked grin. 'Oh, he's a doll. But I was thinking of setting the two of you up, honey. He's Chez. The guy you kissed at the wedding.'

'No, April,' Louise said, with a rush of horror. She tried to be firm. 'I really don't want to see him. And anyway, there won't be any of that. I'm in this . . . non-situation with Niall, I'm still shaken as hell over someone assaulting me, however little I can remember, and . . . and the rest. We're not going to do any setting up. Not for a long, long time, all right?'

April tutted. 'If you say so.' She sat back a little. 'But I bet he won't even remember that whole kissing and running thing. It'll be like you just met.'

'Well, here's to almost having put a case together,' O'Malley said, raising his glass of tonic a little unsteadily. It was wonderful to Hanson how he could simulate drunkenness with the rest of them without ever touching a drop. He told her that he never consciously modified his behaviour. He just got drunk on *their* drunkenness.

'Ugh, thanks,' Hanson said, lifting her glass. 'I just spent five hours today trying to prove that Alex Plaskitt had the knife in time to kill a young woman in London, and I can't seem to do it. She's the one person we still don't have a DNA match for, but I'm so sure it was him. The Viagra. The way she looked.' She sighed. 'He didn't order two knives at once, and the only order that's anywhere nearby was made after she was killed. And given a similar weapon was used, I may have to accept that he didn't do it, even though every other thing fits.'

'But he didn't have that knife on the night of January the nineteenth, either,' Lightman pointed out, 'as he'd given it to Step. We're positive he was the person who attacked Gianetta Jilani. She specifically mentioned a knife. Maybe he was using something else for quite some while, but eventually decided he wanted something more like Step's artistic one from Steel and Silver.'

Hanson hesitated for a moment. 'Yeah, or . . . or what if he took it off Step on the nineteenth? Offered to look after it and then used it, cleaned it and returned it?'

She put her glass down onto the table, quickly, and pulled her phone out of her pocket.

'Um . . . It is Friday night, you know,' O'Malley said. 'You're not actually supposed to be working.'

'It'll only take a second,' Hanson said, grinning.

She took her phone out of the warm pub and into the cold street. It was another arctic night, and there was a sharp, all-penetrating wind tearing down Shirley Road. She regretted leaving her coat on the padded bench inside but made the call anyway.

Step Conti picked up warily, and she didn't blame him. Finding out that your best friend had been at the very least a serial rapist would have made anyone wary. Each phone call from the police so far had revealed a darker and darker truth, and she felt a twist of guilt that she was now in the process of pinning a murder on Alex, too.

'Step, hi,' she said. 'DC Hanson here. I'm sorry to call you on a Friday night, but there's something we need to check with you. It's about that night that Alex and the guys gave you the knife. January the nineteenth.'

'If you'll just give me a second . . .' There was a brief toddler screech in the background. His daughter, she guessed,
up later than she was supposed to be. After that came the
sound of a closing door. 'OK,' Step said. 'Yes.'

'I just wanted to know what happened to the knife after
you were given it,' she asked. 'Did you hold on to it yourself?
Or did someone else look after it?'

'Um . . . oh,' Step said. 'I left it behind the bar. Marc's
brother Charlie owns the club we went to, and he offered to
keep hold of it.'

'Marc's brother,' Hanson said. 'So that's Charlie Ruskin?'

'Yes,' Step confirmed.

'Does he own any other clubs?' she asked, trying to make
the question sound as if it had no importance at all.

'Yeah, he has three. We normally go to the one in Southampton but we did an overnighter in Portsmouth for my
birthday.'

'Oh, right,' she said, aware that her voice sounded not
quite right. 'The one in Southampton, is that Blue Underground, where you were last Friday?'

'Yes, that's the one.'

Hanson was aware that she was shivering, and that it had
as much to do with the adrenaline that was suddenly cours-
ing through her as it had to do with the cold. She tried to
keep her head. To ask all the relevant questions.

'Did you take it home at the end of the evening? The knife?'

'No,' Step told her. 'Charlie wasn't around when I left so I
got it off him the next day.'

'That's great, thanks,' she said. And then she added, 'So it
couldn't have ended up with Alex?'

'No,' he said, firmly. 'No, it couldn't.'

*

April swung herself to her feet and grabbed her handbag. 'I'm going to pee and redo my lip gloss. You coming?'

Louise shook her head, determined not to be a tag-along. Not to be needy, anxious Sober Louise any more. 'I'm good here, thanks.'

But as soon as April was gone, she regretted not going with her. The club turned from a comfortably dim place into a shady, crowded cavern. The men dancing down on the floor took on a predatory shape, and she found herself staring at the closer ones.

One of them glanced round and gave her the smallest of smiles, and she looked away, quickly, ashamed of how wobbly she suddenly felt.

She pulled her bag onto her lap, the big, comforting shield, and pretended to be rooting around in it. When she looked up again, the dancing guy was facing away from her, as though nothing had ever happened, and she sighed.

For fuck's sake, get a grip, Louise. Nobody's looking at you. Nobody cares.

She wondered whether she should have just one more drink. Another gin and tonic. Just to ease the panic.

She looked over towards the bar, which she realised wasn't even that crowded. It was still only eleven fifteen. Early for a club. It wouldn't turn into a real crush until later, at pub kicking-out time.

The barman April had flirted with was speaking to someone, but there was no queue behind them. She could get over there, get herself a drink and get back before April returned. A small victory for independence.

She stood, pulling her bag strap over her head, and began

to walk over. She saw the barman nod in her direction, and the guy who'd been talking to him turned towards her.

And as she took in his face, her whole body felt like it was tipping sideways into some kind of a void.

'You've got a fucking nerve.'

Hanson swung round, the phone still close to her ear, even though she'd rung off. There was urgency thrilling through her, and the person she cared least about just now was Damian. And of course, *of course*, he had followed her to the bloody pub. And of course he'd chosen now to confront her.

'What exactly do you think you're going to get out of this shit?' he asked her. 'Do you think you're going to get me put away? Because I've done nothing the fuck wrong, and you're going to look like a total tit in front of your precious new colleagues.'

She'd thought so many times over of the things she'd love to say to him if she were to confront him. She'd fantasised about it for days. How she'd laugh at him and tell him to talk to her solicitor. Or she'd ask how he'd liked being caught on camera.

But in the end there was no time for anything she had to say. And when she thought about it afterwards, there couldn't have been a better way of pulling the carpet out from under him than what she said instead.

'Sorry, but I don't have time for your bullshit right now.'

And she pushed through the heavy swing door of the pub and said, 'We've got everything, *everything*, wrong.'

It was strange how quickly hours and hours of memory could suddenly replay themselves. Louise was standing in a bar in

Portsmouth with her bag over her shoulder and had faltered for only a second. That was the truth of it.

And yet the truth of it was also that she had been sitting at another bar for almost an hour while a tall, handsome Italian bought her drinks. While he charmed her. She couldn't quite remember his name. And she felt as though he was familiar somehow, but she wasn't sure how and had somehow missed the part where she should have asked.

She had also been thinking about Dina and Niall. Specifically, about Dina's hand on Niall's knee, and she had rested her hand on this man's leg, imagining that she was Dina. That she had that sort of power. And the handsome man had given her a long, slow smile and said, 'Drink up.'

And then she'd been leaning too heavily against the bar. She'd felt too drunk. Sick drunk. She'd become suddenly frightened of it and of herself, and she'd stood up, unsteadily. She found out only then that the man's hand had been right at the top of her thigh. And she was no longer sure that she even knew who he was. What had she been thinking?

'Are you leaving?' he'd asked. And she'd tried to focus on his face. He seemed to be giving her a smile that wasn't quite right.

'Yes,' she'd told him. 'Sorry. I need to – to go home.'

She picked up her handbag and went staggering out into the hall, weaving almost from wall to wall as she went.

And she was still in that second of frozen time on the dance floor, but she had also spent what felt like hours trying to stay steady on her feet and on her stupid fucking heels as she stumbled up London Road. Somewhere during those hours, she'd glanced behind her and seen that not-quite-right smile following her, and she'd felt frightened.

She'd pulled out her phone but somehow been unable to

unlock it. Her fingers weren't working. They had become someone else's. And so she'd started trying to run.

And then, without any time passing, she'd been on her face in the earth, sobbing into the ground as he pressed a knife into her lower back. And she recognised his voice this time. She'd heard the Sheffield lilt back in the club, back when he'd been saying nice things to her.

'Please don't,' she'd told him. 'Please. Please.'

'Shut your fucking mouth.'

Her hair had been over her face as he'd turned her over, and she'd felt like she might vomit through it. She felt dizzy. Unwell. Nauseous.

He was pulling at her underwear, but he couldn't be. This couldn't be happening. She must be able to fight, but it was like a dream where her body wouldn't work. Nothing worked.

'Hey!' It was another voice. A deeper one. One that was full of a different sort of threat. 'What the hell do you think you're doing?'

The tugging at her underwear had stopped, and the weight that was on her eased momentarily, though there was a sharp pain in her left arm still. She could feel his hand pressing down on it.

'Get – the fuck – out of here,' the man who was on top of her said. 'I'm not fucking around.' Louise managed to free a hand and pulled the hair out of her eyes enough to see something. She twisted to see the face of this man pinning her down. The smile had gone, because he was wearing a balaclava now. He'd become faceless. Awful.

There was a tall figure standing a little further away, one that loomed over them both.

'I don't care who you are or what you think you're doing. You need to get off her. Right now.'

'Mate, I told you to go.' There was such coldness in that cheerful northern voice. 'This has nothing to do with you.'

'Please,' Louise sobbed. 'Please don't go.'

There was a brief silence, and then the tall figure strode forwards. The weight on her arm lifted abruptly as the figure above her was hauled away. And then there was a sickening noise as her attacker swung a fist at the tall stranger.

She heard a noise of pain and then a roar. The taller man brought his fist up so quickly that there was no time for the balaclava-clad man to dodge. It connected with a crunch, and then the taller one was kicking and shoving her attacker away, so that he was scrambling backwards. He was fleeing and trying to shield himself all at once.

It was quiet for a moment after that. He'd gone. The awful man in the balaclava had gone.

She could hear the tall man breathing, and then he said, 'Are you OK?'

And then suddenly she was crumpling in on herself and sobbing. Sobbing so hard that she couldn't breathe.

'Shhh,' he said, and he was sitting next to her. 'Shhh. It's all right. It's going to be all right.'

He helped her to her feet, and once she was in front of him she saw that there was something sticking out of his abdomen. She reached out. She touched his dark-stained T-shirt just below it, and when her hand came away, it was warm and sticky.

'You're hurt,' she said. 'You're hurt. He hurt you.'

He gave a laugh, but it ended in a groan.

'Ah, s'OK,' he said, after that, and she looked into his face for the first time and realised that she knew him. Had spoken to him. He'd been in the club too. 'I'll get it . . . doctored . . . Just let me walk you home first.'

He sounded so sure that she nodded, and started to lead

344

him home. Flakes of snow were beginning to fall around them, and everything seemed unreal.

And it was a while later, but all in that same second, that she was up in her room, and kicking her shoes off so she could climb into bed. She was still shaking, but she curled up facing him and felt better because he was there.

He sat heavily on the bed, making her tip and bounce as the mattress moved.

'I don't . . . Is it all right if I lie down?' he asked. 'Just for a minute?'

'Yes,' she told him. 'Lie here.'

He lay down, his face towards her, and he gave a sudden, sharp intake of breath. And then he was struggling with something, until he gave a gasp of pain and relief. It was a knife that had been in him. A knife. She could see it in his hand and a small voice was telling her that this was wrong. That she needed to do something.

But even while it told her that, she was shutting down. Losing consciousness. Losing the world around her in favour of a softer one somewhere beneath all of this.

'I'm cold,' he said, and she opened her eyes again, and saw that he was pale. So pale. And his eyes were frightened.

She reached out to his face and began to stroke it. 'It's OK,' she said. 'I'm here. I'm here.'

38

The scene was so very familiar to Niall. Another hotel bar, with Dina waiting for him, long-legged and intensely glamorous in her short black dress, her hair pinned in a loose bun so that most of it fell in artful, dark brown curls.

She was looking at her phone as he arrived, a drink already in front of her. It was always like this. His ex-wife would always be waiting, perfectly arranged for maximum effect.

He shook his head slightly and closed the last few feet between them. She looked up and smiled at him, her expression rueful this time.

'I'm glad we get to see each other again,' she said. 'I hated being told not to talk to you.'

Niall sat, slowly, and then said, 'We won't be seeing each other again, Dina.'

Dina's gaze settled on him for a moment, and then she laughed. 'Don't be ridiculous, Niall.' She picked up her martini and took a very careful sip. 'We're free to do what we want now. Everything's all out in the open.'

Niall laughed in return, a sound that was totally unlike her relaxed chuckle. It was a bitter sound.

'You're right,' he said. 'Everything *is* in the open. Who you are, and what an idiot I've been.'

He saw Dina roll her eyes. 'You aren't angry with me for obeying orders, are you? What was I supposed to do? Tell her no, we had our own plan?' Dina shook her head, the expression in her eyes a little harder. 'You know it doesn't end well for people who do that.'

'There's not a chance in hell those were orders,' Niall said, flatly. 'Everything you've tried to do from the moment she brought you in . . . wriggling your way into the middle of it all, to get one up on me . . . has been a ridiculous game. And, of course, playing me at the same time. Telling me you missed me, that you regretted ever walking out. Chipping away at my chances of happiness. And for what? To feel like you've *won*?' And then Niall stopped, closing his mouth deliberately. 'Actually, forget that. I don't need to know why. I don't care any more. I'm here to pick up what you have to give me, and then I'm going.'

Dina gave him a long look, and then she shrugged. She put a manicured hand out to the handbag that was hooked over the back of her chair and drew out an envelope.

'It isn't as much as you're hoping,' Dina said. 'Certainly not enough to see you out of debt.'

Niall took it with a shrug and slid it into his pocket without opening it. He wasn't going to give her the satisfaction of seeing his disappointment. 'It doesn't matter. It's all done.'

'Nearly,' Dina said, as he rose. 'She has a few loose ends to tie up, she said.'

Niall paused, his feeling of certainty wavering. 'What does she mean, loose ends?'

Jonah had almost made it out of Southampton by the time Hanson's call came through.

'I'm so sorry, chief,' she said. 'But it looks like – it looks like Alex Plaskitt never attacked Louise Reakes. It was the nightclub owner, Charlie. He's Marc Ruskin's brother, and he was at Rain for Step's birthday, the night Gianetta Jilani was attacked in January of last year. And he had the knife for safekeeping.'

Jonah found his mind slow to process all this information. 'Step's knife?' he eventually managed to ask.

'Yes,' Hanson said. 'He was also at Blue Underground on Friday. I've called the staff there and it turns out he wasn't actually working like he implied. He was the other side of the bar, and one of the staff can remember him flirting with Louise Reakes. He's sure it was her because she came back in asking questions later. Charlie had told him to lie if anyone asked, and say he'd been working. And the bouncers were told to support the idea that he'd been punched by a punter. They thought he actually had been, after Charlie tried to walk home then came back to put ice on it.'

'Right.' And he was turning the car across the crosshatching, swiftly and illegally. He switched the flashing blues on. 'Did they say where he is?'

'In his Portsmouth club,' Hanson replied. 'Rain. And . . . Niall Reakes called me. He's frantic with worry for Louise because she's apparently in danger. He says we need to track her down, but he can't raise her or April Dumont, who he's sure she's with.'

'Right, that's . . .'

'The thing is,' Hanson went on, 'Niall found out they're going to Rain. Where Charlie is.'

He thought back to Louise's accounts of their night out, and how the venue had been April's idea. He felt a run of cold up his back.

'Was it Portsmouth they were going to on Monday when we picked them up at the service station?' he asked.

'Yes,' Hanson said. 'I think so.'

348

And that had been April's idea, too. If Issa hadn't disrupted everything, they would have been off for a night out in Portsmouth. To a club. He was willing to bet he knew which one they'd been headed for.

'OK. I'll be there in five to drive you, provided you've only had a couple of drinks. Tell Domnall to take Ben and go. Now.'

This couldn't be happening again. It couldn't be.

And yet it was. Louise had made no conscious decision to run. By the time she'd surfaced from the terrible waking dream, she was no longer close to the bar. She was running, skidding down the corridor that led to the way out, with her handbag banging uncomfortably into her leg.

There were bouncers on the door. They could help her. She could tell them what was happening and they could protect her until she could call a cab and get hold of April.

But then, as she drew level with one standing in the doorway, she remembered what April had said. Charlie owned this place. Charlie, who she'd wanted to set Louise up with. The same man Louise had once fled from at a wedding, with a better instinct than she'd had when she saw him again, years later.

Fuck, she thought. *Fuck. They work for him.*

And so, as one of them gave her a coldly amused look, Louise ran past them, and out onto the road. A terrifyingly empty road.

She'd expected to find people out here, but it was drizzling now, and nobody seemed to be out in it. She looked frantically for some kind of shop that might be open, but all she could see were estate agents and dry-cleaners, their lights off and shutters down.

What's wrong with this place? Why didn't you stay at fucking home, Louise?

She saw an alleyway to her left, and she scuttled into it. She could at least be out of sight while she called for a cab. She ducked behind a large blue wheelie bin that stood against the near wall of the club. God, it was cold. She wasn't dressed for this. The overhang from the roof above was so small that it barely kept any of the rain off her, and the wind kept picking it up and hurling it around.

She reached for her phone, and then felt her heart drop. A terrible, lurching fall.

Her phone was still in her jacket pocket, all neatly folded up on the padded bench of their booth.

Fuck. She wanted to hit something. Herself. The bin. Anything. *What the fuck were you thinking, Louise?*

But she had to stay quiet and think. She had to get herself out of this mess.

Could she just go back into the club? She might be able to find a group of people to protect her.

But she remembered all of the men and women in there, how drunk they were already. Would they even stop him if he came and dragged her away to somewhere quiet? Some part of the club that only he knew about?

There were voices somewhere on the road, and she froze, trying to catch what they were saying. But whatever had been said had been over too quickly for her to understand.

And then she heard footsteps, and she knew that the bouncers had told him where she'd gone. She'd been too close to them when she ducked down the alley. Of course she had been. She'd done everything wrong.

And while she stayed absolutely still, hoping that he might somehow walk past her without seeing, or turn round and go back to the club, she started to talk to her husband again in her head. She imagined writing to him, safe and warm in their house. She imagined getting out of here and surviving somehow, and she promised herself that she was going to write it all down. All of it.

I'm going to see you again, Niall, she thought.

The footsteps were painfully close. He was walking past the bin. There was no way he could fail to see her now.

She could feel her hand shaking, and she shoved it into her handbag. The handbag that had no phone in but was still unbelievably full and heavy in the way of every handbag she'd owned, despite her having cleaned it out and organised it earlier this evening.

'Louise . . .'

He said it so quietly. So gently. And Louise felt her body try to sob in fear, but she wouldn't let it.

Charlie was suddenly there, in front of her, looking at her, but it was somehow better now that he'd found her. This was the worst it could get, and she wasn't going to die cowering behind a fucking bin.

She stood up straight, and she looked back at him.

'There you are,' he said, and his eyes flickered over her and over the bin, and he smiled.

She understood the smile. He was thinking that she'd brought him to the perfect place. Because after he'd killed her, he could simply tip her into the bin and come back for her later.

'I'm so glad you came,' he said, with a cheerful little laugh. 'I can't believe it's been quite this perfect, but . . .' He glanced over her face. 'You do remember me now, don't you?'

Louise nodded, and said, in a voice that wasn't as steady as she wanted it to be, 'You're the one who has to drug girls in order to fuck them.'

His mouth moved. Tightened. His grin went a little awry.

'Just as much of a bitch as I thought you were,' he said. 'You should watch that, Louise. Men don't like it.'

And here it was. The feeling of strength that Louise had been looking for. She'd pissed him off, and she was going to keep doing it. She was going to make him angry, because she was so very, very done with being afraid.

'Did you enjoy getting thrown around by him?' Louise asked. 'By Alex? He totally owned you.'

Charlie gave a laugh that had no humour in it. 'Yeah, well. He should have stayed out of it like I told him to. Because I totally killed him.'

She could see in his expression that he was thinking of what he was going to do to her. She watched him, tensely, waiting for his move. Was it going to be a knife this time? Had he brought one?

He looked right and left, up and down the short alleyway, and he seemed satisfied. He stepped towards her, and before she'd had time even to think, his hands were round her throat.

'Bye-bye, bitch,' he said, as he lifted her up off the ground with his hands.

It was the worst thing she could remember feeling. It made her want to vomit and kick out at him. And it hurt. Jesus, it hurt.

Her hand was still in the bag. But it was holding a rubberised black handle, as it had been for some minutes. And, in spite of the pain, she put every ounce of her consciousness into that instead of her desperate need for air. She was nothing more than her hand on the handle, and she drew it out and across in the small space between them, and then she drove it up and sideways into the flesh below his armpit.

There was a long second while he did nothing, and then, just as she started trying to pull the knife out, he suddenly let go of her. She fell, gasping desperately for air, but she didn't lose her grip on the handle, and she could feel it levering downwards as she dropped to her knees.

Charlie let out a howl. And then he started to kick her, his feet connecting hard and painfully with her thighs. Her stomach. She once again thought she might vomit, and wondered if her throat might be too swollen to let it out. But she stayed kneeling there and grabbed on to the handle with her other hand, too.

And then she remembered how Alex had died, and with a strangled roar, she yanked on the handle and felt the blade come clear of his flesh. The feeling was followed by an awful pain in her head. He had hold of her hair and was lifting her up by it.

'What the hell?'

She heard the voice. Her friend's voice. April's voice.

At the sound of it a sudden rush of fear ran through her.

She brought me here. She wanted to set me up with him . . .

She'd planned all of this. April had planned all of it.

'No,' Louise said.

But the pain in her head stopped. Charlie was slumping backwards, and it was April whose arm was round his neck.

'Get off her! Get off her!'

Charlie spoke, but it wasn't quite his voice any more. It was a gurgling, cracked sound.

'She – fucking – stabbed me!'

He stumbled backwards, and April shoved at him until he

fell. She looked him over, coldly. And then she met Louise's eye, for a moment. She gave her the strangest smile.

'Goddamn right she stabbed you. She's a stone-cold badass.'

There was little left for Jonah's team to do except deal with the aftermath. They arrived an hour too late to stop Louise Reakes stabbing someone for real this time. Fifty minutes too late to help Charlie Ruskin, who went into arrest before the two paramedics managed to get him to the ambulance.

And when one of the uniformed constables from Portsmouth City asked if he'd really wanted to save an attempted murderer, Jonah had rounded on him and told him of course he bloody had. That a human life had been lost tonight, and another one probably ruined.

Though at present, Louise actually looked the happiest he'd ever seen her. Her neck was already red and purple with bruising, her left leg had a bandage on the knee, and she was holding an ice pack to her right wrist. But she gave Jonah what was definitely a smile when he went to speak with her.

'The crew tells me they want your wrist and neck checked,' Jonah said. 'Let's get you taken to Portsmouth General and we can talk later.'

'You can talk to *me* right now,' April said, from her perch next to her. Jonah was glad she had stuck around. There was an awful lot he wanted to ask her.

'Thank you,' Jonah said. 'Perhaps we can take your statement.'

There was nothing in April's account to suggest that she'd had anything to do with the attack on Louise Reakes.

Nothing to suggest that she might be involved in Niall Reakes and Dina Weyman's drug trafficking, either. Nothing, in fact, to give him any reason to take her into custody. At least not yet.

And counting in her favour was the fact that she'd been the one to call an ambulance, and the one to drag Charlie Ruskin off Louise. She was also determined to come to the hospital, and Jonah told her to ride with him, rather than the paramedics. He shut her into the car, and then watched alongside his team as the ambulance carrying Louise Reakes drove away.

He breathed out in a long sigh. 'What an utter mess.'

'I'm sorry,' Hanson said, looking wretched. 'I should have thought of asking Step earlier. Ben said – well, he was the one who thought of it.'

Jonah shook his head. 'Honestly, I'm not sure yet whether this was our mistake or not. We'll undoubtedly spend a lot of time over the next few weeks trying to work that out. Regardless, you actually *did* work it out.' He gave her a tired smile. 'Which puts you a whole step ahead of your wrong-headed chief.'

He told O'Malley to drive Hanson home, then took Lightman to the hospital along with April Dumont. He glanced frequently in the rear-view mirror at April, but there was nothing in her expression except grim determination.

April stayed with Louise until Niall Reakes arrived, ash-white and frenzied and desperate to see his wife.

There was a curious moment, though, when Niall and April came face to face. Niall faltered, and then gave her a very small nod.

April raised an eyebrow and asked, 'So you're here for her now? I can trust you with her?'

Niall Reakes's voice was very quiet and very raw as he said, 'Yes. You can.'

April smiled, jumped up from her chair and announced that she was going home.

'We'll need you at the station tomorrow,' Jonah told her.

'Sure thing,' April said. 'Just don't make it too early, hey? See you, Niall.'

'Is Niall there?' Louise called from behind the curtain. 'I want to see him.'

And Niall Reakes had surprised Jonah by crying as he cuddled his wife. He had kissed her again and again and told her he was sorry.

Patrick Moorcroft surprised Jonah almost as much by coming to advise Louise in person. He was waiting at Southampton Central by the time she'd been discharged at one in the morning.

Niall had followed his wife to the station and agreed to wait in the relatives' room for as long as it took. Though Louise had told him to get some sleep if he could. That he looked exhausted. She had suddenly seemed like a parent looking out for a child, and it had been a strange thing to watch.

What followed was the first interview in which Louise seemed unafraid. She sat up straight in her chair, apparently unaffected by tiredness or injury except for the huskiness of her voice. And she was calm and rational as she told them what she'd finally remembered about that Friday night.

'I'd seen Alex's face so many times. I looked him up online, watched some of his videos . . . and I suppose, without realising it, I started to overlay him onto other things, so when I began to remember sitting at the bar, I just assumed it was with him.' She shook her head, her mouth tight. 'Probably partly a guilty conscience at work.'

She explained to them April's idea of going out in Portsmouth, and her own terror of being attacked again.

'I just thought . . . that I would never have survived last time if I hadn't got my hands on a knife,' she said. 'And it made me feel like I could face going if I knew I had one.' She gave a short laugh. 'I can't tell you how little I actually believed that I'd use it. But I suppose I became the same as every other terrified knife-carrying adult out there.'

'Weren't you afraid of what you might be capable of?' Jonah asked her. 'You thought you'd killed Alex Plaskitt. Did you not think you might kill again, but without cause?'

Louise shook her head, and said, very clearly, 'I was thinking of nothing more than surviving. I'm sorry.' She frowned, after that. 'Though I'm not, really. I wouldn't have made it if I hadn't taken it with me, would I?'

And then she'd told them about Charlie's attack on her, and how stupid she'd been from the first.

'I panicked, and I did the wrong thing,' she said. 'I should never have left the club. I should have gone to the ladies' and found April.'

Jonah gave her a thoughtful look before he asked, 'Do you feel that you can trust her? She's explained that she knows Charlie. It's possible that . . . well, that she invited you to Portsmouth so he could silence you.'

Louise gave him a smile. 'I thought that for a minute, too. When she turned up at the scene. And then instead of helping him, she hauled him off me and was in no hurry to stop the bleeding. She cared a lot more about if I was OK than about him. Until I said I didn't want to be facing a murder charge.' Her mouth twisted. 'And I do know that I'm facing one now. I do know.'

357

Jonah could only nod, feeling inwardly furious that she had avoided one false charge for killing Alex Plaskitt, only to find herself forced into killing Charlie Ruskin. It seemed desperately unfair, and he wondered what going through all this did to a person. Ironically, he now strongly suspected that the Louise of over a week ago would never have reacted violently. They had all, between them, somehow created a new version of her.

The strange thing was that their wrong assumptions had helped her. Without them, she would almost certainly have been dead before April Dumont arrived. It was possible that April would have been killed shortly afterwards, too.

That said, he still wasn't sure what to make of April Dumont's involvement. She had insisted that setting up Charlie and Louise had been her own idea, not Charlie's, and that it had all been the worst coincidence. She said she'd had no clue what Charlie was capable of. She'd thought, like the rest of them, that Alex Plaskitt was the killer.

She'd also insisted that setting Louise up had been a secondary part of the evening. 'The main thing was to make her feel like she could go out and be herself,' she'd explained, with her customary firmness. 'I didn't want all of this to end up changing her for good.'

They'd also found out that April had known Charlie for longer than she'd known Louise. But a lot less well, she said. He'd run the bar at a conference she'd been to several years running, back when she worked in pharma. They'd got on well and managed not to ruin everything by sleeping together. Jonah had tried not to smile at that. A world where not sleeping with a friend seemed surprising was a very different world from Jonah's.

'You really weren't aware of any of Charlie's crimes?' Jonah had asked her, watching her very closely.

'Of course I wasn't,' April said. 'Jesus, you think I'd try and get my best friend together with him if I knew he'd sexually assaulted her before and stabbed a guy? I love Louise.' She fixed him with a very direct gaze. 'I would probably have killed him for her if it would have saved her life. She's the only one – the only family I have, and it doesn't matter that we aren't blood-related.'

And asked whether she was involved in organised crime, April had laughed, and said of course she wasn't. That she had enough trouble organising her own life.

Discussing it with Lightman after Louise had given her statement, Jonah admitted that he at least partly believed in April's ignorance. Charlie Ruskin had successfully convinced the world that Alex Plaskitt had died poetically at the hands of his own victim. The last thing he would have wanted was to meet Louise. The chance of her recognising him was too high.

The conversation had tailed off in uncertainty. Jonah wanted to grill April again the next day, though he suspected she'd be a tricky customer. Louise, at least, had told them everything readily, and then had been given an overnight cell with as many comforts as Jonah could get organised at that time in the morning.

After that, Jonah had finally headed home. He had to wind the windows down for most of the drive. His eyes were desperately heavy and he was seriously concerned about nodding off. He drew the car into Jojo's driveway as quietly as he could and got himself ready for bed downstairs to avoid disturbing her. And then he climbed the stairs and slid into her very new Egyptian-cotton sheets beside her.

He thought about Alex as he started to drift off. About what a good man he had been, and the unfairness of Charlie Ruskin and alcohol conspiring to kill him.

But at least everyone would know now. Everyone would know what he'd done.

39

By the time Saturday evening came round, Jonah felt like walking right out of the station and not coming back.

It had been a gruelling day, made up of difficult conversations and extensive paperwork. He'd reported to the DCS first thing on Saturday morning, and after a long silence, Wilkinson had asked to meet him for a proper conversation. That second conversation had been probing, and difficult, and had made Jonah feel like he'd failed everyone.

In the end Wilkinson had sighed. 'My personal feeling is that you made the best decisions you could at each stage. I honestly don't think anyone could have been more careful, Jonah.'

'Thank you,' Jonah said, already braced for what was coming next.

'But, as DCS, I'll have to put this all under review. We need to dig into everything and show that we weren't lax in allowing a serial offender to almost kill the woman who might identify him. We need to show that there were no failings. And perhaps we'll all learn something from the process, too.'

'Understood.'

He'd had to call on Marc Ruskin after that, with Lightman, and inform him of his brother's death. Marc, who was a shorter, milder version of his brother, had gradually become pale and silent, and had then gone to be sick for some while in the bathroom of his home.

On his return, he had sat down in front of Jonah, fixed his

gaze on the carpet, and said, 'It wasn't his fault. That he was like he was.'

'Did he . . . was there something in his past?'

'It was our mum,' Marc said, his voice unsteady. 'She . . . we were both abused by her. She used to make us do things . . . Charlie was older, and he often used to talk her into leaving me alone. So he got the worst of it. The worst of all of it. I knew it had messed him up, but I thought that we'd – that we'd come through it.'

Jonah thought of the box planted in Alex Plaskitt's car and asked if his mother had been dark-haired.

'Yes,' Marc said. 'She had long dark hair. She used to make us brush it, before . . .'

Jonah did his best to get the full story out of Marc as gently as he could. He eventually left the house with a heavy feeling in his chest.

April Dumont had been due in to see them after that, but they'd been unable to raise her. Her phone was, in fact, no longer connecting. And when they'd eventually sent someone round to her flat, it was to find her husband distraught. April had left him a full twenty-four hours before, removing her stuff before she'd picked Louise up to head to Portsmouth. She'd told him she was unhappy, and that she wasn't sure if she would see him again.

It became apparent that April had wound up every part of her life. She had closed down her bank accounts, or at least the ones her husband knew about, and had left her passport in the hotel room she and Louise had booked in Portsmouth.

And somehow Jonah knew they wouldn't find her again. That she was far, far too clever for that. And that she must have had an escape route planned for years.

'At least it answers a few questions,' Jonah told the DCS, with an attempt at positivity. 'I'm pretty sure it was April and her ex-husband who recruited Niall Reakes. I have a strong suspicion that she was doing a lot more, too. My guess is that the whole drugs operation was her brainchild, and under her management. And now that she's gone, Niall will probably be happy enough pointing the finger at her.'

There was nothing much else for Jonah or the DCS to do about April, except to pass her details to the National Crime Agency and make tracking her down their problem.

Later, in the early evening, Jonah and Lightman had arrived at Issa's house. They'd come to sit amid his brightly coloured cushions and tell him that his husband hadn't been a killer after all.

'Oh my God,' Issa had said, his hand to his mouth. 'You're sure? You're sure?'

'Yes,' Jonah had said. 'We believe that it was Charlie Ruskin. His friend, apparently.'

'Charlie?' Issa asked, his face blank.

'We think Alex happened on him while he was attacking Louise Reakes,' Jonah told him. 'Charlie was masked, and unrecognisable. Alex stepped in to stop him. Louise is now certain that that's what happened, and that the killer stabbed him and ran.'

Issa was listening to this intently. 'So . . . so he tried to save her.'

'Yes,' Jonah said, and he added, quietly, 'I'm so sorry we were so wrong about him.'

Issa's eyes moved back and forth a few times, as if he was trying to compute all of this. 'But how did he end up back at her house?' His voice sounded anguished again. 'Why didn't he go for help?'

'We think it's because he was very drunk and didn't realise how badly injured he was,' Jonah said. 'And also because he wanted to make sure Louise got home. She says . . . he put her to bed, and then asked if he could lie down, because he felt unwell. Louise did her best to comfort him, not realising that he was dying.'

Issa's mouth twisted, and then he nodded. 'What about – the box? In his car.'

'It was Charlie's, not his,' Lightman said, taking over. 'We think Charlie had a stroke of good luck. Alex had left his bag at the club, and so Charlie had access to his car keys. He planted the box in Alex's car at some point during the early hours of the morning, once you'd driven it home and parked up. And then we think he posted the keys through your front door.'

Which was something Jonah had realised for himself, when he'd finally remembered how Issa had struggled to open the front door to receive news of Alex's death. There had been a set of car keys jamming it, apparently having fallen from the table in the hall, but, in fact, shoved through the letterbox.

'They were actions of desperation,' Jonah added, 'designed to cast doubt if Alex survived, and to frame him if he didn't.'

'We also have accounts of the killer talking to Louise Reakes for some time at the club,' Lightman added. 'And we've placed him at three scenes where other women have been victims of assault.'

'So you think it'll be enough for the court?' Issa asked, his expression suddenly and markedly eager.

'It's certainly enough to be conclusive,' Jonah agreed. 'Unfortunately Charlie died late last night in circumstances we're still looking into.'

For a moment Issa looked as though he might crumble again. But then he breathed out a shuddering sigh and said, 'Good. He deserved to die.'

There wasn't much more to tell him at this stage. It wouldn't have been appropriate to explain the events of the night before, so they took their leave. But as they reached the front door, Issa said, 'Please say thank you. To Louise. For – for comforting him. It means such a lot to know that he didn't die alone.'

Jonah nodded. 'I will.'

Hanson finally managed to get some exercise on Sunday, tired though she was from the day before. She ran until she felt wobbly and slightly sick, and enjoyed the sensation hugely.

Lightman messaged her late in the afternoon to suggest they go for a drink. She wondered whether he was just looking out for her, or whether he wanted to talk something through. It was unusual for him to suggest anything sociable.

They met at the Marriott, the same hotel where they'd last had a drink together. It had seemed the natural place, though she then felt awkward at having suggested it. That last drink had been on uncertain terms. She'd never been quite clear whether they'd purely gone as friends.

She took a good look at him as she approached his table. She thought he looked tired. And possibly, just possibly, like he was sad. It was admittedly hard to tell. She'd known cappuccino art that was more expressive than he was. But she decided she was going to be brave and ask him before he had a chance to sidetrack the conversation.

'How are you?' she asked, putting her bag down and sitting quickly. 'How was yesterday? How's your dad doing?'

Lightman looked up at her and broke into a grin. 'Do you want me to answer all those at once, or shall I take them one at a time?'

She grinned back at him. 'Well, the most important one really is how you are. But I thought that might be affected by the other two.'

He tilted his head back and forth a couple of times, as if allowing that that was fair. 'Everything's all right,' he said, and glanced at her as if checking to see that she believed him. She made it obvious that she didn't. But he went on, anyway. 'It was a long day yesterday but the chief did a great job of talking people round.'

'How did it go at the hospital? With Louise Reakes?' It wasn't really the question she wanted an answer to, but it seemed like safer ground than anything personal.

'It went weirdly,' he said, giving a slow nod. 'Her husband turned up and was, to everyone's surprise, desperately upset about what had happened. And of course I wasn't intentionally listening, but they were only behind a curtain . . .'

Hanson grinned. 'You can admit that you find people's love lives as interesting as everyone else does, you know. Come and tell me at the bar.'

'All right.' Lightman rose and walked with her, speaking quietly as he went. 'He did a good begging act. All about how much he loved her and how much of an idiot he'd been lying to her for so long. He told her it was all about this drug-running mess he'd got himself into. And he added what an awful person Dina is and how much he hopes he never has to see her again.'

'Hmm,' Hanson said, thinking inevitably about her own situation. About Jason. 'Do we believe him?'

Lightman stopped with his hands on the bar and looked

at her for a moment. A look that could have meant anything. 'It's hard to say. Tense situations can make people think they care more than they really do.'

'I suppose so.' Hanson flagged down the bartender. She ordered them both gin. It seemed like a gin kind of day. And then she asked, 'What did Louise say?'

'Somewhere between won over and wary,' he said. 'I'd imagine she'll give him another chance.'

Hanson pulled a face and said nothing for a while. They both watched the bartender pour Tanqueray into a metal measure, and then she said, 'I don't know what I'd have done, in her shoes. Whether there was enough trust.'

Ben nodded next to her. She could feel his eyes on her, but it was easier to keep watching the bartender.

'I suppose what it really comes down to is happiness, isn't it?' Ben said. He leaned further over the bar, resting his elbows on it. He was at her level now. 'My theory is, that's the only thing that matters. Does having that person in your life make you happier than not having them in it? And if the answer is yes, it's simple.'

Hanson gave a small smile. 'Yeah, well. I've pretty much always got that one wrong myself.' She gave him the very briefest of looks. 'Maybe I don't *want* to be happy.'

'You should work on that,' Ben said, and then gave the ghost of a smile in return.

The bartender deposited their drinks in front of them. Hanson paid, and then lifted her glass. 'Well, I'll drink to it anyway. To not choosing to make your life more shit.'

'Cheers to that.'

They were in perfect unison as they lifted the glasses and drank.

*

It was actually on Sunday night that Jonah's worst conversation happened.

He was back at his desk, trying to provide the CPS with sufficient reason to dismiss the case against Louise Reakes. The sound of his phone ringing was a relief at first. He didn't recognise it for what it was, not even when he saw the name of his ex-fiancée on the screen for the third time that week.

He still didn't know what to do. But something in her insistent contact struck him as unusual. Michelle might be in some kind of trouble. Something could be badly wrong.

The ringing took on an urgency he found hard to deny. And so he picked up.

'Jesus, Jonah,' she said, sounding somewhere between angry and tearful. 'Could you just have replied to one message?'

'Sorry,' he said, easily manoeuvred into guilt. 'I've had a really intense case. Are you . . . all right?'

'No, not really,' she said. 'I'm . . . well, in a bit of a state, to be honest. We fucked up. I'm four months pregnant.'

There was a beat, while Jonah's mind did the maths, an instinctive checking to make sure he understood what she was saying, and then he said, 'Oh. Fuck, that's . . .'

'A massive balls-up,' Michelle agreed, and then he heard the sound of her crying down the phone at him, and he wasn't sure he had it in him to comfort her. Not when he could feel everything falling apart.

40

Louise

It's time for you to read all of this. Everything I've written to you. Everything I wrote up until the night that almost killed me. It's all here.

There isn't a lot to add from the last few days. Except that I'm honestly not afraid.

That doesn't mean I'm deluded. I know the CPS is bringing a manslaughter charge against me, and I know it's possible that I'll be convicted. There are a lot of women who have been convicted for killing their attackers in the past. The stats are actually quite frightening now I've looked into it.

I don't know how much Patrick has told you about the case. But he tells me a lot will hinge on my decision to take the knife with me, which implies premeditation. However, he hopes that any jury will understand I had no idea I was going to meet my attacker and was purely thinking defensively.

The other bonus is the trauma I'd already gone through. Legally speaking, that is. I can speak openly and honestly about that when my time comes. Nothing anyone says will change how frightened I felt. Patrick thinks I should allow myself to look vulnerable when the time comes. This is something I am now struggling with, and it's the strangest feeling. I keep somehow coming across as too strong. Too together. What happened to the old Louise?

April has managed to be our star witness even in her absence. The statement she gave was pretty conclusive. Apparently there's no case being pursued against her at present to make that statement doubtful, which is lucky for me. The National Crime Agency is looking into her, but Patrick tells me she's done a remarkably good job of disappearing. I suppose that's the advantage of planning it for a long time. I just feel strangely grateful that she risked it all to spend one last night out with me. It's obvious to me, now, that it was a farewell.

It probably seems strange to you that I feel the loss of her so intensely, given how much she hid from me, and how responsible she was for all the shit you got into with Dina. I know that she essentially blackmailed you into running drugs for eight years. I understand that nobody made her do any of it, and that she must have made unbelievable amounts of money off you, Dina, and every other person dragged into her scheme. And I know that you're still angry as hell with her, for all sorts of reasons.

But I miss her, Niall. It's clear to me that she's cared about me for the past five years more than anyone else, even you. I'm sad that I'm going through this without her now. I'm sad, too, that I won't get to hear her stand up in court to say her piece. I know she'd have done a great job tying the prosecutor in knots. Though I don't feel scared of it. I don't feel like I actually need her to fight my corner any more, however much I might enjoy it.

I found out a little more about her from the National Crime Agency. They asked me if I knew her by any other names, and then they asked if the name Abigail Jones-Rounier rang any bells. She was April's age, the daughter of a Tennessee doctor whose wife left him. April brought up her sister, Dolores Jones-Rounier, pretty much single-handed, and then lost her to a drunk with a gun one New Year's Day. Abigail vanished soon afterwards, but not before the drunk had been beaten senseless with a scaffolding pipe.

So maybe you could argue it wasn't really me she loved. It was her baby sister, Dee. Everything she felt for me might only have been a shadow of that, it's true. And yet I felt like April saw me and understood me like nobody else. Like I hope you will.

There's one more thing for me to tell you about April. I had a card that's clearly from her, even though it isn't signed. It called me 'honey' and apologised for her terrible lack of judgement in Charlie's character.

There was a key taped into it, too. For a Big Yellow storage facility. It has the address on the fob. And she'd circled it and written 'not to be opened until your next, next birthday'.

I'm pretty sure I know what's inside it. That she's left me a comfortable life, and the option of clearing your debts if I want to. I'm not sure yet whether we should take it. Whether I should just leave it and everything to do with April behind.

I'll certainly have to leave it until after all the court proceedings are done, and even then, it might get me into a lot of trouble if anyone finds out. Taking the proceeds of crime. But I'm still glad she sent it. And equally glad that she's out there in the world, unarrested and probably kicking ass.

Anyway, I think that's enough about April. This is supposed to be about us.

Such an awful lot of strangeness has come out of all this. Your fear for me. Your respect for what I did. And your sudden, absolute hatred of Dina for betraying you when things got tough. I actually think you calling her a manipulative cow might have been the most wonderful thing I've ever

371

heard you say. I fully recognise that that's a petty victory, but it doesn't lessen my enjoyment of it one iota.

There was the other thing you said, too. About how worried you'd been that I couldn't cope with a child. How stupid you'd been, in fact, because I'd just coped with something a lot harder, and come through it just fine. You said you should have seen that capacity in me before, but in fairness to you, Niall, I never truly saw it, either. It was hidden from both of us.

Perhaps the strangest thing of all is suddenly thinking we might have a future again. And actually *wanting* us to have one. It's still only a *might*, of course. There's a lot of shit that the two of us have to deal with. Two probable prosecutions and potential jail time in each direction, though Patrick says Daniella's working incredibly hard on a plea deal for you.

We also have a lot to work through and explain and apologise or get angry for. Or to just . . . forgive. But it feels like we might get to build this again, on solid foundations. That maybe, just maybe, if we fight hard enough for it, we might end up the family I've always wanted us to be.

And I want to tell you that I'm looking forward to the fight.

Acknowledgements

A book is created by so many people. It is never, ever just one author sitting alone and writing.

Felicity Blunt is, was, and always will be the reason that this book happened at all. My wonderful human dynamo of an agent. You rock in every possible way.

Joel Richardson was the one who ran with my sudden change of idea for this book, and helped me turn the idea into a real, wonderful reality. The very best of editors, one of the nicest people on the planct, and a huge amount of fun to work with.

Grace Long was my fabulous second pair of eyes, and turned in an unbelievably excellent set of notes to help me through that significant last draft. Also, a constant support and organisational demon. Huge thanks.

To the fabulous cover design team at Penguin Michael Joseph, you have surpassed yourselves once again. I've been so lucky to have such beautiful covers on all my books, and I know just how important they are.

To the wonderful Penguin reps, who are the reason my books end up on any shelves at all. I am so fortunate to have your faith in what I write, and for that to turn into the amazing reality of seeing it in countless shops all over the country.

To Jen Breslin and Ella Watkins, who are just the most amazing publicity and marketing team. The thought, imagination, and constant determination to support have been unbelievable. Also, your patience with my constant questions and ideas. You are fabulous.

To Andrea Walker, US editor extraordinaire. Your faith in me is wonderful, humbling and inspirational. And your team is as warm, smart and exciting as you are. I am so proud to be working with you.

To Beatrix McIntyre, Jennie Roman and the whole wonderful copy-editing team. You provide such smart, insightful comments and save me from huge embarrassment time after time.

To the wonderful rights team at Penguin, who have brought my books to a staggering number of countries across the world. I owe you so much.

To Tariq Joyce, who was there for that all-important conversation right at the beginning. The one that made me realise how this book would work, and that it really would work. Great writers give the best advice.

To Chris Haines, the policing mastermind I go to whenever I want to ask about how some aspect of the forces work. You are just fantastically patient and helpful. It's so heartening to have you there, and I just hope I managed to ask all the right questions in order to avoid any unintentional errors. Any of those are obviously mine.

To David Stubbings and Sarah Preston, who I somehow (inexcusably) missed off my list of the fantastic Girton Players last time. Thank you for every minute of your time and support over huge numbers of plays.

To my fabulous family and partner, who are still the most incredibly supportive bunch. I hope you have the patience for it all with the next books, too.

To Colin Smith for all the cheerleading, support and epic

procrastination. This book would genuinely have been written more quickly without you.

And to all the wonderful members of the crime-writing community I have got to know over the past three years, who are too numerous to name but who have been the most welcoming, fabulous and entertaining bunch. Who knows how such lovely people write such horrific things?

AMERICAN
RADICAL

AMERICAN RADICAL

THE TRUE STORY OF AN UNDERCOVER MUSLIM
FBI AGENT RISKING HIS LIFE TO SAVE YOURS

TAMER ELNOURY

with Kevin Maurer

BANTAM PRESS

LONDON · TORONTO · SYDNEY · AUCKLAND · JOHANNESBURG

TRANSWORLD PUBLISHERS
61–63 Uxbridge Road, London W5 5SA
www.penguin.co.uk

Transworld is part of the Penguin Random House group of companies
whose addresses can be found at global.penguinrandomhouse.com

Penguin
Random House
UK

First published in Great Britain in 2017 by Bantam Press
an imprint of Transworld Publishers

A CIP catalogue record for this book
is available from the British Library.

ISBNs
9780593079744 (hb)
9780593079751 (tpb)

Typeset in Adobe Garamond Pro
Printed and bound by Clays Ltd, Bungay, Suffolk.

Penguin Random House is committed to a sustainable
future for our business, our readers and our planet. This book
is made from Forest Stewardship Council˚ certified paper.

CONTENTS

To my mother.
Everything I am and ever will be is because of you.
Rest in peace, Mom.

GLOSSARY OF ARABIC WORDS

Dunya: this world, Earth

habibi: brother, friend

halal: accepted and allowed in Islam; blessed

haram: forbidden in Islam; against the religion

insha'Allah: God willing

masha'Allah: an expression of appreciation, joy, or praise

mujahid (singular)/mujahideen (plural): one engaged in jihad

munafiq (singular)/munafiqeen (plural): an outward Muslim who is secretly unsympathetic and undermines the Islamic community

Muslim Ummah: the collective community of Muslims

NOTE TO THE READER

American Radical is the story of a group of extraordinary men and women whom I was lucky enough to work alongside for the past nine years and the human toll and sacrifice we make to do the job every day.

Only the first names of the actual agents are used. I do this to protect them from harm by enemies of the United States. I refer to publicly recognized senior agents and FBI management by their true names. I have taken great care to avoid going into specific detail about training, tactics, and procedures used by the FBI and law enforcement.

My intent in writing this book is to ensure that the content gives a clear and accurate account of the events and experiences in which I took part, but it is of paramount importance to me that I maintain the sanctity and secrecy of operational and security issues.

The majority of the material contained within this book was derived from reports and transcripts generated during the investigation. When no documents were available, scenes were reconstructed from my notes and memory. This book is my perception of what happened and when it happened. If there are inaccuracies in it, the responsibility is mine.

This book was reviewed and approved by the FBI, but it presents my views and does not represent the views of the FBI, the U.S. Department of Justice, or anyone else.

AMERICAN
RADICAL

CHAPTER 1

Super High

I was Rico Jordan before I was Tamer Elnoury. Hell, I was a lot of people before I ever got in front of a terrorist. I spent a lot of days looking and acting like a criminal. I had a knack for being able to relate to people. To pull them in and make them feel comfortable, even drug dealers.

I became Rico Jordan as soon as I tied my do-rag.

I stepped in front of the mirror and smoothed out my thick mustache and goatee that grew six or seven inches off my chin. Two hoop earrings went into my left ear. I tucked my baggy pants into my black Timberland boots and slid a pistol between my waistband and the small of my back.

It was close to 6:00 P.M. on September 10, 2001. I was working narcotics in New Jersey, so most of my days started when everyone else was headed home. For months, I'd been looking for the

1

distributor of Super High, a potent batch of heroin coming out of New York. When Super High hit the streets, overdoses skyrocketed.

My target was Kit Kat's crew. She and her two sons ran a network of dealers working the towns and cities in central New Jersey. After months of buying from them, they agreed to let me meet their Super High source. The supplier's street name was Black. We'd heard of him, but we'd never gotten eyes on him. That was my job. Identify him and wait for the SWAT team to make the arrest.

Traffic was thick with the bridge-and-tunnel crowd coming home. Kit Kat's crew worked out of a row house at the end of an alley with lookouts positioned on the roof. I parked my green Mazda 626 behind the house after circling the block a few times. Most drug dealers will make a couple of passes to make sure the block isn't hot, and I needed to look the part. It also let me relay information back to the waiting SWAT team. While I drove, I narrated what I saw into a Nokia cell phone.

"Four guys at the front of the house," I said. "No one on the porch."

Billy, my sergeant, was on the other end of the line. He passed each mental picture back to the staging location, a makeshift command center. At the mouth of the alley, I saw the spotters on the roof watching me. With each step, everything slowed in my mind. I'd come a long way since my first drug buy three years ago.

My first buy was for "dip"—shards of crack cocaine chipped off a bigger rock. My hands were sweating as I approached the dealer. I pressed a twenty-dollar bill into his hand and waited for him to fish out a shard from a plastic bag. I was anxious. I couldn't catch my breath. My fingers tingled with adrenaline. I probably looked like a junkie. The dealer put the shard into my hand. I barely felt it as I ran back to the undercover car.

"How did it go?" Mike, my handler, said.

"Good, man," I said. "Look."

I held out my hand. The dip was just a smear. The rock melted in my sweaty hands.

"That's great," Mike said. "What was his name?"

"Who?" I said.

"The dealer," Mike said. "What was he wearing?"

I stared out the windshield trying to conjure an image.

"Was he black or white at least?"

I didn't know. I found out later the dealer had an enormous eagle tattoo on his neck. I was so full of nerves and fear I missed everything. It was embarrassing.

After that, I started to study. I found a junkie who taught me how to cook crack, cut heroin and cocaine. But the biggest lesson was the power of addiction. Just the thought of getting high aroused him. He carried a razor blade in his pocket. If he got arrested, he sliced up his leg through his pants and poured heroin into the wound. It was the only way to stave off withdrawal in jail. Rico Jordan was born out of those meetings. There was no respect in the drug world for a user. I had to be a dealer.

The key to a good cover story was keeping it close to your own experiences. I was a college graduate, so Rico Jordan had a few credits but no degree. He was a former business major—like me—who'd turned entrepreneur drug dealer. Rico Jordan was all business, which earned respect on the street and avoided the hassle of explaining why I wasn't using.

I'd been Rico Jordan for about a year and a half. People didn't know if I was Hispanic, light-skinned black, or Middle Eastern. All they knew was that I wasn't white. I didn't earn a second glance in the neighborhood.

A guy near the front of the alley—security—was sagging to the left as I approached. He likely had a gun on his right hip. He nodded to me as I passed. Kit Kat's crew knew me and I was ushered into the house.

"G-Money's in the kitchen," he said.

I'd been in the house before, so I knew the way. The house stunk like feet. Weed smoke hung in the air. The TV was on, but no one was watching it. About a half dozen men were too busy joking, talking, and smoking. No one acknowledged me as I walked into the dining room.

Two men—one of the guys was part of the crew—looked up. Money was being counted on the table. Glassine bags of heroin were piled in the middle. One of the guys had a bulge—likely a pistol—in his waistband. They kept talking.

I took a snapshot of each room. This wasn't about protecting the SWAT team any longer. This was self-preservation. If the deal went south, I knew my escape route and each room's biggest threats.

G-Money was leaning against the counter. I have no idea how he got the nickname. Probably because he thought it sounded cool. He was scrawny with short-cropped hair. I never saw him in anything but a FUBU shirt or a baggy sweatshirt and jeans.

Scumbag chic.

"Yo, what's good?" he said. "Where's your whip?"

I nodded toward the back of the house.

G-Money nodded.

"Black should be here any minute."

I looked around the kitchen. No one used it to make food. The counter was grimy and sticky. The sink stunk of stale beer.

"Good looking out putting him in front of me," I said.

"You're good people," G-Money said. "Don't forget me when you start moving up."

I laughed. He didn't have to worry about that.

"How much do you think he'll shave off?"

"If you buy twenty bricks, he'll knock it down," he said. "Just get to know him first."

Heroin is packaged into bags or decks, bundles, and bricks. In New Jersey, a brick of heroin is five bundles, or fifty bags. The street value of a bag of heroin is about ten dollars. I wanted a bulk discount.

I heard Black's Acura pull up outside the back door. I could see the car's rims and spinners from the window. He grabbed a black gym bag out of the back seat. G-Money greeted him with a handshake that turned into a hug.

Black was tall and thin with skin so dark it looked like it hurt. He had baggy black jeans that he had to constantly pull up over his ass. Black wore his tan Timberland boots untied. A comically large gold medallion hung around his neck. When he got to me, we shook hands.

"This is Black," G-Money said. "This is Rico, short for Tarico."

Black's face changed. His hands went to his sides as he eyeballed me, skeptical of what he'd just been told. The look startled me. Did he know me? Had he seen me somewhere? Had he made me as a cop? The mental pictures started flicking through my head. Threats. Escape routes. Seconds started to drag. Then he smiled.

"My name is Tariq," Black said.

"No shit," I said, my stress bleeding away.

Black chuckled.

G-Money had a big smile on his face. It was the best possible ice-breaker. Before we could get to business, Kit Kat staggered into the kitchen. She walked like a sailor on deck in a storm. She smiled at Black and then hugged me. I could feel her skeletal body against mine.

"Hi, baby," she said, kissing me on the cheek.

"What's good, Kit Kat?"

My luck was getting better and better. I could see Black checking us out as the matriarch of the family was hugging me. G-Money was making jokes about my name. Black was relaxing.

"Since we sort of share a name, you have to hook me up," I said.

"I got you," Black said. "I got you."

There were seventy-five cops staged around the house. Everyone was waiting for him to open the bag. This part always got my heart racing. He unzipped the bag and I looked at the bricks of heroin. A calm came over me. We had him.

"Let me grab a couple of bricks now," I said. "I'll get the rest later."

I had money to buy twenty bricks. Once we made the deal, his charge went from possession with intent to distribute to distribution in a school zone. An elementary school was only a block or two away.

"Yeah," Black said. "That works. Here, take these."

He stacked the bricks on the kitchen counter. My heart started to race again, because I knew when I gave the word, SWAT was going to hit the house.

"Want to give me your number?" I said. "I'll hit you up later for the rest."

Black was closing the bag.

"Absolutely," he said.

Every operation had a takedown word and a distress signal. The distress signal meant "Come and get me, I'm in trouble." The takedown word signaled "The deal is done. Take it down." This operation's takedown word was "soft pretzel."

"Man, you guys eat yet?" I said. "I missed lunch. All I had to eat today was a soft pretzel."

Black didn't answer. He just gave me his mobile number. I put it in my phone while Black and G-Money made small talk. Black started to pack up.

Hurry the fuck up, I thought.

Then I heard it.

"5-0! 5-0!"

The spotters saw SWAT coming. Everybody stopped. Fight or flight took hold. G-Money and one of the guys in the dining room bolted for the back door. Black froze. His eyes darted back and forth as his mind tried to figure out his next move.

I pressed my back against the refrigerator. My eyeballs went to Black's hands and waist. If he went for a gun, I was going to shoot him.

I heard the front door open with a crash.

"Police! Search warrant! Get down! Get the fuck down!"

Black's mind finally engaged. He grabbed the gym bag and went out the back door. SWAT officers with MP5 submachine guns met him on the steps. He came barreling back into the kitchen and tossed the bag as soon as he got inside. The heroin went everywhere.

Twelve seconds of yelling. Furniture breaking. Chaos. One of the guys in the dining room got slammed on the table, shattering it.

I knew Bobby, one of my closest friends, was coming for me. A few hours before the operation, I briefed the team dressed as Rico Jordan. That was common practice so that everyone knew what I was wearing. It was an officer safety thing.

"I'm going to put the cuffs on him this time," Bobby said during the briefing.

Bobby was Jewish. I am Muslim. I called him "Jew Boy." He called me "Camel Boy." The unit nicknamed our corner of the office the Gaza Strip. Political correctness had no place in our office. Every day was about the mission and the brotherhood in that order.

I could hear Bobby yelling at suspects to get down. His voice got louder and louder. Bobby hit the kitchen at a sprint. He was headed for me.

"Get down! Get down!"

I stepped to one side and bitch-slapped him. The crack of my hand hitting his face cut through the chaos. Everyone stopped for a second. I tried not to laugh just as hands grabbed me and slammed me to the ground.

"Get the fuck down, asshole."

I covered my head as Bobby and the guys flipped me on my face and cuffed my hands behind my back. You don't hit a cop without getting your ass beat, and I took a few slaps too. But it was worth it to see my handprint on Bobby's face a few hours later.

Bobby took me out to a waiting car. I could see the guys from the living room lined up along the wall. Everyone had their heads down. At the police station, Bobby took me in the back door. Billy, my sergeant, met me at processing. He dressed in old faded jeans and white Reebok sneakers. His disheveled brown hair needed a comb. When he was doing undercover drug work, we called him Charles Manson because of his long brown hair and thick beard.

"You all right? You good?"

I nodded. We spent about an hour going over the buy. It turned out to be a huge hit. We flipped some informants and found the source of Super High in Spanish Harlem. We also broke up Kit Kat's drug ring. After the briefing, Billy led me to a cell where they held the others.

"This fucking guy has a warrant," he said.

The fake warrant was from another town.

"I took care of that shit," I said, playing along.

"The fuck you did," Billy said. "It says it here. They want you."

A sheriff's deputy escorted me out of the cell. Right after we were out of sight, the cuffs were off.

"Just because I'm going home doesn't mean I won't get those overtime hours," I said.

Billy waved as he headed back into police headquarters.

"You'll get it. Get some rest," Billy said. "You've got that crack buy in the morning."

CHAPTER 2

I Am a Muslim

I was back on the street the next morning.

It was before 8:00 A.M. on September 11, 2001. The weather was perfect. Not hot, but not cool yet. The only hint of fall was football dominating the morning sports talk. Week one was over. My Bills dropped the season opener to the Saints, but it was week one. There was still hope.

I was tired as I drove my Mazda to the buy. Even though Billy cut me loose early, it still took me hours to come down. When I finally got to sleep, the alarm went off. I dragged myself to work, praying for a weekend.

It was only Tuesday.

I parked my car after doing a lap around the block. My spotter, James, was set up across the street as I approached the dealer. He was a young black guy. A low-level guy. He was just a cog in the machine. The start of a thread that hopefully led to his supplier.

The crack buy was routine. Money and drugs exchanged in one

fluid motion. The dealer was chatty. I wasn't interested in talking about the weather or if the Seattle Mariners, on their way to winning more than one hundred games, would challenge the Yankees when the playoffs started next month. But sports turned to current events before I walked away.

"Yo, did you hear some drunk guy just flew a Cessna into the World Trade Center?" he said.

"What?"

"Yeah. A plane hit one of the towers."

I didn't believe it. A drug dealer wasn't the most reliable source unless you were looking to score. I got back into my car and tossed the drugs onto the passenger seat. I tuned the radio to a news station. Initial reports had a Cessna striking the north tower at 8:46 A.M., a few minutes before I made the buy.

As I drove back to the office, details started to come in about the plane. It wasn't a Cessna. It was American Airlines Flight 11. The Boeing 767 aircraft had left Boston's Logan Airport headed for Los Angeles. I'd learn later that Mohammed Atta and four other hijackers took control and flew it into the North Tower of the World Trade Center. There were eleven crew members and seventy-six passengers on board.

I got back to the office just as United Airlines Flight 175, a Boeing 767 with a crew of nine and fifty-one passengers, hit the South Tower. I ran into the conference room. Guys from the unit were watching the news on a TV in the corner. A stunned silence hung over the room as the footage of the plane hitting the South Tower was replayed. The pit in my stomach grew each time I saw the plumes of smoke and fire shoot out of the towers.

American Airlines Flight 77, a Boeing 757 aircraft, with a crew of six and fifty-three passengers, crashed into the Pentagon thirty minutes later.

Oh God, please don't let this be a terrorist attack, I thought. That's how naive I was at the time, how naive many of us were.

My cell phone rang. It was my girlfriend. She was crying. Our mutual friend was trapped in the South Tower. He was a few floors above the damage and called his wife. She could hear the sirens in the background as he tried to reassure her.

"I love you," he told his wife. "I don't know what is happening. We're going to try and get out now. Don't worry about me. Take care of you."

That was the last time they talked. Everybody in the office was getting the same kinds of calls. The first reports about al Qaeda shook me out of my stupor. Images of Osama bin Laden in his military field jacket firing an AK-47 filled the TV screen. Then news broke that the hijackers were all Arab Muslims. All of a sudden my religion was front and center. The hijackers had killed thousands of innocents in the name of the most precious and private thing in my life. My gaze was fixed on the TV, but my mind was back in Egypt.

I was born in Alexandria. I arrived in New Jersey in 1977. My father was looking for a better life, so he packed up his wife and two kids and flew three thousand miles to a foreign country. Even at four years old, moving to the United States was a culture shock. My preschool teacher called home after the first week with a good report.

"He is doing well," she told my mother. "He is very talkative. He is a good little boy. But no one has any idea what he is saying."

My father was a medical engineer, but his first American jobs were modest. He pumped gas and worked in a chocolate factory and as a security guard on a department store's graveyard shift. My mother was a chemist. She worked side jobs before getting a job at a chemical company that made fabric dyes. She was lucky. It took my father six years to get a job designing orthopedic implants. His claim to fame was Bo Jackson's hip. Each passing year my family got wealthier. When my father bought a house with a pool in North Jersey, we knew we had settled into the American dream.

Being Muslim in America in the 1980s wasn't a big deal. We lived across the street from a church. A synagogue sat behind our house. I had sleepovers at my Jewish friends' houses. Most people thought I was Hispanic. But at home, my mother only spoke Arabic to me. She never wanted me to lose my culture or religion.

Islam was something I practiced privately. My mother made sure I studied the Quran and made Islam a daily part of my life. I still strive to say my prayers every day. Do I miss a day? Yes. Have I missed fasting during Ramadan? Sure. I'm no different from Catholics who go to church only on Christmas and Easter. That doesn't make me less religious. It just makes me a human who, at the end of the day, is a Muslim.

It was a trip to the mosque with my father that set me on my path. I was in college, struggling to get a degree in business. The prospect of being chained to a desk in a cubicle farm made my skin crawl. My favorite college class was an introduction to criminal justice. I knew it would be a hard sell to my parents. They'd accept lawyer, but not cop.

It was Friday and I was headed home for a visit. My father met me at the house and we went to the mosque together. As I prayed, I noticed a Turkish man in a Bureau of Alcohol, Tobacco, Firearms and Explosives (ATF) shirt nearby. I watched as he prayed with his gun strapped to his hip. I didn't know the man, nor did I talk to him afterward. But seeing him planted a seed. In his own way, he gave me permission to consider law enforcement.

The next semester, I switched my major to law and justice. It was a hybrid prelaw and criminal justice major. I told my parents I wanted to be a lawyer, but my sights were set on federal law enforcement. My grades went from solid Bs to straight As. Right before graduation, I broke the news to my parents that I wanted to be a cop. Not a street cop, but a federal agent. The FBI was recruiting me, but I didn't have a formal offer.

I papered the region's police departments with my resume. I was in the running for jobs in Maryland and with the Secret Service, but a New Jersey police department hired me. They promised me an investigative position and a spot on the fugitive task force. I couldn't say no. The day I graduated from the police academy, the FBI recruiter pulled me aside.

"Can I have a minute of your time?" he asked.

Agent Butler was a former SWAT Team member who was finishing up his career recruiting. I had met him during career day in college. Butler had checked in on me at the police academy, but this meeting was different.

"So, son, are you ready to join the FBI?"

"Let me ask you something," I said. "You and I have been talking for a couple of years now. You don't really know me. Why are you pushing the FBI so much on me?"

Butler smiled.

"I don't really know you," he said. "But you speak a language we need. You're in law enforcement, and before your face is known and before you forget about us, we'd love to have you start the process."

The Bureau was looking for Middle Easterners to help with terrorism investigations. It was the late 1990s, and terrorism was on their radar after the 1993 World Trade Center bombings. The FBI saw a gap in its ability to track and understand the Islamic terrorism threat.

"What are the chances of me ending up in a van in Detroit or in New York listening to a bunch of dirty Arabs?" I was trying to get a sense of how typecast I'd be.

Butler shrugged.

"Very astute," he said. "I'm not going to lie to you. A high likelihood. You're twenty-two years old. We don't hire twenty-two-year-olds to become agents unless they have one of a handful of things that we need. You speak Arabic. You're hired for that reason. They're not going to stick you in a bank robbery squad."

The FBI was one of my career goals, but more than anything I wanted to get my hands dirty.

"Okay," I said. "Can you give me some time to figure out what it means to be a cop? Get that out of my system, and maybe our paths will cross later?"

Butler shook my hand.

"I respect that," he said. "Good luck, son. Stay in touch."

I graduated from the police academy on a Friday in 1996. On Monday, I joined a fugitive task force in New Jersey. A couple of years later, I moved over to narcotics and guns. Back in the conference room on 9/11, I couldn't shake a feeling of guilt. Had I missed my calling? If I'd gone a different route, could I have prevented this? Should I have taken the FBI's offer?

"There's nothing we can do about this," one of my coworkers said. "I'm going back out on the street."

I couldn't move. At one point, a sandwich showed up for me. It sat untouched. People shuffled in and out of the room. But I stayed in my seat. An evidence bag of crack cocaine sat in front of me. All day I could feel the rage building in the conference room. There was a twinge of anger in Peter Jennings's tone as he read the updates. I understood it. But this wasn't Islam to me.

The sun had set when I felt a hand on my shoulder. It was Billy, my sergeant. He didn't put his hands on anyone unless they were getting arrested.

"We know that is not your religion," he said. "I hope they get those fucking animals. Go home. Get some sleep."

It was dark when I finally stood up. I'd been physically, mentally frozen all day. I locked up the office and walked to my car. I didn't turn on the radio. I just drove to my house in silence. I couldn't take any more talk about al Qaeda or the attack. I was angry, embarrassed, and hurt. Some asshole in a cave turned me and my family into the enemy. I hadn't felt this lost since my mother passed.

As I drove home, my mind drifted to 1997. It was July 4th weekend and I'd been a cop for a little more than a year. I was standing in my kitchen when my father called. I could tell something was wrong immediately. There was a hitch in his speech.

"Pop, what is going on? You're freaking me out."

He paused.

"I don't want to worry you, but your mom started dropping things in the kitchen," he said. "Being clumsy. She hit a shopping cart at the A&P parking lot. She clipped the mirror pulling out of the garage. I took her to the doctor. They found a brain tumor."

When my father said "brain tumor," I felt sick to my stomach. My legs felt weak and I sat down. My father sounded confident as he talked about how one of the best brain surgeons on the East Coast was going to treat her. I knew he was being positive for me and I took the lifeline. She was going to be fine, I told myself.

My mother was in and out of the hospital the next few weeks. The biopsy confirmed the tumor was malignant and aggressive. The treatment plan was to use chemotherapy to shrink it, and then the surgeon would go in and remove it. My father called me after one of her stays in the hospital. My mother wanted to have a party.

Our house had a cabana with a fireplace and furniture. I helped set it up for the party. Growing up, my friends spent from morning to when the streetlights went on swimming and hanging out at the cabana. My mother waited on us with drinks and snacks, but she was more than that to many of my friends. They spent hours talking to her. She knew more about their aspirations and problems than I did. I spoke to my mom every single day I was away at college. So did my roommates. They would run to answer my phone just to talk with her.

On the day of the party, guests arrived in small groups. There were lots of smiles. Some tears. Many laughs. I stayed busy helping with drinks and food. It was around dusk when my father asked me to help my mother to the pool deck. The guests were outside and my father wanted my mother to be in the mix. I trotted across the thick green grass of the backyard and in through the back door of the house.

"Dad wants you to come out," I told her.

She smiled and reached for my hand. She clung to me as we walked from the family room to the back door. Each step was a grind.

Left. Right. Left. Right.

I used to yell from the pool for more chips or soda. She had walked these few steps with ease and a smile. Now nothing flowed. Her joints were like hinges in need of oil. She was leaning on me so much that I practically carried her across the lawn.

I had leaned on her my whole life. Now she was leaning on me just to get across the yard. My mom wasn't getting better. She wanted this party to say her goodbyes.

My mother returned to the hospital less than a week later. I lived about an hour south, but I came up a couple of times a week to visit. One evening my father called me and asked if I could keep my mother company.

"I'm going to be late," he said. "I have a meeting in the office."

"No problem," I said.

"Just help her out with dinner," he said. "Sit with her until I get there."

I left work early the next day and headed to the hospital. Traffic was terrible and I arrived about ten or fifteen minutes late. She was alone in her room. Her dinner was on the tray across her bed. She had her knife and fork, but her brain wouldn't let them work together. The fork fell out of her hand. She held the plate with her elbow and tried to cut a piece of meat.

Tears rolled down my face. I froze at the door. I didn't want her to see me because I knew she'd console me. I wasn't there for me. I was there to help her. I wiped the tears from my cheeks and walked into the room. My smile hid the pain. I hugged and kissed her.

"I'm so sorry I'm late," I said.

I made no mention of the fork or knife. I just started cutting her meat and talking. I tried to keep a happy face, but my mother saw right through it. She knew I was hurting.

After her tray was cleared, I sat by her bed. I held her hand. I still wasn't ready to accept what was happening. But she was. She squeezed my hand and told me it was Allah's will.

"It is everything I ever taught you," she said. "You need to believe it in your heart."

She told me to take care of my father and sister.

"One day we will all be reunited," she said, the hint of a smile on her face. "Never spend a day being sad. Remember all the love and the memories we had. Wear them. Use them. Be the good man I know you will be. Help people. Do as much good in this world as you can. I will see you in heaven."

It was calming, yet devastating. Our bond was for eternity. I needed to hear it. But I still wasn't ready for the end.

My father called me the following week.

"You should come up," he said. "Your mother slipped into a coma."

I rocketed up the Garden State Parkway. It was just a setback. It happens. I kept repeating that to myself while I drove. When I got to the hospital, the nurses were standing around crying at their stations. In the short time my mom was there, she knew every nurse by name and everything about them. They adored her.

My father was in the doorway of her room. His arms were crossed.

He was crying. It was the first time I'd ever seen him shed a tear. I touched his shoulder and entered the room. In the corner was my sister in a ball. She was hugging her knees and sobbing.

The doctor was at the foot of my mother's bed looking at her chart. I was struck by how thick it was. He flipped page by page like he was looking for a cure. His eyes never left the chart. I ran to my mother's side. She was wearing her favorite purple robe. She had a breathing tube in her mouth. Her head was leaning toward me. I grabbed her hand and touched her head. My mouth was dry. My head was throbbing. I wasn't sure what to do. There was only silence and the hum of her respirator.

Why weren't we game-planning? Why wasn't this like a war room? I didn't want peaceful. I craved action. A plan. Anything but surrender. I stared at the doctor. He kept his gaze on the charts.

"The tumor clearly didn't reduce in size," I said, struggling to engage him. "It's obviously getting bigger. What if we go in and we just try to take it out? You said it would be like arthroscopic surgery. We can just reduce it, right?"

I wanted him to order the nurses to prep my mother for surgery. I wanted him to tell me he was going to save her. The doctor put down the chart and looked at me.

"Look, kid, it's over," he said. "Say your goodbyes."

"You motherfucker," I said.

Then I dove across my mother's legs and reached for his shirt. My pistol—slid into the waistband of my pants—was visible. The doctor recoiled and stayed just out of my grasp.

Then I felt someone grab me. It was my father. He was in shock. He went from watching his wife die to stopping his son from hurting the doctor. I was screaming and yelling as the doctor ran for the door.

"Call the police," the doctor told a nurse as he left.

Jasmine, one of my mother's nurses, took me to a neighboring room. She was a Middle Eastern woman in her late forties. Not much younger than my mother.

"I was with your mother before she slipped into the coma," she said. "Your mother kept looking at something in the room."

The story calmed me for some reason.

"What was she looking at?" I said.

"She saw light," Jasmine said. "She told me everything was going to be fine. She said, 'I know it is going to be fine. I am so relieved. Tell my family it is all going to be okay.'"

I didn't know what to say.

"It's going to be fine," Jasmine said.

A police officer arrived a few minutes later. He was wearing sergeant stripes and a stern look. Jasmine met him at the door. She said a couple of words to him just out of earshot before he walked over to me.

"Son, are you on the job?" he said.

"Yes, sir," I said.

"Can I see your ID?"

I showed him my badge. He looked at it and put his arm on my shoulder.

"I'm sorry for your loss, son."

My mother died later that day. I didn't sleep for weeks. I paced. I stared out the window. When I got home on September 11, 2001, I felt the same profound sense of loss. But unlike with my mother, there was something I could do to help. The next day, I met Billy in his office.

"They're going to need help," I said.

Billy was confused. "Who is going to need help?"

"The FBI," I said. "I speak Arabic. I know the religion. I know the culture."

I needed Billy's permission to talk with the FBI. Billy signed off immediately. The next day Jim, the FBI resident agent, met me.

"We're a little slammed," he said.

It was three days after the attack. The Bureau was running down every lead they had on the hijackers. There were reports of meetings in a northern Virginia mosque, of trips to flight schools in Florida, and of post office boxes and checks cashed in Virginia Beach. Every FBI agent seemed to be working the case.

"What can I do for you?" Jim said.

He looked haggard. His suit jacket was absent. His shirt was wrinkled and he moved with a nervous energy. He hadn't slept for days and likely wouldn't for the next few at least.

"I speak Arabic," I told him. "I'm Sunni Muslim. If there is anything I can do, let me know. I cleared it through my chain of command. I want to help."

"We really appreciate it," Jim said. "We'll definitely be reaching out to you if we need you."

I got the message. Don't call us. We'll call you. The meeting had lasted less than thirty minutes. I followed up with Jim for weeks after the attacks, but he was always too busy to talk. The FBI was waking up to a new war. They could no longer just be cops. They had to adapt to meet a new enemy.

When I arrived in America, Islam just *was*. Now it was the only thing that mattered.

CHAPTER 3

No Fear

The first rule of undercover work is: The day you're not scared anymore is the day you have to get out.

It was the summer of 2008 and I'd been working drugs for ten years. Rico Jordan's cover story led me from the fringe into the heart of the drug scene in New Jersey. I'd picked up some informants who knew I was a cop. One of my best was Jose, a fat Hispanic guy from the neighborhood. His information got more drugs off the street than most detectives. He also elevated Rico Jordan's profile. In the drug world, you're only as good as who you know. Jose was connected to all the players, so by extension, so was Rico Jordan.

My new target was a Dominican crew led by two guys named Manuel and King, who used their limousine service to bring drugs down from Spanish Harlem. Billy only agreed to take on the case after the DEA asked us for help. They wanted Manuel's crew, but they didn't have an undercover who could do it. My source, Jose, already had an in, so the DEA agreed to front the cash.

We met at the office before the first buy. I sat around the table with Billy; Mike, the case agent who would run our side of the investigation; Steve, who used to work with us before transferring to the DEA; and two other DEA supervisors.

"These guys are pretty badass," one of the DEA supervisors told us.

I was bored from the jump. I knew how to handle myself. I lived it every day. I didn't need a bunch of DEA guys in suits who hadn't made a drug buy in decades—if ever—telling me anything. I zoned out for most of the meeting. Then one of the DEA agents mentioned something about Bangkok.

"Sorry?" I said. "What did you say?"

"We've gotten information about a large shipment of heroin coming in from Bangkok," one of the DEA supervisors said.

I smiled like a junior high school kid. I caught Mike's eye. He and I had worked together for years. He was a big Italian guy with piercing blue eyes. I was his undercover. We had made a lot of great cases together. We also had the same sense of humor.

Mike giggled.

I snorted, trying to hold in a laugh, and covered my mouth with my hand. The DEA supervisor giving the briefing hesitated for a second. I could feel Billy's eyes on me. I glanced up. He had the look of an embarrassed parent.

"What the fuck is going on?" he said.

"Sorry, boss," I said. "He said Bangkok."

Billy and the DEA agents just stared at me and Mike. Steve knew us too well and laughed.

"Excuse me," I said.

I stepped out of the room. Looking back, I'm embarrassed. The DEA was about to trust me with tens of thousands of dollars and I'm laughing at "Bangkok." I was too cavalier going into the operation.

Living up to his reputation, Jose set up an introductory meeting with Manuel at a downtown row house in New Jersey. They were sniffing me out. If this meeting went well, I'd meet the supplier.

The humidity hit me the second I climbed out of my car, but everything else seemed right. My spotters were in place. Jose was waiting in front of the house. He was holding a can of Coke. I never saw him without a can, and never the diet stuff.

Jose knocked and a tall Dominican opened the door. He had a scraggly beard and was wearing a tank top with a pile of chest hair climbing out the front.

"Your boy is downstairs," he said.

We followed him through the house to the basement door. I cased the place as we walked. There were toys on the floor and the table was clogged with mail. The row house looked lived in and not by a bunch of gangsters. A family lived here.

Jose went down the wooden stairs first. I followed. The Dominican bolted the door. Manuel was standing in the middle of the room with another bodyguard. He had a massive gut. It stuck out like a pregnant woman's stomach. A skinny beard framed his face. He was still dressed from his shift driving one of the limos; his dress shirt was unbuttoned at the neck and his black slacks were wrinkled.

The basement was unfinished. Everything had a musty smell, but it was cooler than being on the street. A small table sat in the middle of the room. Chairs were arranged around it. I spotted some trash bags in one corner. The only way in or out was through the bolted door at the top of the stairs, but I wasn't worried. I wasn't going to die in this basement. Something about doing a drug deal with a guy in business casual set my mind at ease.

We gathered around the table. Manuel and Jose made the introductions. I wanted to buy a few ounces of cocaine to start. My goal was to make Manuel believe this was an ongoing thing. Five kilos a month forever and ever, amen.

"Give me the right price," I said. "I don't want it to go up."

Manuel wanted five thousand a month on top of the price for the cocaine.

"Fuck you, I ain't paying that shit," I said.

I was flippant. Dismissive. Cocky. It didn't matter that I was in a basement with only one way out.

Manuel insisted. The extra money was for delivery. He was offering to bring five kilos of coke to my door once a month.

"You're out of your fucking mind," I said. "Why am I going to pay so much? I can drive up to New York myself and buy it anywhere in Spanish Harlem."

The second rule in undercover work is to always deescalate. Don't take control of the situation like a cop. You don't control the room. But I wasn't following the rules. A smirk creased my lips as Manuel explained the economics of drug dealing.

"I get what a delivery charge is," I said, leaning back in my chair. "But you're fucking bending me over."

Jose was looking at me. His eyes asked what I was doing and his face said stop.

"Come on, Rico," he said when I ignored him. "Let's just get a taste to start and work out the price next time."

He calmed everything down with one sentence. Manuel looked at him and then at me.

"Let's get the taste and then we'll see what's what," I said. "We can finalize the price when I meet your guy."

I made the first buy without incident. Now we were in business. Manuel agreed to deliver one kilogram of cocaine and a thousand pills of Ecstasy. He also agreed to bring the supplier.

Billy was pissed when he heard we met in a basement.

"We're not meeting there again," he told me during the debrief. "Find a new place."

We set the next buy in a row house we could control. It was wired with video cameras and microphones. Billy staged the arrest team around the corner. Jose and I waited for Manuel and his boss, King, to show up. They were driving down from New York. We had them under surveillance the whole ride.

Mike picked them up when they got near the house. He was driving a gold Ford Taurus and drove right up behind the limousine as soon as they got close.

"Got 'em," he said over the radio.

Mike was notorious for bumper-locking suspects. Instead of shadowing them on parallel streets, he jumped into their backseat and hounded them like a guy late for a meeting. I warned him about it before the buy, but he ignored me. Mike followed Manuel for a few blocks and then peeled off just before they arrived.

Jose and I saw the limousine pull up. It sat idling for a few minutes. No one moved. I could hear Manuel put the car in gear. He eased it off the curb and drove off.

"Where is he going?"

Jose just shrugged.

"We've been burned," I said. "Fucking Mike."

I lit a cigarette just as Manuel rolled to a stop at the curb again. He walked to the trunk and took out a gym bag. King climbed out of the back and joined Manuel in front of the house.

King was about forty years old with a lean build, short cropped black hair, dark brown eyes, and a scar on his forehead. He was dressed like a drug dealer trying to look like a businessman. Nice pants, but baggy. A designer button-down dress shirt with rolled-up sleeves and opened in front so you could see his Guinea tee and gold chains. He wore a gold pinky ring. His pinky had a very long fingernail—a coke nail—used to scoop and sniff cocaine.

Manuel and King were speaking in rapid-fire Spanish as they walked up to the house. It took Jose a second to figure out what was being said.

"There was a white guy in a gold car," Manuel said to me in English. "He was following us."

"You're talking about crazy Eric," I said, waving my hand like I was shooing him away. "That fucking guy follows people around all the time out here."

To this day, I still have no idea how I pulled that out of my ass. Even now, guys in the department still talk about Crazy Eric. Manuel wasn't sure if I was kidding or not. But it wasn't what I was saying. It was how I said it. I was calm and they believed I was taking the same risk as they were.

"He's a crazy white guy that follows everybody," I said, shrugging and turning to enter the house. "Don't worry about him. He's a nobody."

Jose laughed.

Manuel relaxed.

Ice broken.

We settled into the living room. King's English wasn't very good, so Manuel translated. King took out a kilo of cocaine and started to unwrap the tape. Then the foil. Then the plastic. At one point, Jose handed King a butcher knife to cut through the wrapping. I shot him a glance. Nice job giving the drug dealer a weapon. King got through the tape and plastic, but he couldn't get through the foil. I was losing my patience.

"Who the fuck wrapped this?" I said.

King stopped and looked at me.

"I did," King said.

"Yeah, that's right," I said, nodding like I approved. "You've got to keep that shit tight."

My frustration changed to a compliment in a breath.

King finally got it open enough for me to dip a finger into the powder. Cops can't take drugs. Well, they can in extraordinary situations, but it becomes a lot of paperwork. But I had this trick. I dipped my middle finger into the cocaine and moved my hand up to my mouth to taste it. I turned my head just a bit so King couldn't see my hand and I swapped my middle finger for my pointer finger. The movement sent a subliminal message to King that I tasted it. But I really put my clean pointer finger into my mouth.

"Yeah, that's good," I said. "Jose, why don't you go and get the cash."

We didn't want Jose in the house when the raid happened. Plus, a good drug dealer would never have the money and drugs at the same location, so it didn't seem out of place for Jose to leave.

Jose knew to leave the front door unlocked for the arrest team.

He had a cold Coke in his hand and left the can on a table by the door. I stubbed out my cigarette. I knew once Jose left it was only a matter of time before we got hit. I tried to chat with Manuel and King, but it was hard. I just wanted to get arrested so I could finish up my paperwork and go home. I had plans that night.

The front door opened with a bang. We all froze. I knew they were coming, and it still scared the hell out of me. There's nothing like staring down the barrel of a dozen Glocks and machine guns.

The DEA agents crashed into the table, spilling the soda all over the linoleum floor. Manuel bolted for the front door and ran headlong into Steve. They scuffled for a second and then Steve slipped on the spilled soda. They both tumbled to the floor.

"That is a classified DEA technique," Steve told me later as we watched the video of the takedown back at the office. "I can't tell you any more about it."

Since everything was going to be on video, Billy had reminded us to be professional just before we started the operation. He didn't want his men to look stupid in court.

"Let's put everybody in custody," he said. "Once the house is secure, shut that shit off."

I went right down. No slapping. No fighting. I didn't talk shit. The agents arrested Manuel and King. Both men were on the couch and I was facedown on the floor. Billy was the last one inside. He saw the drugs on the table. A smile spread across his lips.

"Po-lice, muthafuckers," he said, like a true professional.

A few weeks later, I had to listen to all of the recordings. We were preparing the file for court. I sat for hours at my desk listening to myself talk with Manuel. That was when it hit me. I didn't give a fuck. I wasn't scared anymore. Contrast that with my first buy. That was fear. I was so scared I missed an eagle neck tattoo. Somewhere in between, I found the happy middle. Just the right amount of fear to keep me focused and safe. But after ten years on the street, I had traded my fear for arrogance. I refused to acknowledge it because I was the unit's eyes and ears. But I knew it in my heart. I was burned out.

Billy came by my desk the night before we started a new investigation.

"Hey," he said. "You need to go down to the state police office tomorrow at ten and get a new license. It's all set up. They're waiting for you."

The New Jersey State Police had a special office for undercovers. I arrived wearing my scumbag clothes. I skipped the lobby and snuck into the office from a side door. I didn't want to sign in or be seen. The office wasn't far from where I made my buys.

"Hey, Sarge, I'm here for my ten A.M.," I said to the state trooper in the waiting room.

The state trooper waved me toward a line of chairs along the wall.

"Have a seat," he said. "I'll be right with you."

I found a chair near the end and stretched out my legs. Even in our special DMV we still had to wait. A few minutes later, a man stomped into the room in black jeans and motorcycle boots. He looked like the love child of a mobster and a biker. He was Joe Pesci short, with a slicked-back salt-and-pepper ponytail and a huge cross tattoo on his right forearm. He took a seat nearby.

Who the fuck was this guy? Why was he back here with me?

I could feel my blood pressure building. I couldn't believe they let a shithead in here with me. I looked over at the state trooper. He was shuffling papers and didn't notice the guy.

The biker fished a silver BlackBerry out of his jacket and powered it up. He held it at arm's length, like it might bite him. The font on the screen was huge. I could see the screen from where I was sitting. The first e-mail header was from the Department of Justice. I relaxed.

"Yo, my man," I said. "Who you with?"

He took off his tiny round John Lennon sunglasses and looked me up and down.

"Who you wit?"

He sounded like an extra from *Goodfellas*.

"How are you doing?" I said, breaking the ice. "I work undercover narcotics."

"I'm Vinnie," he said. "I'm the assistant undercover coordinator for the FBI's Newark division. Great to meet you. What are you doing here? Is it for a case?"

I shook my head.

"Nah, it's not for a case," I said. "It's all I do."

Vinnie cocked his head. He wasn't tracking. Most local departments didn't run long-term undercovers.

"What do you mean?" he said.

I just do undercover drug work, I told him.

"Really," Vinnie said. "What nationality are you?"

"I'm Egyptian."

He turned his whole body to face me. Ten minutes later he knew I was born in the Middle East. He knew I spoke Arabic and I had ten years of undercover experience.

"When we're done here, can I buy you a cup of coffee?"

"Sure," I said.

I found out later the FBI was having trouble getting Arabic speakers through the undercover program. Vinnie was of the mindset that it was great if you could speak a language, but the undercover skill set was even harder to find.

We found a coffee shop a couple of blocks from the office and took a table near the back. At a glance, we looked like two scumbags enjoying coffee. *The Wire* meets *The Sopranos*.

"It's funny, I reached out to the Bureau right after nine-eleven," I said. "I went in there to offer my services."

"Listen, after nine-eleven, it was a cluster fuck," Vinnie said. "We've come a long way since then."

We talked for a little while longer. He was interviewing me. Finally, he gave me his number.

"We'd love for you to come and help us out with a case," he said.

Back at headquarters, I went into Billy's office and shut the door.

"I met this guy," I said. "He is with the FBI. They want me to help them with a case."

Billy folded his hands. The urgency of the attacks on September 11 had worn off. It was 2008. He wasn't keen on losing his only undercover. But he also knew this was something I wanted to do. It was something I needed to do.

"Have him reach out to me," Billy said.

A few days later, Vinnie called Billy. Vinnie's team was investigating a gang of Turks bringing in Middle Eastern illegals from Mexico. The FBI feared the human traffickers were also bringing in terrorists. None of Vinnie's men could get close to the ringleaders. They needed a Middle Easterner.

Billy knew once I was exposed to the Bureau there was no way I was coming back to drug work. But he couldn't say no to the FBI's request. He knew what it meant to me. So when Vinnie called, Billy had only one request.

"Look out for my boy."

CHAPTER 4

Dirty Arabs Group

I met Vinnie at the FBI office in Newark a few weeks later.

"Kid, you need a legend," Vinnie said.

"What's that?"

"Come up with a name," Vinnie said. "And then leave the rest to us. We'll make you real."

It was pretty much what I did with Rico Jordan, but I didn't know the terminology. I picked an old family name and cooked up a story about a property manager who didn't want to bother with the visa process because getting people in from the Middle East was a pain. I was looking for a way around immigration laws. Vinnie loved it.

The next week I pulled into an abandoned strip mall in southern Jersey, just across the Delaware River from Philadelphia. It was a crisp day in early fall of 2008 and I was going to meet Ali—the gang's leader.

The strip mall was deserted. I pulled around the back. A fleet of government sedans with blacked-out windows and antennas sticking out like porcupine quills was parked behind the empty stores. Everything screamed feds.

I knocked on the back door and an agent showed me to a makeshift command center. Computers and recording equipment were set up on plastic folding tables. All the FBI agents were in 5.11 Tactical pants and blue polo shirts.

I sat down on a folding chair and started to put on my wire. The case agent, Victor, began to go through the operation. I was headed to a hookah bar owned by Ali. He usually arrived in the early evening for dinner. My job was to meet him and start building rapport.

"These guys are your backup," the agent said, nodding toward four guys in polos. "Where do you want us to set up? There is a parking lot in front of the place."

It was culture shock. I was used to my guys. My spotters could blend into the neighborhood. They looked the part and knew the streets. These guys looked like lawyers or accountants with guns.

"No," I said. "How about you guys stay here. If you want to drive up and down the highway, be my guest. Don't pull into the parking lot. Hell, don't get those vehicles near that parking lot. I'm a new face. If they put together a new face with your cars, this case is over before it starts."

The FBI guys looked around. I could tell they thought I was a diva. I was. But I was also the guy going into the bar.

"We'll do it your way," Victor said with a shrug.

The hookah bar was tucked into a modest shopping center with a grocery store, a sandwich shop, and a pharmacy. The place was packed. I checked my watch. It was barely five o'clock.

Don't these people work?

The cacophony of backgammon and card games and the low roar of men arguing sports and politics over thick Turkish coffee hit me when I stepped inside. The clank of spoons hitting cups of the thick brew mixed with the smell of coffee and roast meat attacked my senses. Waitresses moved around the room delivering plates of food and drinks from the bar.

Ali was supposed to arrive in a half hour. I wanted my face seen first. At the bar, I ordered a plate of kofta, a grilled dish of minced meat made from a mix of lamb and beef and served with tzatziki, or yogurt sauce. I met a Turk who ran a construction crew. He was sipping a cup of coffee. I introduced myself. He asked me what I did, and all of a sudden my legend kicked in.

A waitress brought over my food, and I turned and surveyed the room. The only open table was in the back. I walked over and put my plate down. I got looks from everyone in the room.

Who are you?

I sat down with my back to the front door and started to eat. I wanted to look like a guy enjoying a meal, not a cop. As I dipped into my kofta, I felt someone standing behind me. I cut another bite and then looked over my shoulder. Ali had a grin on his face. *Do you have any idea how badly you messed up?* it said.

Ali was in his late forties. His dress shirt was unbuttoned one or two buttons too far. A shock of gray hair peeked out of the fold of his shirt. His more-salt-than-pepper hair was slicked back and his cheeks had a calculated level of scruff—more groomed than missing a razor. Fit and lean, Ali could handle himself.

I heard Rico Jordan in my head. *"What the fuck are you looking at?"*

My new legend said the opposite.

"I'm so sorry," I said. "Is this your table?"

"It is," Ali said. "But you're already eating."

"No," I said. "I'll stand by the bar. I'm sorry."

I started to gather my plate and utensils.

"No," Ali said. "Finish your dinner."

My Middle Eastern manners kicked in.

"Sit with me," I said. "Please. I didn't mean to take your table and interrupt your dinner."

Ali moved to one of the open seats. He signaled the bar with a wave and sat down. A waitress came out a minute later with a plate of mixed kabobs with rice and a plate piled high with fresh vegetables. That spoke volumes and he knew it. Between bites, I told him how I was in town looking at some properties. A friend told me about the restaurant. I decided to stop for a bite on the way home.

"I didn't realize how crowded it was," I said. "I didn't mean to step on your toes by sitting here."

Ali just shook his head.

"Absolutely not," he said. "You didn't step on my toes. How is your food?"

"Spectacular," I said.

And it was. It was the only thing I wasn't lying about. Over tea, I started to dump more of my legend.

"I'm having trouble finding workers," I said. "Good Muslim brothers."

"That is a problem," he said.

Ali told me he owned two restaurants as well as a cell phone shop nearby. We talked about the area and business opportunities. He liked being seen as a player with his hand in as much of the action as possible. So I did what I do. I made him like me. I made him laugh. I made him feel happy to be around me. I made him feel good about himself without kissing his ass. At the end of the meal, he gave me his contact information. Cell phone. E-mail.

"Next time you call me," he told me, handing me a card with a couple of numbers written on the back, "I'll take you to a better spot for dinner. I'm a part owner there too."

"I'll call you when I know I'm coming back," I said, shaking his hand.

An hour later, after making sure I wasn't followed, I sat down at the abandoned strip mall. The 5.11 pants were huddled around me as I debriefed. I walked them through the room, giving them details about the patrons and Ali.

"Should we record this?" one of the agents asked.

"No," I said. "We recorded the meet. I'll write a detailed report of the other stuff."

I saw a couple of agents exchange glances when I got to the part about Ali's table.

"You sat down at his table?"

"There was nowhere else to sit," I said. "What do you want me to do? I went there to eat. I couldn't stand at the bar. That would be weird."

I handed the agents Ali's card.

"Holy shit, he gave you his personal cell?" an agent said. "We didn't have that number."

Victor high-fived a fellow agent. It was so dorky it made my teeth itch.

"Hey," I said. "Let's not start sucking each other's dicks just yet. I just got a phone number."

The air went right out of the room. They didn't get the reference. *Pulp Fiction*. The Wolf.

Two of the agents looked horrified. One guy put his hands in his pockets and looked down at his boots. Victor, who was trying to be cool, looked away. I didn't know what to do. Explaining the joke felt weirder.

"I'm out of here," I said, patting Victor on the back. "I'll get you that report."

I got in my car and drove off. I could only imagine what they told Vinnie. During the investigation, Victor kept him in the loop. He called me a few days after I met Ali with some pointers. He told me if I did well, there was a good chance I could do some work on the dark side of the house.

"The dark side?" I said.

"The FBI is split into two," Vinnie said. "We have a CT [counterterrorism] side of the house and we have a criminal side of the house. Right now, you're helping the criminal side. Do a good job on this case and you'll get a chance at the CT side."

I was used to doing drug operations. In the drug world, it was hurry up and make the buys because funding and manpower were always at a premium. The FBI's mind-set was slower. Undercover work was an art form. I had months to ingratiate myself. Become friends. Be there for them. Then take them down. My legend had to be fully rounded. It couldn't be like Rico Jordan—an attitude with a name. It had to be a real person. A guy Ali liked.

After several more meetings at the hookah bar, we met at his

Turkish restaurant. It wasn't far from the hookah bar but didn't cater to an almost all Middle Eastern clientele. Ali again had the best table in the place, toward the back and away from the noise of other diners.

Dinner was a whole fried fish. It sat in the middle of the table. We picked at it with our hands. Plates of fresh vegetables and bread crowded around the fish platter. As we ate, I had to make up stories about a fake wife and a fake uncle who owned the properties. Some of the stories were taken from my own life with the details switched. At the end of dinner, Ali took out a bottle of raki, or Turkish moonshine. He poured a few glasses, for me and some of his associates. When he added a little water to it, it turned milky.

"*Şerefe!*" he said.

Cheers, or literally, to honor, in Turkish.

We all drank. It tasted like water with a kick. After a couple of glasses, Ali started to talk about his time in prison. He had been convicted of passport fraud. An informant—a rat—dimed him out.

"Fucking rats," I said. "I hate them."

Ali stopped talking and looked at me. I had yelled it so loud I'd startled him. Hell, I startled myself. A silence fell over the table. I took another bite of fish.

What the fuck was that? I thought.

"Excuse me," I said.

I was drunk. It felt like someone tipped the room on its side. I practically dove into the bathroom. Gripping the sink with one hand, I splashed water on my face.

I hate rats? What is wrong with you? Why is your face so red?

The agents listening to the wire told me later they couldn't stop laughing. When I got back to the table, Ali eyeballed me for a second. When it was clear I wasn't wasted, he was ready to do some business. He explained how the immigrants fly into South American countries with no visa requirements. He gets them to Mexico and trucks them into Texas, where he gets them fake identities. That was enough to lock him up. We had everything on tape.

After Ali was arrested, Vinnie called me with an offer. The New Jersey State Police had asked the FBI to do a weeklong undercover school. The Bureau agreed, as long as I could take one slot. As a student. At first I balked. I had ten years of experience. What was I going to learn in a school?

"Yeah, I know," Vinnie said, anticipating the pushback. "But there are some FBI-type scenarios I'd love to run you through. I want my guys from Headquarters to take a look at you in action."

They wanted to see if I could come close to passing the FBI Undercover School. The weeklong course at the New Jersey State Police Academy was intense. We did classroom work and role-playing. The scenarios ranged from drug buys—which were second nature—to murder for hire. I impressed the powers that be and got a formal offer from the FBI. They wanted me to join the Bureau's Joint Terrorism Task Force, a local, state, and federal law enforcement partnership spearheading the fight against terrorism. I had to go through all of the background investigations and polygraph tests before I received my security clearance.

The final hurdle was the FBI Undercover School. It didn't matter that I passed the state version. To work as an undercover in the FBI, you have to be certified. The school has a 50 percent graduation rate. It's a small and elite fraternity.

The location of the FBI Undercover School alternates among

major American cities. It's two weeks of the most intense training I've ever received. Every minute was planned. If we weren't in a classroom learning about techniques, we were practicing them in role-playing scenarios. Sometimes it was a fake bar meeting. Sometimes a meeting in a hotel room. Since the techniques are being used every day to keep America safe, I won't get into too much detail. By the end of the two weeks, I was exhausted both mentally and physically. But I also felt more confident in my abilities. One of the proudest moments in my career was getting pinned.

I returned to the Newark office after training. The FBI is a collection of kingdoms. Each special agent in charge runs his region. Everyone is territorial, and Vinnie kept me on a tight leash. He had one of the few Arabic-speaking Muslim undercovers and wasn't keen on letting me out of his sight.

But Headquarters had other plans. They were putting together a counterterrorism undercover unit. I nicknamed it the "Dirty Arabs Group." It was designed to eliminate the red tape and bureaucracy of getting an undercover in front of a potential terrorist on U.S. soil.

I met the team in Los Angeles. We were headed to the Howard Fine Acting Studio and then to our first briefings. Our acting coach, Howard, had trained some of the biggest names in Hollywood. He shut down his school for the week to work with us.

Howard taught us how to tap into emotions that we already had and use them to be believable. He helped us focus on character so our legends came to life with real emotion. I have no doubt his training saved my life as much as any training I got from the FBI.

Before we left Los Angeles, our supervisor held a final meeting. We gathered around a conference room table as he read down the caseload.

"I need someone in Chicago," he said. "And we need a couple of you guys in Jacksonville. A DirecTV installer saw a map of a military base along with 'religious paraphernalia' in an apartment."

I knew right then I was going to want every case. That this was where I belonged.

CHAPTER 5

Tamer Elnoury

The beach house overlooked Monterey Bay.

Every morning, I took my cup of coffee outside after prayers. I walked down to the sand and stood watching the waves. A pregnant sea lion I named Whiskers lived nearby and usually sunned herself on the beach near the house. The sound of the surf and the sea air soothed me. I could feel the stress drain out of me. It was my few minutes of peace before I rejoined the terrorist living in my guest room.

After working a few low-level cases, I got my first big one. The FBI had a source with connections to al Qaeda's leadership. The group was looking for a financier, and the FBI was happy to provide them with one. The objective was to sell my legend to an Afghan emissary to get face-to-face with his boss. From there, we could follow the chain from boss to boss, eventually getting to al Qaeda's leaders.

Chris, a former marine turned FBI agent, had the case in the San Francisco office. I flew out there a few days before the Afghan arrived. I already had worked up my legend—Tamer Elnoury—a wealthy Egyptian-American real estate developer whose views had become more radical in recent years.

Tamer's story started with his uncle in the 1980s. Tamer's uncle bought two row houses for twenty thousand dollars in New Jersey. He went down to city hall and convinced them his investment would expand the tax base. That investment turned into one hundred and fifty thousand in less than two years. Tamer's uncle sold the pair of row homes and bought more. In five years, he owned more than twenty houses in New Jersey and had created the Elnoury real estate empire. Eventually, Tamer's uncle needed help and he asked Tamer to come on as a property manager after Tamer's mother died.

But I had to change my mind-set. It wasn't enough to be a criminal. I needed an ideology. A reason why my legend wanted to commit terrorist acts.

During our acting training, Howard had urged us to come up with a backstory. We took that idea and created our "point of radicalization." For Tamer, it was his mother's death. I used my own mother as the basis, but twisted up the facts. After her death, Tamer was ready to leave the country, but his uncle convinced him to stay. Run the business and send the profits to al Qaeda in the Arabian Peninsula.

In my legend, Tamer took the business to the next level. Elnoury Investments bought beach houses and commercial property and the profits flowed overseas. Tamer grew the business from slumlords in New Jersey to commercial developers in New York.

Real estate was tricky because so many people know it or think they do. I was on the fence about using it at first. But then I remembered that James, one of my spotters when I worked drugs, was a slumlord. He got into buying homes and flipping them. It was his side business. I stole the idea for Tamer's background.

The FBI unit that backstops our legends brought Tamer to life. They created Tamer's company's website, Facebook page, and financial accounts. All the things that mean you're alive in the modern world. The FBI made sure someone answered the phone at Tamer's office. All e-mails and correspondence had a company logo and letterhead. When the FBI was done, Tamer was a real guy, ready to meet al Qaeda.

The Afghan arrived from the Middle East in the fall of 2011. He was coming to vet me before I met al Qaeda's leadership. We planned to spend about a month together.

The Afghan was tall with a little potbelly. His beard was thick and his eyes were hooded under thick eyebrows, which made him look drowsy.

I took him back to the beach house, which was wired with cameras and microphones in every room. FBI agents monitored the cameras twenty-four hours a day. The first night, I asked the team to disconnect the one in my room. I couldn't sleep knowing someone was watching me. They refused. It was for my security. I hated living in a fishbowl.

The first few days were slow. The Afghan slept off his jet lag and we got to know each other. His Arabic was learned and hard to understand sometimes, but we managed. After three days of being cooped up with him, I took him and the FBI source, who introduced us, to dinner at a nearby seafood restaurant. There were no halal places nearby, so seafood was the easiest choice. The Afghan was dressed in a galabia, the long white Arab robe. Everyone else was in business casual. We stood out.

The waiter came over and I started to order for the table.

"None of us eat pork here," I said. "So if anything has pork in it, will you do us a favor and just let us know? We're going to have water. I'd like to have an iced tea. With extra lime on the side and no lemon."

I stopped and looked at the Afghan.

"Do you want something else instead of water?" I asked in Arabic.

He couldn't muster a word. I was spooked.

"That's it for now," I said to the waiter.

I turned back to the Afghan.

"What's wrong, brother?" I said.

He just shook his head.

"*Masha'Allah,*" he said. "You sound just like they do."

It was the first time he'd heard me speak English. That was the minute I got him. I was what they were looking for—a jihadi, but I talked, dressed, and acted like an American in public.

I spent two more weeks with the Afghan as his people in South Africa, Southeast Asia, and the Middle East vetted me. The FBI was working overtime as they pinged my businesses, checked my records, and made sure Tamer was who he said he was. The vetting allowed us to map their network. After the vetting, the Afghan told me his boss wanted to meet me and Yasser, another undercover posing as a bomb maker. Yasser arrived a couple of weeks into the operation. I wanted the Afghan to know I could recruit.

After a stop in Germany to meet the overseas team, we flew into a country on the Arabian Peninsula. We looked like the odd couple as we walked toward immigration. Yasser was tall—six foot two—with a thick, unruly beard. He was dressed in dress slacks and a button-down shirt. I was the opposite: shorter, groomed, and dressed in a nice suit. As we walked from immigration into the main terminal, I spotted four police officers corralling us.

"Stop talking to me," I said to Yasser.

I thought they were going to grab him. He looked down and I started to move away from him.

"Mr. Elnoury, right this way, sir," one of the officers said.

They were very polite. But they formed a wall blocking me from exiting the terminal.

Keep walking. Keep walking, I thought, as I watched Yasser from the corner of my eye. He walked right past. The police ushered me to a side room. I was met by a supervisor with wavy black hair and piercing eyes that never left my face.

"What brings you here?" the supervisor said, as the other four officers started opening my luggage.

I told him business and pleasure. I was looking for investment properties and on a short vacation. The officer nodded. After he asked me the same question a couple more times in different ways, I realized he was fishing.

"Why did you stop me?" I said after a few minutes.

"You're well dressed," the supervisor said. "You come from America. But you were born in Egypt. You know how Egyptians can get a little crazy sometimes."

He figured I was an Egyptian radical with a U.S. passport, and he was right about Tamer. He knew within the first two minutes not only that I was Egyptian, but from which city and neighborhood based on my accent. He was a brilliant young guy and very good at his job. As we talked, another officer was checking my passport against a database. That was the first real test for my legend and the FBI's backstopping.

The supervisor nodded at my bags.

"Do you mind?"

I smiled.

"No, go ahead."

Three officers started to go through my toiletry bags. The supervisor noticed I had two.

"One man, two toiletry bags?" he said.

"I can't look this good on my own," I said, giving him a smirk.

He laughed. After that, we just made small talk while the officers finished searching my bags. They let me go an hour later and I made it to the hotel, which overlooked the Persian Gulf, around three in the morning. I called Yasser.

"You in your room?"

"Yeah," he said. "You made it? What happened?"

"Come to my room."

"You're all the way on the other side."

"You need to come to my room right now," I said. "You've got to see this place."

My suite made the nicest apartments in New York look like a slum. Each room had a balcony that overlooked the water. Four full bathrooms. The furniture was ornate, decorated with gold accents, and straddled the line between nice and gaudy. The whole country did.

Yasser was floored when he walked into the suite.

"What the hell?" he said, poking his head into the empty rooms. "I thought my room was nice. Do you know you have a bathroom over here?"

"There's a bathroom there too?" I said.

Yasser just shook his head.

"Hey, man, you wanted to be the bomb maker," I said. "I'm the money."

The next morning, the Afghan took us around the city. We saw the malls and the iconic buildings. My eyes darted among the authentic Gulf architecture that seemed to spring up between the glass and steel. Cranes dotted the horizon as newer and taller buildings climbed skyward. Everything was clean and new, like the city had grown out of the desert sand.

We had dinner in a working-class part of town. This was where the guest workers—Bangladeshis, Pakistanis, Indonesians—lived. The Afghan took us to a buffet restaurant with huge silver domes filled with lamb, rice with raisins, and grilled kabobs. Sliced fruit and vegetables took up one whole table. As we dug into our first plate, the call to prayer echoed across the city.

Waiters put cloches over our plates to keep the food warm. People left their bags as we walked across the street to the mosque. For a second I lost myself in prayer. I forgot I was there to meet with a terrorist until we returned to dinner.

"The Sheikh wants to meet you," the Afghan said. "I will pick you up tomorrow afternoon."

The Sheikh was the Afghan's boss, but he answered to the people we wanted: al Qaeda's planners and leaders. We were slowly climbing up the chain.

The Afghan stressed to us this was only an introduction when he met us at the hotel the next day. We picked up the Sheikh around the corner. He was dressed in a suit. Older than the Afghan, he was in his sixties, with a neatly trimmed white beard and deep black eyes.

He climbed into the front seat of the Afghan's SUV and we drove around the city talking about current events, the war in Afghanistan. It was all very vanilla, but I knew the drill. He was checking me out.

"I want to hear your English," he said after almost an hour.

I said a few words to him. He looked at the Afghan and smiled. The Afghan must have told him I spoke perfect English with an American accent. I could tell he was impressed. The Afghan pulled to the curb.

"Let's meet tomorrow in private," the Sheikh said. "We will pick you up at the hotel in the morning."

Every time I left the hotel, the country's security services or al Qaeda tossed my room. They were subtle. Nothing was out of place. But they always missed a piece of tape across the door or something I balanced on the drawer that fell when it opened. I was on everyone's radar, which I took as a compliment. I was doing something right.

But it was also a reminder that, unlike in my drug days, backup wasn't a few minutes away. I was on my own. My only link back home was two proof-of-life calls. Twice a day at a certain time, either Yasser or I had to call our handlers in Europe. This was our signal that we were safe. Code words were in place to relay whatever message we needed to at the time. Missing a proof-of-life would set off alarms. Our handlers would send help, regardless of whether it blew our cover.

After our first meeting with the Sheikh, I didn't sleep. My mind kept running through all the scenarios. I rose at dawn, prayed for the courage to do my job, and dressed for the meeting. The Afghan was out front and we all climbed into his SUV. He drove us in circles for the next hour. Finally, he pulled into a parking lot across the street from a beautiful mosque right on the water and shut off the engine.

"Come on, I want to show you this mosque," the Afghan said.

I shot Yasser a look. Bullshit. The parking lot had only one way in or out. It was easy to see if we were followed. We walked over to the mosque but only visited for a minute before the Afghan ushered us back into the car.

He drove the SUV across the street to a tall apartment building. The biscuit-colored building wasn't shoddy, but it lacked curb appeal. A middle-class workingman's building. The lobby was dark and dusty. The elevator took a minute to arrive. The Afghan hit the button for the twenty-seventh floor and the elevator clattered up the shaft. The door opened into a pitch-black hallway. As soon as the Afghan stepped off the elevator, the lights popped on. Motion sensors.

We followed the Afghan down the hall. He stopped about halfway and opened a door into an apartment. No furniture. Every room was empty. The blinds were open, and we could see the deep blue of the Persian Gulf and the mosque across the street.

The Afghan opened one more door. The Sheikh was sitting on a sectional couch. He stood up when we walked inside. We all greeted one another while the Afghan got a tray with tea and dates. The Sheikh never touched his tea or the dates. I wondered if we were getting poisoned. But to not drink the tea would have been an insult. When the Afghan finally took a sip, I relaxed.

"It would be great if you could support the hospitals and schools in Afghanistan," the Sheikh said.

His cover was the head of a charity, but it was clear before I came that I wanted to support the fight. I was here to help kill Americans. I let him do his pitch. When the Sheikh paused, I cut in.

"Let me ask you something," I said. "You know where I am coming from. You've already checked me out."

The Sheikh nodded.

"We're sitting here and you're telling me about building schools and hospitals," I said. "Let me put it to you this way: You're telling me that one of our brothers has cancer. And you're asking me to buy him a suit. To dress him up. Why don't you ask me to help remove that cancer? We'll worry about what he looks like after."

The Sheikh gave the Afghan a nod. He stood up and left the room. Another door opened and closed. I heard voices in the hall. Yasser shifted in his seat. No one said anything.

The Afghan came back with a twelve-year-old boy in a white robe and kufi—the white skullcap—carrying a laptop. The boy didn't look at anyone. He just sat down next to the Sheikh and put the computer on the table. The Sheikh gave instructions in Dari and the screen soon filled with charts and spreadsheets.

"These are the areas I was describing," the Sheikh said. "But clearly you can be an asset to the brothers in other areas, such as military aid. But these are sensitive areas."

The Sheikh never touched the computer as the boy scrolled through the information.

"We'll have to shield your assets," the Sheikh said.

"Of course," I said. "You have my e-mail. Send me the proposal. If you have a way to receive the money, I'm all ears."

"*Masha'Allah,*" the Sheikh said. "We will contact you."

I was ready to talk specifics, but the Sheikh put his hand on the boy's back, who closed the computer and left. We had an understanding but nothing more. The Afghan stood up and we followed him out.

We were leaving the next night. Our flight departed near midnight, so Yasser and I lounged by the pool the rest of the morning. Just before lunch, I got a call from the Afghan.

"The Sheikh wants to meet," he said. "I'm coming to the hotel."

We met the Afghan in the lobby. There was a seriousness to his movements. This was important and had to be done before we left. The Afghan turned to leave and we followed. He stopped after a few steps.

"I'm going to get the car," he said. "The Sheikh just wants to meet with Tamer. Finish up their discussion from yesterday."

The Afghan walked out, leaving us.

"No fucking way," Yasser said once he was out of earshot.

"Listen, he bought what we were selling," I said. "Let's see what he has to say."

I checked my watch. It was just after 1:00 P.M. and our last proof-of-life call was scheduled for 2:00 P.M.

"I'm not going to make the call," I said. "Make the call for us. Trust me. I'll be fine. We've got to make this happen."

Yasser didn't like it, but he didn't stop me. I jumped into the car and the Afghan drove around the corner to a coffee shop. The Sheikh was waiting there. He climbed into the front seat and we drove a few minutes to an underground garage. The Afghan found a spot in the lowest level. It was dark and quiet.

"Take the battery out of your phone," the Sheikh said as he turned to face me.

I showed him the battery. He smiled.

"Thank you for coming," he said. "You're going to be the reason we win this war."

The Sheikh laid out the plan. They needed money for weapons.

My point of contact was the Afghan. The Sheikh wanted me to wire him money that I raised through my business. I had an envelope with a few thousand dollars in it and handed it over as a goodwill gesture.

"It is very important to me that this money go directly to our leaders," I said to the Sheikh. "Can you assure me of that?"

I also had a message for al Qaeda's leaders.

"I can help brothers come to America," I said.

Our business was done. I checked my watch. It was close to time for the proof-of-life call, but the Sheikh kept talking. We were friends now. The Sheikh asked me to fly to his home in South Africa in a few months. Not for business, but because he wanted to host me at his home. We also talked about setting up bank accounts so I could send them money.

I watched the hands of my watch blow past 2:00 P.M.

A half hour.

One hour.

Finally, the Sheikh thanked me for the money and agreed to pass along my offer to get American visas for like-minded brothers.

By the time I finally got back to the hotel, I was three hours late. The Afghan dropped me off and I walked into the lobby. Yasser was in the same spot as when I'd left. He was a mess. He had tried to call me, but of course my phone didn't work.

"I don't know whether to punch you in your fucking face or kiss your lips," Yasser said.

He hugged me.

"Let's go to the room," I said.

In the suite, I told Yasser that the Sheikh confirmed everything. Tamer was now going to provide money to al Qaeda, and the Sheikh agreed to deliver my visa offer.

For the next few months, I kept in touch with the Afghan and the Sheikh. No money was exchanged, but we were both working toward it. We'd set the trap with the visa offer; now we just had to wait for the Afghan to deliver it. I was working with Chris to set up another trip overseas to visit the Sheikh when he called me.

"Our boy is on his way to Kabul," Chris said. "Looks like they took the bait."

"That's awesome," I said. "We have coverage?"

"Yeah," he said. "I'll let you know."

The very next day I got another call from Chris. The Afghan had been picked up.

"They took him into custody for special conversations," Chris said.

"What does that mean?" I said.

"Don't know," Chris said. "I'll let you know when I do."

Then, in late spring, I noticed a breaking news scroll flash across the TV screen. A drone attack in Pakistan. The target was one of the al Qaeda planners on our list.

My phone buzzed. It was a text message from Chris.

"It's over. I'll call you later."

A few hours later, Chris called. After he was brought in, the Afghan had held out for two weeks before he gave up his mission and Tamer. His confession had led to the drone strike. Because of it, one of al Qaeda's chief planners was dead. The operation was a success.

"What about Tamer?" I said.

"You're good," he said. "The military folks scrubbed everything. Tamer's clean. Your legend is still intact."

CHAPTER 6

"Take His Temperature"

My cell phone rang as I lounged in my undercover apartment in St. Louis.

I recognized the number. It was FBI Headquarters in Washington. Suhel, my supervisor, was on the line. I could tell he needed a favor as soon as I answered.

"Hey, we've got a case out of New York," Suhel said. "It's a Canadian guy in Montreal. We need you to take his temperature."

Shit. I rubbed my temple and took a deep breath. I hated to say no, but I was jammed. I didn't have a moment to spare. Since returning from the Middle East, I'd jumped back into my caseload.

"I'd love to help, but I'm in St. Louis today," I said. "I've got to be in Jacksonville at the end of the week and I've got a case in Tennessee. I've got to be in L.A. for two weeks at the end of the month."

Suhel was prepared for my answer. He must have studied the large board that took up one wall of the unit's Washington office. Each undercover agent had his own row with color-coded magnets for each case he or she was working. The colors—red, yellow, green—signified where each case stood. Next to my designation were two rows. I had six cases across the country in addition to the overseas mission.

"We know," Suhel said. "But we think this is a very bad guy and we need a Muslim and Arabic speaker. He is flying to California for a conference in a month or so. Just take his temperature. It's a three- or four-day babysitting assignment."

"Fine," I said. "I'll drive up to New York and meet with the case agents when I get back from Florida."

I had no choice. I wouldn't be able to live with myself if this guy killed people and I hadn't intervened. This is what I signed up to do.

A week later, I fought the Holland Tunnel traffic and arrived at the Joint Terrorism Task Force offices on the west side of Manhattan. I badged my way in and was ushered into a conference room. I shook hands with the two case agents, who had come straight from central casting: drab suits, conservative haircuts, no regional accent. They introduced themselves and I started the meeting by telling them all about myself, the different legends I had, and my level of experience.

"We think we can get you in front of him," the male agent said, looking at the case file. "Which legend do you want to use?"

I had several. But I needed more information before I could figure out which one would work.

"Do you have any idea when he'll be flying?"

The agents looked at each other.

"No."

That was weird. Headquarters said he was going to California in a few weeks.

"He speaks Arabic, right?"

More confusion.

"We don't know if he speaks Arabic," the female agent said.

"I'm sorry," I said. "I thought he was Tunisian."

"No, he is Bangladeshi," the male agent said.

Now everyone was confused.

"Are you looking for CT-1?" the female agent said.

"Yeah."

"This is CT-4."

I was in the wrong room. I gathered up my notebook and stood up to leave.

"Sorry," I said. "Can you point me in the right direction?"

The male agent shut the door.

"Now you can't leave," he said with a smile. "You're ours now."

I laughed. We talked for a few more minutes about the case. They were investigating Quazi Mohammad Rezwanul Ahsan Nafis, a native of Bangladesh who had links to al Qaeda. I knew the undercover officer they were going to use.

"Listen, the guy you're getting is a great guy," I said. "But I'll make myself available if you need me."

A couple of months later, after meeting with another FBI undercover agent, Nafis was arrested for plotting to remotely detonate a bomb in front of the Federal Reserve Bank of New York in lower Manhattan. He pled guilty in February 2013 and was sentenced to thirty years in prison.

The male agent walked me over to CT-1. Nelly—a short Colombian with coffee-colored skin—greeted me at the door.

"I almost got sucked into that," I said, looking back as the agent from CT-4 walked away.

"Fuck those guys," Nelly said. "You're with us."

CT-1 was the task force's international, extraterritorial squad, known historically as the al Qaeda squad. It worked the 1993 World Trade Center bombing, the 2000 USS *Cole* attack in Yemen, and arrested and thwarted the 2007 plot to blow up jet fuel supply tanks and pipelines at JFK Airport. The squad was known across the FBI as the premiere counterterror unit in the country.

Nelly ushered me into their conference room. A New York City detective assigned to the Joint Terrorism Task Force, Nelly joined CT-1 in 2005 after working in a citywide anti-gun unit. Besides working terrorism cases in the United States, he assisted with cases worldwide, including going overseas after a suicide bombing attempt in Stockholm, Sweden, in 2010.

We were joined by Johnny, another NYPD detective on the task force, who worked homicides and robbery before joining CT-1. His nickname was "mini-Hulk" because he looked like a giant muscle with his short and stout build. His New York accent was so thick, it sounded fake.

Kenny—a barrel-chested Italian from Boston—was one of the primary case agents on the JFK bombing case. He came off as more of a cop than an FBI agent. Most of the other agents were lawyers with guns. A navy veteran, he also maintained all the surveillance equipment. Without him, we couldn't gather the records needed for a conviction.

The supervisor of CT-1 came and popped his head in to say hello just before we started. He reminded me of Karl Childers—Billy Bob Thornton's character in *Sling Blade*. As he talked, all I could hear in my head was *"I like them French fried potaters."*

When he left, I looked at Nelly.

"What's up with *Sling Blade*?"

Nelly's face lit up and he tried to stifle a laugh.

"That's my boss."

We both started laughing. I know in the first five minutes if I like someone. I loved Nelly. He reminded me of Billy, my old boss when I worked drugs. They were both street cops. I found out later Nelly had also worked drugs in the Bronx before he came to the task force.

Johnny led the meeting. He handled all the intelligence on the case. Our target was Chiheb Esseghaier, a Tunisian citizen living in Montreal. Chiheb had popped up on the FBI's radar after he made contact with some al Qaeda operatives online.

"Over the last two years, the target traveled to Iran twice," Johnny said. "We're not sure why he went to Iran, but we think he went there to train."

While Johnny talked, I flipped through a bunch of top secret folders. I stopped on a flowchart showing the guys Chiheb was talking with and how they were connected to al Qaeda's leadership.

"He may be in the pre-operational phase," Johnny said. "The Canadians have seen an escalation of his countermeasures and recruitment."

Basically, once he was on our radar, we had notified Canadian intelligence. They opened up their own investigation and believed he was acting suspiciously.

"What's he doing in Canada?" I said.

"He's going to school," Johnny said. "He's getting his doctorate."

Chiheb was a doctoral student at Institut National de la Recherche Scientifique, Canada's top research university. He was world-renowned for his work in biological nanotechnology. His research was part of a project developing optical and electrochemical biosensors. But his trips to Iran were a red flag, because as part of his research he had access to infectious diseases.

I looked at the pictures of Chiheb. Thick beard. Shaggy, curly hair. He wore glasses that softened up his jihadi look. He looked more scientist than killer. I compared the current pictures with ones shot soon after he arrived in Canada. He didn't have a beard and looked like an innocent kid.

"The Canadians tried to bump him in Cancún, Mexico, during a conference in 2011," Johnny said. "They weren't able to get close to him."

A bump is a casual meeting. It seemed random and was used to meet a target. The Canadians didn't have a Muslim, so they used a Peruvian Christian. Chiheb's English wasn't that good. The hope was a native Arabic speaker would have a better chance.

"What is his family like?" I said.

Johnny flipped through some pages in the file. Three brothers. Mother and father both alive. The family was mainstream.

"What flipped him from 'As salamu alaikum' to 'I'm going to kill your ass'?" I said. "Something happened."

No one could tell me. Johnny had all the facts, but not his pattern of life.

"What does he do on Saturday night? Where does he eat? What does he do after the mosque on Friday? Is he an early riser?"

Everyone looked at one another like I had two heads. Why did I want to know all that?

"You're asking me to get in front of this guy and develop a relationship with him," I said. "We've swung and missed in the past. I need to know how I'm going to craft my legend to make sure he chooses me. I want him to go to bed at night thinking about me. I want him asking himself what he can do for me. How can he make me his friend?"

The lightbulb went on. Nelly and Johnny both nodded in agreement.

"We're on it," Nelly said. "We'll get you a better pattern of life."

The meeting ended with Nelly taking down my list of questions. As he walked me out, he promised to get on the phone with his counterpart in Canada. We agreed to meet a week later to review the findings and work on my legend.

On my ride home, I went over the facts of the case. A lot of these bumps get blown out of proportion. Most times it is just some ass-hole talking shit. All bark. But something wasn't right with Chiheb. His trip to Iran was troubling. He met with and talked online with bad guys.

But first, I had to learn more about him. Did he like to smoke hookah? Was he like the September 11 hijackers and have a thing for strippers? I needed a thread to pull. A week later, I was back in New York in the same conference room with Nelly, Kenny, and Johnny.

"The guy is all about Islam," Johnny said.

"What do you mean?" I said.

"All he does is talk about religion," Johnny said. "But he stopped going to the mosque."

As soon as Johnny said that, my heart sank. It was said in pass-ing, and Johnny was already on to his next point when I stopped him.

"Johnny, did you say he stopped going to the mosque?"

Johnny flipped back through his notes.

"Yeah," he said. "He used to go to a mosque around the corner from his place in Montreal. Every Friday. He stopped going shortly after he got back."

"From overseas?" I said.

"Yeah. Why? What's wrong?"

"Was it a radical mosque?" I asked. "The one in Montreal."

"It's a legit stand-up mosque," Johnny said.

"What about the Imam?"

"Nope. Nothing on him."

"Did he go to another mosque?"

"Nope," Johnny said. "He stays home on Fridays. If he's not at work, he's at home."

Mainstream Muslims go to the mosque. If you're radicalized, Muslims in the mosque who aren't as "dedicated to the cause" are going to drive you nuts. They are an affront to Islam, more so than nonbelievers, because radicals feel they should know better.

"I need you to ask what his dialogue was like in Cancún," I said. "Did he say anything about women on the beach?"

"Women?" Johnny said.

"What was his reaction to women in bathing suits?" I said. "Was he angry? Disgusted?"

I saw Nelly and Kenny exchange a puzzled glance.

"In the eyes of the mujahideen, the women on the beach are the types you grab off the streets," I said. "You cut their throats or stone them for not covering themselves. They're whores."

"We'll call the Canadians tomorrow and hit you back," Johnny said.

But he didn't wait until tomorrow. On my way home, my cell phone rang. It was Johnny.

"I don't know how you figured this one out, but he was spewing all kinds of shit in Mexico when he saw the women in bathing suits," Johnny said. "He said those women are going to rot in hell-fire. He went out of his way to talk about it."

These were all signs that he was already gone, and the only thread I had to get close to him was Islam. Chiheb didn't have any bad habits. My only way in was to be a recruitable asset. I'd have to be a Muslim, but I'd be hiding my supposed jihadi beliefs. I had to convince him he needed me.

A week before the bump, I was back in New York with Nelly. The plan was to intercept Chiheb on his flight to California. Kenny was working with headquarters to set everything up while Nelly and I worked out my legend.

With little lead time, we decided to use Tamer Elnoury. You're not supposed to use the same legend for multiple cases, but this was just a bump. Plus, Tamer was fully backstopped after his trip to the Middle East. Al Qaeda had already vetted him and he had some attractive qualities. He was born overseas but living in the West. Chiheb could relate. Tamer also had money.

"I have to be wealthy," I said.

"Why?" Nelly said.

"For two reasons. One, I'm going to be traveling a lot. I need a reason to go anywhere and be anywhere. Two, I don't know what his intentions are. Does he want to bring people in? Does he want to just recruit? Whatever his reasons are, you're better off having money."

Nelly got it immediately. Money was the world's best superpower.

"I'm down with that," he said. "Tamer Elnoury is the most interesting man in the world."

"Stay thirsty, my friend," I said.

We were ready. Now all we needed to do was get on the plane.

CHAPTER 7

The Bump

Nelly returned from the hotel's breakfast buffet with bacon piled high on his plate.

I was sitting across from him. Unlike during my drug days, my hair was thicker and my beard was untrimmed like the Prophet's. Most days I could pass as Hispanic or light-skinned black, depending on my haircut, but not now. I was an Arab and there was no mistaking how I felt about pork.

Nelly took a bite of bacon and looked at me. The realization hit him as fast as the salty flavor.

"Shit," he said with a sheepish grin. "I forgot I'm eating breakfast with a Muslim."

I laughed. I didn't know him well yet, but I already felt like I was back with my old narcotics unit. I loved that he was already breaking my balls.

"Bro, we're good as long as you're not stuffing it down my throat."

We were in Houston. It was June 2012 and we had a few hours before Chiheb's bump. For the past several weeks, Nelly and Kenny had worked to set everything up. First it was to be in Chicago. Then Minneapolis. Houston was a last-minute change.

We arrived the night before, and Nelly went over to the FBI office to coordinate everything. I stayed at the hotel alone. I was already Tamer. I'd been in legend since I left home. In my pocket was Tamer's driver's license. His credit cards. His business cards. His phone was in my jacket pocket. My FBI work phone was packed away.

My transformation started before I left my house. Like a batter getting ready to hit, I had a routine that always ended with me sitting on the beach watching the waves. It started with a shower. I washed my true identity away and got dressed in Tamer's clothes. I put on his watch, slid his wallet into my pocket, and charged up his phone. From my house, I drove out to the Jersey Shore. There was something about being near the sea. The natural rhythms of the waves helped me focus. I watched set after set of waves crash against the sand, each one clearing my head so I could fill it with Tamer.

"Hello, my name is Tamer Elnoury," I said out loud as I stared into the surf. "Nice to meet you."

I recited his mother's maiden name, his social security number, and his address over and over until it sounded natural. Passersby figured I was nuts. But it was the only way I knew how to get ready. A half hour later, I put the car in gear as Tamer.

At the airport, I stopped at a restaurant in the terminal to get a bite to eat. At the bar, I introduced myself as Tamer. I even handed out business cards and offered some real estate advice.

Usually I traveled alone, but Nelly forced me to straddle both worlds. As we ate breakfast, he started to fill me in on Chiheb's movements from his apartment in Montreal to the airport.

"He boarded his flight early this morning," Nelly said. "He's headed for Orlando now. From there he will make a stop in Houston before going on to California. We're going to get on his connecting flight from Houston to San Jose."

"Okay," I said. "What are you looking for in this bump?"

I needed to know Nelly's goals. It helped me to know what buttons to push once I was in front of Chiheb. For some reason, it always came out in baseball terms.

"What's a base hit?" I said. "Do you want to just figure out if he is jihadi? Are you looking to develop a relationship with him? Uncover a plot? What is a grand slam in your eyes? What would be the greatest thing I could do to make your case go forward?"

Nelly finished a strip of bacon as he thought about it.

"I want to know if this guy is who we think he is," Nelly said. "And if he is, I want you to get close to him. If you do, I want you to find out everything there is to know about his intentions."

Nelly was treating this as more than just a bump to take his temperature.

"Thanks," I said. "That's what I needed."

I pushed my food around my plate for a few more minutes and then excused myself. I wasn't hungry and I needed to reset. I wanted to get fully into Tamer's legend. Back at my hotel room, I showered again and got dressed. Tamer had money, so I wore a tailored shirt, expensive slacks, and Italian shoes. Except for the untrimmed beard, I looked put-together.

I took a taxi to George Bush Intercontinental Airport and went straight to the gate. I was early, so I took a seat in the corner and fished out my BlackBerry Torch. At a glance, I was checking my e-mail. But my attention was on the waiting area. I'd only seen a picture of Chiheb once. I didn't want to see another picture of him, because I wanted it to seem natural when I saw him at the gate.

When my group was called to board, I saw him. He was wearing a button-down shirt and jeans rolled up so his pant legs never touched the dirty ground. He had an overstuffed laptop bag over his shoulder. He was fidgeting with his ticket. There was a nervous energy. He rocked his weight from foot to foot, trying to burn it off.

I relaxed when I saw him. I was no longer dealing with the unknown. He was right in front of me. I could see him. I could almost touch him. He was two people ahead of me as we boarded. I kept looking down at my phone when he looked back in my direction. I wanted to be surprised when we ended up sitting next to each other. Our seats were in the second row just past first class. But when I got into the cabin, a family was sitting in our row. The man was on the end, with his wife seated in the middle next to their young daughter by the window.

Chiheb was staring at them. He checked his ticket and then looked back at the full row. He waved his hand at a male flight attendant helping passengers with overhead baggage. The flight attendant didn't notice him. I turned my back to Chiheb and flagged down the female flight attendant in the first class section.

"Excuse me," I said. "I believe my seat is messed up."

The female flight attendant looked at me and smiled.

"Sir, I'll be right with you," she said.

She had to wait for the line of passengers to clear.

I kept my eyes on my boarding pass. I could feel Chiheb behind me. Suddenly, he stuck his head around my shoulder.

"Do you speak Arabic?" he asked in Arabic.

"Of course," I said.

"*As salamu alaikum,*" Chiheb said.

"*Wa alaikum al salam wa rahmat'Allah wa barakatu,*" I said, the extended Arabic greeting.

It sent a message about who I was and my religious beliefs.

"I knew it," he said. "I could tell you were a brother."

By now we'd moved to the front of the plane so the other passengers could board. I was doing my best to stay out of the way as passengers brushed by us.

"Where are you from, brother?" I said.

"Tunisia," Chiheb said. "Where are you from?"

"Egypt."

"By the grace of God, what are the chances?" Chiheb said, visibly relieved to have someone to talk with in his native language.

"Sorry, dear brother," I said. "They messed up my seat."

"Me too," he said. "Hold on."

"Sir, we need to sit together," Chiheb told the male flight attendant in heavily accented English. "You have to put us together."

He chose me.

The flight attendant found two open seats next to a European guy in the exit row. I took the middle seat. Chiheb grabbed the aisle. The row was right in front of the female flight attendant's jump seat.

As I sat down, I spotted Nelly and Kenny. Two air marshals were also taking the flight. The flight attendant knew four armed federal agents were on board, but not why. She had no idea who I was. When the flight attendant took her seat, I noticed she kept looking toward Nelly and the other agents.

You're here for them, right? her eyes said. *Please tell me you're here for them.*

It was a three-and-a-half-hour flight to San Jose. After takeoff, Chiheb and I picked up our conversation in Arabic. We covered family, my work, his work, and our hometowns. I mentioned that my uncle still lived in Egypt. Before the drink cart got to us, Chiheb flipped to politics. Islamic politics.

"This *Dunya* doesn't matter," he said.

In his mind, everything a Muslim did in this world, or *Dunya*, was a test. He was earning his place in paradise.

Chiheb started to rail against the munafiqeen, Muslims who are secretly unsympathetic and sought to undermine the Muslim community. The Quran calls them the most dangerous enemies of Islam.

"They are worse than the infidels," Chiheb said. "They have been shown the way and have elected not to choose it. As opposed to the infidels who never had the opportunity."

This was classic fundamentalist talk. It didn't mean he was a terrorist. It just meant he took his religion very seriously. It was a flag, but not necessarily a red one. Not yet.

So far, I was able to balance the conversation. It's a very fine line between agreeing and kissing ass. I wanted to push his buttons. Put him in a position to be the Imam and educate me. Show me what it means to be a real Muslim.

Chiheb's demeanor changed when he talked about the drone strikes in Afghanistan and Pakistan. The Imam was gone. There was anger in his voice.

"The West is killing our women and children," he said. "They are raping our women."

I agreed, citing a passage from the Quran.

"'A life for a life, and an eye for an eye, and a nose for a nose, and an ear for an ear, and a tooth for a tooth, and for all wounds, like for like.'"

Something similar appears in the Bible and the Torah. But I left off the last part:

But whosoever forgoes it by way of charity, it will be for him an expiation. Those who do not judge by what Allah has revealed are indeed the wrongdoers.

The Quran makes it clear human beings are not supposed to be judge and executioner. That is God's job. Humans forgive and forget.

But I knew Chiheb rejected any notion of forgiveness. That is what the jihadis do. Edit out the parts of Islam that get in the way. Leaving it out was a signal. In skipping the last lines, I was like him.

As the flight went by, his body language changed. I could feel his passion and excitement building. He knew I was a like-minded brother. He was leaning so far forward he was practically in my lap.

"What started out as a disastrous trip turned out to be a fateful trip," Chiheb told me just before landing.

Chiheb had no idea when he left his apartment in Montreal that morning that he would fly all over the United States. His itinerary was supposed to have been a more direct route. At each stop he got searched.

"What do you mean, brother?"

"I almost didn't come," he said. "I was so fed up. I kept asking Allah why am I going on this trip if you keep putting roadblocks in front of me? And here we are, dear brother. I was meant to meet you. Allah put us together, Tamer. This is Allah's will."

I believed him. Allah put me in his path to take his temperature. The pilot came over the intercom. We were on final approach.

"Where are you staying?" I asked.

He told me his hotel was a long way from the airport. He planned to take a taxi, but I shook my head no.

"Absolutely not," I said. "I've got nothing until late tomorrow. I want to make sure you're okay. I'm going to drive you myself. My job is to protect you and make sure you're safe. If my brother is visiting me in this country, I am going to make sure my brother is okay."

"May Allah reward you for your blessings and your kindness," Chiheb said.

It was close to midnight when we landed. The airport was deserted except for the cleaning crews. Chiheb followed me to the rental car area after we retrieved our bags. We bypassed the desks and went to the VIP area. Nelly had arranged a luxury rental car. Chiheb followed me as I was greeted by a clerk. The car was running next to the curb.

"Hello, Mr. Elnoury," the clerk said. "Your car is ready."

No signatures. No paperwork. He just took our bags and put them in the trunk. I climbed into the driver's seat of the Mercedes sedan and punched in the address of Chiheb's hotel. It was 1:00 A.M. by the time we arrived. I helped him get settled in his room. It was a modest room with two double beds. Chiheb put his suitcase on one bed.

"Look, I have two beds here," Chiheb said. "I insist you stay with me."

He was trying to return my hospitality. I thanked him but declined.

"I've got meetings tomorrow," I said. "I'm going to go to my hotel and check in and get settled."

"Can we have dinner tomorrow?" he asked.

"I'd love to," I said. "I should be done by dinner. Give me a call."

Chiheb walked me to the door of his room.

"Brother, do you need anything else?"

Chiheb shook his head no.

"I'm eating," he said. "I'm sleeping. I'm praying. I have all that I need, dear brother."

CHAPTER 8

Live Amongst Them
to Defeat Them

The streets were deserted when I left Chiheb's hotel.

Before I could go to bed, I had a meeting with Nelly and Kenny. Nelly met me at the door of his room at the Residence Inn Suites in San Jose. I took a seat on the couch. Nelly and Kenny sat in chairs in front of me. We went through the bump and the ride to the hotel.

"What is he doing tomorrow?" Nelly asked.

"The conference," I said. "I'm going to dinner with him afterward. I need a good halal restaurant in the area."

"I'll check in with one of the San Jose guys," Nelly said. "We'll get you a place."

The rest of the meeting we talked about the flight and laughed about the seat mix-up. I left the suite just before dawn and went to my hotel. That morning, I waited to hear from Chiheb. He e-mailed me in the late afternoon. Chiheb's phone didn't work. I fired back a response.

No problem, brother. Let's communicate via e-mail. See you at 6 p.m. for dinner. I'll pick you up at the hotel.

I called Nelly after Chiheb confirmed dinner. He had a restaurant for me.

"Menara Moroccan Restaurant," Nelly said. "It's on East Gish Road. Four stars. High-end."

"It's halal, right?" I asked.

"Definitely," Nelly assured me.

"Perfect," I said. "I got an e-mail from Chiheb. His phone doesn't work here."

Nelly chuckled. I knew what he was thinking right away.

"I'll run it by the team," Nelly said. "See you at the safe house to wire up."

I got to Chiheb's hotel at 6:00 P.M. He was waiting for me in the lobby. When he saw the car pull up, Chiheb got into the passenger side. After saying hello, I handed him a smartphone. Nelly and the team had gotten the phone for me.

"Here, take this," I said. "So you can reach me, brother."

Chiheb wouldn't touch it.

"Absolutely not," he said. "You can't do this. What did it cost?"

I refused to tell him. He reached into his pocket and took out his wallet.

"Let me pay for it," he said.

I refused to take his money.

"While you are in my country, it is my honor to give you what you need," I said. "You need a phone, brother. Nothing else. Just call me this week. It can dial international. Feel free to talk to anyone you want."

Chiheb finally slid the phone in his pocket. He took it because it would have been rude not to, an insult to my hospitality. Plus, he felt like I was being a good brother. But now we had coverage on his calls and e-mails.

"Thank you, brother," he said.

I put the car in gear and eased into traffic. The restaurant was in North San Jose, near the airport.

"Where are we going to eat, brother?" Chiheb said.

"I called a buddy in New York," I said. "I told him, 'Do me a favor, you've been to San Jose. Can you tell me a halal restaurant for a couple of good Muslim brothers?' He gave me this place. I've never been there. I don't know anything about it. But he said it's delicious."

Another rule in undercover work was never pretend to know something or someplace, because it will always bite you in the ass.

I could tell he was uncomfortable with the restaurant. He'd rather eat at a fast-food place and save the money. A true mujahideen wouldn't waste anything. Everything Chiheb did was for Allah. It was a sin to waste money on frivolous things.

I had to justify my choice.

"We kind of have to spend money because my company makes so much money a year," I said. "We have to spend a good amount to have a business write-off. This whole trip. My flight. The car. My meals. Your phone. Everything is being billed to the company. At the end of the year, say we make a million dollars. In order for us to pocket the profits, we have to show expenses. If we don't spend it on ourselves, the government gets it in taxes."

Better to spend it than let the American government use it on guns and missiles to kill the brothers overseas. Chiheb listened carefully. His scientific mind started processing my logic.

"That makes sense," he said, content that he understood it. "So basically, if we don't spend it here, the haram government is going to get it."

"Exactly," I said.

He smiled.

"Bon appétit."

Menara looked small from the outside. But once inside, it opened up into a large, low-lit room with a fountain at the center. I got three steps into the restaurant when I noticed the bar. It was massive, with top-shelf liquor on the shelves. The place was supposed to be halal, which means blessed by an Imam. Chiheb noticed the bar too. My heart sank when I saw his face turn.

"May Allah forgive me," he said quietly in Arabic.

The hostess met us at the podium. She gathered up two menus.

"Can I get a table in the back corner," I said. "We want to be away from the bar area."

She led us through the dining room, which was decorated with a Middle Eastern aesthetic. The tables were low, with pillows or low benches for seats. I took off my shoes and sat on a pillow. Chiheb sat opposite me. He was angry.

"How can a Muslim owner possibly have liquor in this establishment? I don't understand it."

I was trying to calm him down when our waiter showed up with glasses of water. He was an Asian kid. Mid-twenties. Scruffy goatee.

"Can I get you anything to drink?"

Chiheb folded his hands on the table. His inner Imam was fighting to get out.

"No," he said.

Chiheb was angry.

"How can you call this place halal?" he said. "No Imam should bless a place that serves alcohol."

He went on and on.

"Look, man, I just work here."

I cut Chiheb off.

"Yeah, okay," I said. "We'll figure out who the owner is and we can talk with him later."

Chiheb agreed.

I ordered some fruit juices and appetizers. Hummus. Grape leaves. Olives. A feast. When the waiter left, we started talking. He wanted to know about my uncle in Egypt. The one who started the Elnoury Investment Group. We were headed toward my "point of radicalization," the incident that led me to embrace radical Islam, when the lights in the restaurant dimmed. I noticed two disco balls come down from the ceiling. I turned toward the front of the room. Two guys dressed like extras in *Aladdin* were banging on drums.

Are you fucking kidding me? I thought.

I glanced at Chiheb. His mouth was open in stunned silence as a gorgeous Arab woman started belly dancing. She moved around the room shaking and gyrating. Chiheb covered his eyes.

"Stay right here, brother," I said.

I stood up and walked toward the bar. Our waiter was coming with a tray of drinks. I flagged him down.

"Do me a favor, ask her not to go anywhere near our table," I said, pressing a twenty-dollar bill into his free hand. "As you already know, I have a very religious man with me."

"Absolutely, I understand," he said.

He started to walk away.

"Hey, when is she dancing again?"

The waiter started laughing.

"Six o'clock Thursday," he said.

"Thanks," I said, and headed back to Chiheb.

"What did he say?" Chiheb said as I sat down.

"Clearly this owner is munafiqeen," I said. "I berated him. I told him do not let that woman anywhere near our table."

"Good for you," Chiheb said.

The dancer stayed away and the first plates arrived.

"Let's just finish our meal," I said.

I sampled all the dishes. After about a half hour, I stopped eating. I was full. There was plenty left and Chiheb kept eating. For pleasure at first. Then to finish each dish. One of the hadiths tells Muslims not to waste food, water, anything. I watched Chiheb hold the plate at an angle with his left hand as he scooped the hummus into his mouth with his right hand. It was clear he was full. But he couldn't waste a drop. When he was done, the plate was spotless. He did it with every plate. He knew the waiter was going to throw it out, and that is haram. Waste not, want not to the one-hundred-thousandth degree.

While he ate, I talked about my mother. I told him how much she meant to me and how I felt when I got to the hospital on her last day. Chiheb sat quietly as I described the room and my mother in her bed. The doctor was there with some nurses. We were the only Muslims. I ran to my mother's side. I grabbed her hand and touched her head. Everyone was silent. They just stood by and watched my mother die, I told him. I looked at the nurses. They were joking. Laughing. They didn't care about my mother because she was Muslim. I told Chiheb how I could feel my rage building. I wanted to smash the doctor's face against the wall. I wanted to beat the nurses for not helping. For hating my mother and my family for being Muslim. Even telling the fictionalized version of my mother's death was hard. Tears welled up in my eyes. I took a moment and sipped my water.

"I tried to fit in so much," I said. "I lost my religion. I looked like them. Dressed like them. Talked like them. But when my mother needed them the most, they weren't there for her."

Chiheb held my gaze. There was a hint of empathy. He believed me.

"My father died four months to the day after my mother," I said. "I was ready to go back to Egypt. I was done with this country. I was done with everything it stood for. I was disgusted with myself. I wanted to go back to Egypt and dedicate myself to Islam. Then my uncle Ibrahim, God bless him, he put his arm around my shoulder after my father's funeral."

Chiheb leaned in as I explained how Uncle Ibrahim left me the business and went back to Egypt to help the brothers in the Sinai Peninsula. Ibrahim was one of the group's financiers. There was a good bet Chiheb was going to check my story, so making Ibrahim a financier was safe. Al Qaeda's revenue streams were kept secret even from the group's leaders. No one was going to talk about who was funding whom, so it would be impossible to debunk.

"My uncle told me to live amongst them, as them, to defeat them," I said. "I've been helping my uncle with the profits from my company."

Chiheb had a knowing look on his face, like he had found what he was looking for in me. It's a look that I don't normally see so early on in a bump, but it was there. I was hesitant to give him so much so soon, but I felt like I only had a few days.

"Your uncle is a brilliant man," Chiheb said. "He is exactly right."

"I don't know if you know of the true brothers in Sinai," I said. Chiheb nodded. He knew the brothers.

"I don't know why I'm telling you this much already," I said. "I just met you. But I can see Islam is in your heart. I am confiding in you. I beg you to never tell people."

"Of course not," he said. "You have my full trust and confidence."

Chiheb was especially taken with my uncle's strategy to live among the West to defeat it.

"I will tell you hypocrisy is haram in Islam, but it's not during times of war or necessity," he said.

He explained how Muslims can break rules in order to survive—eat pork if it is the only food—and pretend to be American in order to blend in during times of war. Chiheb forgave me for straying from the path of Allah and pretending to be American when I desperately wanted to be like them.

"My God, my brother, how many years younger you are than me and look how well-read you are," I said. "Look how smart you are with your job. Look how educated you are in our religion. God bless you, brother, and may Allah keep you for all the Muslims, because we need you. We need your brain."

I found out later that his al Qaeda recruiter told him the same thing. Al Qaeda needed his brain. As we waited for the check, Chiheb leaned in closer. Now Chiheb felt the need to reciprocate.

"With you in America and me in Canada, we can do great things together, my brother," he said.

Off the cuff, it was an innocuous comment. But it was clear to both me and Chiheb what he meant. He just confirmed what we knew. That was as close as I needed to get.

"Chiheb, I will do anything for you," I said. "You and I think alike. You and I are the same. We have the same thought process. Thank God, it is nice to know that I have a Muslim brother like you, but I don't know you like that brother."

My job was done. We had confirmation that he was a legitimate threat.

At the hotel, Chiheb seemed reluctant to get out of the car.

"We need to spend every night together," Chiheb said. "There are a couple of Muslim brothers in this conference; maybe we can go to dinner, all of us?"

I was due in St. Louis at the end of the week. There was no way I was going to stick around, since he'd already given me what I wanted to know. I had other cases, but it was easier to tell him yes.

"You know, brother, I would love that," I said. "But be careful what you tell them."

"Oh no, I'm not telling them anything about you," he said.

"Get some rest," I said. "Call me tomorrow on your new phone and we can go to dinner."

At the Residence Inn suite, I settled into a couch across from Nelly and Kenny.

"Who suggested Menara?" I said.

"One of the San Jose guys," Nelly said. "Why?"

"There was a full bar when we walked in," I said.

Nelly was stunned. "Shut the fuck up."

I took a sip of my water.

"Yeah," I said. "But wait, it gets better."

I then told them about the belly dancer. Nelly looked at Kenny.

"Holy shit, that didn't happen," Kenny said.

I just sat back and smiled.

"Was she hot?" Nelly said.

"Oh, yeah," I said. "Smoking hot. That was my first question: When is she dancing again?"

"When?" Nelly asked.

"Thursday night at six."

"Nice," he said.

But the joking was over after that.

"So, what is this guy's deal?" Kenny said.

"Better tell the Canadians they have a shit storm on their hands," I said.

"Really," Nelly said. "You're sure?"

"Yeah," I said. "I've been in front of posers. I've been in front of the real deal. This guy is the real deal. He is up to something. He was recruiting me tonight."

I went over the dinner.

"He went that far with you already?" Nelly said.

Both Kenny and Nelly were suspicious. A seasoned sleeper wouldn't reveal himself so easily. I could tell they thought this guy was an amateur. But I saw something different.

"I think this guy is a very suave recruiter," I said. "He asked all the right questions on the plane. All through dinner. I jumped through all of his hoops before he opened up to me. When I gave him my POR [point of radicalization], I think I tipped the scales. They need a full detail on him. I don't know what he is up to or where he is going. I believe he is looking to go operational."

"And then he recruited you," Kenny said, checking his notes.

"Yeah. That's why I pushed him away."

"Why did you push him away?" Nelly said.

"Because he isn't our fucking problem," I said. "He's Canada's problem."

Nelly laughed. "You're fucking right he is."

"I also pushed him away because I'm part of six other cases right now and I was hoping tomorrow night I could leave."

"No fucking way, you're staying the whole week," Nelly said.

Nelly knew what we had. A clean bump on a potential al Qaeda sleeper. I was going to dinner.

"He is going to ask some Muslim brothers from the conference to dinner tomorrow. A Pakistani guy from London and an Iraqi dude from Germany."

"Great, a dinner party," Nelly said.

"Let's see how he deals with others," Kenny said.

The next night, I picked up Chiheb and his friends and drove them to San Francisco. We had dinner at McCormick & Schmick's near Fisherman's Wharf. Chiheb made small talk. They talked about the conference. Politics and religion. But it was all surface talk. The jihadi Chiheb never came out.

After dinner, I picked up the tab and we walked to the car. I was in front with Chiheb. The Pakistani and the Iraqi were several steps behind us. A plane bound for San Francisco Airport thundered overhead. Chiheb looked into the sky and at the buildings nearby. He pointed to one.

"Look at that building right here," he said. "Perfect rooftop. With all these planes coming, get a surface-to-air missile and take them all down. You could probably take down three or four before they knew where you were."

He said it nonchalantly. Like pointing out a nice sunset. No matter what he'd said and done at dinner, he was still focused on his purpose. The look in his eye was pure evil as he watched the plane fly overhead. His purpose from Allah was to kill the infidels. Before I could dig further, the Iraqi interrupted us. I walked back to the car in silence.

When I dropped off everyone at the hotel, I knew one thing: Chiheb loved Tamer. In Chiheb's eyes, Allah had given him what he needed. A wealthy American jihadist with money to fund his operations. I promised to keep in touch but knew I wouldn't.

But it was clear Chiheb was a threat.

CHAPTER 9

Uncle Ibrahim

For my part, I was ready to forget Chiheb. I had to—it was Thursday and I was due in St. Louis on another case. My mind was already transitioning to my new legend when I sat down for my final debrief with Nelly and Kenny.

"I would love to tell you he was all talk," I told Nelly and Kenny. "But I have no doubt this guy is a true mujahideen. You need to tell Canada that this fucker is for real and they can't take their eyes off of him."

"Are you sure?" Kenny said.

In all the years I've been doing this, no one has made the hair on my neck stand up like Chiheb Esseghaier. I had an opportunity to be out in public with him. To be on an airplane with him. To see how he interacted with the public. Interacted with other Muslims. But the look in Chiheb's eyes when he talked about killing infidels was something I'd never seen before in my life. It was a look of hatred and death. It turned my stomach.

93

The debrief took a couple of hours. Most of it was settling up receipts for the hotels, dinners, and rental car. Death by paperwork. When we were done, I grabbed my backpack and suitcase and headed for the door. I had a plane to catch in San Francisco.

"If you ever need a dirty Arab, call me direct," I told Nelly.

"You good? Need a ride to the airport?" he asked.

"No," I said. "I'll take a cab."

"We'll take you. When is your flight?"

"You sure?"

"Yeah," Nelly said. "We're meeting the San Jose guys in San Francisco for drinks after we get Chiheb on his flight. His flight doesn't leave until tonight. We've got time."

Nelly and Kenny dropped me off in front of the terminal an hour later. I was happy to be done with Chiheb, but I'd miss working with Nelly and Kenny. They were good dudes.

"Tell those assholes thanks for the restaurant suggestion," I said as I got out of the car.

After I landed, the St. Louis case agent picked me up from the airport and took me to my cover apartment. It was a spectacular loft with views of the Gateway Arch. Of all my cover apartments, this one is still one of my favorites.

I had a meeting with the target scheduled for the next morning, so I stayed in and watched the Cardinals game. I was about to switch off Tamer's phone when it started to ring. A second later, my FBI phone started to ring. I checked the caller ID. Only Chiheb had Tamer's number. Nelly was on my FBI line.

I answered Chiheb's call first. I heard the sound of a metal detector beeping and the noise of the airport security gate in the background. Chiheb's voice was breathless. Frazzled. He spoke in Arabic. It came out in short bursts.

"Peace be upon you, my brother," he said, still trying to be polite. A brief pause.

"They are trying to touch me on my private areas. You know it's haram. I don't care if it is a man. He can't touch me there. He has no reason. They are not touching anyone else."

I closed my eyes and let out a long exhale.

"Slow down," I said. "What's going on?"

"I'm at airport security and they won't let me on the plane unless they search me," he said. "There are police officers around me. They are threatening to arrest me."

"Chiheb, do me a favor," I said. "Take a deep breath. Calm down."

I knew what was going on, but I had to get through to Chiheb without alerting him that he was under investigation.

"Let me call my lawyers in New York and see if there is a way around this," I said. "I'll call you right back. Don't let go of your phone."

I heard him let out a sigh of relief.

"May Allah reward you for your troubles," he said, and hung up.

I called Nelly. No greeting. He was agitated like Chiheb.

"What the fuck, bro?" Nelly said.

"What's going on?" I said.

I could hear the same background noise on Nelly's phone. He had to be less than thirty feet from Chiheb.

"They are going to lock him up," Nelly said. "It's going to be over unless you get him on this plane."

"What are you talking about?"

"It's protocol," Nelly said. "TSA will not let him on the plane without a physical search. He is wigging the fuck out. As soon as they try to move him out of line, he flails his arms. He is causing a scene. I tried to tin the supervisor, but he isn't getting it."

Nelly had showed the TSA agent his badge, or tin, and asked them to let Chiheb pass. But they refused. Chiheb wasn't getting on the plane until TSA searched him.

"I really didn't want to go down this road with him," I said.

"I know," Nelly said. "I hear you. But we have no other choice. He has to get on that plane or this is over."

"All right. I'll call you back."

I tossed my FBI phone onto the table. If Chiheb got arrested or detained, he'd know he was under surveillance. He'd go underground. His sleeper cell, if he was part of one, would disappear. I took a deep breath. I had to tell him something to get him on that plane. I dialed his number, hoping something would pop into my head.

"Hello, brother," I said. "I just hung up with my attorney in New York. He said it is their right in this country to search anybody whenever they want. You know it's because you have a beard and you're a Muslim. This shit happens to me every time, brother. But you need to take a deep breath. It's okay."

"It's haram," Chiheb said, his voice rising an octave.

I was going to lose him. I knew what I needed to say, but I didn't want to say it. I couldn't push the words out of my mouth. My fist was clenched. My jaw hurt from grinding my teeth.

"Chiheb," I said. "Chiheb! Listen to me. Are you listening?"

"Yes," he said.

"Do you remember what Uncle Ibrahim said to me when I

was ready to leave this country? You're in the same place now. You're leaving this country but you plan on coming back, don't you?"

Chiheb's voice was even again. He understood what I was saying to him.

"Yes," he said.

"He told me to live amongst them, as them, to defeat them. And you told me hypocrisy is not haram in a time of war."

There was a pause. At this point I was pacing. I pressed the phone closer to my ear. I could hear the low murmur of people talking. The beep of the metal detector. TSA officers telling passengers to remove their shoes.

Chiheb was silent. Did he hear me? Was I getting through?

"Are you there?"

"Yes," he said.

"If you draw attention to yourself today by getting arrested, you draw attention to me," I said. "We just spent a week together. You draw attention to us. And then they know who we are."

We were now a team. Two mujahideen. Two brothers doing their part in the war. But no undercover moves this fast. It went against everything I was trained to do. But it had to be done.

"May Allah reward you," he said. "Thank you, my dear brother, for everything. I'll call you when I'm in Montreal."

The line went dead. I relaxed. Chiheb told me later that my speech set a flashbulb off in his head. It wasn't worth fighting now. Better to wait for the greater good. I didn't know it at the time, but his al Qaeda trainers told him the same thing in Iran.

A few minutes later, Nelly was on the line.

"What happened?" I asked.

"He hung up with you and tossed the phone on the x-ray belt," Nelly said. "Then he put his arms out and TSA searched him."

"Okay," I said. "So we're good."

"Yeah," Nelly said. "He just got through security. What the fuck did you say to him?"

"I gave him my uncle Ibrahim's 'live amongst them, as them, to defeat them' speech."

I could feel Nelly's smile through the phone.

"Great work," he said. "I'll call you later."

I hung up the phone and mixed a drink. I wasn't looking forward to Chiheb's next call. After my speech, I knew it was coming.

CHAPTER 10

Gone Fishing

It was just before Labor Day weekend in 2012 and I was headed to the Caribbean.

I had promised some very dear friends a year earlier that I would be around for their destination wedding. It was a swanky affair with rooms at the Ritz-Carlton and a big reception on the beach. My friends knew my job kept me on the road, so they gave me plenty of lead time. I had jealously guarded that weekend.

I needed a break. After St. Louis, I'd worked cases in Tennessee, California, Washington, D.C., and Florida. I'd also taught terrorism indicators to local law enforcement, counterterrorism techniques at the FBI undercover school, and the "mujahideen mind-set" at the FBI profiler's school. The Bureau was getting their money's worth out of me, and I'd loved every second of it. But I was burned out and needed a few cocktails on the beach to recharge.

It was Wednesday and I was off the rest of the week. I planned to bum around the house before I went to the airport. I had just finished packing when my phone rang. It was John, the special agent in charge in New York.

"Hey, boss, what's up?"

"Listen, Nelly tells me you're getting ready to ship out on vacation tomorrow," he said. "What time is your flight?"

I checked my flight confirmation.

"I'm taking a late flight out of New York."

"Any way possible you can run by the office tomorrow?" John said. "We have the assistant director of CSIS flying in. He has a bunch of questions about your new best friend."

CSIS was the Canadian Security Intelligence Service, and my new best friend was Chiheb. Chiheb and I had talked almost every day since San Jose. I'd gotten him out of the country safely—or he thought I did—and it turned out to be the catalyst for our relationship. But the conversations were about keeping up appearances. For the most part, I had punted the case to Nelly and the Canadians.

"Sure thing," I said. "No problem. I can come up."

I was headed to New York anyway, so what was a few hours earlier? I could hang around the city and catch up with Nelly and the guys before my flight.

"Thanks," John said, the relief evident in his voice. "I really appreciate it."

"Formal attire?"

I eyed my suits hanging in the closet.

"Come as you are," John said. "You're on vacation."

The next day, I pulled on some shorts and flip-flops, tossed my bags in the car, and shot up to New York. I hit midtown just before noon and parked at the office.

We were meeting in the special agent in charge's conference room. It overlooked the Hudson River. Artifacts from Ground Zero hung on the wall as a constant reminder of why we did the job. A flat-screen took up the wall on one end. Over the TV were clocks with the local time in different time zones. It was the "Hollywood" conference room, meant to impress visitors.

The CSIS officials were sitting with their backs to the Hudson. Big visitor badges with "Escort Required" printed in huge red letters on the front hung off their suit jackets. They couldn't go to the restroom alone. Nelly and his team were sitting on the opposite side of the table. John was standing at the head of the table when I walked into the room. Everyone was in suits. Nelly smiled.

"He said casual, not beach wear," Nelly said.

I just shrugged and smiled at him. Nelly pulled an empty chair out for me. I dropped my backpack next to it.

"Give me one second," I said. "I've got to use the men's room."

I ran to the bathroom and hustled back to the conference room. On my way back, I clipped my ID badge on and turned it backward so my true name was facing my body.

John waited for me to sit down.

"Are you ready now?"

"Yeah, boss," I said.

We went around the table introducing ourselves. I studied the CSIS assistant director. I didn't catch his full name. He looked like Danny DeVito. His suit was two sizes too small.

"They've got some questions for you," John said after the introductions were finished.

The Canadian looked at me.

"What can you tell us about Chiheb?"

It seemed like a pretty broad question to ask this far into the investigation. I looked at Nelly and then John. Both nodded for me to give them my take.

I turned to face the Canadian.

"He is the real deal," I said, folding my hands on the table in front of me. "He is not a poser or a pretender. I wholeheartedly believe he is here to commit a terrorist attack. I don't know where. And I don't know when. But I do believe he is here to hurt us."

It was clear to me that Chiheb followed the "path of Allah." There was no way for a believer to remain a believer without trying to live a life of total obedience to Allah. This was the path that every Muslim tried to walk every day, but Chiheb twisted it and made it extreme. He brushed his teeth to keep them healthy so he didn't have to waste time going to a dentist to fix them. He ate not because he was hungry; he needed food to continue on the path of Allah. He slept to regenerate his body to do Allah's work. Even his conversations were focused on staying on the path.

Chiheb never mentioned any terrorist attacks on the phone. But he did probe my legend. During one of our conversations, he asked me about the deal I was working on when we met in San Jose.

"I bought both buildings, brother," I told him. "Then I flipped one of them and made more than a million dollars. My uncle was happy. I was able to get most of that to him. My uncle said the brothers are praying for me. I said they should pray for you too. Your face was good on me."

I explained to the Canadians that we were speaking in Arabic and the saying "your face was good on me" was like saying Chiheb brought me good luck. And now he felt like he had a hand in getting the brothers a million dollars.

The FBI told me people connected to Chiheb overseas researched my business, my financial holdings, and my background. They made sure the building deals I mentioned happened. Each verification made Tamer more valuable. He was already vetted by al Qaeda operatives, so to Chiheb's handlers, Tamer was clean. And his wealth gave Chiheb's plans—which he hadn't revealed to me—some serious muscle. I was the jihadi bank. I was the fuel for his jihad engine.

Our conversations fell into a familiar pattern. Greetings followed by talk about family and work. We seemed to always talk about the brothers overseas. I always asked him if he needed anything at the end of the call. His response, like the first night I met him, was the same.

"I'm eating. I'm sleeping. I'm praying. I have all that I need, dear brother."

It was his reminder that he was still and would always be on the path of Allah.

"Thank you very much," the Canadian said after I was done.

But that's not what he was really saying. His tone was off. He was being polite, but his body language rubbed me the wrong way. I felt like we had shared a lot of information and insight, and now I wanted him to help connect some of the dots. What was Chiheb planning? What had they learned about him that we didn't know? I still wasn't clear why they had called me in for this meeting.

But the Canadian was keeping his cards close. It was his nature as an intelligence officer not to share. I was used to working with cops. At the end of the day, all cops are sheepdogs. We want to protect people, and for the most part, we share information in order to do it. But these were intelligence officers. Information is currency to them. Being in the know is more important than anything else.

"We know he is going fishing this weekend," the Canadian said. "We just wanted to get some insight because we don't know the people he is going to meet yet."

I leaned over to Nelly.

"There is no way Chiheb is going fishing."

"No way," he said.

Fishing didn't make any sense. But I did know the guy he was going to meet.

"You're talking about the Palestinian guy, right?"

The Canadian looked at me and then at John.

"Yes," the Canadian said.

"He just told me on the phone last week that he was going to visit a Palestinian brother in the Toronto area."

The Canadian perked up when I said Toronto. He hadn't mentioned it yet.

"How far is it between Montreal and Toronto?" I asked.

Six hours, one of the CSIS staffers said. I started to do the jihadi math. There was no way Chiheb was going to spend twelve hours in a car to go fishing for a day. That would mean being thirty-six to forty-eight hours outside of the path of Allah. He couldn't stand being off the path for ten minutes.

"Sir," I said. "Based on everything I just told you, it really doesn't make sense that Chiheb is going to go fishing."

There was an awkward silence. Both sides of the table looked at me.

"Let me put it to you this way," I said. "If I asked anybody in this room if you had plans this weekend, even if you didn't have anything firm, you'd have something in the back of your mind. Some of you might be going away on vacation. I'm going to the

Caribbean. We all have plans. This is how normal people live their lives. We take breaks. We travel for pleasure. Chiheb does not take a vacation. Every action he takes is to support jihad. There is no way he is going to cast a line and sit and have a conversation with an old Muslim buddy."

Silence. The Canadian was looking at me. He raised his hand, signaling me to stop talking. He turned to face John.

"We know for a fact he is going fishing," the Canadian said. "He rented a boat and we know the area he is going to is a popular fishing location."

Just as he finished his sentence, I stood up.

"I gotta roll," I said to Nelly.

"I don't blame you," Nelly said.

I looked at John.

"Hey, boss, I've got a flight to catch. Are we good here?"

John nodded.

"Thank you so much for coming up."

Everyone stood up. I gave Nelly a hug and shook hands with the rest of the team. I was being an undercover diva. CSIS made it clear they just wanted my insight and that was it. It was a Canadian problem. I had done my job. I hoped to God they got to this guy in time.

"Take care, guys," I said. "Have a good weekend. Enjoy your holiday. Good luck with that fishing trip."

At the airport, I shut down my FBI phone and didn't plan to be sober the rest of the weekend. Two days later, I got a call from Nelly on my private phone.

"Hey, remember when you said it probably wasn't a fishing trip?" Nelly said, trying not to disclose classified information over an open line.

"Yeah," I said.

"You were right," Nelly said.

"What was it?"

"Can you get to Bu space?"

A Bu, or Bureau, space is a secure location. I was standing on a beach with a drink in my hand.

"No."

"We'll fill you in later, but let's just say it is very nefarious."

Nefarious could mean anything. Was he recruiting? Did his Palestinian friend want to head overseas to fight? I wasn't sure what Nelly was getting at, but I did know something was up. There was tension in his voice. A sense of urgency. Whatever Chiheb was up to, he had our attention.

CSIS quickly realized Chiheb wasn't fishing. He was on a recon mission for an attack. The target was a train bridge. That weekend, CSIS dropped the case in the lap of the Royal Canadian Mounted Police, or RCMP. Since Chiheb was now talking about committing a crime on Canadian soil, CSIS was no longer involved. This was a law enforcement matter. In Canada, CSIS and the RCMP operated much like the FBI and CIA pre–September 11. There was an immovable wall between the agencies that existed to protect intelligence agents and techniques from the court system. But after September 11, the wall came down in the United States. Terrorism straddled both sides. The FBI had to learn intelligence, and the CIA had to get comfortable sharing information that could lead to arrests. I was the change personified. When I went overseas, I was a spy. When I worked in the United States, I was a cop. Everyone in the Bureau working counterterrorism undercover operations became this hybrid agent.

CSIS told the RCMP a terrorist was planning an attack and his best friend was an undercover FBI agent in New York. The RCMP called the FBI, and eventually I got the call from Nelly. I spent most of the weekend on the phone. I couldn't even give one weekend to my friends.

My flight landed Monday afternoon and Vinnie, my boss in Newark, met me at my house and drove me to the FBI office. FBI executive management wanted to discuss the case.

"Do I have time to change?"

"No," Vinnie said. "The boss is waiting for us."

I was wearing board shorts and flip-flops. Vinnie shrugged.

"It doesn't matter," he said. "It's Labor Day."

I grabbed my credentials and stuck my gun in my waistband.

"I'm really sorry you had to work through the one weekend you wanted to yourself," Vinnie said.

"It is what it is," I said. "Is the threat real?"

"Very real," Vinnie said. "I listened to everything and it's as real as it gets. They want to blow up a train from New York to Toronto."

I shook my head.

"I'm going to give you some kudos," Vinnie said. "You nailed it. You knew this guy. You put it out there to everyone and no one listened to you. Shame on them. Good for you."

That felt good. But I didn't want to be right. I think deep down I had wanted him to go fishing.

"We've got to figure out how we're going to get you in front of him now," Vinnie said.

"When do I leave?"

I was ready to get on a plane the next morning. But Vinnie warned me there were still some details to be worked out.

"We've got protections in place for you," he said. "The Canadians don't. There are a ton of questions we need answered. The problem is, this attack is a week away."

"How do we know that?"

"Because they called it an anniversary attack," Vinnie said.

September 11 was eight days away. Al Qaeda isn't known for anniversary attacks. It didn't add up. But if they were getting ready to attack, the chatter made sense. The recon made sense.

"Shit," I said. "We don't have a lot of time."

Mike, the FBI special agent in charge for Newark, met us in the conference room. We were all dressed for a cookout, but Mike looked like he had just stepped out of a DeLorean in 1984. He was wearing a pair of corduroy OP shorts. I couldn't take my eyes off his pasty white legs as we shook hands. Bill, the assistant special agent in charge, shook my hand next. He was one of the first bosses I met in the FBI. A cop's cop. He was in charge of the counterterrorism side of the house for Newark.

I took a seat next to Vinnie. Mike wanted to talk before we turned on the videoconference with Headquarters in Washington, D.C., the legal attaché in Ottawa, and Nelly and the team in New York.

"You comfortable with this?" Mike said. "We don't know if the Canadians are going to honor your protections."

Basically, my true name was protected, even in court documents, in the United States. It was unclear if the Canadians would grant me the same protections. If they didn't, there was a good chance my true name would come out if there was a trial. I didn't care. All I thought was—*the clock is ticking*. We had eight days to stop an attack.

"I'm sure," I said.

Bill started the videoconference. Nelly summarized the case for everyone. The fishing trip turned out to be a recon of a bridge used by Canada's VIA rail line. The train line went from New York City to Toronto. CSIS watched Chiheb and his Palestinian friend rent a boat and row it underneath the bridge. They didn't carry fishing poles.

Chiheb talked about the very shallow water underneath the bridge in a recording of their conversation. He didn't want the water to put out the flames as the train derailed and ran off the bridge. His goal was to kill every passenger on the train.

Nelly said the operation came from al Qaeda leaders overseas. Chiheb was getting direction from the highest levels, according to intercepted communications. His contacts were all on the FBI's Most Wanted list. Everyone agreed Chiheb gave us a chance to generate intelligence on al Qaeda operations.

Nobody was denying the evidence. Everyone knew it was real. The question was whether it was worth risking my identity in the process. But that was never a question for me. I knew I was doing it. I just needed to wrap my head around the fact that this could be my last mission.

"I'll clear my schedule," I said when they asked if I was ready. "As soon as you give me the green light, I'll be on a plane to Montreal."

But Bill wasn't ready for the green light.

"Time the fuck out," he said. "No one is taking my guy anywhere until we meet with their brass and they match our protections."

I looked down the table at Bill. What was he doing? I didn't care about protections. The clock was ticking and I had a relationship with a terrorist planning an attack in a few days. There was no time for posturing and politics. People's lives were in danger.

"Well, Bill, I've got to tell you, I doubt they will play ball," said one of the suits from Headquarters.

Bill shrugged.

"If they don't, they're going to have to figure out how to stop these guys on their own, because they're not going to get my guy up there."

The videoconference ended at an impasse. Headquarters promised to work on getting my protections. Bill agreed to have me ready. The screen had barely faded to black when I confronted Bill.

"I have to do this," I told Bill.

I didn't understand what Bill was doing.

"I know you do," Bill said. "And you will do it. But you're going to do it on our terms. They need you more than we need them. Go home and get some rest. You're going to have a fuck of a week coming up."

Bill called Headquarters' bluff. The FBI was under pressure to produce an undercover who could help Canada, one of the United States' closest allies. They also had the juice to make sure I was protected. They just needed the right motivation. Bill's refusal to send me was that motivation.

After the videoconference, Heidi, a lawyer in the FBI's National Security Law Branch, wrote a thirty-three-page affidavit asking the Canadian courts to grant me the same protections I had in the United States.

While she worked, we planned. Since it was Nelly's and Kenny's case, they were headed to Montreal with me. The plan was to get on the ground in Montreal, figure out the conspiracy, and then arrest Chiheb. It was a weeklong operation.

Every major FBI undercover operation has a contact agent who makes sure the undercover has everything they need to be successful. The contact agent is never someone with a stake in the case. His only agenda is the undercover's well-being.

The undercover picks the contact agent. I picked Joey after Vinnie suggested him. We had gone to undercover school together. He was the Italian mob version of me. What made him so talented was his ability to read people. It didn't matter if you were a foreigner or a crack dealer, Joey could figure out your motivation. It was uncanny. I was excited when Vinnie told me he was available.

"That's my family," I said. "Is he okay with it?"

"He can't wait to get started," Vinnie said.

It was almost Tuesday when Vinnie finally drove me back to my house. Neither one of us talked on the way home. My mind was working through all the scenarios. Only one scared me: What if the Canadians didn't give me the protections? The FBI went to extreme lengths to protect my identity. I never had to testify in open court and my true name would never be revealed. I could do my job over and over again without ever having to worry about being compromised. I knew I had to go, but then my true name could be revealed, putting my father and sister in harm's way. I'd signed up for the job. They hadn't.

"What would you do?" I asked as Vinnie pulled into the driveway.

Vinnie put the truck in park and rested his head against the seat. He let the question sit out there for a minute. I could tell he was mulling it over. He was like me. An undercover who had been in the same room as killers. He loved the work as much as I did, but he also understood the cost. This wasn't going to be a simple or quick case. We had an al Qaeda sleeper in our sights. He was a direct link to the organization. A link that could lead us deeper into the network. I was convinced the risk was worth taking. I just wanted to hear him say it.

A wry smile creased Vinnie's lips.

"You're fucked, buddy," Vinnie said. "You're damned if you do, damned if you don't. But this is why you joined the FBI. This is why we recruited you. This case is going to change your life."

Over the next week, the team went to Toronto to work out the details with the RCMP. Three days later, I got word to get packed. The RCMP agreed to protect my identity after Heidi argued that revealing my true name would cause severe damage to the United States' national security efforts.

As she put it, I was a non-fungible asset.

Yeah, I had to look it up too.

CHAPTER 11

Apartment 23

I took a deep breath as the plane made its final approach into Montréal–Pierre Elliott Trudeau International Airport.

It was September 2012 and the air was crisp. I retrieved my bags from the carousel and took a cab to the hotel. I was alone and traveling under Tamer's identity, just in case Chiheb had someone waiting for me at the airport. I had told him I was coming in a day later so I could meet with my team. Nelly, Kenny, and Joey were already set up at the Marriott Château Champlain, a luxury hotel in the heart of downtown Montreal.

"Get checked in and then give me a call," Joey said when I called him from the car.

The hotel was a time warp back to the 1950s. The lobby was all gold and marble. The echo of footsteps bounced off the walls. The bellman took me to Tamer's suite. I called Joey after he left.

"We're in the penthouse," he said.

Joey gave me the room number and the code for the elevator, which took me to the top of the hotel. The hallway was deserted. I knocked on the double doors and a woman opened one.

"Do I have the right room?" I asked.

"Are you Tamer?" she said in a slight French accent.

"I am."

"Come on in," she said, kissing me on both cheeks and giving me a hug. "You're here to save our country. Thank you."

"Man, did I make the right call coming up here," I said, laughing.

The team was sitting in the living room. Benny, the RCMP undercover boss, stood up and shook my hand. He was a handsome guy who looked like he read a lot of fashion magazines. He was wearing a corduroy sport coat and a puffy white shirt. A scarf tied the whole outfit together. My mind went to the *Seinfeld* pirate shirt episode. I stifled a smile and reminded myself to mention the shirt to Nelly.

We nicknamed Benny "the party planner" because he took the team to the best bars and restaurants when we weren't working. Always without me, of course, because I couldn't be seen with them in public. And I made sure to remind him of that on a regular basis.

"We'll get you anything you need while you're here," he said.

Frank was next. He was the RCMP Toronto liaison, a former undercover. Frank's long ponytail from his biker days was now gray. He introduced me to Doug, my RCMP handler. He was lean with a receding hairline that he wore as a buzz cut. Like Frank, he was a former undercover.

"You're doing God's work," Doug said, giving me a firm handshake.

Doug motioned me to a seat near Kenny, Nelly, and Joey, who smiled. Joey shot me a knowing glance as I sat down. He had already figured out the room. Joey looked like George Clooney in both appearance and spirit. He made life look easy, but the façade hid one of the Bureau's best minds. He was a grinder who didn't miss a detail.

The meeting started like all the others. The Canadians wanted all the same information that CSIS did in the New York meeting.

The next evening, I waited until my "flight" landed, then I walked down to the lobby to call Chiheb. When I'd told him I was headed to Montreal, he had made it clear never to call his cell phone because my mobile phone account was tied to my name. It seemed he wanted to protect me. So perhaps it wasn't a surprise that the phone rang and rang. It was after 7:00 P.M. and people walked in and out of the lobby on their way to and from dinner. A generic message finally answered my call. His voice mail wasn't set up. I tried two more times and then sent him an e-mail asking if he wanted to meet up. Chiheb picked up when I called just before nine o'clock. His phone was out of minutes, he told me.

"I was hoping it was you," Chiheb said. "I've been waiting for you, brother."

"I just got in," I said. "Give me half an hour and I'll shoot over."

He wanted to give me directions, but I told him that wasn't necessary.

"I have a GPS in the car," I said. "I have your address from our e-mails."

"That's great," he said. "I'll be waiting for you."

I arrived at his apartment on Rosemont Boulevard at 9:34 P.M. Chiheb lived in a three-story brick building. I circled the block, a habit from my drug days. My GPS told me to make a U-turn. I ignored it and made a left. I went a few blocks and then pulled over.

I watched the cars pass for a few minutes. I studied faces. Did I see the same faces? Who was trying not to look at me? I returned to his building twenty minutes later, confident no one was following me.

I rang his apartment number. Chiheb came over the intercom and buzzed me up. His apartment was on the second floor. Chiheb, wearing jeans rolled up at the cuffs and a light blue button-down shirt, was waiting for me on the landing.

"Peace be upon you," I said in Arabic.

We almost always spoke in Arabic together. By now he'd mastered my Egyptian dialect. To the untrained ear, it sounded like we were speaking the same language. But to a native speaker, it was like hearing English spoken by a New Yorker and by a southern gentleman from Charleston. Same language. Drastically different sound. It amazed me that Chiheb could tailor his accent so that I could better understand him. I could hear my childhood in Alexandria coming from the mouth of a Tunisian.

"Peace be upon you," Chiheb said.

"*Habibi, habibi,*" I said, calling him a friend.

"How are you?" Chiheb said. He was excited to see me. "I really missed you, I swear."

"May Allah keep you," I said.

The apartment building was home to students and low-income workers. I could hear the other tenants watching TV or talking inside their apartments as we walked down the corridor. He stopped at the first door on the left. Apartment 23.

"Why didn't you have me pick you up at the airport?" Chiheb asked.

"I didn't want to disturb you, *habibi*, because I knew they would be giving me a car," I said. "They had a car waiting for me when I arrived, so there was no reason to put you out."

"No, that is not a problem, that is not a problem at all," he said. "Please come in, brother, please come in."

His apartment was small. The front door led into the kitchen. An old mattress was on the floor in the living room. His clothes, a laptop computer, and some random belongings sat in the corner. A sliding glass door led to a balcony. His roommate, a taxi driver from Algeria, lived in the only bedroom. His roommate was in Algeria, so we were alone.

Chiheb motioned for me to sit on the mattress. I hesitated. It was streaked with dirt. A massive brown stain covered more than three quarters of it. I found out later he took it from a dumpster. Why spend money on a mattress? His comfort was second to Allah's will.

"What's all this? I told you when we spoke not to prepare anything."

Chiheb smiled. Next to the mattress was a plate with oranges, plums, strawberries, and dates. He poured me a large glass of milk. He was excited to play the host because now I was in his country.

"No, no, no, it isn't much," he said. "Just cold milk, so it can help you sleep tonight."

Anything given to a guest, especially a drink, is personal in my culture. There was no getting out of drinking it. Thank God it wasn't spoiled and it was cold.

"How was your trip? Was it a long trip?"

I took a sip of the milk and put it on the stool next to the mattress.

"It was a long trip, the flight was a bit delayed," I said. "For about half an hour or so."

Chiheb nodded along. His eyes never left me.

"I really miss you, brother," he said.

"I miss you too," I said, looking around his apartment. "May Allah keep you safe. This apartment is nice."

"Yeah, what do you think?"

"Praise Allah," I said. "Everything you need."

"Tell me, how have you spent the time since Santa Clara?" Chiheb asked.

"Thankfully, things are good in terms of the building; we rented it out already," I said. "It's making money. And as for work in general, it's still very busy, but busy is good. But truthfully, Chiheb, after I met you, I see everything differently now."

Chiheb's weakness was his fatalism.

"May Allah bless you," Chiheb said.

He was staring at me intently.

"You understand," I said. "You understand what I mean?"

"Yes. Thank Allah."

"I know my Arabic isn't perfect, but bear with me for a bit so I can explain this to you," I said. "Right before I met you, I said to myself . . ."

I let the sentence trail off. I paused. I looked away as I pretended to search for the right words.

"I pray every day, and every time I pray, I ask Allah . . ."

Chiheb was getting swept into the moment.

"Tell me what I can do," I said. "I look at all the problems that are taking place in this world and the Muslims being oppressed by the infidels we are living next to and I just wish, O Lord, give me the strength and the courage, give me something more that I can do to help. You understand?"

"Praise Allah," Chiheb said.

"I asked Allah to show me how to help the Muslim Ummah. Give me any sign. Then I went to the airport. So, I got to Houston and then I met you," I said.

"Do you really want to help the Muslims?" Chiheb asked. "I mean, do you wish to help the Muslims?"

"Exactly. I wish to."

I wanted to talk about the plot. We only had a few days before September 11, but I wanted him to lead the conversation.

Chiheb's demeanor changed. His smile was gone. One second he was playing host. Pouring a glass of milk. Trying to coax me into eating some fruit. The next second his eyes got dark. He was still, but intense. He looked right through me and it gave me a chill.

"Is your cell phone on?"

One of two things was going to happen when he asked me to turn off my phone. One, he was going to rip my shirt open and look for a wire, or two, he was going to open up about the attack.

"Let's get the devil out of the room," Chiheb said.

I took my phone out of my jacket.

"Do you want me to shut it off?"

"Yes," Chiheb said, staring at the phone like it was a bomb.

I started to tap out a text message to Joey, claiming to be in touch with an employee.

"I have to let him know that I arrived; let me do it before I turn it off."

"Shutting the phone down," I wrote. "All is good."

I sent the text and deleted it before Chiheb could see. Joey knew the drill. He would never send me anything overt on my undercover phone.

Chiheb got up from his pillow and sat next to me. His chin was almost on my right shoulder as he watched me shut down my phone.

"That's it," I said, letting him see the screen.

"Is it off?" he said.

I put the phone back in my jacket. I had another phone. I pulled it out and shut it down as well. Chiheb smiled.

"It's not that we're afraid of them, but it's a precaution," he said.

"Talk to me, brother."

"I have brothers who I visited who are mujahideen for the sake of Allah."

"Praise Allah," I said.

"Yes, may Allah keep them," Chiheb said. "I visited them at the border."

"What does that mean?"

"The border. The border between Iran and Afghanistan."

"What do you mean?" I said. "They live here or there?"

"They live near the border between Iran and Afghanistan," Chiheb said. "They are in contact with our brothers in Afghanistan who are carrying out jihad for the sake of Allah."

"May Allah be with them," I said.

"The brothers told me, go back to Canada and stay there and, of course, we'll keep in touch, God willing. So I am in contact with them."

He studied me as he spoke. He seemed nervous, like he needed validation. I nodded with each sentence. I leaned in, held his gaze, and offered a slight smile at the end. I acted impressed.

Chiheb took out his passport and flipped a few pages.

"I mean, this is the visa," he said, showing me the page in his passport. "The Islamic Republic of Iran."

I studied the page.

"I went to Iran," Chiheb said.

"Who is that?" I said while I stared at his passport. "Is this one of the brothers?"

"No, that's me."

"That's you?"

I acted surprised, but I wanted him on tape talking about his trip to Iran.

"Yes, that's me," Chiheb said. "I went to Iran in April 2011."

"Praise Allah, you were in Iran?"

"Yes," he said. "Then I went again in February 2012."

"So it was this past February?" I said.

My mind started to put the pieces together. I reached for my passport and handed it to him.

"Hang on a second," I said. "So in February you were in Iran. And myself, let me see, in February . . ."

I let the sentence trail off. I had more evidence that Allah put us on the path together.

"Where were you?" Chiheb asked as he turned the pages of my passport to match the dates.

"I was near there," I said. "I went to see my brothers."

Chiheb was floored. He saw my stamps from February 2012, when I was in the Middle East.

"I mean, there was only a sea between us," he said.

"We were there together," I said.

I couldn't help but think that if he only knew why I was really over there, he would cut my throat right there on his shitty mattress.

"Do you know which city in Iran I was in in February?"

"Tell me," I said.

"In a city in the south of Iran."

"So that means it's not that far," I said. "You were in Iran. And I was meeting with the brothers."

"You?" Chiheb asked.

He was astonished. But I needed him to know I could do more for the brothers. For him.

"When I met with them, they told me that I was an asset to them in America. I know they're right, and I get it. But they also knew that I wanted to do more than just send money. But I'm still waiting. I haven't heard from them. But anyway, look at the path that you and I are on. We were overseas at the same time looking for the same thing. And look at how Allah put us together in Houston.

"Brother, let's keep the devil out of the room," I said. "I know Allah had a plan for us. But I've only met a couple of other good brothers like you."

I rattled off some names—aliases of my fellow Dirty Arabs Group members. I wanted to know if Chiheb had any brothers in Canada. I wanted to know more about the Palestinian he went on the recon with a few days ago. Chiheb had mentioned him in August, but I didn't have any firm details.

"You told me before, there are Muslims you want me to meet," I said. "I told you they have to be like us."

Chiheb nodded. He said we should meet Raed Jaser, the Palestinian brother in Toronto.

"If you want, we can visit him," Chiheb said.

"Of course," I said.

We agreed to drive to Toronto to visit Jaser the next day.

"If you finish at three o'clock, we can go straight to him," Chiheb said.

"Does he know that we are coming?"

"I told him, I said, there is a possibility that a brother from America is coming to pay us a visit," Chiheb said.

"He is like us, correct?"

"Yeah, he is truly into jihad," Chiheb said, smiling. "Don't worry about him."

"Okay, good," I said.

"Actually, him and I, we have projects together."

"You have what?" I asked.

"We have a project together," Chiheb said.

There was no mistaking what he was talking about.

"You mean plans?" I asked.

"Plans. We have plans."

That is all he would tell me in Apartment 23. But we both knew what "plans" meant. We were now brothers against all infidels, with a mission to kill.

CHAPTER 12

The Road Trip

Joey put his arm over my shoulder and guided me into the other room of the suite.

We talked about the road trip to Toronto for hours after I got back to the hotel. Nelly and Doug had a map spread out on the table and were going over the route for the six-hour drive. I made it clear I was not spending much time in a car with Chiheb.

"No way," I told Joey. "It's a forty-five-minute flight. Why would Tamer drive if he could fly?"

When I made the plan the night before, I forgot Toronto was that far away. My Canadian geography sucked. Now I was in a full-on diva shit fit. We already had Chiheb. He'd admitted to planning the attack the night before. There was no reason to spend the time driving.

"Let's just fly," I said. "I can get the Palestinian to admit his role and deliver the case to the Canadians with a bow."

But Joey had other ideas.

"Listen, I hear you," Joey said as we left the room. "I'm with you. I wouldn't want to spend any more time with him than I had to, but think of the evidentiary value of that six-hour conversation. Just the two of you. Phones shut off. Think of what he wants to tell you. Look how quickly you brought him around."

He was right, even if I didn't want to admit it. But I wasn't thinking about the case. I was thinking about me. Spending time with Chiheb required me to put my arm around him. To call him *habibi*. Tell him he was my brother. Plus, I hated who Tamer was. I created him to be recruitable. But a little part of me died every time I had to denounce my country or pervert my religion.

"Think outside yourself," he said, really driving home the point. "It's not a car ride, it's an interrogation. Do your thing. There is nobody that we would want more in that car to save these lives than you."

Joey, ever the smooth one, was basically telling me to shut my mouth and do my job. But doing it by tickling my ego. A little sugar to help the medicine go down.

"You're right," I said.

Just after 4:00 P.M. the next day, I picked up Chiheb in my Chrysler 300. It had a V8 hemi engine. Leather seats. GPS. It was flashy and expensive. It screamed Tamer. All Chiheb knew was that I "rented" it on business travel. But of course it was also wired up so everything we said was in surround sound. I jumped on the highway heading west. The road—immaculately paved—skirted Lake Ontario. There was little traffic and I pushed the gas pedal to the floor.

There were multiple surveillance teams on the road ahead of us and behind us. A plane circled overhead. My phone buzzed. It was Joey asking me to slow down. I was pushing it. I didn't want to prolong the trip. Once we got outside of Montreal, I poured on the speed. The second text was more urgent. What were they going to do, pull me over?

My phone buzzed a third time.

"SLOW THE FUCK DOWN."

I looked at the speedometer. We were going well over one hundred miles per hour. Surveillance vehicles couldn't keep up without giving themselves away. I let the speedometer fall to about seventy-five miles per hour.

About an hour outside of town, Chiheb flipped the switch. I handed him my phone and he shut it off. It was time to get serious.

"The project regarding the train," Chiheb said. "You are included in what we are planning. Do you understand?"

I said I did.

"You are included because we need you."

He told me the brothers in Iran—al Qaeda planners—ordered him to cut a hole in the train tracks and derail a train heading to Toronto from New York. He and his Palestinian friend were going to use jackhammers to cut out the track on a bridge near Toronto. When the train derailed, it would smash through the barriers on the side of the bridge and plunge the passengers into the shallow water below.

"The thing is that it needs two people, you know, the hole," Chiheb said. "When it's dug, there has to be one person on one side and one on the other side."

"Right," I said.

"They start together at the same time and when it starts breaking up, it's all going to fall. Do you understand?"

"Of course," I said. "Definitely."

"So, I mean we need only two people to do the work, but we need a third person as an external partner to watch our back. Do you understand? You are the external partner."

As he talked, I concentrated on my smile. I touched my heart. I wanted him to know I embraced his beautiful plan and that I felt like I was part of something real. It was firing him up that I wasn't appalled. By being quiet yet reassuring, it made for better recordings. The jury didn't need to hear my voice.

"How do you know it's not going to be considered an accident?" I asked.

Chiheb and Jaser planned to shoot a video taking credit and warning the United States and Canada that the attacks would continue until all foreign troops were removed from the Middle East. I asked if they had a target. Chiheb smiled.

"I talked with the brother from Palestine about the operation," Chiheb said. "I asked him, 'Are you going fishing? Did you go fishing? When are we going fishing?' Understand?"

"Ahh," I said.

"He understands me when I say it," Chiheb said. "Like, there isn't fishing."

"No, that's easy," I said, thinking back to the Canadians in New York before Labor Day.

Trust me, we know it's a fishing trip.

Yeah, right.

Chiheb said he was instructed to cut a five-meter hole in the tracks. The hole would be big enough to derail the train, but Chiheb thought it would be almost undetectable to the engineer.

"You are in construction," Chiheb said. "What do you think?"

"Five meters is about fifteen feet," I said. "That makes perfect sense; if you're traveling at what, eighty kilometers, a hundred kilometers, you've got five meters, right, which is a good amount; it's going to drop at some point and it's gonna derail it, just like you said."

With the rail plot on tape, I switched gears.

"What other good ideas do we have to work on, Allah willing?" I asked.

Chiheb said his other plan was to hire a cook and send him to work on a military base in the United States. Once there, he would poison the soldiers' food. He wanted me to help find a cook.

"When you look for the cook you have to be careful," Chiheb said. "When you talk to a person you need to have a reason why you are searching. For example, 'I have some plans for buying a restaurant,' for example."

Chiheb asked me if I understood.

"My business is my cover," I said, which is probably the only truthful statement I made during the six-hour car ride.

Before I got in the car, Doug had asked me to confirm the timeline. We assumed the attack was set for September 11. He wanted to be sure.

"God willing, it'll be in December, when five o'clock at night is dark," Chiheb said after I asked when he planned to attack. "So the train would have no opportunity, no chance to escape, because the vision is poor. Do you understand?"

"Of course," I said.

"Because at night there is no traffic," Chiheb said. "So the train's speed becomes faster."

"It's brilliant," I said, relieved.

When CSIS picked up Chiheb and Jaser talking about an anniversary, they meant Christmas. The anniversary of Jesus Christ's birthday.

We were barely halfway to Toronto, and I had enough evidence on tape to charge Chiheb. With four more hours to kill, we started to talk about his training in Iran. An al Qaeda planner—El Massoul—trained Chiheb in Iran. One of my tasks was to figure out who El Massoul was, since we only had his nom de guerre.

"The brother, the one who is in charge, El Massoul, the Responsible One, that I met in Iran. He told me he has a soldier in the U.S.A. He's just sleeping, you know?"

"Yes," I said.

"Do you know the sleeping cell?" Chiheb asked. "One sleeping cell."

My heart started to race. Did Chiheb just tell me there was an American sleeper? I focused on the road as I regained my composure, because I had to work overtime not to show him I was losing my shit.

"Is he alone?" I asked.

Our Canadian problem had just turned into an American problem.

"I mean, he didn't tell me," Chiheb said.

"Better this way," I said.

"But El Massoul told me 'I will call you and I will make the soldier call you. Either the soldier comes to Canada or you go to him in the U.S.A.' I am asking myself, this soldier, is it you?"

Then it dawned on me why he'd brought it up. He thought I was the American sleeper.

"Praise Allah, may Allah keep you, oh God, God willing, I am a soldier of Allah," I said.

But I told him I wasn't the sleeper. Still, the fact that there might be an American version of Chiheb? That scared the shit out of me.

"Tell me about your time in Iran, *habibi*," I said. "Did you enjoy it there?"

I wanted him to talk about his training in hopes he'd give me something on the American sleeper.

"They had me memorize the symbols, the language. Memorize some of the projects, the plans. They taught me the symbolic language."

"Yes, the codes," I said.

"They taught me the project of the cook. I got the message from our Sheikh, you know him?"

"Our Sheikh?" I asked, hoping he'd say his name.

I wanted it all on tape.

"The Sheikh, the one who succeeded Sheikh Osama, without saying his name."

"Oh, you don't want to say his name?"

"Do you know Sheikh Osama?"

He was talking about Osama bin Laden.

"Of course."

"The one who succeeded him," Chiheb said. "He's from Egypt."

"The Egyptian."

He was talking about Ayman al-Zawahiri, the Egyptian-born doctor and a former deputy to Osama bin Laden. He took over after bin Laden was killed in Pakistan.

"I got a message from him personally," Chiheb said.

"Unbelievable," I said.

"Praise be to Allah," Chiheb said.

"Praise Allah, *habibi*," I said, trying to sound as impressed as possible.

"I got a message from him through the Responsible One," Chiheb said.

He was bragging. But I wanted to talk about the American sleeper.

"Do you know who this guy is?" I asked.

"No, I never met him," Chiheb said. "But I know he was there, because El Massoul talked about him a lot. When I'd do something good he said I reminded him of Al-Amriki [the American]."

"Wow, are you ever going to cross paths?"

"One day, we'll meet when the time is right," Chiheb said.

"Maybe one day I will meet him," I said. "I'd love a chance to meet a good dear brother like you."

We needed to rethink the case. Chiheb was our only link to the American sleeper. There was no way we could arrest him before we identified the other sleeper. About halfway to Toronto, Chiheb got quiet.

"Maybe you can advise me," Chiheb said. "So in the last period, my boss brought in one PhD student from Jordan."

"Okay," I said, not tracking where the conversation was going.

"She is a girl," he said.

It was clear he was uncomfortable. He was back to being the awkward Chiheb. The scientist with no social skills.

"A woman," I said.

"But it's a girl—she's not married," he said.

The Jordanian woman had the office next to Chiheb's. She was Palestinian but grew up in Jordan after her family fled Israel.

"The distance between her office and my office is just seven centimeters," he said. "Can you imagine?"

I tried to act surprised. But I still wasn't sure where Chiheb was headed.

"Almighty God, this is His wisdom. So, why this girl, she didn't come when I was not thinking about all of this stuff? But what makes things more serious, it's a test, Allah makes this girl love me."

"You're kidding," I said, more to myself than to him.

Chiheb needed dating advice. He was attracted to her, but was nervous that his feelings would take his focus off his projects.

"Yes, she tries to always show me that she loves me," he said. "I am very disappointed about this subject. Could you give me some advice about this issue, because I see her every day?"

"Are you sure she loves you?" I asked.

Knowing Chiheb as I did, it seemed strange that a woman would be into him. She hadn't been over to his apartment. I shuddered just thinking about that mattress.

"I am sure. When I talk with another girl, she became very mad."

He told me a story about a female colleague joking with him after he spilled something on the floor of his office. The Jordanian woman saw them laughing and shooed the other woman away and started to clean up.

"Can you imagine?" Chiheb said, smiling at the memory. "Just for the sake to stop the joke. So give me advice please."

It was obvious the Jordanian woman was important to him. Important enough to demand his attention and force him to think about something besides the path of Allah.

"Do you love her?"

"Sometimes I feel that I love her. When she disobeys Allah, I feel that I hate her."

This crush concerned me. I didn't want him talking to her about the plot.

"You can't talk to anyone about the project, because now it's not just you," I said. "It's you, it's me. The Palestinian brother. I know she's not your wife but if she's going to be your wife, think about it—does she have to know?"

"That she married a mujahid?" Chiheb said. "She didn't marry a regular person. She should know that she is married to a mujahid."

I nodded.

"That's true."

"But the issue is not me. I don't want my heart to become deviated."

Chiheb was always on the lookout for obstacles on the path of Allah. He feared the Jordanian was one.

"It's kind of a war inside myself," he said.

"If she loves you the way you're telling me, she knows that you are a mujahid and that's not the problem," I said. "The problem is you're telling me you believe you have a mission, but you're afraid that if you end up falling in love or getting married it will deviate you from the mission."

"Either I cut any kind of relation with her and I leave her forever or I marry her forever. One of the two."

"And if you marry her forever are you going to walk away from being a mujahid?"

"No. And if she pushes me to do this, I will divorce her immediately. So what is your advice?"

"Okay, before I give you my advice I have one very important question that you have to make clear for me," I said. "If you walk away from her and you cut ties or if you go the other way and you marry her, either way, you are still staying focused to go straight ahead with the missions and stay mujahid?"

"Yes," Chiheb said.

"No matter what?"

"No matter what."

"So there is no issue," I said. "Follow your heart."

"You don't think that what is in my heart is just simple desire?"

"You're thinking it's the devil in the path of Allah?"

"Do you not think that what I have for that girl is just simple desire?" Chiheb said. "Because of Satan?"

"That's a possibility, I'll give you that, but let me ask you something. With love comes desire. Marriage isn't haram and it isn't always Satan. If you love someone, you desire them."

"Yes."

"That's not haram and that's not Satan," I said.

Chiheb seemed grateful.

"You are not only professional advisor but you are also personal advisor," he said. "Another advice?"

Chiheb looked out the window. He hesitated before he spoke again.

"She's trying to show to me that she doesn't love me."

I smiled. "They call it in English 'she's playing hard to get.'"

But I wasn't convinced she was even interested. My hope was to force the issue. Get her to reject him and end any chance that he'd tell her about the plot and derail the case.

"When you return to work, ask her, Could we talk? Talk to her. The best route is honesty. Be straightforward with her, tell her, Look, instead of playing any games, you know me, let's be straight. What's your feeling? Where are we going?"

Chiheb seemed discouraged.

"She won't say. She hides her feelings."

"You tell her and then she'll tell you, that's it. No more of this talk, that's it, no more games. You go in straightforward now. You're a man of business, go in straight and tell her, Look, I swear by Allah this is the story and I'll say it to you straight, do you want me or not?"

I laughed. This was kind of fun.

"It's my business mind, okay?" I said. "No games, no more playing games, get to the point. Give me the bottom line."

As we got close to Toronto, Chiheb asked me not to mention the plot to the Palestinian brother.

"No, no, I would never say anything until you tell me we could talk," I said.

Chiheb relaxed.

"Yeah, like, I have to prepare him psychologically. You let me talk to him."

Chiheb tried to call the Palestinian, but his phone didn't work. I handed him my phone.

"Tell him this is the brother's cell phone," I said.

After a few tries, Chiheb finally reached him. It was around eleven o'clock and we wanted to make sure it was still okay for us to visit.

"Of course," the Palestinian said. "I'm waiting up for you."

CHAPTER 13

The Imam Complex

Raed Jaser, the Palestinian, lived in a quiet suburban neighborhood in northern Toronto. His house was a mother-daughter home converted into apartments. Jaser lived in the apartment around the back of the main house.

We arrived a little after 11:00 P.M. and followed the path to his front door. Chiheb was in the lead. I started shooting mental pictures of everything. I memorized the license plate numbers in the driveway and made mental notes of the layout, because at some point the SWAT team would want to know.

Jaser's entry was a sliding glass patio door. Chiheb knocked. A few seconds later, Jaser came to the door. He was wearing a long white robe, a red-and-white checkered scarf on his shoulders, and slippers. He was heavily bearded, with a pronounced nose and dark eyes. He wore a kufi on his head. His face lit up when he saw Chiheb. They embraced and exchanged kisses.

"This is my dear brother from America," Chiheb said, turning to me. "He's Egyptian."

"Welcome, brother," Jaser said, looking me up and down before hugging me.

Jaser's apartment was quaint. There was one bedroom and a bathroom. With men in the house, Jaser's wife hid in the bedroom. Fruit and snacks were spread out on the table.

"Brother, can we use your restroom to make *wudu*?" I asked. "We'd love to pray Isha. Do you want to pray Isha together?"

The Isha prayer is the fifth and final prayer of the day. But before we could pray, we had to clean ourselves, or make *wudu*. Jaser showed us the bathroom, but shook his head no when I asked if he wanted to pray.

"I already prayed," he said. "You guys go ahead."

Chiheb excused himself and used the bathroom. I thought it was strange Jaser hadn't waited to pray with us. He knew we were coming, and you get extra credit from God when you pray in a group.

When I got out of the bathroom, I joined Chiheb. Jaser sat on the couch nearby. Isha requires four *rakk'ah*—the movements and words of the prayer. The first two *rakk'ah* are prayed aloud. I could feel Jaser's eyes on me as we recited the Quran during prayer. He watched my every move. He wanted to hear my Quranic voice. He listened to the way I said each word in the prayer.

This was a test.

Mainstream Muslims pray a certain way. But the mujahideen have little idiosyncrasies, tells that signal to others they are "more religious," like not crossing your legs or spreading your fingers when you kneel and bow. There are certain ways to enunciate the words.

It was hard to pray for real with Jaser watching. It annoyed me that I couldn't concentrate and instead had to focus on making sure I passed the test. Saying my prayers was never an act, even when I was Tamer. But I trusted that Allah understood what I was doing.

When we were done, Jaser relaxed. He poured us each a cup of tea. It was clear he and Chiheb were friends. They jumped into talk of religion and how the brothers overseas were being oppressed by the Jews and America. Jaser started quoting from *Milestones,* written by Egyptian Islamist Sayyid Qutb. He was one of Osama bin Laden's idols.

Qutb called for Muslims to re-create the world based on the Quran. He argued Muslims lived in a "state of ignorance of the guidance from God" because they didn't follow Sharia, or traditional Islamic law. He considered Sharia no different from the "laws of nature," like gravity. Anyone living under any law other than the law of Allah was a *kaffir,* or nonbeliever. He called for the rejection of secular leaders and "the rubbish heap of the West" and wanted to form a "vanguard" that resembled Mohammed's first followers. The vanguard would cut itself off from Western thinking and any non-Muslims. They would inspire people to become "true" Muslims and throw off the shackles of secular leaders and systems.

Sharia Law has become code for oppression in the United States, but for me it was just the rules a Muslim must follow to be religious. It has nothing to do with violence or extremism. Books like *Milestones* created confusion and omitted the parts of Islam that didn't support radical Islam. The Quran specifically states that Muslims must abide by the country's laws in which they reside. That is the word of God, not some Egyptian scholar's interpretation.

I knew Jaser was quoting Qutb even though he never said the

name. With each quote and idea, I responded enthusiastically. When Jaser's testing me was over, we agreed to meet the next day for prayers at a mosque on Victoria Park Avenue.

Back at the hotel, I waited in my room for an hour—to make sure Chiheb was asleep in his room—and then texted Joey.

"You good?" he asked.

"Yeah, but I need to meet."

"Do you want to do it tonight? Is it too risky?"

The plan was to complete the trip and then meet, but I had to dump the audio and make sure they picked up Chiheb talking about the American sleeper.

"We have to meet tonight."

"Stand by for a location."

A half hour later, I grabbed the recorders and drove over to a nearby parking lot. Nelly, Joey, and Doug were waiting in a black SUV.

I jumped in the back.

"Did you hear?"

Nelly nodded.

"Yeah, most of it," he said. "But it was muffled a lot of the ride."

The cell coverage was spotty between Montreal and Toronto, and the audio must have cut out. They had no idea about the American sleeper.

"There is an American sleeper."

Nelly and Joey looked at each other.

"What?" Nelly said. "Are you fucking kidding me?"

"That's why I wanted to meet."

"Does he know who it is?" Nelly said. "Has he met him?"

I shook my head no.

"The American sleeper trained in Iran before Chiheb," I said.

As I rehashed the conversation, I could tell by Joey's face that everything had changed. This was no longer a favor to Canada. The United States had a massive interest in this case. While Nelly and Joey stressed about the American sleeper, Doug chimed in.

"What about the train plot?"

Doug cared about the American sleeper, but it was his job to protect Canada. He had an active cell planning an attack. I didn't blame him, but that was my first whiff that I was now working for two competing masters. The Canadians wanted Chiheb and Jaser. We wanted the sleeper.

I told him the train attack was scheduled for December. We had time.

"I'll get more details about the plot tomorrow," I said. "We're meeting for prayers in the morning."

At dawn, I joined Chiheb for the day's first prayer. Even with Chiheb right next to me, I asked Allah for help finding the American sleeper and protecting innocent men, women, and children. I needed His strength and wisdom to stay the course. After prayers, we agreed to sleep a few more hours before meeting Jaser at the mosque. We drove over in silence. Both of us were tired after the long drive and late night.

From the outside, the mosque looked like a house. Inside, all of the non-load-bearing walls had been knocked down, and rugs and pillows were set out on the floor.

Jaser wasn't there. We prayed with the rest of the group and then went back to the car. An Afghan man flagged us down before we left. He introduced himself as Waleed. He was dressed in the same camouflage jacket worn by Osama bin Laden. His beard was thick but he didn't have a mustache. At a glance, he looked like someone dressed in a terrorist Halloween costume. It would have looked comical, except he was serious.

"Hello, dear brothers," he said. "I hear you are in from out of town. I am a good friend of Raed. He is running late. I'd love to take you out to breakfast."

Chiheb agreed immediately. He seemed taken with the young Afghan. Waleed climbed into the back of the car and we drove to Tim Hortons, essentially the Canadians' version of Dunkin' Donuts. Jaser called me while we ate.

"Brother, I'm so sorry," he said. "I overslept. I just got out of the shower. Where are you guys? Still at the mosque?"

"No," I said. "We met a friend of yours. Waleed."

"Yes, what a great brother," Jaser said. "Why don't you guys come to my house?"

"Great, can we get you anything?" I asked.

"No, I'm fine."

Then he paused a beat.

"Get me a tea," he said.

I ordered him a tea and we headed back to his house. He met us in the driveway.

"Why don't you leave your phones in the car," Jaser said. "There is no reason to bring them in."

Chiheb and I put our phones in the center console.

Jaser took Waleed's phone and removed the battery. We sat around the table. Jaser started talking from Qutb's script. But he never took it over the line. It was all talk. He knew what he could and couldn't say. The whole speech came off polished. Practiced. I'd seen this before. I called it "the Imam Complex." Jaser liked to talk about jihad and quote Qutb, but he wasn't interested in getting his hands dirty. After an hour, Jaser said he had to go to work. He put his arm around me as we walked to the door.

"Come with me, brother," Jaser said as we left the house.

Chiheb and Waleed walked behind us. They were becoming fast friends. It was clear Chiheb still dreamt of fighting in Afghanistan, and Waleed represented everything he wanted to be.

"Brother, why don't you leave Chiheb with me today, since you have a long day," he said.

I had told Jaser about my plans to see a few properties with a real estate agent.

"That's fine," I said, welcoming a chance to get away from him. "You guys haven't seen each other in a while."

Jaser smiled.

"I have to go into the office, and he can come with me," he said.

Jaser was a taxi dispatcher. They could speak freely in the office, since it was Saturday and only he was on duty.

"Yeah, that sounds great," I said.

"Let's shoot for dinner tonight," Jaser said.

"Done. That sounds great. See you guys later."

As I drove off, I called Joey.

"I can't go back to the hotel," I said. "They think I'm going to look at properties. Got a place I could hole up? I need to get some sleep."

Joey sent me the address of a new hotel. Joey, Kenny, and Nelly met me an hour later with Doug and the other Canadians. The Americans wanted to know about the sleeper. Nelly, Kenny, and Joey took turns asking me the same questions and getting the same answers. I still didn't know the sleeper's identity, his location, or if he was operational.

The Canadians were focused on the train plot and my dinner with Jaser and Waleed. They wanted to know if I thought the mosque was radical, if Waleed was part of the attack, and where I planned to have dinner with them so we could set up surveillance. After the debrief, I watched as everyone jumped on their phones. The cacophony of conversations made it impossible to sleep, so Joey and I went into the other room and started to plan the night's operation.

The plan was to pick up Jaser and Chiheb for dinner around 7:00 P.M. I was in the car heading to Jaser's house when he called and switched the location. A few minutes later they switched it again. I was on edge. What was going on? Were they onto me?

I called Joey.

"Get every surveillance body off the street," I said. "If I get burned because of surveillance, I'm going to kill somebody. Tell them to let me do my job."

Joey didn't like leaving me without backup.

"We need to make sure—" Joey said, hoping to change my mind. I cut him off.

"I will do everything in my power to keep you posted," I said. "But shut it down."

I had no choice. Chiheb was my lifeline to both the Canadian cell and the American sleeper. I was either walking into an ambush or they were ready to cut me in on the plot. I knew how to defend myself, but I was more concerned about getting burned because of some RCMP agent. I'd never be able to forgive myself.

Before I could confirm dinner at the third location, my phone pinged. It was a text from Jaser. He wanted to meet at Waleed's house. Before I could respond, my phone rang.

"Brother, did you get the address?" Jaser said.

"Yeah, what's with all the cloak-and-dagger stuff?"

"We don't want to go out," he said. "We'd rather have a more private dinner."

"Alright, on my way."

Waleed's house was in an upper-middle-class neighborhood in southern Toronto. The four-bedroom colonial style house sat on a cul-de-sac. I pulled up to the house and parked facing out toward the exit of the cul-de-sac. The streets were dark, lit by an occasional streetlight. I stayed in the shadows until I reached the walkway leading to the front door.

It was a cool fall night and I thrust my hands into the pockets of my peacoat. I could hear someone shuffling to the door after my second knock.

"Brother Tamer?" an older Afghan man said after he cracked open the door.

"Yes," I said, my eyes looking past him into the house.

"Come on in," he said with a smile.

I stepped into the foyer and kicked off my shoes. There was a pile of men's shoes next to the door. I tried to count the pairs, but the old man motioned for me to follow him down the main hall.

Everything was dark inside the house. The smell of food cooking hung in the air. I could hear the sounds of pots and pans banging around deeper in the house. Something moved in my peripheral vision. A woman's hand drew a drapery closed, but I could just make out a counter and some bowls used for cooking before the room got darker.

The Afghan stopped at a door near the kitchen and opened it. A wooden staircase led to the basement. The Afghan held the door open and urged me to go down first. I smiled and hesitated for a second. I really didn't want to go into the basement. The Afghan smiled. Another beat and things were going to get awkward. I started down the steps.

The Afghan shut the door behind us as I walked down the stairs. The basement was finished and well lit. Oriental rugs covered the floor, and posters showing off various sites of the Middle East hung on the wall. A bar near the staircase was stocked with water and fruit. As I got to the last step, I could hear Chiheb talking. He was sitting at a large picnic table with Jaser and Waleed. The tabletop was covered with a cloth and plates of lamb, shrimp, and hummus. Everything was home cooked and looked delicious.

I started to calm down immediately. Chiheb stood up to greet me. Everyone had a smile. They were waiting for me. I took a seat near the corner and everyone started to eat. Before I could get more than a few bites, Waleed and the Afghan—his father—started asking me about my business.

"What do you do?"

"Real estate," I said.

"Is it commercial or residential?"

Before I finished an answer there was another question. A half hour into dinner and I'd only had a few bites. By now, the main course of stewed meat and rice with raisins was served.

Between answers, I started to look for the exit. The staircase was the only way in or out. Going around the room, I figured the old Afghan would be the last one I'd kill. I'd start with Waleed. He was in good shape and would give me a fight. Then probably Jaser and Chiheb in that order.

But with each question I got more comfortable. There was no malice, at least toward me. It was clear they believed the legend and were curious. I was something new. Jaser, Waleed, and his family lived in isolation. An insular community of Muslims who didn't fit in with their neighbors.

But I was a Muslim brother who spoke English like an American. I was very successful. I had money, my own business, and yet I still had the same values as they did. They were tired of talking to one another. My presence at dinner injected new topics of conversation. I was the entertainment.

After dinner, we prayed. Jaser led this time. When it was over, I pulled him aside. I still had to win him over and knew the best way to do it. Stroke his ego.

"Brother, you have an amazing Quranic voice," I said. "It just takes me over."

I wasn't lying. His delivery was flawless. He never hesitated. He never stammered. Jaser's eyes lit up after the compliment. He pulled out his phone and let me listen to recordings of him reciting other prayers as we ate dessert. When everyone was done, Jaser pulled me aside.

"I'd like to take a walk with you," he said.

"Sounds great," I said. "It's a beautiful night."

Waleed volunteered to walk us out. Jaser was wearing a brown leather jacket. As I buttoned up my peacoat, I asked Chiheb if he had a coat.

"It's cold out here," I said.

Chiheb had only a button-down shirt and jeans. Waleed took off his camouflage jacket and handed it to Chiheb. He refused it until Waleed insisted Chiheb take it.

"Brother, it's a gift from me, it's a gift from me," Waleed said.

"But it's a big gift," Chiheb said, trying to hand the jacket back to Waleed.

He was afraid this was Waleed's only jacket.

"Brother, I have another jacket," he said. "I have so many. I need to get rid of them."

Finally, Chiheb pulled the jacket on, and I could tell he loved wearing it. In his mind he looked like the Sheikh, Osama bin Laden. I thanked Waleed and his father for the hospitality and started for the door. Just before we walked outside, Jaser stopped us.

"Keep your phones in the car and walk in the middle of the street," Jaser said.

By walking in the middle of the street, no one could overhear our conversation and we could spot surveillance. We left the house and walked down the middle of the road. Chiheb was on my right. Jaser on my left.

A few minutes into the walk, I spotted a couple walking a dog. They were trying not to look at us. When Jaser spotted them, they turned and walked in the opposite direction. Jaser kept watching them until they disappeared. It wasn't RCMP. It had to be CSIS. They were keeping tabs on us.

Once we were alone, Chiheb started the conversation.

"The issue is that we would like to tell you what we are planning, me and Raed," he said. "Because me and Raed, we have some plan . . . But of course we need someone to protect our back."

"Of course," I said.

"And this person who protects our back should be someone who is in a very good position, high position. He has the ability to manage the situation by distance. The ability to deviate the attention of the security services."

"Staying careful," I said.

"You understand?"

"I understand," I said.

Chiheb said Canada and America have armies in the Middle East.

"These armies are taking control of our land and they are spreading corruption on the Earth," he said. "They are spreading evil, they are spreading, you know, adultery, they are spreading alcohol, you understand? They are spreading Christianity. So it's our mission to fight those countries that have harmed us. The military power comes from the money power. Because those people who are supporting those evil governments are making war in our land, our home, our lands. So it's our duty to break their economic resources. To make trouble in their homes."

"Destroy their homes, because they are destroying our homes," I said.

Chiheb nodded his head yes.

"An eye for an eye and a tooth . . ." Jaser said.

"A tooth for a tooth," Chiheb said, finishing his thought.

"And the oppressor is who started it," Jaser said.

Chiheb thanked me for supporting the brothers overseas with my profits, but said this time was different.

"This is your time now," Chiheb said. "This is your time and your opportunity to not only support our brothers by money, but also by action."

Chiheb again laid out how they were going to do the attack. Having talked to Jaser about it at the taxi office, he was pretending to tell me for the first time. The whole time Jaser was silent. In order to prove the conspiracy, I needed him to talk. I needed to bring out the Imam in him.

"It's brilliant in its simplicity, but how does that serve our purpose as far as letting the world know?" I asked about the plot. "The important thing is to let the nonbelievers understand. Am I right? To let them know that this will keep happening—we can strike you whenever we want. But they're just gonna think it's an accident. But actually, it's an act of war. You understand, *habibi*?"

Chiheb started to answer. Shielding Jaser, I grabbed Chiheb's arm and squeezed it. He stopped talking and looked down. Jaser stepped in to fill the silence.

"I got the question for you answered," Jaser said.

He and Chiheb told me about the video.

"Because we want to make sure that they understand that as long as they're over there, their people will not feel safe on this side," Jaser said.

At first, I had feared the dinner might be a trap, but now I was the one setting the trap—and Jaser walked right into it.

"God almighty says fight their leaders," Jaser said.

He wanted to launch a string of sniper attacks targeting Canada's leaders. Chiheb was puzzled. How would we get near their leaders? They live in "castles," as he put it. They were protected, but Jaser said local leaders gave public speeches and attended parades. His example was a recent gay pride parade.

"The reason why is because they feel safe," he said. "Bunch of faggots. You know what I mean? Who's gonna attack them? They're just like them. Okay. That's when we hit them. This is the plan."

I stayed silent. Jaser and Chiheb were both committed to carrying out a terrorist attack.

"They feel safe," Jaser said. "We're gonna change all that."

CHAPTER 14

The Christian Burial Speech

Chiheb had to piss.

I could see him squirming in his seat as I drove east back to Montreal. We had spent the last two hours drinking tea and talking with Jaser at Denison Park next to the Humber River.

After our walk the night before, I'd agreed to meet with him before our drive home. Jaser's Imam Complex was in full swing. He agreed to the train plot, but he was more focused on his own sniper attack. It turned out Chiheb was annoyed by Jaser's rants. The train plot was sent from the brothers overseas. It was the priority, but every time it came up Jaser changed the subject. Jaser didn't want to take orders from overseas, from brothers hiding in caves who had no idea about Canada.

He became emotional at one point and shed a tear.

"Islam is a very powerful weapon, okay, and if it's in the right hands, you can bulldoze the whole world," he said. "And the beauty of Islam is that even the ruler or the president or the Caliph who is ruling himself, he submitted to the law of Allah."

It was the first time I saw the cracks in their relationship.

After the meeting, Chiheb and I drove back to Montreal. There were no bathrooms at the park, and we both climbed into the car with full bladders. I watched Chiheb fidget in his seat.

"Come on, we're gonna piss our pants," I said, laughing.

"My Lord," Chiheb said, a look of anguish on his face. "Allah, may Allah relieve me and relieve you. We should look for a washroom."

I searched my GPS for the closest gas station. It was uncomfortable for me. For Chiheb, it was a full-on crisis. One drop of urine on his skin or clothes and he'd be unclean. Making *wudu* wasn't enough. One drop of urine would send him careening off the path of Allah.

"Yeah," I said. "The first washroom I see. We'll stop, Allah willing, even a restaurant or whatever."

The closest one was a couple of miles off the highway. We both leapt out of the car. It took me a few minutes to go and wash up. Chiheb went in at the same time and didn't come out for forty-five minutes. He would urinate and then painstakingly make sure he didn't get any urine on himself. By the time he was done he sometimes had to urinate again. He was an extremist in every sense of the word. I sat in the car and waited. Thirty minutes was common, but this was a longer trip than usual. He looked distraught when he got back to the car.

"Tamer, I think I got some urine on my clothing," Chiheb said. "I had to go so bad that I barely made it."

"No worries," I said. "We'll figure it out."

I had to solve this or all conversation was done. He was already distraught and it would only get worse as we got closer to prayer. I got my phone and found a Gap a few miles away.

"We shouldn't waste money," Chiheb said when I told him where we were going.

"Don't worry," I said, putting the car in gear. "It's tax deductible."

Chiheb exhaled. He seemed relieved.

"God bless you, brother."

Chiheb picked out a pair of boxers, jeans, and a button-down shirt from the Gap. I paid and we went over to a nearby Marriott hotel. He went into the lobby bathroom to clean up. The Gap gave him an extra bag, so his urine-stained clothes wouldn't touch anything.

I walked over to the front desk.

"My friend and I would like to pray," I said. "Is there a place that is quiet that we could use so we don't have to pray outside?"

"Of course," the clerk said.

A few minutes later, I had the key to a banquet room. Chiheb came out an hour later wearing a smile and his new Gap clothes. Suburban dad with a jihadi beard.

"Brother, we have a place to pray," I said.

Once we got back to the car, my mind was stuck on my new mission: to find the American sleeper. The Canadian case, for all intents and purposes, was done. We had all the elements of a conspiracy. It would be nice to have one more overt act, like scouting the location or buying equipment, but it wasn't necessary.

I had everything I needed to convict Chiheb, but I wanted to give him the "Christian burial" speech. I was inspired by *Brewer v. Williams*, a 1977 United States Supreme Court case dealing with waiving the Sixth Amendment's right to counsel.

Robert Williams, who escaped from a mental hospital, kidnapped ten-year-old Pamela Powers on December 24, 1968, at the YMCA in Des Moines, Iowa. She was watching her brother in a wrestling tournament and left to use the bathroom. A fourteen-year-old boy saw Williams carrying something wrapped in a blanket through the lobby. He saw Powers's legs when Williams put her in the car. A warrant was issued and two days later Williams surrendered.

The Des Moines police drove 160 miles to Davenport to pick him up with a promise not to interrogate him without his lawyer present. Detectives knew Williams was deeply religious. Once they reached the highway heading back to Des Moines, the detective gave Williams what would later be called the "Christian burial speech."

> I want to give you something to think about while we're traveling down the road. . . . Number one, I want you to observe the weather conditions, it's raining, it's sleeting, it's freezing, driving is very treacherous, visibility is poor, it's going to be dark early this evening. They are predicting several inches of snow for tonight, and I feel that you yourself are the only person that knows where this little girl's body is, that you yourself have only been there once, and if you get a snow on top of it [sic] you yourself may be unable to find it. And, since we will be going right past the area on the way into Des Moines, I feel that we could stop and locate the body, that the parents of this little girl should be entitled to a Christian burial for the little girl who was snatched away from them on Christmas Eve and murdered. And I feel we should stop

and locate it on the way in rather than waiting until morning and trying to come back out after a snowstorm and possibly not being able to find it at all. . . . I do not want you to answer me. I don't want to discuss it any further. Just think about it as we're riding down the road.

Williams took the police to Powers's body on the way back.

My version of the speech was different. Basically, if Chiheb didn't waver and back out, then there was no defense for his actions. I didn't entrap him. He was plotting to murder hundreds of innocent people. I used this technique as a final nail in the coffin. I was looking to bury him using his own words.

"Okay, so look, thank God, you are a religious man and are more learned about our religion than the majority of Muslims I know," I said, starting the speech. "But I need to ask you something. I don't want you to think that I'm wavering here. I'm thinking ahead a bit. When the news breaks about what we've done, we will see that there were women and children who died. Are you sure this is considered halal? Is this what Allah wants?"

Chiheb turned in his seat to face me. This was serious. He started in English to make sure I understood. He had three proofs that condoned the attack.

"God almighty, He gave us the permission to eat dead animals, and to drink alcohol if you are close to death," Chiheb said. "But when you eat the dead meat or you drink the alcohol, you should do just what you need to survive; not more than that. That means don't fill your stomach. You just eat enough to keep you alive. Right?"

"Of course," I agreed.

His voice was measured and serious. Chiheb wasn't scolding me for doubting, but he wanted to crush any doubts.

"So what does this mean?" Chiheb said, settling into his lesson. "This means that you are allowed to do something haram if there is a necessity behind that haram. And when you do that haram, there are two conditions. You should not do this as you like to do. That means that when I do that haram, inside myself, I should have the feeling of not loving what I am doing. This is the first condition. Second, I should not exceed the necessity. Now please, brother, follow me on this point. If God almighty allows us to do that haram to save your life, what about saving your religion?"

Chiheb slapped his thigh and startled me.

"The necessity of saving religion is much higher than the necessity of saving your life. But God almighty, He allows you to do this haram for a lower level, which is the necessity to save your life. So what about the necessity to save the religion? So of course, you are more permissible to do that haram. This is one point."

For a second, I thought Chiheb might be turning. He admitted killing innocents was haram and that he shouldn't and couldn't like it, but he justified it.

"The second point, you know very well that all the civilian people who are living here, they are paying taxes. But also you know that those nonbelievers, they are attacking and killing our women and our children in our land. God almighty, He said that you should make aggression as they aggress you. You know aggression?"

"Do unto them as they've done to you," I said.

"So if they are killing our women and our children in our country, why don't we kill their women and their children in their country? And God almighty told us in the Quran to do to them as they are doing to you. So, this is the second proof. The first, you get the first, right?"

"The first one, yes," I said. "Of course."

"The necessity of . . ."

"Saving Islam," I said.

Saving Islam from him, was what I really meant. My job was to keep him talking. But in my mind I was arguing. This was not the religion my mother and father taught me. Islam wasn't a religion of violence and revenge. The Quran says he who slays a soul on earth shall be as if he had slain all of mankind, and he who saves a life shall be as if he had given life to all mankind.

"Saving religion, the necessity of saving religion is higher than the necessity of saving a life," he said. "But God, He allows you to do some haram. You understand?"

He was making sure I understood every point. This was jihad 101 and he wasn't sure why I needed to be told why our actions were justified.

"The second is that they are killing the women and children in our land. So why we don't do as they are doing? Now the third point, it's not from religion but it's a practical justification."

This I have to hear, I thought.

"You know very well that the nonbeliever is controlling our land. He's colonizing our land. Tens of years, right?"

"Yeah," I said. "Long time."

"One hundred, maybe more," Chiheb said.

I agreed in hopes he'd get to the point.

"Okay, so are we able to kick out the nonbeliever from our land with military organization? With a military army? Are you follow-ing? Do you get my question?"

"Meaning they have a big army," I said.

No Muslim army could kick the Western militaries out of the Middle East, Chiheb said. The brothers lack resources, technology, and equipment to resist. And when a Muslim nation does gain strength, the West destroys it.

"Look at Iran: Israel is preparing herself to send planes to destroy the nuclear factory," Chiheb said. "So this means that the nonbeliever is not allowing us to use technology. We are not able to kick out the army by fighting army between army. So, in that case, we are in the obligation to use other ways. Are you following me?"

"Absolutely," I said. "We have to fight the only way we can."

"The only way we can for the purpose to remove them, even when you find yourself obliged to do something haram," Chiheb said. "Are you following me?"

I felt his eyes on me.

"One hundred percent," I said.

"Are you following me?" he repeated.

This was the last time he wanted to talk about justifying the attacks.

"Amazing words," I said. "It's never gonna be an issue again. You explained it brilliantly. You said it perfectly. You are right on."

"So the first and the second, they are religious, the third is practical. You understand?"

"Of course," I said. "I'm thinking about the media and what is going to be said about us and everything else. They are going to call us terrorists and they will call us all kinds of bad things. They're gonna show pictures of the women and the babies that died, but they'll never show the pictures of the women and the children that are dying every day back home."

But what I was saying wasn't Islam, and I knew it. The Quran was very clear on the laws of war. A Muslim could only fight against other combatants. The Prophet Mohammed had clear rules. He instructed his soldiers it was forbidden to kill "any child, any woman, or any elder or sick person." Mutilation, scorched earth tactics, and destroying crops and villages were forbidden. The Prophet said nothing about terrorism, because there was only one way to wage war as a Muslim.

There was no question Chiheb wanted to commit an act of terrorism. He was convicted by his own words. My questions must have concerned Chiheb. A little while later, after we'd stopped talking about his proofs, he quizzed me.

"So, can you repeat the three points?"

"I will repeat them right now. Is this my test?"

Chiheb giggled.

"Because you failed your test when I asked you how many brothers you have, but I'm gonna pass my test."

Chiheb had three brothers. When I asked him about his family, he didn't include me as one of his brothers. I never let him forget.

"First proof, God almighty, He allows us in times of need, if we are this close to death, we're allowed to eat a dead animal or drink alcohol, just enough to save our lives. And to do that haram to save our life. Now imagine what God is going to allow in order for us to save our religion. Right?"

Chiheb smiled like a teacher happy with his pupil.

"Number two. Look at what they're doing to our women and children. For dozens of years, and years and years, they are killing our women and children nonstop. Right? So they're killing our women and children, we're gonna kill their women and children.

That's the second proof. And the third, which is what we just discussed . . ."

"Which is not religious, it's practical," Chiheb said.

"It's practical," I said. "They have occupied our land."

"And our brothers, they can't succeed right now," Chiheb said.

"They're winning some battles but they're losing some battles and they're not succeeding, but the point is, they are over there occupying our land. And they are a big military. For example, let's use Israel and the United States. Both of them have huge military armies. We can't get a military army to take our land back, so we have to use any means necessary, any means necessary to fight that evil. And the only way we can is this way."

I was getting into the act now.

"We're gonna have more success doing it this way," I said.

"Yeah," Chiheb said. "But don't forget that the nonbeliever, when he is in our land, he's taking more security procedures than he is in his land."

"Exactly," I said. "Because he feels comfortable here."

"They are ready for them over there," he said. "But here they are not ready for us."

"Can I ask you a question now?" I said.

"Yes," Chiheb said.

"How did I do on the test?"

"One point for you and zero points for me."

"I did well?"

"You are a good player."

"But you're a good teacher."

And convicted, I thought.

CHAPTER 15

Best of the Mujahideen

Back in Montreal, Chiheb wanted me to meet two like-minded brothers for dinner.

We met them at an Egyptian seafood restaurant not far from his apartment. The last two weeks had been a blur. I'd gone from relaxing on a beach in the Caribbean (well, trying to), to being embedded in an al Qaeda plot to derail a train in Canada, to trying to find an American sleeper cell.

It was September 11, 2012, and I was in no mood to be breaking bread with a terrorist. But I put on my best smile and tried to at least enjoy my food.

The two men were actual brothers from Tunisia. They arrived just as we got to the restaurant. Both were engineers who worked in Montreal. Typical Middle Eastern foreigners: young, educated, religious, and generous.

Over fish, Chiheb worked politics into the conversation when he could, but it was obvious that the brothers weren't interested. There were a few times when I was a little embarrassed for Chiheb as he tested their interpretations of hadiths and scolded them when their views were different from his. The brothers failed Chiheb's test.

I paid for dinner and we walked to the Cold Stone Creamery across the street for ice cream. The Tunisian brothers paid for dessert. As we were eating our ice cream, I was making fun of Chiheb about his hard-line views. He knew I was trying to placate the brothers and played along. We said our goodbyes and I drove Chiheb home.

"Those are good brothers," I said.

"But not like-minded," Chiheb said. "They are not like us."

"Few of us are like you, brother," I said as I stopped in front of his apartment building. "I am floored that you were actually trained by our elders, my brother. How did that happen? I'd love to hear that story."

From the beginning, something had bothered me about Chiheb. It didn't make sense that this goofy scientist with a Canadian visa ended up one step removed from the leader of al Qaeda in less than one year.

There was no doubt he wanted to kill Westerners. It never left his heart, even when it was the furthest thing from anyone's mind. But this dark center was hidden from view by a jovial scientist working to cure the world's deadliest diseases. He laughed like Baba Noel, the Arabic name for Santa Claus. It was hard to wrap my head around.

As we sat in front of his building, I wanted to know whether he was evil or someone overseas had turned him into a monster. Chiheb was happy to tell me the story. He was proud of his time in Iran.

When Chiheb got to Canada in 2008, he was lost. Everything

was foreign. He barely spoke the language. The weather was frigid and he recognized few customs. The order he found in the laboratory was absent in his daily life. Exiled from the daily rhythms of Montreal, his focus turned inward. He studied Islam, read the Bible and Torah. He was looking to bring order to the chaos of the real world. But it wasn't until he started to follow the war in Afghanistan that things crystalized.

"I researched their struggles in Afghanistan," he said. "I wanted to die on the battlefield with the mujahideen brothers."

In the spring of 2011, Chiheb emptied his bank account, bought a one-way ticket to Tehran, and planned to drive to Afghanistan.

"Buying a ticket to Kabul was too obvious," Chiheb told me.

"Why didn't you go to Pakistan?" I asked.

Most foreign fighters filtered in through the ratlines in Pakistan's tribal areas.

"Pakistan is a friend to the United States," Chiheb said. "Iran is not."

I still didn't know what pushed him to seek out the mujahideen, but I didn't press it. I wanted him to tell his story.

When he landed in Tehran, a cab driver at the airport befriended him. The cabbie was a Sunni Muslim, like Chiheb, which is a minority in Iran. Chiheb stayed at the cabbie's house for a few days. But his mind was still across the border in Afghanistan.

"I need to get to the border to cross into Afghanistan to help the brothers," Chiheb told the cabbie.

"No," the cabbie said. "Stop talking. That kind of talk will get you in trouble."

Chiheb pleaded for his help, and the cabbie hooked him up with a friend who was more sympathetic. Chiheb paid thousands of dollars for a ride to Zahedan, a town in southeastern Iran that bordered Afghanistan and Pakistan.

"I just told him to drive me as close to the border as possible," Chiheb said.

When they arrived in Zahedan, Chiheb and the driver stopped at a local mosque to pray.

"Everyone stared at us," Chiheb said.

Right after prayer, a couple of young men wanted to know who Chiheb was and why he was there.

"I told them I was passing through on my way to Afghanistan. I asked to speak to the Imam so I could get some guidance on crossing the border."

One of the young men got El Mofti, an old Iranian man in his late sixties. He limped out from the back of the mosque to meet Chiheb.

"Where is the easiest place to cross the border into Afghanistan?" Chiheb asked.

"Are you hungry?" El Mofti asked. "Come, I know a restaurant nearby where we can eat."

Chiheb thanked the driver and followed El Mofti to a restaurant. They took a table in the back and ate.

"I was completely truthful with him," Chiheb said. "I told him that I was ready to die for Allah and that it is my destiny to fight with the mujahideen in Afghanistan."

Chiheb found out later El Mofti had thought he was a spy, but his truthfulness at dinner changed the Imam's mind. El Mofti invited Chiheb to stay at his home.

"El Mofti kept telling me not to go to Afghanistan," Chiheb said. "I stayed at his house for a few days until I needed a new visa."

Chiheb got a cab and started his trek back to Tehran to renew his visa. On his way out, he realized he needed to change his Canadian dollars to Iranian rials. Chiheb stopped at the mosque to ask where he could change money. One of the young boys ran to the back and told El Mofti Chiheb was leaving.

"Don't go, brother," El Mofti told Chiheb. "There is someone I want you to meet. A very special guest."

Chiheb tried explaining that he was just going to get his visa renewed, but El Mofti shooed the cab away and he brought Chiheb back to his house.

"Don't worry about your visa," he told Chiheb.

That night, a tall Afghan wearing a black robe and a black turban came to El Mofti's house.

"The second I laid eyes on him, I knew I made the right choice," Chiheb said.

The Afghan went by the common alias of Abu Hamza. He spent the evening getting to know Chiheb.

"He tested me," Chiheb said. "Like I tested you."

"You passed?" I asked.

"Yes," Chiheb said. "Like you."

Chiheb spent almost a week at Abu Hamza's house. He learned al Qaeda's codes and how to send messages to the brothers overseas.

"I wanted to learn how to shoot," Chiheb said. "I wanted to be a soldier."

But Abu Hamza had other plans. Chiheb had a Canadian visa. He had access to the West.

"Your brilliant mind shouldn't be wasted on the battlefield," Abu Hamza said. "You will be the best of the mujahideen because you will be able to do Allah's work in the heart of the infidel's land."

Abu Hamza told Chiheb to go back to Canada and await further instructions. Chiheb spent almost a year working and studying in Montreal.

"My mother called me months later," he said. "She said strangers came to her house and introduced themselves as my new friends."

Al Qaeda was checking his story. Then in February 2012, Chiheb was instructed to return to Zahedan for his training. He bought a ticket and flew out the day after he got the e-mail. He stayed at Abu Hamza's house.

"Tell me about him, brother," I said.

"Abu Hamza was a general with the Taliban, but I was trained by a general in al Qaeda."

"Who is that?" I asked.

"El Massoul," he replied.

Abu Hamza drove Chiheb to the outskirts of the city to meet El Massoul, who dressed in a long white robe and wore a camouflage jacket like Osama bin Laden.

"It was the Sheikh's jacket," Chiheb said. "El Massoul wore it everywhere. Meeting him was the greatest moment of my life."

Chiheb lived with El Massoul for six weeks, where he learned about the train plot, how to recruit like-minded brothers, and how to resist torture.

"Resist torture?" I said. "Did they actually torture you?"

"No," Chiheb said. "El Massoul explained that it would be an honor to be tortured by the infidels in this life instead of the afterlife and to accept the pain. Because it will be nothing like the pain of hellfire."

"Was there any Islamic studies done during your training?" I asked.

"Not once," he said. "That's not what this training was about."

Of course not.

"El Massoul left for a few days, but promised to return before I went back to Canada," Chiheb said. "When he returned, he had a note for me."

It was handwritten in Arabic, Chiheb said.

"It said 'Focus on your studies and don't argue.'"

"What does that mean?" I asked.

"It's like what your uncle told you," Chiheb said. "Live amongst them, as them, to defeat them. Blend in using my work. The second part, I had to ask El Massoul. He told me it meant not to draw any attention to myself when I was finding good brothers."

"Is that how you found me?" I asked, hammering home the fact that he chose me.

"Yes. El Massoul told me that when you try to bring a brother along and he argues with you, try again. If he argues again, leave him. Don't fight with him."

"That's an amazing story, my brother," I said.

But Chiheb wasn't done. He took out his wallet. It was thick with notes, receipts, a small Quran.

"Tamer, that note that El Massoul gave me was from our Sheikh," Chiheb said.

He held up his wallet.

"I carry it everywhere with me."

He'd mentioned the note during our road trip to Toronto, but I didn't really understand its significance. The Sheikh was Ayman al-Zawahiri, the leader of al Qaeda. El Massoul was one of a handful of people on the planet who could meet with the Sheikh in person, Chiheb said.

"Are you kidding me? *Habibi,* you have a note directly from our Sheikh?" I said. *"Masha'Allah."*

Chiheb returned to Montreal soon after getting the note and continued his studies just like al-Zawahiri ordered. He also started working on the train plot. We met shortly thereafter.

"El Massoul told me to be ready by the end of the year," Chiheb said. "He will send me an e-mail with the code word to attack."

"What is the code?" I asked.

"Akbar."

CHAPTER 16

Pizza with Terrorists

I buttoned my peacoat when I got out of the taxi and watched as the Delta Hotel bellhop loaded my bags onto the cart.

It was late September 2012—ten days after my car trip with Chiheb—and I was back in Toronto to find a safe house and meet with Jaser.

Everything changed when we learned of the American sleeper. Chiheb was planning attacks across the border, but the RCMP was aware. We had our own Chiheb and had to find him.

This had become my only case. The FBI had other undercover agents take over my caseload. Progress on the case was briefed daily to the White House. My four-day babysitting mission had stretched into three months with no end in sight.

While we focused on the American sleeper, Canada wanted an airtight case and pushed me to get the plot's final details.

I called Jaser from my two-room suite. No answer. The RCMP

wanted me to spend some alone time with him. Take his temperature without Chiheb. They were concerned he was just following along.

Jaser had moved to Canada in 1993. His family was forced to leave the United Arab Emirates after his father refused to spy on the Palestinian refugees living there. Jaser, fifteen, arrived with his parents and two brothers—eleven-year-old Nabil and ten-year-old Shadi. His mother was pregnant with another boy. The Immigration and Refugee Board accepted Jaser's family into Canada under an old program that accepted stateless refugees.

While the family fought to stay in Canada, Jaser was convicted of fraud in 1997 and for threatening a pub manager in 1999. Ordered out of Canada, he was finally picked up in 2004 after Canadian immigration issued a warrant for his arrest. He was released from the Toronto West Detention Centre when officials couldn't find a country to deport him to. Being Palestinian, Jaser had no country.

He stayed out of trouble after that. Jaser married and started a limo company. He was pardoned in 2009 and received permanent resident status in 2012. When his limo company failed in 2011, he took a job driving special-education students and working customer service for a moving company. By the time I met him he'd gotten his job as a taxi dispatcher.

Jaser fit the profile of a petty criminal who was now sprinkling a little jihad on his activities. Disenfranchised, he wanted to lash out against the Jews and the government for stealing his country. Jaser was a cliché.

I unfolded two maps of the Toronto area and spread them out on the living room table. We still didn't know the target for sure. Was it the bridge they scouted over Labor Day or another one? Doug came up with the idea for the maps.

"If he sees them, maybe he can walk you through where they are potentially going to do this," Doug said in the briefing before I went to the hotel.

Worth a shot.

My cell phone rang about an hour later. It was Jaser. I told him I was in town and wanted to meet up. I could hear radio traffic in the background as he talked. He suggested we meet at the taxi dispatch office but reminded me that there was audio and video there so we couldn't discuss the plan.

"Why don't you come by the hotel?" I said.

We could have a late dinner and talk in private, I told him. Jaser agreed. I hung up and called Chiheb. He knew I was in Canada and I had promised to check in. When he found out Jaser was coming over, he got upset.

"Any discussion about the projects should be with all three of us," he said.

He was acting like a jealous girlfriend. He didn't want to be left out, but he was busy with his dissertation and couldn't leave.

I sensed some tension after the first trip, but it was clear Chiheb and Jaser were in a power struggle over who was the leader. There was no way Chiheb was going to let Jaser sap my resources with his plans. For now, the tension worked in my favor.

"I could get to Toronto Sunday," he said.

"Perfect, brother," I said. "We will pick you up then."

That gave me two days with Jaser. He arrived around nine o'clock. We prayed and then ordered room service. While we waited for our food, Jaser noticed the maps on the table and started to show me where he and Chiheb were thinking of derailing the train. It was a bridge south of Toronto near Lake Ontario. But he didn't think the plan was doable. There was no way to cut the rail in two hours, the time between trains. He wanted to do it his way. Jaser made a gesture with his hands, like a bomb.

"Boom," he said, hinting that the best way to derail the train was with explosives.

Dinner arrived—fish and risotto—and we talked about renting a safe house as we ate. I told him I had talked to a real estate agent and my company was ready to sign a lease for a condo north of Toronto. Jaser liked the area, but he was concerned my name would be on the lease. I assured him my name wouldn't appear on anything regarding the safe house.

The food was delicious. I picked up the plate of fish and offered him more before taking another sliver. He waved it off but kept eating the risotto.

"This rice is good," I said. "The rice is nice, right?"

"It's good, yeah," Jaser said. "It has a nice flavor to it."

"It's called risotto," I said. "Vegetable risotto."

"Yeah, it's pretty good," he said between spoonfuls. "Mind you, though, if I would make this risotto it would be creamier. And the rice would be cooked more."

I chuckled. That was such a Jaser comment. He was that kind of guy. Everything he did was better. This was his first taste of risotto, but he could make it better.

After dinner, he laid out his ideas. He wanted to train a sniper—likely from the household mosque where I met him on my first trip—and target Jewish businessmen, gays, and local leaders. He told me how we could inflict more damage than anyone in al Qaeda because he knew Canada and Toronto better.

"There is so much we can do," he said. "So much pain we can

inflict. Look at the Prophet, peace be upon him, all the wonderful things he did. He did all of that, but he didn't have a day job. I do, unfortunately, and if I didn't and I could focus on this, I think I can do . . ."

I stopped listening and looked at him. Did he just say if he didn't have a job he could be like the Prophet? A Muslim never compares anyone or anything to the Prophet, or any prophet for that matter. It was haram. But Jaser was as good as the Prophet, except he had to dispatch taxis.

It was getting late and Jaser wanted to go home to his wife. We planned to meet the following day. I told him about my plan to meet with a real estate agent to finalize the lease on a condo on Harrison Garden Boulevard in North York.

After Jaser left, I met the team at a nearby hotel suite. Frank answered the door. Nelly, Joey, and Doug were waiting in the living room.

"Good call with the maps," I told Doug as we talked about the meeting with Jaser.

"I know," Doug said, shrugging his shoulders and sniffing.

It stopped me in my tracks.

"Did you just sniff?"

Doug did it every time he was right or told a joke that made someone laugh. From that moment on, we called it the "Dougy Sniff."

As we talked through the next Jaser meeting, Frank filled us in on the layout of the condo. The living room had a couch and an easy chair with a table in the middle. The whole place was wired with microphones and cameras.

"Hey, Frank, tell me where the best cameras are," I said. "Where do you want them? I can throw my bag on the chair to make them sit on the couch, or if you'd rather have one of them in the chair?"

I was trying to figure out where I could sit to avoid the camera. It made life for their tech guys a little easier because they didn't have to pixilate my face. But Frank looked at me like I'd just asked him for a naked picture of his wife.

"You don't need to worry about any of that," he said.

"Excuse me?" I said.

"Don't worry about where they are. Just get them in there and we'll figure it out."

I looked at Joey and Nelly. Nelly shook his head. Joey cringed. He knew this was something he'd have to fix.

"Is this fucking guy for real?" I said. "Is he really not telling me where the cameras are? Frank, you know I'm a cop, right? I'm not a confidential informant or a source. I'm police just like you."

That was the big difference between how the Canadians and Americans ran their undercover programs. The Canadians kept their undercovers in the dark. American undercovers were in on everything behind the scenes. I wasn't used to working in the dark.

"No, I just meant don't worry about it. You have enough to think about," Frank said, realizing he'd hit a nerve.

"Fuck you," I said. "I don't want to know where your cameras are. It's your prosecution."

I left to put my bag back in my hotel room. I could hear Nelly behind me.

"You fucked up," he said to Frank.

Joey found me a few minutes later in my room. I was unpacking.

"Come on," he said. "I'll tell you where the cameras are."

"Don't worry about it," I said.

I wasn't interested.

"I was making an effort," I said. "I was trying to make their lives easier so they didn't have to redact me for hours and hours. If I sat in a chair and my face was obscured they could use the whole tape."

Their case. Their country. Their rules. But Joey told me where the cameras were anyway.

That night I picked up Jaser and took him to the condo. It had two bedrooms, a small kitchen, and a sitting room. In the foyer, Jaser noticed a fruit basket with a thank-you note from the real estate company. Next to the basket was the lease.

"Please enjoy this place on us," the thank-you note read. "We'd love to do business with you."

Jaser was intrigued with the lease and that my name was nowhere on it. I told him my company got the condo for two months. I gave Jaser a quick tour. He approved of the place and looked forward to showing it to Chiheb.

Chiheb called Jaser from downtown the next day. He needed a ride to the condo after catching a carpool from Montreal to Toronto.

"I know where he is," Jaser said. "I'll go grab him."

I gave him the extra set of keys to the condo.

"I'll get dinner," I said.

There was a Pizza Pizza restaurant around the corner. I got two large pizzas with green peppers and onions and met them back at the condo.

Chiheb seemed happy to be in Toronto. I sensed he didn't like being out of the mix. We gathered around the table and started to eat. When the train plot came up, Chiheb mentioned their first recon trip. This was the Labor Day fishing trip. The bridge sat near

Lake Ontario. Both Jaser and Chiheb started to giggle. They were like two old college buddies telling stories from their glory days.

"We wanted, from the beginning, to get closer to the bridge," Chiheb said. "I mean, there was many trees, many trees. And it was some type of a mountain, very strong to walk . . ."

"Hard," Jaser said.

"Hard, is very hard. There is a lot of trees, a lot of insects, a lot of—" Chiheb said.

"I saw a frog this big," Jaser said, holding his hands about six inches apart.

"Oh my God, you're kidding me," I said, egging them on.

"That was a crazy place," Jaser said.

Jaser said they got lost in some thick grass that was ten feet high. Both made it sound like an expedition to the Amazon. The insects. The frogs. The brush. Finally, they stumbled onto the banks of the lake. Out in the distance was a boat. A young couple with big cameras was paddling nearby.

"We waved at them like this," Chiheb said, waving his hand over his head like he was trying to flag me down. "We would like to see the sea."

I started to laugh. He had tried to flag down the CSIS surveillance team. The same guys who had insisted Chiheb and Jaser were going fishing. I was having trouble keeping a straight face.

"He's calling them over to take us to the other side," Jaser said.

"No way," I said.

One of the agents put down his camera and waved back.

"They didn't understand," Jaser said. "They were just waving back, but they wouldn't move. So I was telling him maybe they're not in a good mood. That's why they wouldn't come."

Jaser and Chiheb fought their way back through the grass but got lost again.

"We ended up in somebody's backyard and they were out having a barbecue," Jaser said.

"Halal?" I said, laughing.

"You ask if it is halal, ask him what they said to us," Chiheb said. "Ask him what they said to us."

I looked at Jaser and then Chiheb.

"What?"

"'Why are those terrorists there?'" Jaser said.

"No they didn't," I said.

Chiheb couldn't keep a straight face as he tried to avoid my gaze. He started to laugh.

"I am testing you if you will get scared," he said.

"No, they were nice people," Jaser said.

"Ah, okay," I said. "What'd they say?"

"We talked to them for a while," Jaser said. "I gave them a copy of the Quran."

"They were thinking that we are camping, because many people come to this place, I mean for adventures," Chiheb said.

Despite getting lost twice, they saw enough of the bridge to look for another target. There were too many houses nearby. The terrain made it impossible to bring the equipment needed to cut the rail on the bridge.

Instead, they set their sights on a new, more isolated location near the U.S. border. The location fit the criteria set out by Chiheb from the start, but they only visited it at night. They needed pictures and video of the rails during the day.

"What do you think, we go visit soon?" Chiheb said to both of us.

This is what I was hoping, that they would ask me to scout the location with them. The final piece of evidence for the Canadian case. One more overt act for the conspiracy.

"What do you think, do you have work tomorrow?" Chiheb asked me.

"No," I said.

They wanted me to come because of my expertise in construction. We agreed to scout the new location the following morning.

Chiheb stayed at the condo for the night, since I already had a hotel room. I left with Jaser. The cold hit us as soon as we left the condo. Jaser zipped up his leather jacket. I left my peacoat open.

"You don't get cold?" he said, shivering. "I'm freezing."

"If you feel my skin, I'm hot," I said. "I'm always hot. When I'm at home, my wife goes to bed with two sweatshirts, sweatpants, socks, and sometimes even gloves."

Jaser laughed.

In legend, I am always married. It would be odd if I wasn't.

"I'm wearing no shirt and I'm on top of the covers. I have a tremendous amount of heat, I'm always very hot. Maybe because I'm Egyptian."

We got in the car. Jaser's smile was gone. He stared out the window. There was no energy to his movements. I noticed his mood changed when Chiheb started talking about the train plot.

"Something's on your mind. I want to know what you're thinking," I said. "Spell it out for me. You're the brains here, *habibi*. You can't hold back now."

Jaser just shook his head.

"Not brains, brother. You know, like I said to you, it seems to be too much work for a very small job."

"You think we should go bigger," I said.

"It's too small," he said, turning to look at me. "It's a big operation, we're setting up for a big operation and we end up doing something very tiny. The setup is nice, but the operation doesn't make sense."

I couldn't tell if Jaser didn't like the plan or didn't like that it wasn't his idea. He hated being one of the workers. My job was easy. Pay for equipment and supplies and upload the video. Jaser and Chiheb had to go out in December and cut the track. If he was going to get his hands dirty, it had to be for his plan. He wanted to do his sniper plot instead, but there was no way Chiheb would go for it.

Unless Jaser convinced me.

"Who are they?" he said about the people on the train. "Slaves. Really, just like you and me, workers. You know? Sheep. We don't want sheep. We want the wolf. We can get the wolf. Brother, we can get the wolf."

CHAPTER 17

The Bridge

Chiheb climbed into the passenger seat of my rental car the next morning. On the way to Jaser's apartment, I worked the American sleeper into the conversation.

"Do you think he would want to meet me eventually?" I asked.

"Without a doubt, without a doubt," Chiheb said. "I mean, once he talks with me."

"How do you make this meeting happen?" I asked. "Do you have to call someone? Do you have to send an e-mail because you don't have his number?"

"When I go back to Montreal I will start making contacts with the brothers, God willing, to make arrangements to make the plan for the meeting with the brother."

"Beautiful," I said.

Jaser was waiting for us and jumped into the front seat, forcing Chiheb into the back. Chiheb put up a fight, but Jaser insisted. He knew the way. Like a human GPS, he spent the whole drive barking out directions.

We were headed to the Highland Creek railway bridge in Scarborough. The Maple Leaf, a train line jointly operated by VIA rail—the Canadian train service—and Amtrak—the American rail service—travels over the bridge en route to Penn Station in New York.

We parked in a lot next to a water treatment facility. A trail ran near the train bridge. I saw a few bikers riding away from us as I got out of the car. Jaser had his leather jacket over his white robe, and Chiheb wore his bin Laden jacket. Both Chiheb and Jaser wore kufis, knit Muslim prayer hats. There was no mistaking we were Arabs.

Chiheb led the way as we walked toward the bridge. We cut through a thicket of trees and walked along the edge of the tracks. A commuter train heading toward Toronto passed us. I could feel the rumble of the cars in my chest.

"That was nowhere near the size of the target," Jaser said.

Soon, the steel bridge came into view. It was a one-hundred-foot drop off the bridge into very shallow water. A steel railing ran the length of both sides of the bridge. A footbridge ran underneath for pedestrians. Before we got on the bridge, I stopped Chiheb.

"Are you sure about the train schedule?" I said.

Once we were on the bridge, we were stuck. There was no place to go if the train came.

"Positive," he said.

There were two sets of tracks on the bridge separated by about four feet. Chiheb got on all fours to inspect the rail. The scientist in him took over. He looked at the attack like it was an experiment. He estimated the thickness of the rail and talked about the different ways we could cut it.

Blowtorch.

Jackhammer.

Jaser suggested a military-grade laser, which we all knew was impossible to get.

It was clear a blowtorch was never going to cut through the rail in time. Explosives were probably the only course of action, something Jaser had pointed out in an earlier discussion. Chiheb was thinking out loud as he tried to figure out if two hours was enough time to cut the rail. He was yelling out his ideas in Arabic.

"*Habibi,* lower your voice," Jaser said.

Chiheb ignored him.

"I'm talking in Arabic," he said. "No one knows what we're saying."

I looked back at Jaser. He was nervous we were drawing the attention of joggers and cyclists using the footbridge and nearby paths. Jaser was supposed to be videotaping the tracks with a small camera, but when he saw bikers or runners, he stuffed it into his pocket.

"What's wrong, Raed?" I asked. "There is something on your mind."

"There are many things on my mind," Jaser said.

"Talk to us, *habibi*," I said.

"When I tell you there is someone looking at you, okay, you don't say to me it doesn't matter," Jaser said. "The devil sent him to spy on us."

"The devil sent him?" Chiheb said.

"Of course, who else sent him?" Jaser said, losing his patience a little.

Chiheb laughed.

"Praise God," he said.

"So why don't you take these things seriously?" Jaser asked. "In a serious way?"

"Because in my mind, what does this person know about our project?"

"Brother, it is not about him knowing or not knowing. Just the fact of collecting information for the devil."

Jaser said if we made a mistake and got caught because we didn't take the plot seriously then we were committing a sin.

"I don't need this kind of sin, man," Jaser said. "So take today's act as a lesson."

Chiheb was still on all fours looking at the rail. He waved me over. I climbed down next to him and put my hand on the rail. It was vibrating.

"Chiheb," I said. "Do you feel that?"

He ignored me.

I stood up. Jaser was frozen. We both saw the train at the same time. There was no outrunning it. I looked at both sets of tracks and then back at the train. There was nowhere to run, but the bridge was wide enough for two trains to pass. Our only chance was to get on the far side of the active track and hold on to the fence. But which set of tracks? We had to decide, because once the train reached the bridge it was too late.

I studied the pair of tracks. The south side of the tracks was close to the water. About 250 yards west of the bridge there was a bend. If the train made the bend and I saw tracks, it was on the north side. If I didn't see tracks, it was on the south side.

Jaser started hopping back and forth from each track. At my

fcct, Chiheb was still talking about the rail. My eyes were fixed on the bend. The train started to turn and the tracks disappeared.

I grabbed Chihcb by thc back of his jackct and hcadcd for the north side of the bridge.

"Grab the rail," I said.

Jaser was already following me. I reached the cold metal railing and hooked my arm around it. Jaser was fixated on the train. He looked stiff and scared. Chiheb's face didn't change. If the train killed him, he believed Allah would reward him. I wasn't going to take that chance. I held on to the rail with both hands.

The train got louder as it approached. The thundering of the engine hit me in the chest. I pulled myself tighter to the rail. Wind whipped at my pant legs. It felt like the train was trying to drag me under its wheels. The shrill of the whistle hurt my ears as the engineer spotted us on the bridge. He was hanging out of the window. His face was a mix of shock and fear.

Our eyes locked.

What are you doing? the engineer's eyes asked.

A few seconds later, the train was gone. I let go of the railing.

"That's the target," Jaser said.

We climbed off the bridge and inspected underneath before walking back to the car. Jaser and I walked back the rest of the way in silence. My legs were a little wobbly as the adrenaline of almost getting hit by a train wore off.

Chiheb didn't stop talking about what needed to be done. He got into the front seat of the car and took out a pad of paper. I got behind the wheel and Jaser got in the backseat. Chiheb was unfazed by the train. Seeing the bridge and the train just energized him. He was already thinking of what had to be done. I was sliding the key into the ignition when Jaser spotted the police.

"There's police over there, brother, but they're just passing by," he said.

I checked the mirror. They weren't passing by. They were getting in position. I knew what a felony traffic stop looked like. My mouth went dry. These cops were just doing their jobs, but if they searched the car and found Chiheb's notebook or Jaser's video camera, we were cooked. The investigation was over. I looked over at Chiheb. He was still writing.

"Put it down, the police are coming to talk to us," I said.

He tossed the notebook faceup on the dashboard. I looked at Jaser in the rearview mirror. Sweat was beading on his brow. He looked tense. Scared. As the officers approached, he stuffed the video camera under the seat.

"Hi, sir," a male police officer said as he reached Chiheb's window. "How are you?"

He was dressed in a dark blue uniform. His hand rested near his belt, within reach of his holstered pistol.

"*As salamu alaikum,*" Chiheb said.

"How are you?" the male officer said. "*Wa alaikum al salam.*"

I was focused on the officer talking to Chiheb when I caught some movement out of my peripheral vision. A female officer was at my window. In the rearview mirror two police cars boxed us into the parking spot.

"So what happened was the driver of the train called in and said that he had to honk his horn to have you guys move out of the way," the male officer said. "That's why we're here."

"Yeah, we thought the pathway to get to the walkway was there," I said. "So we realized when we got there that this isn't . . ."

The officer's eyes scanned the car while I spoke.

"You're in the wrong area," he said, cutting me off.

I smiled.

"When we saw we were in the wrong area," I said. "We doubled back."

"What brings you down here?" he said, his gaze alternating between me and Chiheb.

"We're just sightseeing," I said.

The male officer asked for identification. He noticed Chiheb was from Montreal and I was from New York. We told him I was looking at real estate investments in the Toronto area.

"I'm trying to stay away from downtown but the condominiums are unbelievable down here," I said. "You guys seem to be the only country in the world that's not affected by this economy."

"I know, we're lucky," the male officer said. "Unless you walk into some of the condominiums that we have to deal with; then you'd think otherwise."

We all laughed. We made small talk for a while longer and then the officers left.

"Thanks for your cooperation, guys," the officer said, returning to his police car. "Have a nice day."

"All right, you too," I said.

"Peace upon you," he said.

"Upon you too," Chiheb said.

We waited for the police to leave. I let out a deep sigh and looked over at Chiheb. He was back to work making lists in his notebook.

The police stop didn't register with Chiheb. It was just an obstacle to overcome on the path of Allah.

"Damn them," I said. "As brother Raed said, the devil is always watching."

Jaser's nerves were shot. He was jumpy and his eyes darted between me and Chiheb.

"You guys are stupid, that's why," Jaser said. "You don't listen. Sorry, I'm very upset with you."

"Why?" I said.

"I told you to be serious about this. I told you the devil sends people to locate you. You don't listen."

"But thank God, we handled it," I said.

I looked over at Chiheb and shrugged.

"No, no, no, no," Jaser said. "This is okay, but we just compromised the location. So no worries, we just have to find another place. It's not a big deal, there's a lot of good places."

Chiheb stopped working.

"How would they make the connection?" Chiheb said.

"You're foolish," Jaser said. "And you should be happy and say, thank God that you have a brother like me who is telling you about your faults. You're very foolish."

"What does it mean, foolish?" Chiheb said, partly as a challenge and partly because he didn't know. "I don't understand."

"You're gonna make a video, okay, and then the video is not gonna be aired until after the train derails. Where? About two hundred meters, five hundred meters away from where three Arab guys, one from the States, one from Quebec, and one from Ontario, were found, you know, uh, hanging around and checking things out not too long before this happened. This is what they do. Now they have a piece of information. A piece of the puzzle. They're gonna put it in their database and when the right time comes, they're gonna connect one, two, three and they have our information. So this is what I'm talking about taking things seriously."

"But we said that we are just being tourists, we are seeing beautiful pictures," Chiheb said.

"And they probably bought it," I said. "If they didn't buy it, we would've been out of the car."

Jaser just shook his head. He wasn't going to take part in the attack unless we changed the location.

"You do things according to the reality that's on the ground," he said. "You don't do it according to how they do it back there. Do you see my point? There is a completely different set of scenarios and situations. So, if you wanna do this, fine, we can do it, but we're gonna do it our way, not their way. You see, because we're in Canada, we're not in Kandahar."

"Our mistake is that we didn't leave the place immediately," I said. Jaser sighed.

"Yes. That was a mistake," he said. "We should've left as soon as we got to the car."

"We stay at the car like a stupid person," Chiheb said.

"It doesn't matter, nothing happened," I said, hoping to calm everyone down. "We're good."

The police stop was just the opening Jaser needed to change the plot. He asked Chiheb how long he had lived in Canada as I drove back to Toronto. Chiheb told him four years.

"Okay, that's all," Jaser said. "You've been busy studying."

"Yes," Chiheb said.

"I've been busy living. For twenty years. Okay? Who has more experience?"

"You of course," Chiheb said.

"Okay. Who knows how to hurt these people the most? You or me?"

Chiheb looked at me and then back at Jaser. I could see where Jaser was going, but I wasn't sure if Chiheb was tracking.

"You."

"That's it. Okay? Now . . ."

"But, this operation . . ." Chiheb said, realizing he'd fallen into Jaser's trap.

"This is an operation because they asked you to do something," Jaser said. "Okay? That's it. But we can do our own operation. Okay? And their operation, we could do, if it makes sense. If it's safe to do. Okay? But we can do our own operation. Now, if you want to talk about how to hurt these people the most—"

Chiheb cut him off.

"Now you are making the whole operation in question, right?"

The train attack was important to Chiheb and the brothers overseas because it proved al Qaeda could reach out from the battlefields of the Middle East and attack the homeland. The symbolism was almost more important than the attack. It empowered the brothers and terrified the nonbelievers.

Jaser said no, but no one in the car believed him.

"I'm telling you that they gave us a command to do something," Jaser said. "Okay? We're going to try to fulfill the command as we see fit. Not as they see fit, because they're not here. You are following me, right?"

"I am following you," Chiheb said.

"Okay. So we're trying to work things out according to what we know, what we see, and the reality on the ground. Now, at the same time, I can bring your attention to something that is even more relevant than a train. The train, we can continue to do, no problem, find another location, God willing, you never know."

Jaser was in Imam mode.

"These people, they only understand the language of two things. Death and money. That's it. You hurt them. You hit them where it really hurts. You take their lives. You take their wealth. You do these two, they will go crazy."

Jaser said the real target should be Jews living in Toronto, not a train full of sheep. But the people on the train were giving tax money to the governments killing the brothers overseas, Chiheb said. That justified their deaths.

"They are paying taxes, yes," Jaser said. "But do they mean to pay the tax for the government to go, are they giving the green light to the government to go and kill people? No."

"But they know that their government, they are killing . . ." Chiheb said.

Jaser was getting frustrated with Chiheb.

"They don't know, brother, they don't know, you think they follow the news like you? Okay? They are sheep. The whole thing in their head, I gotta pay the mortgage payment, I use my Visa to buy milk, oh, I gotta pay my Visa bill, what are you talking about, man? Get a hold of yourself. Okay? Stop being so dramatic. Dramatic doesn't do anything for Islam. You are becoming a problem more than an asset."

I pretended to listen. This wasn't my first jihadi bitch fight. The biggest misconception about radical Islam is that everyone agrees. To most Westerners, Islamic terrorists are a bunch of bearded brown guys with one worldview. But a jihadi from Saudi Arabia likely has a totally different grievance than one from Iran or Syria. The only unifying idea is the perversion of Islam.

Chiheb sat stone-faced for a few minutes as his mind tried to grind out a response.

"Raed, we are obeying our elders," he said. "They ask us to do this kind of operation. They know better than us."

"They know better than us over there," Jaser said. "Not here."

"Can I ask you guys something?" I said, trying to defuse the situation. "Why can't we do both?"

Chiheb grabbed my lifeline.

"We do both," he said. "I agree with him. I never say no, but my question, how?"

This was what Jaser and I had talked about in the car the night before. If he brought up killing Jews, he had to have a plan or Chiheb would never accept it. Chiheb needed to know the process, how Jaser could accomplish the plot. Otherwise, it was too abstract. Too wishful thinking to merit debate.

"Brother, listen to me," Jaser said. "Why are you asking me how now? I'm sitting in the car right now, just been interrogated by the police."

"He can come up with a plan," I said, hoping to end the debate.

"You can come back with a plan?" Chiheb said.

He was skeptical.

"Brother, I can come up with a better plan than anybody else in this city," Jaser said. "I know this city inside and out." He said his plan was far easier and cheaper than derailing a train. It took only one gun and a bullet.

"If you kill one hundred people, it's more effective than if you kill one or two people," Chiheb said. "And after that you are arrested or killed even."

It was a circular argument. No one was going to win, because they were both too stubborn to admit both plots were stupid. There was no way two men could cut the rail in two hours. We didn't have the expertise or the equipment. Explosives would work, but they didn't have access to any. Jaser's attack was no better than a mugging and would likely lead to the assassin's death. It was time to put a stop to the fighting. It was counterproductive to the case.

"We live to fight another day and we do more," I said. "I think we all agree they need to be killed, especially because of how safe they think they are, but we have to have a plan to do it so we can continue. If we shoot them or kill them with a knife, or walk up to them in Tim Hortons, there are witnesses. We're done. It's over. Sure, we got one of them or two of them. But why not kill them all, and then when the next head of the snake comes up, we kill him too, because we're not arrested and we're not dead yet."

Chiheb looked at Jaser.

"You understand?" he asked.

"Do you know how hard it is for mujahideen to be in the Western world?" I said. "They fucking hate us. So we have to use our heads. You both have beautiful minds. You both are saying the exact same thing."

"But different way," Chiheb said.

"We all have the same goals," I said. "We just have to organize."

Chiheb was very clear. The location was changing. The target was not. We shouldn't be scared of going to jail or dying for God. That was what we wanted.

"Answer me this question, Raed," Chiheb said. "Why do you care about all of this stuff and the only thing that is the most important thing you didn't care about it?"

It was a challenge. Chiheb was calling Jaser out for being scared. For being unwilling to sacrifice for Allah. I looked into the rearview mirror at Jaser.

"Because Allah doesn't want us to do the operation," Jaser said. "Yeah, don't play that game with me, man."

"If God don't want us to do the operation, why those police they didn't arrest us?" Chiheb said.

The reason was simple, according to Chiheb. Allah protected us from being searched because He wanted us to succeed. I marveled at how Chiheb could twist Allah's will into anything he wanted it to be.

"I don't know if God wants us to do the operation," Chiheb said. "But what I know is that we have to fight those disbelievers. This is what I know. But I think, Raed, you now are a little bit scared about what's happened today."

"Yeah yeah, I'm very scared," Jaser said.

I could tell he was being sarcastic. No doubt the police spooked him. He didn't want to get arrested doing the train plot. It wasn't worth the risk to him. But he also didn't want to get lectured by Chiheb.

"He is joking," I said.

We dropped off Jaser at his house and drove over to the mosque, where we prayed with Waleed. Jaser said he would meet us there.

"My feeling is that he is not afraid, but he feels that you are . . ." I paused, trying to find the right word as we drove toward the mosque.

"Careless?" Chiheb said.

"He wants to do something, but he wants to do it on a much bigger scale," I said. "Meaning in his mind this isn't big enough."

"It's not big enough?" Chiheb said. "If he has another plan, show it to us. He's comparing himself with the brothers? Our brothers? They are sleeping on the ground. In the mountains with the animals. No way, don't say to me any kind of this bullshit things."

"No, you're right," I said.

"I don't want to be harsh with him," Chiheb said.

We were at a crossroads. Jaser or Chiheb. It was a split-second decision, but an easy one. Chiheb had the world to offer me. Jaser didn't. Jaser wanted to kill Jews on the street. But he had no access to the brothers overseas or the American sleeper. I was never going to walk away from the guy who could get me to him.

"I know, I know," I said. "But I can tell it bothered you, and it bothered me because he said they don't know here like we know here."

Then I sealed the deal.

"If we did something with the train and the projects you're talking about, this will be in the news and they will say, 'Oh my God, what did the mujahideen say?'" I said. "They said, 'Get out of our country or we will hit you in your home.' Which is better, this or a Jew died because someone killed him? He is Palestinian *habibi* and for a Palestinian brother, his heart is in the right spot. He hates the Jews to an unbelievable degree, like us. But he has extra hate for the Jews, right? That's why his thinking is such, we can kill the Canadians, we can kill those people, yes, but let's kill the Jews. My opinion is, it would be better after we meet the brother in America, he may tell us. He will be able to tell us do X, Y, and Z or stay with the plan. He will tell us. What do you think?"

"The brother may benefit us, the sleeper," Chiheb said. "But do you think what happened today has an effect on our operation as a whole?"

"No," I said.

"There is nothing," Chiheb said, just making sure the train plot was still on track.

"Nothing," I said as we reached the mosque to pray.

We were partners now and we were going to derail a train.

CHAPTER 18

Team Chiheb

Joey paced in front of the flat-screen television in the living room. Every few steps, he paused like he was trying to figure out a way around an invisible barrier. Nelly tried to talk to him, but Joey held out his hand like any noise would knock a good idea out of his head. He started to pace again. With each step, Joey puzzled through our latest problem.

The Canadians weren't happy that I'd sided with Chiheb. They wanted me to play both sides. But that wasn't an option. It was clear Jaser and Chiheb were on diverging paths, and I had to make a choice.

"We need the American sleeper," I said. "We need the intel from overseas. We need everything that is in that brain."

We were meeting at a hotel suite in Toronto. In a few hours, I had to take Chiheb to the bus station.

"Let the Toronto guys worry about Jaser," I said. "Sorry, Doug. But we've got to focus on Chiheb."

Doug shrugged. He understood what his bosses wanted but also saw my logic.

"I would have done the same thing," he said.

The debriefs after each day were intimate affairs. Joey made sure the core team of Nelly, Kenny, and Johnny were always there. Doug was the Canadian representation. Every now and then if the situation was serious, Joey invited one or two RCMP bosses, but that was it.

I usually got to the safe house first to collect my thoughts. I put a pinch of snuff in my lip and just bullshitted with the guys. When I was ready—sometimes right away, sometimes I needed more time to come down—I went over the day's meeting in minute detail. Nelly and Johnny took notes. Joey just listened. When I was done, they peppered me with questions. After the debrief, Nelly and Kenny sent the highlights to executive management in New York and FBI Headquarters in Washington. Doug briefed his people. Joey paced and we started strategizing for the next meeting.

"Dougy, we have to stick with Chiheb. If the situation presents itself, we'll reengage with Jaser," Joey said.

Joey looked at me.

"As for you, make sure Chiheb knows Tamer is with him," Joey said. "Leave no doubt."

The threat was under control and that was the main concern. Chiheb was convinced, after inspecting the track, another brother was needed to help. No way two guys could cut the rail in two hours, which meant there was no way the plot would be ready in December. Plus, Chiheb and Jaser were under arrest. They just didn't know it yet. The only play was to stay with Chiheb for the intelligence in his head, and his potential connection to the sleeper.

I left to pick up Chiheb around 7:30 P.M. The condo didn't have

Internet, so I offered to let him use my hotel room. He met me in the lobby and we headed to pick up Jaser. Chiheb's bus left at nine o'clock. As we drove, I asked him about his work.

"So you will be a doctor?" I asked.

"Yes," he said. "I am not looking for money or looking for PhD. I am just looking for the PhD because it is good for our projects. You understand?"

"Of course," I said.

"I mean if I am a doctor or a professor, who will catch me?"

"Nobody," I said. "No one is going to look at a doctor." Not true, but it made sense to him. I asked about the safe house. Did he approve? It was a chance to pull Chiheb closer.

"I worked for a week with these idiots in order not to have my name or your name on it, because I know this is what I do," I said, talking about the condo lease. "To protect us. That's my job. You said to me, Tamer, we need you to protect us. Right?"

"Yes."

"I'll give you guys the key. I am in America and you guys are here in Canada, use it. Use the computer, if you need phones, if you need tablets, anything. Just ask me for it. Before you are done asking, you will have it. Whatever you need from me, I will give it to you right away. Because I need us to be on the same page. But he will start talking back and forth, saying, let's do the sniper thing and he wants to do this and he wants to do that. Come on, this is a joke."

Chiheb was still upset after our trip to the train bridge. "We need to focus and be on the same page," I said.

"And maybe while you are focusing on the sniper he comes up with another plan," Chiheb said, laughing.

"Exactly," I said.

Jaser was waiting outside when we arrived. He got into the back and we drove to the bus station. I found a parking spot and we started talking more about the train plot. Chiheb wanted to be ready when El Massoul sent the code word to attack. But Jaser wanted to delay.

"There's always wisdom in patience," he said.

Chiheb let out a long sigh.

"You see?" Jaser said. "So for me rushing into something just because you want to do it, for the sheer fact that you want to do something, doesn't make any sense."

Jaser told us he prayed *salat il Istakhara* after our visit to the bridge. It is a specific prayer asking Allah for guidance.

"I said if this is good for us in this life and the next, He will make it happen," Jaser said. "If not, then no."

But Chiheb saw Jaser's prayer as the move of a coward unwilling to commit to the path of God.

"No, this feeling that you have, Raed, is coming from the devil," he said.

"The devil?"

Chiheb nodded.

"The devil wants you to leave the project."

"I'm not leaving the project, *habibi*," Jaser said. "But we have to be extra careful."

"No, of course I agree with you," Chiheb said.

"Yeah, you agree with me, I tell you I cannot do anything anymore in this operation because you see, unlike you, for me I am very well known in the city of Toronto, okay," Jaser said. "Thank Allah I have no record. I have no problem. But I am very well known in other ways, you see."

"So what's the point?" Chiheb said. "You are scared that you go to jail?"

"Scared of going to jail?" Jaser said. "You are the one who's worried, not me."

"No, I am not worried," Chiheb said. "If I go—"

"We want to live for another day," Jaser said.

"If I go to jail, I don't care," Chiheb said. "If I die, I don't care."

"Why are you talking like this?" Jaser said. "This is not the right time for this. You have to watch what you're saying. You are just not very professional, *habibi*."

Chiheb bristled at the "professional" comment. He was trained by al Qaeda. Jaser had no training.

"So this means that you are scared that you go to jail, right?"

"It's not about jail," Jaser said. "It's about success. There's a difference."

"But I don't care about my security," Chiheb said. "I care about the security of the operation."

I could see the anger on Jaser's face.

"I cannot help you," he said. "Get somebody else. That's what I'm telling you. I cannot help you. That's what I am trying to explain to you. For me personally, it's no good for me. It's compromised, for me. But, I mean, there's many other things we can do in this lovely place, you know."

"Okay then," I said.

I was happy to be done with Jaser. Now I could focus on Chiheb full-time. But Chiheb wasn't going to let him go without a rebuke. It was clear to Chiheb that Jaser was no longer a good Muslim. His true colors were exposed. He cared more about this world and that was haram.

"This is your obligation," Chiheb said. "You are scared that you go to jail, no problem. But I can say to you one thing, if you are scared about entering jail and you are not scared about Allah and your obligation in front of Allah, I say to you, we don't need a person who will do this behavior. We want someone who isn't scared about anything except Allah."

"Praise the Prophet, *habibi*," I said.

I was trying to calm Chiheb down.

"Okay, *habibi,* no problem," Jaser said. "I cannot work with you. You are very rash."

Chiheb was getting worked up.

"Our women, they are raped," he said, his voice almost a scream. "They are raped. They are raped in jail."

"It doesn't do anything yelling and screaming," Jaser said. "Yelling and screaming doesn't work."

Jaser's eyes shot from Chiheb in the passenger seat to the window and back. He was searching for a way to calm Chiheb.

"Do you want that your sister is raped?" Chiheb said.

Chiheb's eyes were dark as he turned to face Jaser.

He radiated hate and anger.

"Pay attention," Jaser said. "Yelling and screaming does not work. Go ahead, go in the street, yelling and screaming, what is it going to do?"

I scanned the street to see if anyone was looking at us after Chiheb's screaming.

"Relax, relax," I said.

They both sat in the car, arms folded, with scowls on their faces.

"We'll clean this up, Allah willing," I said. "The most important thing is to understand we're going to have disagreements. We're going to have arguments. Right now let's just chill out."

Chiheb kept trying to interrupt me.

"Tamer?"

"Yes, *habibi*," I said.

"Tamer," Chiheb said. "We will go search for another believer, okay?"

"Listen, *habibi*, don't talk that way," I said.

"You see, this is the extreme ideology," Jaser said. "That's why I can't work with you, brother."

Jaser didn't mean jihad. He was objecting to the way Chiheb planned the attack.

"No," Chiheb said. "We don't want someone who stops our project. We want to go forward. We want someone who wants to give his blood to Allah."

I couldn't take much more of this.

"Listen, let's get you on the bus, so you don't miss the bus," I said.

All three of us left the car. We found the bus and I bought Chiheb a sandwich and drink. As we walked, Chiheb seemed anxious.

"He wants to work with you," Chiheb said. "I hope that he will not tell you another plan and ask you to leave the project."

I shook my head and put my hand on Chiheb's shoulder.

"We are all brothers here," I said. "I'm leaving my home constantly to come visit my brothers because I feel like I have a purpose, thank Allah. I'm being careful. I'm practicing everything that you guys have taught me from the beginning, and I am trying to do right and then we have one bad day, does that mean we're going to lose focus? Do you think that the brothers who are dying over there daily, what do you think they would do, with an opportunity that we have? This is what I am thinking."

I thought Chiheb was going to hug me.

"They are not seeing police like we see today," Chiheb said, happy to be compared to the brothers overseas. "They are seeing missiles. They are seeing bombs. He just sees three police and he becomes scared."

I looked at Jaser. He just glared at us.

"I don't think that's his issue," I said. "I think he's thinking about the success of the operation."

Jaser shrugged.

"You are too aggressive," he said to Chiheb. "I can't work with you."

Chiheb's bus boarded just before nine. Jaser and I waited until it left. On the way back to his house, Jaser tried to explain why he was out.

"It's too much work," he said. "It's for nothing. At the end, they're going to downplay it. Train derailment, whoop-de-do?"

Jaser was stung by Chiheb's accusations of not being a true Muslim. He spent half the ride proving himself to me using the Quran.

"I need to look right and left before I cross the street," Jaser said. "If I don't look right and left, a car is going to hit me. And especially if I didn't look at the traffic light to see if it's green or red. Allah says do not lead yourselves into destruction, do not go with your own hands into destruction."

Before he got out of the car, Jaser returned the thousand dollars I gave him to buy a new video camera to shoot the message after the attack. He promised to get me a plan for his sniper attack and his plan to build a training compound. But I think we both knew it would never come to be.

It was now just me and Chiheb.

CHAPTER 19

The Responsible One

It was Eid al-Adha, or the Sacrifice Feast, and I was back in Montreal to spend it with Chiheb.

Since the American sleeper revelation, we wanted to get him a visa so he could visit the United States. The goal was to get him to New York in hopes he could facilitate a meeting with the sleeper. I flew up to Canada to take him to Ottawa to get his visa paperwork.

I arrived in Montreal a few days before the holiday, the second of two Eid holidays. The better-known Eid al-Fitr celebrates the end of Ramadan, the month of dawn-to-sunset fasting. Eid al-Adha celebrates Abraham, who almost sacrificed his son for Allah, and signifies a Muslim's submission to God's will. The morning of Eid al-Adha, Muslims sacrifice a lamb. The meat is split among family, friends, and the poor.

A few days before Eid al-Adha, I took Chiheb to an Islamic butcher shop to buy a few lambs. Two for me. One for Chiheb. The butcher shop was at the back of a small supermarket with produce and dry goods. The meat was stored in refrigerated glass cases in the back. One of the butchers—a Muslim—met us at the counter.

"We'd like three lambs for Eid," Chiheb said. "One for me and two for my friend. Do we sacrifice them here?"

The butcher took out his pad and started to take the order.

"Sorry," he said. "Canadian law kicked in this year. You're not allowed to slaughter it yourself. It has to be done by a licensed butcher."

Chiheb looked at me and shook his head. The lambs aren't just slaughtered and eaten. The slaughter is an integral part of the celebration. A good Muslim makes his own sacrifice.

"That is not right," he said, placing both hands on the counter and leaning into his argument. "There are prayers. It is something that I need to do."

"Sorry, that's the law, but you still get your credit from God," the butcher said, smiling. "Your hands are tied. You have to respect the laws of the country you live in."

The butcher sounded like my father, I thought. God would understand, and even the Prophet Mohammed said to follow the laws of the land where you live. We were still fulfilling our obligation. But Chiheb was upset. He looked at me, urging me to protest. I looked away.

"Fine," Chiheb said. "Do you have a piece of paper and a pen?"

The butcher gave up his pad and pen. Chiheb wrote out the prayer that is said when the lamb's neck is cut. He wrote it in Arabic first. Then he wrote it in English and tore the sheet off the pad.

"May Allah force you to do this," Chiheb said. "Make sure you give this to the Imam. Have him recite this Quranic verse while you are slaughtering the lambs."

The butcher looked at me. *Is this guy for real?* his face said. I looked back at the butcher with my best *Please take the paper* face.

"Of course," the butcher said, folding the page up and sliding it into his apron's pocket.

For the rest of the day, I had to listen to Chiheb complain about the butcher and Canada's laws. Another grievance on a long list.

Nelly and Kenny worked with the State Department to get the visa approved; otherwise Chiheb had no chance, given all that law enforcement already had on him. But it was my job to go through the motions. That meant getting the paperwork from the American Embassy. Chiheb knew a Tunisian in Ottawa, so we planned to meet him for dinner and take his temperature on our way there.

We met his friend at a Chinese buffet on the outskirts of Ottawa around 9:00 P.M. When we got there, the restaurant was deserted. The food on the buffet looked like it had sat all day under heat lamps. It was near closing, but the staff was happy to have a few more paying customers.

Over spring rolls and General Tso's chicken, Chiheb ranted about the West and its war on Islam. His friend didn't join in, but admitted he was thinking of moving to Saudi Arabia because he wanted to live in an Islamic country. That didn't make him a jihadist. I scratched him off the list by the end of dinner.

This was normal since Jaser left the plot. Chiheb dragged me into meetings with like-minded brothers ready to help. But most of them were just lost souls having trouble coping with a foreign culture or angry about what they saw in the news. No different from Americans angry at Washington. Conversations got heated. There was real anger. But no one—Muslim or American—was about to derail a train over it. Anytime a Muslim expresses any anger they get stamped a terrorist. But what is the difference between a devout Muslim who doesn't drink and a Mormon who doesn't? Nothing. Same God. Different name. It was easy for non-Muslims to confuse a devout Muslim with Chiheb. But I knew different. Chiheb was a perversion who believed that God wanted him to kill in His name. His friend just wanted to live in a Muslim culture.

On the drive back from Ottawa, we talked about Chiheb's recruiting. He hadn't found another like-minded brother since we met.

"What made you trust me and know I was who I claimed to be?" he asked.

Chiheb was being polite, because what he really wanted to talk about was why he trusted me. But it would be rude not to ask me first.

"No disrespect, brother, but if you recall correctly, I pushed you away," I said.

He started to laugh and smile and rub his beard.

"I do remember that," he said. "That was very telling for me."

"But I could tell every single hadith, every single passage of the Quran you interpreted, the way you saw the world was exactly how I saw the world," I said. "Exactly the way my uncle taught me Islam. I saw me in you. I saw my uncle in you. I saw a true mujahid in you. But as happy as I was, I couldn't trust you. I'd just met you. I believe in fatalism but I had to be sure."

He laughed.

"That is exactly right," he said.

He was smiling, his eyes bright and happy remembering our trip to San Jose. It made me sad. He and Tamer were friends. He'd found a like-minded brother, but he'd also found a friend. Someone to share meals with and talk with in a country so foreign to him. Al Qaeda used his isolation, his awkward social skills, and his naiveté to brainwash him. Part of me wished I could save him. Clean his mind of their filth.

"So, I ask you, brother," I said. "What about me?"

"Your interpretation of certain hadiths led me to believe you were a true brother," Chiheb said. "The fact that you pushed me away led me to believe you weren't government. But what really did it for me that week was that night at the Moroccan restaurant. Do you remember that night?"

In my head, I couldn't stop thinking about his face when he saw all the booze on the bar or the belly dancer.

"Remind me," I said.

"Every test I put you through was good," he said. "But it wasn't until we were at that restaurant when you told me about your mother and how it turned you. How it brought you back to Islam. You cried that night. There was no way a government operative could fake that. I knew that night that you were a true brother."

He was right. I wasn't faking. Even though I'd twisted some of the details to appeal to Chiheb, the foundation of the story was true. My mother's death was a defining moment in my life. Losing her was a pain I'd never felt before. But driving back to Montreal from Ottawa, I realized my mother was a hero. She made me into the man I am and armed me with a story that allowed me to infiltrate this evil and stop it. I was following through with her dying wish to use what she taught me about Islam to do good in this world.

"Speaking of true brothers, tell me about the brothers in Iran," I said. "El Massoul is a brother like us, right?"

FBI Headquarters was after me to get more on Chiheb's training in Iran. In the past I acted in awe of El Massoul and the brothers in Iran. But on this trip, I flipped it. I downplayed him, prompting Chiheb to defend him.

"No, no, no," Chiheb said. "He was like a son to Sheikh Osama. He has been with him since he was a boy."

I urged Chiheb on with "Oh, dear brothers" and *Masha'Allah*. But in my mind, I was puzzled. How did we miss bin Laden's protégé? We had to know him.

"Tell me more about El Massoul," I said. "I'm fascinated."

Chiheb told me he had a bus company. He owned thirteen buses and his twenty-six-year-old son was in an Iranian prison. But El Massoul was proud because every single morning the entire prison was awakened by his son's call to prayer. El Massoul's son had a beautiful Quranic voice.

"How old is he, brother?"

Chiheb said he was around forty-six or forty-seven. He had wild salt-and-pepper hair and a scar under his left eye.

"I looked at it every day," Chiheb said. "I wanted to ask him if that was from him being a mujahid."

These nuggets didn't seem like much at first glance. But to our intelligence analysts, these bits of conversation—the buses, the son, the scar—were bread crumbs to El Massoul.

On our way back from Ottawa, I dropped off Chiheb at his lab in Montreal. The plan was for him to get some work done and we would meet up for dinner later that night. The lab was located in an industrial part of town, and as we drove up to the campus, I started to hear some static coming from the dashboard.

Chiheb noticed it too.

"Tamer, what is that sound?" he said.

Chiheb feared technology because he assumed it allowed the government to listen to us.

"No idea," I said as I fiddled with the radio.

The static stopped and I could hear Nelly and Doug talking. They were in a surveillance car nearby. Somehow, the signals got crossed and the receiver became the transmitter. Chiheb's eyes went from the radio directly to the GPS unit in the middle of the dashboard. It was the only logical explanation. I smacked the GPS unit as I pulled in front of his lab.

"This stupid thing has been acting up," I said as I yanked it off its mount.

"You should replace that one," Chiheb said as he grabbed his bag. "I will call you when I'm done, brother."

I tossed the GPS into the passenger seat and drove back to the safe house. I was angry when I arrived. I wasn't sure if this technical glitch had just fucked up the case.

"Kenny, are you fucking kidding me right now?"

Kenny was checking the transmitter.

"This doesn't make any sense," he said. "It's new tech but that's obviously not supposed to happen."

"You think it was the electrical lines?" Doug said. "It's a very industrial area."

But why it happened didn't matter anymore.

"Get rid of it," I said. "I never want to see that thing again. And tell Headquarters never to use that in the field."

Joey pulled me aside before the debrief.

"What was his reaction?" Joey said.

"I blamed it on the GPS," I said. "We could only hear them for a few seconds."

Joey started pacing.

"Did he buy it?"

I shrugged.

"I don't know," I said. "I think so."

Joey wasn't convinced. He looked nervous.

I hadn't eaten all day. I ordered a feast—Caesar salad, French onion soup, pizza, poutine (French fries with gravy and mozzarella) burgers, and pitchers of iced tea with lime. We spread the food out on the table and started to work. Topic number one was El Massoul.

Nelly grabbed my MacBook.

"What's the password?" he said.

"King Tut," I said, as Joey paced in front of me. "There is no way we don't know who this guy is. I feel like I'm at the point I could give him a photo lineup and ask him which one he is."

Joey laughed.

"You could probably show him your badge and he wouldn't believe you're government," Joey said.

I heard Nelly typing. A few seconds later, he spun my laptop around so I could see the screen. He was on the FBI's Rewards for Justice page. He scrolled through the Wanted photos.

"I bet you it's one of these guys," he said, pointing to a group of photos. "He has to be in the five-million-dollar range if he is that close to bin Laden."

Joey was looking over my shoulder.

"Why don't you just show him this website?" Nelly said.

Everyone was silent. I looked at Nelly and then Joey.

"You know what?" Joey said. "Why not?"

It wasn't a bad idea, I thought. Our relationship was solid. But why would I be on that website?

Joey started pacing again.

"Tamer likes to search for different brothers that he reveres," Joey said. "He came across the site and looks at it sometimes. It's like an affirmation."

"And next time I'm sitting with him, I'll surf over to the site," I said.

The plan was to grab dinner with Chiheb, pick up the meat from the butcher shop, and then go back to his apartment so I could show him the website. After the debrief, I got a call from Chiheb. Everyone knew it was my undercover phone, so Doug muted the TV and Joey put his hand up, signaling everyone to be quiet.

"*Salamu alaikum,*" Chiheb said. "I am home now."

"*Wa alaikum al salam,*" I said. "How was your day, brother?"

"*Al hamdul'Allah,*" he said, meaning "thank God."

"Where do you feel like having dinner tonight? When will you be ready?"

"It doesn't matter," he said. "Come and pick me up when you are ready, *insha'Allah.*"

I hung up the phone. Something was wrong. I told the team that I was going to pick him up later and go to dinner. Doug unmuted the TV and everyone jumped back into their conversations. Joey pulled me into the bedroom because he'd noticed the look on my face.

"What's going on?" he said.

"I don't know," I said. "He sounded off."

"Listen to me," Joey said. "Do not look at him like the Arab Santa Claus. He is a mujahid that would cut your throat in a heartbeat if he suspected you were government. You know how he feels about munafiqeen."

"I know."

"Do you want a weapon?"

"No."

"Then remember your training. Grab whatever you can and defend yourself," Joey said as he grabbed a pen from the dresser and held it like a knife.

"I'm good, brother."

I went back to my room to get changed and left for Chiheb's apartment. As I climbed into the car, I saw the concern on Joey's face. He had been in dangerous situations before and recognized the potential danger of the meeting. It was his job to protect me, but his nerves were getting the better of him. But I was confident we weren't burned. Call it a gut feeling, but I knew the guy. There was something bothering him, but it wasn't me.

I arrived around eight o'clock. It was October 26, 2012, the last day of Eid al-Adha, and we were headed to dinner before picking up our meat at the market.

Chiheb was standing in the foyer of the apartment building speaking with a woman when I arrived. He didn't notice that I was there, so I parked and waited. After a few minutes, I brought him his Eid gifts—a box of dates and a prayer rug provided to me by the RCMP. Chiheb let me into the foyer.

"*Eid Mubarak* [Blessed Eid]," I said.

Chiheb took the gifts and thanked me. I ignored the woman and started for the door.

"I'll wait in the car," I said. "Take your time. We're in no rush."

He finally got in the car, and I studied him as I drove off. I found a seafood restaurant on my phone while I was waiting that wasn't too far away. He barely spoke during the ride to the restaurant. My instincts were right. There was definitely something bothering him. I knew I had to address it.

"How was your day, *habibi*?" I asked, trying to fill the silence.

"*Al hamdul'Allah,*" he said, trying to smile.

I got lost on the way to the restaurant. I was a little preoccupied and couldn't use the GPS anymore. We decided to try a Turkish restaurant downtown, but I could tell it was Americanized and probably had an open bar. I considered pushing him to look the other way so we could eat, but something was already bothering him.

I pulled over and turned to face him. Joey's warnings echoed in my head. I didn't want him to attack me while I drove.

"Talk to me, brother," I said. "I know you. Something is bothering you."

Chiheb forced another smile and crossed his hands between his legs.

"Tamer, you know me better than I know myself."

Right then and there I relaxed. This wasn't going to be about the equipment malfunction. His body language spoke volumes. He was embarrassed about something.

"What happened?"

"Today in the office, she was laughing and joking with a man in our group," he said. "She was doing it very loud so I could hear them."

It was girl trouble again. The Jordanian was talking to another man. Thank God. The wire glitch was forgotten.

"Tamer, you won't believe, she touches his arm when she is laughing," he said, looking like he was about to cry.

"Oh no, *habibi*. What did you do?"

"I waited until he left and then I talked to her," he said.

"What did you say?"

"I told her that what she is doing is against Allah. She is not married to him and she shouldn't be touching another man."

I felt bad for this poor girl.

"What did she say?"

"She got very upset. She was yelling at me and told me none of your business. She shut the door of her office very hard."

"I'm so sorry, Chiheb," I said. "I can tell how much this is bothering you. But now you have your answer, right?"

"I think she did this because she knows I will see. I don't want to be part of her doing haram. I have to forget her. May Allah forgive her."

Chiheb's phone rang, ending the conversation. One of his colleagues was calling to wish him *Eid Mubarak*. Chiheb asked his colleague if he knew of any good halal restaurants nearby. He told Chiheb about Château Kabab on Rue Guy in downtown Montreal. We got a table and had a long dinner. No jihad this time. We talked a little more about the Jordanian girl instead. I managed to shoot a text to Joey during dinner because I knew he was worried.

"All good. Just girl trouble."

After dinner, we got ice cream at Tim Hortons. While we were eating, Chiheb called Jaser to wish him *Eid Mubarak*. It was a short call. Polite but not warm. Chiheb had no respect for Jaser any longer.

"We don't discuss projects," Chiheb said after hanging up. "If I said anything, Raed would hang up. He is fearful of the police. Any true believer should not be worried about jail or death. It would be an honor to die for Allah; why wouldn't it be an honor to go to jail for Allah?"

Jaser was now munafiqeen.

It was close to midnight when we arrived at the market to pick up our lambs. The shop was busy because of the holiday.

"Sorry, guys, crazy day," the butcher said. "It's going to be another thirty minutes. I'm working on it now."

I suggested we go back to my car to wait. I fired up my mobile hotspot. Chiheb opened his laptop and showed me some jihadi sites that posted videos of attacks. I got my MacBook from the back seat.

"Brother, you don't mind if I check my e-mail?" I asked.

I logged on to my e-mail and then pulled up the Rewards for Justice website. The plan was to wait until we got back to his apartment, but I couldn't.

"By the grace of God," I said as I scrolled down the website.

He was talking about one of the jihadi websites, but stopped when he saw my screen.

"What's that, brother?"

My MacBook was on my lap in the driver's side. I turned the screen so he could see it better.

"These are the true brothers, just like you were discussing with me," I said. "I saw this on TV. All the brothers wanted by the Americans are on this website. I wanted to see who these brothers were."

He tilted his head and moved it so he could see the whole screen as I scrolled through the photos. I started reading about Sheikh Ayman al-Zawahiri. He pointed out one of the Pakistani individuals as I scrolled.

"By the grace of God, I know that brother," he said. "I met that brother when I was in Iran. He is helping the Taliban."

"These are the brothers—" I started to say when Chiheb gasped.

He snatched the MacBook off my lap. The screen smashed into the steering wheel as he pulled it into his lap. He tried to scroll up but didn't know how to use a MacBook.

"Tell me what you're trying to do," I said, concerned that he was going to damage my computer. "Relax. What do you need?"

"Go back up, go back up," he said, half handing it back, but clutching it at the same time.

I showed him how to scroll with both fingers. Seconds later, the picture of a barrel-chested man with a mane of thick, wild hair and a bushy beard with no mustache filled the screen.

"Tamer, that's him," Chiheb said. "Brother, that's him."

"That's who?"

"El Massoul. That is the brother I spent six weeks with."

"You're kidding me," I said.

We zoomed in on the picture and I saw the scar under his left eye.

"That's his face," Chiheb said. "Those are his eyes. That is his scar. That's definitely him."

According to Chiheb, El Massoul was Muhammad ar-Rahayyal, one of four terrorists who took part in the 1986 hijacking of Pan Am Flight 73 in Pakistan. After a sixteen-hour standoff, ar-Rahayyal and the others opened fire, killing at least twenty passengers and injuring more than one hundred. Pakistani security forces arrested ar-Rahayyal. He was released from prison in January 2008. The hijackers were added to the FBI's Most Wanted list in 2009 after they were indicted in federal court for the murder of U.S. nationals outside the United States.

As I read his bio, Chiheb agreed with everything until we got to his nationality. The website said he was Palestinian and hiding in a Middle Eastern country.

"He's not Palestinian," Chiheb said. "Every Palestinian speaks Arabic. El Massoul only speaks Farsi and Dari. He doesn't speak Arabic well."

Chiheb said he still had the crazy hair, but he had aged since the photo was taken. The image on the website was from 2000. I checked ar-Rahayyal's date of birth. It checked out. Every single thing checked out. Without him knowing, Chiheb gave us El Massoul. Nelly's idea panned out. Before we moved on, I checked the reward. Five million. Nelly nailed it.

After finding ar-Rahayyal, we were looking at other pictures when Chiheb suddenly had a solemn look on his face.

"Brother, what's wrong?" I said.

"Nothing."

"Talk to me. You seem upset."

He sighed and stroked his beard. He paused for a full thirty seconds.

"I wish I was on that list," he said.

His words hit me like a punch. He wanted to be on a list of murderers. Of men who brainwashed the young with an ideology of hate. He revered these men like bin Laden, who would send their followers to the grave for an ideology they refused to fight for themselves. Ar-Rahayyal wasn't any different. He didn't care if Chiheb lived or died as long as the attack was a success. He was safe in Iran, hiding in the shadows and sending others to die. His jihad was one of safety, if not comfort.

But I wasn't me. I was Tamer. I had to bite back my words as I put my arm on his shoulder.

"God willing, one day, we will be at the top of that list with Sheikh Ayman," I said. "We will be wanted for twenty-five million."

He smiled.

"God willing."

CHAPTER 20

The Radicalizer

Chiheb was under surveillance twenty-four hours a day. We knew his friends. We knew his family. So, when a friend of Chiheb's in Quebec City popped up on our radar, we were puzzled.

Who was this guy? How did he fit into the picture? Why hadn't Chiheb brought him up?

The Canadians wouldn't tell me his name. All they would tell me is that I should consider going to Quebec City and hinted that there may be something or someone of interest there. Nelly told me the friend's name: Ahmed Abassi.

"Why are you going up to Quebec City?" Nelly said, as we strategized a reason to get me in front of Abassi.

"Ski rentals," Doug said. "Tamer wants to invest in some ski houses."

I liked it. It was October 2012 and Tamer wanted to see some properties before winter. Since we needed help for the train plot, I pushed Chiheb to get us in front of as many like-minded brothers as he could.

"Are there any brothers for us to meet with up there?" I said after he agreed to come with me to Quebec City.

Chiheb grimaced and looked away. He had someone, but didn't want to say.

"What are you not telling me?" I asked.

"There is a brother," Chiheb said. "He is the brother that got me on this path."

That was something that had bothered me since Chiheb told me about his training. It was never clear why Chiheb chose radical Islam. Now I had the chance to meet the man who put him on the path. But something was wrong.

"Tell me," I said.

"It is sort of complicated."

"Come on, brother," I said. "Talk to me. Let's meet him."

"I gave Ahmed two thousand dollars for one semester of his school and he never paid me back," Chiheb said. "He can never go to his grave in debt."

Chiheb didn't care about the money. It was haram to not pay your debts.

"Clearly, money matters," I said. "In the grand scheme of things, maybe it is time to forgive and forget. You're telling me he is a like-minded brother. Not only that, he is the like-minded brother that started you on this path. I'd love to meet him."

"He is Tunisian like me," Chiheb said. "He is my age. Very smart. Very religious."

"Is he like us?"

"He is a mujahideen brother," Chiheb said.

Abassi was studying engineering at Laval University in Quebec City. He met Chiheb at a conference. Two Tunisians far from home. It was Abassi who taught Chiheb jihad was part of every Muslim's duty.

"E-mail him," I said. "Tell him you're here with an Egyptian-American brother, a like-minded brother, and we're traveling up to Quebec City because I have business there. Tell him I am a dear friend and you'd love him to meet us for dinner."

Chiheb typed while I spoke. About an hour later, we got a response, which he shared with me.

"I'd love to host you, dear brother," Abassi wrote. "Let me know when you'll be here. I'll make sure I am here so we can go to dinner."

I was sure Chiheb was exaggerating Abassi's intentions. But Abassi was the only person Chiheb ever described as a "mujahideen brother."

I picked up Chiheb at his apartment around eleven thirty in the morning and we headed for Quebec City. We met Abassi for dinner after looking at rental properties all day.

Abassi was tall and thin with a neatly trimmed beard, no mustache, and close-cropped hair. There was a confidence, swagger even, like he knew he was good-looking. Both his English and his Arabic were flawless. He also spoke French fluently. I studied his face after he got into the back of the car. His glasses hid his eyes, but his eyebrows poked up above the lenses. They were shaped like devil horns.

We ate at a halal restaurant on a quiet cobblestone side street near Parliament Hill. We ordered at the counter and ate at one of the many wooden tables. I covered the table with hummus, tabouleh, bread, stuffed grape leaves. We each got an entrée. I got the kofta with rice and salad. Abassi and Chiheb had grilled kebobs.

Most of dinner was small talk about my work, ski houses, and properties in the area. Abassi was recently engaged and I bought him baklava to celebrate. After dinner, we went for coffee at a nearby shop. On the way, we passed the Parliament Building, the meeting place of Quebec's National Assembly. The 125 elected representatives serve as the legislative body for the Province of Quebec. The Parliament Building—constructed between 1877 and 1886—reminded me of Philadelphia's City Hall with its frontal clock tower.

"That would be a great place for an attack," Chiheb said, looking at me.

Chiheb let out an uncomfortable giggle looking for affirmation, but I didn't say anything. My focus was on Abassi. He didn't flinch. Didn't smile. Didn't turn his head to even look at the building.

"No, no, no," Abassi said. "Don't talk that way."

All through dinner Abassi was very guarded, especially when talk veered toward the war in the Middle East or some of Chiheb's extreme interpretations of the Quran. He was savvier and more disciplined than Chiheb. This guy had the right rhetoric, but he stopped short every time. He knew how to run to the line and stop.

Usually I make the target earn my point of radicalization, but I didn't have time for the slow play. I wanted him to know he had an audience ready to listen. We were talking about the war in Syria over tea when I brought up my uncle.

"I have an uncle in Egypt that put me back on the path," I said. "I wanted to go home. I was done with America, but he told me to stay. To live amongst them, as them, to defeat them."

Chiheb had a big smile as I talked.

"Oh, God bless him," Chiheb said. "If you only knew the things he did."

I knew Chiheb would echo my legend and give me the bona fides to be believable to Abassi. I watched Abassi closely. He had a look. A twinkle of recognition in his eye. It was like I hit a chord with him. He looked at Chiheb and then at me. There was no doubt he got the gist. And he liked it. But he said nothing. Then, as we walked back to the car, my phone buzzed. It was Joey.

"Wrap it up. Everything is okay."

My mind jumped to all the worst-case scenarios. Was my father sick? My sister? I had trouble concentrating on the mission. Abassi asked if we'd like to stay up late, but I declined.

"You know what, if we're getting up early to leave, we're going to get going," I said.

I exchanged e-mail addresses and phone numbers with Abassi and promised to call next time I was in town. I dropped off Chiheb at his hotel room and joined the team at the safe house. I was barely through the door when I confronted Joey.

"What's wrong?"

"We need to get a flight back," he said. "There is a hurricane coming."

"We live in New York, bro," I said. "There are no hurricanes there."

"There is one coming," Joey said.

Fox News was on the TV. A reporter was standing on the Jersey Shore talking about how Superstorm Sandy was bearing down on the East Coast.

I texted Chiheb and told him we had to go early because I had to get back to New York to check on my properties before the storm. He agreed to meet at eight for the drive back to Montreal.

"Another dead end?" Nelly said as we sat down to debrief the Abassi meeting.

"No, actually, there is something there," I said. "I can't put my finger on it. He is very good. Not good enough. But very good at disguising things. Something is in those eyes. In that head. It was on the tip of his tongue."

I explained to the team how I dropped my uncle into the conversation.

"Let him chew on that shit," I said. "He'll be thinking about my uncle until we meet again."

"Yeah, exactly," Joey said. "Let's see where it takes us. Let him come to you."

We finished the debrief after midnight and I got a few hours of sleep before meeting Chiheb. We were on the road back to Montreal when Chiheb brought up the project again. He still wanted to derail the train on Christmas, but he needed help.

"Your job is to get back and continue on with your work and do what you are doing," he told me, meaning raising money for the brothers.

"Look, you got the hardest part of your job out of the way," I said. "The funding and access to America, you have it. You have that done."

"You're absolutely right. Now I just have to get the true believers with us, and I will find them," Chiheb said. "Even if this means I have to go to where the munafiqeen are, I will go to all the mosques in Montreal to find the true believers."

"Did you hear from the brothers overseas?" I said, anxious to get the American sleeper meeting set.

Chiheb shook his head no.

"Sometimes it takes a week," he said. "I told them it was urgent."

"Good," I said. "God willing, they will contact you soon."

"God willing," Chiheb said.

I took a sip of my coffee.

"I got an e-mail about the apartment in Toronto," I said. "Do we want to let it go?"

"Could we hold it for a little bit longer?" Chiheb asked.

He was holding out hope that he could recruit another like-minded brother in time.

"Yeah, listen, I could call him back and tell him to hold it for a month. I can probably hold it to the end of November, early December," I said.

"That would be great, and tell him I promise I will have an answer by then," Chiheb said. "Listen, the only place we can do this project, and this project has to happen, is in Toronto. There's no other place to have a possible location as far as this particular project."

"No worries, no problem," I said. "We'll hold it for another month, and we'll go that route. Keep me posted on the brothers."

"Yes, brother," Chiheb said. "You'll be with me every step of the way."

I dropped off Chiheb at his apartment in Montreal before lunch and raced to the airport. The team was waiting for me at the terminal. Every flight was canceled.

"What do we do?" I said to Nelly.

"Shit, we've got to go," he said, looking at his phone. "The storm is hitting tonight. Fuck it. Let's rent a car."

Nelly got a minivan and I jumped in the back. Nelly drove with Joey in the front. Kenny was in the back with me. Joey gathered up our passports as we approached the border.

The Border Patrol agent leaned into the window and took our stack of passports. He shuffled through them like they were a deck of cards. Nelly, Joey, and Kenny all had diplomatic passports with brown covers. Mine was a tourist passport with a blue cover. The border agent looked at Nelly and then into the back of the van at me with my long jihadi beard.

"You know what?" he said. "I don't want to know. Welcome home, guys. Have a safe trip."

"Thanks, bro," Nelly said, smiling at him.

Nelly took the passports and crossed the border. We all waited until the window was up before everyone started laughing.

"That dude had no idea what he was looking at," Joey said. "For all he knew, we just snatched your ass."

We stopped at McDonald's just over the border and I jumped behind the wheel. Fueled on cheap hamburgers and snuff, I drove south like my hair was on fire. We arrived in New York in five hours. I got to my house an hour before the storm hit. Rain was lashing my windshield as I drove the last mile. Three hours later, the power went out for three weeks.

Back in Canada, both Chiheb and Abassi watched the coverage of the storm and flooded my phone with text messages of encouragement. Abassi seemed especially anxious to develop a relationship with me.

The Canadians decided to fly me back to Quebec City in mid-November 2012. This time they didn't want Chiheb there. They wanted me to take Abassi's temperature alone. But without Chiheb, I couldn't record the conversation. Under Canadian law, we could record only when a target of the investigation—Chiheb or Jaser—was present.

I sent Chiheb and Abassi an e-mail telling them I was coming up to Canada. Chiheb volunteered to catch the bus to Quebec City, but I waved him off. I told him I had business and I'd come down to Montreal after I was done.

Abassi responded right away to my e-mail.

"I look forward to hosting you," he said.

We agreed to meet for dinner. Before I left the hotel, I met with the team to go over a game plan.

"My intention tonight is to simply develop my relationship," I said. "We can eventually draw out what his true intentions are."

Joey agreed.

"Don't go down any roads unless he does," he said. "Let him guide the discussion. The Canadians just want you to gauge his religious ideology and his beliefs."

Back at my hotel, I called Abassi's cell phone but got a recording. I fired up my MacBook and sent him an e-mail.

"Are you still free for dinner tonight?" I wrote. "I tried your cell phone but it was out of service."

He responded four minutes later. "Where? How are you?"

I was about to click "reply" when my phone rang. I didn't recognize the number.

"Tamer, Ahmed," Abassi said. "I am so sorry. My cell phone ran out of minutes."

"No problem, brother," I said.

"What are your plans? What are you doing up here?"

I closed my laptop and sat back in my chair.

"Still looking at the ski houses," I said. "But I'm free for dinner. Say around seven or eight?"

"That is great," Abassi said.

"I'd like to take you out," I said. "Think of a good restaurant that we'd both enjoy."

"No problem," Abassi said. "I'll be ready. You just let me know when you're ready."

"E-mail me your address and I'll pick you up."

His e-mail arrived a minute after we hung up. A short while later, he called me from his cell phone to let me know he got more minutes. He called me again at six thirty.

"Dinner's getting cold," he said, chuckling. "What's going on? Are you ready? What's up?"

He sounded anxious.

"Yeah, I'm good, brother," I said. "I'm wrapping up with the Realtor now and I should be leaving here in about half an hour."

"Great, call me when you leave."

I arrived at his house around seven. He was standing outside waiting. It looked like he was holding a parking spot. When he saw me, he waved me over. I rolled down my window.

"Park here," he said.

"Come on, brother, let's not waste time parking and getting out of the car," I said. "Let's get to the restaurant."

"We're at the restaurant," Abassi said. "You're coming to my home. I prepared dinner for us."

This wasn't a social dinner. He wanted privacy.

I locked the car and followed him into the lobby. He lived on the second floor in a small but quaint apartment. I stepped into the foyer. The kitchen was to the left. It was small with a little table in the middle of the laminate floor. A bedroom was to the right of the front door, and the bathroom was straight back. Unlike Chiheb's place, Abassi had a 52-inch LCD screen TV hooked up to a laptop.

Nearby, I saw two other laptops. Al Jazeera news was streaming on the television, and the table in the kitchen was crowded with Middle Eastern dishes.

"My wife cooked," he said. "She teaches Mondays. She is usually out late."

"Okay," I said.

There were pictures of her and her family on the wall. We sat down at the kitchen table and started to eat. Abassi told me about his family. He was the youngest of seven children. His mother and father still lived in Tunisia. Talk soon turned to my meetings in Quebec City. I told him about some condos I was considering and how I hoped to make money renting them out as vacation properties. Abassi seemed impressed. I was setting the stage for another glimpse up my skirt.

"Everything I do is to make money for the brothers and the cause," I said.

Abassi let that go, but it was clear he understood what I was saying. He wanted to talk. The meal. The private setting. It felt like I was being recruited.

"I wasn't as religious as I should have been until my mother died," I said. "My uncle changed my life."

"This *Dunya* doesn't matter," Abassi said.

They were the exact words Chiheb said on the flight to San Jose. But I almost laughed when Abassi said them. Muslims are encouraged to not focus on earthly concerns and possessions. A Muslim's focus should be on the afterlife and earning a place in paradise, which is why Chiheb shared a small, cramped apartment, slept on a used mattress, and never wasted anything. Abassi didn't take it as far as Chiheb.

"Chiheb speaks very, very highly of you, more than anyone," Abassi said. "He said that he loves you more than anybody."

"That's very nice," I said. "I appreciate that."

"Everything happens for a reason; look what's happening in today's day and age. Allah has turned everything against the evildoers in America. Climate, the weather, other governments, politics, every single thing in this world hates America. Look at all that's happened with the natural disasters; it's a sign from God that their time is coming. Look at all the wars that they're starting in our lands. It wasn't just with the Muslim people. Look at what they did in Vietnam. And we're defeating them. We are going to defeat them. Their defeat is imminent."

Abassi was starting to sound like Chiheb. I wished I was recording his rant.

"Look what nine-eleven did to that country. It literally destroyed their economy. They've yet to recover and they're not going to recover. It's only going to get worse for them. The big, bad, evil person, the United States, was toppled by one man: Osama bin Laden."

Abassi's eyes changed with the mention of bin Laden. There was a reverence as he spoke. He told me a story about how in Tunisia they chanted his name to remind President Obama that one man could topple the United States.

I sat in stunned silence. On the surface he looked and acted like a mainstream Muslim, but he was of the same mind as Chiheb. But Abassi was more cunning. He was doing the same thing I was doing. Giving a little, testing the waters, and then going a little further.

Unlike Chiheb, who hated all infidels, Abassi's hatred was centered on the United States. At this point, he couldn't say one sentence that wasn't damning the United States or revering bin

Laden. His wife called shortly after dinner and interrupted his rant. He took the call right in front of me. I'd invited him to New York earlier in the evening to reciprocate his hospitality, and he was excited to tell her. They were traveling to Tunisia in January for about four to five weeks, but maybe when they returned we could meet in New York, he told her.

After he hung up, Abassi started to talk about studying nuclear engineering. He was close to completing his master's degree.

"If Iran had a truly Islamic regime, I would go over there in a heartbeat and study and learn with their nuclear program," Abassi said. "That would be the best way to help the brothers in the long term with jihad."

I'd sat in front of a lot of wannabe terrorists, but this was different. Abassi wasn't just talk. He was selling his knowledge to me because Tamer was the jihad lottery. Win him over and he'll throw money at your plots.

"You know, you can buy anything on the black market," he said. "You can buy bombs, you can buy chemicals cheaply and very easily. Anything you want, right? And you need the brains to operate behind that. But none of that matters if you don't have money. You need money for jihad. The brothers overseas need money for their jihad. You think they could fight the Israelis without money? No. Money is needed for all jihad. Jihad is *fard* [obligatory]. It is Islam's sixth pillar, even though all of the fake Muslims won't acknowledge it. There are a million brothers out there. You could put a gun in their hands, they can go wage jihad. But without money, you don't have jihad. That's what's rare."

Abassi was painting a picture for me. It was almost comical because it was the same technique we use in the FBI. We paint a picture for the bad guy and let him connect the dots. It's extremely cunning. He was preying on my emotions. He was putting it all out there without specifically saying, "I need your money to buy chemicals to build a bomb."

It was time for me to go. I wasn't recording this conversation. I didn't want to go down this road unless I could record it.

"Brother, I don't want to hold you up, I know your wife will be home soon," I said. "I'm getting up early and I'm leaving tomorrow to go to Montreal. I have some business there and I want to meet with brother Chiheb before I fly back to New York. Brother, it was so great to see you, I look forward to seeing you again."

He insisted I stay longer, but I resisted. As I got into the car, I let out a sigh of relief. I'd met many people who claimed to be mujahideen, but this guy scared the shit out of me. It was more of a gut reaction. He didn't say anything overt. He just painted pictures in my head. Bomb making. Exploding nuclear reactors. I knew it wouldn't take long to tease out his full intentions.

Back at the safe house, I was fired up. Joey told me to take my time with my notes so I could capture the conversation. Abassi was dangerous and he wanted to make sure the Canadians understood.

But I had doubts about my decision to cut the meeting short. I pulled Joey aside.

"I made the right call there, right?" I said.

"You absolutely made the right call," Joey said. "You walking away at that point only makes him more eager to tell you the next time."

"There is no doubt this guy is bad," I said. "We need to record our next meeting."

I told Doug and his bosses Abassi was the real deal. The Canadians promised to file a warrant with the court so I could record my next meeting with Abassi. With Abassi done, Doug and the Canadians wanted to talk about a new development.

Chiheb had signed up for a conference in Singapore the week before Christmas, and the Canadian government was going to arrest him at the airport.

The case was over.

We couldn't stop them from locking him up. The Canadians couldn't afford to let him out of the country. Plus, the case was eating up their manpower. They had enough evidence to convict. It was time to wrap it up.

But we had more work to do.

Doug wouldn't look me in the eye as his bosses delivered the news. I did the math. We had three weeks to get something on the American sleeper.

Joey started to pace after the Canadian bosses left. Suddenly, he stopped.

"What is the only thing that will stop him from going to Singapore?"

"Jihad," I said. "Helping the brothers."

Joey shook his head.

"Helping *you* help the brothers."

"I'm not tracking," I said.

"Follow me on this," Joey said, starting to pace again.

"Your uncle needs you," he said. "The banks are all fucked up after the Arab Spring. They can't get money and he needs cash."

I looked at Nelly. He had a smile on his face.

"Yeah," I said. "So I'm putting a delivery of cash together for the brothers . . ."

"Pitch it to him tomorrow in Montreal," Joey said. "Tell him you need him in New York at the same time as the conference. The Canadians can't arrest him in New York, and we'll invite them down to watch the operation."

"That is brilliant," I said.

"You need Chiheb's help with the delivery," Joey said.

"He'll do whatever you need, especially since you're helping the brothers."

CHAPTER 21

Spitting in the Eyes of God

I parked my rental car in front of Chiheb's apartment. I'd made the drive to his house so often I didn't even use the GPS. The streets of Montreal were comfortable. I fished out my BlackBerry and scrolled through my contacts until I reached Chiheb's name. He answered after a few rings.

"I'm in front of your house," I said.

It sounded like he was outside. I could hear him walking.

"I just finished praying and I'm walking out of the mosque downtown," he said. "Let me give you an address so you can come pick us up."

I heard some other voices in the background. *Us?* I thought.

"Chiheb, who are you with?"

"I'm with a good brother that I met at the mosque," he said. "I think you should meet him."

I was silent for a minute. I had to talk about Singapore and there was no way I was going to do that with a stranger present. I didn't

239

have time for Chiheb's recruiting tonight. He was spending time in
the mosques looking for a replacement for Jaser.

"Listen, get a phone number from him," I said. "Tell him you'll
call him later tonight. We need to meet alone to talk about some
things first."

"Yes," Chiheb said. "Yes. Okay."

He gave me the address of the mosque and I picked him up. We
went to a nearby Tim Hortons. He ordered a hot chocolate. I got a
tea. We went back to the car. Chiheb blew on his hot chocolate as
I talked about my meeting with Abassi.

"He said a few things that caught my attention," I said.

"He didn't ask you for money, did he?" Chiheb asked.

"No, no," I said. "Not at all. He just talked to me about his degree and how he knew chemicals and how with that knowledge he
could make anything blow up. He also told me it was our duty to
do jihad. What do you need more than manpower for jihad? You
need money."

Chiheb shrugged.

"Of course you do," he said. "Everybody knows that."

"Well, it caught my attention," I said. "It sounded like he's got
some thoughts."

"Yeah, well, does he have a plan?"

"We didn't go that far," I said. "I didn't go that far because as
much as I feel like you're right—he seems like a good brother—I
don't know him and I can't trust him like that yet. I just can't seem
to bring myself to go there with him just yet."

Chiheb turned to face me to make sure I understood what he
was saying.

"No, listen. He is a true mujahideen. But he doesn't want to do anything right now. I bet he is going to want you to pay for his PhD and get him through so that long-term he'll be able to help the brothers. But you're supposed to be doing projects along with what you're doing, your everyday work. You should run them parallel."

"Okay," I said. "We'll get back to that once I talk to him again."

I told Chiheb I was headed back to Quebec City in February to finish my conversation with Abassi.

"Listen, brother," I said, trying to sound serious. "I need a favor. You know what's going on with my uncle and everything. He's over in Cairo and he's helping the brothers."

"*Masha'Allah,*" Chiheb said. "May God protect him."

I set my tea in the cup holder and turned to face Chiheb. It was important I sold this pitch. If we couldn't get Chiheb to abandon his trip to Singapore, our case was sunk. We'd never identify the American sleeper.

"He needs money," I said. "The banks are screwed up because of the Arab Spring and he needs cash."

Chiheb had a look on his face that said whatever I needed he would provide.

"No, no," I said. "I've got the money. I have it. I'll put it together. But he's sending a brother, a Palestinian brother, over from Egypt to the United States. A brother that I know and he's a trustworthy brother. He's good. But we're talking about a lot of money that we're going to hide inside a suitcase. That kind of money sometimes . . ."

I paused for a second, building up the tension, the gravity of our mission. I wanted him to come to me. Chiheb finished my sentence.

"The devil can come in," he said.

"That's why I need you," I said. "I can put a million dollars in cash with you. I'd leave. I'd come back and it would be a million dollars plus ten thousand. That's the way you work."

Chiheb laughed.

"You're right, brother," he said. "I'm as loyal as you think I am."

"I trust you with my life, let alone my money."

"Absolutely," Chiheb said.

I told him the Palestinian brother was coming to New York in mid-December to pick up the cash. Right when Chiheb was supposed to be in Singapore.

"Are you okay with everything? Your schedule?"

Chiheb looked concerned, like he was weighing his options.

"Well, there was this Singapore trip," he said.

"What's going on with that?"

"Don't worry about it," he said, sipping his hot chocolate. "It's no big deal."

"Well, tell me about it. What's the thought? What were you going to do?"

"I want to go there because it's not just for work," Chiheb said. "It's great for work, but it's also for religious purposes. Look at how I met you when I went on my last conference. But also there's a lot of good brothers over there in Singapore and I was hoping to maybe make some contacts over there."

But we both knew getting money to the brothers was more important.

"Did you pay? Did you buy a ticket or anything?"

"No, no," Chiheb said. "I didn't book anything yet."

But I could still tell he was hesitating.

"What?"

"Nothing," he said.

"What?" I asked again.

"Well, there was the registration fee, but don't worry about that."

"How much was it?"

"Don't worry about it."

"Tell me."

"Three hundred dollars."

I smiled as I imagined handing Doug the receipt. The Canadians were going to reimburse him.

"Do you have a receipt?"

"Yes."

"Great. Here's what you do. See if you can get your money back. If you can, great. If you can't, don't worry about it. Give me the receipt when you come to the States, when you come to New York, give it to me. We'll put it on your trip. We'll write it off."

"You can do that? That's wonderful. That's great."

"Listen, brother," I said. "I'm sorry about the conference. I really appreciate the help. I hate to ask."

Chiheb put his hand on my shoulder.

"Don't be sorry," he said. "It doesn't matter what I have going on. It doesn't matter. If you say you need me, I will be there."

"Thank you," I said. "Now go ahead and get your visa. Do it for a week. Until December 22. You still have the address, the name of the airport, location, my information, everything?"

"Yes," he said. "I'll e-mail the embassy tomorrow."

"How do you feel about eventually inviting Ahmed to New York?"

We both knew that Abassi was going to Tunisia to celebrate his wedding at the end of December. I wanted to get in front of him in Quebec City, get his true colors on tape, and then arrest him in New York.

Chiheb looked up like he was thinking for a second.

"Hear me out," I said. "You're not sure if he's about money or if he's about jihad. You say he's a mujahid."

"Yes," Chiheb said. "He's one hundred percent mujahideen. But I'm afraid that he has some money things as well."

We were back to the loaned money.

"Okay," I said. "Let's put him to the test. We fly him to New York, we have him stay at a nice place, we have him go out with us, see the sights, and then the three of us sit down together. And then you do your thing. You put him to the test."

I could just make out Chiheb's smile in the thick hair of his beard as he let out a deep chuckle like he was Baba Noel.

"We're putting him to the test so we'll see whether he's about the money or jihad," he said.

"Exactly," I said. "Don't give me an answer now. Think about it. If you want to do it, we do it. If you don't, we don't need him. I need you right now. I don't need him."

I could see Chiheb's pride swell.

"Wouldn't it be great if we can get everything lined up with the American sleeper by the time you get to the States?" I said.

"Yes," he said. "I just sent an e-mail a few days ago asking Abu Hamza for the phone number for El Massoul."

"Why don't you let Abu Hamza know you're going to be in the United States to meet with a brother and that you could call him from there," I said. "We'll get a secure phone of some sort."

"I'm not so sure about secure phones, and I can never tell him where I'm going," Chiheb said.

"What do you mean?"

"I'm under orders," he said. "El Massoul said I'm never allowed to tell anyone, even Abu Hamza, where I am or where I'm going. That's rule number one."

"Alright," I said. "So that's out."

Chiheb said the delay was getting in touch with El Massoul. Only Abu Hamza could do it, and El Massoul was still in Afghanistan.

"They are both traveling," Chiheb said. "I'm patient. I'm trying to be patient. We'll give it some more time."

"Okay," I said.

There was nothing else I could do that night. I was happy with my Singapore victory.

"Tell me about this brother you met," I said.

"I met him yesterday," he said. "His name is Mohammed. We met at the mosque. He is from Tunisia too."

Chiheb wanted me to meet him and test him. Mohammed was a promising lead, but I shook my head when he was finished.

"You know what, I don't want to meet this guy," I said. "Why don't you go ahead and meet him. Figure it out yourself. If you feel like this is someone worth talking to, we'll move forward. If not, then there's really no reason for me to meet him, right?"

"Yeah," Chiheb said, his shoulders slumped in disappointment. "You're right."

Chiheb called Mohammed and canceled. I could hear Mohammed on the line questioning Chiheb.

"Why don't you want to meet me?" he said.

I tried to ignore the conversation, but something was nagging me about Mohammed. On the off chance that I might be missing something, I reached out and touched Chiheb's arm. Chiheb asked Mohammed to hold on and covered the phone.

"Tell him we'll meet him," I said. "Where's he at?"

We picked him up near the mosque and went to a Turkish restaurant downtown. Mohammed was a large man with a beer belly. Something was off with him from the minute he got into the back of the car. He always seemed to have something on the tip of his tongue.

We kept the conversation light. Current events. Islam, but not the heavy stuff. Small talk about our families. I kept my eyes locked on Mohammed throughout dinner. He was always trying to say the right thing. He was constantly thinking. Nothing was natural. I could see it in his eyes. His mind was working through the conversation, always looking for a gap to draw out information. He was either a wannabe jihadi or an informant. In the car afterward, Chiheb wanted to know my impression.

"There's something there," I said. "I don't know what it is, but there's something there. That's your job to vet him."

We both were perplexed and quiet because we couldn't figure out his deal.

"One thing I know for sure is he's fat," I said.

Chiheb chuckled. "Yes, he is fat."

We never brought him up again. I dropped off Chiheb at his apartment. Before he got out, I gave him a hug and thanked him again for coming to New York.

"I can't thank you enough," I told Chiheb. "I'll get the paperwork together. Let me know when your visa comes in. Brother, do you need anything? Can we stop at a food store so I can stock up your fridge?"

"No, brother," Chiheb said. "I am eating. I am praying. I am sleeping. I have all that I need."

I drove back to the safe house. The more I thought about

Mohammed, the angrier I got. I was convinced he was an informant, likely put in place by CSIS to keep tabs on the case. This was the second time they'd gotten in the way. The first was the dog walkers who interrupted my talk with Jaser and Chiheb in Toronto.

But this was worse.

Mohammed wasn't a good informant. He didn't actively listen. He tried to steer the conversation. Everything came out forced. We were lucky Chiheb was so desperate for help that he wasn't picking up the tells. I slammed the safe house door shut and slumped into a chair. Nelly looked at Joey and Doug.

"He didn't go for the New York trip?" Joey said.

"No, he is on board," I said. "That worked beautifully."

"What's wrong then?"

I pulled my jacket off and put in a pinch of snuff.

"Fucking CSIS," I said.

"What?" Nelly said. "They had surveillance out there again?"

"No," I said. "The guy I had dinner with tonight is a fucking informant. His body language sucked. He was trying to give us his legend, which was full of holes. Everything was a lie. All he wanted to do was bring the conversation back to jihad. You better call CSIS. This shit has to stop."

Joey looked at Doug and Nelly. Both men hung their heads. No one wanted to look at me.

"Well, the cat's out of the bag," Joey said.

"Calm down, brother," Doug said. "He's not CSIS."

I looked at Joey.

"Don't look at me."

"That was our call," Doug said. "Chiheb was in the mosque talking jihad and this guy walked into our office and said he had information about a terrorist. We interviewed him to keep him from knowing we had an ongoing op. We signed him up but we didn't think you'd meet him. We didn't want to tell you about him so it wouldn't cloud your judgment."

"That motherfucker knew who I was?" I said.

"No, we didn't tell him shit," Doug said. "As a matter of fact, he just called his handler with his assessment. He said you were an evil fuck and we should let the Americans know you're a real terrorist and Chiheb is a danger to everything and everyone. His assessment was spot-on. But we didn't tell him anything."

I understood why they didn't tell me. Under Canadian rules they couldn't. I flew home the next day. Chiheb's New York trip was paramount; that was where I had to be focused. At this point, the team was convinced if we identified the American sleeper, the Canadians couldn't shut us down.

But Chiheb still confused me. He was a bad guy when he was in jihadi mode. But that wasn't all the time. I'd spent so much time with him when he wasn't talking about murder every minute. I knew how much he liked the Jordanian girl in his office. I admired his willingness to help me. That kind of selflessness you don't see very often. I saw him as a human and not just a target. I wished there was a way to keep him from throwing the switch. A way for him to keep his deep, hearty laugh. Keep him in Baba Noel mode. Abassi and El Massoul had poisoned him. I knew he was going to jail and that was where he belonged. But I wondered if we could bring him back to true Islam.

It was Thanksgiving week and I wasn't going to see my father, a tradition we'd held since my mother passed away. I called him as I drove home from the airport.

"How was your trip?" my father asked.

He knew I worked undercover for the FBI.

"It was alright," I said.

"What's wrong?"

He heard it in my voice.

"You know what?" I said. "It just weighs on you."

"I know you can't talk about what it is you do, but if there is anything you want to talk about generally, I'm here for you," my father said.

"Let me ask you something."

"Sure," he said.

I still had Chiheb on my mind. The question of if he could be saved was nagging me. As a Muslim, I wanted to know if it was my duty to try to save his soul. I was stepping out of my cop mind-set when I called my father. I was searching for guidance in the same religion Chiheb perverted. I couldn't go to an Imam, but I could ask my father. I knew few non-Imams who understood the Quran better.

"When someone misinterprets our religion," I said. "When someone is so far gone and uses Islam as a weapon to kill, but that is their only bad fault, is there anything redeemable? Is there anything that can fix that person? Bring that person back to being a true Muslim?"

I heard my father let out a sigh. He was thinking. Searching his memory of the Quran and his experiences. It was a question all Muslims struggle with. Islam is what makes me who I am. So, how do I identify with the same faith as a small group of mass murderers? Being a Muslim didn't make us villains.

"Listen, it has been my experience that it is very rare when someone is so taken by hatred and evil that they've reached the point where they are using God and Islam to take another soul, any soul, even a military soul," my father said. "That person is far gone. Nothing you say or do will bring them back. But the only advice I can give you is to be sure that person is at that point."

In my head, I was thinking about the Christian burial speech. How Chiheb had laid out his justifications for killing men, women, and children in the name of Allah.

"And if I am sure they are at that point?" I asked.

"If that is the case, it is your duty as a Muslim and as an American to not only stop them but stop them dead in their tracks and make an example of them," my father said. "That is not Islam. That is not anything resembling Islam. That is an evil that needs to be wiped off our planet."

As my father was explaining things to me, I became Chiheb. I argued his justifications for the attack, testing my father's assertions. Each time my father shut it down.

"What you are describing is a warped rationalization," he said when I was finished. "It is human. The Quran is from Allah. When you try to change what is black and white, that is human. That is haram. The Prophet said to you, peace be upon him, this is Islam. These are the rules of Islam. These are the rules of war in Islam. No innocent person can be killed. Women and children of your enemy are off-limits. Even the men of your enemy who are not fighting are off-limits. Never to be touched. The only people of your enemy that you are allowed to kill during times of war are the combatants. That is black and white in the Quran. Anyone who colors outside those lines is spitting in the eyes of God. Anytime you change the meaning of Islam, it is a complete desecration of the religion."

Just hearing my father say that gave me the affirmation I needed. I never doubted my actions. I wasn't seeing things in Chiheb's way. I just saw the human side of a monster, and I didn't want to abandon Chiheb if he could be saved.

But I knew he couldn't.

My father was right. Chiheb was gone.

CHAPTER 22

Operation Happy New Year

Chiheb was due into New York in a week and FBI Headquarters wanted to talk about the plan.

They called a meeting at the joint operations center in midtown Manhattan. I sat next to Nelly at the conference table and stared at a wintry, cold Hudson River. Ari, the assistant special agent in charge of counterterrorism in New York, went over the plan. The Canadians agreed to let him travel. Doug and two of his bosses were scheduled to arrive the day before Chiheb to monitor the operation. The embassy in Ottawa granted his visa on our request, and his flight was booked. The last hurdle was the money. We needed to show Chiheb the cash or the ruse wasn't going to work.

Joey waited until the end of the meeting to spring it on Ari.

"By the way, we're going to need two hundred thousand in cash to show the bad guy," Joey said.

There was a pause as Ari chewed on the request.

"We're not going to put that kind of money in this guy's hands," Ari said. "There's no way."

Ari was worried Chiheb was going to steal it, but we assured him Chiheb would never be alone with the money. And even if he was, it would still be safe.

"You don't need to worry, because that money is safer with him than anyone in this building," I said.

Ari cocked his head in disbelief. He was used to dealing with criminals, not terrorists.

"Listen," I said. "He is not a criminal. I understand what he is doing is criminal. But he believes this money is going to help his cause. He would die before anyone touched it, let alone spent it. I'll make you a bet. Not only will he protect that money, I bet he finds a way to add whatever he has in his pocket to it."

Ari just shook his head.

"You're out of your mind," he said.

I shrugged.

"Gentlemen's bet, then," I said.

"No," he said. "Put your money where your mouth is. Twenty bucks."

I held out my hand.

"You're on."

We shook on it and then Ari turned to Joey.

"Approved," he said.

As we walked out of the conference room, Joey patted me on the back.

"Good job," he said. "And it only cost you twenty bucks."

"I think he just made a sucker bet," I said.

Nelly nodded his head in agreement.

"I think you're right."

The day before Chiheb's arrival, I met with Osman, a new undercover officer. I'd planned to use Yasser, my Palestinian buddy whom I traveled overseas with to meet the Sheikh, but he wasn't available.

Osman grew up in the Midwest and joined the FBI right out of college. Prior to the undercover school, he was saddled to a desk. This was one of his first chances to go undercover as the courier sent by my uncle. We met in Brooklyn at a Buffalo Wild Wings near the Brooklyn Nets arena. We ordered lunch and we talked about Chiheb. I warned him to steer clear of religion. Osman is a devout Muslim and had trouble bending his religion to fit into the jihad ideology.

"Listen, this guy is hard-core," I said. "Watch yourself. For the sake of this investigation, you can't let him know you're a true Muslim. You need to be a like-minded brother."

"No problem," he said.

"Do not correct him," I said.

"No problem."

"You're the courier," I said. "You just arrived from Egypt. My uncle sent you to bring back a suitcase."

"The money?" Osman said.

"Yeah," I said, putting down my iced tea glass. "But you don't know what you're carrying. You're just here to get a suitcase and take it back to the brothers."

Osman smiled.

"No problem," he said.

"Good, I'll call you in a few days and set up the meeting with the target."

I kept in touch with Abassi via e-mail. He was still in Quebec City. But he was getting ready to fly to Tunisia. I wanted to firm up plans to meet again. Abassi suggested that we meet the first week in February back at his apartment to finish our conversation.

"Mark it down," I wrote to Abassi. "I will be up there for business and I'd love to meet for dinner, dear brother."

"I can't wait, brother," Abassi wrote back. "We have a lot to discuss."

But first I had to pick up Chiheb. His flight landed at LaGuardia Airport around four fifteen in the afternoon on December 15, 2012. I met him outside the terminal. I could see his smile through the scruff of his beard. He threw his arms around me in a bear hug.

"Good to see you, brother," I said.

"God be praised, how are you, brother?" Chiheb said.

"I'm well," I said, walking him toward the car.

I put his bag into the back of my Mercedes C300. I purposely chose the smaller sedan because I wanted to have a nice car, but not too flashy and certainly not wasteful. I took the Grand Central Parkway to Interstate 278 to the Manhattan Bridge. We were headed for lower Manhattan. Chiheb was staying at one of my rental properties next door to Ground Zero. It was not done on purpose. It was the only apartment the FBI could get on short notice. As I drove, we talked about Abassi. Chiheb had come around a bit and saw some value in meeting with him.

"He is for real," Chiheb said. "Raed is gone and we need to see what he can do to help us."

"We need to talk about that," I said. "That first week in February I'm going back up there to talk to him. I think we should do that together."

That was my backup plan if the Canadians didn't file the paperwork to get a wire for Abassi. If Chiheb was in the room I could
record. Chiheb agreed and then changed the subject to the American sleeper.

"I got great news from Abu Hamza," Chiheb said. "Our dear
brother is back from Afghanistan, but he is now in Syria helping the
brothers."

I was annoyed.

"You're here for a week, brother," I said. "We need to set this
meeting up ASAP."

"I have a number," Chiheb said. "We can try calling him tomorrow."

After dinner, we went back to Chiheb's apartment and made
several calls to the number. None went through. We didn't have the
correct country code. I promised to figure out the right one and left
Chiheb to pray.

The next day we planned to go to dinner near my apartment in
midtown, but not before we went over the plan for the money and
courier.

"My uncle sent his best friend's nephew instead of the Palestinian brother," I said. "He is good. He is just a little green and gets a
little nervous."

I set the stage for Osman to be nervous on his first major undercover operation.

"Do you trust him?" Chiheb said.

"I do," I said. "I trust his family. His heart is in the right place.
He is a good Muslim brother. He is just like us."

If I trusted him, so did Chiheb.

"Here is how it is going to work," I said, quickly moving to the next topic. "This is the way we've done it in the past. We have a guy in customs in Cairo . . ."

"Is he your guy?" Chiheb said.

"My uncle's guy," I said. "My uncle will be there waiting to receive the package, because we've lost money in the past and this can't be lost."

"Okay, what is the plan for us?"

I told Chiheb about my baggage handler at JFK—another FBI undercover—who would make sure the suitcase got on the plane.

"I need you to help me pack the suitcase and make sure Osman doesn't know what is in it," I said. "All he knows is he has to deliver the suitcase. You're going to help me hide the money."

"Perfect," Chiheb said, content with being one of the trusted brothers in the operation.

"We'll count the money once I get it," I said. "You need to watch over it until it gets to the airport."

"With my life," Chiheb said.

He would never question why I needed his help, especially when it was for the cause.

"You're another set of eyes," I said. "I'm trusting you. The brothers are trusting you with the money. We have to deliver it."

I told Chiheb that Osman was around for dinner if he wanted to meet him. We planned to go to the Palm, a steakhouse on West Fiftieth Street. It was only a few doors down from my apartment.

Chiheb hesitated.

"I don't know about dinner," he said.

I didn't blame him. He wanted to talk with Tamer more and not waste time on a courier. I was happy, because I wasn't sure how Osman would do over a long dinner.

"Once we're done with dinner, I'll text him and he can have dessert," I said.

"Okay," Chiheb said.

We got to the Palm around eight. One of the waiters remembered me from past visits and greeted me warmly. He was Egyptian and spoke Arabic. I purposely got to know him prior to Chiheb's arrival in an effort to show Chiheb that I was a regular at a restaurant near my apartment.

Chiheb studied the menu.

"Have the lobster, brother," I said.

He put down his menu.

"I've never had it before."

"You'll love it," I said, ordering him the whole lobster.

There was no way he could eat the whole thing. It was my solution to waste not, want not. I couldn't have him scooping food off of a plate again. The lobster arrived on a white plate. It was bright red and wisps of steam rose from its shell. Chiheb slid the lobster bib over his head as I showed him how to crack the claws and pull the meat out with a little silver fork.

He smiled as he chewed.

"It's good," I said. "Right?"

"*Masha'Allah*," he said. "It is wonderful."

Between bites of my lobster, I watched Chiheb crack open the tail and another claw. By the end of the meal, he was rooting through the pieces of shell to make sure he got every morsel of lobster meat. As the waiter cleared the table, Chiheb grabbed the butter from the bread basket. He held it in his left hand at an angle and started to spoon it into his mouth with two fingers from his right hand.

"You know that's butter, right?" I said.

Chiheb looked at me and then went back to eating it.

"Thank God," he said.

I understood the idea of not wasting food, but now he was eating butter. I took out my phone and sent a message to Osman.

"Come now."

Osman was nervous when he arrived. He wouldn't sit down until I motioned to the empty chair. Chiheb didn't take his eyes off him. The Arab Santa was gone. I had flashbacks to our flight from Houston to San Jose. Chiheb ran through the hadiths, listening closely to Osman's interpretations. When I could, I answered or guided the conversation away from Osman so all he had to do was agree. By the end of dessert, I was exhausted.

"We'll see you tomorrow at my apartment," I said. "I'll call you when we're ready."

"Great," Osman said, shaking my hand and Chiheb's before leaving the restaurant.

As Osman walked out, I looked at Chiheb.

"What do you think?"

"He is a little nervous," Chiheb said.

"I know he is," I said.

"May Allah protect us," he said.

I paid the check and we walked out to the curb. I didn't want to go back to the apartment and have the same conversations over again. Times Square was only a few blocks away and it wasn't too cold.

"Want to go walk this off? I'll show you Times Square."

We started down the street toward the massive video screens.

Chiheb was silent as the lights of Times Square got brighter. We joined the crowd heading toward the pedestrian plaza. Neon illuminated signs and "zipper" news crawls surrounded us. I let it wash over him.

"That's where the ball drops?" Chiheb said, getting his bearings from the countless movies and shows filmed there.

Times Square was crowded with shoppers getting ready for Christmas. Chiheb kept his eyes up at the buildings and the neon. I watched as several times he cocked his ear, picking out some of the languages spoken around us. We stopped near a McDonald's and he started to scan the tops of the buildings.

"This is the center of the universe of the West," he said. "What a brilliant place to have an operation. Operation Happy New Year."

I pretended not to hear as we walked back to the parking garage.

"We'll need multiple bombs," he said. "The best-case scenario would be vehicles, but the security could be tight around New Year's Eve."

I looked over at him as we drove down Eleventh Avenue toward his apartment.

"It's two weeks away," I said.

"Not this year," he said. "Next year. It will take some time. I'm going to have a job for you. Can you come here for New Year's Eve?"

"Sure," I said. "I live here."

"You need to take pictures from an elevated location," he said. "Show me what the security looks like."

"Okay," I said.

I stopped listening before we reached Canal Street. At his apartment, we tried El Massoul's number again, this time with the correct country code. But a recording told us it was disconnected. Frustrated, I told Chiheb I was tired. I suggested that he reach out to Abu Hamza again and figure something out, because we were running out of time.

I picked up my peacoat off the couch.

"We've got a lot of work tomorrow," I said. "I'll pick you up in the morning."

When Chiheb got into the car the next morning, he started quizzing me about who was getting the money.

"Are you sure this money is going to the mujahideen and not the munafiqeen?"

"Absolutely," I said.

"Who is it going to exactly?"

"Al Qaeda in the Arabian Peninsula," I said.

"Not Hamas."

"No," I said.

The divisions among groups like al Qaeda, ISIS, and Hamas are stark. They all use radical Islamic teachings to brainwash their followers, but that is where the commonality stops. Each group has its own goals. Hamas is a Palestinian Sunni-Islamic group whose primary target is Israel. Al Qaeda in the Arabian Peninsula is a franchise of al Qaeda based in Yemen whose primary target is the United States. All the groups compete for the same pool of recruits. Chiheb was recruited into al Qaeda and didn't want to support a competing group.

"I have five thousand dollars in my checking account," Chiheb said after I convinced him the money was going to a group he supported. "I want to give half of it to the brothers."

"Chiheb, I'm sending two hundred thousand dollars," I said. "All due respect, that is plenty."

"Are you telling me I can't do this?" he asked, an edge in his voice. "This is for Allah. I have to. I have an opportunity to send money."

I shook my head. I didn't care that he was about to give the American government money. I just didn't want to add anything to the plan.

"That's too much," I said, turning into the parking garage of my apartment building.

"I insist," he said. "Don't stop me from getting this credit from Allah."

"Okay," I said, closing my door and heading for the elevator. "How are you going to get the money?"

After an hour on the phone with his bank in Montreal, Chiheb withdrew slightly more than a thousand dollars from an ATM across the street, because that was the most they would allow him to take out in one day. We wrapped it up with my two hundred thousand. When we were done counting and wrapping it in bundles, Chiheb took out a twenty-dollar Canadian note and added it to the pile. That was all the money he had in his wallet.

The suitcase had a hidden compartment in the base and we packed the money inside. I called Osman to come pick it up and ordered a pizza for lunch. While we waited for the pizza to arrive, Chiheb watched as Osman transferred his clothes from his suitcase into the one with the money. Before lunch, we prayed. Chiheb acted as the Imam. Osman and I removed our shoes. Chiheb kept his on as he recited the call to prayer.

"He's got his shoes on," Osman whispered to me.

To a mainstream Muslim, that was frowned upon. But to a mujahid, it was accepted. I shot him a look like I wanted to strangle him. No religion talk.

After prayer, we sat around the table and ate pizza. Chiheb laid out his rationalization for killing innocent people. Osman flinched at each interpretation. I could tell he wanted to argue. Finally, Osman had enough.

"Time out," he said.

Osman started questioning everything. He broke cover and stumped Chiheb using my father's rationale. Chiheb had no answer for why his views violated the Prophet's rules of war. I was proud of Osman as a Muslim. But at that moment, I wanted to smash his face. *Shut it the fuck down and finish the operation,* I thought as the conversation got heated.

"Alright, guys, we've got to get going," I said, breaking up the argument.

Chiheb shot me a look like he wanted to talk. I gathered up the pizza boxes.

"Hey, Osman, can you take these pizza boxes to the trash chute?" I said.

Chiheb pulled me aside after he left.

"What's up?" I said, knowing damn well what the problem was.

"Are you sure you trust this guy?" he said. "Can he be trusted?"

Chiheb wanted to know how Osman, who clearly believed in mainstream Islam and was possibly munafiqeen, was chosen for such an important job.

"He is young and naive," I said. "He is on his way. Just like the brothers you introduced me to in Montreal. He is close. He is being converted. He is a good soldier right now, but he is still confused by the munafiqeen mind-set. He is okay. Trust me."

Chiheb didn't say anything at first.

"I don't trust him," he said as he waved his finger in my face. "May Allah watch over us."

Chiheb sat down on the couch as I put the last of the dishes in the sink.

"He probably couldn't find the trash chute," I said, hoping to catch Osman before he came back to the apartment. "I'll be right back."

I grabbed my key and met Osman in the hall.

"No more religion talk," I said.

"I'm sorry," he said.

He looked down at his shoes and started to explain his actions when I gave him a throat-slash gesture. I was still wired.

"Okay," he said. "Okay."

"It's time for us to go," I said. "Got it? Silent ride to the airport."

Osman and Chiheb avoided each other as we rode down the elevator. A car driven by another FBI agent was waiting to take us to the airport. The (FBI) baggage handler met us at the terminal so Chiheb could see him.

"Wait with the car," I told Chiheb. "I'll get Osman checked in and be right back."

The next morning, I called Chiheb and told him the money arrived safely and my uncle was taking it to the Sinai Peninsula to give to the brothers. Chiheb was fired up after being challenged by Osman. I spent hours listening to him rail against everything. It was six hours of hate.

By dinner, I'd had my fill. All I wanted was to identify the American sleeper. But Chiheb was focused on Operation Happy New Year. The U.S. attorney was ecstatic. He had listened to the previous day's recordings and knew we already had a strong case against Chiheb. He'd gifted us by putting his own money in the suitcase and verbally earmarking it for a specific terrorist group. Now he was planning an attack on American soil, and the U.S. attorney wanted audio. I did my best to stay plugged in, but it got harder as each hour passed.

By the time I reached his apartment after dinner, I was fried. I parked around the corner and we walked the half block to the front door. The building sat next to the entrance to the 9/11 memorial. One World Trade Center towered above us. Chiheb stopped and looked up at the building. He slid his arm over my shoulder and pulled me close.

"Tamer, this town needs another nine-eleven. And we're going to give it to them," he said, rubbing his beard. "Come upstairs. I want to tell you about Operation Happy New Year."

I saw red.

I could feel a pen in my jacket pocket. Every fiber of my being wanted to grab it and jam it into Chiheb's eye. I wanted him off the face of the earth. He died in my mind that night. Any concern I had for the human inside that monster was gone. I shoved him away. He looked at me funny.

"You know what, brother, I'm not feeling good tonight," I said, turning back toward the car. "It might be something I ate."

"Are you okay?" Chiheb asked, not sure how to read my body language.

I started to walk away.

"Just an upset stomach," I said. "See you tomorrow."

I got to the safe house on the west side first and sat by the window. I left the lights off. I felt like I had let everyone down. It was my job to separate my personal feelings from the goals of the investigation. My anger was turning to shame. I was not a professional undercover that night.

Joey arrived a few minutes later.

"Can I turn the light on?" Joey said.

"Sure."

"Are you okay?" Joey asked.

"I fucked up, bud."

"No you didn't," he said, failing to be convincing.

"I fucked up. I know I fucked up. Are they losing their shit?"

Joey shifted in his seat.

Everyone in the operations center was listening in on our conversations. A known terrorist was about to lay out a plot to attack the United States and I walked away. I found out later the U.S. attorney listening to the wire lost his shit. He should have. I failed.

"Fuck them," Joey said. "Are you okay?"

"Yeah, I will be."

Joey pulled out a tin of Copenhagen Long Cut Straight.

"Put a pinch in," he said, switching off the light. He sat in silence for the better part of an hour as I collected myself. I didn't want to talk about the case anymore. I didn't want to talk about killing people. I didn't want to be fake.

I finally pulled the wad of Copenhagen out and looked at Joey.

"Tell them they'll have everything they need tomorrow morning."

CHAPTER 23

High Five

I called Chiheb first thing in the morning.

"I'm coming over with breakfast," I said.

"How are you feeling?"

"Feeling great," I said as I headed out of my apartment.

I stopped and picked up some bagels and drove downtown to his apartment. We sat around the coffee table in the living room eating as he explained Operation Happy New Year.

"There needs to be three explosions at different points of a triangle," Chiheb said, looking at his computer.

A Google map of Times Square filled the screen. The plan was to hide the bombs in parked cars.

"They have to be set off between five and ten seconds apart," he said. "As one explosion detonates, people will run away from it. That is when the other explosion will take place. Maximum destruction, maximum fatalities if you do it that way."

I chewed and listened. If he had said that last night, he'd be dead and I'd be up on murder charges. A decent night's sleep saved his life.

"I need you to spend some time there," Chiheb said, leaning back in his chair and taking a bite of his breakfast. "Take video and pictures. Learn the security procedures. What do the police do if you leave a car unattended? Checkpoints and things like that so that we can accurately plan the attack."

I nodded.

"I'll e-mail you the pictures," I said.

"No e-mail. Put them on a flash drive."

"Okay," I said. "I'll have them in February when I come up to meet with Ahmed."

"We'll do it in a year," Chiheb said. "We're going to need hotel rooms nearby so we can see down onto the street. We can set off the bombs from there."

All of this came from one walk through Times Square. The bumbling professor persona was just a façade, and I fell for it, even going so far as talking to my father about saving him. This plot showed Chiheb's true nature. This was his idea, not the brothers'. He was thinking for himself. Forget the train plot. This one scared me because he was using his training. No e-mail. Figuring out security and getting access to Times Square. While in its infancy, this plot seemed more doable than the train plot. I never said it, but this is what Jaser told us to do from the start.

Chiheb's flight left later that day. He was flying back to Montreal and then getting a ride to Toronto. His lease was up at his apartment in Montreal, so I offered him the safe house in Toronto.

"They let me have it for a few more months," I said. "It's yours if you want it."

"Thank you, brother," he said.

I took out an envelope from my backpack and put it on the table. There was five hundred dollars in cash in it.

"What is this?" Chiheb asked.

"For your visa and conference registration," I said. "Thank you for coming down here, brother. I needed you and you gave up everything to come."

Chiheb smiled and rubbed his beard. His eyes lit up as he talked.

"Look at what Allah is doing for us now," he said. "We just sent two hundred thousand dollars to the mujahideen overseas. I was able to give a little bit and look what is happening now. I got five hundred back from you. My apartment lease was up and you give me a place to stay. Your business is doing so well, *Masha'Allah,* God has paid us back already."

Just after New Year's Day, Joey got a call from the Canadians. They wanted me to fly to Toronto and meet with Chiheb.

I balked.

"I'm not getting on a plane," I said. "I'm not being a dick, but what the fuck are we going to gain from me hanging out with Chiheb? Nothing. There is no imminent threat. I don't understand."

Chiheb wasn't going to do anything without me.

"They need to re-up the wire," Joey said.

Every thirty days prosecutors had to prove to the court that a wiretap was still warranted. They had to show significant progress in the investigation, which was simple when you have a terrorist like Chiheb.

"Bullshit," I said. "They have everything from the New York trip. What more do they want?"

"I know, it doesn't make sense to me either," Joey said. "But that's what they are saying. Maybe Canadian courts are different."

"But they haven't been for the last several months," I said. "There is something going on. If it made one iota of sense to me, I'd be on the next fucking flight out. You know that. But it doesn't make sense. It doesn't. We're not going to acquiesce to this bullshit."

"Fine," Joey said. "I'll go back and tell them."

The Canadians backed off and I stayed in New York. Nelly, Joey, and the team flew to Toronto instead to discuss strategy. Joey called me after the meeting.

"Looks like all the cards are on the table now," Joey said.

"What happened?"

"They revoked Abassi's visa," Joey said.

"Are you fucking kidding me?"

I'm convinced that when I told the Canadians Abassi was a bad guy, they decided to pull his visa. They didn't want this case to drag on any longer. But now we had problems. Abassi wasn't just a loose end; he was a threat to the United States. Revoking his visa didn't protect us. And sooner or later Chiheb was going to find out. This might tip him off to the whole investigation.

"Do I need to come up?"

"Don't come up right now," Joey said. "We're coming back. We'll have a meeting and figure it all out back in New York."

A day later we were all sitting around the conference table overlooking the Hudson. Abassi didn't know his visa was revoked, but when he found out, we planned to invite him to New York instead. Ari wanted to make sure it was worth the effort.

"Is this guy the real deal?" Ari said to me.

Nelly walked Ari through my first meeting with Abassi. We talked through how he flirted with the line, talking about jihad one second and then his nuclear engineering degree the next. He was painting a picture for me to connect the dots. Abassi had Chiheb's brains and beliefs, but he knew how to blend in with the West. He kept his true nature hidden.

"He scares me more than Chiheb," I said when we were done presenting the evidence.

"Enough said," Ari said. "Get it done."

As I was leaving, Ari stopped me. He had a twenty-dollar bill.

"You were right," he said.

I took the cash with a smile.

A few days later, Nelly called me. He and Kenny were getting Abassi cleared to enter the United States.

"Listen, they're breaking my balls," Nelly said. "They want you to reach out to Abassi. They want you to invite him to the States."

"Nelly, do you know what I'm going to say to you right now?"

"I know exactly what you're going to say," he said.

"Tell me what I'm going to say."

"It's going to stink," Nelly said. "It's going to look weird if you call him right now on the heels of his visa getting revoked. All of a sudden he is hearing from you with an invite to New York."

I laughed.

"I couldn't have said it better myself. Tell them I'm not making the call. I'm not sending an e-mail. Trust the technique. Believe me when I tell you, the second he finds out his visa was revoked, I'm going to be his first call."

I got a call from Abassi three days later. He was about to return to Canada when the Canadian Consulate in Tunisia informed him his visa was revoked.

"You won't believe this," he said, his voice sullen and defeated. "I just put my wife on a plane. I couldn't get on the plane. It is haram for her to travel alone, but she had to get back. She had her work and studies."

"What happened?" I asked, acting surprised. "Are you okay, brother?"

"I have no idea," he said, his voice cracking. "They are just telling me my visa was revoked."

"Oh no," I said. "Brother, I already booked my flight to Toronto because I was going to visit Chiheb. We were going to fly out to visit you."

"I know," he said. "I was looking forward to that. They messed my life up. And my brother got into an accident. He is in a coma."

There was real pain in his voice.

"Ahmed, I don't know what to say," I said. "I am praying for you and your family."

I could hear him sniffle as he tried to regain his composure.

"Thank you, Tamer," he said. "It means a lot that I have a friend in you."

I offered to send him money and medicine for his brother and told him to call me if he needed anything. I resisted the urge to invite him to New York. That would seem scripted. But he knew I wanted to help him. The seed was planted.

The next day, I flew to Toronto to babysit Chiheb. The trip was planned and it would be weird if I canceled it. I got to Toronto on February 9 and went straight to the condo on Harrison Garden

Boulevard in North York. When I told Chiheb about Abassi, he dismissed his troubles.

"He shouldn't have gone to Tunisia in the first place," he said. "What a waste of time. He deserves what is happening to him. He did not have to go there. Look what happened. You see what we do? We send two hundred thousand dollars to the brothers and Allah opens doors for us. He goes there to waste time and Allah shuts doors for him. It's amazing."

His rant ended as soon as I took out the thumb drive.

"I have pictures from Times Square," I said. "I was able to get on the rooftop. A friend let me shoot some photos from where CNN was broadcasting."

In reality, the New York City Police Department gave me behind-the-scenes access to the ball drop.

As he looked at the images, Abassi came up again. After visiting the tracks with Jaser, Chiheb was convinced the only way to derail the train was with explosives. We also needed someone to build the bombs for Operation Happy New Year. Abassi gave us that capability.

"What if we bring Abassi to New York?" I said. "We'll vet him in New York, see if he is like-minded, and you can test him."

It was an idea I'd pitched a few months before. Chiheb stopped clicking through the pictures and looked at me.

"For one month," Chiheb said. "One-month visa and no more."

Chiheb started to rub his beard.

"Do it so it is the same time of my two conferences," Chiheb said. "I have a conference in Philadelphia in late March, and then I have to be in San Francisco in early April. Between the conferences we will see if he is truly ready."

"Okay," I said. "I'll invite him next time he contacts me."

I walked into the kitchen to get some water. I was tired of talking about the plots.

The next night we planned to meet Waleed, Jaser's Afghan friend, for dinner. Chiheb said he was close to joining the cell to help with the train plot. The hope was that dinner with us would seal it. Chiheb called him.

Chiheb hung up the phone and looked at me.

"No answer again," he said.

"And you're sure he is like-minded?" I said.

Chiheb nodded.

"Yes," he said. "We had the tax talk and everything. He was ashamed that he still paid his taxes."

"Try him again," I said. "If he doesn't answer, let's just go have dinner."

While Chiheb called again, I did a Yelp search. Waleed never answered. I suspect Jaser told him to stop talking to Chiheb, but I wasn't sure.

"How about the Lobster Trap for dinner?" I said.

"I am expert now," Chiheb said.

It was a Tuesday and the restaurant wasn't crowded. It resembled an old fish house inside. The waitress, a bubbly college student with auburn hair and a smile that made you fall in love with her, brought us both whole lobsters. For whatever reason, Chiheb was normal that night. It wasn't jihadi talk. He'd gotten that out of his system at the condo.

The waitress was joking with us all night. Chiheb's plate was a pile of broken shells by the end of dinner. He got every morsel.

"Wow," she said as she cleared Chiheb's plate. "This lobster didn't stand a chance."

Chiheb smiled.

"I've been traveling the world eating lobsters with my brother," he said. "I am expert now."

We all started laughing.

"You the man," she said, putting her hand up to give Chiheb a high five.

He didn't move except for his fading smile.

"High five?" she said, smiling at him.

His eyes got dark and the jihadi returned.

"No, no, no," he said, turning away from her. "I cannot touch you. You are not my wife."

There he is, I thought.

Her smile turned. She wasn't mad, more embarrassed. She wasn't sure what to do.

"We'll take the check," I said, breaking the tension.

She turned and walked back to the serving station. She left the check on the table without a word and disappeared. I left her a generous tip and we left.

Back home, I sent Abassi an invite to New York via e-mail. Chiheb's blessing was all the cover I needed.

"Why don't you come here? I'll have my lawyers look into your situation. At least you'll be closer to your wife if you come. Maybe she can visit you here. I'll take care of you. You can stay at one of my apartments."

Abassi's response was almost immediate.

"I don't know what to say," he wrote. "I really appreciate it."

Abassi was on his way.

CHAPTER 24

The Sixth Pillar

I merged onto Interstate 95 heading south toward Philadelphia.

It was March 2013. Chiheb had landed at JFK a few hours before, and I was driving him to his conference in Philadelphia. Something was different from the moment I picked him up at the airport. He was quiet. Focused.

"I tried to get an earlier flight," he said as we left New York behind. "But the woman at the American Airlines ticket counter told me I couldn't."

I turned to look at him. He was staring at the highway in front of me.

"Why?" I asked.

"I am flagged," Chiheb said, turning to look at me. "That is what she told me. I could only fly on the ticket I had."

"Really," I said. "That's weird."

Shit. Shit. Shit. Think fast.

"You know what?" I said. "It's because you're an Arab. I'm always getting hassled by security. It's happened to me even with an American passport."

Chiheb shook his head.

"No matter," he said. "Even if they are watching they don't know anything. We are going to need explosives. It is the only way we can complete the work on the train in time."

Enter Abassi. I mentioned he was arriving at the end of the week.

"I hope he knows how lucky he is to have a brother like you," Chiheb said.

"It's not about the recognition or the money," I said. "I just want to make sure he is a like-minded brother."

"He is like-minded," Chiheb said.

"How do you know?" I asked.

"I knew when we met," Chiheb said. "It was a conference like I am going to now. We met the first day and he watched as I left the sessions to pray. He stopped me the second day at lunchtime."

"Why?" I asked. "Didn't he pray too?"

Chiheb tipped his head back like he was watching his memories play out on the roof of the car.

"Yes, of course," Chiheb said. "But he told me, 'Brother, you're leaving this conference to pray, but you're leaving out the most important pillar. That's jihad. It's obligatory. Don't you think for a second you are a true Muslim if you are not following every single pillar and every single obligation Allah has put on you.'"

"Allah bless him," I said. "He is wise."

But there is no sixth pillar. Islam has only five pillars. The first is Shahada—the declaration of faith. There is only one God and Mohammed is his messenger. The second pillar—Salat—requires

Muslims to pray five times a day. The third pillar—Zakat, or charity—requires a Muslim to be charitable, and the fourth is Sawm, fasting during Ramadan. The last pillar is Hajj, the pilgrimage to Mecca for Muslims who are able to do it. Islam's pillars have the same theme: peace, submission, helping the less fortunate.

"Yes," he said. "That night we talked about Sheikh Osama and the brothers overseas. Ahmed talked about how much he admired Mohammed Atta. He wanted to wage jihad too once he finished his studies."

"And now he is almost done," I said. "We have operations for him now."

"Yes," Chiheb said. "But after that conference, I couldn't wait. I didn't care about my studies. That's why I went to Iran. That's why I wanted to fight in Afghanistan. Ahmed showed me the way, but El Massoul showed me how to do jihad. But I fear he loves this world too much. We will test him. It will be a surprise that I am here too."

"I Skyped with Abassi last week," I said. "I told him you're coming and we'd all meet in New York."

Chiheb sighed.

"It's no secret," Chiheb said. "I just didn't feel there was a need to say anything. He is coming here for a reason and that reason is to find out if he is ready to help now."

I had planned to prep Chiheb to recruit Abassi on the ride to Philadelphia, but it was the opposite. He was getting me ready.

"I have two projects—one in the United States and one in Canada—that need attention," Chiheb said. "We need his skills. He can do whatever he wants long-term. But I need explosives for Operation Happy New Year and Operation Fishing."

"And we need to meet the American sleeper," I said. "Have you heard from El Massoul?"

Chiheb looked away.

"No," he said. "I sent a message before I left but got nothing back. They are very careful. We must be patient."

I had already burned through all of my patience. The Canadians had pulled Abassi's visa. The ticket agent had told Chiheb he was flagged. It was only a matter of time before the Canadians or FBI management decided the case was over.

I slapped the wheel in frustration. Chiheb looked at me.

"How many of our brothers have died in the last year?" I said, a hint of anger in my voice. "How many infidels? It's too lopsided. They need to know what an amazing job you've done. It would take anyone else years to accomplish what you've done in so little time. Think about it. You've got the money. You've got like-minded brothers. You're the greatest cell leader they've ever sent over, and they're taking their time responding. We're ready. We've got another operation. You have access to the United States. You can do anything and everything. Money is no object. And they can't respond to an e-mail because they are busy fighting in Syria? In Afghanistan?"

"You're right, brother," Chiheb said.

I wanted him to think al Qaeda was failing him.

"You are our leader," I said. "You have the brains. You have the bomb maker. The money. We need direction now more than ever."

I let that sink in a bit. Chiheb's body language changed. He sat up in his seat. He stopped fidgeting.

"How ironic is it that your brother here is the money guy and the man who trained you happens to be their financier?" I said. "Don't you think we should meet or talk or something? Don't you think you should find a way to connect us? Don't you think he needs to know you have a Tamer?"

"You are absolutely right," Chiheb said. "I will send a strong message to Abu Hamza tonight."

I took Chiheb right to his hotel outside of Philadelphia. As he waited to check in, he took out an envelope and tried to hand it to me. I wanted to get it on tape, so I scanned the hotel and spotted some security guards standing near the front desk.

"Hold up," I said, nodding toward the security guards.

Chiheb slid the envelope back into his bag. When we got to his room, he took it out and handed it to me. I opened it and saw a thick stack of American one-hundred-dollar bills.

"It is three thousand dollars," he said. "I want it to go to the brothers in Mali if Uncle Ibrahim can get it there. If not, he can have it for our brothers."

The French intervention in Mali was in the news.

"May Allah bless you," I said. "I will send it to him with my next shipment."

I knew not to argue with him anymore. I took a mobile phone out of my backpack and handed it to him.

"I wasn't sure if your phone worked in the United States, so I got you one," I said. "My number is programmed in. So is Ahmed's. I got him a phone too."

"Thank you, brother," Chiheb said, putting the phone on the bureau.

We prayed and then I gathered my things to leave. I had to get back to New York. Chiheb walked me to the door.

"Make Ahmed comfortable when he arrives, but don't talk about the projects until I arrive on Thursday," he said.

"Of course," I said. "Do you need anything else before I head back to New York?"

Chiheb gave me a hug.

"No, brother," he said. "I'm eating. I'm sleeping. I'm praying. I have everything I need."

Back in New York, Nelly and the team were tracking Abassi as he left Tunisia for Paris. After a layover there, he got on a plane to New York. His flight landed around eight in the evening, but he didn't emerge from customs until close to ten. He looked tired. His shoulders slumped and his eyes were dead. He barely had enough energy to shuffle his feet forward.

I greeted him with a hug and ushered him to my waiting Mercedes. He climbed into the passenger side while I put his suitcase in the back. When I climbed into the driver's seat, he was riffling through the glove box. He shut it and ran his hands over the visor and poked his fingers in the air vents.

"What's wrong?" I said.

"They are listening," he said. "They are watching me."

"Who?"

"The Canadians," he said. "The Americans. Everyone."

"Be calm, brother," I said.

Abassi ignored me. The confident man I met in Quebec City was a distant memory.

"They interviewed me at every stop," he said. "Security guards checked my bags over and over again. In Paris, the Americans almost didn't let me on the plane."

"It has happened to me," I said. "They are always looking at us because we're Arabs."

"No, this was different," Abassi said. "A woman in Paris said I wasn't going anywhere until she spoke to someone in Washington."

"How do you know?"

"I know," he said. "I overheard. Be careful of everything and everyone."

All day his wife was texting me from Quebec City asking if he had arrived. I promised to call her as soon as he did. I dialed her number on his new cell phone. I wasn't about to hand him a phone cold. His wife gave me a reason to offer it to him.

"Someone wants to talk to you," I said as the phone rang. "It's your wife. She has been texting me and calling me."

He took the phone and relaxed when he heard her voice.

"I'm good," he said. "I'm just so tired."

When he went to hand the phone back, I told him to keep it.

"It's yours, brother," I said. "I got one for you and Chiheb from my company while you're here in the States."

Abassi looked at the phone for a second and then slipped it into his pocket.

"My number and Chiheb's number are already programmed," I said. "So is your wife's. Feel free to call her when you want."

"May Allah reward you for your good deeds," he said.

He sat in silence as we drove into Manhattan. If he was impressed with the scenery, he didn't show it. His eyes darted between looking out of the windshield and looking for microphones in the car.

"I still don't understand what happened with your visa," I said, trying to get him to talk.

"It's a long story," Abassi said. "We'll get into that when we get back to the house."

He was still angry.

"It is haram for her to travel alone," he said. "But she had to go. She is almost done with her studies. She had to return."

"You had no choice," I said. "I almost left this country for good after my mother died, but my uncle convinced me to stay. But that is a story for another time. You're tired. We can talk later."

I got him settled in the same apartment building near Ground Zero where Chiheb stayed and left him to sleep off his jet lag.

"I will come by tomorrow," I said. "I'll take you out to a nice dinner."

Chiheb called me the next day. I was on my way to pick up Abassi.

"Talk to him about the projects, but don't give him any money," he said. "Remember, he is a good brother. He can be trusted, but what is important is he wants to help with our projects."

"Okay," I said. "Do you need me to set up a ride back to New York?"

"No," he said. "I met an Iranian brother that will be traveling to New York on Thursday. He offered me a ride."

I stifled a laugh. It wasn't a coincidence that Chiheb tried to contact El Massoul in Iran when he got to Philadelphia and magically an Iranian was available to drive him to New York. It wasn't the FBI. I guess someone else was keeping tabs on him too.

"Fine," I said. "See you Thursday."

It was prayer time when I arrived at Abassi's apartment. I did the call and Abassi led the prayers. When we were done, Abassi asked me about my mother and uncle.

"What did you mean that you almost weren't going to be in this country?" he asked. "What happened?"

I tried to divert the conversation because I didn't feel that he was ready for my point of radicalization, but he wasn't having it. It was clear he wasn't going to dinner until we talked about it. I told him how my mother got sick and the doctors failed her. It was a vanilla version of the story. I didn't get emotional like with Chiheb, because it was clear Abassi wasn't interested in the details. He was interrogating me. Several times he stopped me and we went back over the details.

When I was done, he opened up a bit more. We read from the Quran and a sura about the seven levels of heaven and how a Muslim can never truly understand the beauty of paradise. From time to time, Allah sent down jinns to watch and listen to Muslims. These jinns watch everyone, but they can never know what the true believers are up to because they are the ones on the path of Allah. I learned the sura as a kid growing up. It warned Muslims the devil was always around us and tempting us and that the true believers would never give in to temptation. But Abassi got another message from it.

"Tamer, as we sit here on the floor, between you and me right now, there are millions and millions of bacteria like the jinns all around us," he said. "We can't see them, but we know they're there. We need to take precautions to protect ourselves from these germs, but they won't alter our course."

In his version, the jinns were the American government. He was warning me to be careful. We were getting back to the guy I met in Canada. As we were leaving the apartment, he stopped just out front and stared at the construction of One World Trade Center towering above us.

"Tamer, I can't believe my apartment is only a few meters away from Ground Zero," he said.

I could see his body language change. He no longer slumped. It was like he got energy from being so close to al Qaeda's major attack. It was sickening.

"It's been over ten years," I said. "They're still rebuilding."

"I'd really like to see the memorial and spend some time there," he said.

I shrugged but didn't say anything. That was the last place in the world I wanted to take him.

Dinner was uneventful except that with each passing hour the old Abassi started to come back. When a well-dressed woman in a dress walked by the table, he turned away and shook his head. As we were leaving, a man with liquor on his breath bumped into us. The man apologized, but I heard Abassi mumble "I ask the magnificent Allah's forgiveness" as he passed.

We drove back to my apartment near Times Square. It was too cold to walk. I let the ride pass in silence. His eyes were fixed on all the lights and sounds. Unlike Chiheb, he didn't see evil. He just saw the grandeur of New York and he liked it.

I made tea at my apartment while he looked around. I handed him a cup as he admired a picture of the Kaaba hanging on the wall. Muslims pray facing the Kaaba, a square building that sits in the middle of Al-Masjid al-Haram mosque in Mecca. It is considered the "House of Allah" and one of Islam's most sacred sites.

"My wife's parents have the same picture in their house in Tunisia," Abassi said.

He scrolled through his phone to show me a photo. As he was scrolling through the pictures, he paused. A strange look came over his face.

"Are you looking at some wedding pictures?"

"You won't believe what I'm looking at," he said.

I leaned over and he showed me his phone. It was a picture of bin Laden. The terrorist leader was bathed in an angelic light.

"There was a poster in Quebec City years ago," Abassi said. "Some French author said he must die. I contemplated finding that author and killing him. I took a photo of the poster to always remind me."

I was happy that everyone listening to our conversation in the command center heard him idolize Osama bin Laden. This was the Abassi I'd met in Quebec City. This was the guy I'd warned the Canadians about. He was warming up just in time for Chiheb to arrive the next day.

The FBI got Chiheb an apartment in the same building as Abassi. After a dinner at the Palm—Chiheb had the lobster—we went back to my apartment in midtown to talk. Chiheb asked me to take out my passport. He wanted to show it to Abassi.

"Look at my passport," Chiheb said, putting it on the table between us. "Look when I was in Iran."

Abassi picked up his passport and looked at the entry stamps. Chiheb nodded at me to show him my passport.

"Look at Tamer's now," Chiheb said. "He was in the Middle East at the same time. He was there helping the brothers. I was there training. It was Allah's will that we were both there."

Abassi handed us our passports back.

"That is who we are," Chiheb said.

"*Masha'Allah*," Abassi said.

But he wasn't all that impressed. It was more of a *so what?*

The next night Chiheb laid out both plots. He wanted Abassi to make the bombs. But Abassi stayed silent. He let Chiheb talk but didn't agree to help. He was still spooked. The clock was ticking. If the Abassi I met in Quebec City didn't fully reveal himself, we didn't have a case.

CHAPTER 25

Eyes of Allah

Abassi invited us to his apartment the next day. He wanted to talk. For the past several days he and Chiheb had been in a constant fight. Chiheb thought Abassi was of true mind and heart for the cause, but didn't agree with waiting. He had orders from overseas and wanted to act. But when I got to Abassi's apartment, something was different.

"You're a scientist," Abassi told Chiheb. "You work with hazardous materials. You work with deadly diseases. You can get some. We can grow it in our own lab. Take it to a reservoir and put the virus in the water. It will mutate and grow on its own. They'll drink it and we'll have thousands of dead Americans."

The Abassi I met in Quebec City finally had arrived. Even Chiheb was impressed. But it was the way Abassi explained the plot. He laid it out like someone sharing a cookie recipe. It was no big deal to either of them, and I sat there pretending to be impressed, but I was sick to my stomach.

"Look what I can come up with in a couple of days," Abassi said. "Imagine if we take our time what we could accomplish."

I realized we were at an impasse. Both wanted to kill Americans but disagreed how. I needed a change of scenery, so after dinner I took them to a small hookah bar on the east side near New York University. The scene was pretty mellow. There were a few students studying. A group was sitting at one table smoking hookah. We found a table near the back and ordered tea and baklava.

Abassi sat on a bench with his back to the wall. His legs were crossed and he wagged his foot up and down as he spoke. Abassi was holding court and looked very comfortable as we smoked and talked.

Chiheb was at the head of the table to his right. He was leaning forward like some anxious freak. He didn't smoke. The hookah bar wasn't on the path of Allah. In his mind, we were wasting time.

I was half listening to Abassi as I smoked.

"The U.S. government can never outsmart me," Abassi said, taking a long pull off the hookah and sending a stream of smoke into the air above his head. "I know the FBI is always watching."

He was looking at me as he spoke. I put a puzzled look on my face. Was he suggesting that I might be an informant for the FBI? I was exhausted with all the fighting between him and Chiheb. I needed to put Abassi on the defensive.

"Are you kidding me right now?" I said, keeping my voice measured but stern. "Is this your way of telling me that you are an informant for the FBI?"

I looked around the hookah bar like FBI agents were lurking around every corner. Abassi didn't know what to say. Chiheb looked at me with a puzzled expression. This was the first time he'd seen me this upset. I let the weird energy crackle between us.

Then I snapped.

"Do you have any idea how important my company is to the Muslim Ummah?" I said, staring at Abassi. "Are you trying to tell me that you are bringing them to my door?"

Chiheb tried to interrupt me.

"Tamer . . ."

The other patrons started to notice our table. I kept my gaze locked on Abassi as I put my hand up for Chiheb to stop talking. Abassi uncrossed his legs and put both feet on the floor.

"Tamer, that's not at all what I was saying," he said, lowering his voice. "I would never—"

I stood up and smashed the small tea glass against the wall. I heard someone behind me gasp. Abassi and Chiheb recoiled as I threw a hundred-dollar bill on the table.

"Find your own way home," I said.

This was my last-ditch effort to turn the tables on him. I wasn't sure if it would work, but we were out of options.

I stormed out of the hookah bar and climbed into my car. Chiheb called my cell phone before I arrived at the safe house.

"I'm sorry," I said.

"Don't worry, brother," he said. "I understand. We took a cab home. Ahmed was upset."

"Are you sure about him?" I said. "I don't know if he is a like-minded brother."

"He is," Chiheb said. "But he isn't worth it."

Chiheb wanted to break ties with Abassi, but I still had work to do with him. We didn't have enough to charge him. I couldn't cut him loose.

"Okay," I said. "I know you have work to do for school. I'll spend some time with him tomorrow morning. I will call you after."

The team met me at a hotel suite in midtown. As I told them what happened in the hookah bar, Abassi called me several times. I ignored the calls.

"You should answer it," Nelly said after the third call.

I refused. I wanted him to sweat it out. He was isolated in a strange city. His benefactor just rejected him. Any reunion with his wife felt remote. He was freaking out.

Joey smirked when Abassi called again.

"I love the play," Joey said. "Let him stew in it a bit more."

After the fifth call, I answered. I could hear the fear in Abassi's voice as he apologized. He asked me to come by his apartment to talk. I met him outside the building. He got into the passenger seat and apologized.

"Put yourself in my place," he said. "A few months ago, I was finishing up my doctorate and getting married. My life was perfect. Then Canada takes away my visa. I'm away from my wife. I don't know if I will get my degree. My brother is dying. The FBI almost doesn't let me come to New York. I have no idea what is happening and didn't know who I could trust."

He reassured me over and over that he would never betray me to the FBI, because then he would have to answer to Allah.

"Only Allah knows what is truly in a man's heart," he said.

But even his apology felt like a threat.

The next day, I brought breakfast to his apartment. He was wide awake and working on both laptops. He ignored the breakfast and ushered me over to the computers. On the screens were scientific journals and stories about Mohammed Atta. Abassi was studying the engineering behind how the steel in the World Trade Center towers melted. He talked about jet fuel and melting points. Most of it went over my head.

"The brilliance of that attack was in its simplicity," Abassi said.

Abassi wanted to top it. Chiheb's plans weren't big enough.

"We could do much bigger things that would truly make a difference," he said.

I wanted to foster his excitement and keep him on track, so I asked him if he still wanted to go see Ground Zero. I had resisted in the past, but he refused to let it go. I ran it by FBI executive management. They refused at first but finally gave me the green light after the New York police commissioner's office got on board.

Abassi stopped talking and smiled. He looked like a kid who was just told he was going to Disney World.

"Right now?" he said.

"Let's go."

As we walked through the memorial, a profound sense of loss came over me. It was my first time and I had to hold back tears. I had lost friends, and I didn't want to be there with him. The other tourists had solemn looks on their faces. But as Abassi looked at each plaque detailing the attack, a different look came over his face. It wasn't a smile. It was pride.

My tears turned to rage. I felt the same emotions and feelings I had when Chiheb put his arm around me and told me New York needed another 9/11. But I didn't have time to be unprofessional.

Abassi walked over to the two pools where the towers once stood and looked at all the names engraved on them. He then looked up to the sky as if he was imagining where the towers once stood. In his mind's eye, he could see the planes and the fire. He couldn't hide his smile now. He handed me his phone and asked me to take a picture of him in front of the pools. I handed the phone back to him.

"I don't think we're allowed to take pictures here," I said.

Abassi looked around the memorial.

"They're taking pictures," he said, pointing out some tourists snapping photos with their phones.

I needed this moment to be over, so I didn't argue and snapped a picture. I later told Nelly that he needed to delete that image after we locked Abassi up.

I went into the bathroom as soon as we got back to his apartment. I threw some water on my face and gathered myself. When I came out, he couldn't control his excitement.

"I was part of a study group in Tunisia," he said. "It was during the Arab Spring. One of the brothers from the group is here."

"In New York?" I said.

"Yes," Abassi said. "He is a taxi driver but he is visiting family back in Tunisia. Another is studying in Atlanta. I haven't been able to reach them, but I did talk to a brother studying computer science in Las Vegas."

Abassi had a contact with al Nusra—an al Qaeda offshoot—in Jordan. He wanted to stay in the United States to restart the study group. The underground groups were breeding grounds for dissent in the Middle East, but Abassi wanted this one to be a terrorist cell.

"I will need a visa," he said. "And we can get all of the like-minded brothers together. I will live here, pretending to work for your company while I prepare the attacks."

I left his apartment with a promise to return and take him to dinner. I went over to the operations center so that I could meet with Ari and the team. Nelly and I had an *I told you so* look on our faces when we all sat down to review my conversations with Abassi.

The assistant U.S. attorney didn't share our look.

"He didn't break any laws," he said after we were done laying out the evidence. "His thoughts and opinions, no matter how disgusting, aren't illegal. He hasn't met any elements of any crime. You have more work to do."

I was exhausted. The last place I wanted to be was back at his apartment. Then I got a call from Chiheb. He was done working and wanted me to meet him at Abassi's apartment, where he had spent most of the afternoon. Abassi went into the kitchen to make tea for us when I arrived. As he left the room, Chiheb leaned over and whispered to me.

"I got all of the scientific knowledge that I needed from him," he said. "We are good now."

The conversations must have provided Chiheb with enough details that he thought we didn't need Abassi's expertise anymore. Nothing Abassi said was going to convince Chiheb to work with him.

But I needed him to talk. I needed Abassi to commit to a terrorist act and make an overt act toward it. We had his intentions on tape, but I needed more for a charge.

"Please let him speak," I said. "Then we'll make a determination together."

Abassi returned and we gave him the pulpit. I was having Jaser flashbacks. Abassi began his sermon by explaining the religious justification for committing jihad. Chiheb made comments but let

Abassi speak for the most part. When Abassi said we were three travelers so our prayers could be shortened, Chiheb interrupted.

"Tamer is not a traveler," he said. "This is his home."

When you're traveling, you can combine your prayers and they are shortened.

"Would you please just let the man finish his thought process?" I said, staring down Chiheb. "Let him talk, Chiheb. Stop interrupting and nitpicking every single thing he says. You're harping on shit that we don't need to talk about right now."

Chiheb sat back in his chair and folded his arms.

"Fine," he said. "I will just sit here and not say anything."

Abassi took a sip of tea. He had my undivided attention and knew it.

"You see?" Abassi said. "That's what I'm talking about."

Abassi had pages of notes, but he skipped to point seven after Chiheb's outburst.

"How can we do these projects and expect not to get killed or arrested with irrational behavior like this?" Abassi said, staring at Chiheb. "If you don't tone it down we all will get captured or killed before our work is done."

Abassi waved me over to the laptops set up on the desk. How to build a bomb, how to deliver weapons of mass destruction, how to commit mass killings on U.S. soil.

Everyone was quiet.

"I need to evaluate Chiheb's orders in an effort to coordinate our efforts," he said.

It was an olive branch to Chiheb. By now it was midnight, and I told them I had a meeting tomorrow. Really I just wanted to leave. I thanked Abassi for the tea and told him we'd talk in the morning.

Chiheb left with me. He had a lot of work to do before he went to San Francisco for his conference. We walked up to his apartment together. I knew I had to make up with him now. Once in his apartment, I apologized.

"Tamer, you have to see that he is of this *Dunya*," he said. "I agree with what he is saying, but I believe that he is just buying time to enjoy this world and its possessions."

"Let me ask you something, Chiheb," I said. "If I told you that there was a Jew that could supply us with the bombs we needed for Operation Happy New Year, would you tell me to buy them from him?"

Chiheb considered my question for a minute.

"I would tell you to buy them," he said.

"Then how can you dismiss another Muslim, the one who started you on your path, so quickly?"

"Tamer, you should have seen him after you yelled at him," Chiheb said. "We each went to our own apartments and before I could sit down, he was at my door. He was so upset. He started giving me all of the technical stuff about the projects. That was the proof that he was of this *Dunya* and not the afterlife."

"Sincerity is only in the eyes of Allah," I said. "While you are in San Francisco, I will spend some time with him. I will properly vet him, okay?"

I said it like I was asking his permission. I wanted him to know that he was still in charge.

"I will report back to you and you will ultimately make the final determination," I said.

As I was leaving, I stopped at the door. I wanted to make sure Chiheb knew I was still with him.

"Don't be mad at me, brother," I said. "I lost my cool there a little bit."

Chiheb put his arm on my shoulder.

"I could never be mad at my brother," he said. "The only time I could be mad at you is if I felt that you were losing your sincerity."

"Am I?"

"No," he said. "I'm just saying that that's the only time I will ever be mad at you."

Stay on the path of Allah. That was his shot across the bow.

CHAPTER 26

Stay True to Islam

Chiheb called me the next morning distraught.

He had stayed up the whole night thinking about Abassi and our projects.

"Because we can't see eye to eye, how about I send an e-mail to Abu Hamza to ask his advice?"

Chiheb wanted him to be the judge.

"I would love to hear his thoughts on the matter," I said.

Chiheb didn't say anything for a few moments. I could hear him breathing. Finally, he told me he would call me back. A half hour later, he called and read me a message in Arabic.

As Salamu Alaikum, my Grandfather.

I have a close friend that I like. He has a very big company and a lot of money, and he uses that money to help the Children of the Mother. His opinion is like my opinion and your opinion. I started with him the travel of research of sincere workers. We found a worker that has a difficult material condition and a new marriage. I agree with my friend regarding the two points regarding the state of this worker. One, he has some of this Dunya in his heart and he is not sincere one hundred percent. And two, he has ideas and knowledge that he announced and can benefit the Children of the Mother. And I disagree with my beloved friend about the way to deal with this worker. I say it's necessary to put the worker far from our path because he lacks sincerity and he can cause our destruction if he has serious problems or tests. My friend says it's necessary to use him because the Children of the Mother have an emergent need of workers particularly if this worker has good ideas and is able to help. Please, my grandfather, look carefully on the issue and judge between us what is right. And if the issue is difficult with you, no problem if you take the opinion of someone that you presume is able to give the solution. The disagreement comes between me and this friend. And I am afraid that these issues will go to an ending that we don't want.

"What did you mean by the last sentence?" I asked.

"Many bad things can happen, for example, our relationship could be broken, our work can be disturbed, Ahmed could give us up to authorities or hurt us," Chiheb said, exasperated by the argument. "What if he gets arrested by the police or FBI? What if he gives you to them? I cannot have that."

Then it dawned on me. He was worried about me. Not because

of any loyalty to me personally, but because of what he believed I meant to the mujahideen overseas.

"Don't worry," I said. "Ahmed could tell the FBI anything he wanted. All I did was sponsor a brother to come in to help me with my company. The FBI can never pin anything on me. They could never know my true intentions."

After we hung up, Chiheb sent the e-mail. Later that day, I picked him up outside of his apartment. He was flying to San Francisco for a conference. I grabbed him and gave him a big hug.

"I want you to know that I'm with you, dear brother," I said as I held him. "We're together no matter what."

Chiheb looked at me with a reassured expression on his face. We got in the car and I merged with the traffic heading uptown. I needed him to believe that I was still on Team Chiheb and that he didn't need to go anywhere or do anything without letting me know first.

"You are a trained al Qaeda sleeper and I am just a businessman," I said. "You gave Ahmed all the tests and he is not sincere. He is of this world and not true of heart."

"Yes," Chiheb said, his chest puffing out. "He cares too much for this world."

But Chiheb said I should test him while he was in San Francisco. He wanted me to find his true heart and make sure Abassi understood Chiheb was in charge.

"Even though I am not a trained al Qaeda operative, I promise I will take this week to give Ahmed my businessman test. I will test him. Even though you haven't heard from Grandfather yet."

Chiheb got quiet. I knew he had received an e-mail response

from Abu Hamza. Nelly had offered to let me read it, but I passed. I wanted Chiheb to tell me. I needed my reaction to be natural.

"Tell me something, brother," I said. "Twenty-four hours ago, you were dead set against Ahmed. Now you're giving me specific instructions on how to properly vet him and to make sure he knows who is in charge. What's changed?"

Chiheb smiled and looked away.

"You know me too well, brother," he said. "Grandfather responded to me."

I pretended to be upset with him.

"How could you keep that from me?"

"I had no intention of keeping that from you," he said. "I just didn't feel like the time was right for me to tell you. I don't want to tell you exactly what he said yet, but I will tell you when the time is right."

"Has Abu Hamza ever responded to any of your e-mails this quickly?"

Chiheb shook his head no.

"That's because this is the first time you ever asked him about something of substance," I said. "The first time you weren't whining about talking to El Massoul or the identity of the American sleeper. You weren't needy. You presented him with a well-thought-out argument while pointing out the fact that you now have financial support to fulfill your mission and like-minded brothers around you ready to strike. In his eyes, Chiheb, you are a good worker. Look at all that you have accomplished in one year. That's the image they have of you right now. Don't taint that image with an e-mail littered with counterpoints. Don't come across as combative or insubordinate."

He looked out the window.

"I'm not going to send anything to him until I run it by you," he said.

"Maybe if Abu Hamza knew that you had unfettered access to the West, he would consider hooking you up with the American sleeper," I said. "Right now, he is the one you are in contact with and he is the one that will give you further direction."

Chiheb reminded me Abu Hamza didn't know his location. It was forbidden under El Massoul's rules. But the seed was planted.

He needed a reason to justify breaking operational protocols for the greater good. Chiheb called me from his hotel room in San Francisco later that night. He read me Abu Hamza's e-mail response in Arabic:

My generous brother,

As Salamu Alaikum Wa Rahmat'Allah Wa Barakatu

Thank God for your safety. Thanks to Allah, we are doing well and in good health. I am busy these days in the transportation of the families of the Children of the Mother to some of the liberated countries close to you [meaning Tunisia and not the United States].

Concerning the use of the brother, my generous brother, if we find a person which inside him there is good for Islam and Muslims, we benefit from him according to the need with these difficult conditions and the lack of sincere men who have passed the conditions and who have succeeded the test. And this dear brother, he has the right to use the worker and you should behave with the worker with good behavior to let him ripen and reach a place that he's ready to sacrifice himself for this sake.

We have tested this method many times; replacing men from the beginning is very harmful and brings mistakes. The best thing is to advise them and show them the path and that this is the life. This is the biography of Mohammed, peace be upon him.

More important is to take benefit from this brother just according to the need to allow yourself to bring the good for him. And, insha'Allah in the future, he will be a sincere brother for you.

May Allah give you success. Give Salam to this dear brother, our new friend.

As Salamu Alaikum Wa Rahmat'Allah Wa Barakatu

It was clear that Abu Hamza agreed with me. The only thing that Chiheb was happy about in this e-mail was the fact that Abu Hamza sent me greetings and appreciation for my efforts to the cause. Chiheb still wanted to argue against using Abassi, but I cut him off.

"Don't worry about that right now," I said. "We have his attention. Ask about the American sleeper."

He sent out the following e-mail to Abu Hamza:

As Salamu Alaikum my Grandfather,

The brother who traveled and didn't return back informed me before that one Child of the Mother is staying now in America. Do you know him or know the address of that Child? My beloved friend wants very much to enter the Children of the Mother to America through his big company. If you or anyone else know of Children of the Mother in Jordan, Egypt, or something like that that are trained to produce sweets or are ready to get the training, please send me their names and addresses with the three brothers.

May Allah reward you.

When Chiheb was done reading, I asked what he meant by the "three brothers" comment.

"That is how many brothers I would like," he said, meaning he was looking to recruit three more men to his plots.

"Okay," I said. "Call me when you hear back from him."

I had to focus my attention on Abassi. The next day, I met with the team and the assistant U.S. attorney. Unlike in past meetings, the assistant U.S. attorney was upbeat. Even happy. Abassi had opened the door when we talked at his apartment after visiting the September 11 memorial.

"When Abassi suggested that you help him get a visa to stay in this country under false pretenses, specifically for facilitating acts of international terrorism, that is a serious charge," the assistant U.S. attorney said.

"It's like how they got Al Capone," I said. "Tax evasion instead of murder."

"Exactly," the assistant U.S. attorney said.

It wasn't my first choice. Abassi was a dangerous guy. I wanted him charged with terrorism, but it was better than nothing.

"What's the penalty?" I asked.

"It carries a twenty-five-year sentence."

That sealed it for me. We talked about getting the final pieces of evidence the rest of the meeting. I was scheduled to get together with Abassi the following day. His visa was my first order of business.

"You said a lot to me this past week," I said after we'd met up at his apartment. "Where do we begin?"

"My visa," Abassi said. "I can get the application. Can your company be the sponsor?"

I was hoping he'd say that.

"I spoke with Farris," Abassi said. "He is studying computer science in Las Vegas."

"Should we go see him?" I asked.

"Absolutely," Abassi said.

During the course of the next two weeks, Abassi got the necessary paperwork for his visa application. He lied about his purpose for obtaining it and told me of his plans to recruit like-minded brothers to plan and carry out multiple terrorist attacks across the United States. All of the elements of the crime were met. But I didn't want any confusion as to what was happening. I sat down with him before he signed the documents and did an abridged Christian burial speech.

"Are you sure about this?" I said. "You're lying on federal

documents here. Maybe you should actually get a job and work for my company for real?"

Abassi didn't want to work unless it was on a terrorist attack.

"This is the only way to accomplish our mission," he said.

As he signed the documents, I felt a sense of relief. He mailed the applications out himself, and our charges for visa fraud with a terrorism enhancement were secured.

A few days later, we flew to Las Vegas to meet his "like-minded" brother from the study group. We checked into our suites at the Venetian. Kenny, Johnny, and Joey took a room on the hotel's top floor. We don't like the agents to have rooms in the same hotel as the target, but it was the best we could do on short notice. Nelly stayed behind to finish Abassi's arrest warrant.

Abassi and I met Farris that night in Abassi's suite. He was tall with a thin beard, olive skin, and short-cropped hair. His khakis and shirt were baggy in an attempt to hide his bulging muscles. His English was very good. *Shit,* I thought. This guy was smooth and blended in perfectly.

After we prayed, we sat on the floor and talked. Abassi and Farris caught up. Abassi gave him a quick rundown of what happened with his visa. He was spewing venom about the evils of the West, but Farris never echoed his sentiments. I couldn't tell if he was just being careful.

The next morning, I received an e-mail from Chiheb.

"Call me right away, brother," it read.

Chiheb was back from San Francisco. He was staying at a friend's apartment—who was also an RCMP undercover—in Montreal. I called his cell.

"Tamer, Gidou [Grandfather] sent me an e-mail," he said, the excitement forcing his voice to rise to an uncomfortable level. "He has agreed to meet with us and give us everything that we need."

"Calm down, brother," I said. "What do you mean?"

"Abu Hamza wants us to join forces with the American Child of the Mother so that we could accomplish our mission," he said. "I told him we were lacking proper guidance."

I asked Chiheb to read me the e-mail from Abu Hamza.

> My dear brother, we are very proud of the work you have ac-
> complished. We believe it is time for you to be united with the
> Child of the Mother by you. I am inviting you and your beloved
> friend to meet with us in Dubai as soon as you are able to
> travel. Insha'Allah, we will give you all that you need.

"We need to plan a trip to Dubai now," Chiheb said.

"Is the American sleeper there?" I asked.

"They won't give me that information over the phone or through e-mail," he said.

"So who are we meeting?"

"Abu Hamza," he said.

"I'm in Vegas," I said. "But when I get back to New York in a few days we can book a trip."

"Hurry," he said.

I hung up and called Nelly. He had the e-mail and was waiting for the translation. I filled him in on my call with Chiheb.

"Holy fuck," he said.

Nelly went to meet with FBI executive management about the latest development while the Canadians were also digesting the e-mail. This part is pure speculation on my part, but I know the Canadians got this e-mail as well and they weren't going to let Chiheb go to Dubai. They had their own agenda that wouldn't come into focus for a few more days.

The next three nights I spent with Abassi and Farris, but my mind was in Dubai. We had dinner, walked the Strip, and prayed. When we were in private, Abassi preached about the sixth pillar of Islam. He started out relatively vanilla the first night and then progressed rather quickly with each conversation. Farris would argue about the justification of killing innocents. I mainly sat quietly and chimed in only when asked. I wanted Abassi to do his thing, and I needed to gauge Farris's true feelings. On our last night, Abassi told me that he planned on pushing Farris hard.

"What happened to that guy I knew back in Tunisia? Where is that fire?" Abassi asked Farris.

"My dear brother, we were stupid kids angry at the Tunisian government," Farris said.

"Fuck the Tunisian government," he said. "It was never about them. It's about our religion and every Muslim's obligation."

Abassi told Farris he was resurrecting the study group to carry out attacks on the West. But Farris wasn't buying it. He kept shaking his head as Abassi spoke.

"Nowhere in the Quran does it justify taking innocent lives," Farris said. "No matter what."

Abassi just stared at his friend. "You are very, very wrong," he said.

I had seen enough. Farris wasn't a threat.

"I'm hungry," I said. "Who wants to get dinner?"

The buffet was closed, so we headed for the first open restaurant. I held the heavy glass doors of L'Atelier De Joël Robuchon for

Farris and Abassi. As soon as the doors shut behind us, the cacophony of slot machines and gamblers disappeared. There was red
velvet everywhere. A hostess greeted me.

"Reservations?"

I looked around the dining room. The place was almost empty.

"Do we need one?"

She smiled politely.

"It will be one minute," she said, ushering us into the lounge.
The dining room's red velvet turned into purple suede. The couches
looked so nice I couldn't sit on them. Abassi and Farris checked
the menu.

"Tamer, I think this place is too expensive," Farris said. "Maybe
we should go somewhere else?"

"Don't be ridiculous," I said. "It's tax-deductible."

Kenny, the co–case agent, still laughs about that line, especially
after we were warned to keep costs down on the trip. The case had
already blown past its budget by tens of thousands of dollars.

Farris looked at Abassi, who just smiled. He liked having a powerful friend. Price didn't matter to Tamer. The hostess brought us
to a table near the front of the restaurant. Dinner was surprisingly
pleasant. Abassi tried to sprinkle in some jihad, but it was clear that
neither I nor Farris was in the mood. The bill was more than a
thousand dollars. No alcohol. FBI management was going to lose
their shit.

On the way back to the room, Abassi stopped to use the bathroom. Farris grabbed my arm and pulled me away. He wanted to
be out of earshot when Abassi emerged.

"Tamer, I want you to know that it was truly a pleasure meeting
you and spending time with you, dear brother," he said. "You will

always have a brother here in Vegas if you ever need anything. Anything at all."

I told him the same thing, but he cut me off with a squeeze of my arm. He looked me in the eye. This wasn't about pleasantries.

"Ahmed is a very angry and confused brother," Farris said. "Don't let him take your religion. Stay true to Islam."

It took all my training to keep me from hugging him.

That night I debriefed the team at the Venetian, but no one was thinking about Vegas. All our minds were with Attorney General Eric Holder and his meeting with the Canadian prime minister. After learning about the e-mail, the administration had sent him to Ottawa to talk with the RCMP about a Dubai trip.

Joey checked in with Headquarters before we ended the debrief.

"We won't know until tomorrow morning before our flight," Joey said, wrapping up the meeting.

My mind was already planning the overseas operation.

CHAPTER 27

The End

The next morning the whole team met in the suite. We were hanging around bullshitting when Kenny got the call from Headquarters.

We all watched him talk, trying to read his body language. He said little. His body language was neutral. A bad feeling fell over me. Kenny thanked the person on the other side of the call and hung up.

"It's over," he said. "The Canadians are executing their arrest and search warrants. They're going to wait until you and Abassi get to JFK. Nelly is heading the arrest team in New York."

I went numb.

It was April 22, 2013. The week before, two homemade bombs had detonated twelve seconds apart near the finish line of the annual Boston Marathon. Chechen-American brothers Dzhokhar Tsarnaev and Tamerlan Tsarnaev killed three people and injured hundreds of others.

Everyone was on edge. No one wanted to let a terrorist slip out of our grasp.

"They are aware of the latest intel about the American sleeper, right?" I said.

Kenny nodded.

"They know everything," he said. "It's over."

Joey crashed on the couch and made a blanket out of the *USA Today*. He closed his eyes. Kenny and Johnny sat down and stared blankly out the window overlooking the Strip.

"How could we let the fucking Canadians dictate our national security?" I said, taking Joey's place pacing around the room.

Kenny leaned back in his chair.

"Headquarters actually congratulated us just now," he said. "We should be proud of this case. We saved lives, they said."

While management on both sides of the border were high-fiving, everyone in that suite, along with Nelly back home, felt like someone had kicked them in the balls. I collapsed on the bed and tried to make sense of what was happening. A small part of me was relieved. It was over. I could go back to my life and all the other cases the Bureau had on hold. But mostly I was angry.

I felt like the Canadians and the FBI wasted all of our hard work. We had a platform set up to actively vet any and all known threats on both sides of the border. What about the American sleeper?

Looking back, I understand the impossible position our government was in with the Canadians. We never had any concrete proof of the American sleeper. For all they knew, Abu Hamza was a fifteen-year-old kid in Iran stringing Chiheb along. The cop in me knows that. The boss in me knows the decision had to be made.

The case was done. We took three terrorists off the street, and our government could preserve an important relationship with a foreign partner that was already strained because of multiple extensions.

But this wasn't a victory. Best case, we tied. But really you could say we failed. Every time I hear about someone committing a terrorist act on U.S. soil, I wonder if that was the American sleeper. Chiheb was a lot of things, but he was never a liar. Personally, I have no doubt that there was an American sleeper. My biggest regret is that I couldn't find him.

I spent months imagining what the American sleeper looked like. Every time the image was the same. He was the real Tamer Elnoury in my mind. In my daydreams, he was always in a business suit. I could see him watching the press conference announcing Chiheb's arrest on the flat-screen in his office. Rattled, he dumps his cell phone in the trash outside his building and disappears into the crowd walking down the street.

I was in a bad mood when I met Abassi in the lobby a couple of hours later. He couldn't stop fidgeting as we stood in line to get a cab to the airport. He was giddy with purpose. Even though Farris wasn't receptive, Abassi was energized by the trip. I think he liked being on the road trying to recruit like-minded brothers and making plans.

I pretended to care about all his visions and plans, but it was hard because I knew what was waiting for us when we landed. The more he spoke, the happier I became about ending the case. I couldn't get arrested fast enough.

At the airport, I upgraded to first class as one last fuck-you to executive management. I decided to blame them for the case ending. I was acting out instead of taking the blame. It's embarrassing looking back on it now, but it did make the flight back to New York more comfortable. Besides, it was the only way Abassi and I could sit together.

About midway through the flight, it hit me: I was probably never going to see Chiheb again. We weren't friends and it wasn't like I felt sorry for him. It was just strange knowing someone so well. I knew more about him than his family. I had seen his dark side. But I'd also met a brilliant scientist with girl troubles. A goofy guy who liked lobster. I knew the terrorist and the man. While I was happy the terrorist would never be free, I felt sorry for the man. I felt bad that a man with so much to offer to the world got duped by murderers posing as holy men. It made me sad that they'd used my religion to pollute him. I was still frustrated I couldn't save him. What a waste.

When the pilot told the flight attendants to take their seats for landing, I got anxious. I knew what was coming. Getting arrested is an unnatural act. Even though I knew it was fake and I had been arrested many times, it always left me with a peculiar energy. Not anxiety or stress. A mix of both with a side of adrenaline. My skin started to tingle and my legs felt rubbery as I left the plane and walked toward the gate.

We were first off the plane. It was cold as we entered the airport. Abassi was still talking at me while I scanned the airport. I noticed seven or eight agents dressed in plain clothes following us as we walked from the gate toward baggage claim. I recognized a couple of them. Nelly was standing near the baggage carousel. We made eye contact.

I watched the bags on the belt. Abassi got his bag first. I could feel the agents close in a little when Abassi reached down and grabbed it. A few more suitcases passed me. I shot a glance at Nelly.

He looked calm. My big, gaudy Samsonite silver hard case parted the rubber flaps and trundled toward me a minute later. I took one more look around and noticed the surveillance guys getting closer. I grabbed my bag and started walking to the exit with Abassi. The surveillance guys surrounded us as Nelly blocked our path. He slid his suit jacket open to show us his shield.

"FBI," he said. "Would you folks please come with us?"

"What's this about?" I asked.

Normally, I would have put on a song and dance, but I was exhausted.

"Please come with us and we'll explain everything to you," Nelly said.

Nelly and another agent bracketed Abassi. Two agents I didn't know stepped next to me. They took us toward two different SUVs.

"Where am I going?" Abassi asked. "Where are you taking him? Why are we being separated?"

Abassi gave me a confident look, as if to reassure me that he was in control. He knew the drill. We were taken to separate interrogation rooms at JFK. Nelly left Abassi and came to see me. He took my cuffs off and gave me a hug.

"You good, *habibi*?" he asked.

"I will be."

"What do you want to do?"

FBI protocol was to keep me under lock and key until the dust settled. I knew I couldn't go home till at least the next day, but I didn't want to be around anyone. I just wanted to be alone.

"You have someone who can take me to my undercover apartment?" I asked.

Usually, I would get my gun, credentials, and phones back at this point, but I wasn't ready to plug back in just yet. I took the backpack with my true identity in it but didn't turn on my phone.

One of the surveillance agents drove me to my apartment. The poor guy was feeling pretty good about being part of this "huge success," but he wasn't getting that vibe from me. I didn't say a word the whole ride back.

The agent dropped me off and I called over to the operations center and asked them to take the cameras off-line. I didn't want anyone watching me anymore. I turned the TV on just in time for the breaking news alert. The Canadians were holding a press conference. It felt rehearsed, and no one on that screen had a clue about what had actually transpired over the past year. ABC News was the first to connect the Abassi arrest to the VIA Rail plot in Canada a few days later. But I still wasn't sure why the Canadians were in such a rush to end the case.

The very next week the Canadians announced their version of the Patriot Act, which passed swiftly through Parliament. This was the win they needed and just cause for this new legislation.

I found out later Chiheb was arrested in Montreal outside a McDonald's. He was flown to Toronto and informed of his right to counsel, but he declined. Chiheb told the Canadians he refused to be judged by man-made laws and that he only wanted to be judged by Sharia Law.

During the interrogation, Chiheb spoke freely. He even corrected his interrogator about the plot details. He was trying to find a bridge with as little water as possible to maximize casualties. He pointed to the officer's notepad and told him to write that down. When Chiheb was told that I was an undercover FBI agent, he didn't believe it. He protected me through every interrogation, but gave up Jaser and Abassi. He even talked about Abu Hamza and El Massoul. But he wouldn't give me up. The money Tamer was providing to the mujahideen was critical. It was so important Chiheb dedicated his doctoral thesis—his life's work—to me and my company instead of his professors, family, and research partners. It was his way of thanking me and acknowledging that nothing else matters besides helping the brothers overseas. When they played recordings from our conversations, he just assumed that the government wired us up and I had nothing to do with it. Chiheb was given enough discovery documents to finally believe that I was an FBI agent.

A month after his arrest, Chiheb gave an interview to a Toronto newspaper. Nelly forwarded me the link. Chiheb was savvy enough not to discuss the particulars of the case, but I was confused why he would break his silence to the media, until the last paragraph of the article. Chiheb told the reporter that despite being in jail, he was eating, sleeping, and praying. He had all he needed. Translation: *Fuck you, Tamer.*

Jaser was arrested in his home the same day the RCMP got Chiheb. A SWAT team executed the search and arrest warrants. He lawyered up right away and didn't say a word.

I didn't get much sleep the night of our arrests. I started packing up the apartment before dawn. The FBI told me I was clear to leave in the morning. I took one last look at the white Egyptian porcelain teapot on the stove I'd used so many times to make tea and left shortly after the sun came up. On my ride home, I got a phone call from my supervisor at the National Security Covert Operations Unit—the Dirty Arabs Group.

"I know you must be exhausted, but is there any way you could get to Portland tomorrow?"

In all my years in the FBI, I never said no to any other case. But this time, I did. I didn't even ask what the case was about.

After a few weeks, I came out of my funk and dove headfirst into my caseload. About a year later, I received a subpoena from the Crown Counsel, the prosecutors working the case. Chiheb's refusal to even acknowledge the charges forced the Canadians to give him a trial. He and Jaser were being tried together, despite Jaser's lawyers' argument for separate trials.

I called Nelly.

"Is this for real?" I said. "They're really taking this to trial?"

I'd testified many times in drug cases but never in a counterterrorism trial. The defendants always pled guilty. I stared at the subpoena in disbelief, my heart rate rising. I thought about my family. This was the nightmare I worried about before I took the case. Vinnie's words echoed in my head.

This case is going to change your life.

He had no idea.

I called Heidi in our National Security Law Branch. The subpoena was legit. The Canadians' case was based on my investigation. It was impossible to prosecute Chiheb and Jaser without me. But before I could testify, Heidi told me the Canadian courts had to rule on her thirty-three-page affidavit, signed by the assistant director of the FBI, requesting that the Canadians honor the same protections afforded to me in the United States. The RCMP had already agreed to it, but the court had to now. It didn't take much convincing for the Canadians to agree.

The court let me testify as Tamer Elnoury. The prosecutors,

defense team, and court personnel all signed a nondisclosure agreement promising not to reveal anything about my identity. The media wouldn't be able to cover my testimony in the courtroom, but they could listen to it.

The Crown and FBI were happy, but now I had to be Tamer in front of Chiheb and Jaser, one last time.

CHAPTER 28

T-Bags

The trial started the Monday after the 2015 Super Bowl.

Nelly and I arrived in Toronto the Thursday before for trial prep. We flew out of a small airport near my house on the RCMP's jet. This way, we didn't have to deal with security or any cameras or biometrics. The flight was short and when we landed in Toronto, there were no other planes in sight. The pilot handed me a ski mask and asked me to put it on before he opened the door to the plane. Nelly got out first, carrying one large duffel bag. I climbed down the retractable stairs next and met several large, burly men dressed in all black carrying assault rifles.

When the pilot opened the back, the RCMP SWAT guys started unloading my bags. The team leader, Hal, pulled Nelly aside.

"How many people are on the plane?"

Nelly laughed as the security team unloaded my bags into the back of an SUV.

"They're all his," he said, pointing at me.

I didn't realize they were flying me home every weekend, so I had two large suitcases, a garment bag, a carry-on, and my backpack. I can't pack light. I like options, especially for court. I found out later I earned my code name that day. The guys called me "T-Bags." I laughed every time I heard it on the police radios.

"T-Bags is on the move."

For the next three weeks, I lived in a bubble. Hal and his men became my family. They protected me at the safe house, which overlooked Lake Ontario. On Super Bowl Sunday, they even rigged an antenna so we could watch the Buffalo, New York, feed instead of the Canadian feed without the commercials. It turned out to be an amazing game—New England beat Seattle. Or more like Seattle beat Seattle. At one point, I made a joke about a guy getting used to having a security detail, but I was sexually frustrated and I needed them to address it. The next day, when I got back from court, they had a blow-up doll in the living room with her ass in the air.

She was pretty hot.

The prosecution was led by Croft Michaelson. His cochair, Sarah Shaikh, was overseeing my testimony. Sarah was of Indian descent, and I found out later she was a Muslim, but not practicing. We had met a few months prior in New York to start my trial prep. After I landed, they met me at their office in downtown Toronto for a few days of last-minute prep. I had let my hair and beard grow on Heidi's suggestion. The Crown wouldn't let me wear a disguise—even fake glasses—and I wanted to change my appearance.

"Why the fuck do you look like that?" Sarah asked.

She always cursed.

"You look like a Neanderthal jihadi."

She sent me to a salon to get a haircut before starting trial prep, which lasted twelve to fifteen hours a day leading up to my testimony. Initially, Sarah was trying to put the words in my mouth. I tried to say things the way she wanted me to, but it sounded phony. After a few hours, Nelly spoke up.

"Sarah, I apologize for interrupting," he said. "You need to stop feeding Tamer the answers. Ask him whatever you want and let him be himself. It will come across more natural and he will be a much better witness for you."

He then looked at me.

"No one in the world knows this case better than you do," he said. "You lived it. You were there. Just be yourself and everyone will love you."

That was exactly what I needed to hear. Sarah tried it Nelly's way and the trial prep got much smoother. Nelly saved me, again.

I was nervous as Hal and his team drove me to the courthouse the first day. They ushered me into the courtroom from the jury's door so I could avoid the media. When I first entered, my eyes went right to Chiheb. He was sitting on the opposite side of the courtroom encased in a glass bowl, a goldfish without water. He was wearing the black and blue ski jacket he was arrested in with a blue button-down shirt on underneath it. His jeans were rolled up into thick cuffs.

Chiheb looked me dead in the eye and didn't blink. It was the blankest stare I've ever seen. For a second, I wanted him to smile or say something. I wanted him to understand. My heart sank. I felt sorry for the human inside him. Not the monster. No, the monster was going to jail. It was the lost puppy that I felt sorry for, but it was Allah's will that I stop him and this was the final step.

To his left, closer to me, in another empty fishbowl, was Jaser. He was wearing a suit with a neatly trimmed beard and glasses. I almost didn't recognize him. He looked like a businessman or a lawyer. Jaser couldn't wait to get my attention. His hands were palms down on the desk in front of him as he leaned forward, begging me to look at him. When he caught my attention, Jaser looked around the courtroom to make sure no one else was looking and then looked me in the eye.

"I will find you," he mouthed.

Nelly saw him do it and looked at me with a smirk. I relaxed immediately. Jaser was desperate. He knew we had him. I couldn't wait to get started.

All the attorneys arrived wearing black robes like American judges. Sarah and Croft sat to my left behind a wooden table. To my right was a lawyer the court appointed to help Chiheb. In front of him was John Norris—Jaser's lawyer. Norris came over to greet me before we started. I had no idea what to make of that. The niceties started early.

I arranged my notes and introduced myself to the court clerk—an older man who made sure I always had a glass of water. Justice Michael Code took the bench soon after and court was called to order. Code reminded me of the judge from *My Cousin Vinny*. He had a reputation for being one of the most brilliant legal minds in Canada. I had also heard that he was one hell of a prosecutor back in his day. The judge greeted the court and looked at the cameras and greeted the media sequestered in another room. They couldn't see me; they could only hear my testimony. Code instructed the clerk to bring in the jury. They filed into the jury box.

I was introduced to the jury as Special Agent Tamer Elnoury of the Federal Bureau of Investigation. Tamer Elnoury was burned. His apartments were gone. His company dissolved. Tamer didn't exist anymore, so the FBI agreed to let me testify in that name. My training and experience were discussed without ever mentioning where I was from or where I was currently assigned and without giving away anything that could disclose my true identity. It was a very well-scripted opening that was agreed to by both sides.

I had great chemistry with Sarah from the start. It began the same way every day.

"Good morning, Agent Elnoury."

"Good morning, Ms. Shaikh."

After lunch was the same thing.

"Good afternoon, Agent Elnoury."

"Good afternoon, Ms. Shaikh."

Croft must have said something to her, because after the first couple of days she started right with her questions without the pleasantries. But I interrupted her.

"Good morning, Ms. Shaikh."

She blushed, smiled, and replied in kind. The entire jury laughed. They were waiting for it too. Croft was pissed. I found out later that he told someone I was an American witness but it was still a Canadian courtroom.

The entire trial was about the conspiracy to attack the train from Toronto. Sarah would ask me questions to set the stage and then play a recording for the court to hear. The courtroom was wired with surround sound and multiple flat-screens that showed videos or transcripts. A translator sitting at the prosecutor's table would scroll down and highlight the transcript.

This was the Crown's way of playing the recordings in court

even if the conversations were in Arabic. Very smart, because there's nothing like hearing the words coming out of the defendants' mouths in surround-sound stereo. A lot of it was in English, which just highlighted the horror even more. During some of the recordings when we were laughing and joking, Chiheb sat back and smiled and laughed. He was reminiscing and enjoying it.

After the first few days of testimony, we wrapped up early enough for me to catch the local evening news at the safe house. I hadn't seen any of the coverage so far and was shocked to see what was happening. The focus was on Islamic extremism. Nothing about true Islam. In the media's defense, all they were hearing were Chiheb's and Jaser's interpretations.

The next morning, when Sarah came into the courthouse break room, I told her about the coverage.

"I know, I've been watching," she said. "What can you do?"

"I could state the obvious," I said.

"What do you mean?" she asked, focused more on the day's testimony than my editorializing. "You can't say anything. What are you going to do? What are you going to say?"

We were getting to the Christian burial speech, where I gave Chiheb a chance to back out of the attack. I told her there was a pause in the middle of the conversation. After the pause, I told her to ask me what was going through my mind.

"What are you going to say?"

"I'm going to say that his thoughts and rationalizations are not indicative of true Islam."

Sarah was good with that explanation and agreed to ask the question. We wrapped up for lunch right before the Christian burial speech. After lunch, I was excited to take the stand. This was a point I wanted to make. I needed to make it. Islam was never the cause, and I wanted the jury to hear it. I wanted the world to hear it. Just as I got comfortable, Croft and Sarah walked over to the witness stand.

"Tamer, Sarah mentioned to me what you wanted to say about Islam," Croft said. "I don't think it's a good idea."

"Have you been watching the media coverage?" I said. "They are making it about Islam. The world needs to hear from me that this is not Islam."

"Yes, but that's not what this trial is about," he said. "We're going to leave your personal comments out of it."

I leaned closer because I didn't want the whole courtroom to hear.

"Croft, I am your witness, not your fucking puppet," I said. "Either ask me the way that Sarah and I discussed, or I will blurt it out at some point while I am on the stand, and that could get awkward. Your choice."

Croft backed away. He looked me in the eye and then put both his hands up.

"Ask him what he wants," he said as he walked away.

Sarah smiled at me as she walked back to the table. When the pause came, she stopped the tape.

"I have one more question for you, Agent Elnoury," she said. "You also said prior to the break that this particular part of your conversation with Mr. Esseghaier stuck out in your mind, and you provided a justification for that. What was really the reason that this bothered you?"

I sat up a little straighter in my chair.

"These religious views that are presented are a complete desecration of my religion," I said. "So it stands out to me when I am having a discussion about rationalizing killing innocent women and children."

Chiheb kept quiet for most of the proceedings. He knew to wait for Justice Code's permission to speak, but my comments set him off. I wasn't talking about the facts of the case anymore. I was talking about Islam. He jumped out of his seat and was waving his hand at the judge to get his attention. Code removed the jury and then let Chiheb speak.

"I want to address what that witness agent just said," Chiheb said. "He is very, very wrong. There is no interpretation of Islam. There is only one Islam. Either you get it or you don't."

I couldn't have said it any better myself. *His* interpretation was wrong. Chiheb went on and on about religion but was eventually cut off by Code so we could all get on with it.

"Your religious explanation is duly noted on the record, Mr. Esseghaier," Code said.

The media coverage shifted that night. TV reporters were interviewing Imams at local mosques who echoed my sentiments. That was one of my proudest moments throughout this entire case. The Muslim community had a platform, and their ally was an American FBI agent. Al Qaeda and ISIS weren't the only ones with a voice anymore.

Two weeks after I took the stand, Sarah was done. We were confident in my testimony. I wasn't allowed any contact with the Crown from this point forward. It was now Jaser and Chiheb's turn to defend themselves.

But so far Chiheb hadn't even tried. During parts of the trial, Chiheb fell asleep in the prisoner's box. He didn't cross-examine witnesses and declined to even present a defense. Before the trial began, he argued the Quran should be used in place of the Canadian criminal code. Code asked if the Quran would lead to a different outcome for murder.

"Just wait and see who is in truth and who is in falsehood," Chiheb said.

When Code asked Chiheb if he had any questions for me, he didn't move or say anything. He sat in silence before turning to face the back of the courtroom.

Justice Code asked Jaser's attorney, John Norris, if he was ready. Norris smiled politely as he stood.

"Yes, Your Honor."

Like Sarah, he said good morning before he started. In Canada, defense counsel was a "friend" to the court and he was always polite. That was so foreign to me. Every defense attorney I had run-ins with in our courts had always tried to trick me, yell at me, discredit me. I never met one I didn't want to fight in the parking lot afterward. I welcomed combative, nasty exchanges. I knew how to navigate that. What if Norris lulled me with his kindness?

Norris started with how I met Chiheb.

"There was an ongoing investigation into Mr. Esseghaier?"

"Yes," I said.

"And as part of that investigation, you were tasked with forming a relationship with him?"

"Correct."

"You engaged with Mr. Esseghaier and the two of you exchanged Islamic greetings?"

"Yes, sir," I said.

"You were portraying yourself as someone who shared views with him?"

"Yes, of course."

Norris talked about my five days with Chiheb in San Jose.

"You shared with Mr. Esseghaier how meeting him had had a real effect on you, how fate had brought the two of you together?"

"Well, fate had nothing to do with it," I said.

"Because of meeting him, your life had a purpose now," Norris said.

"Something like that."

"That's the gist?"

"That's the legend," I said.

Norris had been instructed to stay away from any sensitive techniques, so when he asked me if the FBI orchestrated the whole initial meeting, I balked.

"Mr. Norris, I cannot confirm or deny that," I said. "If you would like to know whether or not I knew if Mr. Esseghaier was going to be on that flight, I can answer that question."

This went back and forth for a while. Heidi and I made eye contact. She was fidgeting and Nelly was almost out of his seat. Norris looked to Code for help. Code took off his reading glasses and looked at me.

"Agent Elnoury, any reasonable person can infer what your answer would be in this situation," he said. "I don't think you would be jeopardizing national security by answering this one simple question. I think you are taking your oath a little too seriously."

I could feel my blood pressure rise. It felt like Code was siding with the defense from the start. They seemed to win every objection. He was kicking out our legs at every turn.

Code called for a twenty-minute recess so that counsel could discuss it. He released the jury and I went back to the break room. I was livid. Heidi reworded the question so it better fit the FBI and Norris's agenda. As we were leaving to go back to court, Heidi grabbed my arm and asked me if I was okay. I nodded and she squeezed my arm.

"Calm down before you go back up there," she said. "He's just trying to get to you."

I was more pissed at the judge than at Norris. I had to say something. I wouldn't be able to go on unless I addressed this with him.

"I trust we reached an agreement with this matter?" Code asked when court resumed.

"Yes, Your Honor," both attorneys said.

"Okay, let's have the jury," Code said as he sat down behind the bench.

I interrupted him.

"Judge, I'd like to address the court before the jury enters, please," I said.

He turned to me, annoyed, and said go ahead.

"Your Honor, I want you to know that I was highly offended by your inference that I take national security and my oath 'too seriously'"—and yes, I used air quotes here. It was the most respectful way I could be disrespectful. "Of all the people in the world that I would think that meant something to, I would think that would be you, sir. I do take national security and my oath very seriously."

He was onstage and the cameras were rolling. Everyone in the media was there and this was his show. So he couldn't just apologize to me.

"I never implied that national security or your oath wasn't a serious matter," he said. "I am very appreciative of how serious you take these matters. I'm sorry you feel that way. It was never my intent to insinuate anything like that."

Sarah had a very proud look on her face and Nelly winked at me. I felt like I could breathe again.

"Thank you, Your Honor."

He called for the jury and we continued. Norris asked the question the right way and we moved on from there. It wasn't clear what Jaser's defense would be until we got to our first meeting at his apartment. Norris's argument was that Jaser was a con man looking to get money from Tamer. If that meant pretending to be a jihadi, so be it. He left the train plot because he wasn't going to be able to get any money from me, not because he was spooked by the police and afraid to get caught.

There were two major holes in that defense.

Jaser was part of the plot from the start. He checked out a possible site with Chiheb before I even entered the picture. I got to hammer that home repeatedly during cross-examination. I kept getting nods from Sarah every time it came up.

The second point was going to be trickier, but I needed Norris to open the door. During my testimony, Sayyid Qutb's name came up a few times. He was the author of *Milestones,* one of the founding jihadi texts. I told Sarah after the second day of testimony to ask me who he was so I could explain it to the jury. She did, but Norris objected. He argued I was an expert in counterterrorism and law enforcement but had no literary expertise. Code agreed and Sarah was forced to move on.

I brought his name up every single chance I got, but we never got to explain how his writings inspired jihadism. After a week of questions, Norris was wrapping up his cross-examination by asking me a bunch of short questions that forced me to answer yes. It's a common ploy used by defense attorneys to get the jury to hear the prosecution's witness repeatedly agree with the defense. It sounds stupid, but it works. Toward the end of this barrage, he circled back to my first meeting with Jaser.

"From the moment he met you, he knew you were a wealthy businessman and—"

I cut him off. That was the crack of the door I'd been waiting for.

"No, actually, that's not true, Mr. Norris," I said. "When your client first met me, he had no idea what my legend was. But he made sure to let me know who he was with his reverence of Sayyid Qutb."

Norris's face was beet red and his carotid artery was coming out of the side of his neck. He opened the door and Sarah went through it during redirect.

"Agent Elnoury, we keep hearing about Sayyid Qutb and Mr. Jaser's reverence of him," she said. "Could you explain why, as an experienced counterterrorism operative, that was a red flag to you?"

Perfect. I couldn't have worded the question any better. Norris jumped out of his seat.

"Your Honor, we covered this already."

But Code just shook his head.

"I believe you opened that door during your cross-examination of the agent."

Code then looked at me.

"Isn't that right, Agent Elnoury?"

"Spot-on, Your Honor," I said, without taking my eyes off Norris.

"Your Honor, with all due respect to Agent Elnoury, I did no such thing. He sort of kicked that door open on purpose."

My second proudest moment of the trial. Code allowed the question, but cautioned me to be brief.

I explained that Qutb was a radical cleric seen in the mujahideen community as a founder of the jihadist ideology against the Western world. He was Osama bin Laden's idol.

It doesn't get much shorter than that. I'd been waiting to say that for two weeks, and I didn't have to cause a mistrial to do it. I got to tell the jury that before Jaser even knew who I was, he was quoting excerpts from *Milestones* and telling me about how he aligned himself with that philosophy. There was no con.

Sarah wrapped up redirect in a couple of days. I was on the stand for more than three weeks. After I was done, Code thanked me for my time and professionalism. After the jury was dismissed for the day, Norris came over to shake my hand.

"You were a formidable opponent, Agent Elnoury," Norris said. "I wish you all the best."

My bags were already packed and in the car. Hal and his men ushered me back to the break room, where I changed out of my suit and into jeans and a sweatshirt. Nelly was late getting back there. He walked in with a grin on his face.

"Code stopped me in the hall and asked if I was going to see you," Nelly said. "He wanted me to relay a message. He said to tell you that you're not only a hero in your country, but in his. Your service and commitment will forever be appreciated. He told me to take care of you."

I finally got it. Code wasn't against us. He was giving the defense every benefit of the doubt because he didn't want them to have any grounds for an appeal. The evidence was insurmountable and he knew it. I felt bad for being so angry with him.

It took us a while to get out of the courthouse. I shook a lot of hands. Some of the courthouse staff and the Crown came down to the break room to thank me and Nelly. Each handshake and kind word was humbling.

Nelly and I got on the plane with bottles of high-end Canadian liquor, patches, coins, pins, hats, stuffed Mounties, and maple syrup from the Crown and the RCMP. As the plane started to taxi, I looked out the window. The entire security detail was lined up and saluted us. That's when I cried like a baby.

Nelly did too.

It was finally over.

EPILOGUE

We're Everyone

The jury deliberated for ten days.

I started to sweat after the first two days. Everyone was still positive through day four. After that, I didn't get any more updates. When they came back on the tenth day, Chiheb and Jaser were found guilty of conspiring to commit murder for the benefit of, at the direction of, or in association with a terrorist group. They were sentenced to life in prison.

As of this writing, Chiheb remains in solitary confinement. He refuses to get strip-searched. I think it has something to do with the San Jose airport. It's a fuck-you to me, because I'm a munafiq in his eyes. No more living amongst them, as them, to defeat them. He's now going to die alone. In a way, he got his martyrdom. I was told Jaser is doing well in general population. He finally got to be the Imam with a bunch of minions hanging on his every word.

Abassi was charged with two counts of fraud and misuse of visas to facilitate an act of international terrorism. After seventeen months in jail, he pleaded guilty to lesser charges, including making a false statement to officials upon his arrival at Kennedy International Airport. As part of his plea, he was deported to Tunisia. The U.S. attorney backed off the terrorism enhancements, in part because the FBI didn't want to expose me to another trial.

"I hope that you will think very seriously about the events of the last year and will decide to always abide by the laws of the United States," Judge Miriam Cedarbaum said during Abassi's July 2014 sentencing. It may not sound ideal, but it sidelined Abassi because it put him on law enforcement's radar no matter where he goes.

After the trial, I returned to work. So did Nelly and the team. We are all still fighting the fight. Terrorism didn't go away when we locked up Chiheb and Jaser.

There are about sixty designated foreign terrorist groups on the State Department's list. I would say that more than half of them are radical Islamic factions with the same essential goal: bring down the West. So when I hear people debate whether it's politically correct to call it "radical Islam," I laugh. There's nothing wrong with calling it what it is. I am a Muslim. I am American, and I am fucking appalled at what these animals are doing to my religion and my country.

But giving them a label is just words. How do we defeat an enemy who is willing to die for a cause that they believe in? That is the question I ask every one of my students at the FBI undercover school before I start my lesson on radical Islam. Over the years, I have heard many different answers, but never the correct one: education. In order to defeat your enemy, you must first understand them.

The problems start when every Muslim gets painted with the jihadi brush. Jihadis are using a peaceful religion to further their agendas. That's not religion. It's politics. The reality is that radical Islam is a very small minority that twists the Quran to fit its needs. Just look at Chiheb, Jaser, and Abassi. Chiheb thought the Quran justified the murder of innocent men, women, and children because he chose not to honor the Prophet's rules of war. He knew the rules. He just ignored them. Jaser thought Allah wanted him to kill Jews, and Abassi interpreted Allah's call as a war against America. None of them were right. That is why "radical Islam" is a fine blanket term, but the key to defeating it is learning the differences among those who believe radically—as evident in Chiheb, Jaser, and Abassi. They're not all the same, and understanding the fault lines between the different groups will be radical Islam's undoing.

Banning Muslims from the United States throws gas on the myth that the United States is at war with Islam. I believe there should be a strict vetting process, but our world becomes more dangerous when we shut our doors to immigrants.

I was born Sunni Muslim in Egypt and came to the United States when I was just a child. I remember the day that I became a naturalized U.S. citizen. I missed most of field day. My dad dropped me back at school and I ran through the halls so I wouldn't miss the whole day. My fifth-grade teacher stopped me.

"Congratulations, son," he said as he shook my hand. "Today is a big day for you."

I was ten years old and I will never forget the day I became an American. But my parents still sent me to Islamic school every Sunday to maintain my religion. We traveled back to Egypt almost every summer so I'd never forget my culture. My mother only spoke Arabic to me so I'd always know my native language. None of that made me less patriotic. I've served my country for twenty-two years and counting. Keeping America's doors open ensures that when we are threatened by an enemy, we will always have someone who looks like them to help defeat them. Our best defense is inclusion.

America is everyone.

ACKNOWLEDGMENTS

To my family, who spent most days and nights throughout my career not knowing where I was or when I'd be home. You'll never know how much your love and support means to me. You carried me through every case.

To my father and my sister, thank you for making sure I always knew the true tenets of Islam. I love you both very much.

To my extended family, thank you for always being there for me.

To my lifelong friends—Mikey, Sugar, KB, Chicken, Bone, and Muscle—thank you for your friendship and loyalty over the years.

To my agent, Frank Weimann, who believed in this story and the message and never rested till the job was done.

To Joe Pistone, for being a mentor and showing me the way.

To Ben Sevier, without you, this story would never have been told.

To Kevin Maurer, a brilliant, gifted author and journalist from whom I learned so much. I love the way you see the world, and I am honored to call you my friend.

To the folks at Dutton—Ivan, Christine, John, and Amanda—you took me in and helped me tell my story in the most incredible way. Thank you for making it so easy.

To Billy, Al, Mike, James, and all my Narco buddies, you taught me how to be a cop and what it means to bring a case home.

To Howard, who taught me how to tap into my emotions.

To my home law enforcement agency, for giving me my start and supporting my move to the FBI.

To the Federal Bureau of Investigation, for giving me the opportunity to serve my country.

To my team, in all the years that I have worked criminal and national security matters, this case will always stand out to me for a variety of reasons. But the main reason is the core of our team: Nelly, Joey, Kenny, and Johnny. I miss working with you on a daily basis. It's rare that a group of all-stars is assembled on one case. You are true professionals and American heroes. Nelly, your gut and instincts are never wrong, and, Joey, you were our director.

To the men and women of CT-1, you lived up to your reputation. Thank you for your tireless efforts and for fighting the good fight.

To the National Security Covert Operations Unit, you are the backbone of the counterterrorism undercover world. Thank you for always looking out for us.

To the men and women of the NYPD, especially the Counterterrorism Division, the greatest police department in the world.

To the men and women of the FBI undercover program, our fraternity within law enforcement is unlike any other. Thank you for keeping America safe. It is an honor to do this job with you.

To FBI Executive Management (New York and Headquarters) and the Southern District of New York, you make tough calls every day while always having our back. And a special thank-you to Big Mark for watching out for us every step of the way.

To the FBI legal attachés in Ottawa, Canada, specifically Sho and LJ. Without you, I never would have gotten in front of the subjects.

To the National Security Law Branch, specifically Heidi, for always protecting my identity and making sure I can do my job over and over again. You were always my last line of defense, Heidi, and you never let me down.

To the FBI unit that backstopped all my legends, specifically Dave, thank you for always going the extra mile for me and making sure I was always "real" no matter where I was in the world.

To our FBI forensic accountant, Lindsay, for taking care of our finances and making sure all our audits went smoothly.

To our FBI analysts, especially Brett, for finding our bad guys and keeping us informed throughout the investigation.

To our FBI linguists, who had to endure hours and hours of listening to me and relaying the information to the agents on the ground.

To our Canadian partners the Royal Canadian Mounted Police—Doug, Johnny A., Christine, Frank, Omar, Benny, Brady, Simone, Marwan, and Rich—and the Royal Crown Prosecutors—Croft, Marcy, and Sarah—whose dedication and professionalism was inspiring. Two countries working together for a common goal.

To the Canadian warriors, my security detail—Hal, Souki, Kenny (JJ), Geoff, and the rest of the team—thank you all for watching my back. There's no one I would have wanted doing the job other than you.

ABOUT THE AUTHORS

TAMER ELNOURY was born in Egypt and emigrated to the United States before his fifth birthday. He began his career in law enforcement in 1995. After a brief stint with a fugitive task force, he began working in undercover narcotics. Elnoury worked on more than 2,500 narcotics investigations as well as political corruption, gun trafficking and child abuse cases. In 2008, he began working with the Federal Bureau of Investigation, joining an elite, covert counterterrorism unit. Elnoury has worked on cases all over the world for multiple government agencies.

KEVIN MAURER is an award-winning journalist and the best-selling co-author, with Mark Owen, of *No Easy Day: The Firsthand Account of the Mission That Killed Osama bin Laden*. He has covered war and terrorism for more than a decade.